BOUND

VICIOUS

DEVOTION

Wed in the Wild Series: Books 1 & 2

in the Fangs With Benefits universe

Aveda Vice

Bad Bite LLC

Also By Aveda Vice

Fangs With Benefits

Hunger Duet
Feed
Yours, Insatiably

Lost Touch Duet
Skin
Inextricably Tied

Wed in the Wild Series
Bound
Vicious Devotion

Fear, and Other Love Languages

Headless

THE BREAK
THE EYRIE
VESTAL BATTLE
STEPPES
CHASMS
BROADLEAFS
TIMBERS

Dedication

When your healing is messy and painful and complex:
you are loved.

Author's Note

This book contains spoilers for the book *Inextricably Tied*.

This book contains sexual situations. It is not intended for anyone under the legal age of adulthood. All characters depicted in sexual situations herein are over 18 years of age. This book is not to be used as an informational guide to any type of sex or sexual education.

Some topics within this book may be sensitive or disturbing to some readers. Reader discretion is advised.

For detailed information on the topics addressed, please <u>visit the author's website</u> or scan the codes below.

Bound

Vicious Devotion

BOUND

Prequel to

Vicious Devotion

BOUND

The blood on Pheir's mouth is still wet when they muzzle her.

They clip her wings as soon as they capture her, leaving the ground covered in oil-slick-colored feathers. Her wrists and ankles are bound in soldered metal, talons scraping the dirt as they drag her toward the center of the carnage.

There's no hope of escape. Still, Pheir kicks and screeches when they shove her to her knees, streaking mud across the pale violet color of her skin.

"Pheir, give it up."

The collar around Rhaiden's throat tightens her voice, but Pheir's close enough to hear her. It doesn't matter that they're both trapped, bound on their knees before the Conclave — Pheir knows what Rhaiden is. A traitor. A deserter. An imposter of a leader who doesn't deserve the air passing through her gills.

Pheir's wings beat where they sprout along her back, desperate to land a claw against Rhaiden's throat. Rhaiden snaps Pheir's name.

"*Capheira.*"

Already, Pheir can feel it: power seeping into Rhaiden as their dead Alpha's blood soaks the grass. It halts Pheir immediately, no matter how she grits her teeth against it. No matter how she fights the bonds struggling to form between the only remaining members of their pack, the invisible bindings straining through the bloody stumps littering the field.

Thalea is quiet on Rhaiden's other side. She's only a husk of a dryad now, eyes on the ground, blank and distant as the Conclave deliberates. She looks as lost as Pheir feels, but it's worse for Thalea. She didn't just lose her Alpha; the moment Vesta's head left her body, Thalea was severed from her mate as well.

And Rhaiden hadn't even tried to save them. She hadn't died for Vesta, like Pheir would have. Like Pheir *tried* to. It plays in white-hot flashes behind her eyes: the Conclave's final offer of mercy. The gory pulp of the Vestal pack that lay around them. Vesta's diabolical laughter. Her refusal to bow to any ceasefire, beautiful and proud. Then her inhale to produce another decimating round of phoenix fire....

And the hellhound's fangs tearing through Vesta's throat before her head dropped to the ground.

It ripped through Pheir like her legs were taken out from under her, air slammed from her lungs as Vesta's blood sprayed across the grass. Pheir's harpy screeches split the air. The Conclave creatures who pinned her were the only things keeping her from flying into the fray.

Through the pain and loss of their Alpha, the Vestals' connections struggle to forge again, winding weakly and meeting dead ends in all the slain bodies around them. Alpha power surged into Rhaiden — Vesta's beta, the pack's second-in-command, the siren who didn't deserve to take Vesta's place. Who didn't believe in the vision Vesta had.

Rhaiden proved that the second the mantle transferred to her, when Pheir still shrieked at her to fight. To spit in the Conclave's faces, to poison them with her spires, to do anything but bow down and give in.

Rhaiden didn't move, enemy claws against her throat to keep her from speaking. Then she lifted her hands in surrender and gave them over to the Conclave.

Pheir's screams were for nothing. Vesta's work was for *nothing*. This is what Rhaiden did to them.

Pheir's anger flares at the memory. "That's all you fucking do, isn't it, traitor? *Give up.* Vesta would have *died* before she'd surrender."

Rhaiden's cool eyes stay trained on the Conclave when she speaks. "And she did, didn't she?"

Rage peaks in Pheir's body. She screams, pushing to her taloned feet, but other Conclave creatures swarm and slam her to the ground. Minutes pass before she stops fighting. This time, the creatures don't lift her from the dirt, forcing her to watch through the grass as Lev and the other Alphas approach.

Of course Lev speaks for the Conclave, her eyes ruminating on Pheir in a way that makes her want to claw out of her skin.

"I'll be honest with you…" Lev's wererabbit ears twitch as her gaze flicks over each of the Vestals. "The Conclave still isn't sold on not killing you right now."

"Fucking do it, then!" Pheir lunges, but her fury is no match for the knees bearing down into her back.

Lev doesn't take the bait. "Since we aren't going to come to an agreement on that any time soon, we'll have to make accommodations in the meantime."

A glint around Lev's neck catches Pheir's eye: a vial filled with Vesta's ashes. Smoke still lingers in Pheir's nose, her eyes darting to the matching vials hanging from the other Alphas' necks. After they tore Vesta limb from limb, her bones shattered and skin shredded, the Conclave burned her and separated the ashes. It's the only way to make sure a phoenix stays dead.

And reuniting them is the only way Pheir can bring Vesta back.

Pheir screeches to be set free, landing a claw against one of her captors. Lev looks around her for support. "Will somebody fucking sedate her?"

A prick lands on Pheir's outer thigh. It takes no time before her body stops responding to her rage, chest heaving where it's pressed to the ground and unable to move.

Unable to fight back.

"Now..." Lev's gaze turns back to Rhaiden. "We're faced with three traitorous beings, and nowhere for them to go. Nowhere they can be trusted. Certainly nowhere they can stay together."

The Conclave hasn't picked up on the foundation crumbling beneath the final Vestal soldiers, the dissent and death that would surely follow if they were left alone. The Conclave's only thoughts are of the remaining members of Vesta's pack plotting the demise of every other creature here. Never mind that splitting the final three Vestals will be brutal and painful, bonds stretching to mold together across distance and death. It'll only get worse the further they're dragged apart. The Conclave might as well kill them now; there's no way they can survive being split and unbonded for who knows how long.

But Rhaiden doesn't fight it, content to let the final Vestals suffer and waste away rather than admit that Vesta was right: the four of them together were better than all the other packs combined. They were *stronger*.

Pheir gives a weak grunt of distaste, but that's all her body can manage before Lev speaks again.

"You'll be split just like the ashes." The thought makes Pheir want to gag. "Absorbed by different packs, your loyalties bound by force."

Pheir's laugh sounds more like a snort. Forced how? There's no way to make them submit. Even if Rhaiden bows her cowardly head, Pheir and Thalea won't give in. Lev hardly hesitates, gazing at Pheir's limp form as if she can read her thoughts. "To accomplish that, you'll be wed to the Alphas of three furthest packs."

A ripple passes through the crowd, hushed whispers mixed with gasps of dissent. Nothing's more painful than the choking sound Thalea makes, panicked eyes lifting for the first time. Through the murmurs of the crowd, Lev's gaze hangs on Rhaiden until it quiets enough for Rhaiden to speak. "And how do you plan to keep us from killing the rest of you until the bonds are solidified?"

"You'll be sent to places where you'll struggle to thrive, where there are plenty of people to keep an eye on you." Lev's gaze slides over the three of them. For the first time, Pheir's temper dip into an inkling of fear. "The dryad will go to the plains, since you two have...things to sort out."

Lev's gaze tilts back to the hellhound Alpha who'd laid the fatal blow to Vesta. Thalea's mouth drops open in horror as the hellhound swallows roughly.

"That's fucking — sick," Pheir slurs, trying to find the strength to yank on her chains. "You can't...force her to marry — the person who..." *Killed her mate.*

Pheir runs out of steam, panting for breath as a guarded look settles in Lev's eyes, something heavy that Pheir can't translate. "It's about the only thing we can do." Then Lev's gaze shifts to Rhaiden again with the heady respect Alphas reserve only for each other. "The siren will go under the mountain."

A dragon Alpha watches from Lev's other side. Rhaiden doesn't even turn her eyes to him. Doesn't make a sound. Doesn't fight back.

"And the harpy can return to the forest with the Timbers. It's cooler than she's used to. We have plenty of natural avian predators in our pack. She won't get far."

Pheir's cheek grinds against the grass. "Birds eat...fucking rabbits."

Lev's eyes glow with a fire Pheir wants to snuff out. "We'll see about that."

Pheir refuses, but any pack strength the Vestals had splinters as Thalea trembles and Rhaiden stares straight ahead. They're too broken, too traitorous to fight to stay together. Their pack is already lost, decimated in the span of a few hours, severing every tie Pheir had tethering her. She hasn't been alone in years, and as the other creatures drag her toward isolation, she's drawn further from the only home she's ever known.

How had the most powerful pack become such a miserable failure? There had been no stretch of land the Vestals couldn't dominate, no strip of sky free of their power, no rivers or streams or seas outside of their domain. Vesta hadn't built their pack for fun. It was strategic, something no other Alpha had the guts to attempt, bringing together creatures tired of being mistreated by the Conclave. In the Break, packs live outside the constraints of the cities in the long valley between the V of mountain ranges...but the packs are never outside of the control of the Conclave.

Once Vesta gained traction, beasts came in droves, intoxicated by the freedom of slipping the Conclave's leash. Vesta enticed them all. *You see how we don't need to be controlled? You see what power you have when the Conclave doesn't water us down?* Under Vesta's influence, her pack grew overnight, moving like a well-oiled machine. The Vestals scattered any smaller packs they came across, poaching promising members until Vesta had a grip on an entire sector of The Break...

And they weren't done yet.

Of course, there were detractors. What movement doesn't have them? Vesta made an example of those who couldn't see her vision, and she was more powerful for it. They were *all* more powerful because of the way Vesta led them. The pack grew with an almighty promise that made them all but impossible to defeat.

They had been dangerous for a while. Potent, dynamic, an impressive force that flourished with every passing day — which meant the Conclave had to take notice. Eventually, the smaller packs had no other choice: flee their land or join with Vesta.

If they were smart, they made the right decision.

But the Conclave could have no one questioning their authority. They had to put down the Vestals once and for all. Now, they Vestals are being sold for parts. It's a pitiful auction, given the scraggly number of them left after the battle, but there's a reason they succeeded for so long. Vesta chose only the best to be in her inner council, a fierce beast from every element — earth, air, fire, and water — the most capable and dangerous creatures by her side.

You mean, "the most easily manipulated."

The voice in Pheir's head surprises her. It's just a memory, Rhaiden muttering in their war council while Vesta laid out their tactics. It took three other Vestals to keep Pheir from attacking her. Rhaiden watched Pheir struggle like she was proving a point.

Whatever. Pheir won't be manipulated. She won't bow mindlessly to the very monsters who have taken them hostage. Who slaughtered their pack. Who want the three of them dead. Who are forcing them to marry their captors.

Pheir won't see Rhaiden or Thalea again. No doubt they'll all be dragged away by the cronies of their new Alphas, just like Pheir is now. Her muzzle binds tighter every time she riots against her restraints. Lev's Timbers aren't cowed when they bind Pheir against a post at their campsite.

She doesn't sleep at all. Why would she let her guard down? Certainly not when the Timbers' highest-ranking officers are watching her.

Aren and Caius. Their names burn on her tongue, clashing the way they do on every battlefield. She's always had a taste for their pain, drawn toward them across the chaos with her talons honed on them. They can't take her one-on-one, too preoccupied abiding the rules of war to fight as dirty as Pheir does. All three of them have landed blows, ripping fur and feathers from each other, only spared when someone else gets in the way.

Or when Lev calls the Timbers back.

The Vestal massacre hours ago was no exception. The sight of Caius at the campsite only stokes Pheir's hatred. Campfire reflects in the fury of her glare as smugness sharpens every one of his werewolverine teeth.

All werecreatures are people covered in fur or scales or feathers, snouts and paws and tails belying the heightened shrewdness in their eyes. They're like shifters lifted on two legs, caught between one phase and the next, but weres don't change their forms. They look half-animal all the time. Caius whittles a stick into a spear with only the side of his claws, fur pulling taut across the muscles in his arms and chest.

Pheir wants to rip the piercings from his ears, to dig talons into the patterned cut of his fur and leave him bleeding out on the ground. Feral and explosive, the both of them. The best qualities a pack's combatant can have. It makes sense why Vesta and Lev chose them.

Pheir gets minimal reprieve when Aren takes up the post, the werelynx who barely makes a sound as he watches Pheir war with her restraints for hours. Somehow, he's even more infuriating, never rising to any of her bait. His tufted ears flick, giving little more than quiet replies to Pheir's goading — just like Rhaiden.

Guess betas have some things in common, too.

By the time the sun rises, Pheir's adrenaline has worn off. Her body aches with the weight of everything: the fight. The loss. The lack of sleep. Most painful of all, the Vestals remaining bonds straining to form across the distance.

"Let's go." A paw lifts her roughly, unbinding her from the post before she's shoved to her feet with wrists tied behind her back.

"Caius..." Aren's voice is a warning. Caius only grins and hoists a thick satchel onto his shoulder.

"You're coming with us, little songbird."

Pheir's gaze cuts to the tent Lev disappeared into hours ago. "Thought your floppy-eared friend wanted me all to herself."

"She doesn't want to deal with your bullshit. And while the rest of the pack recovers from the shit *you* pulled," Caius shoves her again, "we're taking you back to the compound."

Pheir lunges for him, but Aren already has a paw on the feathered scruff of her neck, voice calm and even when he looks to Caius.

"Stop being an asshole." Caius scoffs, but he doesn't contradict him. Aren doesn't release his hold on Pheir. Doesn't drop her gaze until he speaks again. "We'll escort you." His eyes are sharp when he pulls them away. "I promise you're in good hands."

She can do little more than snort through the muzzle strapped to her face when she faces the forest edge. "I highly fucking doubt that."

They hike for hours. Only when the sun is high in the sky do they break, panting under the cover of leaves while Aren tries to coax Pheir toward some of the seeds they packed for her. She eats only enough to make her stomach stop growling, which is more than she would have liked. She only realizes how much she's had once Aren's maw twitches up in a smile.

She snaps her teeth at the next handful he offers. He pulls away before she can land a bite.

Every step takes her further from the corpse of the pack her body begs to bond with. Every minute is more painful, like something's strapped across her chest and hindering all her forward movement. The only thing that spurs her on is the blazing revenge inside her. They don't stop again until the light starts fading, warmth replaced by changing leaves and a cool breeze that makes her shiver. She doesn't have fur to keep her warm, just patches of feathers like decoration along her skin. Her eyes narrow to see through the branches. She's at a disadvantage once it's dark, more than she already is with every vicious part of her bound. Her taloned feet catch on an exposed root. Caius jerks the metal around her wrists to keep her upright.

"Stop tugging," she hisses.

He releases her with a sneer. "Stop bitching."

Pheir whirls. She had claws against their throats not twelve hours ago; she should've found a way to drive her talons deeper. "Nice scar," she growls at the gash across his eyes. Years later, and her handiwork still hasn't healed right. "Want another?"

Caius snarls. Aren gets a paw against his chest and quiets them both. "We're stopping for the night."

A bitter laugh boils out of Pheir. "What, tired already?"

Never mind that she's dead on her feet, pulled between overwhelming exhaustion and the thrumming energy of battle she hasn't been able to set loose. Caius forces her to the nearest sturdy tree, a threat in every hard plane of his body when his voice drips in her ear. "We've got some shit to take care of."

She reaches back to grab him, to twist her talons around his dick. He's prepared — but only just, lurching back the same time she's yanked away.

Aren grips the base of her hair, patience worn thin when he grinds out two words. "Step. Over."

She doesn't drop his gaze. Too proud, even as he's commanding her body to contort, to bend so she can loop her bound arms under her ass and legs around to her front. When he releases her, she tries not to think about the way it made her skin prick with goosebumps. It's just unspent energy from battle. Nothing she can control.

She soothes down the ruff of feathers on her shoulders as Caius ties her back to a massive tree trunk, wrists bound above her head, layers of reinforced rope secured across her stomach and thighs. He leaves her ankles hanging down against the trunk before he moves back to help Aren set up camp.

A different tension permeates the air. Even surly Caius goes quiet, winding ropes around posts in the ground, brows knit in concentration. Aren focuses on dinner, heating meat over the fire until he brings Pheir her portion. He's distracted enough that she lands her teeth in him as he feeds her. He jerks back his paw.

She smirks. "Big plans tonight?"

He shoots her a dark look before he moves away, taking the rest of her meal with him. She isn't deterred.

"Don't tell me I'm keeping you two from something."

The fur on the back of Caius's neck stands on end. Aren soothes him with a low sound that Pheir can't quite make out.

"Since you've gotten some of your strength back…" Aren sucks the nick on his finger and hands Caius the rest of her food. "You won't mind if we leave you on your own for a bit."

Pheir strains uselessly against the bindings, even further from escape than she has been. "You sure that's a good idea? Never know what I might get into."

"I can imagine." Aren returns the muzzle to her mouth, easily avoiding her teeth, but that doesn't make her fight any less. She needs to be contrary. She needs to make this harder for them.

"You're just leaving me here? Unsupervised?"

Aren takes a long drink of water back at the fire. "I'm sure the tree will keep you company."

Her eyes narrow. "Where are you going? We're in the middle of a forest."

"Nowhere exciting."

Oh, but it is, the second she's not allowed to know. "Take me with you, then." Her smile is vicious behind the muzzle. "Promise I'll be on my best behavior."

Caius barks a laugh, dipping another piece of her leftover meat into his mouth. "Trust me, you don't want to go."

"I *really* do —"

"We're going to fuck, Pheir."

She blinks. Aren tenses as he cleans the fur around his mouth. Caius devours another slab of meat, unbothered.

"Still want to come?"

Unbidden, her mind jerks through the possibilities: the three of them wrestling to the ground, panting and slick, dragging each other through the dirt. Giving her body the release she's been aching for, all that excess energy from the fight still ricocheting inside her.

It takes too long for her to answer. By the time she realizes, both weres have lifted their eyes and noses to her. She can't move her legs enough to snap them shut. It's unnerving to know they can sense things she can't, the sudden coil of her arousal hitting their senses. She shoves the thought away, but they're both still staring. Her skin prickles when Caius speaks again.

"You didn't answer the question."

Fatigue fucks with her mind. She reaches desperately for the response she should give, but all she can think about is how her body is bound and captive. Dark heat swirls traitorously in her stomach. "Why would I want to fuck you? I *hate* you."

"That's not an answer." Aren cuts sharply through everything else. Even Caius's ears perk. Aren evens his voice, pulling back on the commanding beta tone. "This is not a demand; it's an offer. If you need some place to expel your energy."

It burns through her. Her heart hasn't slowed since the battle. No resolution, too wound up on blood and gore and death, bonds breaking and stitching together. There's been no place to release the feeling. None of them have had a chance to wear off the excess aggression. The other packs had the opportunity to lick their wounds, celebrate their survival, strengthen their bonds with sex...but the three of them have been stuck together since they tied her to the post last night. That's half the reason Lev sent them away before the rest of the group. She was wrapping up loose ends, healing wounds, finding solace in the rest of the Timbers.

But — no. Absolutely fucking not. Pheir hates them; she's always hated them, clashing in every battle, finding each other on the field so they could dig their claws into each other.

Heat pools between her legs. Both their noses twitch.

"If you aren't interested," Aren murmurs, "we'll just leave you tied to the tree until we're finished."

There's a tic in his jaw that surges toward her clit, a flicker of reaction on that stoic face. If they leave her alone for an hour, maybe she could escape. Already, she knows it's fruitless. They'd be listening, and the ropes are too strong and well-placed for her to slip a talon against them. She twists her wrists where they're bound above her, cutting her heated gaze across the space. "Not very gentlemanly to keep me tied up during."

Caius licks the blood of the meat from his jaws. Pheir tries not to shiver when he speaks. "Like it doesn't get you off to pretend you don't want it. Like we're forcing you."

It takes all she has to reign in her body at the thought of them taking their prize while she's bound and screaming for them to stop. Her gaze flits to Aren's ever-watching eyes. She knows he hasn't missed her clenched jaw, her flexing talons, the wind gusting a whiff of her desire toward them.

"Do you want this, Pheir?"

She hisses a breath at her name in his mouth, tilting over his teeth. It's all too much: fighting for hours, being crushed, losing Vesta, the bonds trying to form with the pack Pheir wants to rip herself away from. She's exhausted and frantic, swarming with anxious energy that makes her body vibrate.

If she can't connect with her pack, she needs to bond with *something*.

Maybe this is punishment, her penance for not saving Vesta. For not dying for her. An ache pierces Pheir's chest, but it's dulled by the instincts thronging within her. She wants to stop thinking. Stop remembering. Find that final release and let her body collapse.

And this is a chance to make her escape.

She pants. "Gonna keep me tied to this tree the whole time you fuck me?"

Heat flashes across Caius's face. Pheir fights down a slick feeling. He's distracted by the carnal offering, but Aren watches her like a predator, searching for the reason beneath her acceptance. He's never foolish enough to trust her. "We'll see how you behave once we get an orgasm out of you."

Her feathers stand on end, senses heightened when Aren and Caius prowl closer, watching her with different hungers. Caius laps up the final bloody remnants from his paws, one finger framed by the two piercings in his tongue. Both weres come to a stop before her, close enough to see her chest heaving under the restraints.

"If anyone wants to stop, you say 'mercy.'" Aren's eyes flick to Caius. "And we all honor it."

Caius grunts.

Pheir twists in his direction. "What was that, mangy mutt?"

He sneers closer. "Don't worry, I won't fuck you unless you're *screaming* for it."

She fights to pull her chest back from where it's straining to meet his. "Guess you'll just be fucking Aren, then."

The words send ripples through their expressions, a cord of tension taut beneath the surface.

"Tell you what…" Caius flicks out a claw to trace around the curve of Pheir's breasts, smattered with feathers that quiver under his touch. "I *will* fuck Aren. And you can watch." He laves against her nipple, the metal barbels in his tongue drawing her tight as his breath cools the wet trail. He nicks her with his teeth. She jerks. "Just to make sure you *really* want this."

It sounds courteous, but they all know it's meant to work her up, to pulse her already frenetic mind with blood and heat and want. Her jaw tightens, but Caius is already dropping to his knees, meeting Aren's eyes only a second before he wraps his mouth around Aren's cock.

Aren and Pheir suck in the same breath, both their eyes trained on Caius, Pheir's talons flexing at the same time Aren gets a grip on the back of Caius's head. Blonde fur slips between Aren's white paws, but Caius wastes no time, swallowing Aren with a sloppy sound that makes Pheir shudder.

"Someone's showing off. You like an audience?" Aren rumbles, tugging Caius's fur enough to slow him. Then Aren lowers his voice, so deep that Pheir has to strain to hear. "Or do you just like that it's *her*?"

Caius chokes around Aren's cock, avoiding any glance toward Pheir before he surges forward and knocks Aren back against a boulder. Something burns into Pheir's skin. It's only then she notices how much she's straining against the ropes, digging into her flesh as she arches and grinds against their hold. Desperate for friction. It doesn't matter where it comes from. When Aren's fingers clamp tighter, teeth bared, she knows he's been close to the edge for a while.

"Don't swallow," he commands. Caius gives no acknowledgement, but she knows he'd never refuse his beta. Caius's piercings slip out to stroke the underside of Aren's cock, and Aren comes like that, gripping Caius's head and grinding against his mouth until he's spent. Caius pulls back with his mouth full when he turns his eyes on Pheir.

It's a wonder she can speak with how dry her throat feels. "You should try that more often," she breathes. "Shutting the fuck up."

Even her riling doesn't affect Caius. Not when he's following orders, a combatant to the very end. He stands as Aren winds closer to her, voice even when he speaks.

"Caius is going to put my cum in your mouth." Every nerve inside of Pheir jumps to high alert. "You're not going to spit. You're not going to swallow. You're going to hold it while we fuck with you, and you're not going to spill a drop." His face hovers unflinching before her. "Do you understand?"

A whimper claws desperately up her throat. She refuses to free it, squirming against the ropes, but the lightest pressure of his finger near her clit has her shuddering. Instinct rears its ugly head. She's so far from anyone and anything else, a wounded thing without a pack, keening to follow Aren's powerful demand. He circles between her thighs, never touching where she wants him, the rough pad of his furred finger nearly enough to send her to the edge. She clamps her lips, too afraid of what sounds might spill if she doesn't.

"Yes. Exactly like that." Aren smirks. "Hold up two fingers if you want to stop." His gaze rises to her hands above her head. "Show me."

There's no hiding the tremble before she flicks him off with both hands. He drags his finger against her clit. It grinds a gasp out of her too quickly for someone meant to hate him. Aren only lets it show in the barest twitch of his lip, unhooking her muzzle and turning back to Caius. It's the first time Pheir's jaw has been free outside of feeding in the last day, and Caius is so fucking smug, mouth bulging from Aren's seed.

So Pheir spits.

It lands on the corner of Caius's maw. He pounces, clamping his paw high around her neck and squeezing.

"Pheir..." Aren face appears beside them. Caius crumples her windpipe, leaning so close she can feel the hot breath from his snout. Darkness dances in the corner of Pheir's vision. Aren's voice comes through the haze. "Are you going to behave?"

She wants to fight. To claw her way free, to leave them both with gashes across their bodies, but something in the crush of Caius's hand makes her wetter. She keeps her lips clamped for another dangerous moment, venom in her eyes before she opens her mouth and lays out the flat of her tongue.

Aren smirks. "That's a good girl."

Caius squeezes tighter before he holds his mouth over hers, spilling Aren's cum and letting it fill her cheeks. He spits the last of it in retaliation. It specks across her jaw, and she tries to lunge toward him, but he pulls back with a maniacal laugh.

Aren clamps a paw across her mouth. "Are you going to hold it?"

Acid burns in her gaze, watching every shift in Caius's hateful smile before she nods. Aren steps back, waiting to see if she keeps her word.

She doesn't let a drop out. *Can't* let it out. She knows how to follow fucking orders.

Once he's satisfied, Aren turns away from Pheir again. "Caius, make her spill it."

Caius rushes her before she can blink, grinding the pad of his palm against her clit in a stroke that has her straining.

"Might as well spit it out now." Caius presses harder. "You can't keep that mouth shut for long."

Infuriating how his words only make her lips clamp tighter, torn between spitting it back in his face and proving him wrong. *Besting* him. He traces the sharp point of a claw against the juncture of her thigh, and she holds rigidly still.

"I'm gonna get you off with only a finger." Caius winds his way closer to her clit, leaving the lightest scrapes against her skin. "Can you stand that?" His face is too close, tilting toward hers and making her dizzy. He teases her entrance, but she refuses to move, to look anywhere but him. There's temptation in his eyes to fuck her with his claw — but he retracts just one, enough to slot that finger between her folds. She sucks in a breath through her nose. His bloodthirsty smile etches wider.

"Someone's been holding out on us. How long has this pussy been sopping wet?"

He knows she can't answer, can't defend herself; that's half the fun for him. She fights to hold onto that anger when he sinks completely inside. She nearly chokes. While Caius torments her, Aren only watches, gaze slipping between her bulging mouth and where she stretches around Caius. Caius's eyes slip down to watch the truth she can't hide.

"Give it up, little bird." He fucks her slowly, long drags in and out. "You can't keep holding it; you don't want to."

"Do not spill it, Pheir." Aren lingers behind Caius. Even if Pheir wasn't intent to hold out, Aren's lethal look would have her obeying. She clenches her teeth harder, holding her hips back from bucking against the feel of it.

Caius has caught the scent now. He wants to dominate her. Defeat her. His finger pumps faster. "This is a good look on you, Pheir: can't talk. Can't scream. Maybe you should keep that mouth shut while we use your other holes."

She's torn and twisted, breath ragged and desperate to spit back in his face, to keep holding on, to let the rising swell of orgasm overtake her. Aren is closer now, both men crowding her against the tree and trapping her under the ropes, so hot she can barely stand it. Bark scrapes her back every time she moves as Caius's teeth drag down her chest.

"Come on: be a little bitch and come for me."

Fangs graze her breast before they dig into flesh, making her jerk and struggle to keep her mouth shut. Caius's dark eyes are on hers, Aren's demanding face hovering beside them, honed on her lips. "Don't spill it, Pheir."

Her blood trickles over Caius's mouth, his palm grinding her clit, every claw but one scraping her thighs. She tries to hold it. She *does*, but a ferocious heat barrels through her when Caius slaps her breast and shoves her straight into her release.

Cum spills from her lips when she screams, shuddering and hating every moment of delicious friction. Her breasts are covered, splattered with Aren's seed mingled with her blood, chest rising and falling under the ropes. Caius doesn't stop fucking her, mocking her, a simpering thread through his voice that she'd use to strangle him if she could stop squirming. "*Aw*, you couldn't do it."

"Caius..." Aren murmurs, and only then does Caius pull away, smirking when Pheir goes limp. It takes a minute before she can lift her eyes to Aren's again. "A valiant effort," he murmurs. The humor in his gaze makes her want to claw at him, but she's not sure she can move. He glances at Caius. "Now, clean up the mess you made."

Pheir has to fight back, lifting her chin to spit the final dregs at Caius. He knows better by now, gripping her cheeks so hard it hurts. He laves the flat of his tongue up the column of her throat, dragging down to her breasts, swirling against her nipple and collecting the pinpricks of blood with a devious smile. His cock is hard against her hip. A subversive desire digs into her gut when she tries to arch out of his mouth. Only once she's stained with all of it does Caius return to her lips, meeting her tongue roughly until she sinks her teeth into him. He forces her cheek against the tree with a paw on her face, and she's left a filthy mess strung up before them.

Aren tilts his head as they watch her. "What do you think? Can she be trusted out of the restraints?"

"She can't be trusted *anywhere*," Caius growls. "But I need to get my dick wet, and I'm not looking at her face during."

Pheir bares her teeth. Aren considers it, leaning close to her once more.

"How about we take you down from the tree. Put the muzzle back on. Keep your hands bound...and we'll let you run." A predatory flash darts across his face. "See how far you can get before we hunt you down and fuck you into the dirt."

Heat darts through her. His suggestion barely gives her a chance; she won't get far with no wings, no teeth, only her feet to run or fight back. Either way, it's better than being bound here and waiting. This gives her a shot at escape...

Not to mention the want that flares in her at the thought of grinding them both into the ground.

"And who knows?" As if he can divine her thoughts, Caius grins brutally. "Maybe you'll even slip away."

Pheir fights not to let the prospect flood her expression. Aren glances between them. "Is everything on the table?"

Caius's eyes light up at the promise of bodily injury. "You know I like it fucking rough."

Pheir's jaw clenches, mind cartwheeling through images of everything that could mean. With all of the weres regenerative healing, the smaller pain receptors, the increased speed... She only has one requirement. "Make sure it's wet."

There's the faintest tug at the corner of Aren's lip. "Agreed." Then his gaze cuts between them. "And no killing each other."

"I'm not agreeing to that," Pheir snaps.

Caius isn't far behind. "Fuck no."

It's the first and only time they've been in agreement. Aren accepts the loss, reattaching Pheir's muzzle and unwinding the lengths of rope to free her from the tree. Her wrists are still bound in front of her, too tight to beat her wings freely— not that she could fly, anyway. Only her taloned feet are free.

It's not much, but it'll have to work.

Her neck snaps back when Caius shoves her toward the forest, making her collide with Aren's chest. He grips her forearms to stop her momentum — and her talons — looking down at her with a flicker of...something. She tenses. Tries not to let the scent of him seep into her nose. He grips tighter, then releases.

It's impossible to read what the look on his face is: disgust. Control. Desire.

The weres don't move as she steps toward the trees. They watch her, Caius's eyes licking over her body as Aren meets her wary gaze.

Pheir doesn't back away slowly. She breaks toward the forest, dodging trees and branches as she disappears into the growth. Without wings, she's slower and off-balance, scraping against foliage as she tears through the brush.

Need to get downwind.

She lifts her face, feeling for the breeze, waiting in silence before she changes course. There's no time to make a slow and careful path. When she gets far enough away, she can cover her tracks.

Once she's panting and glancing at the destruction she's left behind, she doubles back to disguise her footsteps. She has to be smarter now. Has to slow the beating of her heart as she trails through a stream to mask her scent.

This is about escape. About finding a place to hide out until she can saw through her bindings. Still, something warm and wet twists in her gut. That smell is a lot harder to cover. She wades up to her waist in the river before she pulls herself onto the opposite bank.

It's tempting to see if she can make a break for it. Even knowing she won't get far on just her legs, a desperate need claws in her chest to take off, to sprint, to put as much distance between them as possible. But she has to be smart. Has to play this out in a way that gives her the best chance of splitting from the Timbers.

What would Rhaiden do?

The thought barrels into Pheir's mind before she can stop it, head snapping up at the thought. No: *fuck* Rhaiden. Renewed anger swells in Pheir, and she finds a copse of thick bushes that she ducks into, biting her tongue as the brambles drag against her feathers. For minutes, she stays frozen. Her legs burn where she crouches, but she can't risk adjusting, not when two predators are combing the woods for her.

A twig snaps in the direction she came. The forest goes silent. Pheir holds her breath amid the blood pounding through her ears.

She was careful. She covered her tracks. She's still downwind.

Around her, the forest settles, thrumming back to life.

Pheir exhales.

A force knocks her sideways, slamming her to the ground, tumbling end over end before she's dragged from the brush. She scrabbles to escape, talons digging into the earth as something wraps around her ankle and jerks. Her chest skids across the ground. She slams her foot back, met with a satisfying crack that jolts up her leg as warm liquid splatters her calf.

"Fucking *bitch*." Caius's growl tears out of him as Pheir scrambles to her feet, leaping and flapping her wings with all she has. A paw finds her ankle again, claws digging into her shin as Caius snatches her out of the air and drags her back under him.

Blood drips from his nose, crooked and broken where she landed her foot against it. He's grinning, red streaked between his teeth when he grips a hand around her throat. He shoves her chest against the ground, grinding her face into the dirt with her bound arms pinned beneath her weight, ass lifted like he might mount her from behind. His breath is hot in her ear when he leans over her.

"We could kill you right now."

"Fucking *try it!*" She rears back to kick him again, but he grips her legs and shoves them apart, trapping her calves beneath his knees.

"What's your safeword?"

She screams in frustration. He doesn't loosen his hold.

It's fucking useless. She *hates* him. "Mercy," she spits.

It's barely past her lips before his snarl is feral in her ear. "And don't you fucking forget it."

Then his mouth smears against her cunt.They both groan, because his blood isn't the only sticky thing between her thighs. "Looks like we've caught ourselves a needy little slut."

Her body jerks when Caius lands a sharp slap inside her thigh. She kicks against him, but he keeps her pinned, dragging his bloody mouth through her slit. It's filthy, like he doesn't give a fuck that his nose is broken, already healing itself and weaving back together while he torments her clit.

A paw jerks up on the feathered scruff of her neck, forcing her onto all fours. Aren stands before her, keeping her eyes lifted with a paw deep in her hair. Humiliation seethes within her. Kneeling for a beta — *this* beta — makes her blood boil.

His dick is right in front of her. Caius sucks her clit viciously again, and she hates the way her arms tremble, eyelids fluttering as her breath catches. Aren watches it all, never speaking, but she doesn't miss the way his cock twitches.

"Do I need to worry about your teeth?"

It's laughable how calmly he asks, tipping her chin up with the lightest of touches. Nothing like the delicious torture Caius inflicts, sucking her clit so hard it hurts. She grits her teeth, already torn in two by the thought of him slipping off her muzzle, guiding his dick into her mouth.

She could dig her teeth in as soon as it's within reach.

She could swallow it into the back of her throat.

"*You* don't," she manages.

Aren's not stupid. He gives her the barest smile before he releases her jaw. "Somehow, I don't believe you."

She doesn't like the way he looks at her like he's keeping something from her, like denying his dick is depriving her. She keeps her glare leveled up at him, even when he fists over himself, stroking slowly over the purple head.

Desire clenches deep in her stomach. Caius laughs that vicious, unhinged sound and spreads her open on two fingers. "Somebody wants your dick in her mouth."

There's no hiding the way her bound talons dig into the dirt. Aren doesn't take his eyes off her, even when he answers Caius. "You sure it isn't you?"

"I had my turn," Caius growls. "Shame some little birds can't be trusted."

A slick thumb teases at her asshole.

Her body lurches, enough that she brushes Aren's cock with her muzzle. He pulls back, tilting his head to watch the tremors run through her body. Pheir shuts her eyes and tries to focus, but that only heightens how Caius teases her ass, so shockingly smooth she hardly believes it's the same brute as before. Her back arches as she tries to keep the ground under her.

"What are you doing?" The words come through the tight grip of her jaw, claws scraping the dirt, but Caius's slick circle doesn't stop.

"You said make sure it's wet." He sneers like the piece of shit he is, but the wiring in her brain struggles between that voice and the touch he's inflicting. "You're pretty fucking soaked now. Don't tell me your ass lubricates, too."

"Don't tell me you've never fucked an avian —" Her jaw snaps shut to bite her whine in half when his thumb presses into her, every reign of control slipping through her fingers.

"You want me to stop?" he asks. He knows she doesn't. Reminds her how much he can see when he swirls through her desire, pumping two fingers deep in her cunt until she groans. He eases his thumb into her ass again, stretching her around it, sloppy with his blood and her wanton desire. "You had so much shit to say before."

He keeps one arm wrapped around her hips, holding her in place. It's only foolishness that has her eyes lifting to Aren, as if he'll help her. As if he'll call off his dog and let her pretend she doesn't want it.

"Don't look at him like that." Caius curls his thumb until her arms threaten to buckle. "He's not gonna fucking save you."

Aren's impassive, watching Pheir like her being taken apart in front of him does nothing to him. The precum leaking from his dick says differently. Aren's grip tightens in the back of her hair. "He asked you a question, Pheir." She tries to think past the lust that threatens to black her out, but Aren asks again. "Do you want him to stop?"

Her clenched teeth press toward Aren's dick, but he isn't scared, dragging his head along her jaw and leaving his scent against the muzzle. All she can do is glare up at him and take it.

"*No*," she answers.

"Good girl."

She wants to tear her teeth into him. Wants to swallow him down and wipe that controlled look from his face. Wants to see how she could make him gasp with the scrape of her teeth or the slow swipe of her tongue. The hand in her hair doesn't loosen. Caius spears both her holes at once. The muzzle muffles her sound.

Aren purrs. "Oh, she likes that."

They talk about her like she isn't there, a captive body for them to fuck into. The desire that swells in her feels like betrayal. Every pump of Caius's fingers is followed by the teasing tap of Aren's dick against her muzzle, and it's only the dark flicker through Aren's eyes that shows he's as caught up as they are. His gaze drags down her body, torn between her deadly glare and Caius's torment between her legs.

Caius's mouth smears against her pussy, and she swears he's smirking. Her mouth opens to start shit again, but every contrary word is lost when Caius pulls his fingers from her cunt and slides them both into her ass.

"Fuck, this would look so good with a plug." He lands a hand against her ass. The stroke of his fingers is slow, like he's watching the way she stretches open, gripping him like she needs it. "Think Lev will make her wear one once she's a pretty little bride?"

Pheir fights every reaction, battling to keep her eyes hard and unyielding, trying to hold onto the fury that heats her veins. Caius is relentless with the hand wrapped under her hips, tapping against her clit until he's smacking.

She scrambles to escape. Neither of the weres allow it, keeping her in place with a hand in her hair, an arm around her waist, knees pinning her ankles to the ground. For all their viciousness, it only drives her hotter, lancing pain bound up with a pleasure she didn't realize the two of them could provide.

She hates them.

She *hates* them.

She *wants* to hate them, but right now, her body pulses with nothing but carnal need.

She's slick and sloppy, reminding all of them exactly how wet she is, the lips of her cunt swollen with arousal. Nothing can be heard over Caius's mouth on her. Even that is barely louder than the whine that tips out of her when he glances teeth against her clit.

Aren tilts her chin up with his fingers. "You want me to take that muzzle off? Stuff my cock in your mouth?"

It jolts through her, deadly and potent next to Caius's assault on her pussy. Her mouth waters at the thought of Aren stretching her lips, filling her and shoving roughly to the back of her throat — the chance to incapacitate him. To make her escape.

Still, pride sits heavy on her tongue, refusing to budge. Aren balances her chin on a single claw. "Beg me."

"Fuck you."

He jerks the scruff of her neck, and she suffocates a needy sound when he yanks her face toward him.

"Beg for it, if you want it."

She wants to spit. Wants to let it drop to the forest floor while she holds his eyes and disrespects him — and a treacherous part of her wants to swallow him down. Show him the clean flat of her tongue to see if it gets his heart racing to know she's willing.

There's only one option. Caius follows Aren's lead, giving Pheir the slowest swipes of his tongue, taunting with his piercings and the torturous pumps of his fingers, just enough to tease the fire in her stomach.

Her voice is little more than a whisper dragged over gravel. "Please."

Aren keeps her head pulled back. "'Please' what?"

She wants to scream. "Please shove your *dick* in my mouth."

Aren's claws caress the skin of her cheek. They linger over the buckles locking the muzzle in place, clicking against metal — and then they drift away. "You can't have it. Not tonight."

A sudden burst of rage burns through her. He had her make a fool of herself for *nothing*. She lunges for him, but it's useless when he steps away, Caius's arm around her hips dragging her back through dead leaves. So fucking predictable. They know all her tells, exactly what will stoke her anger. She screams nonetheless, clawing at the ground to pull herself out of Caius's grip.

Aren drops to his knees, jerking on her bound arms until they're stretched out in front of her, her chest pressed to the ground. She rears back when the mouth on her cunt is replaced by a cock slamming in completely, Aren's hand pinning the back of her neck. A moan rips out of her. Caius keeps her ass up, her breasts scraping the ground with every thrust.

Her sounds are muffled, but there's no mistaking the brutality they hold. Caius's laughter matches every snap of his hips when Aren presses a foot down on the side of her face. They keep her trapped, shoving her muzzle into the dirt. The fingers on her clit know how to play her. They stroke in dexterous patterns Caius shouldn't be capable of, honing her toward her orgasm as Aren's cock leaks onto her face.

Humiliation burns bright in her, heating her cheeks under the vicious thrusts, sweat slipping down her back when the pleasure becomes unbearable.

"She's holding out longer than I thought." Caius slams into her, strain edging into his throat, the filthy sound of where they meet echoing off the trees and into Pheir's ears.

Aren's voice overtakes it all. "Maybe you should try some finesse."

Caius grunts, but there's something cold in Aren's eyes as he watches. Calculating. Seeing. It sends a chill through Pheir...and then Caius pulls out, dragging every inch until she has no choice but to feel it. Such a contrast to before, th furious pace giving way to a slick slide that works in time with his fingers. Every one of her noises can be heard now. When a whimper slips past the vice of her mouth, Aren's eyebrows quirk. "Oh, now we're getting to it."

Caius picks up his pace, spurred on by her sounds. He controls himself, working her clit between the V of his fingers, framing his cock slipping inside her.

She tries to fight, but it's useless when they have her pinned so expertly. Her body begs for release. Caius drips spit down the seam of her ass, slipping over his cock melding into her. They both groan. The cool air against her is bad enough, but then Caius slides a finger into her ass again, setting the pump of his hips and wrist in alternating rhythm.

"Yeah, that's gonna do it." He *laughs*, so confident that it makes her want to curse them both. She can't make any sound, too focused on holding herself together, gripping the ground and fighting not to work her ass back against him. She can't contradict him when she can't trust her mouth, when she's following orders from these fucking bastards. Caius takes his time so languidly that her legs begin to shake.

Every traitorous quiver of her body gives Caius another clue, guiding him further down the path to destroy her. He follows every sign. How can someone so violent and wicked understand anything but sheer brutality? He's putting every tell in her body on display while he decimates her.

Caius pulls out when he feels her clenching. Burying fingers in her cunt, finding her G spot and giving it all his attention as he strokes the pad of his fingers until she feels that swelling feeling. He bears down even more. "That's it..."

It's not the vicious thrusts they both wanted. Maybe that's why the focused pressure undoes her, because the people she hates most are taking her apart in ways worse than death. She digs her talons into the ground, grinding her teeth, but Caius doesn't stop. He shoves her over the edge with a tongue on her clit, her cheek streaked with mud under Aren's foot when a groan splits her lips against the muzzle.

"There she goes!"

The rush of blood in her ears dampens their degrading celebration, crowing when her orgasm squirts over Caius's waiting tongue. His thumb keeps circling her clit until she shrieks and tries to escape, but his claws dig into her hips. She bucks to escape the stimulation. Only then does Aren remove his foot, yanking her hair back to lift her face toward the fading sunlight. His reflective eyes glint when she meets his gaze. "Sloppy little thing, aren't you?"

Shame burns her cheeks, not just from how easily they'd corralled her. Shame at obeying. Shame at trembling. Shame at her want sprayed across Caius's maw.

Even Aren's faux-disappointment brings an impossible surge of arousal between her legs. Caius's clawed hand clamps under her jaw. She struggles against it, but she's trapped on the ground, and their brute force is more than enough to control her. His thick, wet tongue slides across her muzzle, painting the evidence of her desire against it. She has to face it to *smell* it, to live with the proof that she wants everything they're giving her.

He laves lower, down the column of her throat, scraping a threatening flash of fangs against her pulse. By the end, she's filthier than she was when they started, streaked with spit and cum and blood that's only just stopped leaking from Caius's snout.

Caius's fingers meet Aren's in her hair and jerk back to force her to kneel. "Say, 'thank you.'" Caius bares her throat to the precarious scrape of his teeth...but she refuses. His breath grows hot against her ear. It takes all she has not to let her feathers shudder with his broad chest against her back. "Say 'thank you, Caius, for cleaning up the mess I made. Because I'm a filthy fucking whore who can't keep myself clean.'"

Caius doesn't bother waiting for her response. They all know she won't say it, fire burning in her eyes when Aren crouches before them. Next to Caius's unpredictable fury, Aren's calm is just as eerie and no less dangerous. His hand moves between her legs, the pad of one finger circling her clit before his claw enters her.

Barely fucking her, avoiding her walls — but only just. A frightening reminder that she can't fight unless she wants to be impaled. Worse than that, he can feel the slick warmth building from his motions, from the violence, from the shadows of the two of them leaning over her. Only then do the words finally break through the grip of her jaw. "*Thank you.*"

Caius cackles. Aren pulls out of her in a swift movement before Caius hauls her off the ground, slamming her chest into the nearest tree. Bark scrapes her, but she doesn't even hiss in a breath, talons digging into its trunk when Caius presses along her back. "You're only alive because they made me promise not to kill you." His hard cock grinds against her ass. "I wanted to gut you the second we took you down."

"What?" she gasps. "Too chickenshit to go against a fucking rabbit?"

The trunk digs into her cheek when Caius bears down on the back of her head with a snarl. "Don't fucking tempt me."

He knocks her legs apart with his feet, spreading her wider, his dick lingering below her cunt.

"You're fucking *dripping.*" He keeps her neck pinned with one hand, and there's nothing she can do to stop a drop of her arousal slipping down the lips of her pussy. From the frenzied laugh Caius gives, she knows where it lands. She hears him fist over his cock. There's no warning before he sinks inside, her sounds muffled against the tree. He wastes no time slamming into her, snout brushing the back of her ears. "Tell me it's too deep."

She arches back against him. "Fuck you." The hate and vitriol only spur Caius deeper, the sound of fur meeting feathered flesh sickeningly arousing. He finds her clit again like the bastard he is and slams in deeper.

"Tell me."

"*No!*"

"Tell me it's too fucking deep, or I'm gonna make you come again."

Her legs quiver. He could do it; she's not used to this extended fucking, leaving her panting and trembling while the weres show no signs of slowing. "Are you not — fucking *close*?" she grits. It's not a blow to her ego. She doesn't give a fuck about either of them. Doesn't care if they're getting off on this, but Caius shuts down that line of thinking.

"Don't tell me you've never fucked a were like me before." He throws her words back at her, rutting in so deep they both make a strangled sound when he pins her face to the tree. "I get hard, and I stay hard as long as it takes to wear your ass out." He grinds against her. "Now *tell me* it's too fucking deep."

The textured pad of his paw does things to her that it shouldn't, circling until there's nothing but white-hot pleasure and the sound of his thrusts.

"It's too deep," she finally gasps.

His laughter whets her arousal before he lands a slap across her face, and she gnashes her teeth, burying him inside when she slams her hips back. He doesn't pull out. If anything, he angles deeper, her thighs lifted in his paws. It spirals blunt pain deep inside her, the kind that throbs with sick pleasure and twists in her stomach, but Caius isn't done. "Now, tell me to stop."

Sweat slicks her body. Caius knows what he's doing, the impossible line he's drawing in the dirt. Every command he makes grates against her nerves. She has the safeword. She won't say it, refusing to give into another of his demands.

But if she doesn't, it's as close to admitting she wants this. Wants *more*. Wants every depraved thing the two of them will give her.

He lifts her onto the tips of her taloned feet, holding her suspended between him and the rough scrape of the tree. "Tell me to stop, you bratty fucking bitch."

Her talons dig into the trunk, a vicious snarl ripping from her throat. It was Vesta's favorite thing about her, the thing that made

Vesta look at Pheir with love in her eyes. Pheir spits it back at him, smile curling around her pride. "I don't say 'no.'"

There's a pause. A halting drag in the rhythm of his hips. From this angle, she can't see his face. She presses back from the tree.

His grip on her neck isn't tight enough. She lands her talons into his chest until he roars. Her wings beat uselessly, an instinct when she slips out of his grip and sprints toward the trees — until a solid weight collides with her and sends her crashing into the undergrowth.

She's no match for Aren. He pins her on her back, limbs paired with hers, keeping her arching and writhing on the earth. A second set of paws is on her, trapping her wrists above her head as Aren moves back to grip her ankles. Her fight is fruitless, leaving little more than tracks in the dirt, blood dripping across her face from the wound she left in Caius's chest. The grip on her ankles jerks, forcing her eyes to Aren crouched between her knees. There's a glacial look in his eyes, one that threatens to freeze her where she lay. She has to keep fighting, bucking the restraints, striking out wherever she can.

"Do you want to safeword?" Aren asks.

Neither of the weres move, two heads drifting in her vision, watching her amidst the stars starting to dot the sky.

"I told you: I don't say —"

"You can."

Her body is weak. Never recovered from the fight, from losing the beacon of her Alpha, from being stripped away from the only remaining members of her pack. She's exhausted and mindless and reckless, but heat still digs like a spur in her stomach.

"No," she snaps venom on her tongue. "I don't want to *tap out.*"

There's nowhere to look but Aren's piercing gaze, prodding under her skin and watching every tremor of her want. He doesn't call it out. Instead, he pins her legs open, lowering his mouth to the aching lips of her pussy. The textured flat of his tongue swipes between her legs, stroking over the sore swell of her clit until she's squirming against more than their hold on her.

It takes no time for him to bring her to the brink again, swirling that tongue he uses so sparingly. It breaks her mind, trying to hold two opposing thoughts at once — how the enemy she's battled more times than she can count has learned to play her body, tuning her up until she's a tense wire he can snap with the flick of his fingers. All that time spent learning each other's weaknesses is backfiring on her now.

"So pretty," he murmurs against her cunt. She hates it. Hates the humiliating way it binds in her stomach, her chest, making her squirm more than anything else they've done to her.

"Stop," she groans.

He melds his tongue against her ass until she shudders. She knows it's coming: another avalanche of an orgasm, an infuriating release she can't keep herself back from. Her thighs tremble where he holds them open, working the pad of his thumb against her clit. "But you're such a pretty little bird when you can't help coming for me."

"Mercy."

Aren pulls back. Even Caius loosens his hold, though not enough for her to flee. She keeps her eyes on Aren, forcing her gaze to meet his. "Just keep fucking me," she growls. "And stop saying that — shit."

He can't hide the surprise on his face, but a dark look settles over him, claws digging into her calf when he jerks her closer. "You want it filthy, then?" He leaves marks on her thighs, and she hisses when he bends her in half, burying his mouth against her ass. "Want me fucking your ass while he takes your cunt again? Is that what you want?"

She doesn't answer. Doesn't have to, because Aren makes a mess of her, sucking against her asshole and circling the rim before he flattens his tongue and rolls against her. She cries out every hateful thing she can think of. Only then does Aren lean back and tap his dick against her folds, so slippery he almost slots inside.

A hiss darts between his fangs, stretching her ass around the tip of his head once — twice — three times before he pulls back. "We fuck what's ours."

Her brows knit above the muzzle when Caius tightens his grip around her wrists. Aren traps her ankles beneath his knees, fisting over his cock, dragging it up between her folds before he aims at her stomach.

"And you belong to the Timbers now."

That's when she realizes — but it's too late, her body fighting their grips as Aren marks her. Piss streams onto her stomach, dampening her feathers in a humiliating display. Caius follows, both weres tightening their paws around her until all their scents mix on her skin and she reeks of them.

"Fuck you! *Fuck you!*" She screeches, scrabbling with her talons, but they do little more than leave surface wounds.

Aren isn't disturbed. She's tired of him: his calculating eyes, his calm demeanor that belies his power. Even when he lets those instincts take over, he's restrained, no sound except for the low snarl of his voice. "There won't be a single person who doesn't know who owns you now."

Worse than the disgraceful scent is how wet she still is for them, slick with spit and blood and desire until it leaks down the seam of her ass. It should make her furious. Should make her fight. But her mind is too shredded to think of anything but the want to be battered and used, to cross that final stretch and let exhaustion wipe all her thoughts so she can regain her strength.

Aren coats his cock in her desire, fisting down his length before he works three fingers slowly into her ass.

"Just fucking do it," she pants. He doesn't move faster, sinking an inch deeper with every thrust. She can't do anything but shudder until his palm is flat against her.

Aren and Caius's eyes meet over her. Before she can think, Aren pulls her up and pins her back to his chest. They fall to the ground, him holding her hands above her head while Caius slots his hips between her legs. Caius's grip on her ankles pushes them near her shoulders to spread her wider.

It's so slick, Aren almost sinks inside when he guides his cock against her ass from below. He goes slow, forcing her to feel the stretch of the small spines halfway down his length, edging out her whine when he seats himself completely. She can't make any noise now, not when Caius's face is right above her. Tracking every sound, every flutter of eyelashes, every tension in her legs when she sucks in a breath. She forces a glare up at him. He looks like he wants to rip out her throat at the same moment he slots inside her.

Like he's meant to be there. Like it's *his*.

Pheir tries to scratch at him with her feet, but he gets thick fingers against her clit, and her body seizes. An ache builds every time their cocks saw into her, infuriating pleasure that she can't see past, dragging against her walls as one buries deep and the other draws out. They move in sync, like they've done this before. Like they were prepared for this. For *her*. It's as bloody and brutal and exhilarating as every time she's met them in battle, crushed between both their heaving chests and pushing her body to its limits.

The threat of one of them killing the other hangs over them.

Her ruthless release rolls over her, bearing down when Aren and Caius's rhythm threatens to split her in two. When they pull their hips, keeping her spread open, circling her clit like a punishment. Caius's face hovers before her. "I don't give a fuck what Lev does after this." He thrusts deeper and doesn't pull out, stirring his hips inside until she curses him. "This pussy is *mine*."

They grind into her so impossibly deep, Aren's spikes dragging against her entrance and her walls until her eyes slip back. *It's none of yours*, she wants to scream, but the words hold such little weight when they know how she feels clamping around them. How wet she was as soon as they caught her. How she can barely pretend she doesn't want it anymore.

Caius picks up speed, clamping his paws tighter around her ankles when he snaps his hips into her. Light glints off the vicious tips of his fangs, close enough to kiss. The thought disgusts her, but she can't work up the strength to snap. Can't even open her mouth, because all that spills out are moans. Caius catches them in his teeth, grinning maliciously, like he's found his next meal. "I'm gonna fucking breed you like the bitch you are."

Doesn't matter that it's not possible, that their anatomy isn't compatible, the words are enough to make her groan. Her wings spread wide, reaching for anything but the two of them. Caius doesn't slow his assault, driving down into her and never slowing the ferocious circle of his fingers.

He doesn't stop until she screams. Until she comes around him, clenching and milking for all he's worth. He stuffs her as full of his seed as he promised. She's a sweaty, exhausted mess, covered in so much filth she isn't sure she'll ever get clean...and the musk they'd marked her with still drifts to her nose, pungent and unfamiliar.

It takes too long to recover, trapped between their chests, all three of them panting. The moment she realizes how she's sprawled between them, she stiffens — and so do they. Caius pushes off of her, back to his feet while she's still fighting to make her limbs work. He crouches between her legs to watch his cum drip out of her. "I don't think she's running anywhere."

Pheir can't even bare her teeth, managing little more than a glance in Caius's direction. Aren shifts beneath her, trying to set her upright. Her legs threaten to collapse with her weight on them. He catches her under her arms, and she swipes weakly at him, barely grazing his fur.

It doesn't deter him. He lifts her — not completely, and that's one small gift to her pride — his paws under her arms as he carries her to the nearby lake's edge. There's no use trying to stand. It'll humiliate her, wobbling legs and heavy breaths while the two of them watch cum leak down her thighs.

Something knocks against her back. It's only then she realizes Aren hasn't come since this started. That in all their fighting and fucking, he's still hard.

"This was your plan, wasn't it?" she slurs as Aren deposits her in knee-deep water. "Fuck me until I'm too weak to fight back?" She makes the mistake of meeting his eyes. She's a hopeless mess crouched on the ground while he towers above her, barely affected.

He's still prying with his gaze, nose twitching at the scent of her covered in a mixture of all of them. His expression isn't hardened, and that turns her stomach in completely new ways.

"It's something we discussed." His voice is low and raw. Water laps against her shoulders when she turns her back to him, feathers standing on end until she hears the smaller waves of his steps receding to shore.

Of course this was their plan. Why else would they have fucked in the middle of transporting a prisoner? Lev had a hand in this. She predicted what Pheir would do, and Pheir fell for it.

Her teeth grit at how easy it'd been, how well the people she hates most have come to read her. How they can predict exactly how she'll react. How she wasn't faking any of her arousal.

All she can do is sink into the cool waves, dampening her feathers and hissing as water soaks the scratches littering her body. It's a fresh ache to focus on, one that doesn't dig pins of heat into her the way being fucked by Aren and Caius does. Her body still pulses from being stretched and filled and sated. This new ache reminds her what she has to do for Vesta, the vengeance Pheir has to take before she's completely bound to Lev and her pack.

Pheir won't escape her captors through the lake. In the air, she's deadly, but here...

She hazards a glance over her shoulder. On the shoreline, both weres watch her. She can feel Caius's hate, nearly boiling the water around her as their eyes meet. Hers is just as lethal. Wild, uncomplicated, a vow they have for each other. Either she kills him, or she'll die trying. There's some small comfort in that.

It's Aren's look that's more disturbing. Never revealing anything, too locked and level for her to know where his mind is at. Caius is feral, but Aren was always the more formidable opponent: hard to read, hard to predict, calculating every outcome. He watches her with that same focus, like he's trying to uncover some secret she's buried beneath her skin.

There is no secret. The only thing she clings to is revenge.

Pheir holds their gazes as she scrubs the marking on her stomach. Then she turns her back to them, trying to put the mingled scent of the three of them out of her mind.

VICIOUS
DEVOTION

PROLOGUE

Pheir

12 hours before Vesta's death

There's nothing like the night before battle.

Tension. Frenzy. Anticipation. It ricochets under Pheir's violet skin as she stretches her wings on the balcony. Beneath her, the Vestal camp thrums with activity, people loading boats with supplies under the dense foliage. Treehouses and nests dot the canopy of leaves that spread out before Pheir, lamplight glowing in the windows as far as the eye can see.

It's a utopia. Fruit blooms luscious and abundant, weighing down the boughs within Pheir's reach. Floorboards gleam beneath her feet, slick from midafternoon showers. A warm breeze flutters in from the coast and through her feathers.

It's paradise. Their Alpha, Vesta, made it this way. She built this bliss from the ground up, and soon, every corner of the Break will be as perfect as this.

For years, no one suspected a fringe pack inhabited this abandoned island off the coast. No one knew the Vestals lingered outside of the Conclave's control...but in a few hours, the Conclave will know how badly they've underestimated the Vestals.

Tomorrow, all of the Break will see how many people believe in Vesta's mission. How many members she's recruited in the past few years. The Vestals offer power to packs who never had any, who grew tired of living under the corrupt governance of the Conclave. When the Conclave turned their back on the smaller packs who needed them most, Vesta swooped in with open arms to save them.

Once the Vestals overthrow the Conclave, the packs in the Break will kneel to their new leader. To Vesta.

"Pheir?" Thalea hovers in the doorway, fingers curling around the frame. Her branches scrape hesitantly against the wood. "Can I talk to you?"

Pheir leans back against the balcony railing, body tingling with anticipation. "Too excited to sit still?"

Thalea shuffles on the threshold, pushing the vines of her hair behind her ear. The dryad has been tentative for as long as Pheir has known her. Maybe that's why Pheir's developed a soft spot for her — that, or the fact that Thalea is Vesta's mate. Since Pheir's dedicated her life to safeguarding Vesta, it makes sense that Pheir protects Thalea, too.

Thalea wrings her hands as she steps out onto the balcony. "Have you heard what the scouts are saying? The Conclave's numbers have tripled. Rhaiden said —"

Pheir's eyes roll. "Rhaiden's always trying to start shit. Don't worry about the numbers; Vesta doesn't need a huge pack fighting for her. Not when we're devoted. Not when we're *right*. Besides..." Pheir's smile widens, talons digging into the railing as she leans closer to Thalea. "It's thrilling, isn't it? All the packs the Conclave has fighting for them, and they're still gonna lose to us."

The fire from Pheir's eyes doesn't catch in Thalea's. Instead, Thalea averts her gaze, following the people that move below them like ants. Soldiers in Vesta's noble cause. Pheir is so proud, she almost doesn't hear Thalea whisper.

"I don't feel thrilled. I feel...scared. Scared for those people. Scared for Rhaiden." Thalea's eyes lift to Pheir again. The dryad's lip quivers. "Scared for you."

A laugh bubbles out of Pheir, her head tilting back to catch the golden rays of sun. "The only people you should be scared for are the Conclave, and you shouldn't waste any sympathy for them." With an elbow, Pheir nudges Thalea. "It's like one of your story books. Vesta is a hero that fate delivered to us. Nothing can stop her power."

"The power of *love*," Thalea corrects weakly, rubbing her arm. "That's what the books say. But —"

"Come on." Pheir pushes off the railing and backs toward the doorway. "Vesta will be back soon. Then the party *really* starts."

For a long moment, Thalea lingers on the balcony, lips pulled into a thin line. Eventually, she ducks her head and follows. Pheir brims with excitement as they make their way back into the house. Maps and trinkets cover the dining room table, a makeshift war room Vesta and her inner council use to plan their attack. Pheir lifts one of the faceless figurines by its rabbit ears.

Energy thrums through Pheir. War can't come quickly enough. In a few hours, the Vestals will have their chance to make things as they should be. To get revenge on the Conclave and everyone else who wronged Vesta. With Pheir's talons, she slices the wooden figure to pieces and grinds it into the ground beneath her foot.

A sharp voice prickles across her nerves. "I was using that."

Pheir's gaze cuts sharply to the lionfish siren standing behind the kitchen counter. Irritatingly, the siren resembles Pheir — a mostly-human woman covered in scales and fins where Pheir has feathers and wings. That's the only thing Pheir has in common with Rhaiden.

Vesta's beta and strategist, Rhaiden is the only person with cunning to rival Vesta. A cunning that makes Rhaiden the least-loyal soldier, if you ask Pheir.

"Can't fight without your props?" Pheir asks petulantly. She knocks another figure aside as her brow hikes, seeking a reaction. "Some of us don't need them to win."

Rhaiden is undisturbed. Annoying bitch: the venomous spines lining her body don't even quiver. "You'll be grateful for those props tomorrow." Wiping her hands on a dish towel, Rhaiden nudges two bowls of stew on the counter. "Eat."

Jaw pulling tight, Pheir's talons tick against the tabletop. "Not hungry."

This time, Rhaiden's spires give the barest twitch. A righteous sneer settles on Pheir's lips. Thalea cuts in, voice weary. "Please don't fight." She sidles up to the counter, patting the seat beside her and turning her big eyes on Pheir. "For me?"

Pheir tenses, gaze locking on Thalea's hand. Thalea worries her teeth into her lip, but she doesn't retract the offer. If Vesta saw this rare display of softness, she'd correct them. *Don't waste your power on tenderness.* But Vesta isn't here...

Pheir's spine straightens. It doesn't matter; she knows what Vesta would want her to do. Pheir's arms fold across her chest. Thalea wilts before she turns back to the soup. Through it all, Rhaiden keeps her expression schooled, as cold as the dark depths of the sea. "You need the energy."

"I'll make my own food."

Rhaiden grits her teeth. "Pheir —"

"*You* eat it," she spits.

Rhaiden's jaw clamps shut. Thalea blinks between them. For a moment, Pheir's heart pounds, as if Rhaiden might actually do it — show Pheir she's overly suspicious, prove Rhaiden hasn't been poisoning them for weeks...

Until Vesta arrives.

Everything about the phoenix is aflame. Rainbow fire leaks from Vesta's mouth, cascading through her feathers and lighting the iridescent strands of her hair. Her opalescent body glows as she lands on the balcony, wings spread like a holy mural.

Breath catches in Pheir's chest. The two of them could be sisters. Sometimes, Pheir pretends they are. They look similar enough — except Pheir's dark purple feathers reflect light like an oil slick, and Vesta is the spark that ignites her.

Pheir's fists clench in anticipation as she rushes to greet Vesta. "Did you get them? What did they say?"

It's a silly question when Pheir knows no one can resist Vesta, but she asks it to hear Vesta's achievement. The Alpha holds up her hand for patience, but she doesn't make Pheir wait long. With a grin, Vesta puffs out her chest and speaks loud enough for all of them to hear. "The Broadleafs will be at the battle tomorrow."

Pheir crows in excitement.

Rhaiden's voice dampens everything, like water thrown on a fire. "What did you promise them?"

Vesta waves off Rhaiden's worry. It's through years of practice that Pheir clocks the irritation in Vesta's tone. "We've had an ongoing agreement. The Broadleafs want to strengthen their pack, and I showed them a way to do that."

It's explanation enough for Pheir, but Rhaiden can't leave well enough alone. "How?" she questions pointedly.

Vesta glides into the kitchen, brushing back the vines of Thalea's hair. The dryad swallows thickly before she beams as if Vesta is the sun in the sky. Somehow, the light doesn't reach Thalea's eyes.

"What's important is they support me," Vesta assures them. "Support *us*. The Broadleafs understand our mission, and all we can do is rely on the kindness of strangers."

"What does that even mean?" Rhaiden mutters. She dumps the remaining stew down the drain, bracing her hands on the counter before she lifts her head. "Even with the Broadleafs, we don't have enough people to take on the Conclave. We should wait to strike —"

"It has to be now!" Vesta snaps, eyes whipping back over her shoulder. For a moment, she looks different. Tired. Faded, as if the color drains from her wings. Just as quickly, her shoulders pull back, warmth radiating from her body once more. "Now is the time. We're ready." Her tone leaves no room for argument as she turns toward the balcony. "Pheir? Join me."

It's not a question. Pheir brims with satisfaction, turning her back on Rhaiden's scowl and Thalea's wary smile. Pheir steps outside to take her place next to Vesta as the encampment hums below.

This is where Pheir belongs. No matter who Vesta's beta or mate is, Pheir is the one who understands her. The one who keeps sight of Vesta's vision when the others get clouded with doubt. Pheir believes in what they're doing. Pheir *knows*.

Vesta takes a deep breath as her wings spread behind her. "It's finally happening, kid. I always knew it would. We're gonna show the Break how little the Conclave cares for the people under its control." Vesta's face is awash in the fading sunlight. Her breath sparks with fire as the words pour out of her, eyes growing wild. "They didn't give a *shit* when I was thrown out. And they didn't bat an eye when you were abandoned."

The reminder should sting Pheir, but Vesta soothes it over. Without looking, she finds the raised scar on Pheir's wrist, the "V" that aligns perfectly with two of Vesta's talons. Vesta brushes over the mark, admiring it with softness that makes Pheir's chest flutter.

"You were the first person who believed in what I'm doing, Pheir. The first person who gave themself over to me, who was loyal all this time." Vesta trails her hand up over Pheir's heart, pressing her palm against it to feel it beat. "You'll stand by me forever, won't you?"

The words jump into Pheir's mouth. She doesn't need to think; the answer is forever the same. "Always."

A soft smile crosses Vesta's lips. "I know you will."

"Not like Lev," Pheir adds, smile stretching hopefully. Bashing that bunny bitch is the best way to connect with Vesta, to commiserate over their shared hatred, to remind Vesta of the people who've failed her. Not Pheir, though. Pheir would never leave. Pheir would never betray her.

It was the right thing to say. Vesta's teeth seem to sharpen against each other when she smiles. "No: you're not like Leverette at all."

Praise pulses in Pheir's veins. She's barely met Lev, but she doesn't need to, not when Vesta's painted a vivid portrait for Pheir to loathe. Hating Lev brings the two of them closer, uniting them in their mission. One day, Pheir will sink her teeth into Lev's throat. It makes her mouth water.

But that's a distraction from their true goal. Vesta reminds her when she squeezes Pheir's wrist. "We're going to change the Break forever, you and me." The sun dips below the horizon, its golden glow a meek competition to Vesta's flames. She lowers her voice for Pheir to hear. "Tomorrow, we'll get the justice we deserve."

ONE

Caius

PRESENT
3 days after Vesta's death

"If you want me quiet, you're gonna have to rip my throat out."

Pheir's words are muffled by the ground pressed against her cheek. Caius bears his foot down between her shoulder blades when he leans down toward her. "Keep it up, and I will."

In the last two years, he's learned that nothing deters Pheir. To her, threats might as well be pleasantries. Hell, *better* than pleasantries; at least threats give her somewhere to direct her anger.

Or maybe she's aggravating just to be aggravating. Who the fuck knows? Caius can't begin to imagine how her birdbrain works.

It's been a few days since her Vestal pack was decimated in their attempt to overthrow the Conclave. Since the moment Pheir was captured — and the moment she was born, Caius would wager — she's been insufferable. The two of them must be the same age, but she lashes out at him like she's feral. Despite the fact that Aren and Caius clipped her feathers and talons days ago, her wings keep beating as she scrabbles to break free from her restraints. When she shrieks, it echoes across the open field and into the surrounding forest.

Aren will hear her. The thought raises the hackles on Caius's neck. Perfect fucking Aren. Never bothered. Always composed. Caius can picture Aren now, flicking those werelynx ears with disapproval as he speaks without a hint of emotion.

Cut Pheir some slack. She lost nearly everyone she knows. Her old pack bonds are trying to stitch together. Being a hostage can't be easy — especially one arranged to wed the enemy Alpha.

That's the real problem. Tension knots Caius's shoulders as he envisions his Alpha, Lev, standing in front of Pheir and swearing love and loyalty to the harpy hellbent on spilling Lev's blood. It's infuriating and exhausting. More than that, it's setting Caius off in ways that it shouldn't.

He blames it on duty. Even if he hasn't been fully accepted into the Timber pack, he knows his place as a combatant. His job is to protect his Alpha and strike before the enemy gets a chance. That duty makes sense. It's something he's good at. Something that was carved into his bones long before he joined the Timbers.

But how can he protect Lev when her biggest threat is going to be closer to her than Caius has been able to get?

"Your boyfriend's not gonna be happy when he gets back." Pheir's squirming voice cuts through Caius's thoughts as she searches for a place to plant her feet. Vicious little bitch. Her feathers shake loose, scattering the ground in oil-slick colors. "Aren's gonna put you back in your fucking place, werewolverine *pup*."

Caius's teeth grit. *Pheir's* the one making all of this impossible. As if the Timbers didn't have enough to deal with before the hurricane of Pheir touched down in their lives. Caius doesn't know how she's found exactly how to push his buttons, but it leaves him on edge and more aware of the gap between him and the rest of the pack. It makes him feel like he did the first day he arrived here, emotions spiking out of control.

Digging his heel into the violet of her skin, Caius leans down to grip her mauve hair and snarl into her ear. "Count your lucky stars you're still in one piece."

Across the field of crops, the tree line is empty. Aren hasn't reemerged with the rest of the pack returning from the battle the Vestals instigated. Caius's nose twitches — no scent of them, either. There's still time before they arrive. His fingers flex in Pheir's hair. His hand could slip, claws landing across Pheir's throat and letting her bleed out before anyone returns. No one could blame him. She's practically begging for someone to kill her. Idly, Caius clicks the claws of his other hand against each other.

Would it be any surprise if she got loose from her chains, and Caius had to defend himself?

A familiar whiff hits Caius's nose as two scents rise above the rest — rain after a drought mingling with dark, red cherries. Despite himself, the band around his chest loosens.

Aren and Lev are back.

A tawny gray figure melts through the tree line, fur nearly white as winter approaches. Even from this distance, Lev's features are sharp for a wererabbit, long ears erect to give a semblance of height as the pack follows behind her.

The pack is made up of bipedal werecreatures, people covered in fur and scales and feathers with snouts and paws to match. There's no mistaking the intelligence in their eyes, like shifters stuck mid-transformation.

The Timbers fill the compound with life that makes Caius more uneasy than any bloody battlefield. He shifts awkwardly above Pheir's prone form as the pack approaches, leaning against each other and chattering. The pack members don't bristle when one of the others approaches from behind. They wrap their arms around each other's' shoulders, supporting someone else's weight with ease. Despite their injuries, they look relieved to be together.

Of course they are. Caius's fingers flex. None of them worry about breaking everything they touch because they don't know how to curl their hands into anything but fists.

To busy himself, Caius bends to strap a muzzle around Pheir's mouth, knees creaking in the cold. He narrowly avoids her teeth, but for once, he's relieved. The link inside him that's been straining to reunite with his pack is finally soothed.

Battle— and journey-worn, the Timbers are exhausted, their deepest wounds still healing. Werecreatures may have heightened senses, strength, and speed, but regenerative healing takes time against supernatural injuries.

Lev got the worst of it in battle. *As I should*, she insisted. *Sometimes the Alpha suffers for the good of the pack.* With a twinge of a smile, Caius shakes his head. It's only amusing because Lev survived. He doesn't want to look into the black hole of how he'd cope if she hadn't. Truth be told, he wouldn't be coping at all.

A white-tailed deer stumbles beside Lev, his small rack of adult antlers beginning to shed velvet. This deer is a newer member of the pack. Caius hasn't bothered to learn his name. D-something. It doesn't matter: Caius's concern is protecting his Alpha. He doesn't need to get friendly with anyone else to do that.

Still, Lev hoists the weredeer's arm over her shoulder, wincing when he hits the wound still pink across her neck and chest. Caius starts to move toward her, but when her eyes find him, a smile streaks across her face as if her pain's forgotten. "You look tired."

The ember in Caius's stomach flares to life again. "'I've been babysitting your *bride*." He toes Pheir's writhing body as Lev hands the deer off to a passing grizzly bear. Pheir slams her head into Caius's shin.

Lev tosses the curly white hair of her fauxhawk from her eyes, watching Pheir mildly. "Hasn't lost any of her spunk, I see."

Caius rubs his leg with his other heel. "Not an ounce."

The pack files past them, keeping their distance from the rabid harpy on the ground — or maybe keeping their distance from Caius. A few pack members look concerned. Others look bored. Some look ready to gut Pheir, and Caius can't disagree with that.

He inclines his head toward Lev. "About your bride..."

Lev turns the honey brown pools of her eyes up, as if Caius has all her attention. Being in her presence warms him. Her gaze settles on his mouth. The corner of his lip pulls up as he leans closer —

Then Aren comes to a halt beside her. Caius's spine straightens instinctually. Aren's whiskers twitch when he glances at Caius — then down to Pheir.

"You couldn't keep her upright?" Aren asks.

Caius clenches his jaw, pulling Pheir upright by her elbows. Of course Lev's perfect beta shows up to criticize. When Caius gets Pheir on her knees, she lunges for Aren, and Caius barely has time to stop her before he lifts his brows haughtily.

That's why she's not upright.

Pheir's been like this since Aren and Caius returned with her ahead of the rest of the pack. When she's not fighting, she's threatening. When she's not threatening, she's screaming. Sometimes, she manages all three at once. It would be impressive if it weren't so goddamn annoying.

Lev glances over the three of them, nose twitching before her eyes narrow.

Caius's body runs cold. *Fuck.* He'd almost forgotten what happened between Aren, Pheir, and him after the battle. Caius scrubbed himself raw in the days after, but clearly, the scent of their detour hasn't faded enough.

How about we see how far you can get before we hunt you down and fuck you into the dirt?

The memory of Aren's words to Pheir heats the pit of Caius's stomach. Something primal digs into his gut and squeezes at the image of Pheir on her back, covered in mud and blood and cum as she grit her teeth and begged for more. No amount of hate was enough to keep the three of them from giving into their instincts on the journey here.

Lev's tone is indecipherable now. "You marked her?"

It twinges in Caius's chest. The marking was worse than the sex. It was too much like claiming, possessing, making Pheir one of them. In the moment, the thought of her covered in their scent made his dick hard.

Goddamn, it still does...

It's instinctual, he reminds himself. *It's a testament to your nature, nothing more.* The fact that Pheir was the target is irrelevant. Caius is loyal to Lev, despite the fact that they're...nothing. Nothing he can put words to. Nothing that encompasses the devotion he'd give her if she'd only ask...but she never does.

Aren opens his mouth to answer Lev, but Caius darts in before Aren makes him look worse than he already does. "Pheir's here to become a Timber, isn't she? Might as well get started."

Caius lifts his chin, too proud to admit that embarrassment sears up his throat. There's a quirk in Lev's brow, but it's forgotten when one of the pack members waves her over. A crowd is gathering around the campfire beside the main lodge. Children dart between legs as others embrace, the oldest and youngest members reunited with the rest of the pack. All thirty-some Timbers settle into the circle of benches and seats as the sinking sun darkens the water of the lake.

As Lev moves away, Caius hoists Pheir to her feet. Aren extends a hand. "I can take her —"

"I don't need your help," Caius grunts as Pheir drags her talons through the dirt. Aren lingers another moment. When Caius doesn't so much as glance at him, Aren moves to his post on the other side of the group.

Good. Why would Caius show Aren any weakness? It'd be one more advantage the lynx has over him. One more reason Lev shouldn't trust Caius. One more reason Caius doesn't belong with the two of them.

When Lev approaches the front of the group, a part of Caius stills. Firelight flickers across her face, shrouded in the power she truly holds. Her ears straighten until they're sharp as spears. That authority stirs a longing in Caius to be near her. Their moment before wasn't enough. The pack's return has him shifting weight on his feet, antsy with Pheir struggling in her restraints and Aren watching over them...

Lev finds Caius across the crowd, holding his gaze as she sucks air in through her nose. *Breathe*, she reminds him with her motions. *Relax.*

Begrudgingly, he does.

It's confounding how well she knows him after a few years. Cool air settles into his lungs, lingering as they both hold their breath until she exhales slowly. He follows her lead, and the tightness across his chest loosens. His feet settle firmly on the ground. Lev must see the harsh line of his shoulders fall, because she smiles. His tension eases further.

How does she manage the duality? Standing before the pack she leads, and still, finding a moment for him. She's strength and sentimentality, control and kindness, discipline and delicacy. His feelings for her go deeper than pack dynamics, deeper than a duty to keep his Alpha safe. It's...

His mind blanks out the word, one he's heard in passing or between the pages of secondhand stories. Lev shines a light on him that helps lift the heavy weight of his body. He's not the only one disarmed by her. Other packs laughed when Lev took over the Timbers years ago, the youngest Alpha in the Break in years. Caius heard the stories after — how the Conclave sneered down their noses at her. *A little rabbit? How's prey supposed to lead a swarm of second-rate predators?*

But Lev's pack didn't crumble under the Vestal's reign of terror. The Timbers grew stronger until the Conclave couldn't ignore their importance any longer. Now, Lev has a seat among the other Conclave members. She's finally getting the respect she deserves.

That acknowledgement ripples through the pack now, Timbers perking to listen to Lev speak. Despite her exhaustion, she doesn't show it. She's stoic, certain, and intent when she rises onto the boulder at the center of the group. Her voice is a comfort as she chuckles.

"Is anyone else fucking tired?"

Curses and shouts of affirmation rise, weary smiles tugging across the group's faces. Lev presses the heel of her palm to her eye and rubs at a headache.

"I don't think anyone's gonna have trouble sleeping tonight, even if Marius starts hissing from the trees again." Laughter spreads as a hoary bat on the back row flashes their fangs before the group shushes themselves. "It's been a long few months," Lev acknowledges. "Longer still since we started warning the Conclave of what was happening. But it's finally — *finally* time to put the Vestal uprising behind us."

A chorus of cheers spread. It's been a long few *years* since the Vestals started stirring trouble, flying overhead or lingering at the edges of territories to make people uneasy. When the Timbers backed them down, the Vestals would slip out of sight and let things settle before they'd make their presence known again.

Not that the Conclave cared. They didn't hear the Timbers' concerns until the last few months, when the governing body started to take notice of the Vestals gaining power as they recruited and destroyed smaller packs. Only then did the Conclave act.

How fucking proactive.

When Lev's expression settles, all jostling in the group goes quiet. Her voice is heavier than before. "The battle was costly. Every Timber walked away from the fight, but some packs weren't so lucky."

Her eyes soften toward a corner of the seats isolated from the rest of the pack. There are a few people that Caius doesn't recognize, shoulders slumped as they listen to Lev's speech. These people don't cling close together like the rest of the Timbers. Instead, they look dazed and confused, brought out of their numbness by Lev's voice.

"We'll be hosting a few people from neighboring territories as they get back on their feet. Willow will ensure you all have what you need to introduce you to our way of life." Lev's smile is strained but earnest. "If the Timbers are the right fit, we'll have a place for you here. We'll never replace your fallen pack, but we will find a new place for you to call home."

The strangers nod. Lev doesn't keep them under the spotlight of attention. Instead, she turns back to the group at large.

"The packs that fought alongside the Conclave aren't the only ones we lost. All the packs that Vesta poached were wiped out. The Break is still recovering, and it will be for some time. This battle was the *last* of Vesta's destruction, not the first —"

A cold voice rises from the crowd, sharp and deadly and aimed at Pheir. "Then why is *she* here?"

TWO

Caius

The speaker is someone else Caius doesn't recognize, an arctic enfield that must be new. He looks like a white werefox, save for the eagle feathers across his wings and mingling with the fur of his tail. His fists are clenched under the boxing wraps that cinch around his wrists, like he's ready for a fight.

All eyes turn back to Lev. This newcomer isn't the only one wondering why Pheir's still alive. Hell, Caius would love to finish the job himself. Still, his hackles lift at the accusation in the enfield's tone.

Lev doesn't avoid the question. Instead, she turns to the rest of the group. "Who else is wondering why Pheir is here?"

Pheir jostles on the ground, voice muffled by her muzzle. A smattering of hands rises from the pack.

"I figured as much." Lev's mouth twists before she continues. "The Conclave made a decision to spare the remaining Vestals. We're giving them a chance to rehabilitate and change their lives.

As one of the strongest packs, I agreed for the Timbers to integrate one of them among us."

It's not the first time the Timbers present at the battle have heard this, but those who were left behind whisper as their eyes blow wide

"You're a member of the Conclave, right?" Lev's sister, June, lifts her brows as she speaks. Compared to Lev, June's features are rounder and darker. June never hesitates to ask hard questions of Lev. Caius isn't sure if he hates or admires it. "Couldn't you tell them to fuck off?"

Agreement ripples through the group. Lev's mouth twitches. Caius's lips pull back, prepared to shut down any dissenters, but Lev speaks before he can.

"I *am* a newer member, but I only have as much say as any of the other fifteen." Her jaw tightens as animosity flicks across her face. "The five Regents have the final vote." She shakes the irritation away, focused on the pack as her voice softens. "Regardless, I want to speak with each of you. Some of this is out of our control, but I don't take the decision to keep Pheir here lightly. I want to address your concerns and hear your perspectives. I hope you'll hear mine as well."

Murmurs of acceptance spread through the pack. That's all it takes to assuage them — the assurance that Lev has weighed the outcomes and intends to discuss them. The pack has followed Lev through difficulties before. They know she's a woman of her word. Even a modicum of tension drains from Caius's body.

The same can't be said for the enfield. As the rest of the pack settles, he doesn't look away from Pheir, venom seeping across his expression. "It wouldn't be our fault if there was an accident. If she tried to escape. If she disappeared..."

Pheir snaps her teeth in retaliation. There's a chilling resolution to the enfield's tone, like a scavenger circling a carcass. That's not what gets to Caius, though; it's this enfield's blatant insubordination to Lev. That's one thing Caius won't stand for. He moves toward the path between seats, bristling as he bares his teeth —

"What's your name?" Lev's voice brings Caius to a halt. The pack glances between Lev and the enfield, but Aren's all-seeing eyes flick to Caius.

Of course Aren noticed the disruption. Of course he'd never lose his cool like this, even when Lev's being blatantly disrespected. Criticism burns up Caius's neck as he takes a step back.

This is why Lev always worries about you.

The enfield notices nothing, lips pursed before he drops his answer in the chilly air. "Singer."

"You were a member of the Alpine pack, weren't you? Before the Vestals got to them?" Naturally, Lev recognizes him. The Break isn't overly large; outside of the small pockets of insulated communities, most people have heard of each other.

Singer's eyes narrow, jaw clamped before he rations out the words he wants to use. "Not all of us were so easily swayed."

The words leave Caius feeling chapped and raw. *He's* easily swayed. He can't control himself. He can't school his emotions. Shame ignites at the escalation he'd nearly caused — the fight he *always* nearly starts.

His jaw thuds with an old ache. *It hurts because it's a lesson.* The memory raps against his skull like his father's knuckles. *Disrespect is worse than death. It's letting them kill you while you're still alive.*

Lev's voice cuts through the drain of Caius's memories. "The Break lost a lot of people to Vesta's extreme views. Joining Vesta was not a sign of weakness —"

Singer's laughter rises without any humor as he sneers. "Anyone who aligned with Vesta is pathetic."

"Like your brother?" Lev's words land like a strike across Singer's face. His mouth snaps shut. Despite Lev's pained look, she continues. "Like the Brine and Hillock packs? Like the packs we called friends and neighbors, people we never expected to fight against us? They all joined Vesta's crusade."

It's a reminder of how much was lost to the Vestal skirmish outside of the battle. Connections throughout the Break are on thin ice after neighbors turned against neighbors, packs splitting to join Vesta's crusade. If your family could cast you aside for power, how can you trust anyone?

Caius understands that more than most.

"We don't know how Vesta managed to infiltrate so many packs," Lev continues. "Packs we would have trusted with our lives a few months ago. We don't know the promises Vesta made or how she attracted so many people in such a short amount of time. We only have a sense of her end goal, and that's another reason to keep the remaining Vestals alive — to discern her purpose. To understand her appeal. To prevent something like this from happening again."

The rest of the group is silent, heads bowed in remembrance. Pheir takes the opportunity to jerk at her chains. Caius tightens his grip until she's forced to still.

"Vesta was cruel," Lev acknowledges, "but the people who joined her often weren't. That's why we have to gain a better understanding. A month ago, many of her followers weren't Vestals at all. They were friends and siblings and loved ones. There's a reason why they joined Vesta. Why it was so hard to predict. Why it happened in places we least expected it. We *need* to figure out what that reason is, and we can't do that if her entire pack is dead."

Singer's voice boils with rage. "The *reason* is she had a bunch of asinine followers —"

"If you don't mind..." The deer from earlier stands near the front of the group, leaning on a long-tailed mink for support. Lev gestures for the deer to take the floor. He looks empathetically toward Singer, but the enfield doesn't so much as glance at him. The deer continues anyway, waving uncertainly toward the group.

"I'm Darby. I haven't been here very long, but I wanted to speak, because…" Darby averts his gaze, swallowing roughly. "My old pack joined Vesta near the end."

The admittance stuns Caius. Apparently, he's the only one; the rest of the pack seems unsurprised, nodding toward Darby in support. Caius racks his brain. Sure, he knew some of the unfamiliar faces came from splintered packs, but Caius hadn't committed any of them to memory. What's the point? They aren't people he cares to get close to. Still, it makes Caius bristle at how little he's retained about the rest of his pack.

"It's kind of humiliating to admit." Darby's laugh is strained. "That people I grew up with, people I trusted more than anything, could be so different than I thought they were. They turned their backs on the life we'd built for empty promises. Maybe it was silly to think that caring for each other could outweigh Vesta's pull." The smile Darby tries is heavy with sadness. "But maybe this is an opportunity to wrap my head around it."

The rest of the group falls silent. Singer stands sourly. Even Pheir has given into momentary exhaustion as Darby lifts his gaze to Lev. "I don't know if I'll ever fully grasp it," he says, "but maybe understanding the Vestals will give some sort of closure. Not just for me — for all of us." His hooved hands gesture before they fall back to his side. "I don't know if that makes sense. I just…don't want to wash our hands of this, even if it's hard to look closely at it. I want to do what we can to recover. That's all I wanted to say."

Lev shoots Darby a meaningful look as he sits. On the other side of the aisle, an older black bear rises, hands folded peacefully across his stomach. His voice is low and rolling. "The Vestal situation isn't simple. We don't have to act like it is. For now, we do what we can to help each other heal and find a way to deal with what's happened."

Nods spread throughout the pack, leaving Singer a white speck alone in the crowd. Muscles taut in his throat, he lowers back to his seat with disgust. Lev nods appreciatively to the black bear before she continues. "Pheir is my responsibility. Anything she does, I bear the weight of. I'll see to it that she brings no harm to anyone."

On cue, Pheir lunges. Caius yanks her back by her muzzle, and the pack watches warily. Lev clears her throat before she adjourns the meeting. "New members, hang back to meet with Willow to begin your introduction to the Timber pack."

Despite some of the pack's support, they give Pheir a wide berth as they dismiss toward the A-frame cabins and the lake's edge. A few give Caius a polite wave. Singer, however, lingers and fiddles with his hand wraps. "Drew the short straw, huh?"

Caius hoists Pheir to her feet. He hasn't forgotten Singer's indiscretion to Lev, but Caius restrains himself with a shrug. "I'd rather shove her around than get stuck tending to the goats and chickens."

Singer's fangs flash, gaze trailing down to Pheir's chest. There's a glint in his eyes. Viciousness seeking familiarity, a dull claw searching for a whetstone as he meets Caius's gaze. "Maybe I could help you shove her around. Bet we could find out all about Vesta's '*glorious purpose*.'"

Pheir lunges toward this new target with no thought of self-preservation. Caius struggles to keep her in hand as the idea teases the back of his mind. It would be easy to end her life. Caius could let someone else bloody their hands to give them both what they want — a mutually-beneficial solution. If Caius's grip slips, and Pheir charges, then Singer can't be blamed for defending himself.

With Pheir gone, that's one less thing to worry about. One less person bringing out the worst in —

"Caius!" June waves at him from the firepit. "Guard rotation meeting."

Singer's lips curl, as if he's considering his timing and wondering if he could slice fast enough. If Caius would stop him. Disgruntled, Singer meets Caius's eyes. "When you get tired of holding back for that bunny, you know where to find me."

Then Singer slips away.

Caius's body thrums, fingers clamped tight around Pheir's bindings. He wouldn't have let Singer kill her. Of course he wouldn't. It goes against Lev's decision, and Caius would never betray her trust like that.

But if Pheir keeps creating problems…

No. His thoughts jolt sharply. *Forget it.* Better get Pheir out of his hands as soon as he can. He deposits her against a nearby tree, ensuring the cords hold her tight as he returns to the dozen other Timber guards. They jostle each other and joke as Caius lingers near the back.

No one speaks to him, until someone approaches from beside him. His eyes dart warily, but it's June choosing a spot next to him. She stumbles over her own toes, knocking into Caius who gruffly keeps her from toppling. As she rights herself, she chuckles and nudges him with her elbow. "Hey, watch your giant feet."

Caius glares down at her. Is she making a joke? Is she making fun of him?

He doesn't laugh. June clears her throat and steps to the side, leaving a larger gap between them. Across the circle, Aren takes them both in, his expression unreadable. Caius rolls his eyes away and catches a gray wolf staring at him. She averts her gaze immediately, and only then does Caius realize his hackles are raised.

He tries to smooth them down, but his body's still taut with nerves as he rolls back his shoulders. Whatever. It's instinct. Wolves and wolverines are natural enemies. Caius doesn't need to examine why his body responds the way it does, muscles pulled tight and ready to spring. Wind whispers at his back, drawing his eyes toward the tree line.

Take off tonight. Disappear before they know you're gone.

He grits his teeth against the thoughts. Maybe it would be easier, being on his own again instead of struggling to adapt to a place where he doesn't fit in. But the image of Lev saturates his thoughts, digging his clawed feet into the dirt. Fleeing is not what he wants, no matter how enticing the idea is. He gets a hand around his fear and pins it in place...at least, for now.

As the last of the pack disperses and leaves the guard group alone, a warm presence slips between Caius and June. He's tempted to jerk away before he recognizes the soft fur. Lev hovers between them, her shoulder brushing his elbow. With her arms folded, their fingers almost touch. If he lifted his hand a little, they could...

He's so distracted by the thought that he nearly misses what Lev whispers to June. "Have we heard from the Broadleafs? They weren't at the battle..."

June shakes her head with a shrug. "Maybe they were caught up in their own shit. You know how they've been."

Lev's lips twist, but she nods before she weaves back through the small group and disappears from sight. After a moment, she hoists herself to stand on the boulder again. "Thank you, guards, for hanging back. I know we're all tired, but unfortunately, our jobs are about to get harder.

Good-natured groans rise from the guards as Lev quiets them with a gentle hand.

"The Vestals aren't actively causing damage, but there's still a lot to repair. The Break is unstable. We've seen it coming for the last year, and we're ready for it. While the rest of the pack gets back to normal, we have to be prepared for the fallout: skirmishes, schisms, packs changing, territories shifting..." She lists them off on her fingers. "Until things calm down, we'll revert to Schedule B Guard Duty. Sentinels, continue guarding the pack as you've always done. Combatants, shift your focus from offense to pack defense. We don't want to cause further harm over misunderstandings."

Does Caius imagine it, or does Lev look at him when she says it? Caius shifts as she glances away again. It's no secret he prefers being on the attack more than securing the home front.

"As for Pheir," Lev sighs, "I know she's not the most amenable —"

A few yards away, Pheir wrestles against the tree.

"But we're a strong pack," Lev assures them. "She's one person. We can withstand whatever she pulls. Keeping Pheir with us will protect all of the Break. Remember that: we're making choices for the good of our community, not just our pack. Don't worry about getting information from her. Keep her and the pack separated, and don't let either one kill the other."

June tilts her head beside Caius. "Are we adding a post to our rotation to watch her?"

"Yes, add Pheir to the end." Lev points to the furthest A-frame cabin, the point on the two diagonals that stretch toward the entrance to camp. "We'll keep her there. Should be far enough away that her screeching doesn't disturb anyone. Caius, will you help Echo escort Pheir to her cabin?"

Before Caius can nod, Aren steps in. "And we need to bandage her hands." It's as fluid as if Lev said it herself. Caius's nose wrinkles, but Aren continues. "If we don't, Pheir will hurt herself more than she already has. Oberon, can you handle medical?"

The black bear nods as he rustles through the bag at his side. The other guards watch Pheir from a distance. Her talons are worn down to nubs, blood scenting the air as she claws against the tree. Feathers fall from her in a flurry, eyes glassy as she fights with no one but herself. Nothing phases her. Not exhaustion. Not pain. Not the threat of death.

There's a haunting familiarity to it, a warped vision that forces Caius to look away. When he does, Lev is watching him — and so is Aren.

Sharply, Caius boards up his expression and turns away from their eyes. The three of them have spent years dealing with the Vestals. Of course now that things are finally settling, one of Vesta's cronies is still wreaking havoc — drawing Lev's attention, sowing seeds of doubt, showing Aren exactly what Caius is lacking.

Over Pheir's muzzle, her glare hones on Caius. This is his chance to prove he can be trusted as implicitly as Aren, but Pheir's presence fills his world with chaos. He meets her glare with a furious clench of his jaw.

The battle may be over, but this war is just beginning.

THREE

Lev

As the group disperses, Pheir's wild eyes lock on Lev's still-healing shoulder. Two guards hoist Pheir to her feet, wrestling her toward her cabin as she screeches for the last word. Her muzzle dampens it, but it sounds a lot like, "Hope that fucking scars!"

With a wince, Lev rotates her arm. Maybe Pheir will get her wish, but the remnants of talons in Lev's chest hurt far less than the alternative. At least she's still here. At least her pack is still standing.

The Timbers were lucky. They all returned from battle, avoiding the sharp pain of losing a pack member. That pain is worse than an arm pulled out of socket, an appendage hanging limply with no way to reach for what it needs. The phantom pain lingers long after a pack recovers. It's a dead weight. It's a *lack*.

Lev remembers that pain. Now, the Vestals know it, too. Despite the Conclave's order for them to surrender, their numbers were razed in hours. Lev can't imagine that — losing one member is bad enough, but an entire pack? Then to be ripped away from the only people left standing?

No wonder Pheir is uncontrollable. She's been vicious and unruly for as long as Lev's known her, but this is worse. It must be maddening, dealing with the emptiness of losing her pack. Of course she's lashing out; she's driven by grief and loss and a situation out of her control...

Or so Lev chooses to believe. It makes her bleeding heart less apparent.

Speaking of...the scab on Lev's shoulder cracks, as if Pheir's words scraped the wound open again. Blood pricks through the tight skin exposed through Lev's fur. Slipping off the boulder, she waves to the others and makes her way toward the main lodge in search of bandages.

Muscles aching, she searches the cabinets in the medical room. When she crouches, her knees creak. If only Pheir was the extent of her problems. The harpy's certainly a hurdle, one that Lev will spend who knows how long trying to get past —

The rest of your life.

At the mental reminder, nausea roils in Lev's stomach. Her mouth grows sour. She fumbles for an empty glass. Water sloshes as she pumps the sink tap, tilting back the cup and soaking the fur around her mouth. Her arms are rigid as she grips the counter, willing away the urge to vomit.

Not exactly how you want to feel about your impending marriage. Eyes clenched, Lev sets the glass back on the counter and swipes the first roll of bandages she can reach. *Don't worry about the wedding now. Focus on something else.* For once, pack problems are a benevolent reprieve from her conflicting feelings about Pheir.

Singer's going to be an issue. Lev's jaw clicks with frustration as she folds a clean rag. This pack was built on differences, weaving ties and forming a home of people who weren't accepted elsewhere...but Singer is different. Guilt seeps through Lev like blood through the rag as she holds it against her wound, but that guilt is followed by a familiar nagging feeling.

Lev hates that feeling — her intuition, her "hunches," whatever Aren likes to call it. That little tingling has been in her head for as long as she can remember, less like a voice and more like a sensation.

As soon as Singer stood, it spread through her body like warning beacons catching fire.

Something isn't right.

She tries to tamp it down. How can she judge Singer already? Before today, they'd hardly spoken to each other. But that sense won't let its guard down, combing through facts that heighten Lev's anxiety.

Enfields are camouflaging creatures, like chameleons. They can disguise their scent, their footprints, their traces, any natural sign of themselves...

Lev shakes the thoughts away, carrying the gauze toward the kitchen. Singer is new. He doesn't have the same understanding and connection that the other Timbers do. He'll be introduced to their way of life. Both sides will decide if this is the right fit for him. Lev can't hold a knee-jerk reaction against him, even if that reaction keeps needling at the base of her skull.

She cracks her neck to scare it away.

She needs to focus. She can't make a drastic decision on impulse. How can she trust a feeling that pushes her to save Pheir but turns on this new creature in a second?

Besides... Lev's jaw tightens. She pushes the thought to the forefront of her mind so she's forced to face it. *This "sense" has been wrong before.*

With a whisper, that sense curls into Lev's ear and whispers: *Only once.*

Smoke fills Lev's nose. Panicked, she checks the pots and pans on the stove, but there's nothing but cornbread cooling on the counter. The smell is in her mind, the scent of Vesta's cremation clinging to Lev's nostrils. It pulls her back to the battlefield littered with bodies as Vesta's corpse burned on a pyre. Lev couldn't take her eyes off of it. The other Conclave members argued over each other, deciding the remaining Vestals' fate.

* * * * *

"We need to make an example of them," Boreas growls. He's a well-respected elder griffin who's impossible to argue with after years as the Conclave's Head Regent. On either side of him, the four other Regents nod. Once again, his inner council is on the same page. How fortunate the people who have the final say in the Conclave's decisions are in constant agreement.

Lev's eyes roll.

"Well said, Boreas!" A wolf shifter pipes up with a knowing smile. This shifter's been looking to expand his territory, and with the Vestal uprising, one good word from Boreas could set him up nicely. Other lesser Conclave members jump to throw their support, jockeying to land on Boreas's good side. It all sounds the same, congratulatory words with no thought behind them. Lev doesn't bother watching. She can't stop staring at the pyre anyway, the fire burning red and orange unlike Vesta's rainbow flames.

Because Vesta is dead.

The truth sinks leaden in Lev's stomach. She blinks back a prickling feeling in her eyes. It's from the heat of the fire, *she tells herself before she forces her gaze across the field to the remaining Vestals.*

Rhaiden, still and stoic. Thalea, crying silent tears. And Pheir, scrabbling to fight.

Pick your battles.

It's Lev's first thought. Clearly, it isn't Pheir's, because the harpy has chosen every battle she's come across. Even now, she catches Lev staring and gnashes her teeth so hard it makes Lev's jaw ache. It makes no sense why Pheir's still fighting when the field is covered with evidence that she doesn't stand a chance. Isn't she tired? Does she feel anything besides rage?

And why does that nagging feeling keep telling Lev to extend her hand toward Pheir?

It seems to happen in slow motion, an internal part of Lev kicking and screaming as she turns back to the Conclave. Any suggestion from her will be met with dissent, as it always is. Who wants to hear from the youngest Alpha in years, the head of a pack of misfits? Her legs tremble as if the earth is rumbling beneath her.

Pheir's shrieking pain digs into Lev's mind. She isn't sure what possesses her — a literal bleeding heart or an opportunity to pay Pheir back for all of her torment. When the suggestion leaves Lev's lips, somehow, her voice is firm.

"We should keep them alive."

The rest of the Conclave turns to her in shock. Her mouth keeps moving.

"Separate them so they can't retaliate. See if we can get information from them."

Boreas glares down his beak as flames pop in the silence. When he lowers his head toward Lev, his voice is loud enough for the rest of the Conclave to hear. "Why would we take counsel from a leader of failures? We haven't forgotten who you've chosen to stand beside you."

Lev's tongue curls in a scathing response, but her words are cut off when Boreas continues.

"Not all of us are so keen on second chances for the deficient, lest we forget whose misstep initiated this battle."

Humiliation swarms hot in Lev's veins. There's no explaining why she took the first step on the battlefield. Why she crossed the symbolic line that kicked the fight into action. Why she knew Vesta was here for blood with no intention of surrender.

Boreas's beak smacks patronizingly as he raises back to his full height. "You're still young. You don't understand the way the Break works. Entire packs have been killed for such indiscretions —"

"And that didn't work, did it?"

Around Lev, Conclave members suck in their breath. Boreas blinks incredulously at her as the other Regents murmur. Lev's eyes harden before she continues.

"We ended up here again. Perhaps it's time to try a different tack. Death isn't a threat to people who don't fear it."

She swallows roughly, but she doesn't let her expression fall. She hadn't expected to take a hard stance — hell, she never expected to be a part of this discussion at all, but what's the point of joining the Conclave if she can't do anything to change it? The Timbers have grown into a force to be reckoned with in the last few years. It's the thing that forced the Conclave to begrudgingly accept her membership. About time she throws her weight around.

Boreas scoffs to maintain control. "And where do you suggest we send the remaining Vestals? Home with the people they tried to kill?"

"Yes." No. It's ludicrous, but standing amidst the Conclave, Lev can't back down. Not when her peers watch her in disbelief, whispers spreading among the other Alphas.

"What is she doing? Is this a joke?"

Lev's eyes are drawn once more toward Pheir's cracking screech. She's screamed herself hoarse, and still, she keeps screaming. Doesn't she know when to quit?

Doesn't Lev?

Apparently not. She keeps pushing. "We bond the Vestals to new packs. Build new loyalty. Help all of us recover. Set an example that way."

It's eerily quiet. Even Pheir's protests are little more than harsh whispers as Lev's heart pounds in her ears. Another of the newer Alphas — Dante — shakes his head. His hellhound maw is still bloody from the final blow to Vesta. He doesn't disagree, but his gruff voice isn't supportive, either. "The Vestals will never agree to join another pack."

Nods spread through the group. Lev reaches desperately for another solution. "Marriage! We'll marry them in."

The resounding silence is louder now, making Lev's chest tight with nerves. She's too far in to backtrack.

"It's the least painful way to forcibly bond someone —"

Smoke snorts from Godras's snout. The dragon always has some way to dispute Lev. "No one wants a bride poised to slaughter them."

"Speak for yourself," Lev mutters...but he's right. Marrying the Vestals is asking for a morgue rather than matrimony. Still, Lev doesn't miss the way Godras's eyes cling to Rhaiden. Lev can use that. "It's dangerous, obviously," Lev admits with a shrug. "But if it works? The Vestals are some of the strongest creatures in the Break. Aligning them with our packs would be beneficial. Surely a strong Alpha could handle it."

A few thoughtful murmurs bleed through the group. Godras shifts his weight, scales shimmering in the firelight as his eyes narrow down toward Lev. "And if it doesn't work?"

It's a challenge, but not wholly contradictory. Lev's mouth twists. "If it doesn't work, we can reevaluate."

"Three months," Boreas declares. It takes a moment for Lev to realize he's agreed. His smirk stays honed on her. "That's how long each Alpha will be left to their own devices before the Vestals must be fully integrated. In the meantime, the Regents will do a thorough investigation and find any lingering allegiances to Vesta. If the three surviving Vestals aren't unified by the investigation's conclusion, we'll dispose of them."

Dispose. The word turns Lev's stomach, but she nods. Convincing Boreas to keep the Vestals alive was one thing. She should have known getting her way would be harder. His heavy hand falls on her injured shoulder, and she bites back a sound as he leans closer. His voice drags like a fork against a plate.

"We'll see how your little idea plays out. I'd hate to watch the Timbers crumble because their Alpha couldn't keep herself from hoarding rejects."

With force, Boreas claps Lev on the back, sending her stumbling forward as he raises his voice for the rest of the Conclave to hear.

"Of course, since it was your brilliant plan, you can share the happy news with the Vestals. And you'll volunteer to take one of them to your bed, won't you?"

* * * * *

Lev couldn't refuse, but now, the reality of Pheir among Lev's family and friends makes her fur crawl. Not because of Pheir's physical strength — pound for pound, most of the Timbers could take her on. It's the way Pheir fights like she has nothing to lose. It's her willingness to dive into the fire, to die for any reason Vesta championed.

It's the same readiness ingrained in all the Vestals. Before the battle, Lev could see it, even among the packs that sided with the Conclave mere months before they joined Vesta. Faces that Lev recognized were distorted with nothing but hatred glazing their eyes. They were filled with too much fury to stop, mindless soldiers flinging their bodies at anyone who approached them. Those that would have been spared refused to surrender.

Because Vesta convinced them. Because she made them desperate to please her.

Lev chokes on the familiar feeling.

"Is it infected?"

She turns at the voice. From the outside doorway, Aren's gaze lingers on her wound. Lev shrugs, biting down a hiss as she turns back to the fresh gauze on the counter. "It's fine."

The air of the room stills behind her. Her nose twitches, fur bristling on the back of her neck. Old habits die hard, and prey instinct dies harder. She knows it's Aren at her back, but the sense of a predator nearby sends her primal mind reeling.

A floorboard creaks intentionally. Aren can be as silent as the grave, but he teases her with knowledge of his presence, sending her heart racing in her chest. Hot breath gusts the tip of her ear. She shivers.

"Nervous?" Darkness ticks into Aren's voice, a shadow before a flash of fang. He's fucking with her. Her brain knows it, but her body can't help but respond. He's out of her periphery, quieter than her breath.

A claw ghosts the back of her neck. Her mind spasms between the drive to flee and the desire for his hand around her throat. Heat from his body edges behind her. She rises on her toes, prepared for — what? To take off running? To tackle him to the ground? To crash her mouth into his?

Carefully, his fingers slot between hers and find the bandages. His mouth moves against the back of her neck. "Let me."

Her nerves are alive with static. She should deny it, find a way to reroute the conversation and check *him* for injuries. She's the Alpha. She needs to take care of —

"Lev."

Aren knows where her mind goes. Her fingers flex, but his hand clasps around hers, calm but firm. Finally, Lev releases the bandages with a slow breath. Aren unwinds the gauze from the roll and presses his fingers to either side of her wound. It stretches over her shoulder onto her chest and back. "Vesta got you pretty good, didn't she?"

Lev stares at the cabinets, grateful for the reprieve from Aren's perceptive eyes. "She always does." There's a pause before Lev corrects. "Did." What's left of Vesta hangs heavy around Lev's neck, cremated ashes given to each member of the Conclave. Lev takes the vial between her fingers, twisting it until light reflects off of it like Vesta's winking from within.

Who knows if separating the ashes will work? It's the best guess any of them have. Phoenixes are a mystery, and splitting Vesta's ashes may be a futile attempt to ensure she stays dead. She could be gone for good, or she could come back with a vengeance in ways they never predicted. It's just like Vesta to remain a mystery.

Aren reaches over Lev's shoulder, lifting the chain on two fingers until the vial hovers off her chest. His voice is low in her ear. "You don't have to carry it alone."

Emotion rises in her throat. She hasn't faced this feeling in so long. She's kept it buried the same way she wishes she could bury these ashes. Her lips part, turning in Aren's arms —

And the screen door behind him bangs open.

FOUR

Lev

"Your boytoy's pissy," June grumbles as she stalks to the island to snatch a piece of cornbread. "I know you want him to be included, but I don't think *he* does."

Aren steps back for Lev to speak. "Caius? Did he say something?"

"No. He stared at me, same as always." June takes a harsh bite and finds an empty jar to fill with water. "Between you and me — and Aren —" Aren bows his head in acknowledgement. "I don't know about this Pheir shit, either. That girl is brutal." Shuddering, June takes a long gulp of water before she props a hand on her hip. "Do you have a death wish?"

Lev clucks her tongue.

"I'm just asking!" June throws up her hands, lifting her ears to their full height. It's an unsubtle reminder of who the eldest is here. On the second floor of the lodge, the pack bustles around. June steps closer and lowers her voice between them. "Your feelings about the Vestals aren't exactly neutral. Are you sure it's not affecting the way you're handling this?"

A bitter laugh threatens to spring from Lev's mouth. She clamps her teeth instead. Remaining objective with the Vestals is a challenge, sure, but that doesn't mean this is *wrong*...does it? Lev isn't sure of the answer, but she can't accept that the solution is killing them. Not when other possibilities have tugged on Lev's thoughts since the moment Vesta reappeared.

What if I'd followed through with it? What if I'd tried harder? What if I could have stopped all of this from happening?

"I'm not impartial," Lev admits. "But the rest of the Conclave isn't, either. I think it's fair to give the Vestals one person in their corner, even if they don't want me there."

June lifts her brows, casting a glance toward Aren. Lev can't see his expression, but after a moment, June's mouth presses into a thin line. "It's your funeral, then. Just remember *we're* the ones who are gonna have to plan it."

The screen door opens again. All of them step apart, standing straighter when Caius appears. It doesn't go without his notice. June grabs another piece of cornbread before she salutes, slipping by Caius and out the door. The three of them remain awkwardly in the kitchen until Lev manages to speak. "So, how's Pheir?"

Caius grunts as he pulls a stick of dried jerky from a bowl on the counter. "Still a bitch." Old scars from Pheir cling to his face under the blonde of his fur, already lightening for the winter. "I left the wolf in charge. She can handle Pheir for a night..." He scoffs as he takes a bite. "Hopefully."

"Echo, you mean." Aren corrects. "The gray wolf."

Caius shrugs noncommittally.

"They'll be fine." Lev moves between the two of them, offering Caius the tin of cornbread. "You need a break — both of you. Thank you for escorting Pheir here while I brought the pack home."

Caius finds the final dregs of water in June's glass left on the island. He tilts it back with a cocky grin. "You're gonna owe us a few for that one."

Lev finds a smirk of her own. "Seems like you were already well-rewarded for your troubles."

Caius tries to cover his choke with a cough. Aren rubs his eyelids, avoiding both their gazes, but they all know what Lev means. The scent of what they'd done with Pheir still radiates off both men. Lev steps back from the island as her tone sobers.

"I know I don't have to ask, but was everything you did...agreed to by all parties?"

Offended, Caius lowers his glass. "Of course it was consensual! Gods, do you really think —"

"*I know*," Lev reiterates. "But the Conclave's notorious for looking the other way when it comes to mistreatment. What kind of Alpha would I be if I didn't check?"

There's a shift in Caius's eyes, the dark pools opening — but then, he lowers his gaze until Lev can't make out what his look means.

"It was negotiated beforehand," Aren confirms. "I'm certain Pheir would have taken the opportunity to gouge our eyes out, but we ensured she was willing."

"*Enthusiastically* willing," Caius grumbles. "But yeah, take it from your *beta*."

The men's eyes meet. Caius's gaze is sharp, like he's taking a swing at Aren. Aren parries with a cinch of his brows, puzzled when the fight began. Gruffly, Caius braces his arms on the counter and turns his face away.

Scents mingle in the air, Aren's woodsy amber next to Caius's spicy clove. They bind together with a stinging ginger that can only be Pheir. All three of them mix in Lev's nose, triggering the glands in her mouth to water. Disconcerted, she picks up a corner from the bread to stop herself from drooling. "I'm still shocked she let you mark her."

Aren clears his throat. "We may have gotten a little caught up in the moment."

A teasing smile takes over Lev's lips in an attempt to ease the tension. "I knew *Caius* had a thing for her..."

Caius's eyes roll. "Don't start." With another bite of jerky, he mutters under his breath, "She's a vicious fucking vulture."

Lev reaches to chuck him under the chin. "Pot, meet kettle. Match made in heaven."

It cracks a smile across Caius's face. When Lev passes, he swats at her tail, but his levity vanishes as he leans back in his seat. "Singer was talking shit after the meeting."

Opening a cabinet, Lev lifts on her toes to grab glasses. "This is a new life for him. It couldn't have been easy meeting his old pack on the battlefield."

"Didn't *look* difficult. Pretty sure most of the casualties of his old pack were from him." Caius follows Lev with his eyes. "He's not the only one wondering why the hell Pheir's still alive."

Lev lowers back to the ground, setting the glasses on the counter as she turns to face him. "You mean you."

Caius doesn't look away, his gaze hardened. "She's a danger to anyone who gets in arm's reach."

Memories prod mournfully at the back of Lev's mind. *So were you, when you came here.* She bites down on the words. "Are you worried she'll hurt you again?"

"I can handle her," Caius scoffs. "Hell, the pack can handle her, but she's gonna be *your* wife, sleeping next to *you* every night." He leans into the island. "You're gonna let your sworn enemy close enough to kill you?"

It's a thought Lev's pushed to the back of her mind, but she doesn't show it now, finding a pitcher of tea on the counter. "Pheir's never kept her hate for me a secret; I don't think she can. She's certainly not gonna start just to get me alone. Besides, she has three months to be absorbed into the pack. We'll cross the bridge of sleeping arrangements when we come to it — *if* we come to it."

Sinking roughly back in his seat, Caius's head shakes in exasperation. "Why do you want to give her a chance?"

Lev braces against the onslaught of memories before she pushes past them. "Why don't you?"

Both their mouths stay clamped. The questions are an impasse, a precipice to something Caius isn't saying. There's a *reason* buried beneath his opposition, but he refuses to put words to it.

Does he sense the same resistance in her?

Glaring at Aren, Caius pushes up from the island. "Maybe *you* can talk some sense into her."

Before Lev can speak, the screen door clangs shut behind him. He retreats across the field, fur cut low on his shoulders and sides like a mohawk leading down his tail. The scars on his back and chest stand out more when his hackles are raised — like now. With a sigh, Lev settles in front of the sink window as Aren pours two glasses of tea. The silence goes brittle and snaps when she glances at him. "Well?"

Aren takes a slow sip. "I didn't say anything."

"You're thinking it."

"I'm thinking a lot of things."

Lev's voice wobbles more than she expects. "You're thinking he's gonna leave."

Aren sets his glass on the counter, posture and tone perfectly even. People think Aren is impassive and removed, but he knows the way to help people find what they're looking for. He knows *her*. "If you know what I'm going to say..." Aren stands beside her, hip nudging hers. "Do you still need me to say it?"

It lances into Lev's chest, sharper than Vesta's talons. Lev's fingers curl around the sink's edge like she's trying to grab a thread unraveling through her fingers. "I don't know how to reach him. I don't know what he needs. When I try to be gentle, he pushes away.

When I ask him about anything real, he avoids it. It's like he doesn't know..."

How to be soft. How to open up without exposing his stomach. How to trust.

Lev's fingers tap against her glass as her teeth worry into her lip. "You remember the months after we found him? How he refused to sleep in the compound? How he bared his teeth when anyone got within a few yards? I woke up every morning thinking, 'Today's the day he's gonna disappear.'"

Caius was scrawny then, hardly recognizable next to the healthy weight he's put on, vanishing from sight into the dark of his cabin across the field. Aren nods, eyes trained out the window. "I remember I told you not to bring him in."

Lev flinches. Maybe her sense was wrong about that, too — but Aren chuckles when she tenses.

"I'm not saying you shouldn't have," Aren murmurs. "You saw something in Caius...but that doesn't mean he'll stay. It doesn't mean he should."

It sinks like a weight in Lev's stomach. "You want him gone?"

Aren is silent as he chooses his words, claws clicking against the countertop. "I want what's best for him and the pack, but I don't know what that is. I don't know if those two things align. Caius came during a rough patch. By the time he willingly stepped foot onto the compound, the Vesta takeover was beginning. He hasn't bonded with anyone else in the pack. You're the only one he lets close. The only one he wants to be next to."

"And you." Lev pushes back from the sink. "He lets you touch him."

Aren's mouth twists slightly.

Lev knows that look, the uncertainty if he should speak. She taps his elbow. "Tell me."

"I think he only lets me touch him when he sees me as an extension of you."

Lev's brows knit, poised to deny it, but the truth of it settles into her bones. For all the brutal fight Caius shows the rest of the world, there's something sensitive he's protecting. He won't let anyone close enough to reach it — to even *see* it. She chews her cheek in contemplation. "And the only time he lets either of us close to him is..."

Heat flares through her at the memory — the three of them together, roughened bodies and slick mouths used for anything but talking. Sex is bonding. Sex is the connection they have with Caius, but what if it's getting in the way?

Every time, it's so *close* to something, but it always ends with a gap between them that they can't cross. Aren stands on one side of the chasm with Caius on the other. Lev is in the middle, struggling to hold them together. If Aren is reason, Caius is impulse, and Lev can't find a common ground.

But what if there's space for both of them?

It's a risky thought Lev's not sure she can consider. There's an entire pack she needs to lead with Aren. And Caius...Caius makes her want to forget her duty. He makes her want to give into feelings she's not sure she can trust. She's been there before, sucked into emotion when she should have used her head. She tries to shake it from her thoughts, but intuition rears its head again.

What if they're both meant to be here?

It's the same thing Lev felt when she found Caius, the same certainty that emboldened her to make Aren her beta. A strand of yearning coils inside her. What if the three of them could balance each other instead of constantly tipping the scales? Her heart clenches as if it needs them, as if something bigger's drawing them together.

Her eyes slip shut as an ache pounds through her head. She's not making sense. When was the last time she slept? The last time she turned her mind off for a second? The events of the past few years drape over her — strengthening the pack, finding Caius, Vesta reemerging, quarreling with the Conclave...

Aren curls a hand over hers, quelling the onslaught of panic as he assures her. "We meet Caius where he is. Let him choose what he wants to share. Now that Vesta's gone, we can get a sense of what he truly wants. If it's to become a part of this pack, or…"

Or if he wants to leave for good.

Lev can't bear the thought of that. It stops her breath when she imagines Caius vanishing in the middle of the night. Even if they don't know what it is, there's something between the three of them, a carnal desperation to protect that makes her knees weak. She can't watch Caius disappear, can't lose her tie to someone else until they become —

Aren's voice is gentle. "Caius isn't Vesta."

Lev tries to settle her breathing, filling the cramped space of her lungs until her chest aches. "I know he isn't." *I know he isn't.* That doesn't stop the fear from burrowing into her heart.

Aren tightens his fingers. He's the only one who sees Lev like this, as small as she really is, without the certainty or the confidence or the face she puts on to ease the rest of the pack. Here, with Aren, the facade cracks.

"Why do I miss her?" Lev's voice is little more than a whisper. "I shouldn't feel like this. She *killed* people, Aren." Lev runs a hand over her face as if it might erase the image of Vesta. Lev tries to recite the facts. *Vesta was cruel. She was corrupt. She hurt so many people. When I think about her, it's like…*

Lev's heart aches at the memory. It isn't Vesta's sneer or the pain of her talons that appears when Lev first thinks of her; it's the warmth of the day Lev met her. It's the promise of what she could have been.

Aren turns Lev by her biceps to face him. "It's not wrong to feel that." He stops Lev before she can argue. "Shh, no, it's not. You did the right thing by stopping her, but sometimes…we mourn the right decision. It hurts because you have a heart." He lifts Lev's hand to his lips, speaking against her knuckles. "That's what makes you a good Alpha. That's why I came here with you."

A wet laugh escapes Lev. Her other hand swipes at her eyes before she smooths her hair back between her ears. Everything is surmountable with Aren. Between the two of them, she's always said he has the harder job. An Alpha is responsible to their pack. A beta is devoted to his pack *and* his Alpha. They require different accountability, different handling, different nuance. Aren manages them beautifully. When he moves behind Lev and rests his chin on her head, her breath comes easier.

This feeling will pass. We'll get through this.

"Maybe I should go home to visit the Broadleafs," Lev murmurs. "Get some advice. See how they're doing things. They've dealt with resistant members before."

Aren hums in response. He doesn't need to know her ulterior motive. He's already helped her through this crisis. Her concern is silly, anyway, another in her growing list of worries. Her last talk with Diction left her with an unsettling feeling. Diction may be the Broadleaf Alpha, but he was Lev's friend first, and she'd recognize the nervous crack of his knuckles anywhere — not that she's heard them in a while. It's been a year since she spoke with him face-to-face. Since then, the nagging feeling has subsided. The Vestals have been subdued. Everything's returning to normal.

See? Lev reminds herself. *Sometimes your intuition is wrong.*

The thought is comforting, letting her melt into the warmth of Aren's body. She wants to curl against his chest and forget her encroaching doubts. They pound inside her skull like a hundred fists, forcing Lev to hear them — the Conclave's timeline, the screeching harpy, the werewolverine receding across the field...

As if Lev could forget any of that.

FIVE

Aren

8 years before Vesta's death

"No trouble getting here?" Aren asks.

Flint sets two mugs of beer on the table, his gargoyle wings cresting the rafters before he sinks into the other chair. "The direct ferry makes it hard to get lost."

When Flint asked to meet, Aren chose the easiest place. It's a humble wooden bar overlooking the Break's side of the lake that it shares with the rest of the continent of Orena. The dock is a bit of a trek for non-Break residents, but it's easier than finding their way through the dirt roads that go on for miles.

In thanks, Aren lifts his cup. "I don't suppose you're here for the home brew?"

"It's a little more existential than that." With a grimace, Flint rubs his eyelids. "I need some advice, and when I speak with you, a solution always makes itself abundantly clear."

Humbly, Aren shrugs and tilts his mug to his lips. "I'm facilitating you through a problem."

With the difference in their species' lifespans, Flint has over a decade of maturity on Aren. By human standards, Flint has reached his mid-thirties. Aren's still in his early twenties, struggling to make something of himself — but Flint never makes Aren feel like that.

"Don't sell yourself short." Flint gestures to the rest of the bar. "There's a reason someone comes up to pick your brain every time we meet: seasonal prep, personal conflict..." He shakes his head as he takes a drink. "No wonder you live on your own; you'd never get any peace otherwise."

Flint's words are kind, but Aren's mouth pulls into a tight smile nonetheless. "Not everyone trusts my judgment so sincerely." It stings to be reminded of his circumstances. Aren wasn't always alone. He's made progress in repairing his reputation, but there's no erasing the Break's memory. There are still whispers, hardened eyes, and gossip that no longer resembles the truth.

None of it deters Flint from being here, though. With a click of his tongue, he lifts his cup in toast. "I suppose we can't all have good taste."

A smile twitches across Aren's lips.

It's clear the question Flint has is difficult to put to words. After a long drink, he sets his mug aside and steeples his hands. "You know what I do for work, guarding one town or another. I go wherever people need protection. There's usually a few of us doing community watch — arbitrating conflict, breaking up fights, that sort of thing." When Flint speaks, his voice is encouraging, as if he's trying to convince himself. "It's not easy work, but it's important. It's necessary. It keeps people safe."

Aren's brow hikes. "But...?"

Flint's mouth twists into a heavy sigh as he drops his gaze. "But I'm starting to feel like it's not enough."

The confession surprises Aren. Flint looks relieved, exhaling and letting his shoulders fall as he continues.

"I know what I'm doing is meaningful, but it doesn't always feel that way. It's so impersonal. As soon as I start to put down roots, I get shuffled to another location."

Aren drums his claws against the table. "Could you refuse the change in assignment? Stay permanently in one place?"

"I guess I could." Flint's talons scrape the outside of the mug. "I don't know if that's what I want. I enjoy the change of scenery — traveling to different places, helping people where they are. If I stayed in one place, I'd still be coming and going all hours of the night, missing big events, giving all my attention to work...who wants to be involved with someone like that?" Flint catches himself, blanching as he waves the notion away. "Assuming I was involved with someone. Which I'm not. Because of the hours."

Ah, there it is. Flint's frustration isn't humorous, but the root of the problem is never what it seems. Aren leans back as he considers the situation. "Is it fair to say you're struggling with a lack of personal connection more than the job itself?"

Flint looks out over the lake as he mulls over it. "I like protecting people. Helping people. That part isn't the problem."

With two fingers, Aren straightens one of his whiskers. "You could work with a company that travels — transportation, training, consulting — though I'm not sure you'd enjoy the corporate world."

Flint cringes openly. "I'm not sure I could handle less freedom and control."

Aren hums absently. "You could always come here. The Break is quiet and connected; nearly everyone knows everyone, except for the fringe communities. You'd get to know a lot of people. Most packs train their own guards, but some of the smaller ones outsource protection."

Slyly, Flint cuts Aren a grin. "No offense, but I'm not sure my vision's in line with the governance here if they think poorly of you."

With a chuckle, Aren tilts his head back against the chair. Though he's lived in the Break all his life, he's spent time in Orena learning how their institutions work. He racks his brain for a few more moments before a thought comes to him. "What about private investigation? It would let you use your skills, do what you enjoy, set your own schedule. You could take on cases that you want, and your placement would be more within your control. It'd give you the range to meet different people, but the time and situations to get to know them better."

Flint rests his chin in one hand as he stares off. "It does sound nice: traveling to different places, gathering evidence, getting justice for the people who need it. I'm not sure I'm a skilled enough investigator, though."

"One way to find out." Aren lifts a challenging brow and tilts his mug back to finish his drink.

As if by magic, two full mugs appear on the edge of the table. The woman that accompanies the drinks is familiar, her wry smile sending a matching one across Aren's lips. When her dimples dig into her cheeks, her rabbit ears turn up at the ends.

"Flint," Aren gestures across the table, "this is Lev. She's in training to become an Alpha of one of our packs."

Flint blinks at the young woman, clearly impressed. "That's quite an accomplishment."

Lev's a year or so into adulthood, but she's been nipping at Aren's heels for a few years. He's not sure anyone in the Break is more interested in his thoughts than she is. Any time he dispenses advice to someone else, Lev is nearby eavesdropping and taking notes and prepared to pepper him with questions about the Break's unknowable magic.

From the way Lev tests Aren's logic, one could think they're at odds, but he enjoys it. Her curious inquiries and hypotheticals help him strengthen his own thinking, and she always provides a unique perspective. For all of Aren's thorough processing, Lev has a sense of things, an instinct that goes beyond nature. He may reason his way through scenarios based on facts and prior experience, but if Lev has a hunch about something, he's better off trusting her.

She shifts on her feet, glancing between the men and taking a step back. "The Alpha position's actually what I wanted to speak with you about, Aren — whenever you get a chance. We could meet tomorrow. Or I could walk you home. Or we could go into town, if you have anything you need to get done..."

"That's all right." Flint stands and glances toward the boat. "I should get to the ferry. Looks like they're about to head back." He fixes Aren with an appreciative look. "Thanks for talking through this. Let me know next time you leave the Break. Maybe I'll have joined a traveling circus by then."

Aren laughs as Flint exchanges pleasantries with Lev and makes his way down the dock. She sinks into his chair, folding her hands on the table and fixing Aren with a look that's all business. "Is now a good time?"

"Depends..." Aren curls his fingers around the mug handle, pursing his lips to keep her in suspense. "Is this about what I think it is?"

Her smile is undeniable, but her eyes are steady and certain. "I need a beta, Aren."

He figured as much. He lets her down easy, taking a swig from his refilled cup. "I'll help you find one."

"No: I need *you*."

A hot feeling flashes through him. He doesn't know why the words grip him like they do, why the earnest intention in Lev's gaze makes his stomach coil. His grip tightens on the mug as he tries to tamp down on any scent he might be giving off.

They've danced around this topic before, one of Lev's hypotheticals. *What would it take for you to help lead a pack again?* He humored her with outlandish things, requests that couldn't possibly be met. She doesn't present any of them now. She hasn't touched her drink. She's sober.

She's dead serious.

"I gave that up, Lev." He dusts away the memories that cling to his mind like cobwebs. "I had my shot. I missed. Let someone else have their turn."

"But *you* didn't miss." She leans into the table. "Someone used a guise to get you out of the way. That's not on you."

"I miscalculated," he argues. "That's not a desirable quality for a beta."

A sad smile crosses Lev's face, weight settling into the corners of her lips. "You got it wrong once. I need you because of every time you get it right."

Despite himself, a smile tugs on the corner of Aren's lips. It's nice to hear, but the thought of making a mistake like that again...he understands Flint's desire to help people, to improve their lives, but the thought of failing them gnaws at the back of Aren's thoughts.

Lev notices the shift in his demeanor. Her voice softens below the buzz of the bar. "What do you think went wrong? Why do you think it happened? And don't say it's because you're not cut out for it."

Aren traces the wood grain of his mug, following the patterns until they blur before his eyes. No one's asked him that before; they always assume they know the answer. "Maybe I was too young," he offers. "Inexperienced."

"Like me?"

His eyes jerk up. "No, of course not." But she's right, that's how it sounds. Aren sets both elbows on the table, meeting her gaze head on. "You have a sense about things, Lev, an intuition many people aren't blessed with. You have some understanding of the world, or fate, or magic that the rest of us aren't privy to. You're going to make a great leader because of that compass. You don't need me when you can trust that."

A shadow crosses Lev's expression, mouth twisting uncertainly. She pushes it aside and hones on Aren again. He swears the earth beneath him trembles when she sets her eyes on him. "And what if my intuition is telling me I need you?"

It's hard to argue when his own logic is turned back on him — classic Lev. It strikes him that she trusts him so deeply, that she believes in him when many others don't. At least, not publicly enough to instate him as their second-in-command.

She's going to be harder to deny than he thought. She realizes it, too, smirking as Aren leans back with his counteroffer.

"We both know the Timbers are a smaller group," he muses. "You don't have as much pull with the Conclave or the rest of the Break as a more established pack would. That doesn't mean you have to take the first beta you come across." He lowers his voice across the table, glancing toward the people nearby. None of them pay any mind. "You don't have to build your pack out with a disgrace because someone else is hard to come by. I'll help you find someone who's good for you, Lev. I promise."

A sore look crosses her expression. "I know you don't mean that as a slight to my judgment..."

Aren winces. "Of course not —"

"But I have to say, I don't appreciate you insulting either one of us. I don't want you because you're *easy*." Her tone smacks of contempt before tenderness filters in. She presses one pointed finger down against the table. "I want *you*, Aren. You, specifically. I want your brain. I want your agility. I want your strength. I want your silence as you think through a problem. I want your smile when I say something you haven't thought of, because you're happy I brought it up instead of pissed that you didn't think of it first."

That smile crosses his face now. The confidence in Lev's voice never falters.

"I want you because you don't care about power — hell, you *avoid* it. You care about people. You want to give them the best life they can have. And, selfishly," Lev shrugs, "I want you because of the feeling you give me. You don't panic. You don't overreact. You say we'll find a solution when things seem hopeless — and you're always right. We always do." She leans back, letting the facade of conviction drop for the first time. "I want you, because you make me feel like I can trust myself. Because you believe in me. Because whenever I talk with you, I feel better." Her fingers toy with the edge of the mug, her eyes dropping to follow them. "You make me feel quiet, so I can listen to that feeling inside me. And that feeling tells me that I need you with me."

His chest swarms with emotion. No one's ever looked so closely and seen to the heart of him. It's always Aren keeping his eyes on others, noting the things about them that make them tick.

While he's been looking at Lev, she's been watching him, too.

After a long silence, he drums his claws against the table. "My reputation..." His mouth curls around the word. "It won't help. If anything, people will judge the Timbers more harshly. Other packs, the Conclave...you might never have a chance to join them."

A smile breaks across Lev's face. "Fuck 'em. The Conclave only cares for big packs who can do things for them, anyway." Proudly, she extends her hand across the table. When Aren hesitates, she lifts a brow and makes a concession. "We'll try it out and see how it goes?"

With a smile, Aren curls his hand around hers and squeezes as he shakes. "We'll see how it goes."

SIX

Pheir

PRESENT
7 days after Vesta's death

Pheir will kill the Timbers if it's the last thing she does.

She'll slaughter every last one if she has to, everyone who stands in the way of Lev and the ashes. That's the first thing Pheir needs to bring Vesta back.

Then Pheir will kill Lev out of spite to finally give that rabbit what's coming to her. Maybe Pheir will kill Caius too, for fun. And Aren, with those piercing eyes like he can see under her skin. It'll be a fitting end for the three of them.

Once the Timber compound is nothing but ash — a strike of poetic justice — Pheir will rescue Thalea from the hellhound who ripped out Vesta's throat. Pheir will help Thalea kill him, if she wants to — or Pheir will do it herself. Then she and Thalea will collect the rest of the ashes and reunite them so Vesta can return.

In the end, Pheir will kill that traitor, Rhaiden. *Slowly*. She'll draw it out an hour for every year Vesta wasted on her. Rhaiden abandoned Vesta. Abandoned their mission. Abandoned their pack when they needed her most.

One rotten seed will ruin the earth it's planted in.

That's what Vesta always said. Vesta knew Rhaiden was rancid from the beginning. Now, Rhaiden's ruined everything. The Vestals were so close to having what they wanted, so close to Vesta ruling the way she deserves. After years under the corrupt hand of the Conclave, the Vestals were going to set the Break free...

Now, the ones left are being held captive by the very people they fought against.

Pheir remembers the last moment she felt whole, perfect, *loved*, standing in front of Vesta on the battlefield. It's where Pheir belonged, defending Vesta from anything that might try to harm her. They looked out across the Conclave packs, at Aren and Caius and *Lev*. Vesta reached around to lay her hand over Pheir's heart.

Are you ready to give everything for me?

Pheir was ready. She *still* is, her trapped mind dipping into delusions of Vesta bursting through the cabin door and rescuing her. Like the first day they met, the first day Vesta found Pheir with no one in the world who cared for her, as if Vesta was plucked from the romantic stories Thalea read later. Surely Vesta, in her infinite power, can save Pheir again.

These potent cocktails of fantasies get Pheir through the days in the Timber cabin, dulling the excruciating pain in her body. It feels like she's being stretched on a rack. It doesn't matter that Pheir would rather kill Rhaiden than stand beside her again; their old pack bonds don't discriminate, straining across distance to reunite Pheir with the Vestals who are left.

Every second without her pack is pain, survival instinct drilling into Pheir's bones and urging her to move. *Find your pack. Find protection.* She can't shake the chains and cords binding her in Timber territory. Instead, she screams until her throat is raw.

Time passes. Pheir's certain it does. She struggles to keep up with the days, gouging a mark into the floor as the sun rises each morning. Losing time is the least of her worries. She's been locked in worse places than this. The Timbers will have to try a lot harder if they want to *really* scar her.

At first, Pheir hated the windows of her cabin taunting her with freedom every passing hour, but windows are better than the alternative. At least like this, she can get a feel for the layout of the Timber compound — comings and goings, random visitors, guard shifts, how noisy it always is. All things she'll need to know when she makes her escape.

None of the windows are close enough to break. They're not very big, either, one on each wall of the A-frame cabin. As far as Pheir can tell, the cabin is one room with a small deck outside the front door. Throughout the day, Timber guards swap Pheir between a twin bed and a chair, offering food and books and puzzles that Pheir scatters to the ground. Eventually, the Timbers will stop trying. They'll stop bringing her meals and start punishing her by locking her in a tiny room with nothing but darkness as her company.

But through each day of captivity, the fools keep coming back for more. Pheir wants to laugh in their faces. Only a shitty Alpha would put them through this. Vesta was right about Lev; she's weak and ineffectual. She should have played mental warfare with Pheir long ago. She should have threatened Pheir with torture, given Caius a turn with her...or something worse.

The Timbers don't try any of it. When Pheir spits in their faces, they don't withhold her food; they strap her with a muzzle and carry on. When Pheir rips a book to shreds, they don't lock her in a hole; they find something more durable to offer the next day. When she fights the way they dress her in warmer clothing, they don't hit her; they drape her in a blanket and try again tomorrow.

It's madness. It's absolute *fucking* madness. Who treats their hostages like this? The less torment there is, the more Pheir is on edge. Maybe this is how the Timbers plan to break her after all.

It doesn't matter: she'll go on hunger strike next. Her rotation of guards is larger than anticipated with different patience and temperaments. Some are unbothered by her antics, like the grizzly and the deer. Others, like the boar, look ready to wring her neck — but they never do.

Pheir pays close attention to them, scouring them for weaknesses and items that can be used as weapons. The werecreatures rarely wear clothing. It's only for function, loose pants with pockets or bags strapped across their chests. With nothing to protect them, Pheir could get a few shots in if she could free herself from her bindings.

She gets close when a rabbit who looks suspiciously like Lev brings lunch to the cabin. While the rabbit sets the tray of food on the table, Pheir tries to jerk free, but she ends up slamming her head into the other's nose. Pain radiates through Pheir's skull. It's almost soothing, a reminder that she's still alive. Still capable. Still fierce.

The rabbit curses, holding her face as Pheir screams with laughter. Maybe this time, Pheir will finally force one of the Timbers into violence...but instead, the rabbit glances toward the tray. With a bloody nose, she snatches back the dessert and calls Pheir a cunt as she leaves.

Aren and Caius don't come to Pheir's cabin often. It's a shame, because Pheir would love to torment them. To find the buttons that make Aren feral. To carve another scar across Caius's face. She could rile *him* up without any effort, piss him off enough to crush his hands around her throat, taunt him until he slams her back into the wall and buries his cock inside her.

It's a simple plan to escape. Distracting Caius with rough sex is easy. Aren will be harder. *Much* harder. Pheir could barely get close to him after the battle, his dick dragging across her muzzle...

So fucking hard...

No. Not harder. Aren is more...difficult. He doesn't fall for anything she throws at him. Doesn't rise to her bait, watching the fits she pitches with discernment that makes her scream.

Speak of the bastard. On day seven — or maybe seventy — he enters with his infuriating Alpha behind him.

"Aw, you brought your *handler*." Pheir jerks against her restraints, her chair leaving another gouge in the floor. "Is she gonna make you do a trick?"

Lev stares impassively at the floor, murmuring to Aren like they're the only two in the room. "We need to get a rug in here."

Pheir jerks harder against the chains, hungry for a reaction. Her clipped wings beat, teeth gritting as she lunges in the chair. Aren grabs the top rail behind her, keeping her balanced on the two front legs, eyes locked where his paw grips over her shoulder.

They've never gotten this close except in battle, claws and talons swiping. Her eyes dip to his mouth. Something electric jolts her thoughts apart. He's close enough that she could swing her head forward and bloody him. Pheir's tongue swipes slowly over her lips. Or she could...

Then his mouth moves. "Do you need attention?"

The words don't sound like a threat. She blinks, breath gusting his snout and ruffling his whiskers as she croaks, "What?"

"If that's what you want..." Aren lifts all but one finger off the chair, making her wobble for balance. Her body clamps tight, trying to keep herself suspended. Wildly, her eyes search his, but he's cool and collected as she trembles. It's unnerving. It pulls her stomach tight. His quiet voice crawls under her skin and *scratches*. "You don't have to scream for it. You can ask."

It's not an admonishment. There's nothing cruel in his tone, but panic spikes in Pheir's veins all the same. If she doesn't fight for attention, she'll be left alone to waste away; she knows that intimately. Aren keeps a hold on the chair, the fur of his arm brushing Pheir's cheek. Mindlessly, she latches her teeth into his muscle and clamps down.

With a shout, Lev surges forward. Aren doesn't jerk away, as if he expected Pheir to retaliate. His other fingers clasp Pheir's cheeks, forcing her jaw open until her teeth scrape the inside of her mouth. Aren doesn't yell. He doesn't make a sound, taking a rag from the bedside table and pressing it to his wound.

Blood twinges in Pheir's mouth. Who knows if it's hers or his? Copper lingers on her tongue, but there's more than that, something unfamiliar that makes her want another taste. She wants to dig her teeth into Aren's body, to drag her bloody tongue across his lips...

Her thighs clamp together. How is he so unruffled by every attempt she makes to untether him? Red pricks through the cloth he holds against his arm. He barely looks at it, lynx eyes following her like he's tracking prey through the forest.

"How are you feeling?" he asks.

She bursts out laughing. "What is this, a new torture tactic?" She's delirious and dizzy, trying to understand his nonreaction, waiting for the other shoe to fall. Her gaze lands on the ashes around Lev's neck. *That's* what Pheir should focus on. Her teeth snap together when she smiles. "Let me out, and I'll show you."

They don't fall for it. Aren pulls up another chair and spins it so he can rest his arms over the back. Lev stands behind him, her attention washing over Pheir until she might scream —

"What happened in the woods," Lev cuts in, "on the way back from the battle? Between the two of you and Caius?"

"Jealous?" Pheir sneers. Of course they told Lev about the sexual detour. Lev probably knew from the start. She probably encouraged it as a matter of warfare. Pheir leans roughly back in her chair, making the legs jolt against the floor. "Don't bother sending your hounds to seduce me again. It doesn't work."

Lev's brows knit. "Did you agree —"

"Like it matters to you." The spirit of hate that Vesta held for Lev is alive in Pheir, the harpy's teeth gnashing over the words. "You're not a woman of your word. Not with Vesta all those years ago. Not with your cronies taking their prisoner. Not on the battlefield."

It was clear in the twilight as the Vestals assembled for war. Across the battlefield, the Conclave army waited with Lev spearheading one of their formations. Pheir wanted to fly across the space, to snatch Lev up with her talons, but Vesta kept a patient hand on Pheir's back. Vesta predicted it, as she always did.

Leverette will move first.

And Lev did, as if Vesta spoke it into existence.

Standing in front of Pheir now, Lev's lips clamp together like she's ashamed. Good: she should be. "This is not about Vesta," Lev tries again. "This is about what happened after the battle, and if you —"

"Yes, I agreed to fuck your boytoys." Pheir's eyes roll despite the heat creeping up her neck. Melting memories cloud her thoughts, but she keeps her voice sharp, nose lifting in disgust. "I was just trying to escape. I didn't realize the sex would be so...bland."

Aren coughs a laugh, as if he can read her thoughts. Humiliation singes through Pheir's body. "What are you laughing at, kitty?"

He tries to school his expression, but the corners of his lips turn up. It makes Pheir want to vomit. There's no other explanation for the feeling of feathers swirling in her stomach when he lowers his voice patiently. "There's no use lying when we can smell you."

Only then does she realize the heat in her face has spread everywhere else in her body. Her thighs still clamped, her mouth still tingling with his taste. Just like after the battle, when Caius dripped blood over her face before they —

When Pheir's chair scrapes across the ground, it's from her squirming, willing away the vengeful sting of arousal. She can't look at Aren. She needs a new target, something that stirs up nothing but animosity. Mercifully, she finds the dark circles under Lev's eyes. "You look like shit, *bunny*. Haven't been sleeping? Scared these chains aren't gonna hold me?"

Lev turns away, nose twitching, fingers flinching before she pours water into a cup from the pitcher on the desk. "*Someone's* been serenading us with screeching renditions of every song she knows."

Pheir's grin is vicious. "Simple way of remedying that."

Lev lifts the cup, leaning back against the table as her gaze dips to Pheir's throat. "It *would* be very simple..."

That swirling feeling starts in Pheir's gut again. No: she needs to remember how much she hates Lev. That's what Vesta would want. That would make her happy. As Pheir looks over Lev now, Lev looks nothing like an Alpha. Nothing like Vesta. Vesta never sat or leaned around her pack. Vesta was always moving, rallying the troops with her chin high. Magnificent. Unstoppable. Heroic.

Lev looks like...a woman. Even without the lack of sleep, the fur around her eyes has always been dark. *Don't let that little pink nose fool you,* Vesta used to say. *That rabbit has a body built for destruction.* But it couldn't hold up against Vesta. The wound she left in Lev's chest is nearly healed. Pheir's gaze lingers, following the jagged line around the curve of Lev's breast. Pheir's mouth is dry. It takes a moment for her to wet her tongue enough to speak. "Once Vesta's back, she'll kill you for so much as looking at me. She'll —"

Lev tilts her head. "What makes you think that?"

Hatred seethes in Pheir. "Are you *joking*?"

Lev doesn't smile. She doesn't smile, setting the cup back on the table. "What makes you think Vesta would avenge you?"

All Pheir can do is laugh. She looks to Aren for confirmation. All she gets is that damn penetrating look again. Air puffs out of her in indignation. "What do you mean, what makes me think that? Vesta died for me. For all of her pack!"

"Did she?" Lev asks.

Pheir's mouth falls slack. The question is ludicrous. Her mind can't begin to wrap around it, bent out of shape and desperate to snap back. Her head shakes to free her from the disillusion, but Lev keeps talking.

"When Vesta died, did she know that you would live?"

They're speaking different languages. These Timber assholes don't understand. They *can't.* "No," Pheir snaps, "Vesta knew we'd keep fighting as long as it took to take down the Conclave. And we would have, if that fucking traitor Rhaiden hadn't —"

"So, Vesta knew you would die" Aren murmurs.

No.

It's the response that wants to leap from Pheir's mouth, defending Vesta even in death. The Timbers can't grasp it; they've never had a leader like Vesta, a cause as righteous as hers. Pride blooms in Pheir's chest — but there's another, smaller feeling like her head emerging above water.

Did Vesta know Pheir would die? That all of them would? That couldn't have been Vesta's plan. She had a mission, a reason to lead them into battle — because the Conclave failed them all. Because the Conclave is cruel and corrupt.

Something creeps up the back of Pheir's throat, blocking her air until the smaller feeling vanishes. She knows Vesta. She *knows* her. No prisoner-of-war tactics are going to make Pheir forget that. Vesta loved her. Vesta was dedicated to her. Pheir swallows the sour taste, brows knitting with vigor. "Vesta knew we would keep fighting for her cause. For *our* cause. She trusted us. She knew we wouldn't give in."

Somehow, the silence is more disconcerting than their questions. Concern etches into their features, like they're giving condolences. Like they...*sympathize.*

It burns through Pheir like shame. Vesta never looked at her like that. She knew Pheir could withstand anything. She never would have insulted Pheir with something like charity. Venom snakes across Pheir's tongue, lashing like a whip.

"Why do you look *sad*? Don't fucking do that. Don't pity me." Wrath burns Pheir's lips when she finds Lev's eyes. "Vesta cared about us more than anything. I should pity *your* pack for living under such a shitty Alpha."

"Capheira..." Aren warns.

"Don't call me that!" Pheir snarls, jerking against the restraints. "It's *Pheir*!"

Lev's tongue presses into her cheek, like she's biting back a response. At least she's not looking at Pheir anymore.

When they try to pluck the seed out, dig in deeper.

Pheir's ears perk, head whipping around the room. She heard that voice. She knows she did. It was more than a memory, it was...

Her gaze lands on the vial glinting around Lev's neck.

They know nothing about us, Pheir. Nothing of the truth. Keep that belief firmly planted in you.

Vesta's voice slinks into Pheir's thoughts, so close Pheir wants to cry. She strains against her bindings, fighting to get closer to the sound.

Don't let them manipulate you, Pheir. Don't let them distract you from what you're meant to do.

In the ashes, something moves. A flare of rainbow, a light in the darkness, a spark to lead Pheir out of this. She's so close. If she could reach —

Lev clamps her hand around the vial, blocking the light.

"Don't touch her! Don't *fucking* touch her!" Pheir jerks so hard that she sends the chair toppling toward the floor.

Lev jumps to her feet, sloshing water against the table as Aren leaps to catch Pheir. His head whips back over his shoulder. "What happened?"

"I don't know..." Lev's fingers tighten around the vial. The ashes have returned to dull gray, but in their depths, something winks that disappears as soon as Lev glances at Pheir. "Did you see something?"

Pheir clamps her lips shut. It has to be Vesta. It *has* to. It's one shred of hope Pheir can cling to, searching for more in the vial. No voice returns, but Pheir knows Vesta well enough to know what she'd say, her smile curling around Pheir's ear like a snake.

The best magic is a secret.

When Aren sets Pheir upright again, her lips curve cruelly over the words. "You're gonna regret the day you brought me here."

Lev's tongue is poised to respond. She bites down on it, grabbing Aren's rag and soaking up the water on the table. She tosses it aside, setting the half-empty cup upright before she leaves the cabin. Aren gives Pheir an unreadable look before he returns his chair to its place and follows Lev out the front door.

Ashes swirl in Pheir's thoughts, screaming through her more than the pack bonds. She wants that vial. She *needs* it like a salve against her skin to quell the feeling of being ripped away from Vesta.

Only Lev stands in the way. *Lev*, with the vial nestled against her chest. Brushing her fur. Held between her fingers...

Pheir's eyes dart to the glass of water. She jerks her body toward it, nearly sending herself crashing to the floor before her chin rests on the edge of the table. When she twists her face, her cheek brushes the cool glass.

Her eyes finally slip shut. It's not much. Pheir's skin presses against where Lev's hand had been, the same hand that touched the vial. It's a small comfort that soothes the burn Vesta's absence leaves.

For now, that'll have to be enough.

SEVEN

Aren

In the two weeks since the battle, the Timber compound has been abuzz with catching up on daily work and winter prep. The pack neglected some maintenance in the years the Vestals were on their radar, and now they're left to clean up fallen trees and debris before colder weather hits. As Aren saws silently, though, his thoughts wander toward Pheir's cabin.

She's...interesting.

That's putting it nicely, Caius would grumble if he could hear Aren's thoughts. Perhaps "interesting" is a kinder word than Caius would use, but it's far from incorrect. Pheir is unlike anyone Aren's met, yet she might very well have been nearby all this time. Despite the Regents' investigation, they still haven't sussed out Vesta's former headquarters. There's no point asking Pheir. Any time Aren visits her, she's happier to snap his hand off than give him information.

That's what makes her so intriguing: her dedication. Her allegiance. Her devotion to a cause and a leader who's gone for good. Pheir seems to view Vesta as if she's still alive, a permanent fixture that will reappear when the moment is right. Talking Pheir out of her beliefs is like trying to pry fanatical religion from a zealot. Frankly, Aren's not sure it's possible. In a way, he's not sure he should try...but leaving Pheir to believe in Vesta's return seems equally cruel.

It's a double-edged sword, one that nicks the back of Aren's mind as he busies himself responding to overdue letters and outlining the schedule in preparation for the first snow. He hosts Flint and his partners for a visit as they work on a case of missing girls from Orena. Turns out Flint was cut out for private investigation after all.

Once Flint is on his way and Aren wraps up work for the evening, he's pleased to see a small group gathered around the firepit. Their laughter cascades above the other sounds of the compound, children shouting as they sprint through the lodge and horseshoes clanging in the game pit across the way. As Aren approaches the fire, Mari the bat lifts a jar of moonshine. "About time you take a fucking break."

They shove the jar into his hand. Aren sinks onto a vacant bench across the circle, lifting the glass in thanks. Before he can take a drink, though, someone else lingers near the edge of the circle and locks eyes with Aren.

Caius.

Things between them have been stiff since their return. They work side by side, falling into old patterns and easy synchronicity, but they're constantly surrounded by other pack members. The days are long. There hasn't been a night in the past couple of weeks that hasn't ended with them passing out in separate cabins. Between rotating guard duty and daily chores, there's hardly room to breathe, let alone speak about anything deeper.

Not that Caius would talk about it, anyway.

Oberon, the black bear, notices Caius's presence and lifts a glass of honey wine. "Care to join us?"

Caius eyes the empty seat next to Aren. It would be cramped. Aren can already imagine the warmth radiating between their bodies, a reprieve from the chill in the air. He leans back to rest his arm on the back of the bench in invitation. For a moment, Caius's expression changes, pupils spreading on his already-dark eyes. Yearning weaves its way across his features...but then, he returns to himself and walls his thoughts away.

"No," Caius mutters before he pauses. "Thanks." Then he moves off toward his cabin.

Aren doesn't let his face fall. It's difficult with the others watching. Most of the pack knows what Aren, Caius, and Lev are — and what they aren't. Among werecreatures, there are few secrets, especially when scents are involved. The three of them smell like each other more often than not.

Mari takes another solemn sip of moonshine. "At least he said 'thanks' this time."

Aren lifts his glass to give his mouth something to do besides frown. Funny how he and Caius have no trouble fooling around, but the thought of being pressed together casually sends Caius running. It's too intimate. Too soft. Aren would bet money that Caius would rather fight an insurmountable army at Aren's side than sit this close to him.

It's not wholly surprising. Despite the issues they have with talking, he and Caius have never had trouble communicating. If you left it up to their bodies, the two of them might never have an issue. That unison didn't start with fucking; it started with training, preparing Caius for combat so he could take a place in the lineup of guards. He was a natural at offense. Aren suspects it wasn't nature that taught Caius how to fight, even if Caius won't divulge much about his history.

After Caius left his Timber sparring partners with serious injuries, Aren stepped in at Lev's request. "Help him incapacitate without...mutilating," she cringed. So, Aren did.

Maybe that was the first misstep. It displayed the differences between them, Aren's control and finesse next to Caius's brute force. Despite Caius's frustration – and the few scars Aren ended up with – the training worked. Caius learned when to pull back and wait for his opponent to move first. Aren learned to fight against someone with seemingly-unpredictable tactics. Without realizing, the two of them entered into an understanding. The men's combat became more like choreography, as if their bodies could read each other, movements synchronized until they couldn't be beat.

If only the two of them could find that balance in their personal lives. As soon as the fists stop flying, Caius is a different person, using his body as a battering ram and a shield. He throws himself at people to keep them from getting any closer.

Lev's been able to reach past that, but even then, it's rare. It was easier to forget the gap between them in the chaos of the Vestals. There were so many sleepless nights that all the three of them had time for was burying their mouths together and forgetting the stress for a few minutes.

Almost always, it's the three of them, since the first night Caius came to Lev's cabin and found her with Aren. None of them knew what to make of it, but they fumbled their way through it, and now...it's like they're different people in the dark. They spend their days focused on pack work and their free nights rutting into each other.

Rarely is it Aren and Caius alone. Only on hunting trips with no one else around, when they're off of guard duty on the same evening, when Lev's traveling or holed up working late at night. When it's Aren and Caius only, it's awkward. It's rough. It's uncertain, like one wrong word will send them spiraling into a fight instead of a fuck.

So far, it hasn't.

A scream jerks Aren out of his thoughts. It cuts through the night air and across the field, sending everyone around the fire springing to their feet until the scream dissolves into a string of curses. One word resonates through the threats.

Vesta.

Of course the scream came from Pheir. The group groans and settles back into their seats as Pheir's screeches are muffled by her cabin door once more.

June crosses her ankles over the arm of her chair. "That girl has a pair of lungs." She rubs grumpily at her nose. "And a hard-ass head."

"She'd make a good scout if she weren't so..." Mari tilts their glass with a lift of their brows. "You know."

Through the darkness, Lev crosses the field from Pheir's cabin, rabbit ears dipping at the tips. Once Lev reaches the fire, it's clear how dark the circles have grown under her eyes, body weighed down with pack responsibilities.

The atmosphere doesn't change when the Alpha approaches the group. If anything, they get more relaxed. June chews a piece of straw. "You look like shit."

Lev flips her off as she sinks onto the bench beside Aren.

"I'm serious." June plants her feet on the ground, leaning elbows onto her knees. "Have you been sleeping?"

"Almost." Lev stares toward the sky before she settles her weight against Aren's side. "I'll be able to start getting some now. I've spoken with everyone about the Pheir situation."

Mari scoffs. "How'd that go?"

"All things considered?" Lev purses her lips. "Pretty well. There were lingering questions and uncertainties, of course, but there are things we can implement to address them." She glances toward Willow for support. "Echo said the new pack members are taking well to the introductory course?"

"*Most* of the new members," Willow clarifies as her knitting needles clack, squirrel paws making the work look easy. She takes up half of her husband, Oberon's, lap. "Singer seems to enjoy being contrary."

Mari chitters. "He'd better be careful. If he can't make it in the pack of rejects, where the hell is he gonna go?"

Willow swats at Mari. Lev shakes her head as she smiles. "We're not rejects."

"We *are*," Mari counters easily, lifting their glass. "There's nothing wrong with that! At least your new wife will fit right in."

Your wife. Aren's fingers clench around Lev's tense shoulder. For all their pack planning, they've avoided thinking about what's coming. The Conclave gave them three months, but time is passing more quickly than expected. The reminder falls solemnly over the group.

June rolls her glass between her hands before she looks across the circle to her sister. "Will you tell us something honestly?"

Lev's nose twitches. "Always."

June eyes the nervous tic. She doesn't point it out. No doubt that'll be saved for later when June gets Lev on her own. "Why *are* you giving Pheir a chance? Don't give us the diplomatic answer about the Conclave, or second chances, or whatever. This is *us*." June gestures to the close-knit circle, the handful of pack members that serve as unofficial advisors to Lev. "Why do *you* want to keep her alive?"

Lev chews into her lip, but Aren knows she won't avoid the truth. This is her most trusted circle. They've had difficult conversations before, but they always support each other. They help find solutions. They seek understanding.

"This question may seem obvious, but humor me." Lev pinches the bridge of her nose before she meets the others' eyes. "Why *don't* you want to give Pheir another chance?"

Mari's mouth opens. June clamps a hand over their ankle, cutting off a snarky remark. It's Oberon who speaks first. "She's been a threat as long as we've known her. She supports Vesta as fiercely in death as in life — maybe more so." Oberon isn't unkind, but he is frank. What he supplies are indisputable facts. Lev watches the fire as she absorbs it.

Mari shifts out of June's grip and blurts, "And she gave Caius that scar on his face! She'll probably give us a few more before this is through. Marrying her into the pack isn't something to take lightly."

"I know." Flames reflect off of Lev's eyes. "But if the Vestals don't start bonding into new packs, they'll die regardless. It's just a matter of time." Lev rubs her hands together, sitting in silence for a long moment. "Does *anyone* think Pheir should be here?"

The group is silent...until Aren clears his throat.

"Oh, of *course*." Mari rolls their eyes, bat wings stretching as they settle back. "You always agree with her.

"Now, hold on..." Oberon lifts a paw in Mari's direction. "Aren may be closer to Lev than any of us —"

June gags. Mari stifles a giggle.

"But he's never let that sway his reasoning." Oberon points at Mari. "You were there when Vesta reappeared. Don't act like you forgot how the two of them got into it."

A shit-eating grin splits Mari's face. "I've never heard two people argue that quietly — or that long."

Aren chuckles. The others watch him patiently as he considers his words. "I've questioned Lev's judgment at times. Each time, I was wrong; I can admit that. I was wrong about how to handle Vesta. I was wrong about bringing Caius in —"

Mari mumbles against the rim of their glass, "You might have been right about that one."

June and Oberon hiss for them to quiet. It's too late. Mari's eyes widen as Lev shoots them a wounded look. Aren's not sure what possesses him to speak, but the words spring off his tongue before he truly thinks them. "I *was* wrong about Caius. He's supposed to be here, for however long that may be. Bringing him in gave him a safe place, and it added a brilliant fighter to our ranks. Without him, we may not have defeated Vesta. We may have lost more people at the battle — I saw the way he saved you from that snake hybrid, Mari."

Mari's gaze lowers ruefully. Yes, Caius came with his own baggage, even if Aren can't tell exactly what it is — but that doesn't change where he's supposed to be.

Aren tilts his head back. "Caius is..." This time, Aren doesn't put voice to the words. *Caius is guarded. Caius is complicated. Caius is more than what weighs him down.*

"You have a point," Mari agrees sullenly. "But that doesn't change the fact that Pheir killed people. People we were close to."

"So did we." Lev lifts her head from her hands. "All the people who joined the Vestals are dead because our side killed them. If anything, we killed more than Pheir did. I know what Pheir was a part of. I'm not asking that to be forgotten; I'm asking to extend her a little grace. I think there's more to the Vestals than we understand right now."

June props her chin in her hand. "More like what?"

Lev's fingers flex on the arm of the bench, grappling with something she can't make sense of. "Of all the casualties at the battle, the majority were Vestals. They were outnumbered from the start. I don't know how Vesta couldn't see that, but it was like..."

Lev's head shakes sheepishly, embarrassed to entertain the idea.

"Like what?" June presses.

"Like she was trying to kill her pack."

Crickets churn in the distance as the group blinks at Lev. She continues more urgently.

"I know pack strengthening through death is more of a survival mechanism, a way to recover after the loss of one or two members, but it could happen."

"Setting your entire pack up to *die*?" Mari shivers. "That's freaky."

Willow taps her claws against the needles in her lap. "If it worked, though, it would make the remaining members stronger."

"Or remaining *member*." June meets Lev's eyes across the fire, like she grasps Lev's reasoning. "Maybe Vesta didn't plan for her pack to make it out. Maybe she planned for all of them to die, so she could absorb the power for herself."

An eerie silence settles around them. Aren remembers what Pheir said after the battle, a phrase that gave him a queasy feeling even then.

I don't say 'no.'

Pheir never denied Vesta. She would do anything if it meant keeping Vesta alive. Did all of her troops feel the same way?

The fire cracks so sharply that Mari jumps. They shake their head, voice creaking like they're trying to convince themself. "No one could be that unhinged, not even Vesta."

Lev stares into the woods like she's looking down a long hallway. June catches it too, rising to her feet and stretching her arms overhead. "Enough ghost stories." She lifts her glass toward Lev. "Good night to rejects...and to giving Pheir a *modicum* of grace."

"To rejects!" Mari downs the rest of their drink.

Oberon helps his wife gather her half-knitted blanket, both of them groaning laughter as the cold settles into their bones. Lev finally rests back against Aren's arm, sloughing off the weight of the day as she sighs. "I'd like a simple day tomorrow."

"You can have one." His whiskers tease hers, his cheek rubbing the side of her neck as he smears his scent against her. It's been weeks since he's been able to, and it soothes him now. Even if they don't always see eye-to-eye, it's easy between Lev and Aren. Effortless. Comforting. He never questions where they stand. His voice lowers against her fur. "You're off guard and kitchen duty tomorrow. The garden's been harvested. I sent Flint and his partners to the Broadleafs and Conifers this morning —"

Lev's nails dig into Aren's knee as she sits upright. "You sent them to the Broadleafs?"

Aren can't make out her expression when he nods. Her head whips around as she calls across the campfire. "Hey, Mari!" The bat turns back to look at them. "Can you go to the Broadleafs tomorrow morning? I know it's last minute…"

Mari balances empty glasses in one hand. "Any particular reason?"

"Just to check in." Lev forces a smile. "Diction never answered my letter last week. I want to make sure everything's ok, since they weren't at the battle."

Mari salutes and disappears. Lev sinks back against Aren. She looks less relieved and more like the request took the wind out of her. His concern doesn't dissipate. "What was that about?"

Her head moves back and forth, something rattling that she can't shake loose. "It's probably nothing. A weird feeling." Her teeth gnaw into her lip. "I thought it was gone, but when you mentioned sending Flint there…it's probably nothing," she tells herself again, turning to face Aren with a hopeful smile. "Right?"

Firelight casts across her face. Aren's mouth presses into a thin line. Lev's sense is not something he questions, but he can't tell her that when she's searching his eyes like she's trying to scare away a bad dream.

As the flames stretch higher, the shadows on her face grow.

EIGHT

Aren

Lev barely sleeps. Lying next to each other in the dark, Aren watches her stare off into the distance. Worrying does no good. They both know that, but logic does nothing to quell her anxiety. Aren lies silently beside her until she speaks.

"Maybe Flint's car broke down," she whispers. "Or one of the Broadleafs had an accident. Maybe that's what the bad feeling is."

Aren nods supportively against the side of her neck, grooming his tongue over her pulse when it patters too frantically. She catastrophizes as far as she's willing to, imagining things that might have gone wrong that she can live with. By morning, it soothes her enough that she drifts off for a few hours.

Oddly, Aren wishes Caius were there, though Aren's not sure if Caius's brittleness would have set Lev more on edge. Best case scenario, Caius would have distracted her by putting an end to the talking.

Aren's not sure that would have helped.

Besides, maybe nothing's wrong. Maybe Lev's hunch is misguided, and the panic will be laughed off when Mari returns complaining of a cramp in their wing. Aren hopes for that and ignores the stubborn reminder that Lev's sense is as good as truth to him.

Once morning breaks, there's enough work to keep them distracted. It takes until lunch to clean the gathering area outside the main lodge. Lev and Aren eat by the fence around the compound, leaning back against the posts.

"It's a beautiful day," she insists. "We've got to take advantage before the cold moves in." She's not wrong, but Aren knows they're staying outside so she can keep her eye on the sky for Mari's return.

Lev takes the first bite of her sandwich. "Have you seen Caius?"

Aren shakes his head. "His cabin was locked last night when I checked."

With a nod, Lev wipes her hand on her cloth napkin, but her swallow is rough. From the entrance to camp, Darby approaches, velvet shed halfway off his horns. "Letter for you." He extends a piece of paper to Lev. "Courier said it was urgent. It came from the Chasm pack."

Leverette is scrawled across the envelope. Lev's brows knit. There's only one person that insisted on using that name for her, and that person is dead. Still, she takes the letter, slipping her finger under the seal before she realizes the deer is still standing by.

"Is there something else, Darby?" she asks.

The young buck runs a hooved hand through the scruff of hair between his ears. "Do you know where Marius is? I was going to see if they wanted to..."

Darby trails off and averts his gaze. Lev catches Aren's eyes with a knowing smile before she answers. "They went to the Broadleafs. Should be back later today." Her head tilts innocently. "Why do you ask?"

If Darby's cheeks could flush, they would. "No reason."

He stuffs the rest of the mail under his arm and hurries away, leaving Lev chuckling as she unfolds the paper. It's a simple letter, only one page long. Lev scans it before her eyes narrow.

"It's from Rhaiden."

Aren matches her stunned expression, inclining toward Lev so they can speak without being overhead. Reading over her shoulder, his eyes chase the sharp scrawl like he's tracking a creature through the forest.

Over the years, I had my suspicions...

...slipped it into their food for weeks...

...the longer you're under Vesta's control, the harder it is to get out. Pheir was with her longer than anyone.

Another breeze rushes through the trees, fluttering the paper between Lev's fingers. She holds it flat, as if losing sight of the words will make them disappear. Her expression's dazed. "This can't be real."

Aren turns the envelope over again. Stamped into the wax is a dragon scale that he lifts to Lev's attention. "It came with Godras's seal. He wouldn't have allowed it if he thought there was no truth to it."

Still, the letter's appearance is shocking, never mind its contents. For the time the Timbers spent gathering intel on the Vestals, Rhaiden remained a mystery. Aren's not sure they had more than one conversation with her, but that was enough to recognize the danger she presents. Pheir was never subtle. Vesta lived for the spotlight, but Rhaiden worked in the background. She was clever. Aren suspects she's the main reason the Vestals put up as much fight as they did.

Lev doesn't speak. She doesn't move, reading through the letter again. "It sounds unbelievable."

"It does," Aren agrees.

"I can't take her word for it."

"Trusting any siren is risky, let alone Vesta's right-hand." But if Rhaiden is telling the truth...this letter could explain her surrender. It could provide answers on Vesta's rise to power. It could give the remaining Vestal's a shot of surviving the Conclave.

Lev finally folds the paper over itself, as if not looking at the words might be easier. "This still leaves so many questions."

Aren picks up the pieces of what Lev doesn't say. "We could bring Rhaiden here. See what else she can tell us, what she left out of the letter."

"Bring a siren to our compound?" Lev huffs a laugh, but she doesn't discount it. Her voice goes quiet in contemplation. "We'd need a lot of coordination. None of our pack could get close to her. Godras would have to escort her with his guards..."

Aren mulls over the logistics, letting the scenario play out in his head. It seems doable. "We could manage."

Lev isn't enamored with the idea. Her teeth chew into her lip, gaze skirting across the lake toward Chasm territory in the distance. "Maybe I could go to her..."

Aren takes the letter gently, unfolding it to underline a sentence with his claw. "She'll only do this if she can be near Pheir. Take it from me, hauling Pheir across 250 miles once was bad enough. I can't imagine being stuck in a truck with her."

Lev shakes her head, clenched jaw almost slipping into a smile. "Even as a hostage, Rhaiden's strategizing. I see why Vesta chose her."

They stand in silent consideration, watching the other Timbers move about daily tasks: fetching water from the well, tending to the goats, carrying fishing nets toward the lake.

Lev drums her fingers on the letter. "What if this is a ploy? A way for Rhaiden to reunite with Pheir, to bring the ashes together, to cause chaos. Sirens feed off of that; it would be the perfect opportunity."

Aren folds his arms across his chest, rubbing a hand down the fur of his jaw. "There is that possibility."

"And if the Regents found out we were considering it..." Lev folds the letter again, tapping it nervously against her palm. "They're happy for any excuse to kill the Vestals. If the Regents so much as suspect anything, they might use that to exterminate them — or the Regents might take it out on our pack."

Accusations of treason would be hard to overcome, especially in the Vestal aftermath. And yet...Aren braces his hands behind him against the fence as he settles beside Lev. "What if you did meet with her? On the off-chance the letter is true, it could explain how Vesta was so convincing. It could make Pheir marginally more amenable. It could give us more knowledge about how phoenixes operate."

Lev purses her lips with a far-off look. "It could explain a *lot* of things..." Aren doesn't think she means just recent history. Before he can ask, she shakes the thought away. "Once Vesta was gone, Rhaiden didn't keep fighting. She surrendered. She seemed almost...reasonable."

Aren nudges Lev with his shoulder. "What do you say, Alpha?"

Lev lets her hand with the letter fall to her side. "At the very least, it would require logistics. I'm half-convinced the Regents would use this meeting to get rid of all their problems at once — the Vestals. You and me. Our pack." She settles her weight back against the fence. "But to be able to get some answers..."

Overlapping shouts come from the dirt road leading into the compound. Lev and Aren break into a sprint, dust kicking up around them as they race to the entrance to find two guards lifting Mari off the ground. Their bat wings are limp. They gasp for breath. Lev grabs one guard by the shoulder.

"Water," she instructs. He takes off toward the well as Lev checks frantically over Marius. "Are you ok? What happened?"

Mari's chest heaves beneath the white tips of their fur. "I came back — as fast as I could." When their wings stretch, they wince and their eyes find Lev's. "The Broadleafs are gone."

Lev's brows knit in confusion, clinging to reality she can fathom. "Gone? As in, relocating? Diction hasn't mentioned —"

"Dead." Mari gulps between breaths. "All of them."

Air rushes out of Aren's lungs. It's impossible; the Broadleafs are only a few territories away. Aren spoke with one of them last month. Yesterday, he sent Flint...

"How?" Lev's body tilts like the world is off its axis. Aren jerks out a hand to catch her. She rests her own against his arm, keeping her feet solidly on the ground. "Did some of the Vestals survive the battle? Did they go after the Broadleafs?"

The guard returns with a canteen pouch, followed by Caius through the chaos. Mari drains the water before they can speak further.

"Their pack house is gone. *Everything's* gone. There was phoenix fire."

"But Vesta —" Lev splutters.

"I know." Mari wipes their mouth. "It wasn't her. Not directly. It sounds like..." Mari's gaze cuts to the screeches coming from Pheir's cabin. "The Broadleafs were working with Vesta."

Shock ripples through the group. As soon as Aren thinks it, Lev speaks. "Diction would *never* —"

"Diction's dead." The word drops leaden from Mari's mouth. "He's been dead for months."

The last time Aren spoke to Diction, the last time they saw him...it hasn't been that long, has it? Aren tries to pull from his memories. With all the Vestal focus, the dates get further and further apart.

There's a dazed look in Lev's eyes. "How did he...?"

"The other Broadleafs killed him: Diction, his mate, his beta... They wouldn't be a part of whatever the others wanted to do. It was more than Vesta; it was *really* shady shit." Mari shakes their head, bewildered. "Kidnapping girls. Bonding them to the pack so the Broadleafs could..." Mari cuts off, gaze locking with Lev again. "It was like you said last night: killing part of the pack to make what was left of it stronger."

Aren wants to refute it, to insist the Broadleafs could never do this, that Diction wouldn't allow it to get this bad...but the Broadleafs have kept to themselves the last few years, dealing with interpack conflicts. Diction stopped coming to the Timbers as frequently, finding reasons why he couldn't stay long. The Broadleafs didn't join the battle against Vesta.

In Aren's mind, pieces begin to slot into place.

Caius fills in the silence. "How do you know all of this?"

"Some people made it out." Mari looks toward Aren. "Your friends. The Broadleafs took them hostage before one of the pack members set the place on fire. I found Flint and his partners at the outpost, trying to make sense of it."

It's a relief, albeit a small one. Aren tries to let that feeling even his breathing, but it binds tighter in his chest. How could this have gone on for so long right under their noses? The Broadleaf compound was small and remote, but surely someone knew *something*...unless Diction was keeping everyone away from the shameful truth.

"So it was the Vestals again."

Aren's head snaps toward the intrusive voice. Singer leans against Pheir's cabin. When she screams inside, his fox ears flick.

"It's not too late," he murmurs, crossing toward the group and never removing his eyes from Lev. "This is the perfect opportunity to get rid of her. You can say it was a coordinated attack —"

Even Aren's head bows at the authority in Lev's voice.

"Singer." Her teeth grind together, but her eyes are flecked with pain that she swallows to keep her voice steady. "Now is not the time."

His ears press flat against his head, tail dipping between his legs as he slinks back toward the main lodge. Lev doesn't spare him another thought, staring toward the distant Broadleaf mountains as if she might find an answer in smoke rising off the charred remains. It's useless; the Broadleafs are a hundred miles away. With the storm rolling in, the dark clouds hovering above them are filled with nothing but rain.

Mari shatters the frail silence. "I know we're still recuperating, but the Conifers begged me for help. They have to search the remains of the Broadleaf compound, reallocate the territory, deal with the Orena Investigative Division —"

"I understand." As Lev says it, she looks drained, gesturing to the nearest guards. "Get Mari inside. Bring them anything they need: food, hot water bottle, liquids. Assemble a group to go back to the Conifers in the morning...and gather the rest of the pack. We need to tell them what happened." She braces a hand against Mari's wing. "Your scouting is invaluable, Mari. Thank you."

Two Timbers guide Mari toward the main lodge as Lev moves away from the gathered crowd. To no surprise, Aren and Caius fall into step behind her.

"I need to find June..." she mutters distractedly.

Caius doesn't hear her, lowering his voice sharply. "Helping the Conifers is a huge undertaking."

"I know." Lev's pace is sharp but distracted, already planning what they need. Aren sorts through his mental checklist. *Draw extra buckets from the well, smoke fish for the journey, adjust the guard rotation...*

Caius doesn't let up. "We just got back from a massive battle. Let the Conifers deal with this on their own. Our pack needs to recover. *You* need to recover —"

"I *know* that," Lev snaps, turning on her heel. Despite the curl of Caius's lip, one look from her has him biting off a response. She's a good foot shorter, but there's no question who the Alpha is. She doesn't order him to stop. Instead, she breathes out. A fragment of stress slips out of her voice. "We're dealing with a lot — all of the Break is. We can't leave the Conifers out to dry. They're a small pack. If we don't help mediate, things could get worse: territory disputes, packs encroaching..."

Caius lowers his head to plead with her. "Then let me go for you."

"No, Caius..." Lev reaches toward him. When he stiffens, she pulls back, fingers flexing before they drop back to her side. "I need you to stay here to keep the pack safe." Her eyes cut to Aren. "Both of you."

Aren's mouth drops open in surprise. Beside him, Caius deflates. "I don't need a babysitter," he growls.

"I know you don't," Lev assures him. "But you two have worked harder than anyone since the Vestal uprising started."

"Not harder than you," Caius scoffs.

"That's what I signed up for." When Lev shrugs, the angry line of her scar moves. She tries to hide the wince of tenderness. "Sometimes the Alpha suffers for the good of the pack. I'll take the guards who stayed behind during the battle. The rest of you can recover, and it'll give the others field experience."

Begrudgingly, Caius turns his eyes toward the tree line. He doesn't speak further, so Aren steps in and lowers his voice. "We're in the middle of civil unrest, Lev. You're not taking your second with you across territory lines?"

"June and Oberon will be with me." When Lev reaches for Aren, he lets her slip a hand around his wrist. The squeeze she gives is meaningful, gaze locked on his with solemn reassurance. "I need you two here. I trust the pack in your hands more than anyone else. And with Pheir..." Lev's eyes shut with exhaustion. "I don't want her getting her talons in anyone. At least this way, the ashes are out of her reach."

With Lev outside the safety of the pack, it would be much easier for someone to get ahold of her. Before Aren can mention it, she squeezes his arm again.

"It'll be ok. I promise."

"Famous last words." Caius kicks a rock under one of the cabins. Aren can't help but agree.

He barely has a second to spare for the thought of Lev leaving on her own. The rest of the day is a blur sharing news of the Broadleafs, sending another scout, packing bags and prepping for tomorrow. While Aren sits at the firepit to smoke food for the journey, other Timbers pass through in a flurry. They whisper hurriedly to each other as they pull camping packs out of storage. No one has time to slow, the casual drinks of the night before long forgotten.

Things will get back to the way they were. It's a tough time.

Diction told them that a year and a half ago as they sat around this same firepit, talking late into the night. Though Diction wore a smile, there was tension in the shifter's throat as he swallowed one drink after another.

Lev wasn't fooled. "You have to address the issues with your pack, Diction." He wouldn't meet her eyes, so she leaned forward, forcing him to hear her words. "The infighting won't go away. It's gonna get worse."

Soon after that night, the Vestals completely occupied the Timbers' attention. All smaller issues fell to the wayside: the dripping tap in the main lodge. Caius's inability to open up. The Broadleaf pack's personality clashes.

Who could have known it was so much more than that?

Tonight, the compound is abuzz with activity, but the air is still and quiet. No one speaks above shocked whispers, murmuring memories and praying that the Break will settle back into calm. Aren flips the fish on the makeshift grill to smoke their other sides, mind scattering with possibilities.

What if something happens to Lev out there on her own?

What if the Regents get wind of Rhaiden's request?

What if the letter is a trick?

Most bizarre of all, what if it isn't?

NINE

Lev

You were the first person who believed in what I'm doing, Leverette. The first person who gave themself over to me. Who was loyal all this time.

The scar in Lev's shoulder burns as the memory sears across her mind. There's no time for it. Rifling through her cabin, she stuffs a multi-tool into her pack before the weight of everything finally sinks into her body.

There's no time, she reminds herself, but grief doesn't wait. It curls around her limbs, exhaustion seeping behind her eyes as she's forced to settle on the edge of her bed.

A delicate chain sits on the nightstand. Diction made the necklace to match his own when Lev began to lead her pack. Lev lifts the charm between her fingers, a timber tree melded into a simple metal disc.

So you don't forget who you're doing this for, Diction smiled as he draped it around her neck.

Her fingers tighten around the chain. What if remembering isn't enough? It didn't save him. Lev never doubts that she can trust the Timbers with her life, but Diction likely thought the same until the end.

Guilt sits as heavily as remorse in her stomach. She should have done more to help him. She should have pushed harder, asked more questions, held him hostage if it would mean he's still alive. She should have listened to the creeping feeling she got when Diction left the Timber compound for the last time, but it was lost in the shuffle of everything else.

It was nothing like the sense she got last night at the campfire. No other feeling has struck her as violently as that. In the end, it didn't matter. By the time Marius got to the territory, Diction was long dead. Flint and the others had already made it out. The Broadleafs were gone.

Lately, this "sense" of Lev's is out of whack, miscalibrated and uncertain. Her mind itches with a thought she can't scratch. *You know why.* Vesta's return took a toll in more ways than Lev wants to admit, dredging up memories that make Lev feel less like the woman she's become and more like the girl she was. A reminder hums in Lev's periphery, a flash of Vesta's smile in the dark.

Your sense has been wrong before.

But if Rhaiden's letter is true... No: Lev can't get ahead of herself. She needs to focus on the task at hand and deal with the remnants of the Broadleafs. In Lev's palm, the cool metal of the necklace grows warm, as if it lives on in Diction's place.

Lev's fists clench before she flings it to a far corner of the room.

It's fitting that the necklace has been replaced by Vesta's ashes. Impossibly, the weight of the vial seems to change, as if it's alive. Sometimes, the vial is so light Lev forgets she's wearing it before its crushing weight returns. It digs into her chest like it's trying to burrow and sink teeth into her heart. When the wind blows just right, Lev swears she can hear Vesta's laugh, as if she just vanished through the trees. Her scent lingers in Lev's throat: citrus. Ground pepper. Dark copper that Lev can't get out of her mouth.

You don't have to carry it alone.

Aren's voice whispers through Lev's mind, her constant companion. Even before this, his assurances lingered in Lev's head during the Conclave meetings, the war room councils, the difficult decisions. When Lev asks herself, *what would Aren do?,* the answer is often simple:

What he thinks *Lev* would do.

She swings the vial to her back, as if that will dull its oppressive presence. It still throbs like an ache in her muscles, a reminder of her failings. Aren trusts Lev more than she trusts herself. What if that's dangerous? Lev couldn't stop Vesta. She didn't save Diction. And Caius —

"Hope you packed the double sleeping bag."

There Caius stands on the small porch of her cabin, levity struggling under the concern in his eyes. She finds a smile to lighten the mood. "I'm leaving it for you and Aren to share."

With a scoff, Caius steps inside, floorboards creaking as he leans back against the wall. There goes her heart again, thudding at the predator's approach. Their bodies still as they regard each other.

There's an argument they aren't having, one Lev can never find the root of. She reaches for what she knows, instead. "Why does it worry you so much that I'm leaving without you?"

Caius's eyes harden into a wall between them. "I'm one of your combatants. It's my job to worry about you."

Lev shakes her head. "That's not what it is."

There's a war behind his lips, different than the fight that sharpens his words and fangs and snarls. Something battles to escape him. He grits his teeth like he's afraid it might slip out, but there's a flicker of something in his eyes. "If anything happened to you…"

Another set of footsteps approaches. Caius looks relieved for the intrusion, even after he recognizes that it's Aren. Caius glances over his shoulder to the door, jerking his head toward Lev. "Tell her to take one of us with her."

Aren leans against the doorframe. "She doesn't listen to me."

A smirk cuts across Lev's lips. Caius rolls his eyes, scooping Lev's backpack up with one hand. "You're a shitty liar."

She reaches for it, but he holds it above her head, teasing the short length of her arms. Rising from the bed, she steps toward him with intention, but her words are soft. "You and Aren taught all the guards going with me how to fight. This is only a few days."

He gently flicks one of her ears. "We're just supposed to pace until you get back? Babysit that birdy bitch?"

In retaliation, Lev tugs his fur and pulls him down to her level. It's a distraction they both need from everything else swirling around them. His lips part, gaze sliding to Lev's mouth as he waits for her to close the space. Instead, Lev presses their noses together, walking her fingers up his chest. Her breath ghosts across his maw. "I think you want to do more than babysit her."

Lev's not sure what she expects — stubborn refusal, a roll of his eyes, a click of his tongue — but she's met with the unmistakable scent of arousal. Her eyes widen. Caius winces like he's being punished by it, like his body's response is as confusing for him as it is to her. She releases her hold on him, stepping back Aren interjects.

"We have to do the ceremony soon. We need to bind Pheir's loyalty to the pack."

The mood dampens at the reminder. Lev turns back to the bed, tugging the messy top sheet out from beneath the mattress. Caius falls back into a sour attitude he seems pleased to have found again. "Thanks, buzzkill."

Aren's shoulders rise and fall matter-of-factly. "The longer we wait, the more danger we're in —"

"Don't you think we'll be in more danger once Pheir is linked to us?" Caius's thumb jerks toward Lev. "And what about her? She's gonna be tied to a feral fucking freak who'd gut her at the first chance."

Aren lifts his palms to soothe Caius, but it just makes him snort.

"I understand," Aren murmurs. "But what happened with the Broadleafs makes having an enemy in our midst more of a threat. Bonding Pheir with the Timbers will ease the pain of losing her pack as well as shift her loyalties. It gives us a better chance against anything else that might come our way."

Lev folds the sheet against her stomach, turning back to Caius's eyes burning into hers. He wants her to give another answer, but she can't lie to placate him.

"This is the plan, Caius." Lev shrugs helplessly. "Believe me, I've weighed the alternatives. This was agreed among the Conclave."

Caius's teeth grit. That's never been reason enough for him, blown by the strongest wind of his impulses. "We can find something else to do with her."

Lev tucks the sheet under her arm. "Like kill her?"

At least Caius is consistent. He doesn't have a hint of shame in his eyes. "If Pheir was involved with the Broadleaf shit? Hell yes. You think the Regents are gonna let her live after that?"

It's a fear Lev's been avoiding. Could the woman slated to become her wife have been involved in the death of Lev's oldest friend? The details of the Broadleaf fire are still murky. What the Timbers do know doesn't add up. What other shady things were the Broadleafs involved in? What benefit did it give to Vesta?

You don't know how to get your hands dirty.

Lev shuts her eyes, forcing the memory from her head. "As much as Pheir believes she was in on Vesta's plans, I don't know if that's the truth." Lev's eyes cut to Aren. They need to speak with Rhaiden — and help the Conifers — and bind Pheir to the pack. It's an ever-growing list of responsibilities with dire consequences for one wrong decision. Lev lets her breath out slowly between her teeth. "As long as Pheir stays in our custody, we can learn more about what she knows. It's not going to be resolved with one conversation. She's harder to crack than that."

Aren bows his head in deference, but Caius doesn't look any less fired up. They stand before her on either side, two ends of a sliding scale — Aren's reasoning comforts her, while Caius's passion begs her to give into her most carnal impulses.

It incites Lev. It thrills her. But it also reminds her of the last person that enticed her to be led by feeling.

Earnestly, she meets Caius's eyes as gently as she can. "Give me a little time. There are a lot of moving pieces. We'll deal with it when I get back."

He doesn't look happy, but he gives a begrudging nod. It's all Lev can ask for. Aren steps aside, and the three of them leave the cabin with Lev's gear in tow.

This late, the compound is asleep, candles no longer flickering in the main lodge. The usual bustle of noise has settled to a low hum. Guards scan the compound's perimeter, conversations muffled by the distance as Aren, Lev, and Caius approach the truck parked at the dirt road entrance. Bags and boxes are stacked in the bed of the pickup, ready to leave before first light. Lev pulls down the tailgate as Caius swings her bag into place. Aren rearranges a few satchels next to the wheel well before he steps back.

"That's everything."

Lev will be gone in a few hours. She should really get some sleep...but she doesn't move back to her cabin. Neither do Aren and Caius, drifting at her sides as if proximity might bridge the gap between them. As if lingering close enough will change the indisputable facts they can't agree on. As if it will soothe the burn of her leaving.

She turns to them behind her. Longing branches through the air between them as she looks over the two of them. Broad shoulders, soft fur, thick chests she could bury all her thoughts against...

For once, it's Caius who knows what she's thinking. He sinks to his knees, holding her gaze as Aren follows suit. The scents of heat and sweat assault Lev's senses, arousal twisting through the air. It's not like the tinge moments ago in the cabin. This is overwhelming. Intoxicating. Both men's eyes reflect sparse moonlight as Caius reaches forward to drag a hand down the back of her leg.

"Do you want to think about other moving pieces?"

His offer makes her tremble. It isn't the perfect solution; grappling for physical connection won't solve every problem between them, but she needs to be *close*. She needs to show them how much she hates to leave. She needs to touch someone with desire instead of grief.

Slowly, Lev sinks back onto the tailgate. Her foot lifts to press against Caius's chest, taut with muscle under the golden fur of his winter coat. Under Lev's heel, his pulse thuds.

"So eager." She can't deny her smile. "It almost has me thinking you missed this."

Caius rises on his knees. Lev braces herself against the truck when her thigh comes back against her chest, like Caius might stand and take exactly what he wants. The thought stirs in her. He never looks away, scraping teeth up her calf as his eyes dart hungrily between her legs. That's when she stops him, applying pressure with her foot to keep him in place.

Her head tilts in silent challenge. He edges closer, mouth ducking between her thighs, but she holds him back. Reading Caius like this is easy, the same way it is in battle. He's fierce. Focused. Devoted. Fucking is like fighting, the three of them dancing without missteps.

It's the moments when their bodies aren't moving that Lev loses sight of him.

Aren climbs up behind Lev in the truck bed, easing her back against his chest as his thighs brace outside of hers. The tension in her shoulders eases when she can sink back into the promise of Aren behind her. Caius watches them, air fizzing with friction, like a rope fraying as it's pulled in two directions.

A question flies into Lev's mouth before she can think better of it. "What was it like, when it was the two of you after the battle?"

Caius's mouth halts against Lev's knee. His gaze flicks to Aren with a heat Lev can't place. It's like separate flames converging into a roaring fire. He doesn't speak. His mouth never moves when his body can.

Aren fills the gap instead. "The two of us and Pheir," he reminds Lev, digging teeth into her shoulder.

Of course: even when Aren and Caius's only choice was the enemy, they found a way to use her as a bridge. The image of the other woman between them should do something to Lev, incite anger or jealousy or laughter. Instead, it spawns more burning questions that scorch her tongue. "What was it like with the three of you, then?"

The reminder does something to Caius. His lips curl into a snarl as his grip tightens, jerking Lev to the edge of the truck like he wants to bury his mouth between her thighs. She keeps her foot against his chest, fighting her own desire when Aren digs claws into her hips as the men pull her in two directions.

In this moment, it works, a hot tug of war that gives and takes like the tide. When Caius mouths closer to Lev's clit, Aren pulls her out of reach, teasing until she aches.

"It was lawless." Aren's voice makes Lev's head swim, torn between his gentle claws and Caius's blunt teeth. Aren breathes against the base of Lev's ear until she squirms. "Like pouring gas on a fire. Starting a riot. It was irrepressible."

Lev's nails dig into Aren's knees, hips rocking toward Caius's mouth where he finally lands his tongue. His barbel piercings flick her clit. They both groan at how wet she is, his paws pulling her closer for more, faster, *hotter* —

Aren purrs against Lev's neck. "Caius told Pheir that her pussy was his."

Caius freezes over Lev's cunt, mouth curling into a snarl. *"Bastard."* But Aren's antagonism fans Caius's arousal, scent permeating the air.

Lev eases Caius back with her heel, trying to think past the want between her legs. "Is that so?" Her ass swirls back against Aren's cock. He groans into her shoulder. Caius's gaze darts to where they meet, to Aren's claws trailing around her breasts before Caius's head snaps up at Lev's voice. "Tell me the truth, Caius."

His jaw clamps, fighting the confession, his dick hard under their attention. He tries to shrug it off. "I was talking shit."

Lev hums at the nonanswer, reaching behind her to fist around Aren's cock. His growl rumbles against her shoulder. Caius tries to move forward with a snarl that sounds more like a whimper. A smirk dips into Lev's voice. "I thought you didn't want to babysit her."

"I *don't*," Caius barks despite the way his hips rut into the air, hungry under the reprimand. Aren shakes his head to make Caius surly and snarling. It works; he's ready to pounce. Lev doesn't remove her foot from his chest as she leans down toward him.

"If you ask me, you've been desperate to get inside Pheir since she gave you that scar."

It's a risky move playing with bitter memories. This close, Lev can search Caius's eyes for discomfort and measure his reaction. There's nothing but wanton truth in the brown depths of his eyes. They follow her mouth as it curves low and dark over the words.

"If that's your cunt," Lev coos, "that means you want to be there when I fuck my new bride. Is that it? Is that what's got you all riled up?"

It's all pretense. Pheir would never let Lev touch her. Lev would never *want* to, but this is the closest she's gotten to digging under the wall between her and Caius. He doesn't flinch from the words, rising up to his knees until Lev nearly topples. Aren's weight behind her is the only thing that lets her push back against him.

"Oh, you can watch, Caius," Lev assures him, fingers closing in the fur of his chest to draw him right in front of her. "I might even let you play with her. But that pussy is *mine*. Even if you make her come. Even if she rides your cock and screams your name." Lev's lips part against his, the heat of their breath mingling when he whines. It digs into Lev's gut with desire. She doesn't stop. "Even if you fuck her full of every ounce of your cum."

The thought lights a fire in him. He lunges for Lev, desperate to slot their mouths together. She kisses him fervently, tongue battling his for a trace of what happened that night.

Did Pheir make them work for it? Did she dig in her talons? Did she come with the same unbridled fury she does everything? It's a vision Lev wishes she could grasp, moan spilling into Caius's mouth. She has to hold back. She can't give herself to it completely. With a gasp, she pulls out of his reach.

"I'm sorry, Caius," she pants. "We've been teasing you." Control. Lev has to keep a hand on control, or this will be over before it starts. Her body throbs with desire as she tries to keep her thoughts in line and pull the three of them together. "Aren will apologize for the both of us."

That gives both men pause as Lev scents the arousal drifting hesitantly between them. Caius doesn't show deference, rising to his feet and caging Lev against Aren's chest. "You sure you don't want to say sorry yourself?"

Gods, she wants to. She wants to apologize for anything he'll allow, even the pains before she knew him, anything as long as it means him staying next to her. Everything about him tempts her — the danger of his fangs, the war he wages with himself, the chase he gives her pleasure. But Caius won't let her touch him like that, not with anything gentler than a scrape of her nails. Her eyes trail the muscles in his abdomen, tongue slipping over her lips.

"Tempting..." Heated silence falls over the three of them, chests rising and falling as their faces hover close. Lev wraps her fingers into the thick fur on the back of Caius's head. "But I think you should show me with Aren's mouth how sorry I should be."

Caius grunts in response, but he moves back to make room for Aren to slip down onto the ground. The three of them swap their positions, Caius leaning back against Lev's chest on the truck and covering her torso entirely. He's warm and broad, weight easing the tension from her lungs.

None of them reach for their safeword.

"On your knees," Caius sneers.

Aren doesn't comply. Instead, he sinks to all fours and prowls in a wide loop around the back of the truck. Even as bipedal people, werecreatures move fluidly like this, reminiscent of beasts. Aren's much bigger than the lynx he resembles, his body powerful and honed as he slips into the shadows between foliage.

Caius's breath grows tight. Lev's fingers clench, heart hammering in time with his. Losing sight of Aren was a mistake. He moves silently through the bushes. Adrenaline and arousal spike in Lev and Caius, a reminder of the true apex predator among them.

There's a shift in the brush. A flash of teeth. Caius and Lev press back against the truck, two targets cornered by a stronger creature. When Aren lunges from the darkness, Caius and Lev cling to each other. Satisfied, Aren bites back a smirk, sinking prostrate in the dirt even further than demanded.

The relief makes Lev laugh breathlessly. Her hands drape down over Caius's chest at the sudden thrill. Caius tries to pretend Aren's predatory movements didn't frighten him. That they didn't make him hard. When Aren rises to his knees, mouth lingering an inch away from Caius's cock, Caius shudders. "Catty fucking asshole."

His discontent turns to a bitter groan when Aren noses against the base of his cock. "Then let me apologize properly."

TEN

Caius

Any of the guards could find them like this. From scent alone, it's clear what they're doing, but Caius isn't stopping, not when worries slip from his body like leaves off a tree. He sheds the thought of Lev leaving tomorrow, of the old fractures in his bones that never set right, of Aren always a step ahead of him. Those doubts drift away, letting Caius sink into the animal part of his brain where there are no thoughts — only feeling.

The warm pressure at his back, Lev's pulse thudding an assurance into him. He's protected. His back is covered. His head doesn't have to stay on a swivel. She's a shield large enough to cover the most sensitive parts of his underbelly with her hands.

The beast in him recognizes Aren. Caius tries to resist it, to swim out of the carnal current to find his thoughts again. It's a losing battle. It's too good to give into what the animal inside him supplies, the notion that Caius's better kneels before him. That Caius's beta has lowered to serve him. As loathe as Caius is to admit it, that's what Aren is: *his*. Caius's blood surges with primal instinct.

Hot. Hungry. Safe.

Caius tilts the lynx's chin up with a claw. "About time you pay me back for the shit you gave me after the battle."

Aren's words swim hot through Caius's mind. *You like an audience? Or do you just like that it's Pheir?* In the forest, Aren's comment had Caius nearly feral. There's no remorse in Aren's eyes now. No doubt it was meant to rile Caius up. It's *always* to rile him up, to smoke him out of his cave.

On his knees in front of the truck, Aren laves Caius's cock until Caius writhes at the rough scrape of tongue. Aren takes his time, swirling hot around the head until Caius snaps.

"Come the fuck *on*." He fucks the air in desperation.

Lev holds him fast against her chest, her teeth against the piercings in his ear. "Don't move your hips."

Caius shudders against the Alpha control in her voice, watching Aren like he'd love nothing more than to maul him. That's all the encouragement Aren needs. He slows his pace, stroking a fist over Caius's length before Aren drags his tongue down to Caius's ass.

"*Gods*, fucking..." Caius's eyes roll back as Aren toys with him, flicking against Caius's tight hole. Caius can't surface for air. He doesn't want to, brutal noises escaping him. "This is supposed to be an *apology*."

Arousal saturates his words, Caius's head leaking against Aren's tongue. Then Aren pulls back his lips, exposing fangs that nick Caius's cock the way he likes. "Don't I seem apologetic?" Aren murmurs on that level fucking voice of his, lips encircling Caius for one slow moment before he pulls away. The lack of his mouth makes Caius growl, but Aren smacks his lips. "I need to show you how sorry my mouth is."

Lev chuckles against Caius's neck. His head falls back, a frustrated growl building in his chest. "I want an apology from the back of your *throat*."

Laughter puffs out of Aren, blowing cool against Caius's dick. His roughened tongue flicks out again. "Maybe if you ask nicely…"

"Don't dom me from the bottom." Caius reaches for the back of Aren's head, but Lev pins Caius's arms at his sides. The sound he makes is almost a whimper, sending fire spreading through Aren's eyes. Caius knows that look; it clenches in his stomach. Aren wants that sound again. He wants to draw out Caius's helplessness until all that's left of him is a molten puddle.

Aren will have to try harder than that. Caius clamps his mouth shut, intent to deny Aren any pleasure at Caius's expense. It's nearly impossible when Lev and Aren move like they share a mind. Lev drags her nails up Caius's chest and encircles his throat. He hates the way his eyes roll back. Hates the way his dick twitches against Aren's tongue. Hates how she teases him with pressure, mouthing his ear as she speaks.

"Is the big, bad beta being mean to you? You can always beg for *mercy*."

It's their constant safeword. Caius doesn't speak it, and still, Lev waits for cues that he wants more. She waits until his mouth tilts back toward hers, his hips grinding with another needy sound until Lev's laugh scrapes so low that Caius nearly comes right there.

"You like that?" she coos. He's like a dog in heat, panting against Lev's lips and fucking into Aren's fist. It's pathetic and frantic, unbridled want making Caius forget to keep his claws extended. When he reaches back to pull Lev closer, her fingers tighten around his throat. "Let's see what gets you there first…" Lev pricks her tongue on one of his fangs so he tastes a heady drop of her blood, licking into his mouth as she speaks. "My hand around your throat — or Aren's throat around your cock."

Caius has no time to think before Aren swallows him down. There's no fighting the roll of Caius's hips, but Aren digs his claws in to keep him in place. It does nothing to stop Caius from arching, caught between the heat of Aren's mouth and the pressure of Lev's hand. It's fucking perfect being trapped between them, giving into animal desire when he can think of nothing else but *Alpha, beta, control, hot, mine, mine, mine...*

If Caius can't be close any other way, he can be close like this.

Aren's growl vibrates up Caius's cock until Caius's claws scrape against the truck bed. Sparks fly. Aren doesn't stop until Caius gasps into Lev's mouth, the muscles in his stomach tensing

—

He can't give in that easily. He can last longer; he's built to do it. If he can extend this moment of mindless pleasure a little further...

Caius shoves Aren's head away. Aren stops his motions as Lev freezes behind Caius. He knows the fear they've upset the balance of his moment, that Caius has tripped over an old land mine in his mind, something that's left him feeling wounded. Not this time. Despite the halt, Caius's sneer drips with heat. "Keep going, and you're gonna make me come."

Tentatively, Aren brushes his lips against Caius's cock. "That's the point."

Caius curses his name, slipping off the tailgate to stand. "The *point* is an apology..." Then he turns and grabs Lev's hips to toss her onto his shoulder, making her squeak as he jerks her folded sheet onto the ground beside the truck. A half-empty bottle of lube skips across the dirt. With a whistle, Caius bends to retrieve it, swatting Lev's cottontail where it hovers beside his face.

"Gonna get freaky on your trip?" he calls to her slung over his shoulder.

"It must have still been on my bed." She fights back as best she can, scratching at the fur of his haunches. "From last time, with *you.*"

He deposits Lev onto her chest in the middle of the sheet. She scrambles for the edge, but he pounces and pins her face to the ground in a brazen display of power. His voice curls against the back of her ears. "Little rabbit, caught in a snare..."

He should feel abashed speaking to his Alpha this way and manipulating her body, but he chases the edge of recklessness because he knows Lev runs it with him. Their pack positions mean nothing when Aren and Lev are pulled into this animal place with him, past the point of restraint and uncertainties. It's an indescribable high when they fall into rhythm, too lost on scents and sounds to hold back when they can give into each other.

It's hard to tell if Lev is fighting Caius's hold or working herself back, fur streaked with wet remnants from Caius's cock. Her ass cheeks frame his dick as he grinds down against her, her body small beneath his. A flash of Aren's predator instinct darts behind his eyes. He wants this just as fucking badly, but he tries to cling to the logical side of his mind.

"I want this ass to tell me she's sorry." Caius lands his hands against Lev's cheeks when he glances back at Aren. Caius refuses to let Aren sink back into reason. Caius is going to have Aren exactly the way he wants him. Caius's tongue slides along his lips. "I want to watch her mouth around your cock. Let her *apologize* for not taking us with her."

They've played with power before, but Caius has never been so blatant with his domination. With claiming what's *his* — save for marking Pheir in the forest. Aren glances at Lev to see if she calls for mercy. Instead, her legs tremble enough to catch Aren's attention.

Hunger sweeps over his face, expression shifting into the predator he is. Muffled groans slip when Lev grinds back against Caius. He pins her hips, cockhead dragging against her clit. It's a deliberateness he so rarely possesses, teasing her entrance as his shoulders flex. "Gonna tell me you're sorry?"

This is easier than admitting that it hurts. Easier than putting words to the unfathomable things he feels. He couldn't if he wanted to. He doesn't have the language for it, but this...using his body is freeing. His body is strong. His body is consistent. His body is built to withstand whatever's thrown at it.

If it came down to it, Lev could pull out of his grasp, summoning the Alpha strength she's imbued with — but she doesn't. Caius's mouth waters at the way she gives herself to him. She trusts him with this, if nothing else. She trusts him with her body, and he knows he won't fail her with that.

Her nails dig into the sheet, leaving tears in the fabric as his claws dig into her hips. Rather than submit, she rises to his challenge, circling her ass against him as she looks back over her shoulder. "You gonna *make me* sorry?"

Her motion drags the wet heat of her cunt against him, teasing closer and closer until his cock slips inside. A feral sound rips from him. She's irresistible. He slams fully inside, fucking a gasp out of her as he sets a brutal pace.

Aren moves in front of them, sinking to his knees and settling muscled thighs to frame Lev's face. She buries her mouth against the sheet, as if hiding her sounds will keep any of this a secret. With every thrust, Caius fucks her closer to Aren until her groaning mouth is nearly buried against the base of his cock. She reaches for Aren, but he's stuck in the carnal mode that Caius is ravenous for, two predators playing with their food. Like this, Aren finds a streak of cruelty, stroking over his cock out of Lev's reach.

Her teeth grit in warning. "Aren..."

It plays out on Aren's face. There's a tug inside him to obey her, to bend to his Alpha, but there's thrill in denying her. Like this, Caius feels like the men are on equal footing, like it's Aren and Caius together, forgoing rules and regulations to just *be*. Toeing over lines to see what happens, like that night in the forest with Pheir.

Aren must remember it, too. The men's eyes lock over Lev's body as Aren takes her jaw in his hand. Caius slips a padded paw against Lev's clit to make her squirm.

Aren twists his fist slowly over himself, so out of time with the way Caius fucks her, another way to tease her. "Tell me what you need," Aren murmurs in that even tone, belying the spiteful way he works over himself. Lev's hands grapple for the sheet, but she can't find purchase. How frustrating for her, not getting what she wants...

Caius smirks.

Lev looks like she wants to scratch Aren up or swallow him so deep he can't think. He doesn't give in, slowing his fist until it's still. "Tell me, Lev," he purrs.

Now she sounds as out of control as Caius wants her. "I want your cock in my *mouth.*"

Aren taps her lips with his head. Her mouth opens — but Aren only smears across her lips. Caius howls with laughter, remembering the way Aren dragged his scent over Pheir's muzzle. It lights a fuse in Caius's stomach.

"You *want* it?" Aren asks Lev.

All their instincts are heightened. Lev doesn't get a chance to lunge for Aren before Caius drags her hips back to meet him, angling so he can fuck down into her. Her stomach scrapes the ground. She's further from Aren than she started, panting and trying to climb out from beneath Caius. There's no escaping his hold.

Aren clicks his tongue, still fucking his fist. "Looks like you've lost ground."

A scream tears between Lev's teeth. It makes Caius's dick harder, hips slapping her ass as he buries completely inside her again and again. "Aw," he simpers, chasing the sounds he fucks out of her. He laves a messy trail up the fur of her neck. "Don't like it when you can't get what you want?"

Lev shudders, but a different calmness settles over her. She doesn't move toward Aren. Doesn't fight Caius's grip. He opens his mouth to taunt her again when she starts working back against him. Filthy, wet sounds echo off the trees. Caius hisses, distracted by the way her hips rock to meet him.

"It could be so good, Aren," she breathes. Her innocence is fake under a put-on pout of her lips. Aren's dick twitches at the sight. Jealousy streaks through Caius. Suddenly *he* wants to be the one in front, watching Lev with Aren behind her — but then, Lev brings Caius into it.

She presses up on all fours to shift the angle. It makes Caius's head spin, falling forward to brace his hands on either side of hers. With one hand, she loops behind Caius's neck, turning her head to press her mouth to his throat. Her voice hums through his fur. "Tell him, Caius."

It forces Aren and Caius's eyes to lock. Exposed and vulnerable, pulsing desire through Caius. There's always been someone between him and Aren, someone to play off of, someone to use as an excuse. This is the closest they've come to looking at each other. To facing whatever is between them.

Caius bottoms out inside Lev, gripping her hips like he's scared what he might reach for if he doesn't. He grits his teeth, willing the thoughts away. His mind chants possibilities.

What if, what if, what if...?

When has Caius ever restrained himself from the reckless rush? He lets the words fall the way his body begs him to, following Lev's lead. "Come on, *beta...*"

The honorific makes Aren's head tilt back. The pack bond between them cinches, enticing Aren and Caius closer as he toys with the connection. Each thrust plucks the strands of their bond until the vibrations hum through Caius's cock. Aren must feel it, too. His eyes slip shut, like he can feel Lev through Caius.

It's too much. It pulls them too close, humming through Caius's body like he might shake apart. He can't focus on Aren. He can't call him that again, not when they're too close to each other already. Caius releases the thread between them, letting it grow slack when he pins Lev down between them. She's the bridge. She's the safe link between them, one Caius can focus on without feeling like he's spiraling out of control. He keeps his eyes honed on the back of her head when he growls.

"Don't make her wait. Give your Alpha what she's asking for."

ELEVEN

Aren

The shift in Caius stings Aren, but it's not unexpected. No matter what Aren felt surging through their bond, it doesn't change the way things are. Caius doesn't reach for Aren. Caius withstands Aren's presence as a matter of courtesy. Caius keeps his hands on Lev, bearing harder thrusts into her and focusing all his attention.

It's Lev who extends her hand to Aren, bridging the gap between them and pulling him from his thoughts. Her eyes meet his, glazed with lust when she curls her fingers against his thighs and breathes, "I need you."

It's the same way she said it that day in the bar when she convinced him to join her. When she changed the trajectory of his life, giving him more than he dared hope for. Her words are not, *I need your cock. I need you to fuck me.*

I need you.

Aren doesn't keep her suspended any longer. Relief seeps over her expression when he glides his thumb into her mouth to draw her chin up. She presses up on her palms, his finger dragging down her bottom lip before he draws her eyes to his and speaks. "That's what I want."

She gives the barest nod, as if she understands. As if she can scent how much deeper this goes than a fleeting fuck. That's enough for now. When her lips part under Aren's finger, he lets the head of his cock sink into her mouth.

All three of them groan, Lev's body rocking between them as both men surge together to fill her completely. If nothing else, they know how to move together. While Aren rolls into her mouth, Caius keeps his rhythm, squeezing lube over her ass and working her open on two fingers. When Aren pulls back until he nearly slips out of her mouth, Caius curses as he sinks into the tight heat of her ass. The men's opposing rhythms settle into tandem until they're drawing out of her at the same time, burying deep enough that her groans are muffled by how full they have her. She's wet and wanton around both of them. They take control of her. She gives it to them, the hair between her ears curled in both their fists as they fill her from both ends.

Her gaze stays on Aren, a pitiful plea as pleasure overtakes her body. Caius picks up the pace, fingers working against her clit as he leans down to press his chest to her back. "I want you to smell like us," he snarls, hips snapping into hers. "I want everyone to know what the fuck you've been up to. Who the fuck's in your bed."

It shudders through her. Aren can't fight his own tremor at the words. There's no mistaking the heat that sears them together, drenching all three of them in each other. The smell will cling to Lev for days, no matter how far she goes from them. There's no way any creature in the Break will make the mistake of thinking Lev is unprotected or unspoken for. It's exactly what Caius wants.

What *Aren* wants.

Possessiveness streaks through him. His paw slides along Lev's throat, cupping where his cock nudges inside her. She takes him deep, mouth stretching around the spines halfway down his length. It's filthy and feral and fucking delicious. The thread of Aren's control begins to unravel.

"You gonna let Caius come inside?" he asks. Rather than answer, Lev swallows around Aren's cock, making his fangs dig into his lip. Caius grinds in deeper, tugging back on her hair so he can watch Aren disappear inside her mouth. The new angle sends a jolt of desire through Aren, growl rumbling from his chest as he ruts toward her mouth. "You gonna let *me* come inside?"

It spurs her on, body bent to take them both as Caius drives into her. Who needs teeth and claws when Caius works her clit like he could tear her apart? It's useless for her to fight, body trapped between them when her eyes squeeze shut. Her groans vibrate through Aren's cock as she comes. Caius doesn't stop, caging her against the ground as he hunts the trail of her orgasm. His voice is hot with need. "Don't forget who you're coming back to. Don't forget who makes you feel like this."

When his teeth dig into the side of her throat, he looks up at Aren with unflinching ambition. It's like Caius doesn't have to try, dragging Lev through her orgasm as Aren approaches his own. Aren could hold out longer, but there's a fire in Caius's eyes. Aren's not sure what it means. Not sure if it's Caius asserting dominance or giving Aren exactly what he needs to tumble over the edge.

Caius stretches against Lev's back, bringing his mouth closer to hers as she whimpers...then his tongue drags against Aren's cock. Anywhere Lev can't reach, Caius mouths against. He laves over Aren's base with their eyes locked together, tongue barbels rolling against Aren's sack. The sight of it sends Aren over. Gripping Lev's head, he comes deep in her throat until he's buried completely. She swallows every drop, rolling her tongue against his spines to make Aren shiver until he slips out of her mouth.

Caius grabs her jaw, holding her still as he licks the taste of Aren from her mouth. Aren swears he could get hard again from that, but Caius doesn't let the moment linger.

"Knew you couldn't outlast me," he taunts Aren, digging claws into Lev's hips before he picks up speed in her ass again. All her sounds spill into open air as she clings to Aren's thighs. Aren shifts closer, lifting her hands against his chest as Caius fucks her on her knees. Caius takes his brutal time with her. Aren tilts his head pityingly. "Is he gonna make you come again?"

Lev whimpers into Aren's neck, as if that will save her from Caius's desperate hunt for her pleasure. While Caius fucks her hard, Aren brushes a hand through her hair and speaks against her ear. "He says he can last, but I don't think he's thought this through."

It's loud enough for Caius to hear over the sound of their fucking. His ears perk, hardened gaze darting to Aren. Caius doesn't speak, as if he's waiting to hear how Aren will correct him. Aren's mouth tips up in a smirk, keeping his eyes on Caius. "I don't think he's ready for you to beg him to come. For you to ask him to give you all of it." Aren cradles Lev's head against his chest, turning her chin so she can look back at Caius. "Tell him what a good job he's done."

Caius's eyes snap shut, hips stuttering as he curses. Lev is starry-eyed, mouth falling open through the daze of arousal. She's cock-drunk and hazy. "Caius…"

"Don't fucking —" But Caius can't speak more than that, hips picking up at the pace as he tries to break her first. Tries to be the last one standing. Tries to keep his emotions from tearing across his expression.

Lev arches back against him, and Aren knows it's over. She lowers her head to Aren's lap, ass in the air as Caius takes her, her eyes clinging to his as she whimpers. "It's so good. It's so fucking perfect."

Caius shudders, hips pumping faster as his finger fumbles for Lev's clit. He's in too deep now. She slots her hand between her thighs, guiding Caius's fingers gently against her. It's a clash that meets like lightning, Lev's guidance next to Caius's stuttering heat, a sight that coils in Aren's stomach.

"Please come in me," Lev whimpers. "Please fill me up, please…" She gasps when Caius follows the rhythm she set with her fingers, his hand and hips moving in time. He can't pull his eyes away from her, gritting his teeth like he's trying to keep from falling over the edge, but he can't deprive himself of the sight of her. She knows it, too, voice curling in a desperate plea. "Please let me have it. Please let me watch you, Caius, please don't keep it from me —"

It's inevitable. Caius's hips stutter, buried as deep as he can go, dragging tracks of his claws through her fur. She gasps when he sinks completely, both their lips parting as their bodies notch together. Caius can barely hold himself upright, arms giving out when he tries to brace on the ground beside Lev's shoulders. He collapses on top of her, but Aren holds their heads in his lap. All their heartbeats thunder out of time as Caius mouths against Lev's neck, his hips stirring in a mindless rhythm that fucks his cum deeper into her.

Lev's laugh is weak as she tries and fails to shove him off of her back. Her voice is hoarse, content and sated as she curls fingers into his fur beside her head. "There. No one's gonna question who I smell like."

There's fuzzy delight in Caius's expression. He's so spent he forgets to be surly. Only once he's satisfied with the cum dripping from Lev's ass does he retract. "Don't bathe before you go," he warns, rolling onto his back. "Or we'll have to do it again."

They don't return to the cabins right away, sprawling out together on the sheet. Stars prick through the dark of the night sky, the sounds of the forest swelling around them. Aren listens for anything unusual. There's nothing but patrols on the border and nocturnal creatures scurrying through the brush. On the other end of the blanket, Caius situates himself on his side, facing the forest as Lev traces patterns through the thick fur on his back.

"If you do that," he mutters sleepily, "I'm not gonna be able to keep watch."

Lev doesn't change her movements. "Then don't watch."

He gives a grunt of distaste, but with the swirl of her fingers, his breathing evens. The three of them stay like that, silent and slow, so long that Aren's surprised when Lev whispers.

"We've found one time he'll be soft."

Aren huffs a laugh, eyeing Caius's broad back. "When he's unconscious?"

Lev's fingers keep brushing through Caius's fur. Even in sleep, he jerks, as if he's trying to get away from the soft touch. His hair grows in unevenly, whorls beneath his fur where scars curve and slash. Lev's fingers hover over them. When Caius's sleeping form gives another twitch, she drops her hand back to the sheet, head tilting toward Aren over her shoulder. "Do you still think he sees you as an extension of me?"

Aren rests his head against the sheet. Tonight, there was something different, some piece of Caius emerging that's never been there before. It doesn't change how Caius will settle back into isolation once there's not sex to devote himself to. He's fearless. He's stronger than any opponent they've faced, but it's when there's no physicality that Caius looks out of his element. When his body doesn't know how to hold itself. In the midst of all their heat, Caius pulled away as soon as Lev opened the space between them. That hasn't changed in the span of the evening.

Aren curls his arm around Lev's waist, pressing his mouth to the back of her neck. "I do."

Lev sighs, but she doesn't contest it, resting her hand over his as silence settles between them. Aren pulls himself closer to the two of them until he's pressed against Lev's back. Until he can watch Caius's side rise and fall as he breathes, close enough to touch and still out of reach.

TWELVE

Caius

3 years before Vesta's death

Maybe Caius should have stayed with his family.

Not that he had a choice. He squats in a shallow cave, arms wrapped around his knees and his hackles lifted to half-mast. It's been like this since he left home a few months ago, constantly on edge no matter where he sets up camp.

It shouldn't be this hard. *Another thing you can't do for shit.* He scuffs his foot against the ground, knocking dirt on his poor attempt at a fire. With winter on the way, he has two options: learn to survive on his own, or die. From the way his joints creak, he knows which of those are more likely.

His body was his saving grace for so long. Now, it's pathetic, full of aches and pains, old injuries flaring, fur thinning and dull. In the time since he left home, his body's burned through stores of muscle and fat until he's little more than skin and bones. Beating the shit out of other people is one thing. Stringing up traps is quite another, and sneaking up on prey is next to impossible when Caius has always gotten by on intimidation.

Survival should be easy. It should be natural, but he's been rudely awakened to how little he understands the wilderness.

Told you you had a cushy life.

Caius can practically smell the tobacco leaking between his father's lips. Caius's stomach turns as he grits his teeth, trying to put the man's yellowed sneer out of his mind.

Not the big man you thought you were, huh? Should've listened to what I fucking told you —

Caius winces — but no blow comes. Still, his ears ache, but he can't be sure if it's from all those years of taking hits or this new exposure to cold.

At least the scenery is...something. Outside the mouth of the cave, brilliant red and orange leaves shiver in the wind. Despite spending his entire life in the Break, Caius has hardly stepped outside the small village of his home. They didn't have these "packs" he's heard about, groups of creatures living together and maintaining their territories. There certainly wasn't anyone looking out for *him*. All his life, he was either training in his hometown or making the trek through the mountains to the underground cage matches in Orena.

He could return there and find an Orena city he can survive in, join one of the rings he's familiar with, but Caius winces as he rotates his shoulder. He's in no shape to fight these days. Even if he were, he can't take the daily assault on his body. Loathe as he is to admit it, he can't do anything else, either. From the odd jobs he's found around the Break, he doesn't possess the temperament they require.

Maybe his father was right to kick him out. He should've done it sooner, a few years ago when Caius reached adulthood. Maybe that would've given Caius a better chance to survive.

Who knew spending years becoming the biggest threat in a room would bite him in the ass?

Bushes rustle in the distance.

Caius's weight settles onto his feet, ears honing in the direction of the noise. Whomever it is makes no attempt to be quiet, two voices floating above the forest sounds as they walk. They're happy — a man and a woman, conversation flowing between them.

There's a pang in Caius that isn't hunger.

He buries that yearning. He has to be careful. Different packs monitor different territories. They each have their own way of handling things, but an intruder will hardly be welcome. Claws unsheathing, Caius keeps his eyes on the mouth of the cave.

"I'm not cooking it again." The man's voice rumbles with humor, low and easy like a stream weaving around rocks. "Mari said they've eaten better bugs from a rotting log, and I'm inclined to believe them."

The woman laughs, bright and open. It makes Caius feel like sunlight dappling through the leaves — *no*. He jerks the thought away, claws clacking as he clenches his fist. *Get it the fuck together.* He's tired and hungry, dazed and confused. Any warmth from the voices is imagined.

Footsteps stop twenty-five yards away. Caius's heart thuds, wolverine ears flicking as the woman sniffs and lowers her voice. "Do you smell..."

Caius has to get out of here. The cave is too shallow to hide in. If he gets cornered...creeping to the entrance, his eyes dart for an escape route, somewhere he can sprint —

A twig snaps on his other side. He whirls, teeth bared —

"Hey!" The wererabbit holds up her hands toward Caius as the lynx blocks her with an arm.

Caius snarls. The man growls louder.

Despite the tension, the woman pushes in front of her partner. He barks her name. She moves slowly, keeping her hands raised and maintaining distance from Caius. "We're not gonna hurt you."

Caius's eyes flash to the lynx, who's thoughts seem to match his. *Not unless we have to.* Caius's back brushes one wall of the cave. His gaze darts toward the nearby stream. If he can make it to the water, he can swim for it — but this lynx can, too.

As if she reads Caius's thoughts, the woman speaks again. "You don't have to leave. I'm Lev." She reaches behind her. "This is Aren."

Aren's not happy they're exchanging pleasantries. He steps forward to be closer to her. Caius keeps his lips curled back over his teeth. That doesn't deter this woman — *Lev.*

"I'm gonna reach in my bag." She lifts the strap from her shoulder. "It's for food."

Now is when Caius should run, take off and pray the lynx doesn't spring at his back. *No one else will fight for you the way you will.* It's one rule from Caius's father that's served him well...but Caius doesn't run. He doesn't know why. Maybe his self-preservation instincts are as shitty as his others.

When Lev reaches into her satchel, his eyes flicker between her hands and Aren's face. The lynx's teeth are still bared, but he looks less like a tight coil. His tufted ears flick, nose twitching as Lev removes two wrapped packages and sets them at her feet.

"I have water, too."

Caius knows what Lev must see, a scrawny creature shaking in the cold. An animal useless to keep himself alive. There's not pity in her gaze, though. Her head tilts curiously.

"Are you lost? Are you in trouble?"

Caius doesn't answer, but he does take a better look at her. She can't be more than a few years older than him. Aren must be slightly older than that. The partners hardly look at each other, yet they move in sync. When Lev extends her hand backward, Aren unwinds the canteen from his body and hands it to her. It's as if they know each other, as if they sense each other, communicating in a language Caius can't fathom. It's the same way he would read an opponent in the ring, searching for their tells and weaknesses, but Aren and Lev are working together.

Despite Caius's silence, Lev nods, as if he's told her what she needs to know. "You can stay here, if you want. You're in Timber territory; Aren and I lead the pack."

"You're the *Alpha*," Aren clarifies. The distinction is for Caius's benefit, a reminder of the respect he should show her. For the first time, Caius's vicious expression shifts enough for his brows to knit. He can't decide if the way this man speaks about Lev is impressive or infuriating.

"If you run into anyone that gives you trouble," Lev continues, "tell them we've spoken with you. I'll come back tomorrow and bring you more food, some blankets..."

"You can't come on your own," Aren hisses. Lev looks at him over her shoulder as if she trusts Caius not to lunge at her. The gesture surprises him so starkly, his body relaxes a fraction.

"You think he's dangerous?" She jabs her thumb toward Caius before she glances back at him and winks. It draws out a dimple in her cheek. "Please. I could take him."

It's ludicrous. Even in Caius's sorry state, he's a predator, and she's prey, but the comment has the desired effect. The muscles in his mouth aren't sure what to do — bare his teeth or laugh — so he lowers his lips back over his teeth.

Her entire face brightens at that. The charming gap between her front teeth makes Caius's stomach flip.

"Then we'll both be back tomorrow." She takes a step back before her glance catches on the cave behind him. "You shouldn't build a fire inside there. It'll trap the smoke and heat. You need smaller kindling, too." After a quick search, she pulls up a bunch of brittle grass. "Try these. Fill in the gaps of your twigs and light them first." She sets the grass on the wrapped food. Then, she waves goodbye, tugging Aren away in the direction they were headed.

Caius's eyes follow her before he realizes Aren is still watching him carefully. The lynx doesn't turn his back on Caius until they disappear from sight.

Once their footsteps have faded, Caius risks leaving the cave, snatching up the supplies and sulking back under cover. Beneath him, he swears the earth hums warmly. He must have been closer to starvation than he thought. He doesn't register what the food is before he inhales it, licking the wrappers for every crumb. He shouldn't take handouts. He shouldn't trust these people. He should move on to another location.

But how long can he keep this up?

When Lev and Aren return the next day, the food wrappings lay crumpled next to a fallen tree...and Caius hovers at the mouth of the cave with a fire crackling before him.

Lev smiles at him again.

THIRTEEN

Caius

PRESENT
16 days after Vesta's death

Lev is gone when Caius wakes.

Half-asleep, he takes stock of his body. His joints ache from laying on the ground, back cold and muscles sore. A smile flickers across his mouth. *Worth it.*

Seeking the warmth of Lev's body, he rolls over, but his fingers curl into empty sheets. Through the open cabin doors, light streaks pink across the sky. Drowsily, he recalls being half-carried back to Lev's cabin in the early morning hours. It was Aren's doing, of course. It's tempting for Caius to curl tighter into himself, but another weight on the bed shifts slowly in an attempt not to wake him.

"I'm already up," Caius grumbles.

Aren loops a satchel over his shoulder. "Go back to sleep. I'll do morning checks."

"No point." Caius pushes up from the bed. Aren's amber eyes are still on him, making Caius bristle. *"What?"*

There's hesitancy in Aren, the kind that follows the nights when the three of them do whatever this is. Each second of silence is like claws picking at the raw scab of Caius's emotions until he wants to scream.

Mercifully, Aren speaks. "Lev was right when she said you've been working overtime. You should take a day off. At least take a break."

"She said '*we.*' That includes you. That includes *her.*" Caius cracks his neck bitterly. "Guess none of us know how to relax."

"Let me take breakfast detail, at least. You check in with the overnight rotation. It should only take a minute." Aren stops in the doorway, fingers lingering on the frame. "Keep an eye out for any Regents. Hopefully they won't go back on the timeframe they set, but let me know if you spot any."

Caius sets his feet on the ground. "Why?"

Aren's mouth presses into a thin line. Clearly, it's something he and Lev discussed before she left, yet another reminder that it's not the three of them together; it's Lev and Aren on one side, and Caius making a fool of himself on the other.

He gives up hoping for an answer. "Is that a command, beta?" Caius drawls before he thinks better of it. Suddenly, the room is saturated with remnants of the night before.

Come on, beta...

Heat rushes through Caius's body. Last night was a slip. It was *almost* a slip, but Caius caught himself before he fumbled his pride. It was sex. It was dirty talk spilled without thinking, the same way he did with Pheir in the forest. Gods, he needs to get a grip on the shit he says in the heat of the moment, or someone's going to think he means it.

Still, his pulse follows when Aren's mouth hitches upward. He knocks on the doorframe before he leaves. "Take it however you want, as long as you take it."

Caius flops back on the bed. He knows Lev will return, but he can't fight the panicky feeling in his chest. At least she left the sheet they used last night. Burying his face into the blankets, he inhales deeply. No doubt she left it on purpose, knowing Caius would want a comforting reminder to curl up in. Eyes rolling, he covers his face with a pillow, but he can't deny the smile that presses into the pillowcase.

In the absence of a few Timbers, there's more work to be done, but the day still passes slowly. More than once, Caius stares off toward the tree line as if Lev might reappear. In his fantasy, they don't have to talk when she bounds up to him. It's simple when she flings her arms around his neck. *Caius* is simple, returning the gesture like he knows how, like his body doesn't tense at the slightest touch.

It wouldn't happen like that in real life. Instead, Lev would skirt around him, unsure what movements would startle him. Aren would watch down his nose, waiting for Caius to make a mistake. Because Caius is fragile like two tons of dynamite waiting to blow, and he can't decide if he wants anyone next to him when it happens.

He tells himself he doesn't trust Aren and Lev — except when he's strung out on lust, dick hard and pressed between their bodies to feel closer. If only bridging the gap was as easy as fucking their smell into each other, bodies slamming together so there won't be any space left between them.

It's no surprise Caius wanders back to Lev's cabin at nightfall. He lingers on the wooden steps outside. After the night before and the day's work, he's ready to smear his face in the sheets that still smell like the three of them.

"Thought you might come back here."

Caius whirls — but it's just Aren drifting onto the deck. Unlike the intimidating lumber Caius moves with, Aren is silent and graceful. Another of Caius's failings put into bright focus next to Aren. The cabin reeks of the three of them, and still, Caius feels like an intruder. Tail tucking and ready to run, he steps down off the porch. "I'll leave you to it." He can bury his head in his own scentless sheets that he'll shred in frustration.

"Caius..."

Blame it on pack dynamics, beta power, whatever lets Caius off the hook when he turns back at Aren's voice. Aren's mouth stays closed, choosing words carefully. Doing *everything* carefully. Caius want to scream at him to have a single fucking unplanned emotion —

Finally, Aren finishes. "There doesn't have to be someone between us."

Caius's heart pounds harder than it has on any battlefield.

"Aren!"

Both their ears perk, whipping toward the wolf bursting from Pheir's cabin. The two men are halfway across the field before they can make out Echo's words between panting breaths.

"Pheir! She escaped!"

Aren shifts immediately into action. Even though Caius knows it's his duty, it stings. Whatever Aren meant moments before wasn't enough to get caught up in. It wasn't enough to throw Aren's precise voice off kilter when he calls out instructions. "Alert the guards in the pack house. Make sure everyone's accounted for. Search every corner of the compound."

Echo sprints toward the main building. Aren glances to Caius. He nods in return, and the two of them shift into sync as Aren moves toward the A-frame cabins. Caius nearly follows — but his eyes dart toward the tree line again. He's not sure what pulls him toward it. As Aren and Echo run to opposite ends of the field, Caius bounds toward the border.

As soon as he reaches the forest, his feet slow. His snout lifts toward the breeze. Every sound makes his ears twitch, croaking frogs amplified when all he wants is silence. It doesn't make sense for Pheir to make a break for the woods. She won't get far with clipped wings and poor nocturnal vision, and that spiteful bitch is more likely to maul an innocent bystander to send a message.

So what makes Caius think she's here?

Focus. He shuts his eyes to block out the ambient sounds — an owl hooting to his left, wind rustling in an indiscernible pattern. Fifty yards away, leaves shift by a hollowed log, followed by desperate footsteps making no attempt to disguise themselves.

There you are.

Caius takes off, careening between tree trunks and leaping over stumps as wings flash between shadows. Purple feathers get stuck on brambles. That doesn't slow Pheir. There are a dozen feet between them now. He extends his hands toward her. She ducks sharply, but Caius is faster, colliding and sending them both skidding through the dirt.

Her talons seek him in the dark, her chest slamming to the ground and knocking out a scream. As soon as her legs are underneath her, she fights to stand, but he uses her force against her. With a *crack*, he swings her back against a tree trunk that echoes through the forest.

Copper scents the air. Pheir claws at him, blood slipping down the gash on her face to his hand around her throat. She doesn't notice, mindless and wild, tongue catching a rivulet of red as she scrambles to get free.

Her wrists are still bound — but not her feet. He realizes it a second before she scratches, giving him enough time to slam his hips between her legs and force her thighs apart. He reaches behind him to grip her ankles as she writhes. She won't accept that she's trapped, fury boiling over as she lunges toward him. Caius crushes her back against the trunk and snarls. "I was gonna offer you a scar. Looks like you're already working on one."

Her body barely moves as she jerks in his grip. "Come on!" That bloody smile slips across her lips, as vicious as the way she grinds against his cock, finding friction where there should be none. "Fuck me into submission again. I *promise* I won't tear out your throat."

"Is that the best distraction you've got?" He tightens his hold on her throat, leaning close until they're sharing the same air. "At least offer me something appealing."

"Like fucking you in the bed of a truck?"

Caius freezes. Pheir latches onto the surprise in his eyes, hips swirling into his in a filthy figure-eight.

"I saw you out my window. Couldn't help yourself, could you? You didn't even bother to hide it."

He doesn't know why he reacts like this, knowing Pheir saw the three of them last night. His dick hardens like the sick fuck he is, head swimming at the scent of their arousal mingling with blood. Pheir drags along his length, eyes dark and deadly — but Caius doesn't give in. He doesn't ask the barbaric questions that swarm his mind.

Did you get wet for it? Did you like what you saw? Did you wish we were fucking you, too?

He's jerked out of his reverie when she screams in frustration. "*Kill me*, then! You want to!" Her body strains uselessly, pupils blowing wide. "Fucking do it, like your little friend wanted!"

When she circles her hips again, Caius bares his teeth, digging her head back into the tree bark. "Don't tempt me..." It would be easy. Effortless. Barely a lie when he tells the others that she swung for his neck...but no matter how simple it would be to slash her throat, something stops him. Lev's face in his mind and Aren's voice in his ear. Caius pulls his hand back. Pheir tries to jerk free, but Caius keeps her pinned. "Goddamn, Pheir, *give it up!*"

For an impossible second, her eyes clear. Clouds lifting, glaze dissolving, body falling slack in his grip. It's a trick of the light, though, because her fury reignites like a match.

"*Fuck you!* Vesta will destroy you once I —"

Caius slams Pheir back into the tree. "Why are you killing yourself for someone who never gave a shit about you?"

Words echo off the rocks as the fire in Pheir's eyes flickers. Her mouth falls open, silent for once. Her bundled rage leaks like there's a hole in her, like he's found her soft, vulnerable skin. Despite his instincts, he's tempted to retract. To set her on the ground and dress the wound across her face...

Until her dizzy look disappears, replaced by a film of rage. "You fucking *liar!*"

Her fight returns, but she's too weak to do more than struggle. Her escape is over, and she knows it.

It's a chore getting her back to the cabin. By the time Caius hauls her out of the trees, two other guards hoist her inside. "Make sure she's fucking restrained this time!" Caius shouts after them, rotating his arm as Aren approaches. "How the hell did she get out in the first place?"

"Not sure." Aren stares after Pheir. "During guard change, Echo heard a scuffle in the room. Pheir bolted as soon as she got on the porch."

The cabin door muffles Pheir's screams. Aren lifts Caius's hand, examining the blood and dirt matted in his fur.

Caius jerks his hand back. "It's not mine." It'll still smart tomorrow, as will his knees and back. Caked blood cracks when he flexes his fingers, and he remembers when his hands were much smaller. When he first started to feel numb to bloodying his fists on someone else. When his father's proud voice rattled through him.

My boy never misses.

"Come on." Aren tilts his head toward the bathhouse. "We'll clean you up."

Caius shrugs out of his grip. "I'll be fine."

"*Caius.*"

This time, Aren's voice brooks no arguments, infused with a command he so rarely gives. Caius's lips pull back over his teeth. Aren doesn't cower. Doesn't flinch. Doesn't blink.

Emotionless bastard.

"Let me help you," Aren finally says.

Caius could fight him on it. He could suffer through his tense shoulders, his tight jaw, his fingers curled into fists...but he's fucking exhausted. Maybe a few minutes won't be the end of the world. With a curt nod, Caius follows Aren toward the baths on the other side of the crops. It's an outdoor building with few walls, a wooden frame under a clear, vaulted roof that gives view into the trees overhead. Homemade soaps line the rickety shelves next to metal basins dotted with vines and potted plants.

Some of the water in the buckets is still warm. Aren pours it into a basin, and Caius has no recourse but to get in. He steps inside and sinks down slowly, blood and dirt turning the water a murky brown.

It's disturbing being with Aren like this. Caius's eyes follow him around the space as Aren finds a glass bottle of soap and pulls up a stool. He settles behind Caius. Caius can't relax in the warmth of the water. *Your back's exposed*, his thudding instinct reminds him. His toes curl against the basin, claws extending —

"You can put your hackles down." The low rumble of Aren's voice does strange things, washing Caius in heat stronger than the bath. Willing down the fur on his back, Caius keeps Aren in his periphery.

"Can I touch you?" Aren asks.

Caius barks a laugh. As if they haven't fucked. As if they haven't fought next to each other — but Aren still waits for a verbal response. "*Yes*," Caius finally snaps. Aren lifts a nearby cup to pour water down Caius's back. He lathers soap into Caius's fur with dexterous fingers before he finds a knot at the base of Caius's neck. When Aren kneads his fingers into it, Caius bites back a moan.

"You caught Pheir quickly," Aren murmurs.

Caius curls a hand around the rim of the tub. "She's not as smart as she thinks."

Aren's hands dig in deeper. "It's like you knew where she would go."

Defensive anger swells in Caius. "Are you accusing me —"

"No." Aren guides his fingers up the back of Caius's neck, hovering next to his pulse. Caius is tempted to clamp teeth around Aren's hand as Aren pours another cupful of water, rinsing out splattered blood. "I mean you knew what she would do. I never expected her to run, not when revenge is the thing that drives her. I was certain she'd storm the lodge, attack anyone she could, take someone hostage...but you went straight for the tree line."

Caius has a destructive need to be angrier. To threaten. To make Aren scared to touch him, but Aren's ministrations feel too fucking *good*. An odd mix of comfort and unease floods Caius. "I don't know. It seems obvious now that she'd go for the lodge."

"But she didn't," Aren reminds him. "You were right."

Caius's eyes narrow, head turning to catch a glimpse of Aren. "What are you getting at?"

Aren's palm lays out next to Caius's head, waiting for Caius's paw. Instead, Caius dips the scrape on his knuckles beneath the water.

"It's fine."

Aren doesn't retract. After a long moment, Caius tosses his hand up toward Aren, splashing water over the edge of the tub. Aren doesn't seem to care, scrubbing between Caius's fingers as he speaks. "It seems like you understand her, how her mind works. I don't think any of us can read her like that."

That's a horrifying thought. Pheir is rabid and frenetic, a beast no one could love. What does that say about Caius?

He pops his neck to fill the silence. "I don't fucking understand that bitch." But if that's true, why had he known where Pheir would go? How could he possibly predict someone that wild? He shifts his knees toward his chest like he's covering his most vulnerable parts. "Maybe I smelled her — but she was *weird* when I caught her."

"Weird how?"

"I don't know. She's just fucking *weird*. Like she wasn't all there." Caius gestures in front of his face. "Like she had film over her eyes."

Aren pours water over Caius's wounded hand. Caius hisses, but Aren grips tighter to keep him in place. "That gives more credence to Rhaiden's letter."

"Letter?" Caius's eyes whip over his shoulder. Aren pauses, mouth pulled taut, like he's shared something he shouldn't. Yet another secret Lev and Aren have. It digs between Caius's ribs, a throbbing reminder that they are not the same. That Aren is trusted in ways Caius isn't.

"Rhaiden wrote to Lev," Aren finally says. "She has suspicions of what went on with Vesta. Of what might still be going on."

Another cloud of dirt stirs in the water as Caius shifts. "Like Vesta's still alive?"

"Not exactly. If what Rhaiden says is true…" There Aren goes, shuttering his expression, packing up the serious conversation for when Caius isn't present. "We'll see if Lev invites her to speak about it."

The distance between them grows again. It's as if Caius watches from afar, Lev's head bowed with Aren's. Fucking Alpha-beta bonds, leaving no room for anyone else. They bear the weight of duty together. They share all their secrets. They see every part of each other.

If Caius can't reach them any other way, maybe it's time he shows them he can carry the pack as well.

As Aren dries his own paws, Caius sinks lower in the tub. Waves splash against the sides. "Don't compare me to that birdy bitch again." Then he holds his breath, dipping under for as long as he can, the surrounding noise muffled until there's silence.

When he resurfaces, his lungs burn under the ringing of his ears, and Aren is gone.

FOURTEEN

Pheir

The Timbers might as well let Pheir bleed out.

Why not? They want her dead. Caius could have finished the job moments ago. Hell, they could have suffocated her with a pillow as soon as he brought her back to the compound. Instead, they're drawing out her torture.

It's like it's a game to them, more twisted than she gave them credit for. It's psychological warfare. The cabin is darker than before, curtains drawn tight with no candles lit. And to think, this morning, the guards removed her ankle chains for some breathing room. Now, those bindings have returned with extra lengths to match her wrists and chest.

She can't run. She can hardly move when she's trapped in this prison, so she does the only thing she can: scream. Because she hates the Timbers. Because she wants them to suffer. Because the broken Vestal bonds still *hurt*.

"You're fucking lucky —" Her throat cracks, raw and aching. On the front porch, voices murmur. She can't see outside. She can't see *anything* in the dark, so she shuts her eyes against the cold shuddering through her.

Dried blood cracks around her nostrils as the gash on her face leaks. Her tongue slides out to taste it. It's a reminder of why she's doing this.

Because they spilled Vesta's blood on the battlefield. Because they'll do anything to keep her from me.

Pheir tries to grab ahold of the hatred to keep her afloat, but the darkness threatens to swallow her. The voices outside become a long hum that she can't differentiate from the forest.

How long has she been here?

Only minutes. No more than fifteen.

But her rational mind gets lost in the dark tunnel of time until it's little more than an echo in the distance. The Timbers will leave her like this, blood trickling down her face, dirt smeared in her wounds. Why wouldn't they? It's all by their design.

As someone trained for war, Pheir underestimated the Timbers. *Rookie mistake,* Rhaiden would sneer. *Never think your enemy won't sink as low as you. They'll sink lower.*

The Timbers have, playing with Pheir like she's a wounded animal, extending her suffering until they grow tired of tormenting her. Vibrant anger floats through her mind, something to cling to when all her other senses are deprived. The memory it stirs couldn't have happened more than an hour ago, but in the darkness, it seems like ages.

* * * * *

Guard rotation will happen soon. Good: Pheir's tired of the way the deer looks at her, like he feels bad for her. Like he pities her. He tried to sneak her extra dessert for dinner, so she stared him in the face before knocking the whole tray onto the floor. That doused his smile. He avoided her eyes for the rest of the evening, ducking out the front door a few minutes early once he'd cleaned up the mess.

The clop of his hooves fades off the front deck. Pheir's ears perk. In her weeks held captive, she's gotten good at distinguishing footsteps, the same way she did with her parents. Instead of determining moods, Pheir now determines which creature is approaching for duty next. Her brows knit as she strains to listen.

The claws ticking against the wood now are new, not as sturdy as the wolf's and without the bounding quality of the rabbits. This sound is near-imperceptible, drifting and darting over the deck like a leaf tossed by the wind.

The cabin door opens a crack, enough for the creature to slip inside. The room is cramped when he shuts the door. A few candles on the table cast light enough to see.

It's the arctic fox with wings. Singer, Pheir remembers, because she hates him. Not because he wants to kill her — that's a given in a place like this. It's because he talked shit about Vesta.

Pheir's expression remains astringent. "Finally pulled the short straw for guard duty, huh?"

Singer doesn't reply, stepping toward her with a strange look. Pheir's eyes narrow as he comes to a stop before her, inspecting her like she hasn't lived up to her reputation. His long snout wrinkles. "I'll never understand why she chose you over everyone else."

For a fleeting moment, Pheir's heart soars. Are they talking about Vesta? But of course, they aren't. He means Lev, her wife-to-be. The woman intent on keeping Pheir alive instead of letting the Timbers kill her.

Pheir's lip twitches in a smile. "She must really hate the rest of you."

No argument from Singer. He lifts his hands to the soldered metal wrapped around Pheir's chest, keeping her pinned to the chair. The chains don't move. Pheir snaps her teeth and nicks the side of his finger. Singer hisses, jerking back as Pheir grins.

Her voice is smug. "You'll learn fast —"

A hand lands across her face, knocking the words from her mouth and leaving her cheek stinging and raw. Her ears ring. She turns back to Singer staring down at her with disgust. Something warm trickles down her face. Four lines of pain throb under her skin, matching the lengths of his claws.

Without another word, he moves behind her, fiddling with chains at the back of her chair. She's stunned. None of the other guards have hit her. None of the others have...

She's still dazed when one of the chains slips off her chest. The others still bind her, but her torso is no longer restricted. She can breathe fully. Singer moves back in front of her, clamping a hand around her throat as he shifts the bindings on her chest aside. Pheir squirms, mouth opening to scream.

When he tightens his hand, no sound comes out. His other claws form a circle over her chest, as if he plans to dig out her heart.

She swings her legs, sending Singer flying into the nearby candles. Light scatters across the room, wicks snuffed out by the motion as Pheir hurtles forward. The room goes dark as she crashes to the ground, struggling to unwind the rest of the chains as Singer's claws clamber against the wood beside her.

Chains clatter to the ground, chair knocking against the floor before Pheir escapes her bindings. Claws dig into her calf. She kicks until she lands on something solid. A curse comes through the darkness. Scrambling to her feet, she sprints toward where she hopes the door is, bound hands scrabbling for the knob.

There!

She flings the door open to near-darkness, fresh air filling her lungs for a moment of bliss. She wants to shut her eyes. She wants to enjoy this, but there's a shout from a few yards away. Pheir doesn't stick around to see who it is, sprinting into the darkness and praying Singer isn't close behind...

* * * * *

The door to the cabin creaks open. Past the darkness, a hovering flame casts rainbow colors across the room. In Pheir's delirium, excitement builds in her chest. *Vesta!* But as Pheir's eyes adjust, the flame returns to an orange glow illuminating Aren's face.

Pheir's heart sinks.

"Sorry for the wait." He lights the other candles, pulling a satchel off his shoulders. "You roughed Caius up more than he realized."

"I'll get him better next time." Pheir's strained voice is barely more than a whisper, words tripping over themselves in a rush. "When Vesta comes back, she's going to..."

She trails off as Aren withdraws vials and bandages from the bag. He pauses, brows lifting. "Yes?"

Pheir swallows around the ache in her throat. There's no one jumping to interrupt her tirade. Her words feel petulant under his quiet attention, far less heroic when no one is silencing her. Aren pulls up a chair to face her and lifts his hand.

On instinct, Pheir jerks, prepared for a fist against her face. That's what the Timbers are doing now, isn't it?

Aren retracts. She sees the rag of antiseptic in his hand. "I think we can make this work, Pheir, at least for the next fifteen minutes. That cut is going to get infected. We need to make sure it heals right. Can you allow me that?"

"I'd rather *die*," Pheir seethes. In a way, she wants more pain. She can push Aren to his limits. She can make him hit her the way Singer had. At least it's *something* she understands.

Aren leans back casually. "You *might* die if I don't clean it. It'd be slow and painful, weakening you until you can't lift yourself out of bed." There's his damn knowing smile again. Pheir wants to crash into it. He leans close like he knows. "I imagine you want to go out swinging. At least let me get you back in fighting shape."

She stares, unblinking, trying to wrap her mind around Aren's unnerving grin. It's too easy. Too calm. There's nothing sharp or deadly about it, no threat of violence lingering in the corners.

Who the fuck *smiles* like that?

Unmoving, Aren waits. Silence stretches between them, waiting to be filled by Pheir's response. When's the last time anyone waited to hear her speak? The last time anyone waited for her permission? It's unnerving. Maybe that's his strategy, after all.

After a long moment, her jaw unclamps for a single word. "Fine."

Aren wets the cloth again, lifting it to Pheir's face and waiting to see if her teeth try to land. It's tempting, but Pheir glares, following the cloth with her eyes before it touches her nose. She hisses at the sting. Pain tremors through her, but it's secondary to the Vestal pack bonds. Her body aches to be reunited, thoughts blooming with images of Thalea sitting in front of her like this. She'd wrap a bandage around Pheir's hands. And Rhaiden — fucking *Rhaiden.* Even in Pheir's hate, she can picture Rhaiden without effort, criticizing Pheir's fighting technique...

"How did you manage to escape?"

At Aren's words, Pheir's eyes narrow. Is it part of the Timbers' game to make Pheir question her sanity? Is it possible Singer was working outside the rules? He's never been assigned to guard her. He's the first to actually strike her. If Aren doesn't know about it...

Is this an opportunity to watch the Timber pack crumble down from the inside?

Pheir doesn't know what to believe. It's of no benefit for her to tell the Timbers what she is and isn't capable of. Besides, Singer's misstep was the closest she's come to getting out. He might make that mistake again. This time, Pheir will be ready for him. She can handle whatever he tries with her. She doesn't need any of the Timbers pretending to protect her.

Her chin lifts beneath the scratches. "Guess your compound's not as secure as you thought." Inwardly, she gives a bitter laugh. Wouldn't Rhaiden be proud of her for keeping her strategy a secret?

Skeptically, Aren sets the antiseptic aside. He seems to understand that he won't get more from her. *Good: leave me alone.* Placing hands on his knees, he pushes to stand. "You thirsty?"

Pheir swallows around the scratch in her throat. She wants to say no, to spit something vicious and cruel. All she can manage is a begrudging croak as if her body's rebelling to get what it needs.

A smile flits across Aren's face. "Echo?" he calls over his shoulder. The wolf peeks her head in through the door. "Will you bring us two bottles of lemonade, please?" Suspiciously, the wolf nods, disappearing as Aren turns back to Pheir. "I'm going to see if you need stitches, all right?"

Pheir presses back against her chair, glancing at the medical supplies in the satchel. Her eyes drift over each piece before she realizes he's still waiting for her to answer. To give permission.

Why?

Once she gives half a nod, Aren leans in close. Too close to be smart; she could bite him. She could incapacitate him any number of ways. Her mouth pulls back in a snarl —

His fingers brush her lips, like it was an accident. The fur tickles her chin, his hand hovering to tilt her cheek, catching the light across her wound. Her jaw is slack, eyes wide as his fingers trace the curve of her lip.

"Sorry…" His hand is gentle on her face. "With werecreatures, I don't deal with a lot of skin injuries. I want to make sure I treat it properly." His thumb brushes the skin of her cheek. Pheir doesn't realize he's pulled away until he turns back to the bag, clearing his throat. "It might scar, but a few bandages should keep it in place."

Her mind is reeling, a different feeling than being left in the dark. She's off balance and lost, but she can see everything he does. He unpacks butterfly bandages from the kit. Muscles in his back shift, more than she'd expect for a menial task. When his hands flex, his tendons jump, drawing her eyes to his forearm...

Echo reenters with two bottles of dark pink liquid, the same color Pheir imagines her cheeks are. Aren lifts his head cordially toward Echo. "Thank you. Would you like to join us?"

Echo's gaze darts to Pheir. "Looks like you have your hands full," the wolf answers. When Pheir bares her teeth, Echo backs out of the room and pulls the door shut behind her.

With a claw, Aren pops the top off both bottles. "You don't have to scare everyone off."

Pheir's nose wrinkles. "Have to keep trying until it works on you."

It brings another half-grin to Aren's face. Pheir hates that she wants more, that there's some driving force inside her hungry to draw out his reaction. When he lifts a bottle to her mouth, her lips clamp. Aren's brows knit before he tips the drink to his own lips, taking a large swallow before he holds it out to Pheir again. Cautiously, she lifts her mouth to the rim and takes the smallest sip.

FIFTEEN

Pheir

Cool liquid coats her throat. It's heavenly. She nearly shuts her eyes at the first hint of relief, but she can't let Aren out of her sight. Lining her expression with daggers, Pheir opens her mouth for more. Aren tilts the bottle back. She guzzles it all.

A few rivulets drip down the corners of her mouth. She licks them clean, watching Aren's eyes as it dips to her throat when she swallows.

"Do you need more?" he asks. Her head shakes despite the pins and needles already spreading through her throat. His brow lifts. "You sure? You look like you're in pain."

Her teeth grit, failing to bite down on her irritation. "Because I'm bleeding from my face, and it's cold as shit, and these bonds fucking *hurt.*"

A smile flits across Aren's face. He pumps sanitizer into his hand before he peels the backings off the bandages and sets them on the ends of his claws. When he turns back to face Pheir, he's still smiling.

"*What?*" she snaps.

"You remind me of someone." He presses the sticky bandage to the skin on either side of her cut. As her skin tugs together, she winces.

It's all a little too friendly. Pheir searches for a way to establish distance between them again. "I don't think your boss would like you offering her prisoner cocktails." Pheir glances over his shoulder. "Where is Lev, anyway? Shouldn't she be breathing down your neck?"

Aren places another bandage, smoothing it against Pheir's skin. "What makes you think she wouldn't like this?"

It's a perfect opportunity. Pheir's facial muscles pull up in delight as she recalls countless conversations with Vesta. "Because Lev has to control everything. She has to maintain her image as some selfless sweetheart, to make sure she looks innocent in case anyone figures out how underhanded she is."

There's no reaction from Aren. Pheir presses further.

"Lev started the battle. We all saw it. There's no denying it, but you keep acting like Vesta's the one who's wrong."

Aren nods thoughtfully. "Sounds like you have a pretty solidified image of Lev in your mind."

Pheir doesn't like the way he says it, as if the image is *hers* and not reality. "Of course I do," she spits before she leans back in her chair. "Vesta told me all about what your girlfriend was like before you knew her."

Pheir waits haughtily for the blow to land, for Aren to recoil in shock. He never does. In fact, he barely reacts at all, sticking another bandage into place. After Pheir's expectant silence goes on too long, he glances down at her. "Please, continue."

Her scowl deepens, skin hot with shame. How can this man make Pheir tongue-tied when he's barely speaking? She tries again. "Isn't Lev embarrassed? She thought her history was buried when she got rid of Vesta, but I know who Lev really is."

"And who is that, exactly?"

Nothing Pheir says ruffles Aren, not even a flicker of anger. Where the fuck is Caius? Telling this to *him* would be rewarding. "A power-hungry bitch who doesn't care what's best for the pack." Pheir strains forward against her restraints. "Vesta should have taken over the Timbers. She was a better Alpha than Lev could ever be."

Aren pulls back to examine his handiwork with the bandages. "So Vesta told you about their...falling out."

"Of course." Pheir smiles wickedly. "She told me everything."

Aren turns back to the table. "How did Vesta become your Alpha?"

The subject change throws Pheir off. Of course she wants to talk about Vesta, but she likes tearing Lev down as much. As she considers her response, Aren lifts his full lemonade bottle toward her lips. She jerks her mouth away. "Vesta built our pack from the ground up. I was her first recruit." Pheir's chin lifts proudly. "Then Vesta brought Thalea and that traitor, Rhaiden. Vesta spent years honing each of our skills before we started taking on other people."

Aren takes a sip from his drink. "So Vesta formed a pack where there wasn't one?"

"Exactly." Pheir beams. "She made something from nothing."

Aren sinks back into his chair, crossing one leg over the other. "How do you think Lev became an Alpha?"

Deep in Pheir's skull, an ache begins. It burrows at the base of her neck. Her brows knit, trying to will it away. The pain doesn't subside. She shuts her eyes, speaking past the dull throb. "Lev turned everyone against Vesta. She threw Vesta out of the pack, so there would be no one to challenge her."

Pheir's mind is taffy, stretching and tugging her apart. If not for the bandages, her skin would rip, like her mind is splitting in half.

Two hands grip her face. Aren comes into focus, eyes flicking between either of hers. "Are you ok?" he asks. The pain dulls enough for Pheir to snap her teeth toward him. He releases her and settles back into his chair. "Is that what Vesta told you?"

"Yes," Pheir spits. "That's why Vesta formed our pack. Because the Conclave did nothing when she was run out of her own. Because the Conclave never protected any of us. Because the Conclave doesn't give a shit."

Aren is quiet for a while. There's no emotion crossing his face, but it's the longest he's gone without tripping Pheir up. His gaze stays on hers, but it's distant, as if he's considering something beyond her. Eventually, his voice comes as a low murmur. "That's not the story I know."

Pheir manages a laugh. "Bullshit." But an inkling gnaws at the back of her mind. She wants to ask the question, to know the answer even as something tries to keep her mouth shut. Her lips crack as she parts them, dry and chapped. "Tell me what really happened, then. If you're so sure, tell me what happened between Lev and Vesta. Tell me why Vesta left the Timbers."

Aren shakes his head, a drop of pity in his gaze. "You wouldn't believe me."

Frustration shrieks out of Pheir. It doesn't matter if he's right. She *hates* the way people watch her, as if they know something she doesn't. She flings her body back, trying to topple the chair until Aren grabs a hold of the legs and sets the feet back on the ground.

"What's your obsession with Lev?" she snaps. "You think she's so righteous. You weren't there when Vesta left. Lev could be lying."

"And Vesta could have lied to you."

Pheir jerks again. Aren holds the chair steady, keeping his gaze pinned to hers as he speaks somberly.

"I trust Lev because she's proven herself. That's why this pack voted for her to become Alpha. When Lev's pushed to her limits, she maintains the same morals. She doesn't cause harm out of anger. She doesn't judge people by their worst mistake — you being alive is testament to that. And me being here is proof that Lev doesn't care about power."

Pheir tosses back her head and cackles. "What could you know about that?"

Aren doesn't answer, releasing the chair and planting his foot against the bottom rung. "If you ask me, you're the one who's obsessed with Lev."

"Because I hate her," Pheir seethes. Lev's name is all the invitation she needs to lash out, spilling vitriol that bubbles up inside her. It's a constant chant in her head — *Lev, Lev, Lev* — running an endless loop around Pheir's mind. Finally, the words have an excuse to escape. "Because she's the worst person I've ever met. Because she'll never be half the Alpha Vesta was."

Talking about Lev is a high that leaves Pheir dizzy with delight. It's brighter than the pain of the slashed bonds of her pack. Thoughts of Lev scream through her like adrenaline, swirling in vibrant color of all the things Pheir could do to her. She could pin Lev to the dirt. She could tug back Lev's ears. She could claw Lev until she *screams*.

A chuckle escapes Aren. Pheir's eyes dart to him, prepared to hear his defense. They can go like this for hours, Aren painting Lev in a positive light, and Pheir tearing down every effort. Her mouth practically waters — but that isn't what Aren says. Instead, he folds his arms across his chest.

"Despite your strengths, Pheir, I can do some things you can't."

Pheir scoffs, eager to get back to insults. "Like what?"

"Like fuck Lev."

It shocks the air out of Pheir like a slap, but it stings worse than Singer's blow. These new words sear into her mind in the reddened shape of Aren's hand, burning her from the inside out. Pheir's thighs clench with something hotter than hate.

"More pertinently," Aren continues, as if Pheir's body isn't trembling, "I can smell when someone's mood changes."

Shame creeps through Pheir's body. She tenses at the reminder of the things she can't do. She can't mask her scent. She can't control her reactions. For werecreatures, Pheir's body is a conspirator, whispering in a language that Pheir's harpy senses can't translate.

Aren's brows knit, nose twitching. "Are you…"

Fight screams through Pheir. What is he thinking? What does he know? What is she telling him without permission? Her heart thuds. "Am I what?" she barks.

His tongue ghosts over his fangs. Pheir's eyes follow, honed on his mouth as it moves. "Do you think about Lev like that?"

"No." It lashes out between the clench of Pheir's teeth, as stubborn and instinctual as her defense of Vesta. "Never."

"Never?" Aren asks.

Pheir shakes her head so sharply it throbs.

Aren leans closer to brace his elbows on his knees. "You've never thought about grinding Lev into the dirt?"

The words shiver through Pheir. "That's different." The image lives inside her mind as it always has, Lev's face smeared in the mud as Pheir pins her to the earth.

Aren doesn't move, amber eyes flicking over her. "Never remembered her body under your fingers?"

Of course Pheir has. It's imprinted from the first time Lev wrestled her to the ground, Lev's impossibly soft fur over the thick muscles of her thighs.

"Never…" Aren's eyes dip to the bob of Pheir's throat. "Fantasized about getting her between your legs?"

"That's *different*," Pheir croaks, but the images whirl through her mind — Pheir locking her ankles around Lev's. Pheir pinning Lev to the ground. Pheir tormenting Lev for hours. At Aren's words, the visions change. A tight cord weaves through Pheir's gut. The Lev in her mind circles her hips. The tight hold Pheir has on Lev's hair turns to crushing their mouths together. Dirt smears from Lev's face onto Pheir's.

It's not true. *Aren* planted these ideas, convoluting Pheir's thoughts of revenge into something molten. Every ache in Pheir's body — the slashed bonds, the gash in her face — is overshadowed by the tightening coil in her stomach.

She can't breathe. Aren doesn't look away, focused on Pheir's face. Her pupils blow wider. Her teeth dig into her lip. The air is scented with things she can't comprehend. She cinches her eyes shut, willing the sights and sounds to disappear. "I don't want Lev. I fucking *hate* her!"

Aren rises to his feet in one slow motion. He doesn't believe her. He *has* to believe her. When Pheir shivers, her chains clatter against the chair, but she's not sure if it's from the cold or something else. She wants to deny it again, to tell Aren how completely *wrong* he is. All that comes out is a scream.

Aren speaks over her, packing his medical kit. "Your wound should heal. I'll redress it tomorrow. Get some rest."

Then he leaves her alone.

Her throat aches too much to make any more sound, but it's her only recourse. If she can't escape, she'll keep the whole compound awake, screeching until her throat is bloody. Eventually, no further sound comes out of her, mouth open in a silent scream. Every part of her is sore and weak, mind so wiped she barely puts up a fight when Echo moves her into bed. The quilts keep Pheir from shivering. She wakes in the morning covered in sweat with remnants of a cottontail darting through her dreams.

There's a new pile of things on her bedside table: a sweater and jeans with two open bottles of lemonade next to a note.

Not poisoned.

No doubt they're from Aren. Against Pheir's better judgment, she tips one bottle to her lips and takes a hesitant sip. It's perfect. It's better than the night before, coating the ache of her throat and soothing the dryness of her mouth.

In relief, she shuts her eyes and basks in the bliss.

Then she rears back, flinging her chains to shatter both bottles to the ground.

SIXTEEN

Pheir

3 years before Vesta's death

"Again."

Pheir grunts in response, pushing to her feet. Her chest heaves, arms and face sore from being thrown to the ground again and again. In front of her, Rhaiden hasn't broken a sweat as she watches Pheir down the bridge of her nose.

"You're not listening," the lionfish siren sighs, leaning her weight onto one leg.

"I fucking *am!*"

Pheir lunges again.

Rhaiden side-steps easily, letting Pheir tumble to the dirt as Rhaiden props a hand on her hip. "No, you're not. Because if you were, you'd stop flinging your body at every opponent."

A scream tears between Pheir's teeth. With all her strength, she shoves to her feet and whirls in the opposite direction.

It doesn't fool Rhaiden. She grabs one of Pheir's arms, letting the momentum carry Pheir back to the ground. Mud splatters her feathers as she screeches, "Fucking *bitch*!"

Thalea blanches from the sidelines, hands flitting to her mouth above the story book open in her lap. "Oh, Rhaiden…"

Chest heaving, Pheir pushes to her feet, ready to leave Rhaiden with gouges through her gills. It's Vesta's return that saves her. When the glow of rainbow flames descends to the practice battlefield, Pheir immediately brightens. Forget Rhaiden. Pheir and Thalea rush to the edge of the clearing as Rhaiden lingers behind.

"You're back!" Thalea bounces on her toes, reaching eagerly for Vesta's hand. "We didn't know where you went this morning?" The words titter into a question, as if the dryad isn't sure she should mention it.

"Aw, were you worried about me?" Vesta plants a kiss on Thalea's temple. Thalea blushes under her attention before Vesta taps her nose gently. "Don't you worry. I can take care of myself."

Behind them, Rhaiden wipes dirt from her hands. She takes a swig from her canteen before she speaks. "I didn't know you had a meeting today. I thought I was attending all of those with you."

Pheir's eyes roll. Vesta sends them on plenty of missions to spy on other packs and gather intel. They've started collecting specific books for Vesta, too. Of course, that's not enough for Rhaiden. She has to insert herself everywhere.

Vesta drapes an arm over Thalea's shoulder, tucking a vine behind her ear. Although Vesta's face is warm, her voice blunts toward Rhaiden. "You weren't needed. I'm making investments for the future. People who will sing my praises for years to come."

"This future is for all of us, isn't it?" Rhaiden's tone dances with insubordination, pushing the boundaries of Vesta's will. "Why couldn't I go with you? If I'm going to help —"

"Gods, Rhaiden, *shut up!*" Pheir's ready to pick up the sparring where they left off, but Vesta places a placating hand on her shoulder.

"We all need a reminder sometimes…" She turns Pheir to face Rhaiden as Vesta leans her head over Pheir's shoulder. When Vesta's chin digs in, it's a comforting ache, her voice a singsong that's played hundreds of times before. "What's the best kind of magic?"

"A secret!" Thalea and Pheir answer. For good measure, Pheir sticks out her tongue. Rhaiden scoffs, but Vesta doesn't linger on the dispute.

"Besides, you all need the fighting practice. The Conclave's got a herd of power, and guess who just got initiated into the club."

From the way Vesta's vicious eyes cling to Pheir, she knows the answer. *Lev.* A laugh breaks through Pheir's lips. "No way they accepted that bunny bitch."

"Can you believe it?" Vesta's smile is two rows of sharpened teeth. "Of course they did. The Conclave never gave a shit when Leverette forced me out. She's getting all that power she was hungry for." Vesta flicks out her talons on one hand, tapping them methodically against each other. "She'll get what's coming to her."

"When can we go after her?" Pheir bounces on her toes, itching for violence. "I want to make her —

"In due time." With a shake, Vesta eases the tension from her feathers, letting them fan out behind her. "We're beginning to build a real army — which I can't do if my most trusted soldiers aren't up to snuff. You three will have to teach the others and set an example of how things work." She turns back to the practice field with an inquisitorial eye. "What have you been working on today?"

When Rhaiden clears her throat, it sounds suspiciously like a laugh. "Throwing Pheir into the dirt."

Pheir hisses, lifting an arm to swing at her, but Vesta tugs gently on her hair. "Ah, ah, ah: dirt is where the seed grows."

Pheir shuts her eyes, trying to breathe through the anger and remind herself of one of Vesta's mantras. *Suffering creates strength. It'll all be worth it.* "Besides," Vesta chirps, settling her hands on her hips, "maybe she needs a good partner." With a beam, she glances toward Pheir. "What do you say, kid? You and me?"

As if Vesta had to ask. Pheir nods happily, smirking at the others as Vesta gestures between them.

"Two on two: Thalea and Rhaiden versus me and Pheir."

Thalea glances uncomfortably between them. Rhaiden looks sour before she shrugs and turns to move into position. It's disrespectful, as if Pheir isn't a threat to her back. Frustration boils inside Pheir. "What, you scared?"

Rhaiden plants her feet as she turns back to face them. "Of you? Please."

Pheir doesn't get a chance to respond before Vesta shoots up a spray of fire.

The fight begins.

Pheir rushes toward Rhaiden, launching into the air and soaring toward her target.

"Haven't learned a thing, huh?" Rhaiden snaps, whirling when Pheir swings close. Pheir avoids the spires on Rhaiden's back. A few yards away, Thalea and Vesta circle, vines branching from Thalea's body and darting toward Vesta from both sides. Vesta flutters out of the way, laughing playfully, but there's none of that between Rhaiden and Pheir.

Pheir circles back, colliding with Rhaiden's chest and sending them sprawling in opposite directions.

"Glutton for punishment?" Rhaiden growls. There's a cut above her eye. Pheir swipes the blood trickling from her own nose. It drives her harder. She doesn't back down, springing back toward Rhaiden immediately.

Across the field, Thalea giggles. Her match with Vesta is far from heated. Thalea twists her vines in configurations, sneaking past Vesta to tap on her shoulder. Vesta gapes, surprised that Thalea slipped past her. Thalea doesn't use it to her advantage, tickling Vesta with the vines — until Vesta singes them with fire.

Thalea gasps, retracting the burnt ends with shaky breaths.

Rhaiden looks toward her partner. Pheir takes the opening, rushing with the full weight of her body — and still, Rhaiden blocks her. They spin until Pheir's back is pinned to Rhaiden's chest, the spines at the base of her knuckles pricking Pheir's throat. The spines aren't poisoned at the moment – probably. Pheir fights to escape, wings flapping as she claws.

Rhaiden yawns. "Give it up."

"*Fuck you.*" Pheir swings her legs, trying to land against shin.

Siren persuasion dips into Rhaiden's voice. "*Stop fighting, Pheir.*"

Rhaiden's power has never fully worked on their pack, yet Pheir's body wants to obey, relaxing in Rhaiden's grip. The siren power surrounds Pheir like a riptide, dragging her helplessly toward Rhaiden's will — but Pheir can't give up so easily. She *won't.* Her teeth grit, body straining against the supernatural control, chest heaving as she struggles to escape.

"You're gonna pass out breathing like that," Rhaiden chides her. "Just surrender."

Pheir bucks again. "Not until we win."

Beside them, the other match is heating up. Thalea narrowly avoids Vesta's blast, diving away before a scorching mark is left in the earth.

Rhaiden lifts Pheir's feet off the ground, swinging them both to face Vesta. "I have your combatant," Rhaiden calls. The spires on her knuckles press harder against Pheir's skin. "Surrender now, and I'll make her death swift."

There's a teasing lilt in Rhaiden's voice. Humiliation courses through Pheir's veins, hot and prickly. It's bad enough to lose to Rhaiden, but in front of *Vesta*...

Pheir squirms, elbows jostling for a place against Rhaiden's ribs. Vesta turns toward them, scanning their position before she shrugs.

"So do it."

Rhaiden laughs. It dies in her mouth, withering the longer Vesta stares at them. When Pheir swallows, spires dig into her throat. She winces at the sting, but it's nothing compared to the apathy of Vesta's gaze.

"Go on." Vesta circles closer, the battle forgotten behind her. Thalea hovers in the cover of nearby bushes, eyes wide when Vesta stops a few feet from them. Her eyes are honed on Rhaiden, sharp as the talons folded across her chest. "Kill her."

It's like Rhaiden and Pheir are one body, chests rising and falling in time. This is a joke. Their heartbeats thud. Pheir tries to laugh, but she can't muster up a sound.

It doesn't matter; Vesta doesn't look at her. She's focused on Rhaiden who stays still behind Pheir. Vesta steps closer, leaning forward to speak.

"Let's not make idle threats, *Bubbles*."

Rhaiden flinches at the name. Vesta reaches for her wrist, shoving Rhaiden's spines against Pheir's chin until she draws blood.

"If you want to be in charge, you have to get your hands dirty. And you can never, ever hesitate."

Eerie wind creaks and groans through the trees. The Vestals don't move. They don't breathe. Pheir searches for an emotion or a sign, but there's nothing but assessment in Vesta's face — until Rhaiden's grip loosens.

Fear pulses through Pheir, like the threat of death still hangs over her. She finds the leverage she was looking for, whirling and slamming into Rhaiden's chest until the siren skids across the ground. The spires of her back dig gouges into the dirt as Pheir pants dazedly above her.

Vesta's cackle breaks the silence. She slaps Pheir on the back with a grin. "Nice work, kid."

Thalea rushes past them toward Rhaiden. Rhaiden pushes up to sit as Vesta slips an arm around Pheir's shoulder and shoots Rhaiden a deadly look.

"Don't help her up," Vesta calls back to them. "She needs to think about her mistake."

Thalea lingers a few steps away. Rhaiden grinds her teeth. Vesta leads Pheir away, guiding her chin forward again.

"Perfect timing!" Vesta ducks under an overhang of leaves, tugging Pheir closer. "You'll be kicking Rhaiden's ass in no time."

Pheir tries to swallow past the lump in her throat. A smile pries its way onto her lips. "You really set me up for it." When Vesta hugs her, their heads knock together. It's evidence of their closeness. It's proof that Vesta loves her. Pheir shouldn't forget that.

"Of course." Vesta lowers her voice like they share a secret. "You know you're the most important person in my world, right? I love you all, of course," she adds, waving the thought away before she pulls Pheir closer. "But I see what you can become. What everyone else neglects to look for."

Pheir's voice is almost a whisper clinging to Vesta's every word. "What's that?"

Vesta plucks a leaf from one of the bushes. "Focus, Pheir. What can you learn from that fight?"

Pheir's eyes hone on the greenery like it might provide an answer. In her periphery, Thalea and Rhaiden blur, fading into the background as Vesta blows a gentle line of flames. The leaf between her fingers goes up in smoke.

"Don't get captured." Vesta answers her own question. As the leaf turns to ashes, she places the same hand over Pheir's heart. It thrums at her touch. Vesta grins. "And always have a backup plan."

SEVENTEEN

Lev

PRESENT
16 days after Vesta's death

The Broadleaf territory is little more than charred remains. Skeletons of trees stand tall, their foliage burned away. Beneath them, the grass looks like dunes of sand on a backdrop of scorched hills. At the mountainous peak, a haze hangs overhead like a fog Lev can't quite breathe through.

Any memories she had here are impossible to place. This was her home before the Timbers took her in to train, but she recognizes none of it. There's no telling where the Broadleaf pack house was. Where goal lines were dug for countless games. Where Lev pushed June out of a tree and broke her wrist.

Where Diction was murdered. Where the Broadleafs took their hostages. Where, Lev now knows, countless girls were sacrificed for power.

A chill darts up Lev's spine. It's unfathomable to imagine Diction among the ash, to picture the remains of the girls mingling with the people who sacrificed them. The Broadleafs became a power-hungry monster no one could have predicted, and still, Lev carries the guilt.

June and Oberon stand beside her. There's no wind whistling through the trees, no birds calling, nothing but ghosts and smoke. Oberon brushes ash from his black fur. "The adjacent packs will have to expand patrols to cover this area."

June toes a heart into the ash with her boot, a rare occasion when clothing is more a necessity than a hindrance. This was her home once, too, before she followed Lev to the Timbers. "The land's not gonna survive," June sighs. "Not unless the Conclave creates a new pack to oversee it. Right now..." She shakes her head. "It's unlivable."

"The forest will heal itself," Lev murmurs. Oberon hums in agreement. Perhaps they can will it to happen. In the distance, there's a bloom of color, a field of wildflowers sprouting impossibly through the dead earth. Lev doesn't take her eyes off of it. "Residual magic has a way of showing up when we least expect it."

It's not a completely foolish hope. The mountains and canyon outlining the Break have trapped unexplainable things here, leftover Faerie magic that reappears when all seems lost. Stories pass like legends through the land — crops flourishing the final day of harvest. An entire pack waking with quilting knowledge before a harsh winter blows in. An Alpha reappearing on the threshold of his home after being injured hundreds of miles away.

Faerie magic is how they came to be here at all. When the Land of Faerie withdrew from the continent, mountains sprung up and a canyon sank around uninhabited land. Land where people suddenly appeared, fully-grown adults with no knowledge of where they'd come from or who they were, werecreatures and dragons and nymphs forging packs together. People still speculate how they came to be here — time travel, teleportation — but the mystery persists.

As do the tales of residual magic.

If it can do all of that, maybe it can bring the land back to life. Lev's eyes sting from the smoke as she squints her eyes. *Maybe it can bring the girls back. Bring Diction back.* She wipes her face on the back of her arm. June reaches out to grab her hand as they look over the remains of their first home.

For the next four days, they clear the territory as best they can in daylight. Once night falls, they return to camp at the Conifer border with the other packs that came to help. It's difficult work, not least of all because the memory of what happened hangs over their heads. Rumors whisper through the groups as they reseed native grasses.

"I heard the Vestals were in on it."

"I heard the Conifers were, too."

"I heard Diction was the one behind it."

"Diction would *never* do that," Lev snaps over a stream. The jabbering group on the other side grows silent. Oberon leads her away to find a drink of water. June drops a rock into the mud so it splatters on the others' faces.

Most troubling of all is Lev's gnawing suspicion that eats at her the longer she's away from the Timbers. She knows without question that Diction had no part in this, but she can't say the same for Pheir. Lev defended her, but in private, she has her doubts.

Vesta told me everything. That's been Pheir's resounding truth since she came to the Timbers. Lev doesn't fully buy it, but she has to wonder. Did Pheir know what Vesta was doing with the Broadleafs? Did Pheir have a hand in it?

And why does the possibility bother Lev so much?

At camp in the evenings, the dark cloud over the group finally lifts. Larger, prominent packs shoot clipped glares at anyone who dares to intrude on their hushed conversations. It doesn't deter the Timbers. At their smaller fire, Oberon discusses plans for his apiary as June regales them with terrible impressions of the Regents. It's their way of coping. As the nights go on, smaller packs linger at the edges of conversation until the Timbers invite them to join with drinks and storytelling. It's a nice reprieve from everything else…until the final night.

It rains. It's a good sign that the surviving seeds can germinate, but any camaraderie the working group established scatters when they're forced to huddle under erected shelters. Once the others turn in to bed, Lev crawls into her cot. June and Oberon sleep peacefully, her drooling across her pillow as he snores soundly. Lev stares up at the tarp. She wonders if Aren and Caius can see the stars back home. She wonders if they're together…

A large figure takes cover under the Timber tarp, wings stretching and crowding the space. For a moment, Lev swears she sees the lick of rainbow flames, but it's a trick of the light. Boreas's beak gleams golden under the campfire, dipping to a point Lev doesn't want to get close to. His eyes narrow when he recognizes whose space he's encroached on. "How's your bride?"

Lev gives a tight smile. "Pheir's not my bride yet."

"For the best." Boreas slicks back the feathers of his head, dripping with rain. "We'll have to kill them all now."

Lev sits stark straight in bed, fingers clenching the blanket at her waist. "What? Why? Because of the Broadleafs?"

"The Vestals must have known." With a talon, Boreas picks at this beak. "That kind of insolence can't stand."

Tangled in her sheets while Boreas stares down at her, Lev feels incomprehensibly small. "They might not have," she says hurriedly. "There's no proof of it…" Her jaw clenches in realization. *Pick your battles*, she reminds herself. Again, she chooses the hardest one. "You don't care what the Broadleafs did to those girls. You don't care that they killed Diction. You only care that the Broadleafs weren't loyal to the Conclave."

With a wave of his hand, Boreas disperses the notion...but he doesn't deny it. "The Break cannot function without central allegiance from every pack. Clearly, the Conclave hasn't been scrutinizing the community closely enough."

Lev's voice hisses through the silence. "That we can agree on." That's how the Vestals came to be in the first place, smaller packs scattering and falling to her regime long before the Conclave bothered to get involved. It was the Timbers trying to fend her off, trying to dismantle her pack, trying to get the Conclave to give a shit about the threat she posed.

It's clear Boreas understands Lev's meaning. His arms fold over his chest, voice low enough that she nearly loses his words under the patter of rain. "I suppose you think we owe you thanks. That you deserve our adulation because you managed to fail into a correct assumption for once. Don't think I've forgotten who your beta is."

That's what it always comes back to — Boreas's faulty hate for Aren, the Conclave's grudge because the Timbers don't cower in their place.

"I haven't forgotten, either," Lev snaps proudly. She knows the truth. Boreas's teeth grit, but she doesn't give him time to retaliate. "We don't need a reward for doing the right thing. But since your failure to listen led to where we are now, maybe you should take heed of what I'm saying."

Boreas's mouth draws tight. Lev's heart pounds, but she doesn't stop.

"Don't waste precious time on the remaining Vestals. They're three people, and they're under constant surveillance. They'll still be there at the end of the three months. The Regents are better suited investigating Vesta's other ties to the region. If you didn't suspect the Broadleafs, who else might be slipping under your nose?"

It's a last-ditch effort to direct Boreas's attention away from Pheir, but there's truth to it. Boreas recognizes it, eyes narrowing in contemplation. He won't admit defeat. Certainly not to Lev's face, but at least the threat in his voice is directed at her instead of Pheir. "Yes...who else's loyalties might be slipping out of place?"

The rain slows to a drizzle. With that, Boreas takes his leave, prowling to the most isolated structure at the edge of camp. A breath rushes out of Lev. It's not much, but she hopes it's enough to keep the Regents distracted for a while. She readjusts her pillow to keep Boreas in sight, barely blinking as she curls onto her side.

Eventually, sleep overtakes her. She struggles against it, but her body finally gives into the rest she's deprived it of. It's hours before her eyes slip open. Above her, a shape is outlined in the dark, wings blocking out the firelight. Lev tries to scream and fight. Her body is weak. When the beast opens its mouth, Lev holds her breath. The creature exhales a gust of rainbow fire. Lev's mouth opens — but the fire doesn't burn. It kisses over her, lifting her fur on end. Through the fire, there's a flash of teeth. It's Vesta's smile winking through the dark — but it's Pheir that leans down toward Lev.

We can rule, Leverette. You and me, together.

Lev's stomach knots. The voice is wrong. It doesn't belong to Pheir. Lev gets her hands free, grappling for the monster's throat — but when Lev pulls Pheir down, their lips crash instead, the ginger taste of Pheir heady on Lev's tongue. Their mouths bruise each other, elbows and knees knocking together like they aren't sure if they're fighting or something else.

When Lev wakes in the morning, there's a heavy ache between her legs that doesn't subside.

As camp clears out, Boreas lingers with a cup of coffee, watching the Timbers dismantle their shelter. It's his attempt to unsettle Lev. After the dream last night, it works. The Timbers load into the pickup in record time, Lev's eyes on the rearview to keep Boreas in sight. As they pull away from the Conifer border, a line of wood-boring insects feast on a burnt tree. The ground vibrates beneath the truck as they drive.

Lev exhales a modicum of relief.

By the time they make it back to the Timber compound, there's been no sign of griffin wings following them home. Aren and Caius wait by the entrance, an awkward distance between their bodies. Still, a smile stretches across Lev's lips as she bounces out of the truck.

Aren catches her pack before it slips off her shoulder. "How was the trip?"

"It's gonna take some time before we see if our plans work." She lifts on her toes, stretching after the journey before her voice lowers. "Boreas was there. He made some comments about Pheir. I think I put him off the trail enough, but if he shows up —"

"Speaking of Pheir..." Aren clears his throat uncomfortably. "We had an incident."

Lev's heart jumps. "Is everyone —"

"Everyone's fine," Aren assures her. "No one was hurt. Well..." He glances at Caius, who's intently focused on the lake. "Nothing more than a few scratches."

"What happened?" Lev tries to meet Caius's eyes. He doesn't budge.

"Still can't be sure," Aren answers. "Pheir managed to escape, but Caius tracked her to the forest. They both got a little banged up in the scuffle."

Lev's mind whirls. If Boreas had been here to see that...but he wasn't. She tries to focus on reality. "All right, at least they're —

Aren winces. "There's something else."

Her fingers press to her eyelids. One day. She'd like *one fucking day* where shit doesn't go sideways. "What else?"

Aren doesn't answer. When Lev lifts her gaze, she catches him watching Caius. Caius, who still won't look at them. She's about to ask why when Aren lowers his voice. "Rhaiden is here."

Lev's mouth falls open, panic streaking through her. "You invited —"

"*I* didn't." Aren's mouth pulls into a thin line. It's the truth, but he's unhappy to be sharing it. His head shakes slightly.

Before Lev can press further, Caius finally blurts. "*I* did. Aren mentioned her letter. It seemed important for you to speak with her, so..." He flings his hand out, letting it drop heavily to his side.

There has to be more, something Caius isn't saying, some *reason* he would do this. Lev can't find anything to land on. Gods, if Boreas *does* show up now... Her head shakes slowly, rife with confusion. "Why would you...?"

Caius shrugs, clearly wounded. Aren steps forward and lowers his mouth near Lev's ear. "If you're going to speak with her, we need to do it now. They've been in the cottage since daybreak to ensure they weren't seen."

Lev glances toward the cliffside, trying to piece together some semblance of a plan. "Her voice. She has to wear a collar —"

"She came with one," Aren answers.

"And the ashes —"

"Godras left his vial with his wife. You have the only ones here."

Everything feels uneven. Between the Broadleafs and Boreas and the dream, Lev can't get her feet under her. Returning home to chaos has thrown her completely off balance. Caius turns away, but before Lev can reach for him, Aren speaks again.

"Rhaiden came here. There's no getting around that fact if the Regents find out. They're already suspicious of us, but we can take advantage of this opportunity while we have it."

Dazedly, Lev nods. It's as close to prepared as they're going to get. As Oberon and June onload the truck, the other three set off in silence, hiking across the compound toward the cliffside.

There's a temptation to press Caius further, to get at the root of why he did this, but Lev needs to focus. Meeting with another pack can give away more than what they say to each other. Lev focuses on the two-story cottage in the distance. A balcony on one side overlooks the lake while the rest of the building backs against a rock wall. As they walk, Aren leaves space for Caius between them, but Caius lingers a few paces behind as if each step is an effort.

Once they arrive, they enter a wide room with an open floor plan. To the right, couches and chairs nestle against the bookshelves where the Chasm pack waits. The dragon Godras is flanked by a few of his guards. He's taller than all of them where he stands behind the loveseat, yet the woman who sits in front of him is infinitely more threatening. Her scales and hair are striped white and orange, one leg crossed behind the other as if her wrists aren't bound in her lap. The collar clamped around her throat does nothing to temper the lionfish spires sticking out from her body.

As a siren, the woman doesn't need claws to keep everyone at a distance...and she doesn't even need her voice to be deadly. Her eyes are sharp as spikes when she speaks.

"You look well, Leverette."

EIGHTEEN

Lev

You look well, Leverette.

Lev grits her teeth, fighting the urge to sink back into memories. "It's Lev."

"Apologies," Rhaiden offers. "Vesta always called you by your given name." Her head bows, but Lev can't tell if she's truly sorry. It doesn't matter; that's not what they're here for.

Lev folds her arms across her chest. "Funny: that's not what Pheir calls me."

A smirk darts across Rhaiden's lips, like a fish tail flitting above the water before it disappears into her depths. "I don't think she wanted to give you the honor."

For a moment, Lev considers standing hostilely at one end of the room, but a splintered front is never a good idea. Godras and Rhaiden don't know Lev didn't ok this meeting. Leaving space for Aren and Caius, Lev sinks coolly onto the couch furthest from their guests. "Your letter seemed incomplete."

"I hoped it would."

Lev scowls at Rhaiden's admittance. "Was that part of your plan to get near Pheir?"

"Yes." Rhaiden's anything but ashamed. Worry digs into Lev's gut. If Rhaiden doesn't need to hide the truth to remain a threat, what else is she capable of? But Rhaiden seems unconcerned as she finishes her thought. "Not for the reason you're thinking."

Lev's head tilts. "What reason, then, if not escape?"

"To soothe the pack bond."

It makes sense. Proximity is the easiest way to calm the pack bonds straining to connect, and the Vestals have been split for over two weeks. Granted, Lev doesn't know much of Rhaiden, but the siren seems the most relaxed Lev's seen her. The line of Rhaiden's shoulders is flexible, breathing slow and even.

"It should ease Pheir's pain for a bit," Rhaiden continues. "If she notices, tell her Thalea was here. She'll take it better that way."

"So you know Pheir hates you."

A heavier smile crosses Rhaiden's lips, impossible to read. "We've always had a...complex relationship."

"Given that...." Aren settles behind the couch. "Why would you do this to help her? She thinks you're the greatest traitor the Break has ever known. Speaking with us about Vesta won't put you in a better light."

With a heaving sigh, Rhaiden leans back against the cushions. "Despite what Pheir believes, my intention is not to help you or make your lives easier. It's to protect her. If you gain any benefit in the process, so be it, but don't mistake my presence here as anything more than selfish sentimentality."

Lev blinks to hide her surprise. The Vestals' internal workings have long been a mystery, assumed to be a bond between heartless soldiers. Truthfully, Lev wasn't sure any of them were capable of affection, least of all Vesta's calculating second-in-command.

Intrigued, Lev sits up straighter. "What are you trying to protect Pheir from? Vesta's dead. The Timbers won't harm her.

The only threat to her are the Regents." Lev shrugs. "Nothing stands in her way except herself."

A shadow darts across Rhaiden's expression, like something moving beneath water, unseen until it's too late. "There are things that transcend death, especially with a phoenix."

"Enough cryptic bullshit."

It's the first time Caius has spoken, stalking across the room. The Chasm guards pull in tighter, and Aren follows, but Rhaiden doesn't flinch. Caius leans down toward her, lips curling over his teeth as a threat rumbles through his voice.

"You said you had shit to say, so *say it*."

Aren reaches for his arm. Caius jerks out of his grip and skulks back toward the far edge of the room. Once he looks close to steaming, Rhaiden finds it in her to continue. "Pheir was the first person Vesta recruited. Well..." Her eyes glint toward Lev. In her periphery, Caius glances between them. Lev can't bring herself to look at him, body hot with scandal as Rhaiden continues. "First *successful* person. It was years before I came along."

Lev speaks past the tightness in her throat. "To where?"

"The old avian village on the edge of the Break. You know the one: the Eyrie, abandoned after that hurricane."

Lev's eyes narrow. So that's how they stayed hidden all these years. Idly, Rhaiden waves her fingers.

"By the time I arrived, Vesta had established herself with Pheir and Thalea. Pheir was so far up Vesta's ass, there was no light at the end of the tunnel."

Aren rolls one of his whiskers between his fingers. "So Pheir was always vicious and violent? That's not new information."

"As long as *I've* known her," Rhaiden corrects. It's a puzzling distinction, so she clarifies. "I don't think she was always this way. I had suspicions from the beginning, but they were hard to place. Harder still when you're dealing with a creature unlike anything you know."

"Is this more Vesta worship?" Caius grumbles, leaning sullenly against the wall.

The spires on Rhaiden's skin hike. "I don't mean it the way Pheir does," she snaps. "Phoenixes are built on mystery. There's no way a kid who..." She trails off, poise flickering. Quickly, she straightens her spine and reroutes the conversation. "Every species ages differently, but Vesta...I don't know if her body aged much after I met her. Still, her mind was too advanced —"

A pit forms in Lev's stomach. "Like she'd lived other lives before this one."

Rhaiden meets her eyes with understanding the two of them share. "Exactly. She had prior knowledge to call on, a well of wisdom none of us could access. Her skills were too advanced for her age — her *apparent* age, I mean. She was nineteen when I met her, but her harness on power and control, her ability to read people, they seemed like they were built on memories or experiences she couldn't have had yet."

"So phoenixes age strangely." Aren leans his palms against the back of the couch, considering the hypothesis. "It makes sense, given their mythos of being reborn."

"But it's more than that." Frustration seeps across Rhaiden's expression. Lev catches a glimpse of what her letter described — Rhaiden following a secret suspicion with no way to prove it, ducking Vesta's prying eyes and the tight control she kept on her pack. "Phoenixes are so unknown. So rare. Their capabilities aren't understood, even by those of us who spent years with her."

Aren tilts his head. "You think there's more to them than the stories? More than fire and immortality?"

Rhaiden's eyes flash when she nods. Now they're understanding. "There's a reason Vesta was able to pull so many packs apart, why she targeted the ones she did — smaller packs with enough infighting to split with a few well-woven words."

A lump swells in Lev's throat. *Like the Broadleafs.*

"Vesta tore those packs apart because you helped her," Caius rolls his eyes. "You're a *siren*. That's exactly how you operate: persuasive voice. Causing chaos. Wreaking havoc."

"I can persuade on a small scale," Rhaiden snipes. "Short periods of time, one or two people. There's just enough power to get to my next feeding. What I'm suggesting is that there's a creature stronger than that. One who can command dozens of people for months at a time, sowing seeds of control. It takes longer to work, but once it does, it's overwhelming."

The room is silent save for the rush of blood in Lev's ears, eyes glazed as she stares out the window. Could it be? Lev stood right here on the cliff's edge with Vesta before the cottage was built, the two of them glowing in the setting sun. Vesta leaned close, tongue curling over the words as the waves crashed below —

"You think Vesta had persuasive power?" For the first time, Caius's words sound more like a question than an accusation. "Stronger than sirens?"

"I think Vesta had the ability to plant mental seeds, or eggs," Rhaiden answers. "Foster them. Protect them. Encourage their growth until she was ready for them to hatch. That's what she did with the three of us." Rhaiden's features sharpen, gills fluttering on her neck as she glares into the middle distance. "Honing us until we were single-minded shells. We were an arsenal more than a pack, mindless drones she sent out as she wanted, no personality except the weapon she wanted to wield."

Rhaiden gestures down the hill, where she can surely sense Pheir's presence.

"You've seen it with Pheir: her brutality. Vesta did the same thing with Thalea's obedience. By the time I came along, Vesta needed someone to help her plan. She had people willing to stand by her, to fight for her, but she needed more. She needed a strategist." A quaint smile makes its way across Rhaiden's lips. "She didn't realize the mistake she was making, letting me keep a broader scope of my mind intact."

"Then why didn't you stop it?" Resentment builds in the line of Caius's shoulders, claws clenching into his fists. "If you knew what Vesta was doing, why didn't you fight back? You could have done *something* instead of watching her hurt people."

"Caius..." Aren murmurs. His head dips forward shamefully. Lev's heart clenches, but Caius doesn't look toward Aren. She can't place where Caius's anger comes from. Fur rises on the back of his neck. Godras braces a hand by Rhaiden's shoulder, but Caius keeps his distance this time.

Rhaiden doesn't fight his claims. Her gaze slips to her hands, fingers brushing the inside of her wrist. "I couldn't leave them behind — Pheir and Thalea. They would have died fighting for Vesta. Maybe they still would. I wasn't in control most of the time. As soon as the fog cleared enough for me to make a plan, Vesta would suck me back again. I couldn't find my way out."

"But there is a way out?" The silly, hopeful words jump from Lev's mouth. "You were giving Pheir and Thalea something in their food. Pheir said you were poisoning her."

"It wasn't poison." Rhaiden's eyes roll, but a fond smile flits across her face. "Not for her. Once I caught onto Vesta, I had to try something. The closest thing I could think of was siren's tongue. If it works to prevent a siren's influence, I thought it could work on a different kind of persuasion." Her eyes cut to Godras. "*He's* already added it to the Chasm pack meals, but it's not a simple plant to find on your own. I could barely get enough for Pheir and Thalea, let alone the other packs Vesta poached. I couldn't ingest any myself, obviously, so Vesta retained some control over me. It took weeks to have any effect on the others."

Caius huffs a breath. "Why not tell them what you were doing instead of slipping it into their food?"

"It would have been useless." She pins him with a knowing look. "You've met Pheir. Would she willingly take anything meant to break her devotion to Vesta? And Vesta had these sayings she'd repeat, mantras she taught us to live by to keep us from questioning her." With a flourish, Rhaiden spans her bound hands in front of her face in mocking imitation. "*'Rely on the kindness of strangers.' 'The best magic is a secret.' 'One rotten seed ruins the soil.'*" Her smile flickers bitterly. "That was her favorite for me."

Every word is familiar, the old wound on Lev's shoulder aching with recognition. Above the thoughts clamoring in Lev's head, Rhaiden continues.

"I don't know if it was a code, but I think it had to do with her abilities. If you believe the myths, phoenixes *rely on the kindness of strangers* when they're reborn. They have to hope someone finds them in their ashes to help them get back on their feet. As for the rest..." Rhaiden shrugs. "Vesta never said exactly what she meant. No matter what words were coming out of her mouth, there was something behind it. Something deeper. Something she never explained."

Lev mulls over the words and glances at Aren. He rubs the fur of his chin before he asks the very question she's thinking. "At the battle...do you think Vesta planned for her pack to be killed? To make the remaining members stronger?"

For the first time, Rhaiden's surprised by the question. Brows knit, she leans back against the couch, gaze tracing the ceiling for a long moment. "She could have..." Her voice is low, as delicate as bare feet over a rocky shore. "That would explain why she didn't want to wait. I knew we couldn't win if we fought the Conclave as we were, but Vesta insisted. I thought..."

Rhaiden swallows roughly, clearing her throat before she brings her gaze back, avoiding whatever thoughts distract her.

"I thought it was because Vesta stretched herself too thin, bit off more than she could chew. In the beginning, she'd build her persuasion on one of us for years and weave her way inside. The more people she added to our pack, the thinner her control got, until she was barely hanging on. That's why the Broadleafs didn't show up at the battle. She couldn't compel them. She used up too much of her ability and got impatient."

Lev's jaw tightens. It's the truth she feared. "So you knew about the Broadleafs. What they were doing. Who they killed."

For the first time, Rhaiden's gaze dips remorsefully as she chews the inside of her lip. "I knew Vesta spoke with them. They had an agreement, but she never told us her plans, no matter what Pheir believed. The only person in Vesta's inner circle was herself." Rhaiden's jaw clicks, her eyes honing on Lev. "You know that better than anyone."

In this room, only Rhaiden and Aren know the history Lev's been running from. Blood thrums through her, hotter than Caius's burning eyes on her, louder than his footsteps as the front door swings shut behind him. Aren follows after him. Lev stands too, but Rhaiden speaks before she makes it to the door.

"Vesta never told us exactly what happened between you two, Lever-" Rhaiden stops herself. "Lev. What you did or didn't do. Why she was so devoted to taking you down. I know you think the worst of us. That we're cruel and corrupt, but the choices we've made haven't been choices at all. Our lives haven't followed the same path yours did."

Despite the sharp tongue and conniving mind, there's an innocence in Rhaiden that Vesta never had, a remorse beneath her expression. It bobs to the surface when she talks about the other Vestals, eyes softening.

"If you have mercy for no one else, have it for Pheir. Maybe one day she'll tell you how Vesta found her."

Lev could wonder about that for hours. With a nod, she leaves the Chasms behind as she steps outside. Aren returns with a somber shake of his head. "I'll deal with the Chasms. You go after him."

When Aren passes back into the building, Lev peers down the trail where a dust cloud is settling back to the ground.

Caius is nowhere in sight.

NINETEEN

Aren

Despite the days apart, Lev and Aren work seamlessly as they split off. She makes her way down the trail, and he ignores the pang that he isn't the one going after Caius. It's best that Aren doesn't. Caius would rather speak to Lev, anyway. Given their history, Aren following would inflame whatever's bothering Caius.

There's no time to dwell on it. When Aren returns to the Chasms, he's the picture of cordiality, bracing hands behind his back. "Thank you for coming. You've shed a lot of light on things."

"Hope it helps."

Godras looks blasé. He's always treated Aren with disregard, but he treats everyone that way. Compared to the way the rest of the Break views Aren, it's almost pleasant. But then, Godras narrows his eyes.

"I was surprised that the invitation came from Caius."

Aren gives a tight smile, revealing nothing otherwise. The Timbers are a united front. That's what they need to maintain for outsiders as well as themselves.

In the center of the room, Rhaiden drifts toward the stairway to the second floor. The Chasm guards tense, but Godras lifts a hand as he and Aren follow to the upper landing. She pushes out onto the deck overlooking the cliff's edge with a view clear across the lake.

There's a small island at its center. Past it, forests cover the hills that wrap around the lake and back to the cottage. Aren wonders if Rhaiden's going to fling herself over the railing into the water below. Instead, her voice carries back to them over the wind. "Pheir would like this — being this high. Looking out across the water."

Godras keeps his eyes on her. There's more than watchfulness in his gaze, a fiery ember smoking in the depths of his eyes. Aren fights a smirk, tilting his head for Godras to hear him. "I assume bonding Rhaiden to your pack went well."

"We haven't," Godras answers gruffly. "She's even more dangerous than we predicted. Clever as a demon, and twice as pretty."

Aren turns his gaze back to Rhaiden. There's an ethereal quality to her, scales shimmering in the sun before the light catches on her sharpened eyes. Aren keeps a respectable distance, rocking on his heels. "So coming here truly was her idea, out of no obligation to you?"

Smoke dispels from Godras's nostrils when he snorts. "Why would you think a deadly siren is beholden to anyone, bonded or not?"

Aren purses his lips as he fights a smile. "Because she smells like you and your wife."

When Godras clamps his mouth shut, the smoke halts.

Aren escorts them down the outer stairs to their takeoff point. Rhaiden's eyes don't leave the water lapping against the shore. Once the guards join them, Godras jerks his chin toward a smaller pool of water nestled between rocks. When Rhaiden wades up to her ankles, she sighs in relief.

"We brought some siren's tongue for you," she murmurs. As if following her orders, one of the guards hands a bag to Aren. Rhaiden digs her toes into the sand, head tilted toward the sky. "Now that Vesta's not here to obstruct its effects, I'm not sure what it will do to Pheir. A change could happen rapidly, or other things could get in the way." One of Rhaiden's eyes cracks open to peer at Aren. "Like wedding bonds."

Aren's face remains neutral. "I'll keep that in mind."

"There is one last thing…"

Somehow, the siren sounds foreboding. Aren lifts his brow in silent interest as she drags a foot through the water.

"Vesta planned for everything. Every possible outcome." She plants her foot back onto the ground, watching waves ripple out around her. "It doesn't make sense that she would die so easily."

Uneasiness spreads through Aren's chest. He wouldn't call the battle "easy." Afterward, they did everything they could to prevent Vesta's return, cremating her body and separating the ashes. That's the assurance he clings to, but it's difficult when the person who knew Vesta best has doubts. He tries to maintain a level of surety for himself if no one else. "I suppose we finally got ahead of her."

When Rhaiden smiles, there's no humor in it. "I wouldn't count on that."

The Chasms take their leave before any Regents discover them. Things are tense enough among the Timbers without disputes of treason. Unfortunately, they still have to deal with everything Rhaiden revealed. It's possible it's a misdirection, but if so, it's elaborate, and what she told them makes sense. It would explain why so many packs turned against the Conclave. Why the Vestals seemed mindless. Why Lev struggles to understand her own history with Vesta.

Selfishly — *foolishly*, Aren wants what Rhaiden told them to be true. Lev has put so much on the line to bring Pheir into their pack. If this gives them an opportunity to break the chain Vesta holds, that can make all the difference.

And Pheir...he can't deny the pull to dig deeper with her, to try harder, to fight past her defenses. Maybe he sees the same thing Lev does — someone clawing to reach the surface, buried in armor that drags her down, who doesn't know how to function without sworn duty.

Sounds like someone else you know.

Aren's chest clenches at the guilty thought. If they can get to the heart of Pheir, maybe they can figure out Caius, too. Who would have thought she'd be the one they have a better chance of reckoning with?

By the time Aren makes it back to the main lodge, there's no sign of Caius or Lev, but there is the unmistakable sound of Pheir's squalling. After a pit stop in the kitchen, he approaches her cabin to Oberon stationed on her porch. "She started screaming again," the bear shouts over Pheir, fingers plugging his ears wearily. "I thought we were past this..."

"Take a break," Aren calls. "You've earned it."

Oberon doesn't need more invitation than that, lumbering away as Aren slips inside the cabin.

Rage permeates Pheir's muzzle, heightened as soon as Aren appears. Nonetheless, exhaustion swells in the hollows of her eyes. Muscles wither on her body from lack of food and sleep, both of which are her own doing. The wound across her face is healing, but it's not doing any favors for her haggard appearance, not to mention that dazed look in her eye.

Like she's under someone's control. It's too real in the wake of everything Rhaiden said. Maybe there's credence to her hypotheses. Aren moves closer, setting the tray of food on the table as he removes Pheir's muzzle.

"Feeling better?" he asks.

She doesn't scream, glaring up from her chair. "Fuck you." Her voice is rough and parched, water growing stagnant in the glass by her bedside. Although she hasn't lost her spunk, it's clear it's hanging by a thread. Rhaiden's presence at the compound must have brought some vigor back, but Pheir's too drained to realize it.

"You have to start eating consistently," Aren sighs. "I know you're ready to starve for your cause, but you're never going to get revenge if you're weak from a hunger strike. There's a middle ground, if you'll meet me there."

Pheir scoffs, trying to disguise the way her eyes dart toward the food. As soon as Aren catches her, she glares toward the rafters.

He pulls up a chair in front of her. "We have to negotiate."

"I don't negotiate with my *captors*," she seethes.

"You need to eat," Aren reiterates. "It's only a matter of time before the first snow. You need energy and fat to keep your body warm."

"No, I don't."

"Our environment is —" *Different than the Eyrie.* Aren cuts himself off. No need to expose what he's learned; gods know it would set Pheir off. Instead, he tilts his head. "Have you seen snow?"

Pheir scowls stubbornly. "It can't be that bad. I don't need your 'food.'"

Aren tries a different tack. "Despite what you might believe, we don't want to torture you."

"Is that why you've kept me locked in the dark?" Pheir's voice borders on delirium, pitching higher as she rambles. "As soon as Caius caught me in the woods, you left me to rot. You want to fuck with my head. You left me in here for *weeks*."

Slowly, Aren's feet settle on the ground. An unsettling feeling filters through him. "It's only been a few days, Pheir."

She doesn't believe him, eyes darting the walls as panic ruffles her feathers. Somberly, Aren reaches back for the tray.

"How about..." With his claws, he peels an orange. "You start eating your meals, and we find you a room with a view. A place you can move around."

There's no hiding the way Pheir's face lights up at the prospect. She snuffs it out immediately. "And why would I agree to that?"

Aren shrugs. "It would give you a better chance to escape."

Leaning back, Pheir mulls over the thought before she decides on her price. It's a negotiation, after all. "I want to stay in Lev's room."

Heat thrums through Aren at the memory of the last time he saw Pheir. *Do you think about Lev like that?* It's lingered in his mind for days, along with the heavy rise and fall of Pheir's chest and the sharp tang of her arousal. Gods forbid he bring it up and isolate her further. Mouth twisting in consideration, he drums his claws against the tray. "I'll see what I can do, but you have to eat first. Every meal."

Pheir's eyes narrow. "Once a day."

He doesn't budge. *"Every meal."*

"Why, so you can poison me like Rhaiden did?" There's that hysteria whipping through Pheir again. "I know she was slipping shit in my food. I know she was trying to kill me."

"What do you think she was giving you?" Aren asks calmly. It's not a denial. Not an admittance, either.

"Doesn't matter." Pheir clamps her teeth shut, chin lifting petulantly. "I'm not eating."

For all Aren's patience, it's wearing thin, setting a blunt edge in his voice. "If we wanted to kill you, we'd do it."

Pheir's posture straightens, knees knocking where her thighs clench together. Aren drags his gaze back up to hers. *Don't get distracted.*

"We had a perfect excuse the other night. Gods know Caius could have done it easily. No one would have asked questions if you died in an escape attempt, but you didn't, even when it was the two of you." When Aren leans forward, Pheir's body meets her restraints, edging closer to him. His tongue slides over his lips, voice smoothing back into a soothing bass. "Loan us a little bit of trust."

Her gaze dips to his mouth. It takes all he has not to let his nose twitch, scenting the subtle twirl of her desire slipping into the air. It should bother him more the way his body reacts to being alone with her, as if she wouldn't kill him at the first chance. As if she doesn't tease out a reckless, wild part of him that walks the line between animal and man. It's the same way Caius does. It's the same way Lev did the other night, when Caius took control.

Amidst it all, Pheir's eyes slip toward the orange in his hands. It's clear she's starving, but she won't reach for it. This is a negotiation.

Aren has more bargaining chips up his sleeve, gesturing across the spread of food. "I'll eat this with you. All the guards will eat with you from now on. You choose the tray to ensure there's nothing harmful in it."

His face is placid as she looks for a tell that he's lying. Finding none, she sniffs and eyes the tray. "The almonds don't look *completely* inedible."

It takes the better part of an hour to feed her, avoiding her teeth when she regains some of her strength. Once she gets started, he has to force her to eat slowly instead of scarfing it down. When she finishes the last of her lemonade, color returns to her face, violet eyes sharpened like talons. Callous excitement bubbles over her words. "So when are you taking me to Lev's bed?"

She barely hides her glee at the thought of being close to Lev. Whether it's to kill Lev or fuck with her, Aren's still not sure. He fights down the conflicting swell as he packs up the trash. "Her *room*," he reminds her. "And I'm not sure."

Pheir blanches, jerking in her restraints. "You *agreed* —"

"I'll speak with her. Loan me some trust, remember?" Aren places his full bottle of lemonade on Pheir's bedside table. "It involves some planning, like figuring out how to keep you quiet so you don't irritate everyone."

"Lev has two perfectly capable guards already." Past the viciousness, Pheir's smile is brilliant, a glimmer of the woman that fought Aren and Caius so fiercely the night they brought her back here. "Surely they're up to the challenge of one meager prisoner."

Aren's not sure what possesses him. He's not sure why he braces an arm against the back of her chair, leaning toward her and tempting every molecule of fate when the fur of his forehead brushes hers. His voice lowers with a hint of humor. "You're enough trouble for an entire army."

Her scent hits him fully for the first time, sharp and fresh like tangerine. Her head turns slowly, almost teasing when her lips part next to his as if she's waiting for him to stop her.

He should. There are too many complications already, with the Regents holding a sword over Pheir's neck and Rhaiden exposing powers that the Timbers never imagined.

Aren shouldn't lean closer. He shouldn't let his whiskers drift across Pheir's cheeks until she sucks in a breath as slow as the desire mounting in his stomach. There's a flicker of life in her eyes, a flame that's nearly overshadowed by the darkness, casting rainbow colors across her iris.

Then she clamps her teeth in Aren's lip, drawing blood before he pries himself away. His fingers press to the wound in his mouth. He expected it. Why wouldn't he? Most disturbing is the fact that he'd *known* she'd do it, and he leaned in, anyway.

Maybe he's a glutton for punishment, after all.

Copper tastes sweet when he tongues the wound. It's sweeter still when Pheir laps the reward from her lips, his blood staining her tongue. She's proud and weak and defiant and needy and every contradiction known to man. Her head rests back against the chair, but her body presses against the restraints. "You would've been better off letting me die."

Aren can't help but wonder if it's true.

TWENTY

Caius

Caius would have made it past the tree line if he weren't so damn sentimental.

Instead, he lingers for too long in his cabin, giving a final look to the things he's not taking with him. His sheets lay tangled from fitful sleep, like every night he's not pressed against Lev. Misshapen wax lines the shelves from his early attempts at making candles. A ribbon of Lev's fur is tucked beneath his pillow, one she left to make it easier to settle into his cabin. If some of Aren's fur is mixed up in the bunch, too, then so be it.

None of it comforts Caius now. Not when he fucked up yet again, making impulse decisions that look preposterous in hindsight. Why would he invite the Chasms here? Why would he try to prove he can be trusted when it's clear he can't be? Aren never would have made that mistake. He never would have put Lev in that position, floundering because Caius couldn't cool his heels for a few days.

Why is everything he does to prove he's strong enough to be here shining a bright light on his imperfections?

Leaving is easier. It's better than whatever Lev will say when she dismisses him. Better than Aren's knowing eyes on Caius's back, reassured that he was right about Caius all along. Better than the confusion that clouded Lev's face when Aren attempted to explain without blaming Caius. There was pity from both of them. Caius can't stand that they see him like that, as something soft enough to need sympathy.

He doesn't need it. He *doesn't*. He's not weak.

He's been here before, making a fool of himself trying to stay where he isn't wanted. He won't let that happen again.

You didn't even fucking place. After all I've done for you —

Caius winces at the memory of a glass bottle shattering against the door frame, splattering his nose with the sharp sting of alcohol.

Get the fuck out, you worthless piece of — !

A board creaks on the deck. Lev arrives in the open doorway, trying to piece together the firm grip Caius has on his bag. She doesn't look wholly surprised that he's making a break for it. She reads him better than he wants to admit. When her eyes take in the untouched room behind him, though, her lips part in shock. "You're not taking your stuff?"

Avoiding her gaze, he hikes the satchel higher on his shoulder. "It's not mine. I got it all after I moved in."

"Of course it's yours." She hesitates, like she's got her hands over a broken bone that neither of them knows how to reset. Her voice is tight and small, not the assurance she reserves for the rest of the pack. "Can we talk? Please?"

Fear creeps into his throat. Why bother? He fucked up by inviting Rhaiden here, trying to fill Aren's footprints when all Caius has is shoddy impulse.

When he shoulders past Lev, she spins, panicked voice rising behind him.

"I want you to stay, Caius."

It stops him in his tracks. He yearns to turn back. He's never heard those words before; he may never hear them again. It's not something he knew he was longing for. Hearing the sentiment from her tugs on him like the magnetic force of a compass guiding him where he desperately wants to be.

I *want you to stay.*

Lev doesn't realize the impact of her words, voice cracking like a branch underfoot and exposing her position. "Please don't go yet. If you still want to leave after..."

Caius's hand tightens around the strap of his bag. Behind him, the Timber compound is loud with daily activity. Before him, the forest is yards away. He could melt into it, disappear and leave the Timbers behind...but the wind picks up, ruffling the fur at his back and engulfing him in Lev's scent.

The hold he has on his bag and his pride loosens.

Sinking down on the porch steps, the satchel clatters to the ground as he runs claws back through his hair. At least his cabin faces the edge of the compound. No one will see him like this. Lev sits on the other side of the steps to leave a gap between them. Thank the gods she speaks first, because Caius still struggles to pull words from his flurry of emotions.

"I'm sorry if I made you feel like..." Her voice trails off, searching his face for a sign. He keeps his eyes on the ground, too afraid of what she'll see. "I was surprised that Rhaiden was here. I needed to talk to her. *We* did, I just..."

There's strain in Lev's voice as she seeks the right words. Caius hands them to her, elbows resting on his knees. "You didn't want me involved."

Lev's head whips toward him. "No! No, that's not..." She pulls her feet up a step to wrap her arms around her knees. No matter that Caius can't face her, she keeps her eyes on him, voice softer than he's heard in a long time. "Is that what you think?"

He shrugs. It's the easy response. He could leave it at that, but the emotions thrumming in him push past his lips. "You don't trust me like you trust him."

It takes a moment for Lev to understand. "You mean Aren?" There's a hitch of surprise in her voice. Caius doesn't know why; there's no part of Lev that Aren can't touch. Aren is the perpetual yardstick Caius measures himself against. Aren is everything Caius wants to be. Aren is everything Caius is not.

Carelessly, Caius gestures toward the cottage on the cliff. "You share everything with him. When people talk about your history, he's never surprised by it. Hell, our worst enemy knows more about you than I do. I knew you had history with Vesta, but the way Rhaiden talked, it's like you two were..." What, exactly? Caius still can't comprehend it. "When there's a problem, Aren's the first person you look to. When you need something, he's the one that takes care of it." Caius lets his hands fall between his knees, words tearing from his chest. "How am I supposed to compete with that?"

"You're *not*," Lev splutters. Confusion muddles her expression, as if she can't follow his line of thinking. "Aren is not your competition. This is a pack. We work together for the good of the group. No one is comparing you to each other." Her mouth slips shut before she rephrases. "None of *us* are comparing you."

Caius hears her unspoken words: *Only* you *are comparing yourself.* He scoffs. That can't be true. No one could look at the two men and not see Caius is fighting above his weight class. It roils in him, overflowing now that he's finally opened his mouth to speak. He forces his gaze to meet Lev's, a bitter smile across his face. "You expect me to believe you don't see the contrast? You don't see which one of us doesn't stack up?"

An angry flash crosses her face, brows furrowing. "No. I don't see that."

Caius rolls his eyes.

Lev leans closer, chasing the truth that Caius has finally put words to as if she's afraid he'll lock it up again. "I'm not saying you two aren't different, but that's a good thing. You have strengths that balance each other. That balance *me*."

"Like what?" Caius scoffs.

"Like your instincts!" Her voice raises louder than she means. After a glance around, she lowers it again. "Aren can reason his way through anything, but sometimes, you know the solution without thinking. Nature doesn't always act with the logic we understand; it's emotional. It's reactive. You help me see that. You help *Aren* see that."

Aren's voice comes trickling back into Caius's memory like the water down his back in the baths. *It seems like you understand Pheir. How her mind works. I don't think any of us can read her like that.*

It still stings like an insult. Caius grits his teeth.

"'Instinct' is why I'm always fucking up. I don't want to be like that, I want..." Words threaten to tumble out of him. *I want to make up for the chance you took on me. I want to make it worth your while.* They feel pathetic in his mouth. He swallows them down and settles on something less damning. "I don't want to be like that if it means you don't trust me."

Lev leans back against the steps, staring toward the cottage on the cliff. From here, they can't see it. It's hidden behind the growth of trees lining the hill. "I do trust you, Caius. But the responsibilities you're asking for don't happen overnight. Aren and I have known each other for a long time. We've learned we can trust each other to make choices for the good of the pack. We can trust each other to show up. To *stay*."

Caius winces at the word. Next to his feet, his bag glares up at him. *Aren would never leave.* Another way Caius doesn't measure up.

Despite the voice in his head, Lev softens as if she can hear it. "That doesn't mean you've missed an opportunity. It means we have room to grow."

It's easy enough to say, but living it...Caius presses his face into his hands. Every day is sand slipping through his fingers. There's time he's missed out on, relationships he can't break into.

This isn't what he was trained to do. He was trained to fight. To make people wary. To bully and strong-arm.

"If we're being honest..." Lev's feet rock uneasily. This time, she's the one that struggles to meet Caius's eyes. "I don't think I'm the only one of us who isn't fully trusting."

There's a moment of silence before a laugh bursts out of him. "You think I don't trust you?"

It's ludicrous. Lev is about the only person he *does* trust, the only one he lets himself close to. But there's no humor on Lev's face.

"I know you don't, Caius." There's no levity in her tone, palms up like she's helpless. "You say you don't know enough about Aren and me, but we don't know you, either. You haven't told us anything. When I ask an open-ended question, you shrug. When I wait for you to elaborate, you make an excuse to leave. When I reach out, you turn your back. It's hard to take that on faith, Caius."

There it fucking is. His eyes slip shut. It's exactly what he expected, exactly what he's always known, but hearing the confession digs so much deeper. He's a chore. A difficulty. A liability. A trap snaps around his heart, so loud he almost doesn't hear the rest of Lev's words.

"That doesn't mean I want it any less."

Surprise makes him look at her. Her chin rests on her knees, uncertainty creeping through her gaze. She wets her lips, ears drooping like she's hesitant with what she wants to say.

"I want you to stay here. *So badly*." With an exhale, her eyes slip shut as if she can't stand to face him. As if it's too much for her to contain. "Sometimes, I think it clouds my judgment — how you make me feel. What would happen if I gave into it and..."

Her eyes open to him, gaze as hot as summer sun through the window. His ears perk, body straightening. Her lips part enough to show the gap between her front teeth that makes him forget the aches in his body. Forget the urge to leave. Forget anything but the way she looks at him. He leans closer, palm pressing against the stairs as he inclines his head. When she breathes in, he knows she smells him and how he wants her. They both stay like that, lingering in each other's air until she breaks the silence.

"That's just it." Painstakingly, she pulls away enough to let her head drop. Her forehead brushes his. It bores straight into him when she shakes her head against his. "We end up here every time. We can't keep doing this."

He wants to argue. Wants to pull her closer, to bury themselves in each other where they don't have to speak. They can fall into sync, breathing and pushing and pulling and fucking where there's no question how either of them feel. When her hand presses gently to his chest to hold him back, he realizes that's what she's trying to avoid.

"I want you...so badly," she breathes. Her fingers curl into the fur of his chest. He tries not to whine at the lack of further contact. "But I don't just want you when things are hard, or when you need a release, or when you don't want to talk. I want *all* of you. I want you to make a life here. I want you to be a part of this pack. I want to build that with you. After every argument, after every mission, I want you to be here. I don't want to be afraid you'll disappear."

Funny how the prospect of being beaten bloody scares him far less than putting words to the feelings in his chest. How opening a wound on his body pains him less than opening his mouth.

His lips stay clamped. He could make promises. He could parrot whatever words would assure her, but the thought of it pains him. When her eyes search his, it's like she knows. She understands. She smooths her hand over his shoulder.

"It doesn't happen overnight." It's like she's reminding herself as much as him. "Maybe until we figure something out, we should stop sleeping togeth-"

At the notion, his entire body shudders. "Please don't..." It's hard to speak, but harder to imagine losing the one point of connection they have. His hand closes over her knee, head pressing down to it as he struggles through the words. "Please don't take that away."

He can't bear to look at her when he's this weak at the thought of something so insignificant — but Lev doesn't make him feel like it doesn't matter. Her fingers close around his, a physical gesture that grounds him. "Ok. We don't have to stop, but we do have to do more. More effort with the pack. More..." A nervous breath escapes her. "More responsibility. More *talking* outside of sex."

Caius nods. It sounds impossible, but her next suggestion nearly knocks him over.

"And you need to talk to Aren about how you feel."

Caius groans, paw dragging down his face. "I don't want to talk to Aren."

Lev twines her fingers with his to pull them away from his face. "It doesn't have to be right away, but it does have to happen."

It's a rare occasion where Lev puts her foot down with him. Deep down, he knows she's right. Whatever the fuck this is between them is only complicated by his confusing feelings for Aren. Still, Caius doesn't relish the idea of any conversation with the man.

With gentle fingers, Lev weaves her fingers through the back of Caius's hair. "We'll see how it goes?"

Resigned, he sighs and rests his cheek against her leg.

TWENTY-ONE

Aren

The downside to Pheir eating again is that she's regained her strength. The Timbers assigned to cooking duty found a way to incorporate siren's tongue into her meals. For the fourth time, Aren scans the instructions that Rhaiden tucked into the bag as June stirs the pot of stew.

"It doesn't take much," he reads. "Cook it down with some of the stock, and put it in both the bowls that are going to her cabin."

June's nose wrinkles. "What's it supposed to do to her?"

"Pry her mind out of Vesta's control. Physically, that may mean she suffers withdrawals: sweats, chills, body aches."

Steam wafts off the pot toward June's face, her eyes glowing in the candlelight. "And you're sure it won't harm us if we eat it?"

Aren folds the note away. "Not unless you're being magically manipulated."

Mystically, June wiggles her fingers before she sniffs the two bowls that she ladles out. After a moment, she tastes one, smacking her lips theatrically. "It does *nothing* for flavor."

Pheir doesn't notice anything suspicious with her food, but she does continue her quest to be moved into Lev's room. Honestly, Aren thought it would be harder to convince Lev, but she agrees immediately.

"If that's her requirement for eating, then so be it." Lev shrugs, avoiding Aren's knowing look. "Whatever it takes."

Caius is less happy about it, sulking as they prep Lev's small cabin. She hands one end of a flannel sheet to him before they tuck it over the cot in the corner.

"You know," she muses, "if Pheir's gonna be here, she'll still need an overnight guard."

Caius's ears perk.

Lev takes a pillow from Aren and tosses it onto the temporary bed. "If the two of you want to stay here to make sure —"

"Done." Without question, Caius sinks onto Lev's bed, using his foot to press the cot further into the corner. At least it brings a begrudging smile to his face. "Guess we're having an extended sleepover."

The first night they move Pheir into Lev's single-room cabin, the harpy doesn't speak. For the others, it's been a long day of harvesting autumnal crops and planting winter ones, cleaning the stoves and canning food. When Aren's back hits the bed, exhaustion seeps from his body. Thank the gods Caius is taking first watch. Aren can barely keep his eyes open...

And then, Pheir starts screaming.

She takes every opportunity to drive them up the wall — scooting her bed across the floor, screeching through her muzzle, pissing Caius off until Aren has to take over. One night was bad enough, but Pheir reserves her energy all day to torment them once the sun goes down. When daylight breaks after a second night of tortured sleep, the three Timbers shuffle groggily into the lodge kitchen.

June chews a mouthful of bark. "You look like shit."

Lev throws a dish towel at her as Aren leans back against the island. Caius hovers near the door, gaze darting warily over the group gathered for breakfast. Oberon shoots them a pitying look as Marius steals an apple slice from Darby's plate.

"I heard Pheir from the trees last night." Mari bites the slice in half. "I think she's getting louder."

"She's not hoarse anymore." Oberon sips his tea thoughtfully. "She actually finished her tray when I took her dinner last night — although, she did make me take a bite of everything first." He watches Lev measure out heaping cups of coffee. "Do you think the siren's tongue is working?"

"Currently?" Lev rubs her eyes. "It's only been a few days. It might take some time."

"Can you give her *more*?" Mari grumbles, popping the last bite of apple into their mouth. "Tell her it's a vegetable or something. Give it to her raw."

As the group leaves the kitchen, June pauses in the doorway with a glance at Lev. After a moment, June steps back inside, holding onto the frame.

"Hey..."

It takes a moment for any of them to know who she's speaking to, but she looks directly at Caius. His body tenses. June doesn't let that deter her, tilting her head and narrowing her eyes.

"Do you want to help me compost today?"

Caius's mouth pulls tight like his mind's short-circuiting. Aren doesn't know the last time Caius exchanged more than a few words with anyone else in the pack. There's a streak of panic in his eyes when he looks around for help.

Aren suddenly finds the wood grain of the counter fascinating.

"Yeah, I'm talking to you," June confirms Caius's unspoken question. "I need someone big and strong."

Awkwardly, she taps his bicep with her fist, her smile more of a cringe as her hand falls back to her side. After a moment, she exhales, and the pretense falls away.

"Look, I'm supposed to do it with Mari, but they always make me carry the bags. Plus, they complain about the smell the whole time. I thought you might be better to work with. You don't say much. Plus, you can probably carry the bags in one trip with no problem."

Aren traces a claw around a knot in the wood, resisting temptation to look toward the conversation. It's quiet for a long time before Caius answers.

"Ok."

It's as much a shock to Aren as it is to June, relief pitching into her voice. "Ok? You'll help me?"

Caius nods. June bounces on her feet as she bounds out the door. From the way Lev observes over the brewing coffee, Aren suspects she had a hand in nudging her sister to reach out to Caius.

She pulls the coffee pot off the stove, shifting focus. "So, Pheir's screaming is bothering everyone. We can't keep her in my cabin if that's the case."

Caius takes a seat at the island next to where Aren leans, body slumping against the counter from lack of sleep. "Sedating her is a fucking option."

"We don't know what effect that might have on the siren's tongue." Lev slides three filled thermoses onto the counter. "Gods help us if it makes it worse."

Aren passes the first thermos to Caius before spooning sugar into his own, keeping his eyes on its depths. Maybe Caius is onto something. Getting Pheir to stop tormenting them of her own volition will be tough, but maybe they don't have to convince her to stop. Maybe they need to make her as exhausted as they are after a long day of work. In the past, when Pheir has screamed, it's been for attention. If they could find a way to combine the two...

After a long drink, Caius sets his thermos down on the counter. His gaze hones on Aren. "You're quiet this morning."

"I'm always quiet," Aren answers. He slips into the seat beside Caius.

When Aren lifts his gaze from his thermos, Lev stands up straighter in recognition of what his silence means. "You have an idea?"

Aren turns up his palms on the table. "I don't know if I'd call it that."

"What would you call it, then?" Caius turns in his chair, propping his chin lazily in a hand.

Aren leans back in his seat, tipping his gaze toward the ceiling. "A thought." It's half-formed. It's ridiculous, but the more he considers it, the more he wonders if it could work. Eventually, he turns a knowing look on Caius. "We've tired Pheir out before."

Confusion knits Lev's brow. It takes Caius no time to understand, as if the thought has been hovering in the front of his mind, too. "You can't be serious."

"It worked *before*." Aren holds up his hands. "That's all I'm saying."

Upstairs, feet pad back and forth as pack members shout down the long hallway. Lev's voice lowers to a hiss. "You mean having sex with her?"

Aren taps his spoon on the rim of his thermos, shrugging casually. Caius blusters beside him. "I'm not sticking my dick in her again! She'll probably claw it off!"

"Don't act like it's a chore," Aren chides. "Besides..." When he lifts the spoon to his mouth, his tongue trails along the coffee residue. Despite Caius's best efforts, his eyes follow it. Aren politely ignores the scent of arousal in the air. "If it doesn't interest you, you don't have to participate. Only one of us would need to tire her out."

That shuts Caius's mouth. There's no mistaking the shift in his demeanor, pupils spreading with desire. "Four of us trying that in one tiny cabin?"

"We could relocate her to the cottage on the cliff." Aren swirls his thermos, staring out the window toward where Pheir is now. "It would give us more space. Keep her constrained. Prevent her from disturbing everyone else. Rhaiden said Pheir would like it up there on the balcony overlooking the water. Giving her a view might distract her enough to give us a break."

A contemplative moment passes before Lev drums her nails on the island. "Pheir won't let me near her — not that it matters," she adds quickly, pressing off the counter to stand straight again. "I'm sure she wouldn't miss a chance to make me watch her with one or both of you." Usually, Lev is simple for Aren to read, a well-loved story he knows the intricacies of. Now, though, her teeth worry into her lip as if her mind is somewhere else. She shakes the thoughts from her head. "Pheir would never go for it, anyway. Sex, I mean. It's too close to admitting defeat."

"We thought that last time," Aren reminds them. "If we ask her, we may be surprised."

As ludicrous as the idea seems, the pieces fall easily into place. The three Timbers have taken routine protection potion for years to prevent sexually transmitted infection. There's no risk of pregnancy with Pheir or Lev, due to incompatible anatomy and infertility, respectively. The most insurmountable hurdle may be Pheir's hatred for them, but given the night after the battle, an enthusiastic "yes" is far from out of the question.

"And if Pheir rejects the idea?" Lev looks between them. "What's our backup plan? How will we get her quiet enough to sleep?"

"Gag her," Caius offers dryly.

Aren's lip turns up at the corner. "There's more space to work with at the cottage. At least we have distance and walls to put between us. We'll figure something out." Surprisingly, the heat in his gut says he hopes they won't have to. Hands circling his thermos, he's not sure if it warms him more than the thought of what they're about to try.

He's been with Pheir once. It was a necessity. A strategy. A way to bring order to chaos, but the memories hang in his mind like holiday decorations he should have packed away long ago. For all his planning, fucking Pheir didn't feel like he was in control. It felt like all his baser instincts came to a head, rising to the surface to pull him under. He sinks back into it now, smelling sweat and heat and blood over the fresh dirt ground into their bodies.

And Caius...it twinges in Aren's chest, the reminder of how free Caius seemed. How he released the hesitation that he reserves for Aren. Seeing Caius like that again, *getting* Caius like that again, is an opportunity Aren doesn't want to miss. Plus, the thought of Lev being there this time, overseeing it all, watching and directing what they do with someone else...

It would be explosive. Aren's not sure if that's good or bad.

Lev clears her throat, pulling Aren out of the pool of desire he dipped into. The flicker of a smile on her face says she can smell it. "We'll try it. Just you and Pheir?"

Aren glances at Caius, who adjusts gruffly in his seat, as if that'll hide the scent of his arousal. "I might as well help."

Aren gives him a pointed look over the rim of his thermos. "Wow. Make me twist your arm a little."

Caius shoves his shoulder before Aren glances back to Lev. Despite the agreement, her fingers tap nervously against the counter. Aren reaches a hand across the space to close over hers with a reassuring squeeze. "Sex is bonding. It could work."

The three of them know that better than anyone. They leave it at that, as if continuing the conversation is a jinx of its own. Caius goes to find June, and Lev and Aren lose track of the day to other duties. Once twilight falls, he gets a chance to breathe. It's short-lived as he, Caius, and Lev gather at the base of the hill.

"Is Pheir up there?" Caius stares at the cottage like it's haunted, its windows glowing with candlelight.

"The guards escorted her after dinner." Lev winces, voice strained. "They said she's in rare form tonight."

"Of course she is." Caius rotates his shoulder with a hiss. "On the day June and I set a record for spreading compost."

"Do you still want to do this?" Lev turns to face him. "It's not a requirement. You don't have to."

From behind Lev, Aren can see Caius's expression. His eyes flick to Aren before he tears them away, the faint tang of arousal hitting the air like a broken clove. "As long as I get some sleep tonight, I'm in."

When Lev glances back to Aren, he nods. She steels herself. "Then let's get started."

When they enter the cottage, Lev dismisses the guards for the night. One of them claps Aren on the shoulder as they leave, as if dealing with Pheir requires its own solidarity. The three of them linger in the foyer where they met the Chasms days ago, listening to the silence of the cottage. The quiet is a threat in its own right, a reminder of the peace that Pheir will soon shatter.

Climbing the stairs is eerie, rife with apprehension that Aren can't place. It's like the moments before battle, the three of them moving in tandem, eyes and ears flicking at every sound. Lev leads them, soft footsteps along the hardwood as Caius and Aren flank her. Adrenaline knots tension into their shoulders, a contradictory desire to spring forward and fall back all at once. When they reach the main bedroom door, Lev presses her hand against it for a long moment before she turns the knob.

Pheir sits chained to a chair. Her grin glints like a blade, an assassin lying in wait more than a prisoner. No threat she presents is enough to disguise that she's wearing the jeans and sweater Aren gave her. Beside her bound body, a food tray sits empty, crumbs licked clean.

He fends off a smile.

"Turning in for the night?" she coos, dragging a clipped talon across the floor like nails on a chalkboard. Naturally, she waited until they arrived to begin her routine. Caius busies himself unloading the small bag they brought, but he's already bristling at her voice, his motions barely restrained. Aren hangs back by the door as Lev sinks into the seat facing Pheir.

"Tired yet?" Lev asks, propping her foot against Pheir's chair. Lev jerks out of reach before Pheir can nick her.

"Not even a little," Pheir sneers. Despite her brusqueness, Lev nods and moves back toward the men as if she's mulling over a thought. Pheir's gaze follows, agitated by curiosity. "Why?"

Boredly, Lev turns back to her. "'Why' what?"

"That's a weird *question.*" Pheir's tone drips with mockery. "Why do you ask?"

Lev shrugs, turning down the sheets on the massive bed. "This would be easier if you were. Now you're gonna have to entertain yourself for a few hours."

When Lev bends over, Pheir's eyes cling to her ass. "You aren't going to sleep?"

"Not quite." Lev leans back to inspect her work, bearing weight on one leg so her hip curves invitingly. Aren strangles a laugh. She knows exactly what she's doing when she turns back to Pheir with a simper. "Don't let us bother you, though. I'd hate to disturb you trying to get some rest."

You would think Lev bestowed Pheir with a great honor from the smug smile spreading across the harpy's face. "Uh-oh..." Leaning back, Pheir pouts. "Someone woke up on the wrong side of the bed."

Almost imperceptibly, Lev's nails dig into a pillow before she forces her fist to soften and fluffs it casually. "I never went to sleep."

Irritation slips into her tone. Caius's muscles pull taut as he slows his motions. Pheir sets a smile on Lev that fills Aren with an urge to drop to his knees and crawl.

He locks his legs in place. What is he thinking? Why did that thought cross his mind? There's little time to spare for it, because Pheir's chains clink as she shifts in her seat like she hasn't a care in the world, head lolling maliciously.

"Get to bed, then, little rabbit."

Lev's mouth twitches.

Caius freezes.

Aren holds his breath.

It's not like Lev's never been given instructions before. She's never had an Alpha complex, never struggled to take someone else's advice. With Caius and Aren, she submits to their control on plenty of occasions. The patronizing can be a delicious sting...but the order has never come from someone like Pheir. Never an enemy. Never a captive bound in front of them.

It's defiant. It's bratty. It's *hot.* Everyone in the room feels it, Pheir's legs dropping open as she reclines in the chair. She's taking up space and making demands. Unabashed, she basks in her insolence.

But Lev's dealt with worse than the likes of Pheir. Caius turns to face them, static shifting in the room. When Lev smiles this time, Aren digs claws into his fist to keep from groaning. That's the smile Lev gets when she makes Aren and Caius beg to get inside her. That's the smile she wears when she edges one of them and won't let the other stop coming.

"I don't think I will," Lev purrs. Maybe Pheir has more animal instinct than she realizes, because her eyes widen like she recognizes that tone. Her knees snap together, body straightening as Lev rounds the bed closer to her chair. "In fact, we're not planning to sleep for a *long* time."

It's the same way Aren and Caius enticed Pheir the first time, dropping hints to wind her up. She catches on quickly. Maybe her mind has been wandering over the memories, too.

"You're going to *fuck*?" she spits, as if it's disgusting. As if the werecreatures in the room can't scent desire throbbing through her, her clamped thighs doing nothing to staunch the crescendo of her arousal.

Lev is a patient woman, examining her nails without a glance toward Pheir, paying her back with the same obstinance. Feigning disinterest, Lev's dark eyes flick up. "Don't tell me that's a problem for you?"

TWENTY-TWO

Lev

Somewhere in her mind, Lev knows this is wrong. She shouldn't toe this line with Pheir. She shouldn't play games when there's nothing between them but hate, yet that vicious smirk Pheir wears makes Lev want to smear it against the ground.

Wiping it from her face will be its own reward.

When Pheir hears what the three Timbers plan to do, it throws her off balance. She forgets to fight against her chains, arousal wafting through the room, but she still can't release the hate she has for Lev. Pheir has to cling to it. Pheir has to make Lev work for it.

Lev doesn't know why that gives her a grim satisfaction.

Pheir lifts her chin, looking down her nose. "What if it is a problem?"

When Lev moves toward Pheir again, she can feel every eye in the room clinging to the sway of her hips. She takes her life in her own hands, pressing her palms to the arms of Pheir's chair when she leans down. Pheir forgets to lunge forward. Forgets to snap her teeth when Lev lowers her voice.

"I don't care."

Aghast, Pheir's mouth falls open. Lev's already got a hand on the back of her chair, spinning it to face the wall.

"Now, if you don't mind — or even if you do —"

"Wait!"

Pheir's shout rings in the silence. She's helpless, fighting to get a glance over her shoulder. Lev's smirk grows. It's exactly where she wants Pheir, warring with desire past her tense shoulders and taut restraints. *The second Pheir's not included, she has to be a part of it.* Aren noticed that long before they had Pheir captive. She can barely hide her desperation to throw their plans off course, no matter the cost.

Lev leans on the back of the chair, breath gusting Pheir's ear to piss her off. Pheir jerks with a snarl. Behind Lev, Aren and Caius tug at the end of their control, trying to cage the carnal desire prowling through their bodies. Lev can sense it, so she leans down further until her tail lifts invitingly in the air.

Caius snarls. The predatory threat runs through Lev, but she won't let them off that easy. Her thighs brush together, giving the slightest bit of friction as her wanton scent permeates the room. In her periphery, Aren holds Caius back from pouncing.

Pheir won't admit defeat that easily. She turns her head to get a look at Lev, and Lev's struck by a hot vice clamping deep in her gut. This is how it would look if Lev fucked Pheir from behind, her hands in Pheir's hair, hips slamming together, strap buried in Pheir's cunt...

Lev bites back a groan as Pheir's voice lowers with vengeful heat. "I already fucked both your *boys* during their security detail." Her lips curl into a smile over the words, so close Lev could sink her teeth into them. "You sure you want my sloppy seconds?"

Gods, Lev wants to make Pheir pay. Make her take back every snarky remark she's made. Watch her deny how badly she wants this while she's coming on Lev's fingers — but Lev has to maintain control. She clicks her tongue. Pheir's eyes dip to it.

"If anything, Pheir, you got *my* leftovers."

Lev jerks the chair to face her, edging into the space so suddenly that Pheir doesn't have a second to strike.

"But I think you liked that, didn't you?"

Lev steps between Pheir's legs, forcing them open with her knees. Growling, Pheir jerks the restraints, but her hips rut forward. Lev lowers her eyes to Pheir's so there's no escape from the truth.

"You liked getting one over on me. You liked putting that pussy where mine has been."

Pheir's teeth snap. Lev grips her cheeks and squeezes, holding Pheir in place. There's no space between them now, nothing to keep them from doing more than fighting. Their breathing's ragged, like they've been running from something — running *toward* something — and the finish line is finally in sight.

"Say it." Lev tightens her grip on Pheir's cheeks, hard enough to hurt. Lev can't stop herself now that they're this close. Her voice slows to a crawl. "Open your mouth...and admit it."

A hazy look crosses Pheir's eyes. It's different than it has been, desperation to obey under a hot cloud of lust...

But this time, the longing is to obey *Lev*.

An ache clenches between Lev's thighs. Pheir jerks her head out of Lev's grip, shaking off the daze so she can sneer. "If your *officers* were satisfied with you, they wouldn't have come to me. They wouldn't have *fucked me*." Words lash from Pheir's tongue like a whip. All Lev can feel is pleasure through the pain. "I can show you how it's done, since you need the help."

Almost imperceptibly, Pheir's hips shift, rutting as they seek something to grind against. Heat curls in Lev's throat as she leans back to stand. Pheir's eyes narrow, trying to calculate Lev's next move as Lev chuckles.

"It's cute what you're trying to do." Lev turns away from Pheir, taking a few steps across the room to sink onto the edge of the bed. One leg crosses over the other as she leans back on her palms, a strand of white hair falling over her eyes. "If you want to fuck them that badly, you can just ask."

Pheir's body tenses. She refuses to look at the men, as if that might betray her thoughts. Lev's foot bounces idly as she raises her brows.

"Well?" With a spark of challenge, she gestures behind her. "*Ask.*"

Pheir's jaw clenches. No matter how she tries to avoid her desire, it heightens in the room. Lev knows the test she's presented. Either Pheir keeps her eyes on the woman she hates most, or she's forced to face the men who picked her apart piece by piece, tearing into her like a juicy slab of meat. Lev would wager it's the only way Pheir can let herself have this, framing her hunger for them in carnal terms that lets her pretend this is nothing but violence.

The silence in the room is as stifling as Pheir's arousal. She won't admit it. Lev's brow knits. Despite Pheir's refusal to back down, Lev didn't think she'd deprive herself of an opportunity to rub Lev's face in this. With a shrug, Lev rises from the bed. "Then we're going to put you in the other room —"

"*Okay!*"

The word rips from Pheir's mouth, jaw clicking as she strains against her impulses. Her desire wars with her pride, deadlocked behind her lips and stubborn to the last. She can't bear to humble herself to the request, even when everyone in this room knows the truth. Frustration prickles up Lev's spine. Pheir will deny all of them pleasure out of spite. She'll deny her desire and keep them waiting all night if she has to.

So be it. Lev turns to the door, heat thrumming through her body. If Pheir wants to keep them dangling off the edge of whatever this is, then —

"What's the safeword?"

All eyes snap toward Aren when he speaks. It's the first sound he's uttered since they arrived. His gaze stays on Pheir, focused enough to make her sweat. Lev's breath catches. She's never seen him so openly fixated on anyone but her. Caius would never accept the attention, but in this moment, he's drawn to watch Aren — the twitch of his lynx ears as he eases off of the wall, the shift of his whiskers as he takes a step toward Pheir. He's controlled. Slow.

Caius's throat bobs in time with Lev's.

Pheir's not immune to him. She nearly bites her tongue in half, but one word chokes out. "Mercy."

It's more than she's given so far. Unhurried, Aren crosses the room, coming to halt in front of Pheir. "So you do remember how to make this stop."

It's not her eyes that follow him. It's her entire head, tipping back to keep him in sight. When he braces hands on his knees, her chest sinks back against the chair like a student caught throwing paper balls at the teacher's back.

Aren's voice is wickedly level. "Is that why you've been acting out? You want to get fucked until you can't move again?"

When she shivers, her eyes slip shut. "I am *not* —"

"Yes or no," Aren demands.

Pheir's lips press into a thin line. Aren begins to pull away before she grinds the answer out: "*Yes.*"

With a hand, he grips the chair behind her head. "That's a start."

A look passes between them, the barest shift of Pheir's mouth under the subtle twist of his head. When she doesn't bite, he braces his other hand against the seat between her legs, wrist turning toward her as his fingers curl over the edge. Subtly, she struggles against the restraints in an attempt to bring herself closer. Another inch, and she'll reach him. She'll be able to grind the seam of her jeans against him. Light as a feather, Aren lets his arm brush against her before he pulls away from the chair entirely.

"You're gonna have to tell us more than that."

Conflict rages in Pheir, hips snapping as she seethes. How she's not exhausted from fighting, Lev doesn't know, but she seems to have stores reserved just to war with the three of them. When Pheir's eyes find Lev's again, Lev knows what's coming. She still can't deny the sting when Pheir speaks.

"Without *her*. She can't touch me."

Another attempt to get under Lev's skin, to exert control over the Alpha. Aren's mouth opens to deny her, but Lev refuses to give Pheir the satisfaction of being ruffled. "Fine."

A triumphant sneer crosses Pheir's face. Lev doesn't give her time to enjoy it.

"But just know..."

Lev moves behind Aren, dipping her arms around his waist. He opens easily for her, shifting his arms out of the way. Lev drags her nails down the tight muscles of his abdomen. She peers around his arm, locking her gaze on Pheir as her hands slip down the fur of Aren's stomach.

"When you're taking their cocks?" Lev murmurs. "When you're grinding against their tongues? That's me fucking you. They're an extension of me. Anything I want, they'll do to you." Despite the venom in Pheir's gaze, her body pulls against the restraints. Lev stays out of reach, as Pheir wanted, but Lev's smirk is sharp. "When you come? It's for *me*."

Pheir screams behind her teeth. There's no way for her to avoid it now. Letting Aren and Caius fuck her means admitting Lev is capable of breaking her. Aren doesn't wait for more of Pheir's stalling, lifting the chair with Pheir in it and kicking open the door to the deck. As he carries her into the chilly night air, Lev turns to Caius, who's been nearly silent through it all.

It's not like him to restrain himself, but any worry Lev has is quickly set aflame at the look in his eyes. It's molten heat hammered into a weapon. He watches Aren and Pheir like Caius has been here before, like he knows what's coming, and he's *hungry* for it. It makes Lev's fur stand on end, seeing the unadulterated desires when Caius doesn't know anyone is watching.

Then he catches Lev's eye and tries to douse the flames, setting his mouth in a grim line of duty. When he moves past, she stops him with a gentle hand on his chest. "You don't have to do this."

The look on his face is a lie, the same denial Pheir tried to force. Lev knows better. There's hunger swelling in the dark depths of his eyes. His expression tries to pass this off as obligation. "It's fine. I'll do it." He tries to move past her again.

Lev applies more pressure to her palm, forcing Caius to stay in place. She doesn't let him shoulder past her. Doesn't let him look away. "I need to hear it, Caius." There's a touch of command in her voice. He could deny it if he chooses. Past that, though, her chest is tight, words little more than a whisper as desire pulses through her. "I need you to tell me that you want it."

It's exactly what Aren did to Pheir, insisting on *words* before they proceed. It would be easy to let Caius avoid speaking, to give into physicality again, but they agreed when she caught him in his cabin. More talking. More putting words to the things he wants, the things that scare him, the things that are one and the same.

His jaw clenches, voice tight with truth. "I want it."

Hearing it from his mouth makes Lev's lips part. His eyes dip to it, head inclining like he wants to taste the gasp from her, like the two of them might fall into it right here –

But she can't. This is about Pheir. There's a reason behind this that's more than want.

Lev needs Aren. He'll keep her head on straight when all Caius and Pheir do are drag Lev into animal desire. She clenches her fist in Caius's fur, pulling her mouth away to turn toward the door. A breeze wafts in from outside where Aren sets Pheir near the edge of the balcony. For the moment, her struggle stops, and the three Timbers stop too.

Wind blows hair back from Pheir's face. Even with Aren next to her, she seems to forget anyone else is there as she strains to see through the dark. There's a softness around her eyes that Lev hasn't seen before. When Pheir takes a long breath, her shoulders relax. There's no urge to run or escape. It's a different desire, one that sends her eyes shut.

For all of the view in front of them, the three Timbers watch Pheir. Aren lowers his voice to keep from disturbing the moment. "Better than the cabin?"

Whatever spell the view cast over Pheir is broken. She grits her teeth again, collapsing back into the chair. "Fuck you."

"That's what you want, isn't it?" Hoisting the chair into his arms, Aren deposits her face down on the outdoor daybed. It's a flat cushion longer and wider than Pheir's body. On the other side near the railing, Lev sinks into an armchair so Pheir is forced to watch her and the view at once. Aren pulls Pheir's hair back, working one chain loose as he bends to her ear. "Maybe you'll actually get away this time."

Like clockwork, Pheir makes an attempt to scramble away. It's a wasted effort. In moments, Aren frees her of the chair and her clothes, hogtying her with rope from their bag. She squawks and curses as Caius joins Aren behind her.

Lev's voice rises above Pheir's fighting. "Is there anything we should know before we start?"

As if they haven't started something already. Aren's eyes rove Pheir's bound form. Caius licks his fangs. Pheir can't see any of it, her furious gaze on Lev.

"For fuck's sake," Pheir pants. "You're always talking. Just *do it!*"

Clearly, there'll be no answers from her. Lev turns her gaze to the men. "Do either of *you* know anything she should share before we continue?"

Caius hoists Pheir an inch off the bed by the rope between her ankles before he drops her back down like a pig on a spit. "No praise," he sneers. "Nothing kind."

Like someone else I know. Lev and Aren share a look as Pheir huffs a strand of hair from her face. "Don't act like anything's changed," she snaps. "I still hate you. You don't have to play nice." Her head jerks toward Caius. "Don't tell me he's the only one who isn't putting on an act."

A knowing smirk crosses Lev's mouth. "You prefer Caius's manners?" He flips her off, and Lev wonders how Pheir will look around that finger. Lev lounges back against the seat. "Fine. Nothing nice. Is that —"

"And don't piss on me!" Pheir whips her head back to glare at Aren, but she can't get her chin to her shoulder. "I swear I'll make you —"

"We won't," Aren assures, brushing hair off the back of her neck. The feathers on her body lift to meet his touch, her knees trying to clamp together. The ropes hold her fast. Her captive body squirms with desire when Aren leans closer, words slipping against her ear. "But I think you liked it."

Before she can land her teeth, he withdraws, a different electricity settling over them. The three Timbers lock eyes, nodding together as if they're preparing for battle.

Take your positions.

It's filthy entertainment on display, leaving Lev to watch like a queen on her throne. If she's the regal audience, she's going to give them all what they desire. Her eyes find Caius, her body thrumming at the memory of his words moments before.

I want it.

Then Lev will do anything to give it to him.

"Since Pheir likes you so much, Caius...you're up."

TWENTY-THREE

Pheir

It's pathetic how easily Pheir succumbed to this. *It's boredom,* she tells herself as Aren pins her to the daybed. She lashes out at him with her talons behind her back, body fighting on autopilot.

Being captive has left her with little else to entertain herself. Of course she's imagined fucking them. Of course she's replayed the scenes a hundred different ways in a hundred different positions. It doesn't mean anything. Her growing arousal has nothing to do with Aren or Caius. Absolutely *nothing* to do with Lev.

Or maybe it does.

That thought shocks Pheir enough that she stops scratching at Aren's face behind her back. *It doesn't mean anything,* she reminds herself again. It's a strategy. Fucking the people closest to Lev is the simplest way to fuck with her, especially when there's already tension.

The Timbers have their own issues. Even without instinct, even when Pheir is face down and ass up, she can sense their orbit around each other. Caius's movements halt. Aren's weight shifts. Lev's gaze flicks.

It's different than the night Aren and Caius transported her, falling back on pack ranking so they both knew their place. Now, they seem uncertain how to move, how to take control, how to touch each other. Pheir can almost dig her talons into the cracks of their foundation.

If she slipped her bindings, she could take Lev out. No matter the Alpha's power, it's no match for the deadly parts of Pheir's body, talons and teeth and mind all desperate for the second the Timbers slip up. Still, there's something beneath Lev's surface, something dangerous in that small, soft package. It lingers in Pheir's mind as she plays out the inevitable fight between them in endless combinations.

Should she go for the throat?

Could Lev's powerful thighs do any real damage?

Would Lev leave claw marks down Pheir's back?

With each new question, Pheir's clit aches. That's how badly she wants to destroy Lev. Pheir's hips rut as Caius circles behind her, making the feathers at the back of her neck stand on end. Of course he's first. He's meant to wear Pheir down, to leave her mangled and mauled as he decimates any pride she has left.

Her jaw sets. She won't be broken. She won't give them any humiliating confessions — but with her knees forced apart, more than sweat slips down the inside of her thigh. Her cunt is bared when Caius's claws grip her ankles and yanks her back to the edge of the bed. She writhes, but there's no leverage where she's laying on her chest.

His fangs brand against her ass, making her body jerk. She tries and fails to kick him, to ignore the heat curling in her stomach. All she can see is Lev before her, sitting righteously on her throne. Gods, Pheir *hates* her. Pheir's mouth opens in a snarl.

"You —"

Caius drags the back of a claw between her folds, making her bite off her words. His hand comes away wet, voice making a mockery of her. "Fucking predictable, birdy."

The balcony reeks of desire, no matter how Pheir tries to cut it off at the source. Is her mind that weak? Is her body this much of a traitor? If she fights harder, if she screams —

All her plans are scattered when Caius lowers his mouth to laugh against her cunt, breath almost cool next to the heat of her core. "Not gonna make it a challenge?" he goads. She knows what he means. Between her thighs is humiliating evidence of her desire. There's no denying how wet she is. There's no disguising it like this.

Her teeth dig into the cushions, shoulders shifting to give her a vantage point behind her. All she can see are wild patches of blonde fur that move when he drags his rough tongue against her. The two barbels frame her clit, toying it until she wants to scream. She fights a shudder as her ragged voice escapes. "It's gonna be a challenge to *stay* wet."

He should slap her. *Fuck*, she wants him to, she's *ravenous* for it — but it doesn't come. That lack of pain is so distracting, she isn't prepared for his tongue dipping inside her. Long and solid, curving down over her clit and nudging between her folds as she fights to keep from bucking her hips.

She can't look at him. Can't let him see the carnal need in her eyes. Her gaze searches for somewhere, anywhere else to land. There's only Lev in front of her. Lev, unmoved by Pheir's torture. Lev, staring into the depths of Pheir's eyes like she can see her soul. Lev, watching Caius with a vibrant heat like they're sharing the same thought, settling into a dynamic they both know well. It's a conversation in the twists of his tongue, as if the curls and flicks he gives Pheir are a language Lev understands.

Gods, why does it make Pheir's cunt clench around him?

She hates them. She fucking *hates* them.

She wants to come.

"'*Hard to stay wet...*'" Caius repeats. He sucks sharply on her clit, barbels knocking pain and pleasure against her. The muscles in her body tense while his voice is sharp and easy. "Is that the line you're gonna stick with?"

She can't scream. She can't open her mouth for fear of what might escape: a groan. A pathetic, pitiful plea. When Caius pulls back the hood of her clit and scrapes his teeth against it, she can't keep her hips from snapping back against him.

Cruelly, he chuckles against her slit. "Say it like you fucking mean it, then." His claws dig into her ass, pulling her back to *feel* him talk against her clit. "Tell me how hard it is to stay wet."

There's no time to adjust before he works sheathed fingers into the tight ring of her ass, already slick with its own lubricant. Rage tremors through her body, but all that comes out is a moan.

"I remember this," he taunts. Remembers that her ass lubricates as easily as her cunt, because he fucked her once before. Because he made her come again and again until he let her stop. His fangs drag around the swell of her pussy, two fingers curling in her ass as she fights to stay still. "You love being on the end of my teeth, don't you?"

If she shifts an inch, he'll nick her with the sharp point of his fangs. As if that will deter her. As if that will make her scared and pliant. Instead, frustration funnels into her voice, body jostling against the ropes. "Why are you going so *slow*?"

Pain pricks her folds, making her throb with want. Caius doesn't move any faster, his hate for her constrained to his tongue on her clit. He licks up the spot of blood his fangs drew out. Every stroke and breath is focused on ruining her at his Alpha's command.

When Pheir thinks he's about to let loose, he pulls away until he's barely touching her. She's perfectly spread, bound legs wobbling as he inflicts his torture on her. No brute force, only honed malice in his tongue flicking her clit. She's not going to last. She can't stand all this focused attention. Her teeth shred into the cushion, hips trying pitifully to work back. "Fucking *do it*. Harder! Come *on* —"

When his mouth collides with her cunt, it slams her forward. He wraps his hands around her bindings, slick and hot, gripping her ropes to keep her trapped against his mouth. Her sounds are dampened by nothing in the night air. Lewdly, Caius eats her out as she tries to bury her screams against the pillows.

"Tell me you're sorry for being a bratty little bitch," Caius snarls, pumping two fingers into her ass. He sucks roughly against her clit. "Say you were wrong. I want to *hear it*."

He knows better than that. She'd never give him anything he asks for. Arching when he buries his tongue inside her cunt, a smile spreads across her face, delirious with the pleasure of denying him. "You're not gonna get it from me."

He gets something else when he reaches under her, finding one of her breasts pressed against the rope. The braided lines pull against her skin, leaving indentations that throb with the perfect amount of pain. It's nothing compared to Caius taking her nipple between his fingers and tugging, forcing her to bite back a string of curses when he twists his hand.

"Don't cover your sounds," Lev admonishes. Immediately, a hand jerks back on Pheir's hair until she can't disguise anything. Forbidden desire surges through Pheir as Lev pouts pityingly, her voice as dark as her eyes. "Give me every pathetic little whimper."

Pheir bites her tongue until she tastes blood — then Caius teases his tongue against her ass. It's enough to make Pheir flinch before his mouth fully replaces his fingers there, vulgar and vicious as Pheir trembles like a wire.

"Come on..." Lev leans back against the cushions. It's infuriating. It's *hot*. "When have you ever held those vicious sounds back? Don't start now."

It's Aren's hand in Pheir's hair, tightening his grip. All her expressions are bared to them. There's no disguising what pushes her toward the peak. She doesn't speak. She barely *breathes* when

Caius tongue-fucks her ass to the edge. No matter how she muffles her noises, she can't keep her hips from jerking each time he laves his pierced tongue over her.

Aren's mouth lowers to her ear, a low rumble that makes her shiver. "You're going to pass out if you keep straining like that."

Already, she's light-headed from the desperate hold she has on her pleasure. She tries to keep it walled behind her mouth. She can't let her tormenters see what they do to her, how they've learned her body, how they bring her something worse than pain. It's a fate worse than death; Pheir refuses to give into it.

Her eyes are proud before Aren guides his other hand to her throat. "If you don't want to breathe..." Fingers press against her pulse, slowing the blood racing through her veins. When Caius slides his tongue against her clit, Aren lowers his head to do the same to her mouth, like he can taste the moans she's holding back. "Then we won't let you."

The peak is building too wildly for Pheir to stop, head swimming as Caius devours her. Aren makes a mockery of her restraint, cutting off her air as her hips grind helplessly back against Caius's mouth. She's held captive between them, used as something wet slips down her face.

It's salty and warm. Aren licks the tears into her mouth. Pheir doesn't know when she started crying. Doesn't know when everything held inside her boiled out of her eyes. She swears she can hear Lev *laugh*. It's what the Timbers have always wanted, a way to destroy Pheir's body, to humiliate her, to control all her pain and pleasure at once —

Orgasm races through her, gasp ripping between her lips as Aren releases his hold on her throat. It's pitiful and pathetic, aborted sounds and phrases that are halfway to real words. Her body squirms to escape their eyes, but there's no hiding when she's locked between Aren and Caius's mouths. Her squeal smears over Aren's lips as Caius keeps eating from her, tormenting her sensitive clit and driving her to the edge of sanity.

"*Stop*," she groans.

He doesn't. He won't, claws digging into her ass as he overstimulates her.

"Stop!" It's too much. She can't think, dragged toward a jagged peak. She can't admit defeat — but she can't take *this*, grappling for the safeword —

"That's enough."

TWENTY-FOUR

Pheir

Lev stops them with a fiery glint in her eye, as if she could see how close Pheir was to calling it. It fills Pheir with indignation. Why would Lev care? It's all fake concern when she's kept Pheir tied up for weeks.

Caius withdraws, giving Pheir no reprieve from her shame as he moves to stand beside Lev. Now Pheir's forced to see them both, the evidence of her arousal soaking the fur around Caius's mouth. Pheir's cheeks are still wet, too, skin flushing with embarrassment. If she can't deny them with her body, she can deny them with her mouth. A cool breeze gusts between her legs, goosebumps pricking along her skin. Her fury hones on Caius. "Did that get you hard, you fucking freak?"

"A little brat coming all over my face?" Caius surges back toward her. "Nah, I *hated* it."

Lev's hand settles on his arm. Despite the hate foaming in his mouth for Pheir, he turns back to Lev. No matter how he towers over her, Lev is imbued with power as she looks over him. He's sloppy with remnants of Pheir's desire. When Lev's fingers curl in his fur, he leans down to brace hands on the arm of the chair and cage Lev between them.

She doesn't cower, gripping the back of his neck and dragging his head to hers. She's not quite touching his mouth. Not quite *letting* him touch, gaze roving over him like she's gained some understanding.

"Couldn't help yourself?" Lev's voice is almost too low for Pheir's ears, but Caius is tuned to Lev, body ebbing and flowing like water pulled by the moon. Slowly, Lev trails her tongue around his mouth and licks him clean, tasting Pheir from him before she hums. "Her pussy's that fucking good, huh?"

Pheir can't tear her eyes away from them. It ignites in her stomach, an intimacy she shouldn't be privy to. The people she's fucked in the past were chosen by Vesta, people Vesta wanted something from, people Pheir could please. They never shared a look like Lev and Caius do, desire boiling beneath the surface until it threatens to overflow.

It makes Pheir *want*. Lev speaks about her like she's not here, and still, every word is made to sharpen Pheir's desire. It's an act to torment her, to snap a trap around her arousal and drag her out into the open.

There has to be a reason Pheir burns at the sight of it. She tries to find an excuse — it turns her on because Lev is finally showing the cruelty Pheir always knew she possessed. It's arousing because they hate each other the same way. It's hot because they delight in each other's misery.

Behind Pheir, Aren sheaths the claws of his fingers. She tries to pull away, but she can't tear her eyes from Lev and Caius's mouths molding together. It's more than hot desperation. It's the space between vulgar kisses when their foreheads press together, breath scarce and shared between them. Pheir's never seen anyone pour into each other like this, as if Lev is the very air Caius needs.

As if her touch is the one place his ferocity falls. As if Lev could forget her control when Caius gets close enough to her.

When Aren sinks two fingers into Pheir, she whines. His voice lowers to her ear. "I told you about her." Pheir tries to writhe away. All her hips do is follow his fingers, rolling in time with his strokes. His teeth graze her ear, nose cold and making her body twitch with sensation. "Lev fucks like it's her duty. Like she can't rest until you're sated. Like she'd give you any part of her if it would please you."

Pheir's mind can't take it. Can't think of Lev as anything but an obstacle, but Aren's words worm their way inside her. Pheir wants to sink her teeth into Lev. She wants to sink her claws into her. She wants to sink her tongue and groans and fingers into her.

"I don't care," Pheir grits.

Caius sink to his knees, smearing his mouth against Lev's cunt. He smears *Pheir* against her. Lev forces him to still. He doesn't curl his tongue. He doesn't circle it, laying it flat for Lev to start a slow grind against. She takes what she wants when she rides his mouth.

Pheir's cunt clenches. With a slick finger, Aren eases past the tight rim of her ass. She takes him easily, and he hisses a curse as he spills filth into Pheir's ear.

"Lev rides us both at once and makes us beg to come." Aren's palm brushes the curve of Pheir's ass, stroking with his dexterous fingers that make her mind spasm. "We beg, because it's so fucking *good*. Because her tongue is the softest, sharpest thing about her. Because when we take the power back, and she submits…"

Pheir's traitorous groan binds up with Aren's as he fucks her open. A thousand images pass behind her eyes: Lev forcing Pheir's legs open, eating with those dark eyes honed on her. Lev with her face to the ground while Pheir pounds into her until she screams. Aren and Caius and Pheir filling all of Lev's holes until she's a crying, pleading mess.

It's for vengeance, borne of hatred. Pheir can't accept anything else. She wants to fuck Lev to humiliate her. To wreck her. To destroy her in a way Vesta never did.

That thought alone wrestles another orgasm out of Pheir.

It's blazing, body arching as Aren pumps her through it, lowering his textured tongue to lave at the mess he made.

As Pheir struggles beneath the haze, Lev's smiling face swims into her vision. "I think you wore her out, Aren."

"I'm not — fucking tired," Pheir pants. Never mind that she can barely lift her eyes, body shuddering under the restraints.

"Not tired, huh?" Caius's voice circles behind her. Before she can look, his mouth is on her ass again. He laps it all up, Aren's spit and Pheir's desire smeared with traces of Lev's cunt. A filthy tribute to the Timbers plucking sounds from Pheir like strings on a guitar.

Lev watches Pheir with an intensity she's only seen across the battlefield. This time, though, Lev's look probes deeper. She scents the shift in the air. An amused curiosity crosses Lev's face. "I think she's gonna come again."

"I'm not," Pheir gasps.

It's a pitiful excuse for her voice. She can't accept it. Can't lie here silently while they strip her to her most animalistic parts. They don't show her any pity. Caius tilts her to lie on her side.

"Not gonna come, huh?"

A cockhead nudges against each of her holes, Caius with Aren right beside him. *Lev rides us both at once.* They have to work around each other and Pheir's bound limbs, but they manage. It's filthy, pressing Pheir closer to the edge with every inch she takes of them.

Lev would look bored if not for the fiery ember in her eyes. "I give her two minutes." When Caius eases his dick into Pheir's ass, Aren stretches her cunt around him. They both groan, gripping Pheir's ropes to pull her back against them. She pants for breath, so fucking *full* she can't see straight. When Aren gets his finger against her clit, her head lolls. Lev clicks her tongue, blurry in Pheir's vision. "Or maybe one..."

Heat branches through Pheir's stomach. They fuck her as hard as they hate her. The men's claws scrape her thighs as they pry her bound legs open. Every thrust stretches her around the spines halfway down Aren's cock. Caius picks up the pace, hips slapping her ass as he bounces her against him.

"You love being a Timber whore, don't you?" he growls. There's no denying the way she clenches around them, drawing another curse from Caius. The ropes tighten on her wrists and ankles when he clenches his fist, dragging her back over both of their cocks. "You like being used. A little toy for your enemies to breed, fucked until you can't think from all the cum dripping out of your tight little holes. You're a part of this pack, you get fucked by the pack. Isn't that right, birdy?"

She wants to fight back. She wants to deny it, but her legs quiver in the restraints as she tries to find some feeling to hold onto. Anger. Rage. Vengeance. All she can grasp is pleasure, slipping through her fingers before another wave pulls her under.

"That's why you've been acting out." Lev picks up speaking where Caius left off, leaning her elbows forward onto her knees. She inspects Pheir like she's an experiment. "You were desperate for attention. For the two of them to shove their dicks into you until you learn how to obey. Until you're cum-drunk and useless. Is that why you're always after them for a fight?"

Shame heats Pheir's skin. If she opens her mouth, nonsense will come out. Lev seems to know it, lips forming into a pretty pout like Pheir isn't being fucked open on two cocks.

"You wanted to roll in the dirt with them. Wanted to piss them off enough to fuck you again. Wanted to be tossed like a bone between them."

"*No,*" Pheir groans. It can't be true, but her mind flashes through every moment they dug each other into the dirt. Claws slashing, her body singing at the sight of them. She thought she wanted to have the pleasure of killing them by her hand, but now —

Her eyes snap shut. Pressure builds like steam breaking through the cracks of the earth as blood rushes through her ears. It's almost enough to drown out the dark, demanding heat of Lev's voice.

Almost.

"Come, bitch."

When Pheir screams, there's nothing to hide it. Nothing but agonizing pleasure piercing the night air, sending birds flying up from the trees. Her body tremors, a mess of sticky, warm holes as both men spend themselves inside her.

She came on Lev's command. They *all* did, like they couldn't help themselves, grinding against each other in a pitiful heap.

When you come? It's for me.

A shudder races through Pheir, warming her against the cold. That's not right. It's not *right*. In an instant, every feeling she put on hold for pleasure comes clawing back. She's supposed to hate this. To hate *them*. What has she done instead? She's slipped into weakness and given them a glimpse at a needy part of her.

The tears on her face are humiliating, no longer paired with the sting of arousal from moments before. She's a traitor. She failed Vesta once. With this, she's failed her again. She's no better than Rhaiden.

An uncertain hand reaches for Pheir. She shrugs away from it. The hand lingers next on the cushion as Lev's voice softens. "We should —"

"Don't *touch me*," Pheir snarls. She can't stand how different Lev's voice is in the aftermath, no longer the affected cruelty she'd directed them with. A chill spreads over Pheir's body, legs beginning to numb from the restraints. Everything is wrong — the angles of her body and the temperature of the air and the suffocating swirl of emotions that makes Pheir feel like she can't breathe.

"Pheir," Aren says from behind her, "we can't —"

"I said, leave me *alone!*"

It comes out an angry sob. By some small miracle, the others act like they haven't heard her tears. Quietly, they untie the ropes from Pheir's body. She curls in on herself. She doesn't open her eyes. She *can't*, not when they'll look at her and see more than they already have.

Warmth drapes over her, a blanket blocking her from the cool night air. Weight settles into the chair a few feet away to give her the illusion of space. When Pheir sneaks a glance, Aren does his best to pretend he isn't watching her.

The seat Lev occupied moments before now only holds her indentation. Two sets of footsteps recede behind Pheir, the door to the deck swinging shut behind them.

That leaves Pheir colder than anything else.

TWENTY-FIVE

Caius

2 years before Vesta's death

"Is this a good idea?"

Lev doesn't answer Aren directly, surveying their supplies with distraction. She bites at a ragged edge of her claw. That happens more often these days. "She said she'd be there for the next hour."

"And you believed her?"

The look Lev gives Aren is significant. Something unspoken passes between them, some memory Caius wasn't present for. It soothes out the defensive hike of Lev's shoulders. Gods, will Caius ever be able to do that for her?

"We might not make it in time," she acknowledges as Aren leans against the utility vehicle, "but we have to try."

Aren inclines his head. "Do *you* have to try?"

"Yes, Aren!" It's the first time she's snapped at her beta, at least in front of Caius. Her teeth grind together. "I'm not sending you without me, especially not —" Her eyes dart to Caius. His gaze jerks away fast enough not to be caught. Lev steps closer to Aren, but Caius can still make her words out across the distance. "Yes, this may be a ploy for Vesta to attack the compound, but I think she'd rather come after me. The Conclave isn't going to treat her like a serious threat until we get a better idea of what she wants."

Vesta. Caius learned the name a month ago, but it's been popping up with increasing frequency.

"The others will protect the compound," Aren assures Lev in a low voice. "But Caius won't leave your side. Is it a good idea to put him and Vesta in the same place? Especially if she brings her new guard dog..."

Hackles lift on Caius's back. Of course Aren finds a problem with him. It's been a year since Lev found Caius in the forest, and he's only just been sworn in as one of her combatants. Aren never lets Caius out of his sight. Never trusts Lev alone with him, as if Caius would make a thoughtless mistake and leave her vulnerable.

Thankfully, Lev waves the concern away. "Caius will be fine." It warms him as she hoists a bag into the back of the UTV and glances at the main lodge. "I think everyone involved will feel more secure if he's with me."

A different heat blooms in Caius's face. It's no secret the rest of the pack isn't keen on him. As long as Lev trusts him, he doesn't care. Aren grabs the top rail of the vehicle and hoists himself into the seat. "Fine. Then I'm going, too."

Lev starts to argue.

"It's a fair compromise," Aren points out. Leaning back in the seat, he turns the key in the ignition as he pins Lev with a meaningful look. "We have to be prepared for anything."

Her lips part before they clamp shut again. After a moment, she nods and gestures for Caius to join them.

They rumble out of the Timber compound, pushing the vehicle to its limits as they drive through hills and forests. Where they arrive is isolated, inaccessible to most roads and vehicles of the Break.

"Once we find Vesta, do *not* move." Lev checks their coordinates against the sun's placement as her leg jiggles anxiously. "Don't step forward. Don't make threats." Pointedly, she looks at Caius. "Don't even speak. I don't want to give her any reason to try something."

Aren pulls into park and turns off the engine. "Does she ever need a reason?"

Lev doesn't answer that.

In the apple grove, they forgo the leather armor they packed. "We don't want to incite her," Lev insists. Aren slings the bag over his shoulder just in case. Any other day, the walk through the orchard could be serene, flowers in bloom as birds chirp in the branches. Now, though, the Alpha and beta are more on edge than Caius has seen before. Ambient sounds draw Aren's eyes. Lev's nose lifts to catch a scent, twitching before she stiffens.

"She's here."

Around them, the trees are laden with fruit...and nothing else. No *one* else. Caius holds a hand up against the glaring sun — but the light comes from somewhere else, rainbow colors cast over them like light bending through a prism. A winged woman lands at the top of the nearest tree, beaming down as she takes a bite of an apple.

"Leverette..." The woman takes her time chewing before she swallows with a smile. "I wasn't sure you'd make it." Her voice is a mix of delicate notes played with sharpened spears, flames seeming to swim under her skin.

Caius's fur lifts on end. So this is Vesta.

"And you brought a little group!" Vesta gapes in mock offense, pressing a hand to her chest. "Don't tell me you were worried about me playing fair."

Lev doesn't give into her game, unblinking in the oppression of Vesta's light. "You said you wanted to make an agreement. Let's hear it."

"Oh, don't tell me you came all this way without a little curiosity." Vesta's iridescent wings spread, letting her glide down to the forest floor. Aren and Caius squeeze in tighter on Lev's either side. Vesta's gaze flicks over them. It doesn't go without her notice, but she has eyes only for Lev, sauntering until she's a few yards away. "It's been so long, Leverette. Surely you want to hear what I've been up to."

"It's Lev." Lev doesn't give more than that, but Caius senses her heart picking up speed. His lips pull back over his teeth. Whoever this Vesta bitch is, she knows exactly how to push Lev's buttons — or maybe she's the one who sewed them on.

Vesta's head tilts like she expected the resistance, talons clicking together. "Mm, I prefer your given name."

It's blatant disrespect. Lev's jaw ticks. Caius can't take it. "What the fuck do you want?" he snarls.

As soon as he does, he knows he shouldn't have.

"*Caius*," Lev hisses — but his outburst has the desired effect. Vesta's gaze lands on him like she's seeing him for the first time, an eerie smile drifting across her lips. Her new target's been acquired.

"Who's this? A new *friend*?" Vesta's eyes cut jealously to Lev before she turns to Lev's other side, contempt lining her lips. "And you must be Aren. *My* friends have told me all about you."

"You said," Lev raises her voice, trying to reign the conversation back, "you wanted to come to an agreement. What are you after? Why are you back here?"

"Bunny..." Vesta pouts as she flicks her talons out casually. Lev sucks in a breath through her teeth. "It hurts me that you couldn't tell I never left."

Every phrase is a puzzle, layered with complexity that Caius can't make out. Vesta grows bored with it, holding out her hand like she's presenting something.

"No matter. I've been making new friends of my own."

The only warning they get is a feral screech aimed straight toward Lev before Caius leaps in front of her. Talons slice into his chest, purple feathers scattering around him as he skids across the grass with the wild beast.

She hardly looks real, eyes glassy and teeth gnashing as she claws at Caius. No amount of his werewolverine strength stops her as they roll through the brush.

"Stay out of my fucking *way!*" she screams, pinning him to the grass. She kicks off the ground, wings beating to take flight again. Caius snatches her ankles and yanks her back down.

"Stay away from Lev!"

The name sends the woman into a rage. Talons extended, she clamps onto his face and drowns out his screech with her own. Blood pours from his nose as he claws to escape.

You've had worse, his father's voice reminds him, blood pooling in Caius's mouth. Pain thuds through his face. *Get up. Get up!*

Fangs bared, his teeth snap, but he can see nothing through the river of red. Spitting blood, he grapples for the woman's hands, desperate to pull them from his face — until she goes flying off of him into the nearest tree.

It cracks sharply. Through the blood, Caius can see nothing. Two hands jerk him back as something heavy crashes to the ground and shakes the earth. Caius swings his claws wildly. Against Caius's back, Aren's voice rumbles. "It's me! It's me." Wiping the filth from Caius's face, Aren checks both his eyes. "Are you ok?"

Caius shoves out of his grip. It's humiliating being bested by some birdy bitch in the first five seconds. When he gets back to his feet, Lev is pinning the woman to the earth, each appendage paired with one of hers. The tree they'd flown into lies broken on the ground where Caius had been. The woman screams beneath Lev, but Lev bears all her Alpha strength to keep her from struggling.

"Stop fighting," Lev grits through her teeth. "I don't want to hurt you." Her body is tense, arms locked in a constant battle with the other woman. There's blood splattered through Lev's fur, but Caius isn't sure if it's his, or hers, or all three of theirs.

His eyes whip back to Vesta for another attack, but she's leaning boredly against a tree. She gives a wave of her hand. "Let it go, Pheir."

The woman's tense limbs tremble on the ground, straining against the order. If her scream is any indication, Pheir would like nothing more than to keep lunging for Lev. Both their chests heave. Lev doesn't loosen her grip, doesn't trust that Pheir won't strike again until Lev slowly releases and rises back to her feet.

Pheir pushes to stand, glaring at Lev as she backs away and circles behind Vesta with a deadly look in her eye.

"Pheir," Vesta murmurs over her shoulder like she's speaking to a favored pet. "What did we say?"

Blood drips over Pheir's lip. It's like she doesn't even feel it. "Lev is yours."

Vesta nods with a smug smile. Pheir resumes her place, pacing behind Vesta like a caged animal. Vesta slinks in a slow circle to make the Timbers squirm as they pull in closer.

"The agreement I'm proposing..." When she stops, so do the Timbers. It brings a wicked grin to her face. "Is that you try your *very* best to stop me when I do what I'm about to do."

It's another of her puzzles. Lev's fists clench at her sides. "What does that mean?"

Vesta doesn't answer, choosing only the questions that entertain her. "If your Conclave is as righteous as you claim, you should have no trouble getting their interest on me."

Lev steps forward. Everything in Caius screams to stop her. "You don't have to hurt anyone," she grits. "Whatever it is you're after, it doesn't have to happen like this."

Lev's mouth twitches, resisting the urge to plead. It doesn't stop her voice from quivering, shoulders sinking forward in a much smaller version of herself. It's not the Alpha Caius knows. It's someone younger and uncertain, brought out by Vesta.

"Why are you back here?" Lev whispers to her. "What are you trying to do?"

When Vesta smiles, it's bright and warm. Somehow, that's more sickening than the cruelty. "What we always planned, Leverette."

Lev's mouth clamps shut, gaze turning to Pheir as if Lev might be able to reach her. "You don't have to do this. You don't have to live —"

Vesta drapes an arm around Pheir's shoulders, never removing her eyes from Lev. "In due time." It's foreboding. The harpy looks positively bloodthirsty, body tense like she's barely holding back. Vesta doesn't seem to notice, leaning her weight onto Pheir. "Until then, it was *so* lovely seeing you."

"What do you *want*?" Lev's composure cracks, clawing desperately for explanation, but this was never about that. There was never an agreement or negotiation. This meeting was for Vesta to see Lev, to torment her in a twisted way Caius can't fathom.

Vesta doesn't answer, gaze flicking like a lighter to the wound still bleeding across Caius's face. A smirk settles on her lips when she looks back to Lev. "Good to see you've stopped hesitating."

Caius growls. "I'll show you *fucking* hesitating —"

When he moves toward Vesta, Pheir lunges. Lev jerks Caius back, prepared to take the blow until Vesta snaps her fingers. Pheir comes to a grinding halt. With one hand, Vesta guides Pheir away and calls over her shoulder. "We'll be in touch!"

Pheir sneers. "Hope that fucking scars!"

"Come back and see!" Caius snarls, but the two women have already taken flight, Pheir's middle fingers lifted toward them.

Once they disappear from sight, Lev takes a rag from Aren's bag and reaches for Caius's face. "Are you ok?"

He snatches the cloth before she can get there. "It's nothing," he grumbles. How fucking embarrassing. What kind of combatant has to have their Alpha save *them*? He presses the cloth to his face, surveying Lev as she sinks down against the nearest tree like her legs have given out. It's silent for a long moment as the three of them catch their breath. Nothing about the interaction makes sense, a history lesson Caius has half the notes for. "So that's Vesta," he tries.

"That's Vesta," Lev breathes, staring into the distance.

Clearly, it's a sore subject. Caius doesn't know where to begin, so he holds the cloth to his wound and hisses at the pain. "Who the fuck was that harpy? She's berserk."

Lev leans her head back. "I haven't seen her up close before." It's a shift in focus that Lev is grateful for, turning her gaze back to Caius. "She really got you, huh?"

"Feral fucking freak." He jerks an arm toward the sky. "She's practically rabid! Someone needs to put her down."

Aren folds his arms dryly. "Oberon can check you for rabies when we get back."

Caius tosses the rag in his direction. "Hilarious."

The corner of Lev's lip tilts up. Despite the blood-soaked towel, Caius feels a little lighter. At least it gives her something to focus on besides Vesta. When Lev pushes up from the tree, a teasing lilt sneaks into her voice. "I don't know, Caius. It could be the start of your love story with her: first blood at first sight."

A laugh bursts out of him. Sure, he'd love to get his hands on Pheir...to slam her into the ground and drag her through the dirt. Although the blood has stopped flowing from his face, it still throbs with pain and a taste for retribution. That taste is sweeter than the copper in his mouth.

"Yeah. Real fucking romantic."

TWENTY-SIX

Pheir

PRESENT
25 days after Vesta's death

Pheir dreams in darkness. Her body remembers what to do when she can't see. Instinctually, she feels around the cramped space like she's searching the inside of a coffin. Above her, jagged lines are dug into the wood. If she reaches further to the side, she finds the metal hinges of the door.

She tries to bend her legs. There's not enough space, her knees knocking against wood, making her curse when footsteps sound overhead. They're unrecognizable. Pheir keeps fighting, voice rising to a shout as she kicks and claws with everything she has. The footsteps stop, metal clanging as the door pulls back. Pheir shields her eyes against the brilliant rainbow flames...

But it's Lev looking down at her this time. "You're still in here?" Lev asks. Then the door slips from her hand and slams shut.

Pheir wakes with a start. There's no wooden box around her, nothing preventing her from sitting straight up in bed. Morning light streams through the window. Drowsily, she remembers being brought in from the cold, furry arms cradling her sore body.

Her lips curl in disgust. She must have slept through the night. The room she's in now is small, enough space for a bed and a closet with little else. It's not the main bedroom from last night, but it is a change from the one-room cabin in the middle of the noisy compound.

Change is good. Change gives her a chance to escape.

As soon as she lifts onto her knees, footsteps come to a halt outside her door. Her dull talons scrabble to open the window, but Aren's voice reaches her before she can. "Sleep well?"

Her hands freeze on the frame. She glowers over her shoulder to where he stands in the now-open doorway.

"You brought me inside last night," she complains.

Aren doesn't seem to care. "The other option was letting you freeze to death, which I have no doubt you would have preferred out of spite."

Pheir realizes the blanket curled around her waist is the same one from the balcony, covered in feathers and fur from the four of them. It reeks of what they did. Her skin heats. With two fingers, she lifts the blanket off her legs and tosses it aside with a tempestuous wrinkle of her nose. "Where are the others?"

She doesn't deign to say their names. "Breakfast," Aren answers. "We'll take you in shifts. Caius will be back for lunch."

"And what will you be doing during your shift?" It's an innocuous question, but it's more a distraction than anything. She needs to calculate the best opportunity to break free. If Aren doesn't stay in the room, and Caius won't be here for a couple of hours...

As always, Aren sees straight into her mind. "There are still a few guards on the perimeter." He leans against the doorway.

"We've removed everything in the house that could be a danger. Don't bother trying anything."

Goddammit. Bitterly, she bats her eyelashes. "All that for little old me?"

Aren's lip twitches. Pheir's gaze drifts past him out the doorway. The corridor seems small, but this cottage is bigger than her cabin by a few hundred square feet and a second floor. Feigning disinterest, she jerks her chin toward the interior of the cottage. "What is this place?

Aren steps into the room to take in the view from the window, the cliff's edge and the lake below. "It's a cottage for pack members who want a break from the main compound. A getaway of sorts. For the time being, it'll house you. Congratulations: you're ruining someone else's attempt at peace."

A smug smile settles onto Pheir's face.

"If you want the tour..." He gestures out the doorway. Pheir considers being obstinate before she stands. Aren guides her down the stairs in the center of the building to the open library and kitchen stripped of anything useful. "As long as you keep eating, you have free reign of the house. You have access to the food here. If you need anything cut, you'll have to request it."

When he leads her back to the second floor, she gets a better look through the long wall of windows to the terrace outside. Any conflicting memories she has from last night are drowned out by the view. It's more breathtaking in daylight — not that Pheir enjoys it. She refuses on principle, but she can make out fish jumping and splashing in the lake.

Aren pushes open a door to the deck, voice lowering with sympathy. "The terrace, however, will require supervision."

That stings more than being held captive. It's not a surprise, though. She doesn't squander the opportunity to step out into the fresh air. A breeze ruffles through her feathers. She moves toward the railing, fingers curling as she lifts on her toes. With a little height, she can make out the tops of red and orange trees.

Instinctually, her wings spread like her feathers aren't clipped, as if she could leap from the railing and fly instead of falling.

When she turns, she notices the disarray on the deck. Furniture skewed, couch crooked, daybed cushions tossed about with tears through the fabric. Heat coils through her alongside hostility. She hated every second of last night. Every roll of Caius's tongue. Every filthy word Aren ground into her ear. Every time Lev —

"Still thinking about it?"

Her eyes snap back to Aren when he speaks. Jerking back from the railing, she resets the snares in her expression and brushes past him and the furniture. "Hard to erase something that awful."

He hums in response.

Her feathers bristle. Smarmy fucking cat. She needs to make a point. Pausing in the doorway to the interior, she gives him a sullen look. "Where's the shower? I need to get the stench off me."

Her words have no effect except to make his smile deepen. He takes her to a small bathroom off the main corridor. While she steps into the hand-pump shower, he waits inside the bathroom with his amber eyes on her. If he were Caius, maybe she could tempt him, lathering soap over her breasts until he's close enough to incapacitate. Aren, on the other hand, doesn't get close to the open shower. The only reaction he shows is an exasperated head tilt when she rinses thoroughly between her legs.

There's an unasked question in his gaze that makes Pheir's skin crawl. She's prepared to snap at him to spit it out when he broaches the topic. "You know the agreement Lev made with the Conclave? Why she brought you back here?"

Pheir tilts her hair back beneath the stream of water and considers drowning herself. "To force me to marry her? To turn me into a mindless drone for your pack?"

"*Incorporate* you into a new pack," Aren corrects. "Give you a chance at life."

"Semantics." Soap stings Pheir's eyes until she's forced to shut them. "What about it?"

"We have three months to accomplish that. We're coming up on the end of the first thirty days."

Pheir's stomach sinks. It's been almost a month since she lost Vesta. Grief twists in her chest — but that's not right. Pheir's brows knit beneath the water. She's not supposed to be sad; she's supposed to be angry. She's supposed to get revenge, to make the Timbers pay, to use her hatred to fuel her. Deep inside, she reaches for the rage that's always kept her warm. It's still there, but it's a dwindling flame she struggles to reach.

Fuck that. Last night was a distraction. She fought to get away. She has to try harder and keep her head on straight. The little voice inside her pinches at her nerves.

Don't forget what you're doing here.

The water from the pump runs out. Rivulets travel down her arms, dripping off the tips of her fingers and leaving her cold again.

"You're telling me this *why*?" she snaps acridly. Vesta would be proud. *There's my girl.* "Because the Conclave is gonna — what, kill me at the end of this?"

"It's a possibility," Aren answers.

Pheir rings the water from her hair. "I'm not worried."

"Because you'd rather die than join us?"

Naked, she turns to face him, gaze settling proudly onto his. "Because I'll be long gone by then."

When she steps out of the shower, he extends a towel toward her, expression unreadable. "Guard shift changes in a few minutes. As long as you're in this building, you don't have to wear chains...for now."

She snatches the towel, drying off as slowly as she can. Aren's too smart for her. He waits patiently, hand outstretched for her to return it. *Removing everything that could be a danger.* Jaw tight, Pheir places the towel in his hand. When his fingers close around it, she jerks. He doesn't move, eyes locked on hers.

They both keep a tight grip on the towel. It pricks heat across her skin, irritation and something more. Water drips from her hair onto her bare shoulders. A droplet travels down her clavicle. She refuses to wipe it away as it kisses across her skin. Aren doesn't so much as glance at it, but he knows it's there. He has to, ears flicking when it trails down the center of her chest.

The room is suddenly cramped. There's a foot of space between them. Her mouth shuts to keep her breath from being the loudest sound in the room. The droplet follows the curve of one breast, darting suddenly down her stomach. She tries to keep her gasp behind her teeth.

Aren hears it. He gives the barest twitch of his nose, pupils widening, fingers tightening around the towel. Then the droplet trails lower, between her thighs where the night before his fingers —

He pulls the towel from her slack grip, moving toward the door. "I'll give you a few minutes alone. Don't maul Caius as soon as he arrives."

With that, Aren's footsteps fade down the stairs.

Only after he's gone does she remember to breathe. She doesn't move until the front door shuts beneath her. She needs to focus. There's no point in getting dressed; clothing will snag when she makes her escape. Instead, she tries the doors and windows. All of them are locked, including the sparse inner doors leading to other bedrooms. She surveys the perimeter of the cabin. There aren't many guards, but their sightlines are positioned perfectly to piss her off. After exhausting her efforts, she rifles through the kitchen downstairs. She leaves drawers yanked open. The most threatening equipment she can find is a pot holder.

Something bangs into the front door, followed by a string of curses as Caius wedges it open. Standing in the wreckage of her scavenging, Pheir makes no attempt to help as he struggles with wooden crates. Behind him, someone picks up the pieces he dropped — the other wererabbit, June. Pheir's eyes narrow.

"Here." Caius kicks the door closed behind them, dumping the crates on the counter. "Eat whatever."

Cucumbers roll toward the edge, followed by sticks of jerky and homemade cheese. When June approaches with her arms full, Pheir hones in on the best chance to get a weapon. "I need to cut the fruit."

"Then you'll have to wait," Caius grumbles. He picks up one of the crates filled with blankets and makes his way toward the stairs.

June inspects the food on the counter, lifting an apple between her fingers. "Here, I'll do it."

When she dips into her satchel, Pheir's eyes follow. Beneath the flap of the bag is a glint of a multi-tool. June pulls it out, flipping the knife as Pheir's hand darts for it. June is faster, jerking out of the way with a suspicious look in her eyes. "Watch it, birdy."

Pheir's heart thrums like the minutes before battle. This may be her chance. Again, she reaches for the weapon. June jumps back out of reach and aims the blade toward Pheir. There's a vigilance in June's expression, a restraint that's hard to place when she grits her teeth just like Lev does.

"I'm trying to be patient with you, but you're making it fucking difficult."

Pheir's eyes flick to the knife. It stays pointed at her, ready to swipe if Pheir makes a sudden move. She could take her chances. Maybe she's strong enough to ram into June, fast enough to grab the blade and yank it towards her...

Pheir's stomach rumbles.

Both women stop, glancing toward her abdomen before their gazes return to each other. June narrows her eyes. So does Pheir. Slowly, maintaining the distance, June sets the knife against the apple in her hand. The blade digs into the flesh, cutting lines beneath the surface all while June keeps Pheir in her sights.

This is Pheir's chance. She can strike and snag the weapon and force her way out of here...but the apple glistens, crunching with every slice until June dumps the pieces on the counter and returns the tool to her bag.

Pheir swallows. Her stomach rumbles again. She glances toward the pile and itches for an argument. "I like green apples, not red."

"Oh, fuck off," June mutters. Spitefully, she pops one of the slices into her mouth. Pheir bares her teeth. June sticks out her tongue, crunching as she backs toward the front door and disappears through it.

It's their most cordial interaction yet. Still, Pheir can't miss the opportunity to try the front door. The handle doesn't budge in her hand. Locked. With a heaving sigh, she meanders back into the kitchen, slapping an orange back toward the center of the counter pile.

The pain from her fractured pack bonds has dulled, but it's been replaced by nausea alongside her hunger. Maybe she increased her food intake too quickly — or maybe they *are* poisoning her, even when the guards eat with her. Skeptically, she lifts an apple slice between two fingers. If she stops eating, it's back to the dark cabin again, away from the balcony and the ashes. And, if she's honest, away from the three people she wants to torture most...

"If it isn't the birdy bitch."

At the voice, her head whips around. She's heard that crawling drawl before, the night in the cabin when she managed to break free. The arctic enfield is here again. Singer slips in the front door, still wearing those ugly boxing wraps as if he's seconds from stepping into the ring. He tosses a bruised apple in one hand, flicking out his claws and letting it land squarely atop the middle one.

Pheir scoffs, unimpressed. "Get a hobby."

With his other paw, he pops the apple off, discarding it across the floor as he eases closer. "You're looking at it."

TWENTY-SEVEN

Pheir

Pheir's weight shifts onto her other foot. It's barely noticeable, but she knows what this fox is after. This gives her more leverage to strike before he gets a chance. "Pretty sad you keep coming back to get your ass kicked."

"Says the combatant who couldn't protect her Alpha."

Shame burns up Pheir's throat. Her mouth clamps shut, rage simmering behind her gaze. What does he know? He wasn't on the battlefield. Pheir did everything she could to save Vesta. She dedicated her life to it. She's still fighting to find a way to bring Vesta back, but a guilty feeling gnaws at her as queasily as before.

Not when you're fucking your worst enemies. Not when you're distracted by the things they do.

Her back hits the kitchen island. She didn't realize she was backing away, leaving space for Singer to encroach on her. His head tilts cruelly as he muses. "What was it like, watching Vesta die? Did you realize what a failure you were?" His claws tick together, something wild in his eyes. "Did you know what a *mess* you were leaving for someone else to clean up?"

Gods, Pheir's heard it all before — how the Vestals threw the Break into chaos, how they created problems for everyone else. She doesn't care. One of her taloned hands lift — but the sharp points were dulled by the Timbers weeks ago. Feathers quiver on her back, but they're useless for flying. Her heart picks up pace in her chest. Her body is no longer a weapon. It's not a threat to anyone.

There's no way to defend herself.

She takes off the second before Singer lunges, sprinting up the stairs and colliding with a wall. Thundering footfalls drown out the sound of her nubbed talons scraping the wood floor. She darts down another hall. She knows all the doors are locked. Only one is open. Flinging herself into her bedroom, she collides with Caius's back. He whirls, primed to attack —

Then he takes in the look on her face, ears perking as the sounds in the hall behind her grow louder. There's no way he can understand, but before Pheir can speak, Caius shoves her into the closet and presses a hand over her mouth. "Keep your smartass mouth shut."

Then the door slams and engulfs her in darkness.

Footsteps screech as they approach the room, halting on the other side of the wall. Pheir leans her ear against it, trying to stifle the thrumming of her pulse.

"Just who I was looking for." Singer's muffled voice strikes panic into Pheir's throat. It's outweighed by Caius's surly reply.

"What do you want, Singer?"

The wall creaks next to Pheir's ear. She pulls back with a start before she forces herself still. Singer must be leaning against the door jamb. "You see Lev's prisoner run by here?" There's a sharp sound of his teeth clacking together in a smile. "I want to give her a little treat. Thought you might want the first shot."

Silence is the response. Pheir's legs burn as she crouches. She should spring out of the closet before Singer gets a chance to gut her. It doesn't matter if it's useless; it's better to fight than cower.

It'll be a matter of seconds before Caius opens the closet door. He has her trapped, backed into a corner, perfectly debilitated before she's handed over. She should strike first, come out swinging at both of them so she has a chance at escape —

"I don't fucking keep track of her," Caius grumbles.

Pheir's brows knit. Her poised hands clench. Surely she heard wrong. Surely —

"You don't know where she went?" Singer sniffs once, an exaggerated show before his voice drops. "It smells like her in here."

Pheir clamps a hand over her chest, willing her thudding heart to quiet.

"She slept in here," Caius answers.

Singer's weight shifts into the room. "You know the smell's stronger than that."

This low to the ground, Pheir's at a disadvantage. She's out of options. If they want a fight, she'll give it to them. Maybe give Caius another scar —

When the floorboards creak, she readies to pounce — but Caius crosses the room away from her, tone snapping with irritation. "Because she came on my dick all night. If she's good for nothing, she's good for that. You want to smell it to make sure?"

Pheir's body runs hot. She stays rigid, straining to hear Singer's reply. After a long moment, he huffs a deprecating laugh, pulling his weight off the door frame. "What am I thinking? Of course you'd take care of the problem yourself."

"Damn straight." Caius's tone is lackluster, like he's holding his breath.

A shadow passes over the strip of light beneath the closet door. Singer's voice is louder than ever. "So why haven't you?"

Pheir's fingers itch toward the door handle. She can fling it open, make him stutter, land a few blows — but Caius's voice stops her. "Why haven't I what?"

All the light under the door is blocked when Singer steps in front of it. "Taken care of her."

A lump lodges in Pheir's throat. She doesn't dare swallow. Slowly, the closet door starts to open, light spilling through the crack.

This is it. She starts to stand, but Caius's voice comes low and dark. "Have to make it look like an accident."

Light spills across one of Pheir's eyes, but nothing more. Her arms burn where they brace against the wall, prepared to push her up and out, trembling as she fights to hold herself still. The sliver of light doesn't move further — but it doesn't disappear, either. Her head swims from holding her breath.

"Find me later," Caius directs to Singer. "We'll talk."

After a long moment, the closet slips shut again. The light beneath the door reappears.

"Fine," Singer replies with a hint of acid. "But don't fuck with me."

It takes time before his footsteps recede. Pheir still doesn't move until the front door opens and shuts downstairs.

The bedroom door clicks shut before the closet door swings open.

"Get out."

Pheir squints against the light before a hand closes around her wrist and jerks her into the room. Her chest collides with Caius's, a mix of hard planes and soft fur. It's like the first day they met, bodies tumbling across the orchard ground.

Caius glares down his snout like he'd love nothing more than to rip her in half. She doesn't flinch. She doesn't back away, matching his expression until she realizes they're both still gripping each other.

"Why didn't you tell him?" she asks. Even without heightened senses, she can smell herself on Caius, wet and filthy where she ground against his mouth. Her clit throbs at the memory. His fingers tighten on her arms.

"You heard me." His vicious eyes dip to her mouth, voice tight and angry. "Have to make it look like an accident."

Her lips purse. She tries her luck, stepping close enough to press fully against his chest. His eyes narrow, but he doesn't stop her. Slowly, she eases him a step back. Then another. Then again, until the backs of his knees hit the bed. This is her chance — but he moves too quickly, spinning to pin her face down on the mattress, like the forest when she made her escape. This time, the carnal feel is undeniable, hidden under no other pretense. Her ass grinds back against his cock, as hard and ready as he was last night. She grits her teeth, working against his length. "You told him I came on your dick."

Caius's hot breath against her ear spurs a new surge of arousal. He growls. "So what?"

Arching, she presses back with a steady wind of her hips. "You didn't want him to know what you spent most of your time doing? Mouth buried in my cunt, getting nothing out of it?" Caius's cock slips between her cheeks, dragging down between her thighs before it springs free and nudges her clit. They both suck in a breath. She can't help herself. Can't keep from pushing back until he's almost inside her. "It doesn't *feel* like you hate me."

He tenses — then he drags his cock in circles against her clit, forcing her to bite into the sheets. It's been seconds, and she's already wet enough that he could slip inside and take his choice of whichever hole he wants. He snarls against her ear, searching for restraint.

"I like eating your cunt because you hate it." When he rocks forward, she lifts onto her toes, gasping at the pressure. "Because to you, there's nothing worse than how desperate you get for my tongue on your clit. My fingers in your pussy. My mouth on your ass." When his cock teases her entrance, stretching her around it, she groans — but he never slips inside. He taps his dick against her clit. "That's why I do it. Because you're a little bitch for it. I don't give a shit if you like it."

She almost believes it, that the reason he fucks her is to torture her, but she catches his teeth tracing the pulse in her throat. His claws curl around the back of her neck, snout trailing her hairline and breathing in her scent, brutality building a cage around something softer.

A foreign feeling rockets through her. Her voice comes hoarse. "Liar."

She braces for more. Wants more. *Needs* more, body trembling with anticipation.

Caius releases her, leaving her a pathetic mess on the bed. The bedroom door slams open harder than it needs to when he makes his way out without a look back. "Stay in this room. It already reeks of you."

TWENTY-EIGHT

Caius

Caius wills his hard dick away as he descends the cottage stairs. What the fuck was that with Pheir? He can't shake it out of his head, keeping an eye out for Singer as he crosses the first floor. The enfield is nowhere in sight. Thank the gods: Caius doesn't need to deal with being turned on and brawling at the same time.

You do that with Pheir.

He drags a hand down his face, bursting out the front door where Darby blinks in surprise. Caius holds out his hands for the keys. Darby hands them over without question, and Caius locks the door before he turns back to the deer. "Did you let Singer in?"

"Yes," Darby stammers. His antlers tilt away from the cottage. "He left. He had some food you dropped down the trail. He said he was bringing it to you. I thought..." The stag bows his head in deference. "I'm sorry. I didn't realize..."

Frustration simmers in Caius, lip curling back to berate Darby — but Lev's voice weaves through Caius's consciousness instead. *I want you to be a part of this pack.* He forces himself to breathe.

Tension eases from his shoulders as he begrudgingly searches for what Aren would say.

It was a simple mistake. The boy's clearly apologetic. He's young. He's new to guard duty.

"It's fine," Caius manages. "Don't let Singer near Pheir again, no matter what he says. Matter of fact, don't let anyone in the cottage that isn't a guard. Pass that along to the others."

Darby nods sharply. Caius turns to leave before Darby speaks again. "Anything else, sir?"

It gives Caius pause. Dubiously, he looks back to Darby. Caius searches for someone else nearby, but they're the only people here. There's no Aren waiting in the wings, no Oberon passing by. For once, someone's looking to Caius to lead. It's a role he only views Lev and Aren in, giving instructions that the others jump to follow.

This time, it's Caius making the call.

He clears his throat, shaking his head. "That's all."

Resolutely, Darby pulls out a two-way radio, pressing the button to relay Caius's message to the others. It's surreal. Caius moves down the trail in a daze, trying to sift through the emotions bumping against each other in his chest. Darby's respect is the least surprising. Singer's attack is its own problem, but Pheir's reaction to it still has Caius's head spinning. Her voice creeps back into his mind, burying him under a swell of arousal.

Why didn't you tell him?

That's the closest to honest he's seen Pheir be. Aside from the fear on her face when she fled Singer in the first place, her eyes wide and clear, looking to Caius like she needed to be saved.

It's bullshit. She doesn't want shit from him. The reason Caius didn't hand her over is because he's following orders. Because Pheir feels good wrapped around his cock. Because he's waiting for the right time to get rid of her.

Liar.

His claws rake down his arms as he walks, scratching an itch that can't be soothed. There can't be another reason Pheir is still alive. He can't deal with that. He has enough trouble figuring out his place among Aren and Lev, two people who *don't* want to kill him. People who don't take every opportunity to threaten his life the way Pheir does.

Beneath his feet, the dirt trail turns to wooden planks as he ascends the porch steps to the main lodge's library. No surprise that Lev's inside; in Caius's distress, he followed her scent without realizing. He makes sure the door shuts behind him before he speaks.

"Singer's gonna be a problem."

Lev looks up from a map of the Break on the large table. All the territory lines are defunct now, scattered after Vesta's uprising and the Broadleaf betrayal. The paper is covered with pencil lines, scrubbed out and redrawn. Lev sets the eraser aside, wiping her hands clean of pencil shavings. "More than before?"

"He was hunting Pheir."

Concern crosses Lev's face. "Is she alright?"

"She's fine. Still a bitch." *Convincing, Caius.* "Singer decided to take matters into his own hands."

Lev's look sharpens, puzzled and disturbed. "What's his obsession with her?"

"I don't know, but he's not gonna stop." Caius folds his arms across his chest. "Even with me there, he was going for it. I had to throw him off the trail to get him to leave. I promised I'd talk with him later."

Lev's eyebrows knit in thought, gaze drifting to the door. She's looking for Aren. She realizes it too late, snapping her gaze back. Hope plummets in Caius's chest.

Lev shifts awkwardly across the room. "Ok. Thank you. I'll handle it."

Words spill from Caius's mouth before he can stop them. "You can ask me to take care of it. I'll get him in line."

"That's not..." Lev shakes her head, warring with her thoughts.

Things have been precarious between them since the day he almost left. She's trying. He knows she is. They *both* are, but this new compromise is still uncertain. It's a struggle for him not to stalk off upset, but he forces himself to stay still.

"I know you want to take on more responsibility," Lev begins, "but this is more serious than a passing threat. Singer needs to be dismissed. That's not something an Alpha should pass off to someone else."

As she speaks, she's distracted, hand running back through her hair. Caius hones his ears to the trip of her heart, listening as it fumbles over itself. "There's something else," he murmurs. "Something you're not saying."

He should let it go. Let Lev deal with this how she sees fit, but he can't deny the helpless feeling surging through him. Another secret for Aren and Lev to have. Another thing Caius can't be trusted with.

Lev leans her palms against the table. Caius nearly leaves it at that, another gap between them that he can't cross — until she answers him. "The Regents are coming."

Regret seeps into Caius's chest. "Because I invited Rhaiden —"

"No," Lev assures him, moving around the table like she's afraid he'll run. He can't really blame her. "I don't think they know Rhaiden was here. You remember when I went to the Broadleafs, how Boreas mentioned the Regents might move up the Vestal timeline or disregard it entirely?"

Caius nods before Lev continues.

"I thought I'd bought us a little more time, but when the courier stopped by today, he said he's heard rumors..." Lev pauses like she's not sure she should continue.

Caius closes the space between them. "Tell me."

"I'm afraid they're coming soon," Lev breathes. "I'm afraid they'll kill Pheir when they get here."

It digs like talons into his chest. It shouldn't shock him; the Regents never wanted to spare the Vestals in the first place. Hell, *Caius* doesn't want to...but hearing the threat is coming sooner than later makes it real.

Lev's ears flag, helplessness wearing down the line of her shoulders. This isn't the Alpha presence she puts on. This is Lev, the person Caius has been desperately clawing to get closer to. Even if it's a glimpse, she's sharing it with him.

That realization is staunchly overshadowed by another, the caveat that Lev agreed to when she brought Pheir here. Caius's throat tightens. "You have to marry Pheir now."

It's not a question. Lev doesn't lift her gaze from the table. They both know the truth. Lev has to marry Pheir before the Regents arrive. Before they have a chance to kill Pheir for what she's done.

Caius's heart sinks.

When Lev finally speaks, it isn't a denial, like she's trying to convince both of them that it's not a mistake. "Marrying Pheir will help ease her pack bonds. It'll deter Singer and make it harder for the Regents to try anything. I just..." There's a strange look on Lev's face, a part of her that isn't focused on the rationale. A part of her that *feels* something. A part of her Caius can understand when she lifts her eyes to his. "I never thought marriage would be like this."

A steady feeling thrums in Caius, pulling him toward her, hand settling next to hers on the table. "Be like what?"

Her lips turn down mournfully, watching Caius more openly than she has before. Her gaze skates down his face. It gives him the chance to see her, too, to look at the part of her that's been cracked open by all of this. Hair falls over one of her eyes, brushing her round cheek. When she's like this, the hardened lines of her face fall away, like she's finally removing her armor. Undressing for him.

His fingers curl closer to hers.

"I never thought marriage would be a duty," Lev whispers. "I never thought it'd be a strategy. I thought it would make me feel like..."

Her throat bobs when she swallows. Caius leans closer, snout brushing the column of her neck, rubbing his scent over her pulse. Her fingers curl over his, her other hand reaching the back of his head to bring him closer...

The door creaks open. With a huff, Caius turns to see Marius leaning through the doorway.

"Sorry to interrupt." Mari wiggles their eyebrows before they look past Caius to Lev. "You remember when you told me to keep an eye on Singer?"

Lev nods. Caius snorts a laugh. Clearly, the enfield built for stealth hasn't gone completely undetected.

"He's down at the boathouse," Mari finishes. "I don't know what he's doing, but he was acting sneaky."

Lev lifts her hand to wave her thanks. Before they leave, the bat blows a wet kiss toward Caius. A laugh startles out of him.

Discarding the pencils and erasers on the table, Lev turns to Caius. "Do you want to back me up?"

It's not a responsibility of his own, but it's something. He falls behind Lev to let her lead the way. She worries with the vial of ashes around her neck as they trek to the far edge of the compound, past the crops and animal pens to the boathouse situated on the lake. Noises drift out from inside, objects scraping the wooden dock as Singer toes at the motor of the boat. He turns swiftly when they approach.

"Well, well, well: Little Miss Alpha." Singer's arms fold across his chest. Caius would like to rip them from their sockets as Singer grins smugly. "To what do I owe this pleasure?"

Lev's smile pulls taut. "We need to have a conversation."

"Ooh, sounds like I'm in trouble." Singer sinks down on a wooden crate, resting his arms behind his head.

Caius snarls. Threatening Pheir's life is one thing, but he draws the line at disrespecting Lev.

She keeps her voice level. "You've been trying to get alone time with Pheir. At the fire the first night, in the cottage today…"

Resentfully, Singer's eyes lock on Caius. "Never took you for a tattletale."

"Enough." Lev cuts him off. "*I'm* speaking to *you*, Singer. And you're being released from this pack."

He scoffs, eyes rolling as sits up straighter. "*Relax.* She's a prisoner. No one's gonna fucking miss her."

Lev's jaw clicks. "She's my *wife.*"

Any sense of cordiality dissipates when Singer pushes to his feet, slowly enough that it isn't an outright threat. Caius tenses to spring, but Lev splays her palm out by her side. *Stand down.*

They both keep still, honed on Singer as he shifts closer. It's agonizing, watching his white tail flick as he lowers his snout by Lev's ear. Any closer and he'd graze Lev's fur. Any closer, and he could snap her neck. His smirk exposes sharpened teeth. "Not yet she isn't."

With a shove, Caius forces Singer back. They both bare their teeth as Singer swipes at Caius's throat, honed straight on his jugular —

It should hit. It should land. It should slice into Caius's flesh, but instead, Singer lands on his back. His claws scrabble, clutching at the hand that pins him to the dock.

Lev kneels next to him, fingers crushing his windpipe as she dips his head toward the water. It's rare to see Lev's Alpha strength, but it courses through her now. Singer gapes up in shock. Caius looks the same. *He's* the one built to take hits, the one meant to defend his Alpha, but Lev moved without a second thought. Without a concern for which one of them needs to be protected.

Lev's voice is smooth. "Do not touch him." Her fingers tighten. Singer's eyes begin to bulge. "*Ever.* Do not touch anyone in my pack. This is your final warning."

Singer's breath rasps, struggling to find a way into his lungs before he nods. Lev releases him, stepping back as Singer coughs and snarls from the ground. "That bitch has to die. It's a matter of time."

"That's not your choice to make."

Singer searches for a chance to strike back. He's outnumbered. Outmatched. There's nothing that could give him an advantage. "Don't you think that's hypocritical?" he seethes. "Giving a second chance to some cracked harpy while you're kicking *me* out?"

"I have to run this pack in a way that I can live with." Pointedly, Lev wipes off the hand that was wrapped around his throat. "Caius will ensure you're escorted to the next outpost. We'll report you to the Conclave. Maybe they can find a new pack for you."

When Singer laughs, it's harsh and wicked. "All this for a fucking prisoner?"

"I'm giving you an opportunity," Lev snaps. "There are plenty of other packs to choose from, cities beyond the Break, an entire world you can find your place in. That place isn't here. You aren't welcome in Timber territory any longer."

There's a darkness in Singer's eyes that makes Caius's blood run cold. Singer holds up his hands in defeat, but there's intention curling into the daggered edges of his smile, as if he isn't done with this at all.

"Whatever you say, *boss*."

TWENTY-NINE

Lev

Weddings are meant to be happy. The Timbers know this, but when Lev gathers the pack to explain what's about to happen, they're kind enough not to mention it. At any rate, the pack seems pleased with Singer's dismissal, offering Lev earnest congratulations and a squeeze of her hand.

The youngest pack members pout. "We'll have a *real* celebration with everyone later," Lev assures them. "The ceremony has to happen quickly." That's enough to placate them as they run off, tittering about which foods they'll eat at the feast for their Alpha's marriage.

Not everyone is so easily fooled. In the main lodge, Oberon and Mari prep flowers as June runs a brush through Lev's freshly-washed fur.

"You're supposed to do this with your bride," June points out.

Lev keeps her eyes on the standing mirror and tries to crack a joke. "I think Pheir would beat me to death if I put a brush in her hand."

It's supposed to draw a laugh. Instead, Mari sucks in a breath, shaking their head as June sets the brush aside. She turns Lev to face her on the stool. "I know I don't get...this whole thing." June gestures to Lev, bracing her other hand on the seat. "Romance. Sex. Whatever. But you used to talk about your wedding day: what it would be like, who would be there. I don't think it looked like this."

Lev swallows roughly. She *has* dreamt about this day, less in preparation and more a fantasy. The person at the altar was a secondary detail. All Lev knew was that she would be head over heels. They'd be surrounded by the people they loved, the pack gathered to dance and sing and feast in the forest.

They would be incandescently happy.

Tonight, there will be no happiness. No music. No games. No June, or Oberon, or Diction. No other guests, save for Aren and Caius to perform the ceremony. It's too short notice to plan the celebration that the Timbers are used to, too rushed and political to imbue the compound with elation late into the night. This wedding is a bastardization of what it's meant to be; Lev doesn't want anyone else to have to see that.

She gives a roll of her shoulders. "Sometimes the Alpha suffers for the pack."

June's mouth twists. She turns Lev back to face the mirror, meeting her eyes over the top of her head. "And what if other people suffer, too?"

In the reflection, Aren and Caius wait on the porch outside the window. They've done everything to prepare for the ceremony, but something keeps Lev from looking them in their eyes, as if this lie of a marriage will be too big to contain if she sees what waits silently in their expressions.

While June and Mari weave flowers into Lev's fur, Oberon takes longer than he needs to braiding pieces of her hair. His eyes never leave his work. "You know," his voice rumbles, "you don't have to do this. The pack would do anything for you. We'll protect

Pheir from anyone trying to harm her, whether or not she's your wife."

Lev's lip quivers. "You shouldn't have to."

"But we would."

Her teeth dig into her lip. It's tempting to call this off, to avoid this union and spare herself, but the risk is too great. If Pheir is the Alpha's wife, the pack will have less to worry about. They won't *have* to defend anyone, because the title alone will dissuade others from attacking. Marriage is safer for the pack and safer for Pheir; the only one left in danger will be Lev.

Once they're finished, June braces both hands on Lev's shoulders. When June pulls her into a hug, Lev squeezes tighter. "Make sure the border's secure tonight, and —"

"We'll take care of it." June pulls back to look over Lev. "Try and find a *moment* of enjoyment on your wedding night, please."

Unfortunately, that seems less possible when Lev steps onto the porch. Aren and Caius turn to face her. The look they give her breaks her heart twice over. There's a moment before both men fight to school their expressions, the awestruck widening of Caius's eyes at the sight of her before the pained tick through his jaw at the reminder that this isn't for him. And Aren, his features softening in the saddest happiness she's ever seen.

"You look beautiful," he murmurs.

Lev has to clamp her mouth shut to keep from crying, tearing her gaze away from the most openly Caius has looked at her. As they make their way down to the boathouse, the air between the three of them is a second away from snapping.

The pack meets them at the docks at twilight, lining the pathway to touch Lev's shoulders and offer words of encouragement. Lev smiles gratefully, squeezing their hands and making her way down the line.

When she catches sight of Pheir, her steps falter.

Pheir's already waiting in the boat, bound in her seat as she glares at the others. Cool air darkens her cheeks, but she refuses the fur cloak draped across her lap. Past the simmering rage, she looks like a bride. Beautiful and windswept, the light violet of her skin contrasting with the dark green of her dress. She reminds Lev of a field of wildflowers, like Pheir fits here among the pine trees and lapping water. When she looks up, there's a flicker in her gaze, like maybe she's seeing the same possibility in Lev, too.

That's wishful thinking. As soon as Pheir realizes Lev is staring at her, she sours her expression. With Aren's help, Lev steps into the boat as Caius pushes them off from the dock. The rest of the Timbers wave, calling well-wishes beneath lamplight as Aren paddles toward the small island in the center of the lake.

Once it's too dark to see the shapes on the bank, Lev lets her hand and face fall. It's better this way. Maintaining a strong facade for all of the pack would be a struggle. It's easier to promise they'll celebrate in the future when Lev has her doubts that it's true. What's to celebrate? A lie? A bride that hates Lev as fervently as she loves Vesta?

If all goes to plan, this will be Lev's only wedding. Her only marriage. The thought tightens her throat, the wind across the lake growing colder the further from the pack they get. Eventually, they reach the island. It's quiet under a copse of trees, frogs croaking in the distance. Both men slip into the shallow water, pulling the boat ashore onto the small bank before they extend their hands for Lev.

Staring up at them in the dark, her fingers curl around the side of the boat. More than a party, more than a celebration, she suddenly understands the feeling she missed in all her wedding daydreams. Emotions high and heavy in her chest, yearning keeping her locked in place as if she might stop time just to keep this moment. As if Aren and Caius might always look at her like this, like they see and desire all of her. As if 'forever' is less like a task and more like hope.

You're not marrying them.

The reminder comes like a punch to the gut, knocking the air from Lev's lungs. On shaky legs, she forces herself to stand, gripping both their hands tighter than she needs to. When they guide her feet to the ground, she prepares herself to release them, but Caius doesn't let go. His fingers curl around her wrist, eyes clinging to hers before he finally lets his hand fall away.

Everything is heavier than before.

By some miracle, Pheir is silent. When Aren hoists her out of the boat, she doesn't kick or scream. "We'll get set up," he murmurs, leaving Lev and Pheir on the bank as he leads Caius away. Across the lake, hills stand out against the stars that blanket the sky. Pheir stares toward them like she might escape.

Chains clink around her wrists as she sinks down onto a rock. Purple feathers drift lazily to the ground around her, cheeks chapped from the wind where she's stood on the balcony any chance she gets. Maybe the siren's tongue has had an effect. Rhaiden warned it could make Pheir ill. Currently, her shivering has given way to a sheen of sweat across her skin, face pale, hollows deeper under her eyes —

"Can you stop fucking staring?"

Lev blinks out of her thoughts, meeting Pheir's eyes in the water's reflection. The harpy's voice is hostile, but her wings lay flat, not puffed out in anger. Distracted, Lev unloads a crate from the boat.

"Sorry, you look..."

Different. Compelling. Captivating. The words crowd Lev's mouth, leaving her puzzled. None of those words are right. They're things she should say to her *wife*, but never to Pheir. Somehow, the two oppositions are becoming one. Lev's neck is hot, ears perked awkwardly as she rifles through the box. She knows Pheir's eyes are on her. She can *feel* them. Pheir doesn't give Lev the relief of pulling them away.

"You went all out for this sham, huh?" Pheir is hoarse from her weeks of screeching. The scratch in her voice catches on Lev's mind, making her hand itch to press against Pheir's neck as if she could soothe it.

Instead, Lev swallows past the ache in her own throat as she unwraps flowers. "This is far from all out."

"What?" Pheir taunts. "I'm not worth it?"

Lev's fingers slow over the flowers. They both know the truth is far more complex, but it's the first time Lev has considered that more than one person is losing something in this marriage. *We were an arsenal more than a pack*, Rhaiden said. *Mindless drones.* And Lev tricked herself into believing it was true, that Pheir is a woman without hopes and desires for her own future.

Lev's face stings with shame. How thoughtless of her. She looks at Pheir now. "We can still have a celebration later —"

"I don't give a shit," Pheir snaps, as if letting the thought linger is dangerous. She pulls her knees up to her chest, huddling for warmth. Her fur cloak lays discarded on the ground as her hardened eyes find Lev. Pheir's gaze is as cold as the water before them. "I never dreamt about this 'wedding day' bullshit. I just don't want to be stuck with *you*."

It shouldn't sting, yet it does. This isn't a choice for either of them. Lev clears her throat, returning to the string of flowers. "We're out of options, Pheir. Marrying into the pack will make things easier for you. It'll ease the pain of your pack bonds. As an Alpha's wife, you're protected, whether that's from the Conclave or Singer or anyone else."

In Lev's periphery, Pheir stills. "What do you mean, protected from Singer?"

Lev binds a strand of flowers before she lifts her gaze. "He threatened you this morning, didn't he? Hunted you through the cottage?"

Pheir's brows knit skeptically. After a moment, she nods.

Lev returns to work on the flowers. "He's gone; I dismissed him. But should he return, the marriage will ensure you have more protection. Not just from him. Like I said, the Conclave —"

"What else did he do?"

With her teeth, Lev straightens a piece of thread binding the flowers as her brows lift in question.

Pheir clarifies. "What else did Singer do to get dismissed?"

Lev shrugs in confusion. "He went after you. That's all he had to do."

The women stare at each other as if they're speaking different languages. The fur on Lev's back begins to rise, torn between the threat of an enemy and a strange heat. It's the same kind Aren and Caius spark in her. She has to pull her gaze away, back to the flowers before Pheir speaks again.

"Why do you care?" Combativeness returns to her tone, a guarded sense of apprehension. Sweat spreads along her hairline, cheeks flushed, but her gaze won't let Lev avoid the question. "Why do you care if I die?"

A snowfall of answers begins in Lev's mind, nonsense and emotion she can't begin to reason with as it coats every other thought.

Because Vesta's my fault.

Because you're the wildest person I know.

Because I was you once.

Because I hate you — and if you die, I might not any more.

The avalanche evaporates from the heat in her mouth. She can't say any of that. It doesn't make sense, so she rises to her feet, careful with the florals in her hand. "Brides-to-be typically weave flowers and braids into each other's hair. Can I do yours?"

Pheir rolls her eyes, turning to face the water, but her hair angles ever-so-slightly toward Lev. Lev doesn't miss the opportunity, settling behind Pheir to guide the flowers into place. In the dark, it's hard for Lev to make out the mauve color of Pheir's hair, chopped unevenly at her shoulders. The strands have been washed recently, slipping like feathers between Lev's fingers. Under the moonlight, she manages short braids, guiding petals of yellow and orange and pink into place.

When Lev brushes over Pheir's shoulders, Lev sucks in a breath at the strange feeling. Skin is rare to come by in a pack of werecreatures. Lev's never really felt it under her fingers. Hesitantly, she brushes her hand against it, marveling at the bumps that rise under her touch.

Pheir shivers, chin turning back toward her shoulder. Lev can make out the profile of her face, the slope of her nose, her dark eyelashes, her breath warm against Lev's fingers. Neither of them moves, but Lev imagines —

It can't be true, but she almost thinks Pheir leans into the fur of her hand, momentary relief against the cold.

Lev tries to move her mouth. "You should put on your…"

Then her gaze lands on the raised mark on Pheir's wrist, two lines that Pheir runs her other thumb over. For so long, the parts of Pheir that Lev noticed were the ones threatening to dismember her, claws and teeth and eyes ready to slice her in half. But the burn mark over the vein in Pheir's wrist looks angry and red, though it's long-healed. It's the same place Rhaiden ran her fingers over during their meeting, a scar in the shape of a "V" burrowed like a brand.

When Pheir catches where Lev's eyes go, she jerks away and hunches protectively over the mark. Lev steps back, fumbling for an apology when Aren's feet crunch quietly onto the sand.

"Are you ready?"

He has no idea what he's walked in on. Hell, *Lev* doesn't know what that moment was, if it was anything. She jerks her gaze away from Pheir, too afraid of what she might see: seething hatred. Abysmal suffering. Or something as convoluted as the feeling binding in Lev's chest.

When Aren gestures Lev aside, it's a welcome distraction. They move further down the bank, out of earshot before he turns to face Lev and block her from the rest of the island. It's the two of them now. No Pheir. No Caius. No pack. His voice is soft. "You can still call it off."

Lev's lip wobbles. To hide it, she sniffs, fighting the tears threatening her eyes. "Are you telling me that as my friend or my beta?"

Aren tilts his head, a knowing smile settling onto his face. As her beta, he should tell her this is the right option. It's the only option. They both know there's no avoiding that. Instead, he steps closer until she has no choice but to look at him.

"I am your friend. I am your beta." His fingers trail down her arms, bringing her hands into his. When he leans close, the breeze floods her with his earthen scent, grounding her in her body again. He calms her with a look. "But I am *yours* first, before anything else."

Her lips part, heart thudding so loudly she knows he can hear it. Finally, her eyes slip shut, giving into the overwhelming feeling she never expected this moment to bring. When she offered to spare Pheir by marrying her, Lev never thought it would fill her with such uncertainty. So many questions about her feelings for Pheir, and Aren, and Caius, things Lev doesn't know how to begin to decipher.

Stopping this wedding doesn't change their position. It won't spare any of them, should the Regents arrive at the compound. It won't save the rest of the pack from becoming collateral damage if they protect Pheir, as Lev knows they would. For her.

Marrying Pheir is the way to protect all of them. As if Aren can sense it, his forehead lowers to hers, hands smoothing over her shoulders. "It isn't real," he reminds her.

Lev breathes slowly, basking in his presence. The wedding won't be real. She knows that. If they don't complete the ceremony with blood-sharing, the marriage won't tie Pheir's allegiance to the pack. It's risky. It could have deadly consequences, but so could binding Pheir in the midst of the siren's tongue's effects. Combining the two could pull her loyalties in multiple directions, making her more unpredictable...if it doesn't kill her first.

No one outside of Lev, Aren, and Caius will know the truth — not even Pheir. She'll be Lev's wife in name, protecting her and the pack from anyone who might harm her. No matter the lie, they will be each other's firsts — first wedding, first marriage, first spouse. Given the danger Pheir presents, they will likely be each other's only.

Pain pricks the back of Lev's eyes, forehead resting against Aren's. Her throat tightens like she can't find enough air. It's not that she was ready to marry anyone else, but with Aren and Caius...there was hope. Hope that one day soon, things would calm down enough for them to take time to themselves. To sort through everything. To open up and see if being together like this was something they wanted. To find the balance they were so close to striking. To see if this was a chance they all wanted to take.

Now, it slips through Lev's hands, swirling out of her grasp like snow on the wind. Her fingers curl into the fur of Aren's chest. His face falls, pulling Lev closer when her chin trembles. She doesn't know how to say it. How to put words to the enormity of what she feels, so she buries her face against his chest and fights not to let her voice shake.

"You're my best friend."

His arms tighten around her as he smooths a paw over the back of her head. If they could stay like this, if they had more time, maybe...but if Lev doesn't do this now, she fears she never will. She'll give into the mounting feelings for Aren and Caius and forget her duty to the pack. Wiping at her eyes, Lev pries herself out of Aren's arms.

"We should start. I'll get Pheir."

Behind Lev, Aren opens his mouth. She shakes her head once.

"Please don't." It takes all she has not to look at him, not to find the gaze she knows will fracture her resolve. Her voice cracks. "Please don't say anything else, or I won't be able to do this."

THIRTY

Aren

The look Lev gave Aren cut straight to his soul, past bone and muscle and into the part of him that beats for her.

You're my best friend.

They've known this is coming for weeks. A marriage to someone else isn't the end of the world —

But it's not *nothing*.

No number of his assurances can erase that. No matter what logic and rationale he tries, there's no subduing the wounded animal in his chest howling and grieving like it's losing its mate. Lev and Aren made vows as Alpha and beta long ago, swore to protect each other in battle and life. This wedding is a different promise, a romantic commitment neither of them felt the need to reach for, but now...

Now Aren's careful consideration and reasoning shatters in the face of emotion.

The ceremony isn't real, he reminds himself as he makes his way back to the grove. *It's political. It's strategic.* But Lev's marriage will do more than secure Pheir and the pack's safety; it ensures Lev and Aren will never be able to tie that knot together.

And Caius... Aren's eyes shut for a helpless moment. Things are complex enough between them, a tangled web of conflicting emotions and thoughts that they still don't have names for. Maybe nothing would come of it, but this wedding removes the opportunity. It obliterates the chance. It shatters the hope Aren has foolishly been clinging to when Caius looks at him like he wants to say something. When Caius shifts closer to Aren in sleep.

Lev binding herself to Pheir has consequences that ripple. Despite not fully tying Pheir to the pack, Lev will respect the sanctity of their vows. There will be no more Aren, Lev, and Caius, unless Pheir approves, and gods know she'll do anything to make them miserable. Without Lev between them, there is no Aren and Caius.

It digs straight into Aren's heart. The two of them can't seem to reach each other. After the wound of losing Lev to this, they can't wait Pheir out. She'll be beside Lev until the day one of them dies. Aren and Caius have to make peace with that — or at least a truce.

"She's going through with it?" Caius's gruff voice greets Aren as he returns. The werewolverine waits with folded arms beneath the arch assembled from branches and twine. He flicks a flower dangling from it, feigning apathy.

Aren takes his place next to Caius, toeing the small wooden crate of items for the ceremony. Unlike Caius, Aren can keep his expression impassive, staring down the grassy path to the shore. "Did you expect anything else?"

In Aren's periphery, Caius shakes his head, lips pulling back bitterly. "Did you even *try* to talk her out of it?"

Aren grinds his teeth. How can he explain his understanding of Lev? The two of them know each other, *respect* each other enough to let the other make their own choices. There's no point in trying to put words to it.

Caius doesn't understand anything but lashing out.

At the thought, Aren's body heats with shame. That's not true, but he can't keep the residual emotions from simmering in his throat like a tea kettle beginning to scream.

It pulses so loudly, he nearly doesn't hear Caius continue, the other man's hackles lifting. "It's like you don't care about her. Do you even *want* to be with her? Because all these years of fooling around, and you've never tried —"

It breaks a dam Aren hadn't realized was building — Vesta's rampage, Diction's death, Pheir's screaming, Lev giving herself to someone else, Caius touching but always keeping his distance. It bursts through the wall Aren's tried so hard to keep it behind, flooding the space between them.

"What's this chip on your shoulder?" It's the most bite Aren's put into his voice. Caius blinks in surprise. Aren doesn't walk it back, keeping his gaze trained on the path. "If you have something to say, then say it. I know you're dying to fight about *something*."

Nothing Aren can put a finger on. Whatever it is, Caius won't come right out with it. He'll make surly remarks and underhanded comments before he stalks off, and this impossible gap between them will grow bigger.

Shoulders tense, Aren stares into the forest, waiting for Caius to snap as his footsteps recede — but there's silence. Has the blood pumped so loudly in Aren's ears that he missed Caius's retreat?

When he looks back beside him, his eyes widen on Caius still rooted in place. There's something simmering in him, fists clenching at his sides as he glares toward the beach. His jaw clicks like he's trying to work it open despite its best efforts. "It's always the two of you, isn't it?"

For the first time, Caius lacks the heat that typically fuels his voice. Rage, anger, and irritation are diluted by something wet and heavy, almost...sad. The surprise leaves Aren stuck in silence before he manages to speak. "Me and Lev?"

Caius doesn't answer directly. Frustration brews in the tight curl of his lip as if he's cornered, keeping Aren in his periphery like he can't be trusted. "She looks for you," Caius mutters. "Even when it's just me and her, like you're this shadow I can't get out from under."

A shadow. It claws into Aren's heart, as if he's not meant to be there. As if it's not the three of them. As if he's interrupting whatever Caius feels for Lev instead of being a part of it.

Aren clears his throat. No need to make a fool of himself after Caius's admission. Instead, Aren keeps his voice level, eyes trained in the distance. "I'm not what's stopping you from having more with her."

Caius scoffs indignantly. "What is, then?"

"*You.*" It comes more sharply than Aren means it, emotion sneaking through the cracks of his facade. Moon reflects off Caius's eyes as they avert. It's harsh, but they both know it's true. Aren's head shakes in disappointment. "You never put your heels down. You're always waiting on your toes, like you're ready to run at the next strange sound. To be honest..." Aren exhales before he says it, "I'm surprised you haven't tried to take off yet. I'm not sure you'll look back at us when you do."

Caius's mouth falls open as he glances toward the shoreline. "She didn't tell..."

Aren's brow lifts, waiting for more.

Caius doesn't follow the thought. Instead, he tilts his face toward Aren and almost looks at him. "It's not just about her. It's about *you*, too."

It's the most forthright Caius has ever been, so direct that tension knots into Aren's throat. He tries to swallow around it to even out his voice. "What about me?"

For the first time, Caius meets his eyes. They never look at each other like this, not without someone else to distract them. Right now, there's no one to temper the curling scent in the air, molten heat hammered into jealousy that wants to shatter into something different. The depth of Caius's brown eyes pulls Aren in dangerously quickly. Aren can't stop himself. Looking at Caius,

Aren's mind blanks, losing hold of any sense that tells him he shouldn't —

"Do you feel anything at all?"

Caius's question makes Aren's mouth dry, forcing him to the surface of the wave of *feeling* Caius pulled him into. "Of course I feel..." Aren stops. Met with Caius's unflinching intensity, Aren stumbles over his words, tongue feeling heavy and useless. "What do you mean?"

"Do you feel *anything*?" With a hand, Caius thuds Aren's chest. "Because you never show it. You don't get angry, or scared, or upset. You don't *care*." All the emotion Caius finds lacking in Aren flows through his own voice. "You have it so fucking together, Aren, and I can't be that. I can't turn it off like you can. I *feel* things. It affects me, even when I know you don't feel anything for me."

It wounds Aren. Mouth falling open, he grapples for words, but Caius doesn't stop. Now that the dam has broken, he can't keep it from flowing.

"You think I see you through Lev, but that's how you see me, too: her pet project. A kid trying for someone out of my league. Not good enough to fit in here. Not good enough for her. Not good enough for you."

Aren's breath comes shallowly, a puff of fog in the space between them. For all his careful consideration, he's never been confronted with emotion like this. Never met someone who asks for a glimpse at the unrefined version of Aren. It's enough to make his head swim, instinct spinning like a faulty compass. In the end, there's only one thing he can manage. "That's not what I think about you, Caius."

Wind rushes through the trees. Caius turns fully toward Aren, so close the clouds of their breath become one before they fade. The dark pools of Caius's eyes are deep and hot and brimming with untapped potential. "Then what do you think about me?"

Two figures emerge at the forest edge. Caius steps back as Aren's heart thunders recklessly, and the moment is jerked away.

He has to focus. He has to get Lev through this wedding before he unpacks what he never thought Caius would ask of him.

The marriage could have forgone tradition entirely. They could have tied Pheir to a post and sped through the necessary words, but Lev deserved tradition. Moments of quiet. Moments that meant something.

The women step onto the path lined with torches and candles. It's the first time Aren's seen them in the light and taken them in together. Pheir is still guarded, never letting the others out of her sight, her skin pale and slick with sweat. The siren's tongue must be having an effect; the lines of her body have softened. In the torchlight, her feathers shift between blues and purples and greens, chin lifted so sharply Aren almost forgets the chains around her wrists.

And Lev is...his chest cinches. With the three of them to witness, she glows like an ember, yet she watches Aren and Caius as if they shine brighter than the torches. As if she's walking towards them for a reason that isn't marrying someone else.

A fur cloak drapes around Pheir's shoulders, dragging behind her until she looks like she belongs among them. It stirs in Aren's stomach, his eyes tracing her thighs slipping through the slits in her green dress. Lev is completely bare save for the wildflowers braided through her pale fur.

If Pheir is the breath before a scream, Lev is the sigh of relief that follows after. A selfish animal streaks through him.

Mine.

But they aren't his.

Caius's face holds the same reverence. Aren fears — *hopes* — one of them will speak, call and end to this and find a way to make it right. The island remains silent, save for the bullfrogs near the shoreline and crickets chirring in the underbrush as Pheir and Lev come to stand under the wooden arch.

Wife in name only. It's what Aren's told himself to get through this. As he watches the women who've sworn to hate each other, it's hard to remember what's real and what isn't. His voice lowers between them. "Ready?"

Lev nods. Her eyes don't leave Pheir, as if Pheir might attack or disappear entirely. In this moment, Aren's not sure which would be worse. He tries to recall the vows, searching for words past the emotion that floods his throat.

"Marriage is a risk taken together. It is a step into the unknown, but it is also an agreement of equals. It is letting go of who you are for the chance of who you can be together. It is the belief that the possibility is worth the plunge."

It should feel like a mockery to make such promises, but the grove buzzes with meaning as if the earth hums under their feet. It must be a trick of the night, frantic energy thrumming between them.

Lev swallows before she speaks to Pheir. "Even as you entrust yourself to me, I will never possess you. You are your own, so I will give what is mine to give."

There's nothing for Pheir to say. These aren't vows she's familiar with, but the way she keeps her eyes on Lev says more than words can. Aren forces himself to continue.

"Your lives will converge into a single path, but the union must not diminish either of you. You will grant all to each other, and still, become more than you were."

It's painful to imagine the truth in those words, a partnership they could have in some other life, a vicious devotion dedicated to love between them. Fighting a tremble, Lev extends her hand to Pheir.

"I offer you the first drink from my cup and hope the nectar tastes sweeter from my fingers. I rise before you at every danger. I stand behind you when the threat is greater at your back. I carry you in suffering. I chase your happiness as fervently as your desire." She swallows to get the last sentence out. "I pledge all my living and dying to you."

Pheir doesn't scoff at the words. She doesn't spit in Lev's face. Their gazes stay locked, like the vows are a precursor to battle and not a lifelong promise. Firelight winks off the vial of ashes around Lev's neck. Even in death, Vesta manages to insert herself between them again.

Until Pheir's eyes cut to Caius, sharp and sudden, like a snake sinking in its fangs. Neither of them moves. He looks like he hates her — for taking his place, for getting closer to Lev than he can — but there's more than animosity. It's like Pheir's a mirror, scattering light back toward him...

And then she looks at Aren.

She's impossible to read, seething fury contained in her body, chest rising and falling shallowly. For once, there's clear certainty in her eyes. Aren doesn't know what to do with it. Incomprehensibly, he nods, as if it might be of any comfort to her. As if it might reassure her that Lev will stand by the promises she's made.

Only then does Pheir lift her hand as they all hold their breath, before she wraps her fingers around Lev's forearm. Past the chains on Pheir's wrists, it locks them together as Aren takes the length of ribbon and slots it between their connection.

"You must seek to know each other," he continues. "Honor each other. Challenge each other." He winds the ribbon around their hands, weaving them together. It would be easy for them to break free of it, but both are still. "Give your love freely. Walk together through the tides of time and change. Be each other's friends, lovers, and future."

As the ribbon winds around them, Lev's fingers tighten, her voice quiet in the night air. "I take you as you are. As no one other than yourself. I love what I know of you and trust what I have yet to learn."

The ribbon comes to an end. Aren tucks it between their palms until there's no way to separate them. His voice catches before he finishes. "What fate joins together, no being may separate."

Candles flicker in the wind. When Lev speaks, Pheir breathes in time with her, both their eyes locked on each other. "You are my blood and bone."

With the scissors, Caius cuts a tuft of Lev's fur. When he turns to Pheir, her jaw tenses. He waits until she turns her face away, giving him access to the side of her head. As gently as he can, he clips a small lock of hair. Both pieces sit in his palm until he twists them together, winding purple and white until they're impossible to separate. With twine, he binds them together before he secures them to the small wooden hoop hanging above them on the arch.

It's the first physical sign of their commitment, an endless loop representing unending dedication. All four of them stare at it, flames shivering behind them. Lev shuts her eyes, as if the fear of what Pheir might do to her can't be more daunting than this. The final words escape her on a breath.

"This is my vow to you."

THIRTY-ONE

Aren

1 year before Vesta's death

Aren lays back across the bed with a sleepy smile. "I don't believe that."

"I'm not lying!" Lev's teeth dig into her lip, trying and failing to hide her grin.

The first streaks of light will soon spread across the sky. It's Aren's turn to replace Lev on guard duty, but Oberon let her leave a few minutes early to wake Aren. Naturally, he was waiting in her bed.

He shakes his head, resting a hand behind it before a chuckle rumbles out of him. Lev leaves the cabin door open, standing between his knees and smirking down at him. "I had a thing for you before we met."

Despite the way his eyes roll, the sentiment warms him. "How could that be?"

"I heard the rumors: disgraced beta, lone lynx..." Lev bends to press her palms against the mattress on either side of his hips, warm gaze slipping over him like honey. "I was expecting more of a bad boy, but I'll gladly accept my mistake."

The words don't sting Aren like they used to. In the time since Lev recruited him, the Timber pack has doubled and continues to grow. What was once a small pack has strengthened. Despite the Conclave's best efforts to the contrary, they've had to take notice of the Timbers' prestige and accept Lev among their ranks.

It happened because of her. She insists that Aren had a hand in it, but she's been the true catalyst. Her former Alpha was right in choosing her to take over. She's got a strong head on her shoulders, and an even stronger heart. Her intuition is second-to-none, but she's thoughtful and inquisitive, seeking opinions and weighing them in her decisions.

Aren's glad he didn't let his uncertainty stop him from joining her. He's far from the only "reject" Lev has taken in, and the Timbers are all the better for that. The pack has grown because Lev found people looking for a home, looking to build something bigger than themselves, looking for another chance. Because of Lev, the pack is safe. Happy. Healthy. Because of Lev, the Timbers can keep opening their arms to new members.

As Aren's paws settle on Lev's waist, his claws trace through her fur. It's easy to lift her on top of him. On the bed, her knees settle on either side of his hips, her fingers weaving through the fur of his chest. When his voice comes, it's low and hot, tinged with amusement. "Do you still have a thing for me?"

She leans forward, smile hovering over his. "A bigger one, if you can believe it."

When she captures his lips, he wraps his arms around her waist, pulling her tight against him. It's always been easy like this, the trust between them developing into something more. It's simple. It's sensical. Her mouth molding against his soothes him, their bodies winding like the gentle rocking of a boat. No one calms his spirit like Lev. No one twines through his bones and muscle, fortifying him against anything they face, wrapping around his heart the way her fingers weave between his and pin him back to the bed —

A watering can clatters outside. They both freeze, turning toward the open doorway. Caius fumbles in the dark. He tries to make a quick exit, but he knocks against a potted plant and steadies himself against the deck railing. It would be easier to walk if he weren't watching them, gaze stuck like a creature caught in a trap. As he stumbles down the stairs, Lev pushes off and bounds after him.

With a sigh, Aren pushes up to sit, rubbing his fingers against his eyes. It's not that he and Lev have been hiding what they are from Caius, but the wolverine is still one of the newest members of the pack. They may have met him two years ago, but it was six months before he started taking part in the lifestyle — sleeping within the Timber compound, harvesting crops, eating in the same vicinity as the others. If Aren were a betting man, he'd suspect Caius doesn't care much for the pack at all. He cares for *Lev*.

It's no surprise. From the moment they found Caius, Lev was the only one he'd let close. Aren tried to warn her against it. *You can't bring in every stray you find.*

Her brows lifted. *Why not?*

Aren didn't have an answer for that.

Caius is different than the rest of the pack. He's brittle and hostile, a reminder of Aren's former failings like he's living them again. Lev sensed it, finding Aren's hand and squeezing. *Caius is not taking your place. You're my beta. That will never change.*

As easy as it is to trust Lev, trusting Caius is a different story. Where Lev soothes Aren, Caius rouses him. There's something about Caius that makes Aren feel wild and untamed. It's a dangerous place for a beta to be.

If Aren gave into passion, to some emotion out of his control — anger, defensiveness, carnality – it wouldn't be safe. It doesn't make sense to Aren's logical mind. He can't understand the impulses Caius is given to, the feelings that lead him. If Aren can't reason through it, following that intensity would be dangerous. No matter what Lev sees in Caius, he's a threat to the blockades and control Aren has spent years putting into place.

Aren shuts his eyes, steadying his breath to blur the sound of Lev and Caius outside. Aren's heart slows. The fur on his arms eases back down. *Calm. Use your head.*

From Aren's seat on the bed, he can see Lev touching Caius's arm softly. Caius avoids her eyes. He doesn't cry. For all the emotions whirling within him, sorrow has never been one of them. Yet when Lev guides Caius back to her cabin, he looks like he might break, fractured by something before he saw Lev and Aren together.

Aren stands when they enter, bowing his head before he moves around them. "I should go check —"

A hand clamps around his wrist. The grip is hard enough to hurt, but Caius doesn't release it. He doesn't loosen. He doesn't look at Aren, either, even as Aren searches his face for some sign of what he's thinking.

Caius gives nothing away. His hold is firm, but there's no threat in it, like he's clinging to a cliff's edge to stop from plummeting. Slowly, Aren steps back into the cabin and settles his weight on his feet. Caius finally lets go of him.

It takes little effort for Lev to ease Caius down onto the bed. Over his head, she meets Aren's eyes, speaking without talking. When Caius lies down the rest of the way and curls on his side, Aren and Lev follow suit.

Lev faces Caius, eyes darting worriedly over his face. Behind him, Aren lays on his back, too hesitant to reach out and touch. Who knows if it might set Caius off, make him lash out with swinging claws? The bed is big enough to leave space between them, but Caius reaches back to dig into Aren's thigh, demanding him to move closer.

Or pleading for it.

Carefully, Aren shifts until his chest is barely brushing Caius's back. When Aren breathes, the motion brushes against Caius. Somehow, that lowers the hackles on Caius's neck. Aren can't make sense of that.

It's treacherous to be at Caius's back at any time, let alone when he's on edge like this, yet that's how they stay, quiet as birds begin to chirp outside. The three of them keep their hands to themselves, tucked against their bodies as Lev whispers in the dark. "Did something happen?"

There's no answer. Nothing but the shallow sound of Caius breathing, until he reaches for Lev's waist and pulls her close. He buries his face in her neck. Over his shoulder, Lev's eyes are wide on Aren, both of them waiting with baited breath.

Caius isn't crying. He isn't shaking, taking deep breaths against Lev's throat, like the scent of her alone is enough to ease whatever weight he's carrying. If Aren makes sense of nothing else about this, he understands that — the way Lev flows like warm water over his body and eases out the tension. Gingerly, Lev places a hand on the back of Caius's head. He burrows in tighter. It's a risk, but Aren shifts forward inch by inch until he's lined completely against Caius's back. The other man curls into the shape Aren makes.

Caius's voice is little more than a growl, like a part of him can't accept the vulnerability the rest of him has given into. "It must've been a dream..." His fingers flex into a fist behind Lev's back. It's the most he's exposed himself, giving a glimpse into his head, but it can't be that easy. Caius won't finish the thought, face buried against Lev's throat.

That's when it changes. When Lev sucks in a breath, nails digging into Caius's shoulder. Then Caius's tongue laves against her, small flicks that become strokes from her collarbone to her ear.

It's brazen, but it's not unheard of. Packs find solace in physicality more often than not, whether that be platonic or something more sensual. From the scent in the room, Aren knows it's not a power play, not an attempt to make him jealous or rub this in his face. Between the melancholy that radiates off of Caius, there's a desperate yearning for closeness that binds with arousal.

As Caius mouths against Lev's neck, he grips Aren's thigh, keeping the three of them pressed together. Lev's mouth hangs open in surprise, but her eyelids flutter, breath becoming shallow. Caius continues his motions, grooming her until his hand clenches around her waist and pulls her hips into his.

"D'you want me to stop?" he murmurs.

It's not the first time they've found themselves in a confusing mix of hostility and desire, but it is the first time it's become...more. In the silence, Lev's breath and Aren's heartbeat are the only sounds. She stares at him. Caius must sense it, because he pulls his mouth back enough to speak to Aren.

"Do *you* want me to stop?"

There's no answer Aren can find. No reasonable response when his mind is screaming that this doesn't make sense at the same time his body aches to get closer. Lev's expression holds the same surprise, but there's no denying the sharp scent waking as it burrows hot into Aren's stomach.

He wants more. He wants to know how Caius opens up. He wants to see if Caius fucks like he fights. He wants to see if he and Caius move in sync the way they do in battle.

Aren's not sure who he's speaking to when he says it — to Caius, or Lev, or himself. "It's ok."

Lev squeezes Caius's arm, keeping her eyes on Aren. "It's ok," she repeats.

Relief washes over Caius, paws scrabbling to bring Lev closer. He drags her hips against his, hitching her leg over his side until it drapes against Aren. A whine escapes her when Caius grinds against her, rolling painfully slowly so every inch of him drags hard between her legs.

Aren swallows her sound, capturing her mouth in a kiss like moments before, but this is different. This is wanton, unrestrained, needy, his teeth finding her lip until she keens and spurs a bodily desire inside him.

This is what Caius does to him. He makes Aren lose his head and fall into instincts that he doesn't trust, heat and want and craving overriding every thought. It's unstable like a glass hovering at the end of a table as an earthquake begins to rumble. Aren wants to ride this edge until the glass topples and shatters on the ground. The jagged edges will dig into his body and prick him with pleasure, the same way Caius's teeth do now.

Aren will clean up the pieces tomorrow.

THIRTY-TWO

Pheir

PRESENT
25 days after Vesta's death

It's no surprise being married to Lev makes Pheir's body revolt.

She sweats, but her teeth won't stop chattering. Her skin is hot, but not even pride keeps her from wrapping the cloak around her to stop shivering. Her body aches, warring with the nauseous turn of her stomach. All this suffering is thanks to her new *wife*.

If Pheir's honest, the tremors started before the wedding. It was days ago when she began to wonder if she was coming down with a fever. Now, she recognizes that the symptoms crept in when she started eating as Aren insisted. The Timbers are poisoning her like Rhaiden did.

And yet...

It doesn't feel exactly like the poisoning before. The Timbers are much better at it. Pheir's impressed they pulled it off at all, since she takes a scrupulous amount of time choosing her tray and forcing her guards to finish their meals first. There's no rhyme or reason to the way Pheir chooses, and the guard is different nearly every time. Are they poisoning both meals? Have all the Timbers developed an immunity to whatever they're using? Do they take an antidote after every meal? None of it makes sense. If they want to kill her, why not just do it?

Regardless, the effect the poison has is strange. It doesn't eat away at her muscles or discolor her skin or make her vomit. It doesn't make her feel foggy and confused. In fact, impossibly, it makes her head clearer, like she's surfacing from a murky lake, as if she spent her life remembering sensations from a dream and is now experiencing them for the first time.

Wind is cooler. Pine needles are sharper. Caius's fur is slicker. Aren's paws are bigger. Lev's smile is brighter.

Nausea rises in Pheir again, but it's fake and forced, her body attempting to fabricate the feeling she desperately desires. She *wants* to feel sick when she thinks of them. She wants to bite back vomit at the sight of them — but she doesn't.

It has to be the wedding bonds, forcing her full of Timber love and peace and shit. Between the wedding, poison, and exhaustion finally catching up with her, it's no wonder Pheir can't determine how the fuck she feels. Her mind wanders off course from things that used to soothe her. The thought of gutting the Timbers used to be a lullaby; now, those thoughts drift into something else.

In her visions, Pheir tackles Caius to the ground, and he pins her beneath him. She lunges for Aren, and he catches her against his chest. Most disturbing of all, Pheir reaches for Lev in the dark, and Lev's mouth presses softly to the back of Pheir's head.

It vibrates through her body. *It's the bonds*, she insists as she grits her teeth. There's no other reason for this unexplainable desire to be near the three of them.

But if Pheir's honest with herself, these thoughts started before the wedding, too.

After the ceremony, her legs trembled with the weight of what they'd done. It's disgusting, being forcibly bound to someone, but her body had more trouble reckoning with the meaning of it. Of the power in Aren's voice. Of the weight in Lev's gaze. It made Pheir tremble.

Speak of the rabbit. Lev approaches through the darkened woods, canteen in hand with a look of concern that makes Pheir want to scream.

"How are you feeling?" Lev asks.

Pheir refuses to answer, head resting back against a tree. "Where are your lackeys?"

It doesn't get a rise out of Lev. "They're finishing up. Caius is gathering everything, and Aren is weaving..." Lev's throat bobs, gaze drifting into the distance. She doesn't finish the sentence. After a moment, she lowers herself next to Pheir. "You need to drink some-"

"If you're expecting me to fall in love at your feet, then I hate to break it to you, but your 'wedding bonds' had no effect." Pheir hardens her gaze enough to keep Lev from seeing past it. "I still hate the Timbers, and I still hate *you*."

Infuriatingly, Lev doesn't look surprised. With a nod, she sets the canteen on the ground within Pheir's reach. For a long time, Lev stares at the campfire, as if she's comfortable beside Pheir. It burns Pheir from the inside out.

Why can't she find the right chord to strike? Why does nothing Pheir does get a reaction? Why doesn't Pheir know what reaction she *wants*? Her tongue aches with thirst, but she refuses to drink, spitting out the first thing that comes to mind. "Are you here to consummate it?"

This time, at least, Pheir manages to surprise Lev. Her head jerks toward Pheir. "What? No..." Lev's pupils dilate momentarily before she shakes her head, as if she's chasing away a thought.

It's the first glimpse of reaction Lev's shown all night. Pheir rises onto her knees, swooping like a bird snatching a creature in its claws. "Why not? If I'm your *wife...*" Pheir sneers, "we have to make it official."

Every word is cruel and callous — at least, Pheir wants them to be. Her mind swirls in half-delirium, pulse thrumming. *This isn't me,* she assures herself. *This isn't what I want.* It's the poison or the wedding bonds or the color of Lev's eyes in the firelight that makes Pheir's body fight to be closer. Her stubbed talons claw the ground, neck straining, teeth diving dangerously close to Lev's.

Pheir isn't sure what she'll do if she lands. What happens if Lev grabs her hips? If Pheir pushes Lev's thighs apart? If Lev tells Pheir to get on her knees, and Pheir obeys?

Before she can think, Lev eases her back. "We don't have to do that," Lev breathes. Her chest rises and falls, but not from exertion.

Heat tremors through Pheir. It's not from the illness. "But is it real if you don't stake your claim?" Pheir's gaze darts over Lev's face. Eyelashes. Cheeks. Mouth. Pheir's lips tingle. "If you don't see this to the end? If you don't remind me that you own me?"

It's goading and reckless. Pheir follows through with her words, gripping Lev's fur wherever she can reach. With her wrists chained, Pheir manages to force herself into Lev's lap, slotting one leg between hers and crushing their lips together. It's a bastardized kiss, sloppy and mean, intent on one response only. This is a way for Pheir to pour out her fury. This is a way to torment Lev.

Until Pheir catches a taste of something. It slows the scrape of her teeth, tension easing as her tongue traces the corner of Lev's lips. She's sweet like fruit, warm like summer meeting the tip of Pheir's tongue. It's hypnotic, drawing her deeper until she licks into Lev's mouth.

A whimper escapes Lev, like an animal caught in a trap. Pheir's body seizes, hands clenching as she grinds against Lev's thigh. Pheir wants to hear that sound again, to follow the wounded cries until Lev is laid out like a feast before her, whining and pleading on the end of Pheir's tongue.

She's forced up for air when Lev pushes her back, both of them panting as they stare at each other. Pheir's hips seek aborted circles in Lev's lap. There's a confusing mix of emotion in Lev's eyes, one that matches what Pheir's trying to snuff out. She wants to hurt Lev. She wants to hunt her down. She wants to chase her until she gets a taste of how badly she hates her.

Lev doesn't let it go further. With a firm grip, she holds Pheir away from her body, but she doesn't untangle their legs. "You don't have to do that," Lev murmurs. Unthinking, her fingers brush the hot skin of Pheir's shoulder, Lev's gaze following the path they take. Now she's the one getting lost, the one with glaze over her eyes before she blinks back to Pheir's mouth. "If you don't want to."

Pheir always searches for explosive reactions, venomous hate or screaming frustration. Things she knows. Things she can pinpoint. She's never been this close to someone when there weren't teeth and claws at each other's throats. She's never been quiet enough to hear someone else's breathing.

She watches the rise and fall of Lev's chest as if she's trying to match it. Whiskers tickle Pheir's cheek, then eyelashes take their place when Pheir inclines her head closer. Warm air ghosts across her lips. It settles into sync with her breath, as if she and Lev are here in the same moment. Same connection. Same side.

Traitor!

The familiar voice makes Pheir jerk out of Lev's lap.

Traitor! the voice shrieks in Pheir's head, sending her sprawling to the ground. *You're a fucking traitor!* The words fight through Pheir's blood, shearing her heart in two as her head pounds. *Disloyal! Deserter!*

Lev reaches for her. Pheir smacks her hand away, edging back toward the tree and burying herself inside the cloak. It's stiflingly hot, but it's better than meeting Lev's gaze. Does she see the want in Pheir's eyes? The yearning on her tongue? The animal hunger to taste Lev again?

Vesta's voice in Pheir's head grows louder. *It's not real! You felt nothing! You're sick and desperate and weak. It's the poison! It's the wedding! It's the pain!*

Lev retreats to the other side of the fire. Pheir shuts her eyes as her mind splits like an atom.

Louder than Vesta's voice comes another. This one sounds like Pheir, rising from the heat of her stomach. The voices screech and circle each other, tearing each other to shreds. Pheir doesn't know which she wants to win. Her head aches. Inside her, her voice grows louder, drowning out Vesta's screams until one thought fights to the forefront.

It's me. I want it. I want them.

THIRTY-THREE

Lev

Maybe Lev is drunk. She hasn't had any alcohol, but it's the only explanation for why her legs are wobbly, lips tingling where Pheir kissed her. Lev nearly stumbles as she circles back around the campfire, body flaring hot despite the chill.

This is the first night since Pheir arrived that there's no screaming or threats. There's nothing but croaking frogs and water trickling through the reeds and the memory of Pheir's breath catching where she pressed against Lev's chest.

Dazedly, Lev sinks back onto her sleeping bag. It's tradition to camp outside after a wedding, but Lev isn't sure why she insisted. Nothing about this is normal. Nothing about it is *real*, yet her fingers curl into the dirt when she risks a glance toward the pale violet skin of Pheir's calf peeking out from the slit in her dress.

Maybe Lev fucked that up. She doesn't know how. She doesn't know what happened, a scrabble of claws suddenly turning to clutching hands and winding hips before Pheir jerked away. It's troubling given the sheen over her body as she shivers under her cloak. Sweat isn't something the others are well-versed in, given the Timber pack of werecreatures, but this much of it isn't good. From the way Pheir bundles in her furs, she's freezing, but Lev remembers how hot her skin was. How it grew hotter when she slotted her leg between Lev's thighs —

"Is she still sick?"

Caius's appearance makes Lev jump, sleeping bag rustling beneath her. He raises a brow, depositing the used torches and candles in a pile next to them before he sinks down beside her. All evidence of the wedding has been cleared away, save for the union between Lev and Pheir. Lev can't bring herself to say the word now. *Wife.* It hangs like a guillotine above her neck.

"Not according to her." Lev pulls her knees to her chest. "She wouldn't take any of the water. She wanted me to leave her alone." Holding her breath, Lev bunches the sleeping bag around her feet. "It seemed like I was making it worse by trying to help her."

Maybe Aren can make sense of the way Pheir reacted. The way *Lev* did, flushed and wanton and barely thinking enough to stop. In the distance, she can make him out at the shoreline, constructing the wedding hoop and twining it with mementos from the ceremony.

Flowers from their hair, the handfasting ribbon, dripped wax from the candles, fallen feathers from Pheir's wings. It will all be bound in a circle, a wreath displaying their devotion. Meanwhile, Lev can't get within arm's length of Pheir without them fighting.

That's the truth of their position. What if this ceremony was a wasted effort? What if it's another step in the wrong direction? What if Pheir's hate for Lev will be the only thing that grows over time?

Suddenly, the rest of Lev's life seems insurmountably long.

She should go to Aren — but as soon as she gets her feet under her, the fur on her neck stands on end, straining toward the warm breath of Caius behind her. There's space between their bodies, but not so much that Lev can't feel his presence solid against her.

It eases the tension from her muscles, his hands kneading into her shoulders like he can see the stiffness there. As if he knows what she needs. As if he's beginning to read her as well as Aren can. Her eyes flutter closed, fire heating her face as Caius warms her back. They're quiet as he works his thumbs against knots until her head rests back against him.

When he speaks against her neck, she shivers. "You didn't tell Aren I tried to leave."

She sucks in a breath, chest swarming with cold. "Did you talk to him? About how you feel?"

"Didn't make a difference," Caius grunts sullenly, but it morphs into something else. "But I did it."

There's almost pride in his voice, surprise that he'd confronted a topic he hates and survived. A smile slips across Lev's mouth, cheek grazing Caius's snout. Claws trace the outside of her thigh as Caius laughs, a gravelly thing Lev so rarely hears. After a moment of silence, he rests his chin on her shoulder and takes a slow breath to brace himself.

"I don't want to leave. I want to stay here."

Her rabbit ears perk as she sits upright. His fingers trail up the back of her arm, the weight of his words settling over both of them. He nods against the side of her head in reassurance that she heard correctly. She twists to see him over her shoulder, but he digs claws into her hips to keep her in place. *Baby steps.* She stays facing away, staring at the fur cloak across the circle. Pheir's side barely rises and falls as Caius speaks.

"Something brought me here. I want to understand it. I want to know if there's more." Mouth pressed to the side of Lev's neck, his voice rumbles against her throat like he's testing the words out loud for the first time. "I want to earn your trust. I want to do what you need. What the *pack* needs. I want to learn how to tell what that is without thinking." It's the most he's put words to, voice ragged and slow. His nose drags behind her ear. Her eyes slip shut, fingers clamping on his knee to keep from shivering. Slowly, he exhales, earnestness seeping into his tone. "I want to be good for this pack. I want to find my people. I don't want to be alone. I'm tired of fighting it every day."

Lev's gaze stays on Pheir. Without looking, Lev knows Caius is staring at her, too. Lev doesn't know why. She doesn't understand anything about Pheir, but maybe the strange feeling that's been tugging Lev toward her is tugging on Caius as well.

"Is it because of her?" Lev breathes it almost too quietly to hear. It seems ludicrous. No moment with Pheir could have pushed Caius toward this, but at the ceremony, something shifted, even without binding Pheir to the pack. Call it intuition or residual magic or tension finally snapping, but Lev can't be the only one struggling to find her footing. She can't be the only one trying to understand why the wedding felt more than fake, uniting more than the two of them.

Caius sighs hopelessly. He's tempted to shut himself off, forehead pressing to the back of Lev's head before he takes a slow breath. "I don't know why." There's no way to put it into words. Lev understands that helplessness. "I hate her. I fucking *hate* her, but sometimes the hate feels like..."

There are no words for it. That's the only way to describe what Pheir stirs in them, a desperate thing that has no care for battle lines or years-long grudges. It hungers. It *wants*.

Lev turns in Caius's arms, smearing their lips together and pouring everything that she couldn't give to Pheir. Every convoluted emotion, every confusing moment, every chemical reaction they can't make sense of. When Lev's fingers tangle in his fur, it's like the first time, as if something has opened and spilled between them —

And then the chains rattle.

Their bodies still as they look toward Pheir. She isn't scrambling to escape, writhing on the ground as light reflects off the sweat of her body. For a panicked moment, Lev fears the siren's tongue has poisoned her, but Pheir's eyes are clear and direct. Her jaw clamps, like she hates the word that pries its way out. "Please…"

Neither Lev nor Caius move. Frustrated, Pheir's chains clink as she digs her heels into the dirt and tosses her head back on a strangled scream. Her back arches, sprawled across the cloak beneath her, the slits of her dress hitching high on her thighs. Lev shouldn't look. Shouldn't be thinking about that, but when the muscles in Pheir's thighs flex, Lev swallows.

"Do you need water?" she croaks. She pries herself out of Caius's arms, both of them keeping their eyes on Pheir.

The harpy hisses through her teeth, skin somehow flushed and pale as if her body's withdrawing. As if she needs something to replace the control she's escaping. Carefully, Lev rises to her feet, crossing the campsite until she kneels next to Pheir.

"What do you need?" Lev searches Pheir's face for a sign of what she's lacking. Maybe it's a mistake to try to help her. Maybe there's nothing Lev can give — but when Pheir meets her eyes, there's more than hatred there; there's an ache. A regret. A clarity. When Pheir's mouth moves, it's with the same desire that Lev felt pressed to her lips.

"I need you to touch me. Please."

THIRTY-FOUR

Caius

It's like Pheir knows they're talking about her. The second Caius gets close to Lev, Pheir squirms and draws Lev's attention away.

Caius should hate that as fervently as he hates Pheir. He should despise her for getting between them, but his body runs hot with something else. It's not an intrusion when Pheir pleads for Lev; it's an invitation Caius can't pull his eyes away from.

There's pitiful desperation in her voice that he wants to answer. It darts through his mind like a wounded animal, begging the predator in him to give chase and rousing the broken creature he hides inside himself. He wants to hunt her. He wants to protect her. He wants to cover her body with his own.

It's an impossible mix of instinct, the same ones he feels for Lev and Aren. How can Caius want Pheir the same way? It's impossible. His blood boils, thick with more than anger. It's like Pheir *knows*, tugging her chains and catching his eyes.

"I need it," she pants. Never has Pheir asked anything from them. Now, the plea strains through her teeth as her thighs clamp together. Her arousal burns hot in Caius's nose as she grits her teeth. "I need you to touch me. I need to feel…"

A branch snaps near the edge of the clearing. Lev and Caius whirl toward it, caught up in the sight of Pheir, but it's Aren returning from the shoreline. Aren, who said nothing to Caius's confession. Caius doesn't want to remember that. He wants to block it out the way he has been for a year.

Aren's nose twitches, ears flicking as he takes in the scene of Lev and Caius on edge as Pheir arches in the dirt.

The sight of Aren heightens Pheir's desire, her body writhing. "I need to be *close*." Her talons dig into the dirt, straining like she's reaching for the three of them. There's no denying how their bodies react, fur rising on end as their pupils grow wider. When Pheir's arousal swells, all their noses twitch sharply.

Lev is a beacon of self-control, fingers clenched where she kneels next to Pheir. Caius rises to his feet like he's in a trance. Pheir is a crying creature begging to be put out of her misery. Caius will give her what she needs. When Lev looks back to him, her legs tremble, sending heat darting through his gut. Aren's eyes follow Caius's tongue as it drags across his maw. Caius wants to devour all of them, to taste their blood and sweat and cum —

"It can't be like last time." Lev shakes her head, fighting to focus on Pheir. When Lev's legs steady, her voice hardens. "We're gonna take care of you after. Are you gonna fight it? Because I don't trust you not to."

Pheir hisses as if it's torture, as if she can't stand to bare herself to them a second longer than it takes to fuck. She begs to be touched, but she jerks away as soon as they reach for her. She throws her body at them, but anything softer is too much for her to take. It rings through Caius like a hammer striking an anvil.

She's just like him.

His head spins. *Fuck*. They are the same.

"Those are the terms, Pheir." Lev's voice makes Caius's ears prick. She's talking to the woman in front of her, but she's watching Caius with Alpha control that makes him want to sink to his knees. He bites back a whine. It's too fucking *much*. He holds his ground, fighting to think past the wind lifting the others' arousal to his nose. The campfire is nothing next to the heat spreading through his senses.

Chains clink as Pheir rolls in fury, body arching as it heaves. It's like she hates herself for needing it. "Just don't be – fucking *nice*."

After a moment, Lev nods, as if she understands. Eyes darkening, she snatches Pheir's jaw in hand. "Beg for Mercy now, *bride*, or you're gonna take whatever I give you."

It's Pheir's explicit chance to use her safeword, to deny the others, to laugh at their hunger — but she doesn't speak. Her teeth snap like she gets off on pretending she hates this. Of course she does...because Caius does, too. Because they want the same thing. Because they can't bring themselves to admit it.

"If that's how you want to be..." Lev drops Pheir's jaw as she steps back. Pheir whines like a petulant child. Lev's voice is cold as ice. "Hold her down."

Caius moves without thought, crossing the space the same time Aren does. Their bodies always know what to do even when the rest of them fumbles and stutters. Pheir's too weak to fight them off as they hold her chest to the ground and pin her arms outstretched before her.

There's no hiding the scent of her desire with her ass in the air. A growl rumbles in Caius's throat, desperate to bury his mouth against her cunt.

"Caius..." Aren warns quietly. Caius snaps his jaws but forces himself to remain in place.

Lev sinks to her knees behind Pheir, wrapping hands around Pheir's ankles to keep her spread. Despite herself, Pheir's tail lifts, desperate to be mounted as her green dress shifts up around her hips. Lev's tongue clicks pitifully. "What a needy little bride. Your wedding night with no one to fill you up. That poor little pussy must be so lonely. I bet you'd take one little finger, wouldn't you? One little breath…"

Lev leans forward, blowing cool air against Pheir's clit. A shudder wracks through Pheir, cheek scraping the ground as her hips buck for something to grind against. There's nothing but cold air and Lev's torment. A whine slips out of Pheir's grasp.

"Is that not enough?" Lev mocks. "I bet we could make you hump that fur cloak and pretend it was us. You'd do it, wouldn't you? Just for some relief."

The thought makes Caius's dick press hard against his thigh. All his body's aches from the cold are forgotten. A wicked glint captivates Lev's eyes. She reaches for a length of extra chain from one of their satchels. Carefully, she wraps one end of the chain around Pheir's thigh. Pheir's body jerks at the cold metal. Lev circles the chain around Pheir's other thigh to match. Pheir's legs tremble, but there's no denying the heightened tang of her arousal in the air. Caius's dick twitches, hips threatening to rut against her before he restrains himself.

The chain stretches in a straight line beneath Pheir's ass, tugged higher until it brushes Pheir's clit. She gasps, keening through her teeth as she scrambles against the ground. Caius and Aren don't release her. She doesn't beg for mercy, nearly foaming at the mouth as she tries to clamp her thighs together. Lev holds her ankles fast, keeping the ends of the chain pulled taut against Pheir.

"It's fucking *cold*!" Pheir screams.

There's no sympathy in Lev's eyes. "Warm it up, then."

Every part of Lev makes Caius shiver. He could lose himself in her casual cruelty, but there's more beneath it. She gives Pheir exactly what she's been after — an enemy to fight. A villain to pin her hate to. Pheir would never accept softness, so Lev drapes her benevolence in malice. She uses the language Pheir can stand. She gives Pheir the closeness she wants in the callous package she'll accept.

The same way Lev does for Caius. His fingers curl tighter around Pheir's arms. Goddamn, he wants Lev *more*.

Behind Pheir, the chain teases her cunt. The harpy struggles, fighting not to tremble when she drags against the chain. Her hips rut without permission. A humiliating moan escapes her, face smeared against the dirt.

"There you go," Lev murmurs, dark eyes honed where the chain meets Pheir's body. Pheir's skin is hot under Caius and Aren's hands. He's never felt her like this. Never taken time to realize how easily her skin changes temperature, how soft it is under his fur. His fingers curl tighter around her arms.

Painstakingly, she shifts her hips again, dragging her clit against the chain. With every motion, the metal pulls slack and then taut again, clinking loud enough for all of them to hear.

"Take what you can get." Lev pulls both ends of the chain tighter around Pheir's thighs until the metal at the center grows slick from her desire. If Caius leans, he can see the chain glistening as it dips lower, heating with every rock of Pheir's hips until she settles into a pathetic rhythm.

"It's almost enough, isn't it?" Lev guides one end of the chain up to trace the lips of Pheir's cunt. Pheir's body spasms, breath huffing before Lev teases the cold end of the chain inside her. "What if I just…"

Pheir bites back a groan and tries not to fuck back against the little that Lev is giving her. It's pitiful. It's pathetic. It makes Caius fucking *hard*. Never before has Pheir been so needy, desperate enough to humble herself before the three of them. Caius wants more. He wants to consume her. He wants to lap at this vulnerable part of her and see if it tastes the same as her brutal strand.

It's deliciously cruel how Lev fucks the end of the chain into Pheir's pussy. "It's not enough, huh?" Lev pouts. Pheir tries to scratch at her, but Aren and Caius tighten their hold.

Pheir seethes. "Fucking…" She bites off her curse as she writhes against the dirt.

Lev tilts an ear toward her, grabbing the center of the chain and dragging it against Pheir's clit. "Tell me what you want."

Pheir screams as she digs her talons into the ground. "Fucking — *touch me!*" She's panting and wild, ass growing brighter from the cold wind.

"Finally begging for your wife, are you?" Lev loosens her hold on the chain, letting it fall to the ground to leave Pheir with nothing to grind against. Nothing to console her cunt as it throbs with need. It assaults Caius's senses, making him salivate as he snaps his teeth.

"I guess it's fair I get a little bit." Lev's soft paws run down the backs of Pheir's thighs. "First taste of the virgin bride…" Lev traces the swollen lips of Pheir's cunt and chuckles. "Oh, that's right: you fucked my guards twice already. Traitorous little pussy…but never traitorous enough to fuck me."

Caius can't see exactly what happens when Lev lowers her mouth, but the sounds set the hot coal in his stomach alight. Pheir squeals so hard her voice cracks. Lev hums beneath wet suction. Aren curses at the slippery sound that makes Caius's hips rut against Pheir's cheek.

"You're a fucking *bitch*," Pheir groans at Lev, too distracted to notice Caius's dick leaking onto her face. At the sight of it, Aren has to pull his hips back to keep from doing the same.

Lev's tongue drags between Pheir's folds, loud and sloppy as she smirks. "Ride my face about it."

No matter how Pheir wants to resist, her body can't. Her wings shudder. What starts as a stubborn roll of her hips turns to her fucking back over Lev's tongue and smearing desire across Lev's cheeks. Lev keeps a tight hold on Pheir's ankles, circling her lips on Pheir's clit until Pheir's arms shake. It's barely been fifteen seconds when Pheir's body tenses, eyes snapping shut as her chest drags against the ground. "*Fuck*, don't make me —"

That's the only warning they get before Pheir comes. Her body seizes like it was waiting to blow from the second Lev touched her, a screech tearing from Pheir's throat as she squirts across Lev's face. It stuns Lev, but it doesn't stop her. She buries her mouth against Pheir's clit and sucks until Pheir fights to escape the sensation.

None of the others move. Liquid drips down Lev's chin as she pulls back and blinks at Aren and Caius. Her shocked breaths become labored, pupils blown wide as she lifts her thumb to her lips. Slowly, she drags through the evidence of Pheir's desire and licks it clean.

Primal thoughts slam into high gear. They can't be contained, a feral drive setting off through the Timbers' synapses. Pheir's scent mixes with theirs, the remnants of the wedding ceremony clinging in the air. Pheir is a creature in need with a carnal desperation to be filled, a creature that smells like *them*, a Timber who has marked their Alpha as her own.

They need to make Pheir theirs.

Everything else fades as carnal desire overtakes them. Blood pulses through Caius's ears as he jerks Pheir's ass toward him, forcing her up to her knees with her back against his chest. It takes no time to tear her out of her clothes, the slit of her dress ripping up between her breasts until it hangs useless from her body. He jerks the fabric away, slotting his cock into the wet heat of her cunt. She reaches her chained wrists back over her head, tightening them against the back of his neck until his face is pressed to hers.

"You want to fight me?" His claws lift to her throat, tongue dragging up the side of her neck. "You'd better fucking fight me, then."

Her pussy clenches around him as she snaps her hips back against him, making them both moan.

"Feral fucking *freak*," he cackles, jerking her chin to face him. Fire blazes in her eyes. She's wild, overcome with the same irresistible urge. Her dull talons curl in the back of his fur, tugging him closer as she drags her teeth into his lip. He snarls, jerking her back to sink completely over him. Their moans grow hot in their mouths. Between them, her wings spread, feathers arching on her back in a lurid display that drives his hips faster.

There's a part of Caius that knows he should slow down and get his thoughts in order. When Pheir digs her talons into him, he forgets everything else.

Lev appears before them as Pheir and Caius debase themselves. Lev looks like a goddess of the forest observing their carnal offering, moonlight spilling over the woven braids and flowers of her head. Caius buries his mouth against Pheir's neck as Lev lifts Pheir's chin with her fingers. Stuttering with every slam of Caius's hips, Pheir can barely speak past her groan.

"I hate you."

It tastes like a lie in the air.

Caius tightens his hand around her throat, stifling her breath as her head falls back against his shoulder. One of Lev's hands dips down and circles tight against Pheir's clit. Everything's *wet*, Caius's cock nearly slipping out as he fucks her with abandon. He releases his hold, and Pheir gasps air into her lungs. The pleasure's enough to make her sob as she whines. "I *hate* you!"

Again, Caius chokes her, her breath wheezing under his palm as she fucks back against him. Lev's undisturbed, fingers tracing Pheir's jaw so gently next to Caius's brutal fucking. He releases Pheir's throat again, hand dragging down to her breast to twist her nipple between his fingers.

She cries out. Lev sinks completely to her knees. Across the clearing, a voice drifts toward them.

"Careful..."

It's Aren, watching from a distance. Caius would laugh if he weren't so gone already. Always Aren holding back, Aren putting space between them, Aren trying to force them to slow down. The lynx isn't immune, though, fisting his hard cock as he watches the three of them.

Caius needs to taste it. Needs to taste all of them mixing on his tongue, a cocktail of what belongs to the animal inside him. That possessive beast overrides all Caius's thoughts as Pheir's body pulls taut.

"*Kiss me!*" she demands, straining toward Lev as Caius holds her back against his chest.

Carefully, Lev tilts her mouth. She's out of reach no matter how Caius thrusts into Pheir. It makes Pheir whimper, old pride and grudges falling away in the wake of her desire. Lev parts her lips — but she doesn't kiss Pheir, doing little more than sharing breath as Pheir's forced closer to her second orgasm.

"Do it!" Pheir pleads, eyes dipping to Lev's mouth. It's cruel the way Lev turns her head, letting Caius lick the remnants of Pheir's arousal from her lips. Pheir cries out, struggling in Caius's hold when he lowers his mouth to her shoulder. His teeth scrape against her.

Aren's voice barely makes its way to Caius's ears. "*Careful...*"

How can Caius hear anything when Pheir's brutal, perfect cunt is wrapped around him? He's let his thoughts get as far as destroying her, never discovering how much he truly wants to break her. To taste her pulse as it kicks higher. To rip every cruel word from her mouth until all she can scream is his name.

He wants to mark her. He wants her blood in his mouth. He wants to taste her on his tongue. He wants to dig his teeth into her in an imprint everyone will know is *his*.

Lev has the same thought, guiding her mouth to the other side of Pheir's neck. Lev grips Pheir's hair to expose her throat. The three of them move in sync like this was meant to happen, as if their bodies understand things their minds don't. Pheir pants, staring up between the trees. Moonlight cascades over the curves of her body as she groans. "Do it. Gods, fucking, *please* —"

Her eyes are glassy and wanton. Lev and Caius open their mouths, bodies grinding together in a magnetic pull they're helpless against. She has to be theirs. They have to *make her* theirs —

"Stop!"

The beta command makes Caius's mouth flinch around nothing but air. His jaws snap shut in the quiet above their panting breaths. Lev looks like she's surfaced from beneath water, blinking as she falls back. Pheir's the only one not affected by Aren's voice, hips circling over Caius's cock as she moans. "Don't *stop!*"

Aren's teeth grit, hand still tight around his cock. He's frozen in place. Solemnly, his eyes find Caius and Lev before she speaks again. "You can't mark her like that."

It takes a moment for Caius to remember. This is all for show: the ceremony, the wedding. They can't share Pheir's blood this soon after the vows. If they cross that final line, it would make this real. It would bind her to the pack. But *fuck*, it was so easy to fall into, losing themselves in the reverie as they let their bodies do what they yearn to and make Pheir one of them.

That's why Aren kept his distance, as if he knew what the others would get themselves into. Lev forgot herself, dragged down into the pit of passion with Caius. She blinks between him and Pheir now, shock across her face as she tries to catch her breath.

And Pheir...Pheir begged them like her body wanted to be bitten. There's no way she could know what it means for their tradition. No way she would plead for them to make the wedding real, yet she craves their teeth sinking into her. She fucks herself against Caius and glares across the space at Aren. She doesn't understand the gravity of what's happened, voice hungry and wild. "Always so careful, Aren," she gasps, swirling her hips over Caius's cock.

Aren tries to keep his composure, amber eyes locked on Pheir's no matter how her body arches. No matter how her wings spread, feathers shivering as Caius dips his hand between her legs again. When he finds her clit, her hips settle into rhythm with his.

Maybe Aren stopped them from making a mistake, but it serves to remind Caius of his grievances with Aren. The words replay through Caius's mind as he watches Aren over Pheir's shoulder. *You don't care. You have it so fucking together. Do you feel anything at all?* Aren would never have gotten so caught up that he nearly slipped like Caius did. Aren would never move on impulse. Aren would never give himself over to desire.

It's like Pheir can sense the tension, body rolling in time with Caius, like they have a score to settle. "Scared to touch me, kitty?" she mocks.

Aren doesn't so much as move a whisker, as if shifting a centimeter will make him lose the handle he has on his control. "That's not what it is." His hands flex at his sides. All the restraint in his body can't hide his cock hard against his stomach, reddened and slick with desire. Caius's tongue drags over his lips, teasing the skin of Pheir's neck.

That magnetic pull between them strains to unite, Pheir and Caius on one side with Lev and Aren on the other. Lev's breath comes shallow, eyes clinging to Caius and Pheir as he fucks slowly into her. It's their very nature — the chaos of Pheir and Caius swirls wider to pull Aren and Lev in. Caius traces teeth against Pheir's ear to make Aren suck in a breath.

With Caius behind her, the apple of Pheir's cheek bobs as she smiles. "Prove it."

THIRTY-FIVE

Aren

Aren *is* scared. Scared of how easily this night could've spiraled. Scared that they nearly lost themselves to carnal desire. Scared that this woman who's meant to be an enemy reads him with a glance.

Scared that he wants all of it.

It was divine fortitude that pulled him away when their blood started pumping, scents flowing as instincts took over. There was a nagging feeling at the base of his skull, but he could barely hold back as he watched the three of them together. They weren't Lev, Pheir, and Caius. They weren't separate entities with walls and uncertainties. Their colors blurred until Aren couldn't distinguish their scents, until they became a whirling refrain as loud as his pulse.

Mine.

He almost lost his mind watching them together, mouths and tongues and teeth yearning to mark each other. As if the forest itself willed it to happen, wind whistling and water churning and crickets chirping until he could feel desire alive in his bones.

One slip, and the wedding could've become real, consummated by blood sharing so soon after the vows. Aren knew they were dangerously close when Caius's fangs scraped Pheir's throat, closer still when Lev dragged her mouth against Pheir's shoulder.

Aren let it get too far. He knew he should stop it…

But he didn't *want* to.

Impossibly, the moment felt *right*, so natural it was blasphemous to break. No matter how Aren held himself back, he felt the pull to join them, to mark each of them as his own, to satisfy his need.

He doesn't know how he stopped them. His chest was heaving, fist circling his cock as a growl built in his chest. His claws dug into the earth to keep him from closing the gap, body heating to a fever pitch when their fangs started to sink in.

Now, he stands across the clearing, trying to think through his mind flooded with want. Lev looks shocked, panting as she leans back on her palms like she's broken out of a spell. There's worry in her eyes. They've never experienced anything like that. They've never let their hearts get carried away someplace that their heads couldn't follow, a call so strong that both of them almost gave in.

Caius and Pheir are undisturbed. Their eyes glow under the moon, reflecting light as they watch Aren. If he didn't know better, it would seem like they're conspiring, Pheir's hips stirring as Caius guides her.

There's ten feet of space between the two of them and Aren, but it does nothing to stop their arousal from slamming into him. Aren fights to keep still, but the seductive spark in Pheir's eyes threatens to drag him under.

Scared to touch me?

How does she see to the heart of him? Pheir, who weeks ago was a mindless drone. Pheir, who would as soon maul him as fuck him. With Caius behind her, it's like they share the same lens; they know Aren's always watching, always at a distance, always holding back.

Her words are a challenge: *Prove it.* Despite the control in Aren's expression, a wild creature inside him snarls to escape. If he lets it loose, he wouldn't think when he got his claws into her. He would drag her across the ground, fuck her raw and dig his teeth into her skin. He'd make every inch of her smell like him again and again, only stopping for Lev and Caius to claim her, too.

A smile curls Pheir's lips, like she can feel how badly he wants it. Like she's intent to draw him out and pry his hands off of control. Like she wants him to give into the pulsing desire as badly as he does.

He has to restrain himself. He *has* to.

"We can't mark her like that..." Aren's voice rumbles in his chest, rewarded by the shiver of Pheir's feathers. "But there are other ways."

Laughter slips between Pheir's lips, skin slick with sweat and desire. "Come on, then, kitty cat. Show me."

Aren's heart thunders, jaw set in a tight line. He should stop. He should stay back. He should keep himself from the edge of this slippery slope before he ends up right at the bottom with them. When Aren looks at Lev, her pupils are wide, honed on him with a desire that makes his toes curl. She nods, like she needs this just as badly. She needs to watch Aren cross that line.

"Mark my wife, beta."

Lev's voice sends a shudder through him, lifting his fur on end. It's half a command, teasing his ear like a reassuring whisper that he yearns to fulfill. She knows what her Alpha power does to him. It's so rare that she uses it. When she does, he can feel her on an entirely different level. Her voice is like a tongue tracing up his spine, directing him exactly where she wants him. He could resist — or he could sink fully into desire and give them all what they crave.

There's no warning before he springs, ripping Pheir from Caius's arms as Aren tackles her to the dirt. Caius snarls at the loss, prowling behind Aren as Aren pins Pheir's bound wrists above her head.

Her lips part to torment him, but her words are lost on a gasp when Aren sinks to the hilt inside her. It's filthy how wet she is, used and wanton from Caius and Lev. Aren rolls deeper as he catches every needy shift in Pheir's face.

A mewl escapes her as she stretches over the spines of his cock, her thighs locked against his hips. "You're still scared," she gasps.

His claws dig into the dirt around her wrists. Slowly, he drags out of her, fucking shallowly so his spines drag against her entrance. She bucks at the stinging pleasure. He stirs the swell of his cock against her G spot, his rough tongue flicking against her ear. "Does that feel scared to you?"

Above Pheir, Lev and Caius pin her bound hands. Not that Aren needs the help; Pheir's helpless beneath him, no matter how she needs to believe otherwise. Yet when Aren rolls into her again, her gasp gets lost in a breathy laugh. Her head tips back, eyes dreamy as the tension eases from her, like the orgasms have wrestled away some of her hatred. When she looks up at Aren, his rhythm falters as he strokes deep inside her. He's never seen her face so open, lips parting blissfully as her back arches.

Too often, she's been mindless with hate, but now, she's delirious with pleasure. Her heels dig into his ass to bring him closer. Beneath her sounds, her voice tunnels to the very heart of him. "You're still holding back. I feel it every time you fuck me." A gasp slips out of her, so needy that Aren has to fight not to snap his hips harder. "Like that night after the battle, when you wouldn't let yourself come with me."

When Aren tries to drag out slowly, Pheir squeezes her knees, accentuating the tension in his thighs. He tries to shake it, but every thrust follows the same pattern until the clench of Pheir's legs predicts what Aren will do. No matter how he tries to change the pace, Pheir knows what motions he'll make. It sears through him, lewd and lascivious.

"Like when you fought me," she teases, rolling her hips to disturb his rhythm. "Pulling your punches. Never giving into it. Trying to keep from losing yourself."

With her legs around his back, she does her best to hold him in place, working her hips to meet his. Every swirl is unpredictable, pace speeding and slowing as she chases her desire, switching the angle until his cockhead's dragging against her G spot. Her clit grinds against his pelvis. It makes stars burst behind his eyes, head hanging forward as his chest heaves.

Beneath him, she watches like she's the predator and he's the prey, her voice dragging like a white-hot dagger in his gut. "All that time on the battlefield, and you think I don't know you?"

He doesn't know why that sends him over. His release was a dull roar in the back of his mind, but now, it rages like a sudden storm. It would feel *so good* to lock their hips together, to spend himself inside her, to feel her clench around him when she comes —

But that's not what this is about. He can't lose himself.

Mark her.

Aren jerks back, spines tugging at Pheir's entrance. Her pussy tightens around him to keep him close, a whine building in her throat when he pulls out of her grasp. His orgasm stripes white across her cunt. Pheir makes a strangled sound, hips rocking against nothing as she tries to clamp her legs together.

Aren doesn't allow it, forcing her knees apart with his hand as his cum drips down the magenta lips of her pussy. *Fuck.* His eyes snap shut, dick twitching in his hand. He'll get hard again looking at his mark slipping down the seam of her ass. Every inch of her is wet with sweat, dirt clinging to her chest and hips. Aren's seed joins the mess between her thighs in a heady mix of the four of them.

It hits Caius too, ripping a snarl out of his chest. "God*fucking*dammit." He jerks Pheir toward him, burying his mouth between her legs with desperate need.

The mix of them is potent and irresistible. Pheir digs fingers into Caius's hair, but he eats like a man starved until her eyes roll back. Her voice is high and tight, a whine that barely gets past the words as she tugs Caius's fur. "Fucking — *breed me.*"

Caius grips her hips in his hands, watching her face as he covers her cunt with his pierced tongue. In seconds, he's on his back, dragging Pheir on top to ride him. "Such a fucking slut for us, aren't you?" he growls. Her cunt grinds against his hard length, desperate to sink over him. He hisses as he smears his cockhead along the outside of her cunt. "You smell like a Timber bitch. I'm gonna stuff you so fucking full, you'll never get us out."

It ricochets through Aren, dick already hardening again as he bites back a moan. Pheir can't even manage that, shuddering where she straddles Caius as she grabs his face and presses it down against the dirt. "Don't fucking *look* at me." She works her hips over his cock with renewed force.

A feral sound escapes Caius. He doesn't fight her, guiding her hips in both his hands until the head of his cock starts to disappear inside her. It's torturous watching her stretch over him before she's pulled off again, never taking him fully. Aren's cum is sticky between Pheir's legs, smearing across Caius's head as their bodies rock together. When Caius sinks into Pheir's slick ass instead, they both moan, her hands slipping where they hold his face.

"Forgot how fucking *wet* you are. *Everywhere.*" Caius braces his feet on the ground to drive up into her.

A strangled sound comes from beside Aren. Lev's eyes are wide and glassy, thighs clenched at the sight of Caius and Pheir together. They have no trouble giving into their desires without restraint. That's all they know. Aren can't fathom it. Lev's body strains to be near them, to take what's hers, showing the same fears Aren has.

What if they slip again? What if this is a mistake? What if they're not thinking clearly?

Aren grabs the back of Lev's neck to bring her face to his. She won't falter again. He knows that the same way he knows her, the same way he trusts her more than himself. When she kisses him, he nearly forgets the rules he made, caught up at how desperately she clings to him. It's like the night at the truck, so out of her mind with want that a barrier nearly broke between the three of them. Aren wants more. He wants to see Lev give herself to pleasure, wants to watch her let go and know someone's there to catch her. Her hands tangle in his fur, their tongues twisting together around the taste of Pheir.

A curse cuts through the air. When Lev and Aren pull apart, Pheir's watching them, bracing her hands on Caius's stomach to grind in a tight rhythm. Even chained, she could gut him — but she doesn't, chasing her desire to the sight of Lev and Aren. Caius arches beneath her, trying to make this last as long as he can.

"Get on my fucking face, Lev," he demands. Nothing else will satisfy him. She doesn't make him wait, settling her thighs on either side of his head as she faces Pheir. When Caius lifts his mouth to Lev, her body jerks, voice pitching in a groan as she scrambles to hold on. Caius is relentless, gripping one of her hips as he buries his mouth against her. Her fingers tangle in the fur of his chest, fingers overlapping with Pheir as they ride him.

All Aren can smell is the four of them, scents mingling until they become one. Until he could forget Pheir isn't one of them. Until he could believe this was real.

"Aren...you owe me," Pheir breathes. It takes a second for him to remember what he'd taunted her with the first night in the forest, dragging his dick across her muzzle without letting her taste him.

It's tempting to give into the thought of those vicious lips curving around him. Getting that close to her teeth is walking a razor's edge. Aren fists over himself, cock hard as he steps closer.

Once he's within reach, he teases toward her mouth to watch her lips part for him.

He doesn't quite touch her. Pheir groans, taking her frustration out on Caius as she fucks him harder. He growls against Lev's cunt, making her gasp and tip forward. It's intoxicating to see the reaction, desire flowing through all of them like waves crashing against each other. Aren wants to see it again. Holding Pheir's fiery gaze, he lets a string of spit drip from his mouth onto his cock before he instructs, "Lick it off."

Her cheeks darken with humiliation. Teeth bared, she lunges toward him, but he snags the back of her hair in one hand. When he tightens his fist, her eyes are forced up toward him.

"Your tongue," he commands her. "Let me see it."

Her lips pull back over her teeth, body fueled by rage…until finally, she lays out the flat of her pink tongue. It's pristine and untouched, one of the only parts of her that isn't covered in them. He'll take care of that. Stepping closer, Aren smears his head back and forth, pre-cum glistening as it strings across her tongue. If he didn't have a grip on her hair, he has no doubt she'd snap at him. Like this, she's forced to stay still.

Aren taps his cockhead against her lips. "Now kiss it."

"Fuck y-" Pheir squeals as Lev gets fingers on her clit. Pheir tries to snap her legs together, but Caius won't let her, driving up into her until she screams. It leaves her breathless and off-balance, clinging to Aren's thigh as his cock drags across her cheek like the night after the battle. Pheir remembers it, too, holding Aren's gaze as she lets the tip of her tongue slip out to taste him.

"You want to fuck me?" Aren asks as Pheir bounces on Caius's cock. "You want him in your ass, and me in your mouth? What about your lonely little cunt — or did we fuck it raw?"

At the words, Pheir's eyes slip shut, teeth grit to keep from moaning. Lev teases her clit, working two fingers inside until Pheir's head lolls in Aren's hand. She tries to hide the way her hips rock to take Lev and Caius at once, but Lev doesn't miss it.

"Mm, she can take more, can't you, birdy?" Lev smirks. Pheir told her to be mean, and Lev is, mouth dragging hot against Pheir's jaw. "Little pain slut can always take more. If she wants us to fuck every hole she has, she'll do what Aren says." As Lev grinds against Caius's mouth, she strokes her fingers inside of Pheir and enunciates each word with a sharp tap to her clit. "Kiss...his...cock."

Squirming, Pheir's eyes flash open with furious need. Aren keeps stroking over himself, toying with his spines until Pheir can't resist any longer. Bitterly, she leans forward, puckering her lips. With every inch she leans closer, Aren stops her with the hand in her hair until he finally lets her swollen mouth press against his cock.

"So you can follow orders." He smiles smugly. It doesn't last for long — not when Pheir parts her lips but doesn't take him inside, dragging her mouth to the bottom of his shaft. She doesn't care about the mess, sloppy and slick as she licks him with no hands. Her mouth buries at his base to tease her tongue against his sack until she pulls back with a breathless pop.

Her jaw is caked with spit and remnants of Aren's desire. His dick twitches against her cheek, struck with a primal urge to lick her face, to make her filthier, to coat his tongue with her taste. Pheir knows it. *Gods*, she knows it, because she holds his gaze when she spits on his dick and lets it drip onto her bare breasts.

Her hips set a frantic pace, riding Caius and Lev like she can't get enough. The four of them are racing to the peak, clawing and climbing and shoving each other towards the cliff's edge. Caius fucks sharply into Pheir, knocking her forward until her mouth hovers next to Lev's.

The one place their mouths haven't been.

Pheir grips the fur of Lev's chest like she wants to push her away. "I hate you," Pheir whispers, words buzzing against Aren's cock between them.

It sounds like a confession. It sounds like a plea.

Lev drags her tongue against Aren's dick, keeping her eyes on Pheir. It makes Pheir curse and Aren groan. Slowly, Lev licks Pheir's spit from his cock before Lev speaks against it. "If you hate me, then don't come."

Pheir's head tilts back. Caius's claws dig into her hips as Lev toys with one of Pheir's hardened nipples, fucking her with her other hand in a frantic rhythm that Pheir tries to fight. She tries to focus on anything else, taking Aren deep into her throat so none of them can hear her scream.

It's brutal. It's inevitable. All of them feed off each other like every battle before this. They know when to push and pull and drag each other to the edge of what their bodies can handle.

Pleasure eclipses everything, ripping through Pheir faster than she can take. She shrieks when Aren pulls her off his cock. "Fuck you, fuck you, *fuck you —*"

She tries to muffle her sounds, but he keeps a grip on her hair as she buries her face in the juncture of his thigh. Her moan vibrates up his length. He's not gonna last. Teeth gritting, he guides her willing mouth back around his head as his release tears through him. A hungry fire lights in Pheir's eyes, cheeks hollowing to swallow every drop. He can't bear to look at her, her perfect mouth wrapped around him as she drains him with a molten look in her eye.

It's only a matter of time before the others follow. Lev groans at the feel of Pheir pulsing around her fingers mixed with the swirl of Caius's tongue. Once Lev grinds down against his face, it sends him over the edge as he holds Pheir tight against him to fill her with his release.

They're a mess of panting bodies atop each other. Pheir's dress and sleeping bag are shredded. The ground is covered in gouge marks, all their fur matted and sticky. Aren can't imagine what the destruction would be like if they'd bitten her.

Pheir is the biggest mess of all. Her breathing is ragged, body slumped as the flush fades from her skin. For a moment, she looks sated, eyelids heavy as her head rests on Lev's shoulder. Then Pheir's fingers clench, eyes flying open as she pushes up to wobbly legs.

"Where are you going?" Caius grumbles from under Lev's thighs.

Aren extends a hand, but Pheir rejects it as cum drips down the inside of her legs. "I need to clean this shit off," she offers hoarsely.

"You can barely walk." Aren follows as she steadies herself on a tree. "You remember the terms. We take care of you."

A blush spreads over the back of Pheir's shoulders as she glares back at him. "I *will*. Can I piss in peace first, at least?"

Aren says nothing more, watching as Pheir makes her way toward the shoreline. Caius licks a line up Lev's cunt before he calls after Pheir. "I told you; you're never gonna get us out."

THIRTY-SIX

Pheir

As soon as Pheir finds the shoreline, she falls to her knees, water splashing around her. It's freezing cold. She hardly feels it, shaky from satisfaction and covered in the stench of *them*. Even to her near-human nose, Pheir can smell the sweat and spit and cum. Caius was right; anyone she comes across will know exactly what they've been up to.

It's different from the night after the battle. Remembering that now makes her stomach clench with heat she's been denying. Back then, Caius and Aren marked her like the beasts they are. Pheir wanted nothing more than to dig the scent out. That was revenge, but this time...

Fucking them wasn't an excuse. It was something she needed. She begged and pleaded for it, desperate to be close to someone. Already, the pieces of herself that felt like they were tearing are weaving back together. Touching the three of them has done something to her, filled a hole she doesn't understand. It must be something with the wedding, the new pack bonds taking hold. She told them what she needed, and they gave it to her, because she's part of their pack now.

Her body tingles. Already, the sweat has started to dry on her body, settling back into a consistent temperature, as if the Timbers making her theirs was the antidote to her ailment all along.

When they fucked her, it wasn't to get under her skin. It happened when their bodies slotted together, mouths smearing, fur rubbing against her throat, covering her in their scent and them in hers.

She tries to find a reason for how desperately she wanted them. She was delirious, teething an insatiable need to get close to *something*, but they didn't fuck like it was to sate an urge. They fucked like they were claiming her. Like the ceremony didn't make her theirs half as much as giving her what she needed did.

Her brows knit on her murky reflection in the lake. It should disgust her. It *should*, but when she tries to cling to that emotion, her skull feels like it's being ripped in half. Hate slips through her fingers as easily as water, mingling with desire until she's not sure what she's reaching for.

There is one certainty she can cling to. There's no mistaking the solid glass in her hand. Fingers uncurling, she stares at the vial of ashes in her palm next to the *V* branded on her wrist.

She hesitates, waiting for the vial to vanish or scream or shatter, but it doesn't move. Pheir's not sure why she expected more. Days ago, Vesta's power still felt alive enough to do the impossible, but now, Pheir isn't sure. Beneath the vial, water laps gently at her legs, distorting the ashes until a muted rainbow flashes through its depths.

I knew you'd save me.

Back with the others, Pheir's body had moved on its own, a trained soldier completing a mission. When Lev leaned close, Pheir barely registered the necklace in her hand, fingers clamped tight until she was at the shore.

The ashes are what Pheir wanted — so she tells herself. They're the real reason she begged the Timbers to fuck her, to get close to her and let their guard down. The ashes are a reward for all her patience and suffering.

At least...the ashes *should* be the reason. When Pheir reaches for triumph, she finds confusion, mind fogging around the razor-sharp mission she's spent weeks preparing for. Because when Pheir pleaded with the Timbers to fuck her, she wasn't thinking of the ashes. She was thinking about her aching *need*. Once they touched her, she remembered nothing but desire screaming through her. Nothing but Caius's claws in her hips, Aren's gaze pouring into her, Lev's breath on her lips.

Pheir's head shakes, pounding with contradictions. She needs to escape, to take Vesta's ashes and find the others — so why does her body feel stuck to the ground?

In Pheir's memories, Vesta's smile hangs like a prize Pheir was desperate to win, but the image is distorted. Vesta had once beamed golden and warm. Now, it's scorching. The clever row of her teeth has sharpened to points. The butterflies she caused now swirl into a swarm until Pheir's stomach turns over. Nausea roils through her, mixed with a sickly swell of pride.

Air is crushed from her lungs. Pheir's on her back before she can think, water surging around her. She claws the attacker, body weak and gasping for air when Caius jerks her to the surface.

His eyes land on her clenched fist. His face sinks, but he hides it behind anger. "She has them!" he calls over his shoulder, snagging the vial of ashes from the choppy water.

"Get the fuck off me!" Her dull claws dig into his arms. He doesn't flinch, pinning her back to the shore.

"This was your plan?" He grips her wrists above her head, pinning her ankles with his knees. His voice cuts like a jagged knife. "Fuck us so you could get the ashes? Is that what that was?"

Her chest heaves. She writhes to be free, shutting her eyes against the words. Aren pulls Caius off, but Pheir doesn't stand, cold water dripping down her body. If she swings her talons out far enough, she could wound Caius. From the hardened look on his face, she already has.

Pheir fights the sinking feeling in her stomach. Lev appears beside them, lifting the vial from Caius's grip. "I wasn't careful," she says tightly. She won't look at Pheir. She won't get any closer. "We should have expected it."

Caius shrugs out of Aren's grip, ready to spring at Pheir again. "What are you *doing*?!" he shouts. His clenched fists are the only thing keeping him back, frustration straining through his voice when he flings out his hand. "Don't you know who you're trying to bring back? What you're doing for someone who doesn't give a shit about you?"

His words lance through Pheir sharper than claws or teeth. Those, she can take; she's suffered them countless times before, but she's never seen betrayal on Caius's face. Why does it hurt? Why does it sting as badly as Lev's pain and Aren's disappointment?

What's happening to her? Why does she feel like...

It's frightening. It's terrifying feeling so much when all she's used to is rage. Pushing to her knees, Pheir's body pulses with instinct to react, to be as cruel as Vesta liked her to be.

Hit them. Make it hurt. Doesn't matter if it's true.

"Did you think I'd actually —"

"*Capheira*." Aren's warning shoots down her spine, dunking her back in the icy water. It sobers her, the red around her vision fading as Lev turns away, keeping Pheir from seeing her face.

"Can you give me a minute?" she asks the men. If Pheir didn't know better, she'd say there was a crack in Lev's voice. "Before you bring her back?"

Aren and Caius nod, and Lev moves back up the bank, receding into the forest. Silence spreads along the shore, like smoke clearing after an explosion. The full force of the cold hits Pheir as water drips off her feathers. She wants to wrap her arms around her knees, to curl in on herself, but that would be weak. She can't take anything worse than the feeling she has now.

Caius tremors with rage, pacing through the sand. Aren is unblinking.

"What?" she snaps and prays her voice doesn't break.

"I know this is confusing, but I need you to hear this." His voice is so quiet that Pheir wants to cry. She clenches her fists to keep from making a sound. "Vesta did not protect you."

Pheir's throat is dry. She tries to summon a laugh, but it sounds more like a sob. It cuts off in her throat.

"'*I don't say no.*'" Aren repeats Pheir's words back to her, the ones that had once brought her so much satisfaction. Now, they make her face burn with a shame she doesn't understand.

She hates how her voice croaks. "*What?*"

Aren crouches before her. "Is it that you *wouldn't* say no, or that you couldn't?"

"I didn't want to." Pheir means to say it with conviction, but it rings hollow as she stares up at him. Panic slips into her pulse, like there's something coming that she doesn't want to hear. "I did what I wanted. What *Vesta* wanted. It was the same thing."

It should feel good to say it. That was what Pheir was most proud of, that her desires always aligned with Vesta's, that they were so in sync that Pheir knew what Vesta was thinking before she spoke. Now, the words leave Pheir's tongue heavy, pain radiating through her head. It's deeper than where Caius tackled her, a spike driven down her spinal cord like a string pulled through a puppet.

"She was controlling you, Pheir."

Aren's voice swings like a hammer into her skull. She shuts her eyes, head jerking to make the pounding stop. "*No.* We cared about each other. I protected her because I *wanted* to." It's an explanation. It has to be a way to stop Aren from looking at her like a wounded bird fallen from its nest. He nods as if he's heard something she hasn't said. Pheir's ears ring.

"And who protected you?" Aren asks.

Pheir is queasy, gripping the sand between her thighs, taking deep gulps of air to stop the ground from spinning. The voice in her head claws to escape her mouth.

"You act like Vesta was wrong, but Lev is no better. You do the same things for her."

Pheir has to be right. It *has* to be true, because she can't live in a world where it isn't, where the most important pieces of her life didn't happen the way she remembers. She grits her teeth. Hating Lev is her connection to Vesta. It was the easiest way for Pheir to make Vesta love her. She grapples for it now.

"It was Lev who betrayed Vesta, Lev who started the battle —"

"She started the battle because Vesta was going to kill you."

It comes so suddenly, Pheir swears she misheard it, pressing hands to her ears to quell the ringing. The chains around her wrist smack her face, more painful in the cold. Aren doesn't look away. It sinks in like a bomb as he waits to collect the pieces.

Caius stops his pacing, stunned into silence right along with Pheir. Her head gives a halted jerk, goosebumps pricking along her skin. "That's not true. That's not *true*."

"Vesta stood behind you so you wouldn't see it." When Aren recites it, Pheir remembers that day. How glorious she felt, how perfect standing in front of Vesta like it was her place. Like Pheir would give anything to keep her safe. "Lev saw Vesta open her mouth. She saw the fire starting. She saw it glowing off the back of your head."

"You're *lying*!" Pheir screeches. Aren doesn't say it again. That's how Pheir knows he believes it. Because his lips press into a pitying line. Because when he extends his hand to pull her out of the water, she wants to cry like she never has before.

She smacks his hand away. He steps back to take a seat on a fallen log, moonlight reflecting off his eyes. Caius is still for a long moment before he walks down the beach and disappears around a bend of trees. The forest is dark with Lev inside it, crowded with ambient noise that makes Pheir feel more alone.

She stays in the water until her legs are numb."

THIRTY-SEVEN

Lev

2 hours before Vesta's death

Where there's smoke, there's fire.

The proverb has served Lev well over the years, but it doesn't cover everything. What if you *know* there's fire, but there's no smoke? What if the air is clear, but you'll be choking on ash in seconds?

As the sun sets, Lev shields her eyes, trying to make out the position of the Vestal camp in the distance. They're hidden somewhere in the forest across the massive clearing. The open field is the last thing between the Vestals and the group of Conclave packs behind Lev.

The Conclave established their position hours ago, sending representatives to negotiate a ceasefire with the Vestals. An armistice could stop the violence before it starts. Lev tried to share her insight with the Boreas, but the Head Regent brushed her aside as he left. An hour passed. Then two. Then three. The Conclave packs grew weary as the day dragged on, yet the anticipation keeps everyone alert, bodies tense as they mill about and speak in quiet groups.

Three figures appear across the clearing, flying out of the trees toward the Conclave. A hush falls over the group as Boreas and two other Regents return. A crowd forms as soon as they land. Lev pushes to the front, heart thudding in her chest. This could be it, an end to the battle that's been mounting. Lev is hopeful. Naively, foolishly hopeful...

Boreas takes that hope and crushes it.

He lifts his beak to look over the gathered packs, gleaming in the hour's golden glow. "We have given the Vestals time to make a peaceful surrender. They've rejected that offer."

Murmurs spread through the creatures as Lev's heart sinks. Breath escapes her in one short burst. "What did you offer?" She can't help herself, can't keep quiet when this means war.

Boreas's eyes narrow in displeasure. "We offered to accept their surrender in exchange for their lives."

"Who did you negotiate with?" Lev's mind whirls with conditions, with the delicate balance any interaction with Vesta requires. She tried to tell him before. "If Vesta —"

"They rejected the chance for peace." Boreas's tone brooks no arguments, eyes flaring as he stares Lev down. "They're itching for a fight. This is more than frustration; this is a thirst for violence that won't be satisfied any other way." He turns back to the waiting crowd. "Alphas, prepare your packs to approach. We move in half an hour."

With that, the crowd buzzes with activity, dispersing into separate clans to relay the plans. Lev lingers where she stands, peering through the trees to search for any sign of smoke, desperate for an indication that a fuse has been ignited...

The distance is eerily still. There isn't a cloud in the sky.

Boreas stops as he passes. "And make sure your beta knows his place. We can't have any more costly mistakes."

When Lev turns to respond, the griffin folds into the crowd. A few feet away, Aren waits, watching her closely.

It makes her heart ache. Aren isn't ruffled by Boreas's words, but Lev hates the way people whisper about him. Behind her, she can hear them now. Anxiety spikes through her, desperate to do *something*. She's prepared to shout at the others, but Aren speaks her name.

"Lev."

It's a reminder to focus. They're about to enter battle. They have bigger problems waiting for them, and Aren knows Lev. He understands Lev's fear. His nose twitches. Lev can only imagine the complex emotions wafting off of her.

"Can you do this?" he asks quietly.

Her teeth dig into her lip. The question isn't cruel or doubtful, but there is no other option. It doesn't matter if Lev can face Vesta again — she *has* to.

When Lev nods, Aren matches her, but he keeps his eyes on her as she passes. When it's just the two of them, she can't stop the panic hitching into her voice. "If the Regents had listened when we warned them about Vesta, we could have stopped this *years* ago. We could have prevented everything that's about to happen: the fighting, the bloodshed —"

"I know." Aren squeezes her arm. "But the Regents didn't."

He's right. There's nothing more to say about it. No way to turn back the clock, and gods know Lev has wished she could more than once. With Aren beside her, she moves toward one edge of the tree line where the rest of the Timbers wait. There are fifteen or so of them here — the pack's strongest fighters. A loud silence falls over the group as they tie on leather armor, sharpening claws and beaks and antlers as Lev and Aren approach.

The Timbers stand when they see her. She swallows, stabilizing her voice above the chaos behind her. "Prepare for battle. Take the time to get your head in the right space. We leave in thirty minutes."

The Timbers nod, a tense calm settling over them amongst the frenetic energy of the other packs. Near the back of the group, armor sits at Caius's feet as he rolls his neck. His gaze is far off, narrowed and honed on the distance, but he isn't looking for the Vestals. Lev isn't sure what he's looking at, but she moves toward him with Aren behind her.

She scoops up his leather breastplate. "No skipping the armor," she reminds him. Caius huffs a laugh, but he allows her to lift on her toes to drape it over his head. He stares down at her with a depth that he rarely exposes, the scars on his body highlighted by the lack of other covering.

"I can take hits without it."

"I don't care." There's no snap in Lev's words, only tense protection. Caius warms to it, the corner of his lips lifting as Lev laces his armor like it might be the last time.

She forces the thought out, fingers lingering against his fur. It won't be the last time. Caius will not die on the battlefield. None of them will —

As if he can read her thoughts, his hand closes around her wrist. "I've faced worse than this."

A wet laugh escapes her. She's not sure if it's because she doesn't know what else Caius has seen, or because he doesn't understand what Vesta is capable of. "Act like you haven't." Lev knots the final string, staring up at him with intention. "Don't let your guard down for a second."

Caius doesn't drop her gaze. She hesitates as she pulls away. She has to remind him. She has to say it, lest the universe laugh at her later.

"You're playing defense. Don't forget that. Don't get pulled into a fight for the sake of it." Her hand thuds against his chest. "Don't let Pheir get a rise out of you and draw you off course."

He scoffs, but Lev clenches her fingers around the straps of his armor.

"And stay out of Vesta's path. *Please.*"

His mouth sets into a firm line. "Not if her path leads to you."

Lev tightens her fingers, pulling him a fraction closer. "I'm serious, Caius. She has fire and ranged attacks. Leave her to the creatures who are equipped for that."

His mouth twitches. He doesn't speak. He doesn't need to. Lev knows what that look means. *No promises.*

For now, that'll have to be good enough.

With a final squeeze, she steps back. Caius's gaze shifts to Aren now draped in his own armor. Aren extends his hand, and Caius takes it, their gazes locked when they squeeze each other's forearms. It's as if they're linking together, making their bodies aware of each other, tuning their weapons to each other's frequencies.

Something ignites between the men at the first hint of danger, like an orchestra Lev can't hear. It's bigger than whatever confusion they may feel when it's the three of them alone. Right now, they're united in a common goal, giving themselves over to the trust they need to keep each other alive.

Lev doesn't let herself get hung up on what that means. Why the heat of battle is the time they don't struggle to find common ground. As the other packs settle into formation, Lev gathers the attention of the Timbers and clears her throat to be heard.

"We've trained for this. We studied the Vestal's strategy. We are as prepared for this fight as we could be." Her eyes land pointedly on Darby, the deer who tries to hide the quiver in his antlers. Lev softens her voice a fraction. "Let your body do what it remembers, and don't neglect your mind. Fight smart." She taps her temple. "Remember how to read your opponents."

Caius and Aren have taught all of them well. Lev glances at Oberon the bear, who nods soberly. He claps a reassuring hand on Darby's shoulder. Finally, the deer exhales, meeting Oberon's look with a grave nod as Lev continues.

"Do what it takes to protect yourselves and your pack. Trust yourselves, and trust each other. Remember what we're fighting for. For ourselves, for our families, for our community. To have a home that's safe for all of us." A wave of nods spread throughout the group. With a slow breath, Lev lifts her chin and her voice. "Timbers! Into formation."

The group moves fluidly behind her as she settles on the front line, eyes forward as all of the Conclave begins to move. The Timbers keep pace with each other, senses honed on their perimeter, adjusting the space between them like a single moving beast. They're one with each other and the other Conclave packs as they move onto the battlefield, beginning a steady march across the clearing.

Nerves bite at Lev's heels. She keeps her eyes focused ahead, pushing down the fear and uncertainty nipping at her. This is the end. Lev knows it the way she knows most unfathomable things. There's a feeling deep in her bones. For all the years she's spent trying to forget Vesta, it's all come down to this.

Vesta will never surrender. She'll never be taken alive. Either this is the end for Vesta...or this is the end for Lev.

Despite everything, it makes her throat tight to imagine the scale tipping either way.

As the Conclave marches out of the forest, a rainbow light grows amidst the falling darkness. Lev's heart jumps into her throat. Beside her, Aren's gaze flicks in her direction. From the opposite tree line, Vestals spill out, chaotic and frantic with energy. Shouts and jeers rise from the group as they swarm around each other.

Creatures continue to erupt from the forest. The Conclave still outnumbers them, but the Vestals have recruited more people in the last few months. Lev scans the group, a knot forming in her throat. She recognizes many of them — friends of distant packs, people she's worked beside — but there's something different about them. A wild rage in their eyes makes them salivate with hatred. Where the Conclave is stoic and serious, the Vestals are frothing at the mouth to lunge, rabid animals with glassy eyes and no thoughts but retribution.

Front and center stands Vesta, feathers fluttering like candles flickering in the wind. She looks pleased. Ecstatic. Around her are the three people she's kept close for years: Rhaiden, Thalea, and Pheir, standing in front of Vesta's body like a shield.

The Conclave comes to a halt. The Vestals are barely hanging onto control, scattering in uneven numbers before the Conclave. There's no rhyme or reason, instinct thudding through all of them like a pulse Lev can feel rising up from the ground.

At the head of the Conclave, Boreas raises his voice. "This is your last warning. Surrender now, and we'll spare your lives."

Pheir screeches, fists clenching as she fights to surge ahead — but Vesta keeps a hand between Pheir's wings, holding her in place. Vesta doesn't bother responding to Boreas. She doesn't glance in his direction. Instead, she smiles at Lev.

It makes Lev's knees weak. She forces them to lock as Vesta lowers her mouth to Pheir's ear. There's no telling what she says. Lev can't make out the movement of her lips, but Pheir nods, her body thrumming with promise.

Vesta pulls back to ensure Lev's looking. Then Vesta forms a circle with her mouth. Light begins to glow in her throat, mouth lowering to the back of Pheir's head. Phoenix fire flickers over Vesta's tongue, preparing a decimating blast that lights Pheir's hair —

"*No!*"

It happens before Lev can stop it, her hand extended toward Pheir. Vesta's mouth snaps back into a smile, locking the fire behind her teeth. Lev pants, throat ragged from the scream when she turns to look beside her.

There's no one there. It's only open field.

Behind her, Aren's rooted to his spot. His eyes search her for an answer. Caius's knees are bent, poised to follow, but he stills at Aren's hand against his chest. Every eye is on Lev where she stands, ten feet past the line of battle. Boreas gapes, shocked and enraged as the rest of the Conclave begins to move.

Lev took the first step. She started the battle, as Vesta wanted.

The clearing erupts into chaos. Vestals scream at the shoddy victory as the Conclave streaks across the field. Lev tries to force her thoughts back in order, mind racing as she takes off sprinting toward the Vestals.

Vesta was going to kill Pheir, her most loyal soldier, before the battle began. Why?

The answer is simple: she wasn't. Vesta knew Lev would stop her. Because if anyone remembers what Vesta does to the people closest to her, it's Lev.

Bodies clash at the front lines, Vestals and Conclave meeting in a flurry of claws and fur and feathers. Fire bursts amidst twisting vines and winged creatures taking to the sky. In the center of it all, rainbow flames drift effortlessly from Vesta's mouth as she lifts into the air.

Then she finds Lev again.

Lev tries to move, to draw Vesta away from the crowd, but it's no use. Vesta is on her in seconds, blasting a stream of fire that sets the ground aflame steps behind Lev.

Lev keeps her eyes ahead, running with all her might. A pair of talons snatch into her arm. She bites back a scream, gripping Vesta's leg to keep her body intact. The added weight drags Vesta to the ground, sending them both tumbling across the grass. Pain radiates from Lev's shoulder. She forces herself to her feet, ignoring the blood across her chest.

Vesta watches it drip, tongue slipping against her lips. "Couldn't help yourself, huh, bunny?" Her voice rises above the chaos, eyes wilder than when Lev saw her months ago. Vesta's chest heaves, teeth sharp as laughter bubbles out of her. "Couldn't stop your bleeding heart." Vesta's talons glint in the firelight coiling from her mouth. "I'm gonna help you drain it!"

It would be easier to light Lev on fire, to burn her alive, to make her suffer, to cut this fraying cord between them — but Vesta won't. She wants to do it by her own hand.

Behind Vesta, the Conclave wars with the rabid Vestals. Their numbers are small, but the Vestals fight with fervor like a beast possessed. Lev is too far to shout for help. Vesta has chased her back, putting herself between Lev and her pack. With a hiss, Lev presses a paw to her wound as blood seeps into her fur. Her heart hammers.

This is the end.

A smirk crawls up Vesta's face as she circles closer, tongue clicking with disappointment. "I knew you'd never be the one."

Then Vesta's knocked sideways, body slammed into the earth. Her teeth knock together so hard, they clack above the screams of battle. There's a flurry diving toward her before it's lost in a burst of rainbow fire. Fur and flames swirl together, impossible to make out among roars and screeches.

Then Lev catches sight of Caius's scars under Vesta's talons, and Aren's tufted ears diving after him.

Lev screams before another body slams into her, and she loses sight of all of them.

THIRTY-EIGHT

Aren

PRESENT
26 days after Vesta's death

Morning comes quietly to the island on the Timber lake, as if the sun itself is keeping its distance. Aren didn't sleep, offering to take first watch and never bothering to switch. None of them closed their eyes all night. Caius and Lev curl in sleeping bags on either side of him, backs toward each other, air stiff with the thoughts whirling in their heads.

Aren struggles to make sense of his own. Across the clearing, Pheir is buried in extra blankets, shivering against the autumnal chill. Aren could warm her. He could wrap his arms around her and cover her with the heat of his body, but that might be more painful for her than what he said last night.

Pheir didn't speak after he told her about the battle. He'd thought her screams were the most disconcerting thing about her, but her silence is worse. Her lip trembled, eyes welling as her teeth chattered in the water. She wouldn't cry in front of them. As soon as Caius returned, she locked up her expression and rose to her feet to walk back to camp.

Aren built a fire as close to her as he could. It helped marginally. By daybreak, the flames are nothing but smoldering ashes, and Pheir's teeth are still chattering.

In silence, they clean the campsite. Caius's motions are sharp, mouth clamped at Pheir's betrayal. He and Aren haven't finished their conversation from before the ceremony, but addressing it on this island is jinxing it further. Lev moves like a ghost, eyes hollow and brows knit, a weight of shame draped around her shoulders. Pheir pretends to be asleep until Aren finally rouses her to get into the boat.

Steam rises off the lake. The newlyweds sit with white knuckles as Aren rows, aching to speak. He fears anything he says will make things worse and end with one of them in the water. There's no celebration from the pack when they return at first light; only the gray wolf, Echo, meets them at the dock, breath clouding the air as her nose twitches.

Gods, what she must *smell* on them.

"Congratulations," she murmurs in surprise. "I guess that went better than..." Her voice cuts off as the group avoids each other's eyes. "Oh," Echo starts again. "Sorry. I thought..."

Awkwardly, she winces, pulling Aren aside.

"Is everything...?"

"It's complicated." With a hand, Aren waves it off. "What do you need?"

"We checked the stores last night. A few of those barrel seals finally cracked, and coyotes got into the meat. If we leave now, we should be able to wrap up a hunting trip before the first snow."

"Now?" Aren's gaze flicks back to Lev and Caius stiltedly unpacking the boat. Pheir sits on the grass overlooking the lake, draped in her cloak. It's a gloomy scene.

Uncomfortably, Echo shifts on her feet, eyes darting to the others behind him. "I didn't mean to intrude, but I already asked Mari. They said they'd come along to scout."

When it rains, it pours, but Aren can't stand the thought of abandoning this group when things are so precarious. He can't just take off. "It'll have to be night-trips only," Aren concedes. "I need to be back on the compound during the day, in case the Regents show up."

"That works." Echo heads back toward the cabins. "We'll pack the truck and meet you at dusk."

When Aren turns to Lev, it's clear she overheard. "Should I have turned her down?" Aren asks seriously.

"No..." Lev drifts closer to where he stands away from the others. "It needs to be done...but the timing sucks."

That's putting it lightly. "How are you feeling about all of it?"

With a puff of air, Lev shakes her head. "I'm not surprised, I guess. I just..." Her eyes glaze as she stares back toward the island.

It's impossible to quantify last night. Nothing about it seems real, but they have the scents to prove it. Things felt *different*, like something changed, like a line was crossed – and then, Pheir took the ashes. That should be enough to prove everything before that was a fraud, an act she put on to fool them, but it didn't feel like that. Their desperation for each other was real. So was the hurt when Pheir learned the truth of the battle. As tempted as Aren is to cling to rationale, emotion nags at him. It can't be trusted, but that doesn't stop it from lingering.

"It's complicated," he says again.

Lev nods. That's the closest they'll get to explaining it. Her hand squeezes his. "Don't worry about us. I'll swap shifts with some of the other guards, let them watch Pheir. Caius and I will move into a different rotation that gives us the best vantage point for incoming Regents." As if Lev can't help herself, her gaze slips back to Pheir on the grass. Lev forces herself to look away. "Maybe some distance will help us make sense of it."

That refrain plays in Aren's head as he makes his way to his cabin and tries to sleep. Twilight comes too quickly. He spends the next few days running on fumes, catching naps between the final autumnal chores of the day and hunting at night, constantly watching for signs of the Regents. Being on a different schedule than Caius and Lev is harder than Aren expected; he's only gotten glimpses of them since they returned from the island. Understandably, he's distracted, but the small group of hunters almost manages to make up for the meat they lost.

On the second to last night, Echo carves a moose for transport. "How about we wrap this up a little early and call it done?"

Aren lifts his brow. She matches it with a smirk.

"I think we've got enough meat," she teases. "And your head has been elsewhere the entire time."

"Yeah!" Mari calls from the fire, toeing a rock back into place. "Keep it up, and I'll have to lead the next hunting trip."

Aren laughs, but he can't deny the relief that washes through him. "No argument here."

In truth, he hasn't stopped thinking about the wedding. He hasn't scared off the nagging feelings, either, the ones that swarm incessantly through his head.

Did Caius mean everything he said?

Did something change between them all that night?

Was it more than Pheir's betrayal?

No matter how glad Aren is to get back home for good, he struggles with the knowledge of what he needs to do to set things right.

When the hunting group arrives at the Timber compound the next morning, they make quick work of unloading. June meets them near the end. "Boy, am I glad to see you all."

Aren leans against the tailgate, brows furrowing. "Did something happen last night? With the Regents?"

"No. Everyone's just fucking mopey." After a moment, June reconsiders, hoisting a crate under her arm. "*Lev and Caius* are fucking mopey."

Mari chitters a laugh. "From missing sweet Aren?"

Aren sidesteps the question, climbing into the truck bed and loading folded tarps into another wooden container. "And where are they moping?"

"Lev's getting the morning rundown. Caius is...I don't know. Chopping wood." June shrugs, shifting the weight of the crate. "He didn't seem to want to be around people this morning."

"Shocker," Echo grumbles, tossing a sack over her shoulder.

June looks toward the distant wood shed, her face softening. "He did sit with us last night at the firepit. Didn't *say* anything, but he was there." Furtively, she glances at Aren before she turns back to the others. "He's trying, at least."

Mari grumbles. Echo plays with the strings of the bag before she glances toward the shed as well. Aren grabs the final crate, stepping down from the truck bed. "Has he or Lev spoken to Pheir?"

"I don't think so," June answers. "I've been keeping an eye on her. She's mopey, too, but at least she's not screaming." June's head tilts in thought as the group makes their way to the main lodge. "I started teaching her card games the other night."

Inexplicably, the thought warms Aren. Marius cackles, arms overflowing with supplies. "She's gonna take you for everything you've got."

With a scoff, June shakes her head. "She's shit at cards. No poker face. You can read exactly what she's got in her hands."

Echo huffs under her breath. "You sure she's not doing it to try and escape again?"

Slyly, June watches Aren from the corner of her eye. "We gave her extra chains after the wedding. She hasn't tried to slip them. And she's getting better at cards." Carefully, June elbows Mari. They curse, scrambling to keep everything in hand. When a metal mug clatters to the ground, June laughs, kicking it up and catching it in her crate. "Might actually beat you one of these days."

Mari knocks her with a shoulder. "We'll see about that."

After depositing the supplies, Aren lingers by the cellar. He knows what he *should* do, but he can't help looking for excuses. Maybe the caretakers need help with the younglings? Today could be the last warm day for a while. Or maybe he should go with June and Echo...

Stop stalling. You've had days to prepare for this. You knew it was coming. Yet Aren is still out of sorts. Funny how after all the talk about Caius avoiding his feelings, he's the one that came to Aren first. Tension twists low in Aren's gut. When was the last time he was nervous like this? It reminds him of feelings long forgotten, the early day he'd spent by Lev's side when she'd smile at him and lower her lashes.

The word 'crush' is insubstantial, but it disturbs the butterflies in Aren's stomach. He runs a hand down his face, taking a steadying breath and setting his shoulders as he makes his way to the woodshed.

As expected, Caius is bringing down the axe harder than he needs to. For a moment, Aren considers turning to leave, but the axe radiates through Caius's arm to make his teeth rattle. Aren can't help himself from speaking. "You shouldn't use dangerous tools when you're upset."

Is that *really* how he wants to start this? Caius doesn't seem surprised, tossing both halves of a log onto the pile. "Don't start."

Aren fights the urge to clear his throat. "How was everything here?"

"Same old shit."

Caius lines up again. Aren can see the tension in his shoulders, the urge to block himself off again. Goddammit, Aren shouldn't have waited to talk. He should have said something before the ceremony, before the ashes, before he left —

"I don't give a shit about what happened," Caius grumbles.

It's far from an admission, but it's something. Aren sinks onto the nearest bench. "Which part of it?"

Caius hefts a new log onto the cutting block. "All of it: the wedding, the ashes..." When he pauses, he keeps his eyes on the wood. "You."

Guilt pierces Aren't chest. He should say something *now*, but his tongue is heavy and clumsy, just like that night. This is what Caius meant, how it seems like Aren feels nothing, when the truth is he doesn't trust himself to act on his feelings. They make him uncertain. They make him stumble.

Aren ducks as Caius tosses a scrap of wood toward him. Caius swings the axe again. It gets caught in the block beneath before he wrenches it free.

Maybe Aren was looking in the wrong place all these months, waiting for Caius's mouth to move instead of looking at the truth screaming through his body. Caius tries to hide it now, tries not to care in the same way he thinks Aren doesn't.

You have it so fucking together, and I can't be that.

"You can be upset, Caius." It's not exactly what Aren wants to say. He tries again. "Just because we show it differently doesn't mean the way you show it is wrong."

Caius shakes his head, raising the axe above it. "I told you, I don't care."

"Caius —"

"Don't 'Caius' me!" The axe slams down, wood splitting as Caius comes undone. "How can Pheir do that? The whole time, it was a fucking plan to get Vesta's ashes again. Am I that fucking naive?"

THIRTY-NINE

Aren

After his outburst, Caius avoids Aren's eyes. They're not addressing what happened between the two of them, but this is a start. They can get somewhere with this.

"You're not naive," Aren murmurs.

"Then why did I fall for what she did? Why did it feel like..." Caius's hands fall.

Aren holds his breath. "Feel like what?"

"Feel...*different*." A pained look crosses Caius's face. "It wasn't like the night after the battle. It wasn't like the night on the balcony, either. It wasn't hate. It wasn't mindless. It was like Pheir was *there* this time. It was more than fucking. She was *ours*."

Aren's throat tightens. He felt it, too, when Pheir looked up at him like she didn't have her back to the wall. Like she wasn't poised for the worst to happen. Like the thought of being theirs drove her over the edge.

It felt *real*.

"Maybe it *was* different," Aren offers.

With a scoff, Caius retrieves the axe from the block. "She took the ashes. It was a plan. You saw it."

"Can it be both?"

Caius grits his teeth, like the thought is too much to bear. "No. It can't."

"Maybe she was ours and someone else's." Aren fights not to let hope slip into his voice. "Maybe she was struggling with that. Maybe the ashes weren't the only thing she wanted."

As impossible as it seems, if what Rhaiden told them is true, Pheir could still be struggling to escape Vesta's hold. That's something. If she struggled with it at all, that's *something*.

When Caius swings the axe again, it's more controlled. Aren's tempted to keep his uncertainties locked away...but Caius hadn't done that. Caius approached the most difficult thing for him. For all his ideas of Aren, *Caius* is the one who took steps to fix this.

Caius sees the Aren who's certain and sure, the Aren who's battled his hopes and fears into submission. It's what his beta position requires, reassuring the pack that they're safe and protected...but Caius isn't just part of the pack. Caius is more than that.

Aren lets the words slip quietly. "That night felt different to me, too."

Caius rests the axe against the chopping block, rotating his shoulder. He keeps his eyes on Aren. Aren's tempted to turn his gaze away, but he forces it to remain on Caius, as unguarded as he can be.

When Caius looks away, it's with a shared sadness. "Guess we were both wrong."

A soft laugh escapes Aren. "The Pheir I knew would have clawed you off of her when you caught her with the ashes. She wouldn't have cared if she could escape. She would never have stopped at the shoreline. She would have dived into the water without thinking — but she didn't. She didn't fight at all."

Caius's mouth pulls taut. "That doesn't mean anything."

"Did it mean nothing when you stopped fighting every touch?"

Pain settles into Caius's features. His eyes slip shut, body tense as breathes through his nose. "I don't want to be like her. I don't want to be — *capable* of that." It's clear he's spent days thinking about it, trying to make sense of it. "I don't want to let people close, and then pull the rug out from under them, let them get their hopes up and then…"

It dawns on Caius. He winces, fingers pressing to his eyelids.

"That's what I've been doing, isn't it? With you and Lev. *Fuck,* I'm just like Pheir."

Chucking the axe aside, Caius sinks down roughly next to Aren. Aren leans back against the bench, voice low. "It's not a bad thing that you and Pheir have similarities. You found her when she escaped. You knew something wasn't right when she went to the shore after the wedding. Without you, Lev and I wouldn't *have* our shit together. We wouldn't even have Pheir."

Their bodies nearly touch, wind teasing their fur together. Caius holds out his hand for the canteen hanging on Aren's other side. When Aren hands it to him, Caius pours water into his hand, smearing it over the back of his neck. "I guess I hadn't thought about it like that."

Companionable silence passes between them. Aren presses his tongue against the point of his own fang, hoping the pain will spur him into speaking. *Caius told you how he felt. Now you need to do the same.* "Do you know why I never advocated getting rid of Pheir?"

"Because you hate agreeing with me," Caius grunts.

"No." Aren's heart thuds. "Because there was a time when I was wrong about you."

Caius blinks in bewilderment. Aren can't bring himself to look at Caius, but if he stops speaking, he's not sure when he'll start again.

"I believe in Pheir because of you. Because when you came, I told Lev I wasn't sure if this was the place for you. That it could hurt all of us more than it would help you." A bitter smile crosses Aren's face. "I couldn't see you as you were. I was too jaded by things that had happened to me..." His head shakes, willing the memories away. "I don't want to be wrong like that again. Because if you hadn't stayed..."

Carefully, Aren's hand inches toward Caius. Caius flinches, but he doesn't pull away. Aren's finger traces over Caius's knuckles, running over the ridges of scars. "I don't know your life before us, Caius, but I know it's not what you deserved."

Caius stills under Aren's hand. A lump lodges in Aren's throat, but he forces himself to speak around it.

"Without you, we wouldn't know what was missing. Things changed when you got here. Lev and I are so similar; we understood each other's thinking. We got comfortable. We got complacent — and then you came."

Caius shifts on the bench, jaw tightening. "Sounds like I really fucked it up."

"No, Caius..." Aren grips Caius's arm to keep him in place, but Caius doesn't try to leave. It loosens the pressure in Aren's chest. "You challenged things. You had a different way of viewing the world, and I resisted it. If you hadn't been here, we wouldn't have been prepared for the Vestals. We wouldn't have known how to fight against Pheir or the others. You're a reminder that impulse and emotion have as much place here as logic and reason."

Caius's teeth clamp together. He's quiet for a long moment. A storm cloud hangs above them, threatening to spill. "Well," he finally manages. There's tension in his voice. "I'm glad me being here is good for you. Strategically."

The last word sticks between them. *Goddammit.* Aren shuts his eyes, throat tightening with the words trying to flood out of his mouth, emotions and feelings and messy things he doesn't know how to make sense of.

But Caius doesn't care if things are messy. Caius understands that. He deserves to hear it.

"It's not strategy, Caius."

Caius doesn't speak, waiting to see how far Aren will take this. Despite his rocky exterior, there's an earnest hope in Caius's eyes, like he can't help himself from yearning for something. It breaks Aren's heart. He's kept Caius hanging alone, left in uncertainty about what's between them. Aren can't keep him waiting any longer.

"You make me feel like…" Aren shakes his head. "You make me *feel*. You make me feel things out of my control, like something's awake in me. Like my body knows what to do. Like I don't have to think. That's…scary for me." Aren tilts his head back to look toward the sky. "I haven't done that in so long. I don't trust my instincts that way…but I trust *you*." Finally, Aren looks Caius in the eyes. Caius doesn't flinch away from it. Aren's heart picks up in his chest. "That's why we're always paired together. It's not to keep you in line. It's because I don't want anyone else beside me, and I want to be the last thing standing between you and the enemy."

It leaves Aren as bare as he's ever been. An ember glows in Caius's eyes, igniting in Aren's stomach. He lifts his hand, claws tracing along Caius's jaw.

"You are a perfect balance of impulse and intuition, Caius — but you don't have to be perfect to belong here. You never did."

When their mouths collide, Aren finally grasps the intensity that makes Caius run hot, the fervor in him overwhelming everything in its path. There's a hunger in Caius that Aren wants to feed, an irresistible ardor honed on Aren. *Finally*, he's held to the fire of Caius's attention —

"Are you two still — *oh*."

When Aren pulls back, Lev is halted a few feet away with June smirking beside her. June lifts smug brows toward Caius. "So you like lynx too, I see."

"Shut up," Caius mutters into Aren's neck, but Aren can feel the smile against his fur.

"Sorry, I didn't know you were..." Lev's teeth dig into her grin, brightness spreading through her eyes. "*Talking.*"

It's not lost on Aren that his arm's still at Caius's back, and the other man is leaning against it.

Lev presses eagerly onto her toes. "Does this mean —"

"What did you want to talk to them about, Lev?" June interrupts, nudging her sister forward.

Lev's nose turns a darker shade of pink, flustered as she fumbles with the letter in her hand. "A courier came today. The Regents finished a visit with the Steppe pack."

Aren rises from the bench. "Investigating the Vestals?"

"Apparently the Steppes tried to explain the theory about phoenix brainwashing, but the Regents are loathe to believe it. If they're coming here soon, I want to know what we're up against. And if Pheir's not here, it might buy us some time, especially after..."

The ashes. Aren swallows. In the moment with Caius, he'd forgotten what they're up against. Pheir's devotion to Vesta threatens more than their convoluted feelings. If the Regents question her, and she proclaims allegiance to Vesta...it's better if she's unavailable.

From behind the letter, Lev pulls out another piece of parchment outlining a map of the Break. "I think we should take her back to Vesta's old headquarters." On the map, Lev points to a small island off the coast of the continent. "I don't know if the Regents have searched it yet, but maybe we can find something to break Vesta's hold faster."

"Is that a good idea?" Caius's voice darkens, the bitterness from after the wedding returning. "She doesn't seem interested in anything that goes against Vesta."

"It's worth a shot." June shrugs from beside her sister. "Maybe if you find good intel to give the Regents, they'll give Pheir more time. Plus, she's traveling as an Alpha's wife now. That should keep people at bay if you run into any trouble."

Lev looks toward the cottage, teeth worrying into her lip. "If nothing else, visiting the Eyrie might give her a sense of closure. We can offer, at least." There's a quiet wound in Lev's voice, remnants from the wedding chipping away at her. "On the way back, we can stop at the Steppes. Trade some supplies so it doesn't look suspicious. If Pheir reunites with her friend, maybe it'll make her more..." Lev searches for the word. "Amenable."

It's as good a plan as any, especially if the Regents are headed toward the Timbers. Letting the Regents get a closer look at Pheir right now could be deadly.

Caius glances toward Aren. "You want me to go with you?"

Lev stops Caius with a hand on his shoulder. "Actually...I was thinking you could take her."

Caius blinks between them. "By myself?"

A proud smile crosses Lev's lips. It makes Aren's stomach flip; he can imagine what it does for Caius. "Choose a few people to take as backup. Aren and I have things to take care of here. Someone's been camping across the lake without notifying us..." She waves it off. A random camper is child's play next to what she's asking of Caius, but there's no hesitation in her eyes. "You've been finding your place here. I trust you to do this."

Shocked, Caius takes the map from her hands. When Aren smiles, his fangs dimple his lip, shoulder knocking against Caius's. "Is that a 'yes'?"

"*Yes*," Caius answers swiftly. Lev dangles the truck keys from one finger. Caius snatches them before he stops and catches Lev's hand in his. "Thank you." He looks down at her, giving them all a glimpse at the person he's kept behind a wall for so long, emotions behind his rage. There's humility in his shoulders, joy squeezing Lev's fingers, adoration in his gaze. "I mean it."

"All right, *enough*." June rolls her eyes.

Caius turns to her next. "Are you coming with me?"

Pleased, she salutes with two fingers and bounds back toward the lodge. Aren grips Caius's forearm in the same link they make before battle. "See?" Aren squeezes him. "Perfect."

Grinning, Caius shakes his head. "You're a fucking sap." He jerks Aren into his chest. It's a soft touch that's not quite practiced, but it's there among the delight running wild and free in Caius. He scoops Lev into his arms next, a crushing hug that knocks laughter from her before he deposits her back on the ground.

When Aren steps back next to Lev, he presses a finger to Caius's chest and nudges him toward the truck. Their eyes lock together, and Aren sees what he was missing for so long. "Come back home, Caius. No running."

FORTY

Caius

Caius tries to ignore the impossible thought. He puts it out of his mind as the Timbers pack the truck and fill the canteens, but when Echo hoists Pheir into the bed of the pickup, the nagging feeling is impossible for Caius to fight off.

Maybe the ashes weren't the only thing Pheir wanted.

Aren's voice plays on a loop in Caius's mind. That night on the island seemed so simple from where Caius was standing. At the wedding, he thought something was changing. Turns out it was all in his head. Pheir betrayed them. Done deal.

But if Caius and Pheir are the same...it's possible everything that happened after the ceremony wasn't just betrayal. Caius has spent years shoving Aren and Lev as far away as he could, but it wasn't the only thing he wanted; it was the exact fucking opposite.

As the Timbers finish loading the truck, Pheir's expression is taut. Her wrists are chained over her stomach, her jaw set proudly. A month ago, her violet eyes were wild and frantic. Now, they keep Caius shrewdly in her periphery. When he mentions Thalea's name, Pheir gives nothing away except for the spreading of her pupils.

In the years he's known Pheir, she's had a one-track mind: defend Vesta and destroy anyone who gets in her way. The Pheir sitting in the bed of the truck doesn't look like the woman he knew. He's not sure who's more dangerous, a Pheir with everything written on her face, or a Pheir who holds more beneath the surface.

He hauls himself into the back of the truck and slaps the metal siding for Echo to crank the engine. They roll out of the Timber compound. Behind them, Aren and Lev lift their hands in goodbye as Caius and Pheir jostle among the supplies.

Being trapped in a cab with Pheir sounds like a nightmare, but the two of them alone in the back is somehow more cramped. Despite the landscape stretching endlessly around them, Caius's eyes are drawn back to her, as if there's nothing else to look at. As if the rolling hills and evergreen trees can't hold his atten-

"Stop staring." The knit in Pheir's brow tells she's irritated.

Damn the winding road, making his stomach flutter. He leans back against the other wall. "I'm making sure you don't jump out."

He expects her to bite back, to shoot off at the mouth, to give into the antagonizing back-and-forth. Instead, she holds his gaze until his fur stands on end. "You're a shitty liar," she finally says.

It's like being under Aren's knowing watch, like Lev biting her lip before she smiles at Caius, as if Pheir *sees* something when she looks at him. When he tears his gaze away, his heart won't stop tripping. That's more unsettling than Pheir's rage could ever be.

By the time they reach the shoreline at the opposite end of the Break, they set up lunch on the hood of the truck. June reclines on one hand next to Echo while Caius stands on the ground. Pheir picks at her food beside him.

"You don't like it?" June gasps in mock offense. "I made it myself, hunted and gathered and shit."

Pheir glares beneath her brows before she squashes a blueberry with her thumb.

"Bet you'd like it if you were biting into my finger, instead," June grumbles. To prove her point, she snaps into a carrot.

Echo hoists herself off the hood. "*I'd* like it if she ripped your vocal cords out, so you won't sing the whole ride back home."

June flings a carrot at Echo's head. Something tugs at Caius's lips. He's surprised it's a hint of a smile. More surprising, though, is the matching tilt of Pheir's mouth before she shoos it away.

After walking the shore, the four of them find a rickety boat and cast off toward the island. It's small but densely forested, trees thick and tall and obscuring sight lines. No wonder the Vestals managed to keep hidden for years. The Eyrie's long been considered abandoned, at least from what Caius gathered from the others. Now, there's something almost ghostly about the Eyrie, no sound but water sloshing against the boat. As they approach the island, Caius waits for Pheir to capsize them, but she stays hauntingly still as they reach the bank.

Sand dunes lead up to the foliage, so impenetrable it seems almost purposeful. As Caius tugs the boat ashore, June combs through the thicket. After a few moments, she steps back breathlessly and looks to Pheir. "Is there a path?"

A few paces away, Pheir's arms fold across her chest. Caius cinches the final knot in the boat's rope with a shake of his head. "Don't bother asking —"

Pheir steps forward, extending her wings toward a seemingly random patch to hold back the bush. Hidden behind the first few feet of brambles is a trodden path stamped into the earth, leading deeper into the forest.

Pheir doesn't look at them when she speaks. "Don't touch anything on the outer ring of houses."

Eyes wide, June and Echo wait for more. Pheir doesn't elaborate. Eventually, June tilts her two-way radio toward Caius. "Call if you need anything." Then she and Echo file deeper into the trees until Caius and Pheir are left on the beach.

It reminds him of the night she escaped her cabin, like he can sense her body being pulled in another direction. She's desperate to dart away from the island. Away from history. Once someone's spent their life fighting, all that's left to do is run. Running is easier than battling the memories that latch on.

Rising from the boat, Caius brushes sand from his hands. "Is this gonna be hard for you?"

Pheir stiffens at his voice, but her gaze follows the others down the path. For a long moment, he doesn't think she'll answer, then her response comes a fraction louder than the waves. "Not harder than anything else."

An old soreness twinges in his chest like an overworked muscle. He steps toward her, replacing her wing to hold back the brush as he stares down at her. "That's not saying much."

She doesn't face him — but she doesn't pull away, either. All this wide-open space, and they're crowded next to each other until he can make out the length of her eyelashes. She blinks slowly, keeping him in the corner of her eye. Maybe she'll spring. Maybe she'll swipe at his throat.

Humid air crackles between them. Her chin lifts so she can meet his face, eyelids drooping when her gaze falls to his mouth —

Then she steps away and starts toward the center of the island.

At first, there's nothing but flora and foliage hanging over the path. Caius pushes brambles out of his way, avoiding leaves that snap back as Pheir moves through them. It would be easy to get lost. It doesn't help that he keeps being distracted by Pheir's bare neck in front of him. A bead of sweat forms at the base of her hair, slipping down the pale purple of her skin. Caius's tongue swipes over his lips, tasting salt in the air.

At the middle of the island, they break through the dense foliage. A canopy of trees hovers meters above them, and on the ground, there are charred-out fire pits and rotting rinds of fruit. Plenty of signs of life without any shelter — until he tilts his eyes up. Wooden boards hang from frayed ropes, unraveled ladders disappearing into the trees. He reaches for the bottom rung of the closest one.

"Not that one." Caius turns toward Pheir's voice. There's an odd twist to her mouth, like she's reconsidering warning him. "It's trapped."

His brow cocks, hand hovering off the rung. "I'm supposed to trust you?"

She shrugs noncommittally. "Go for it, then." Then she takes an exaggerated step back.

His eyes roll, casting up into the trees. After a moment, he notes the sharpened spikes that nearly blend into the trunks. Carefully, he leaves the ladder untouched. "A little dangerous, don't you think?"

Pheir starts toward the center of the island as she recites, "*The best magic is a secret.*"

Sun dapples through the thick canopy and onto the ground. It's clear the ladders were meant to help the Vestals go undetected and recoil back up into the trees, yet nearly all of them are unraveled. It turns Caius's stomach. Of course they are; the people who lived here expected to return home and climb into the trees...

Now, the ladders clatter like skeletons hanging in the breeze.

Pheir barely looks at them, weaving over tree roots and discarded wheelbarrows until they come to the largest tree trunk. It might take ten of Caius to wrap his arms around it. Head tilting back, he hikes his bag higher on his shoulder before he glances at Pheir. Resentment burns in him at the memory of the last time he trusted her. "You gonna try to escape again?"

He expects resistance, for her to sneer and rub his face in how foolish he'd been. Instead, her jaw tightens, gaze leveling with his. "We're on an island. You clipped my wings. I can't swim back to shore."

His mouth opens to contradict her. *Same as the last island. Same as the wedding.* He stops himself, tongue curled in his mouth as she stares at him like she knows what he's thinking. Like she's trying to tell him something.

I wasn't going to leave.

His mouth slips shut. There's no way she could mean that. There's no way he could believe it.

Gaze dropping, Pheir says something else instead. "I'm not going anywhere."

It's the most Caius can expect. Unbinding her cuffs, he stuffs them into the bottom of his bag. She rubs her wrists, staring up at the canopy with a hesitancy he hasn't seen before. He holds the bottom of the ladder for her to step onto.

"Go on." He nudges her. Warily, she grips one of the rungs and hoists herself up. Her legs wobble, but Caius's pressure keeps the ladder still. Once he releases the bottom, she sways and curses, locking her arms and legs around the ropes.

"You act like you've never used a ladder before," he laughs. She tries to flip him off, but it makes her shriek as she spins.

"I *didn't*," she snaps. With much effort, she pulls herself up another rung. "I could *fly*."

He takes pity on her, tying off the ropes to posts in the ground before they both begin the long climb to the top. An old wound in his shoulder aches from the effort, but he persists. It's dizzying being this high. Definitely a village built for birds. Caius keeps his eyes focused until he can make out wooden boards through the leaves above him. As they near the top, they pull themselves through a hole and onto a circular deck.

From here, they can see the Eyrie as it's meant to be seen. Across the treetops are a multitude of houses, wooden shapes floating above the foliage and fashioned like treehouses or massive nests. Each house is encircled by a wooden deck. A spider web of swinging bridges connects each deck to its neighbor. At the edge of the island, a ring of taller trees keeps the houses blocked from view of the Break.

Clever.

Beside Caius, Pheir stares into the distance toward a back corner of the island that looks more weathered than the rest. Hands clenching, she steps toward it, boards shifting beneath her feet —

Caius reaches across her before her feet find the edge of the platform. "Don't get too close." He lowers his head to find her eyes. "You can't fly. Remember?"

Blinking, she looks at him before she notices the arm across her chest. Slowly, she steps back from the drop as if she's coming back to herself, but her eyes stay wide like she's seen a ghost.

It's quiet at the top of the trees, wind rushing through the leaves like waves roaring past. It ruffles Pheir's hair, tossing mauve strands and teasing Caius with her scent. It singes his nose, burning and impossible to get out. *Horseradish*, he'd once compared her smell too, back when she bloodied him every chance she got. Now, though, her scent makes his mouth water, sharp and delicious.

Caius clears his throat to escape the taste, rotating his shoulder. "Where did you live? I want to see what's so much better than the Timber cabins."

It's an attempt at a joke, but there's an eerie stillness to Pheir's body as her eyes stay focused on the far corner of the island. She jerks a thumb toward the treehouse behind them. "After Vesta came, we stayed in the center."

After Vesta came.

Caius's brows knit, but he doesn't press further, turning with Pheir to face the house. It's the largest one on the island, wooden floorboards and walls forming a circular home built for the long-term. Fabric hangs over the holes that serve for windows, pulled aside with tiebacks that match the floral pattern.

Pheir rubs the curtains between her fingers. The fabric is dingy and faded, but Pheir looks at them like they were once bright and familiar. Her voice sounds almost dreamy. "Thalea picked these."

Pheir lets her hand drop back to her side. Caius should inspect the residence without her interference. He should make sure he gathers any information Vesta might have left behind. Instead, he waits beside Pheir for her to push the front door open.

There's a damp smell from sea air blowing through the windows. Sunlight gives the house a hazy quality, bright and cheery amidst the emptiness inside. There are no walls in the entryway, giving full view of a simple kitchen and sitting area. A few bowls sit in the sink, chairs pushed out of line, as if someone had just been sitting in them. Pheir circles to a wooden table by the door, covered in an outdated map and carved figurines. She lifts one, pressing fingers to the spikes on the siren's back.

Rhaiden. "Battle planning?" Caius asks.

Pheir curls her fingers around the figure. "Obviously, it didn't help."

She moves as if she's in a dream, viewing something familiar through a smeared lens. There's a short hallway to the back of the house with three rooms. Caius leans inside both the open doorframes to check before he glances back at Pheir. "You didn't have doors?"

"Only Vesta needed one," Pheir says by way of answer. "Well — Vesta and Thalea." Pheir approaches one of the open rooms, staring into a sparsely-decorated bedroom with everything in place. "Rhaiden didn't like that. She said it gave us no privacy, but if you have nothing to hide..." Pheir trails off, as if she's repeating a line that now fits strangely in her mouth.

Caius moves toward the only closed door at the end of the hall. When he turns the handle, it doesn't budge.

"Vesta kept it locked," Pheir lingers a few feet behind him. "Not sure where she put the key last. Probably somewhere near the battlefield."

The words escape Pheir like air from a slow leak, coming shallowly from her throat like it pains her. Arms crossed over her stomach, her weight shifts uncertainly.

"I'm going to have to break it down," Caius warns.

Pheir's shoulders tense, dull talons extending as her arms fall open. Caius braces for her attack. She doesn't move as she stares at the door. Hypnotized, like it's been ingrained in her to protect this space and all of Vesta's secrets.

"I feel like you shouldn't." She stares at the door with puzzled apprehension. "I feel like you shouldn't, but I'm not sure why."

FORTY-ONE

Caius

Caius and Pheir watch each other a moment longer, deciding if the other is a threat.

"Is there a trap on the door?" he asks.

Pheir shakes her head.

Carefully, Caius steps back for some momentum. Pheir doesn't move. Finally, he lowers his shoulder and rams into the wood.

With every blow, Pheir winces like he's chipping away at the foundation of her being. It doesn't take long for the door to give, splintering open by the lock and swinging inward. Caius braces for a trap to spring, but nothing comes.

It's surprising how much bigger this room is compared to the others. Larger floor space, attached bathroom, items sprinkled throughout. It's like a cave, bed and shelves piled high with torn maps and dinged knick-knacks as dust floats through the light from the window. Interspersed throughout, there are a few softer hints that Caius imagines belonged to Thalea — a worn pink blanket hanging off the massive bed. A short stack of romance novels with well-loved spines. A tiny potted plant on the corner of the desk.

Its leaves have shriveled. One drifts to the ground as Caius eases into the room. "Any other traps?"

"Under the mattress." Pheir leans around the doorframe. Caius searches through a much larger stack of books on the far bedside, pages yellowing as he thumbs through antique titles.

Immortal Beings and Ancient Powers.

Foster the Seed: A Case Study in Influence.

A Brief History of Phoenixkind.

Not titles he's familiar with. Behind the bed frame, the corner of another book catches his eye. Careful not to disturb the mattress, he tugs out the leatherbound journal. It's plain and brown, neat with angular handwriting scrawled across the pages. Entries are dated, filled with names Caius recognizes — Thalea, Rhaiden, Pheir. In the front are charts and training schedules interspersed with perplexing quotes.

One rotten seed ruins the soil.

If the garden does not thrive under the best conditions, look to the seed.

He turns the book sideways. "Vesta was really into this seed crap, huh?"

"That's not her real journal."

Pheir hovers by the broken door, as if she's not allowed to enter. Words seem to escape against her will, her brows knit like she's warring with something. Her gaze skirts the room before her eyes shut, forehead pressed to the doorframe.

"She kept that fake journal in case anyone broke in — and to throw Rhaiden off. But I think Rhaiden was catching on..."

Caius doesn't move. It's too precarious, like a sudden sound will startle Pheir back into defense. Suddenly, her hands jerk to her ears like she's drowning out a shriek. Caius moves toward her, but she yanks away.

When she opens her eyes, she realizes where she is and what they're doing. Cautiously, Pheir exhales and steps back into the hallway. "She kept the real journal in my room."

It stuns Caius that she would offer without provocation. His ears twitch to listen to her heartbeat. Could it be a trick? Pheir warned him about the traps thus far, but maybe breaking into Vesta's room has pushed her over the edge. Carefully, he follows her, but she stops and points him toward the romance novels on the ground.

"Bring those."

Caius does as she instructs, slipping the books into his bag as he follows Pheir toward the other open doorway. They stand beside each other in the hall to take it in.

Pheir's room is exactly as expected. Chaos in every corner, trinkets scattered magpie-like across the floor and pillows. There's no order to anything. The blankets in the center look more like a nest than a bed, random items tucked into the folds.

"Did Vesta leave her journal here because no one could *find* it?" Caius mutters.

A smile flits across Pheir's face. "Shut up." Then the glimpse of humor is gone as she steps inside.

Floorboards creak underfoot. Pheir walks as if they might collapse, as if the solid trunk of the tree isn't holding them aloft. She moves like she isn't in control of her body — or she isn't sure if she is. When she kneels at her bedside, her hands drift toward the covers before she pulls back.

"Vesta said she left the journal here because she trusted me." Pheir's palms rest on her knees, head tilting like the thoughts are coming to her for the first time. "But I think maybe it's because...I would defend her secrets better than she could."

The realization sits strangely on Pheir's face, delicate and slippery as her talons tick against the floor. Laboriously, she pushes her mattress aside, feeling for a loose floorboard that catches on her finger. She pries it open, hand flexing as she stares down into that hole. Shuddering, she reaches down and snatches a small book from the depths before she shoves the floorboard back into place.

The book rests in her lap, white leather with gold and black designs Caius doesn't recognize. Pheir's fingers clamp around the edges as if she's trying to keep it closed, to protect it.

It's not like Caius to be gentle, to ease anyone into anything, but he keeps his distance by the doorway. "Did you read it?"

Pheir shakes her head. "Never even peeked. Maybe that's why she kept it here. She knew I would never betray her trust." Pheir's lip quivers when she scoffs, knees tucked beneath her. "Look at me now."

Despite his instincts, Caius sinks down inside the door and leans back against the wall. He understands the feeling of treason, of dedicating yourself to one person for so long that going against their most ingrained lessons feels like betrayal, even if they aren't there to see it. His elbows prop on his knees. "Do you want to read it first?"

Maybe it's a bad idea. Maybe Pheir will tear the book to shreds before Caius can reach it. Maybe she'll find a weapon hidden in her sheets to stab him with. But she makes no move, fingers brushing over the cover of the book to trace the embossed feathers. Slowly, her talon slips under the front corner —

Then she sharply extends the book toward him. Her eyes stay averted until the stress gets the better of her, making her jerk the book in his direction again. "Take it!" Her hands stay tight around the book until he pries it from her grasp. She keeps her eyes down as he settles back and turns the journal over in his hands.

It's worn from use near the bindings. When he flips to the middle, pages of hectic scrawl jump out at him. It seems to be written by a different person than the one in Vesta's bedroom. These pages are frantic, less formal, rambling thoughts and drawings scribbled in the margins. It's like a code Caius can't make out, words strung together in sentences that don't make sense.

Rebirth means relying on strangers to get me back on my feet. It's fucking bullshit; I've found another way. Pheir will come through for me, even if she doesn't know it yet.

There's pages and pages of the "seed," mingled with mentions of eggs and shells. It's like reading Vesta's plans for harvest.

Pheir has always kept me safe. She's never needed to know my secrets. That's why she's the perfect shell. She'll keep protecting me until the sleeper's awake.

It's nonsensical and confusing, the rantings of a madwoman descending into chaos. There are no dates, ramblings that continue in a steady stream. Caius tries to flip back to the beginning when Pheir's breathing shifts. It's slow and shallow, the space between each breath growing shorter. Her chin tucks to her chest, eyes shut like she's trying to outpace a memory.

Caius rises to his feet, lowering his hand to her shoulder. She jerks, but her eyes turn up with a plea he understands.

"We have enough," he murmurs. "Let's go."

Her arm is shaky when she places her hand in his so he can pull her to her feet. Her legs wobble, but when Caius tries to catch her, she refuses to give him any weight. They make their way back to the entrance of the house. Pheir can't seem to cross the threshold, looking back like an accident she can't tear her eyes away from.

"It looks so different than what I remember." Her gaze scrapes the walls for every detail, like she's saving it all to piece together later. "It feels different, too."

"Different how?" Caius asks.

Her brows knit at the impossibility. "Like I'm seeing it for the first time."

As she lingers at the entrance, Caius steps out onto the porch and clicks his radio near his mouth. "June?"

Static crackles before her voice returns over the radio. *"Go ahead."*

"Vesta's house is the large one in the center. Check it when you get a chance. There are books in the back bedroom we'll want to take. Don't lift the mattress — it's trapped."

"Copy."

Caius tucks the notebook into his bag as Pheir joins him on the deck. She turns to the far reaches of the island again, its wood weathered and gray against the green of the leaves. It's the same place she'd been hooked on before.

"If *this* house seems different..." Pheir doesn't finish the thought, as if speaking it aloud might take her somewhere she doesn't want to be.

Caius stands beside her, watching the leaves sway like waves breaking on the shore. He lowers his mouth next to her ear. "What's back there?"

She shakes her head. It's the first time she's looked scared, face paling as her arms wrap protectively across her chest. "I don't know why I care." Her eyes narrow sharply. "I haven't been back there in years. I never even thought about..." Her jaw clenches. She curses in frustration, stamping her foot like she's annoyed with herself. "Come *on!*"

Seeing Pheir like this solidifies it. She fights with her fear the way she does everything else, rage and fury bottled in her body, trembling as she wrestles with uneasiness. It's the same way Caius does when he has to work himself up to enter the animal pen, when the barbed wire across the chicken coop digs into his skin.

We are the same.

When Pheir moves, Caius follows without question across the hanging bridges. Houses near the center of the Eyrie are filled with lives that he can make out through open windows, bookmarks in final pages and laundry lines heavy with clothes. It's a ghost town of things left undone, making the fur rise on Caius's neck like someone is around the corner — but no one's coming back for the half-finished cup of water molding on the table.

No one's coming back for any of it.

When Caius and Pheir round a corner, he startles, jerking Pheir behind him. Vesta stares down at them, teeth gnashing and claws outstretched — but it's a picture on the side of a house, chalk weathered by the elements until it's faded and sallow. Despite the wear, Vesta's eyes are as piercing as they were in life, watching anyone who walks beneath her.

Tentatively, Caius peers across the other houses. Now that they're closer, he can see the faded marks on nearly every building, Vesta splashed across rooftops beneath one of her favorite mottos, Vesta chipping away in paint on one of the decks, a tribute to Vesta spanning three houses. She's everywhere, watching them from every angle.

It makes Caius's skin crawl. Pheir hardly seems to notice.

They continue to the outer platforms where the houses begin to change. Well-connected bridges turn into rickety knotted ropes, decks filled with holes and missing planks. There's nothing in the houses but a few essentials: sleeping bags, water, rotting food. On this outer ring, it looks like these houses were campsites more than homes.

Pheir slows as they pass a ladder dangling by one frayed rope. She runs her finger along where it unravels. "We only had one ladder in the beginning — in the middle, for Rhaiden." Pheir's voice sounds far off, like she's speaking through a film. "When Vesta brought more people, we built new ladders. They were shitty, but Vesta didn't care. *They don't have to last; there just have to be enough.'"

Pheir's lips twist, trying to find a path between what her eyes are seeing and what she remembers. Her mouth's left to try and explain it.

"I thought Vesta meant the ladders, but maybe she meant the people, too. I don't think she meant any of them to be long-term." A cracked mug sits in a windowsill. Pheir lifts it in her hands, trying to place it in her memory. There's no recognition. "Back then, I didn't care. All these people in our pack — I lived with them every day. I *fought* beside them —" She traces the mug's handle, lifting it on a finger. "But I don't know who this belonged to. I couldn't tell you any of those peoples' names." Her fingers curl around the mug, arm tightened to shatter it against the platform. "I didn't care about anything but Vesta. None of us did. It's like we were —"

She stops. Caius can guess the final word.

Brainwashed.

That word is too far for Pheir to admit, asking too much of her, so she sets the mug back into place. She doesn't stop at any of the other houses they pass. Eventually, they reach as far as the bridges allow and circle the final platform. There's no sign of a connection, yet across the gap at the edge of the trees, there's a worn house on a shabby deck.

This house is more weathered, wood rotting and faded as if it hasn't been touched in a decade. The campsite houses are in bad condition, but this house is far worse. From its construction, it looks like a massive ball of sticks above a round deck, a spherical nest with a jagged hole as an entry point.

Pheir watches it like it might spring to life, as if it's more threatening than the dizzying drop feet away. Trees sway beneath them, boards creaking as Pheir tilts toward the edge...

Caius snatches her back against his chest. Her body tremors, skin lined with bumps as her feathers stand on end. His fingers clench around her arms, a shock of concern slipping through the gruffness of his voice. "You're shaking."

FORTY-TWO

Pheir

Being this close to Caius is the least jarring thing about returning here. This village is the only home Pheir's ever known. Now, it doesn't feel real.

The thought sends a chill down her spine. She's being ridiculous, but she can't escape the notion that this place is nothing like what she remembers. All around her loom poor excuses for homes, frantic Vesta tributes, and scraps that barely count as food. In the month Pheir's been away, things shouldn't have fallen into such disrepair.

Even Vesta's central house was wrong. When Pheir and Caius climbed the ladder to it, there was no golden glow, no sweet scent welcoming Pheir in. What happened to the feeling it used to give her that everything was safe and right, that this island was a respite in an awful world?

Blossoming flowers and ripening fruit that once filled the Eyrie now reek of decomposition.

Maybe the old days weren't real. Maybe this was always the truth.

It's too painful for Pheir to grapple with. If the Eyrie wasn't paradise before, that would mean her life has been a lie. Her memories feel like they don't belong to her, a ghost brought back to life to see things without a veil over her eyes.

What once seemed like an oasis is cracking and rotting beneath her feet. The empire Vesta built crumbles all around Pheir, its essence seeping through the holes in the walls and leaking roofs.

Vesta is still alive here. In her bedroom, her voice screamed through Pheir's head, fading with each of Pheir's betrayals. In the other houses, Vesta's name is scrawled in open notebooks, her likeness painted everywhere that arms could reach. Always images of Vesta, but no mention of the cause they were fighting for. There's no self-expression here. No sign of a life beyond the most basic needs.

Every house reflects what Pheir had once been — a shell with nothing but Vesta inside.

Including this final house. Its long-fallen bridge flutters in one of the trees below them like a torn battle flag. Vesta destroyed the link when she rescued Pheir. *Stick with me, and you'll never have to come back here.*

So Pheir stuck with her.

Caius's heart thrums under Pheir's palms. It's the thing that brings her out of her head, turning her back to the dilapidated nest across from them. She has to go in. She needs to know if all her memories are fake, if every moment was manufactured. Nausea swirls in her stomach as she steps back from Caius. His fur is soft and warm beneath her fingers. She doesn't want to let go of the reminder that there is *something* alive here besides Vesta, but Pheir pries her fingers away. After a moment, Caius finds a long board to lay across the gap to the other nest.

When Pheir steps onto it, the board teeters as Caius tries to hold it steady. The threat of plummeting makes her legs tremble less than the building before her. She keeps her eyes on the ground until her head spins, feeling for the deck beneath her feet until she reaches the other side.

Her footsteps sound hollow. She steps toward the jagged opening of the nest and stares into the dark. Tree limbs have fallen from the ceiling, breaking through floorboards in a haphazard path. The holes let light in, highlighting patches of rotted wood and gouges from furniture scraping the floor. In the far corner of the nest, she can still make out a metal handle attached to an open trap door —

Pheir's eyes snap shut, body buzzing like the walls are closing in. This was a mistake. She wants to leave. She needs to *breathe*.

Stumbling, she circles the platform to the back of the house and crouches on the deck. She tries to press her hands against her pounding head, to suck air in through her nose – until she sees it. From here, she can make out the hole beneath the floorboards through gaps in the nest's outer twigs. Sunlight trickles through the open trap door and into the crawl space beneath it. Time has not been kind to it. At Pheir's weight now, climbing into that hole would send her crashing into the forest below.

"Pheir?"

Caius's voice comes from so far away, she doesn't startle at it. The space between her brows is pinched. She's holding her breath, tilting dazedly before she sucks in a gasp like she might not get another chance. Caius grips her arms from behind, turning her to face him, away from the house. His gaze is hard. Worry flits over his expression before his fingers tighten.

"You need to sit down."

For once, she doesn't fight him.

He guides her to the edge of the platform where there's less rotting wood. Her feet dangle over the edge. With her back to the house, she recognizes everything before her. These were the trees she smelled when she was trapped, the ocean she could see through the holes in the nest. It still stretches as far as the eye can see. Back then, Pheir imagined flying and soaring into the sun until she disappeared...

"Is this where you lived?" Caius takes the same position beside Pheir, leaving a few feet of space between them. "Before Vesta?"

That was how Pheir divided her life. *Before Vesta*, the childhood Pheir would rather forget. And *After Vesta*, the golden age when everything was perfect, years of the two of them before Thalea and Rhaiden came along. Amazing how it all took place in the same village, how Vesta could make Pheir forget everything that happened before.

Her legs swing idly, one of her fingers picking at a splinter in the wood. "You'll be a dick if I tell you."

Caius scoffs, but his gaze casts guiltily away.

The splinter digs into Pheir's fingertip. "Maybe that's good, though, because it is stupid. Maybe I need you to tell me that."

* * * * *

It's dark and damp. Capheira's feet slam up against the trap door. The sound is suffocated by the wind screaming outside. Around her, the crawl space is cramped, keeping her breath tight in her chest. She needs to make herself heard, but it's useless. Her throat is raw from hours of screaming already, lip bloody where her knee jolted back after her feet slipped.

"Let me out!"

Her legs burn from exertion. This is the longest her parents have left her beneath the floorboards. Her mother and stepfather are getting better at waiting out her tantrums. Because that's all Capheira's screaming is: an outburst without reason. An annoyance. Her parents mutter when they finally storm over to the trap door, flinging it back and yanking Capheira out by the feathered scruff of her neck.

Irritating. Trying to provoke us. Making us fucking miserable.

When her parents started putting her into the crawl space, it was a punishment for tantrums. Now, it's the natural consequence of her smartass mouth. Of teenage angst. Of backtalk. No matter Capheira's age, there's a reason she needs to lay in the crawl space to think about what she's done.

From the guilty weight in Capheira's chest, her parents are right. She is a bad kid. Bad baby. Bad toddler. Bad tween. Her parents must have been right all this time, because in the last year, she's developed a taste for cruelty, seeking that twitch in her father's eye. Drawing out her mother's frustrated shout. At least then Capheira knows they remember her beneath the floorboards. They have some reaction to her presence. They feel something at the sight of her instead of apathy.

If screaming is the way to draw out their reaction, then Capheira will scream until her lungs burst. Her fists slam against the trap door, rattling the metal handle on the other side. "You're such a fucking bitch!"

It draws no response. Soon, Capheira will be too big to fit in this hole. Her parents will have to stop shoving her in here, won't they? They'll have to find some new punishment for whatever slight Capheira causes, spilling her drink or asking too many questions or using that tone she still can't put a finger on.

She doesn't enjoy pissing them off, but it works. Some days take longer than others, as if Capheira and her parents are at war, seeing who will drive the other to exhaustion first. Once her parents put her in the crawl space, they can sometimes last through the night and into the next morning with Capheira's screaming. In the end, Capheira always figures out which buttons to push. What she has to do to get them to open the door. To yell at her. To look *at her.*

Fighting with them is sweet relief from the hole's deprivation.

But this time, her parents haven't responded to her in hours. Capheira has no sense of time under the trap door, watching slices of sun through the floorboards. That light has become a darkening shade of gray as the wind whirls violently outside. Her parents locked her in here before the storm, before the tree their house is built on started swaying, before rain smacked against the side of the house like it's falling horizontally.

Water collects in the bottom of the crawl space, soaking Capheira's feathers. The tree sways again, sending furniture screeching across the floor above her. Water sloshes into her mouth as she's knocked against the wall. She splutters, coughing through the grime. She can't sit upright to clear her airway. She turns on her side, choking out what's left in her windpipe until she can finally breathe again.

The wind grows louder. Capheira won't be afraid. She can't be. In the dark, her fingers trace the gouges in the trap door that were clawed during her hours spent beneath it. Tally marks to count the days. She ran out of room for them long ago. Near the door's hinges, she finds the circular heads and stick bodies of the family she carved to play pretend.

There's four of them, including her. She's not sure why — siblings, perhaps. Someone to take the heat off of her. Someone to withstand her parents' rage. Someone to protect her from them, or the howling wind, or anything else that comes her way.

Capheira dreams of them. She doesn't know when she falls asleep. Her eyes are crusted together, teeth chattering in cold water as her body wakes with a painful shiver. The wind has stopped. She's suspended uncertainly, tilted at an odd angle as water pools in the corner near her head.

Capheira presses her mouth to one of the walls where a crack in the wood has opened bigger, giving her a glimpse outside the nest. "Let me out!" Her voice is raw and pitiful. What else is there to do? She claws at the hole, trying to break off larger chunks, but splinters dig into her hands. She shouts again. She sounds more like a vulture than a person.

Above her, someone steps on the floorboards. Capheira freezes and strains to listen. It's not the same weight as her parents. It's not stomping angrily toward her, not following the usual worn paths. These footsteps are light and unfamiliar, dancing across the floor as they search for something…

For Capheira.

She slams her fists against the trapdoor, voice cracking. "I'm down here!"

The footsteps pause. They return again in a beeline for Capheira. Furniture shuffles above her, nudged off of the trapdoor until the metal handle drops against it like a knocker. Like someone's teasing her.

Then, the trapdoor flings open. Sunlight pours inside. Capheira shields her eyes — but it's not the sun at all. It's the girl above her, feet planted on either side of the hole, beaming down at Capheira like this girl has conquered a new land. Capheira can hardly look at the girl's brightness. Rainbows reflect around the room like the girl's body is a prism, feathers spread out from her back as light trickles through them like flames. The girl tilts her head. "How'd you get in there?"

Her tone is musical. She smiles as she looks down at Capheira's bruised body. Capheira coughs a laugh. Maybe it's dehydration, or exhaustion, or the ache in every one of her limbs, but the girl's face is the first joyful expression anyone's had when they looked at Capheira.

The girl extends a hand. Capheira has to sit up to reach it, joints cracking as she winces. The girl doesn't lower further, waiting for Capheira's fingertips to brush hers before she pulls Capheira out of the hole. Her body is soaked and shaking, nose running as the girl crouches before her and extends a hand. "I'm Vesta."

She can't be much older than Capheira, yet she seems much wiser. Capheira takes her hand. "Ca-pheira." Her teeth chatter.

Vesta glances behind her for a blanket. When she doesn't find one right away, she turns back.

"You're awfully lucky I found you. I came to check out the island after the storm, to see if there was anything useful in the wreckage. I was about to leave when I heard you."

Sunlight peeks through the clouds. Capheira shuts her eyes and leans back into the light, desperate for warmth on her skin. Her arms wrap around her knees. "The — wreckage?"

Vesta's eyes narrow — but they don't stay that way. Not like Capheira's parents. Instead, Vesta brightens again before it turns into sympathy. "That storm tore half the houses here apart. Boards everywhere, branches broken. I wouldn't be surprised if the people that lived here never came back."

Cold seeps into Capheira's bones, her eyes cracking open. "N-no one else is h-here?"

Her stomach roils. Deep down, she knew it. Her parents didn't stay through the storm. They didn't get stuck on the ground. They didn't come back to the island at the first opportunity to retrieve her.

Vesta's mouth presses into a thin line, fingers finding Capheira's arm in an attempt at comfort. "No one else. Just me."

It's an odd feeling, having someone touch Capheira softly. It's warm against the goosebumps of her skin, and she doesn't know if that's from Vesta herself or the simple heat of another person. Capheira leans into it. Vesta looks surprised before she tucks Capheira under her arm.

"Was someone supposed to be here?"

The question sinks like a rock in Capheira's stomach. Despite everything, she thought her parents would take her with them. That they'd come back for her. There's still a chance they will. They could still be coming back. They'll chide her for not being louder in the crawl space, for not letting them know she was still trapped.

Capheira clings to that fragment of hope so tightly it cuts her. "Maybe they f-forgot...I was down there."

"Oh, sweetie..." Vesta's tongue clicks pitifully. She gives a reassuring squeeze, talons tightening in Capheira's shoulder. "They didn't forget."

Capheira tries to swallow around the lump in her throat. It scratches and aches. This wasn't an accident. This wasn't an oversight. This was intentional. Next to Vesta's broad wings, Capheira is shriveled and small.

Vesta doesn't let her dwell on the thoughts, though. She jostles Capheira's shoulders. "We should get you some food. Find somewhere to warm up for the night. You can tell me more about who was supposed to be here."

Capheira can't speak past her chattering teeth. At least Vesta rubs her warm hands over Capheira's arms, making heat bloom as she continues.

"We should stay out of sight, though. Because anyone who would leave you like that?" Vesta's head shakes in disappointment. "They don't deserve to have you. They've betrayed you. And we don't need them." Vesta beams again, as if she's assuring herself. "The best magic is a secret, and we can keep this one together."

In the breeze, the house tilts uncertainly. Capheira needs water. A blanket. Sunlight. A good night's sleep. The world is foggy around the edges, but Vesta's hands are sure and certain, working heat back under her skin. Capheira likes that. She likes how sure Vesta is. How quickly she's accepted someone as shrill and ungrateful as Capheira.

Is this what friendship is like?

Tentatively, Capheira nods. It brings a grin to Vesta's face. No one's ever smiled at Capheira like that, like she's done something beautiful. Brilliant. Like she's done something right.

She wants to make Vesta smile again.

When Vesta helps Capheira to her feet, brushing dirt and grime from her legs, Vesta pauses to take her in fully. Capheira's a scrawny child, knobby knees and legs too long for her body, adolescent feathers still growing awkwardly into her wings. When Vesta looks at her, she doesn't seem to see that. It's like she sees something else — what Capheira could be.

"You don't look like a 'Capheira'..." Vesta brushes wet hair back from Capheira's face, tracing the bloody split of her lip. Capheira winces — but she doesn't hiss. She doesn't pull away from the pain. A light goes on in Vesta's eyes. She leans closer, conspiratorial, like they share another secret. "How about 'Pheir'?"

Capheira's never had a nickname. Never had anyone speak to her with a light in their eyes, excitement and pride Capheira doesn't have a name for. Vesta circles behind her, painting a picture with a swoop of her hands.

"It's fierce. Intimidating. It strikes fear into the hearts of anyone who hears it." Vesta stands before Capheira, planting her hands on her shoulders. "No matter how many times you get knocked down, you always get back up for more."

In an odd way, it makes sense. It's not the way Capheira would have described herself, but it makes her hopeful. She could become that. It's something to strive for, another stick drawing on the bottom of the trap door, a fantasy about a life she might have.

When Pheir smiles, her bloody lip cracks. "Yeah. Call me Pheir."

FORTY-THREE

Pheir

Once Pheir finishes speaking, it's silent. Good. That means no pity. This story hasn't changed the way Caius sees her. But when his voice comes, it's knotted with astonishment. "Your parents punished you...by locking you in a box? They left you there to die?"

Pheir rests back on her palms like she's sunning herself the same way she had under Vesta's attention. The crawl space looms behind her. "It sounds fucked up when you say it like that."

"It *is* fucked up."

Pheir's stomach stirs. It's one thing to know the truth. She doesn't have to acknowledge it. Every thought is an excuse, an explanation, a reason for why things happened the way they did. *Everyone has bad days. You deserved it. It was an accident.* Hearing her life from someone else's perspective is like realizing the nectar she's been drinking is actually poison. She wipes her clammy hands on her thighs. "Doesn't matter. Vesta came after that."

Caius tosses a broken stick down into the forest. "So that's how she found you."

He doesn't sound like Vesta's a hero. He doesn't sound the way Pheir felt that day. One of her eyes cracks open, a defensive urge darting through her. "What are you trying to say, *how* she found me?"

Caius bends one knee toward his chest as the other dangles off the deck. His arm swoops out in front of him. "You were trapped and defenseless. You were a *kid*. You needed someone, and she knew that. That's why she kept you with her. So you'd be indebted to her."

Fury boils through Pheir's blood. "Vesta was the best thing to happen to me."

"After your parents?" Caius's gaze bores into hers with a rage that matches, but it's not directed at Pheir. It's *about* Pheir. It's *for* Pheir. "It'd be hard to find something worse."

She doesn't know what to do with that. Anger sparks in her throat, but her words feel as hollow as the rest of her. "It was better with Vesta." Her fingers curl around the edge of the deck. "She saw something in me, something my parents didn't."

She saw you were easily manipulated.

That's what Rhaiden said, back when Pheir was too drunk on Vesta's praise to consider anything else. Why is Pheir questioning it now? Why is she telling Caius? Why does she keep talking?

"So, Vesta took care of you." Caius leans back on his palms. "Because she knew you'd stand by her if she did."

"That's not why she did it!" Pheir hisses. Her talons dig into the boards, teeth clamped so tightly they might break. She sucks air through her nose, staring down at her knees as if the world will stop spinning. As if this will start making sense.

Talking about Vesta should be heaven. It should feel like the first bite of ripened fruit, like sunlight on her face, like the glorious way Vesta first appeared to her. Instead, a leaden weight sinks in

Pheir's stomach. This island is not what she remembers. The golden lacquer is worn and faded away, leaving nothing but ruins.

Are Pheir's memories of Vesta the same? Was every moment doused in candy coating to hide the chipped and brittle truth?

Pheir turns her face away from Caius, praying the wind blows her quiet voice away. Maybe he won't hear. Maybe *she* won't. For the first time, these words aren't practiced. They weren't taught to her. They're *real.* "*Is* that why she did it?"

A month ago, it would have been unthinkable, a question that never crossed Pheir's mind. Now, her vibrant memories are tainted with smog, covered in soot she never noticed before. Feathers bristle on Pheir's body, shame heating her face. She doesn't want to believe it. If she truly loved Vesta, she wouldn't question her. That's what Pheir always told Rhaiden, but now…

Pheir grits her teeth. "Am I that fucking naive?"

Caius sighs, like it pains him to say it. "You're not naive." It's the least-hostile thing he's said in her presence. That makes it worse. It's proof that her foolishness is on display, and she's too pitiful for him to make fun of.

"Yes, I am!" she seethes. "All these years, I thought Vesta was protecting us. That the four of us were together because she cared. Because she wanted *us.* Because we were special." Pheir's lip trembles. That's enough to staunch her words. Worst of all, if Vesta reappeared, Pheir would still believe in her. Pheir wants to believe in her now. It would be easier. It would be so much fucking easier.

Vesta's voice in her head is quieter, no longer splitting her in two, like it's calling from a distance. *I was protecting you! You know you're special to me. He's lying. He can't understand what we have…*

An ache starts in Pheir's chest.

"If you're stupid for believing in her…" Caius pauses for so long, Pheir thinks he isn't going to finish. "Then I'm stupid, too."

"That's not really a comfort."

It makes Caius smile momentarily before it's lost again, buried under his surly expression like he's preparing for a fight. Pheir wrinkles her nose. What are they doing? Since when have they been within five feet of each other and not pounced?

Awkwardly, she shoves at his shoulder. It makes him brace his other hand against the deck, snapping teeth in her direction. It's not playful, but it's not violent, either.

"Come on." She shrugs. This isn't her forte, wading through emotions and encouragement. Where's Thalea when she needs her? Pheir does her best to channel the dryad. "I told you my shit. You have to tell me yours."

It's not quite Thalea's voice, but it works. Caius leans forward, elbows resting on his knees as if he's blocking his face from her. He seems somehow smaller, a younger version of himself without the brutal strength. In the sun, his scars stand out against the blonde of his fur.

"Before the Timbers…" Each word comes from him slowly, as if he's not sure he'll continue. Sharply, he exhales, running his hand back through his hair. "Fuck, I don't want to tell you."

"Fair's fair," Pheir insists, knocking his foot with her own.

"Yeah, well, your bullshit was relevant."

Pheir looks toward the ground. Maybe a fall from this height would be less painful for him than sharing. Caius shuts his eyes and flexes his fingers, balling them into fists. His knuckles stand out, the musculature separated from bone. Pheir tilts closer to look. Even with accelerated werewolverine healing, there's lasting trauma to the joints.

Her chin jerks toward them. "Is it about those?"

Caius opens his eyes to where she's staring before he lets out a long breath. "I was in a fighting ring."

"For fun?"

He shakes his head. "Money. Supplies. For my family"

A tiny crease forms in Pheir's brow. "How'd you get into that?"

"I didn't." Caius finally wears past his initial resistance. "It was a part of life. When you learn to walk, you learn to fight. You have to contribute to the family. You have to pull your weight. The more fights you lose, the less you have. Less food. Less shelter. Mom and dad can't pour money into a kid that's not bringing anything back."

"That's fucked up," Pheir echoes.

Caius snorts a humorless laugh. "When you put it like that..." His smile falls, gaze drifting toward the horizon. "It seems weird telling *you* about it when no one else knows. I guess they were right; we are the same. That's why you're so..." His lip curls in frustration. "Irritatingly predictable."

Pheir breaks off a splinter of wood. "Is this an excuse to insult me?"

"I don't need an excuse to insult you."

When she flicks the splinter toward him, he doesn't flinch, bracing his hands by his thighs.

"Anyway," he continues. "That's what I did: train, fight, find new ways to hurt people."

It sounds like Caius, but there's something in his expression that Pheir doesn't recognize, a pause she's not used to. "Did you like it?" she asks.

His mouth twists. "At the time, I did. I was good at it. It felt good to win. Winning made everything else worth it: the sleepless nights, the meals I couldn't have, the bruises from my dad taking me to the ground... When I was the last one standing and the referee lifted my hand, my dad looked so proud. It was like you with Vesta, like the sun was shining on me for the first time."

When Caius's head tilts toward the sky, sun casts through the lighter strands of his fur. Pheir's stomach flips before his mouth moves again.

"I had a purpose. I was good for something. Everything else about me was less disappointing. I had to keep winning. If I could, maybe my parents would care about more than what I could do for them."

Pheir's never heard someone else put words to it — how she got hooked on one of Vesta's smiles, chasing her reassuring squeeze and searching for a hint of praise. Pheir would have done anything to get that, anything to feel that warmth on her skin again.

Caius picks a leaf from the tree beside them, tearing it into strips and letting the pieces drift down. "Of course, it doesn't work like that. No matter how much I practiced, I couldn't win every time. No matter how good I got, my parents wanted more. My old 'best' wasn't good enough. I had to keep improving, keep giving more, keep throwing myself at fighting until there was nothing left. Where else can you go once you reach the ceiling?" He tosses his hands in frustration. "You keep pushing until you die? Quitting isn't an option, so what else is there?"

Pheir's throat tightens. How does he know the feelings she's never put into words, thoughts so vague and unreachable she didn't realize she felt them until this moment? Her life was spent in service to Vesta. Professing it wasn't enough; Pheir had to prove her loyalty. She had to do more, give more, *be* more. How else could Vesta trust her?

In the end, what could Pheir do but die for her?

"The most fucked up part is..." Caius huffs a laugh, "I would have kept doing it forever. I would have spent my whole life fighting until my body gave out, as long as it made them happy for a day. But my dad kicked me out before it got to that. I think he realized I was bigger than him, and he didn't want to risk me figuring out my punches could hurt him, too. At the time..." Caius shakes his head. "I didn't imagine fighting back, no matter what size I was. It was like some mental block. When he hit me, I didn't hit back, like I was still the weak kid he told me I was, who couldn't bear to disappoint him. Who wanted him to smile at me one fucking time. Not because I proved myself. Not because I did something for him. Just because..."

He loved me.

Every bright moment of Vesta's attention glows around one thing — Pheir beating the shit out of Vesta's enemies. Pheir pinning an opponent to the dirt. Pheir putting her body in front of Vesta's.

Transactional. Conditional. The more Pheir gave, the harder Vesta loved her.

We're the only ones who truly know each other. Vesta said that over and over, tucking a strand of hair behind Pheir's ear. *We're the only ones who understand. We have to stick together. No one else gets it.*

But Caius's voice plays a song Pheir didn't realize she'd forgotten. It's discomforting. It's weird. It's...different. She didn't think Caius had anything left to surprise her.

"I guess we are the same," Pheir murmurs.

They both look out toward the horizon, trying to settle this strange connection. "Except Lev found me," Caius finishes, "and Vesta found you."

Days ago, that would have filled Pheir with pride. Now, her chin rests on her knees as she tries to make peace with this new feeling.

The radio crackles on Caius's hip. It's almost a relief to be interrupted, although Pheir couldn't say what they're being interrupted from. June's voice comes over the airwaves. *"Caius? We got everything we could find. Do you need more time?"*

He pulls the walkie from his side. "No. We'll be down in fifteen."

The radio goes silent. Caius doesn't stand. Neither does Pheir, heart thrumming with the fear that when they leave, everything will return to the way it was. Same old Caius. Same old Pheir. Same old chaos between them.

She should like that. It's familiar. It's what they know how to do. She doesn't know why she clings to this strange new connection, despite how it makes her world tilt.

"I didn't think what my parents did was strange," she blurts. "I never thought anything was wrong with Vesta, either. I thought it was normal...until I saw you all. The Timbers."

The first time she'd seen them, Pheir had laughed from her perch in the tree beside Vesta. The Timbers were weak. They didn't try to steal Vesta's followers. They didn't demand dedication. They didn't bite their tongue when their Alpha spoke. How could a pack run on anything but vicious devotion to their leader?

"More members, more power, more compliance...that was Vesta's goal. That's what I tried to give to her." Pheir's mouth twists. "The Timbers aren't like that."

"No," Caius sighs. "They're not."

Pheir's eyes shift toward him. "You didn't say 'we.'"

He runs his tongue over his teeth. "Honestly? I don't think I was a Timber. Not before. I always had one foot out the door. I guess I was waiting for their disappointment, too. Waiting for them to dismiss me. Maybe I was trying to make it happen, so I would know what was coming."

Pheir's wings fold against her back. "But you're still here."

Caius's smile wrinkles the scar on his face. "I'm still here."

Electricity tingles in the air. Vesta was golden from first sight and branded in all of Pheir's memories, but this is the first time Caius has seemed that way. Bathed in sunlight, he looks warm and soft like fruit cracked open. Pheir forgets to breathe, focused on memorizing every detail of his face — the cowlick behind his ear. The crooked tilt of his smile. The fang that protrudes longer on one side.

With Vesta, Pheir wanted to worship, unworthy to touch her. With Caius, Pheir wants to drag her mouth over every imperfection until his taste stays on the back of her tongue.

His weight shifts on the wood as he turns to her. "Stop staring."

He's close enough that she can make out the scar across his face, the one she dug into him in the orchard. Her hand lifts.

There's a flicker in Caius's eyes, a carnal temptation to strike. His body poises to spring. They both still until she moves slowly, brushing her talons against the mark. It drags up past his eyes. He doesn't close them as she finishes the trail and follows it back to his snout.

She doesn't want to pull her fingers away. Her throat is tight. "You kind of deserved that one."

His gaze stays on hers. "Not the worst thing someone's given me."

Unfamiliar feelings gnaw in her gut. Guilt. Sympathy. She'd long forgotten how to feel them, if she ever knew.

They're close enough to kill each other. It's a hard habit to break, tempting like a spark waiting to ignite. At least, that's what the spark used to mean. Now it's an urge to dig her claws into him, to pull him closer, to move before she bursts out of her skin. Still, they both wait, breaths mingling to see who gives into instinct first.

Problem is, Pheir's no longer sure what that instinct is telling her to do.

She wants his teeth in her. Wants him branded into her the same way she's embedded across his face. Wants him to scratch the itch she didn't realize she had. Wants to claw his eyes out. Wants him to keep looking at her when he speaks.

"I don't think you deserved any of it."

She swings at him. Surely she means to hit him. Instead, she grips the fur behind his neck and pulls him toward her. Their mouths knock as they try to catch their breath above the frantic pace of their hearts. She lifts her chin too sharply, her lip scraping his fang. He grips her jaw and forces her into place. It burns hot through her stomach, molten and dangerous.

Their bodies don't know how to act. They crash together, an instinct for violence that gives way under the crush of their mouths. All that fight has nowhere to go but teeth and tongue and lips. He slams her onto her back on the deck, bearing his weight along her body as his torn confession rumbles into her mouth. "I want you so fucking bad, I can't stand it."

Her other hand lifts to strike before he catches it in his. He pins her wrists above her head, both of them panting as she rocks her hips. They know each other. They see each other. They are the same. For the first time, she craves it. Her thighs tighten against his hips, locking him in place.

"Then don't stand it."

He kisses her better than he hates her, raking claws along her skin to patch the holes of her broken memory.

FORTY-FOUR

Pheir

Back at the shoreline, June and Echo recline against a tree as Pheir and Caius approach. June's nose twitches above her smirk. "Working hard up the trees?"

Caius nudges her with his foot. June shares a conspiratorial smile with Pheir. Pheir doesn't realize her mouth has returned it until moments later.

"Did you find everything?" Caius asks.

June waves a bouquet of wildflowers. "Even found these."

Pheir recognizes them. Past the distorted memories of the island, she knows Thalea tended to those flowers every spring, vibrant orange and cool indigo and bright pink. Back then, Pheir rolled her eyes. *What use are flowers? You can't fight with weeds.*

"Here." June extends a bundle of purple flowers to Pheir. There's a variety of flora, round and sharp petals, long and short stems, vibrant and muted colors. Pheir blinks before June nudges the bunch toward her again. "They're your colors."

Surprisingly, they are. The lighter violets blend against Pheir's skin, while the darker flowers match her hair. Long petals billow like feathers in the breeze. Maybe that's why Thalea chose them.

Pheir takes one between her fingers. It's delicate and soft, just like Thalea. After a moment, Pheir grips the stems and pulls them against her chest.

Caius offers June a hand so he can pull her to her feet. She trips over a tree root, but he holds her steady. "Watch your giant fucking feet," he mumbles.

Is he...teasing? Pheir prepares for June to lash out. Instead, a huge smile captivates her face. She kicks his ankle playfully before she takes off with Echo toward the bank. Caius and Pheir bring up the rear.

"One more stop on the way back," Caius reminds her. They've fallen into step. It's almost strange enough for Pheir to break the rhythm on purpose.

Almost.

She's going to see Thalea. Strange feelings ripple through Pheir, the residual Vestal bond twinging like a tender muscle. It's easier to bear now. It's not an overwhelming pain like it was in the beginning. Now, it's fond. Yearning. Missing.

Pheir guesses she has the wedding to thank for that. It alleviated the pain of the broken Vestal bonds, but it's done more than that. The reminder makes her stomach sink. That's the reason she feels conflicted about the Timbers. That's the reason she and Caius got carried away in the trees. The wedding bonded them as it was supposed to; the Timbers have started viewing her as one of their own.

Her jaw sets. She has to resist the pull to ensure she's thinking clearly. It can't be that difficult. She spent years hating the Timbers. What's a little longer? Although when Caius holds the boat for her to step into, looking up at her with the heat from before, she sits down heavily so her legs don't wobble.

After they cast off, Caius takes his seat in front of Pheir to row them across the channel. There's no escape when they're stuck staring at each other with Pheir at the back of the boat. She keeps her eyes on the rocking waves, but she's drawn back to the muscles shifting in Caius's arms as he maneuvers the oars. His shoulders rotate, biceps flexing under his fur —

"Staring?" he asks. There's amusement in his tone.

Pheir scowls. "I'm making sure you don't row us in circles."

His sharp smile makes her feel like the boat is tipping. She forces her eyes back toward the water, sitting in silence as June and Echo chatter at the front. Oars dip into the water, displacing it as the boat moves along the channel.

"Do you *want* to see Thalea?" Caius finally asks.

It's still strange being asked what she wants. Pheir's desires were long tied up with Vesta's. Even if they hadn't been, she's not sure she could have denied Vesta anything, not when the simple act of agreeing made Vesta love Pheir more.

Or, approve of her more — whatever happened between them. Pheir gets a sickly feeling in her stomach when she tries to work it out. She doesn't realize she's left indentations in the boat until Caius pries her grip off the edge. "Is that a no, then?"

Her fingers tingle where he touched her. She jerks her hand back and rubs it against her leg. "It's not a 'no.'"

Once they reach the shore of the Break and load the truck, Pheir sits in the back with Caius. Vesta's books are piled in a box between her legs. The covers look familiar, colors and shapes that drifted in the periphery of Pheir's life, but she's never truly looked at them. It feels wrong to do it now. Her fingers drift over the spines. She could dump the books over the edge of the truck to keep Vesta's secrets. If she goes slowly, the others won't notice. Her teeth dig into her lip, fingers flicking back and forth along the corner until she gets a paper cut.

She could do it; she just has to take the first step...

But it doesn't feel like it used to. Before, Pheir would have tossed the books without thinking, but she hesitates now. Has she ever hesitated in her life? The feeling's foreign, just like the questions bubbling inside her. She leans away from the books, resting her head against the cab of the truck and blaming her queasy stomach on the bumpy road.

After a couple of hours, the truck pulls down a long drive, kicking up dust as they approach a farm. Behind the ranch house are rolling hills and green pastures next to a worn barn where cows and chickens mill about. When the truck parks, Caius hops down and holds out his hand. Pheir eyes it skeptically.

His eyes roll. "Don't worry. I'm not gonna take you to the ground."

"As if you could."

When she reaches for him, he tugs her closer, gripping her hips and swinging her feet down to the dirt. She struggles to catch her balance, grabbing onto his arms. He doesn't release her, lowering his mouth to her ear as he holds her upright. "Believe me: I could."

A shiver fights through her body. Gods, the wedding bonds are no joke. It seems like they've heightened in the days since, making her dizzy when she stands this close to Caius. When he pulls back, he smirks, and Pheir has an undeniable urge to pull his fangs against her throat...

The truck door slams as Echo and June exit. Pheir steps back to breathe, turning toward the house situated before them.

Nerves worm through her chest. Everything is unfamiliar. She hasn't felt anything but anger and rage for years. In the last week, other emotions have crawled to the surface — things she can't put names to, things she barely remembers from the days before Vesta. Pheir doesn't know how to read the sweat on her palms and the skittish patter of her heart.

When the Timbers start toward the house, Pheir's feet drag in the dirt. Before long, Caius turns his head over his shoulder to catch sight of her. She walks behind him like a shield.

"You're hiding," he notes.

Pointedly, Pheir steps out beside him, but she doesn't move forward. He tracks her movements, brows knit as he listens to tells that she can't regulate. Her scent, her sounds, her body shifting. Her breath is choppy. Her weight switches between her feet. That must tell him something, because he asks, "You got the urge to run?"

It's unnerving how he predicts her. She swats at the air like he's a gnat. "Can you stay out of my head, please? Gods, you're worse than Aren."

There's a pride in Caius's smile when he turns to face her. "What are you afraid of?" It's not a gentle question, but it's not meant to torment her, either. He waits for the answer as Pheir's gaze slips toward the house.

What happens when Thalea reappears? The last time they saw each other feels like ages ago. Pheir was enraged. Thalea was crying. They were covered in blood. They'd both lost the most important person in their lives. Thalea lost her *mate*. What will she think of Pheir now? If she knew how Pheir betrayed Vesta in the month since...

The two of them spent years together. If Pheir knew happiness outside of Vesta, it was with Thalea. They didn't always understand each other, but sitting next to Thalea was warm. When Pheir bled, Thalea covered her wounds. If everything else Pheir remembers is wrong, what if these memories are, too? What if there's nothing left between them? What if the bond they shared is broken?

"What if she's not the same?" Pheir swallows roughly. "What if *I'm* not?"

Despite Pheir's resistance, Caius urges her forward, lifting her so her heels can't dig into the ground. "You're not. That's not a bad thing."

Somehow, when the front doors open, his words are a comfort.

FORTY-FIVE

Pheir

A few other creatures spill onto the Steppe's porch to greet Echo and June. Pheir holds her breath, lifting on her toes to see past them. She looks so intently for the delicate girl she knew that she doesn't recognize the woman making her way across the yard.

Grass blooms beneath Thalea's feet, hair lush with leaves and vines as flowers frame her face. Pheir double-takes. Has Thalea always looked like this? She's been beautiful all their time together, but now her stride is bright and certain, sweet without any of the timidness Pheir knew before.

Thalea stops short a few feet away. Pheir fights the urge to touch her, to wrap her arms around her, to grab her hand. That's not what they did before, when Vesta was here. "You look really..." Pheir grapples for words before she blurts, "Alive."

It can't be the right thing to say, but it's the singular word that hangs in her mind. Despite the dry heat around them, Thalea looks more vibrant when she smiles. "Thank you." Her gaze flicks to Caius, then back to Pheir. "So do you."

Panic hitches into Pheir's pulse. There's no way Thalea can know, can she? Awkwardly, Caius clears his throat and leans closer to Pheir. "Don't try to escape." Then he hoists the satchel off of his shoulder and onto Pheir's.

It sits weighty against Pheir's side as Caius departs. Thalea curls fingers around the basket in her hands, rocking on her heels and gesturing to a lone tree by a small pond. "Should we sit? I made a picnic."

Nervous laughter bubbles into Pheir's throat. Imagine that, Vesta's strongest soldiers reclined beneath a tree. It's ludicrous. Pheir nods before she thinks better of it.

They lay out a quilt beneath the tree, unloading the picnic basket of blue-checkered wrappings. It's a mixture of nuts and seeds; biscuits with jams, jellies, and honey; berry cobbler; fruit juices of every variety. With each new package, Pheir blinks in surprise. "Do you even eat half of this stuff?"

The flowers in Thalea's hair blush a shade of pink. "No. But when I heard you might be coming, I got a little carried away."

Pheir's teeth scrape into her lip when she smiles. It doesn't feel fake. It doesn't curl at the ends like a snarl. It's so foreign, Pheir clamps her mouth shut, gaze darting around with nowhere to land.

Thalea folds her hands awkwardly in her lap. They sit in stilted silence for a long moment before Thalea cringes and gestures to the gap between them. "It's kind of weird, isn't it? This whole thing."

This whole thing, like the two of them having a picnic yards away from where Thalea is held captive. Reuniting and not immediately fighting their captors. Talking about anything but Vesta. It feels wrong, but the alternative doesn't feel right, either. Pheir itches like she wants to be free of her skin. Do they have anything in common without Vesta? *Should* they? Should they be angrier? Sadder? More violent?

Thalea holds out a jar of moonshine just as Pheir reaches for it. An uncomfortable laugh escapes them both. It eases the tension in Pheir's shoulders a fraction.

Maybe some things haven't changed.

Pheir's hungrier than she realized. She eats until she's full to bursting just to see Thalea smile. With each dish Pheir tries, Thalea points out the old favorites she incorporated among the new recipes she's learned.

"I almost forgot..." Pheir reaches for the satchel, emptied of everything but Thalea's worn romance novels. When Pheir retrieves them, Thalea's mouth falls open, eyes clinging to the covers like she can't believe they're real.

"You went back?" Thalea asks quietly and hugs the books to her chest, watching Pheir with a pinched face. "What was it like?"

That nauseous feeling pricks in Pheir's throat again. She turns her eyes away. Across the field, horses stampede to the barn and flatten grass under their hooves. Pheir picks at a thread in the blanket, biting back the question until it can't be held inside her.

"Do you miss her?"

Even unnamed, Vesta strikes like lightning between them, leaving the air crackling with static. It almost seems like she could reappear. Pheir should be desperate for that, but the thought is less like a reassuring squeeze and more like a bear trap.

Thalea worries her lip between her teeth. "Yes," she admits. "I do miss her." Her mouth twists in thought, as if she's not sure going any further is worth the trouble. She gives Pheir a sideways glance before continuing. "But I miss her less than yesterday. And yesterday, I missed her less than the day before. Every day, it's less."

An alarm sounds inside Pheir — *Traitor! Betrayal!* — but it fades until all that's left is an empty instinct that she can't muster up any more.

Is that all you think of me now?

Vesta's voice weaves between Pheir's ribs and twists. She pries herself out of the guilt, drowning it in another swig of moonshine. "That's what it felt like for me." Her mouth moves fast, hushed around a secret she can't believe she's sharing. If she stops, she won't start again. "When the Timbers first took me, she was all I could think about. She wasn't gone, she just had to be brought back, but now..." Pheir trails off. Her thoughts don't stop swirling. *But now, what?* Pheir doesn't know how to finish.

Thalea doesn't, either. She holds her breath for a long time before she speaks again. "I don't think it's her I'm missing." Her eyes flit toward the sky, as if Vesta might swoop down herself. When nothing strikes Thalea down, she exhales like a weight has been lifted. "I miss being together. Being united in something. I miss you. I miss Rhaiden."

Pheir fends off the urge to roll her eyes. She doesn't call Rhaiden what she *wants* to, not when Pheir's questioning herself. Instead, she forces herself to focus on Thalea, tongue heavy with guilt. "It must be harder for you, losing your mate. It's like what your story books talk about."

Thalea fingers her books' pages, but her eyes drift toward the house as figures move crates to and from the truck. "I thought it would be, too."

Thought it would be? Pheir's brow kits. Before she can ask what that means, Thalea returns her gaze to her lap. Her fingers trace the embraced couple on the book's cover. Pheir's heels dig into the earth, body resisting the question that threatens to break through her lips —

"Do you think she cared about us?"

The words are barely a whisper hanging in the air between them. It's blasphemy. The longer the silence stretches, the more Pheir feels like a traitor for thinking it.

Wind ruffles Thalea's leaves. Maybe Pheir didn't speak at all. Maybe she kept the question in her head —

Thalea gives a pained sound. She leans back against the tree and watches its branches as if she's plucking careful words from them. "In a way? I think she cared about us. She cared if we were alive. If our bodies were healthy. If we were content enough to stay with her. But I'm starting to wonder if that was 'caring' or investment. Indifference, just better than what we were used to."

Pheir chokes on a handful of nuts. It's frightening that Thalea's been thinking about this, because if Pheir wasn't the only one...she wipes at her mouth with the back of her hand. All those years can't boil down to that. It can't be that Vesta was building an army instead of a pack, assets instead of friends, resources instead of family. Vesta taught them to defend themselves. She showed them how to fight off any dangers, to keep from being taken advantage of again...

Or did Vesta teach them to guard against everything but her?

There's a heartbreaking look in Thalea's eyes. All those years, Vesta told her they were partners and mates, entwined with a love nothing else could conquer. Thalea's lip trembles. "Do you think she cared?"

Pheir's throat aches. The answer comes easily, the same way protecting Thalea always has. "Yes, she cared." Pheir's eyes clench shut. "I need to believe that. At least for now."

Thalea twines a vine around Pheir's hand. She stares down at it and flexes her fingers. They rarely touched each other unless they were sparring. Vesta didn't like them to be soft. *It'll cause problems in battle. Don't comfort each other. Get better at fighting, so you don't have to.*

Tentatively, Pheir wraps her fingers around Thalea's vine and squeezes.

In the distance, the Timbers finish loading supplies into the truck. Caius leans back against it, finding Pheir with no effort. His gaze heats her, dark and possessive, until she notices the two Steppes standing beside him — a burly minotaur and a hellhound.

The one who killed Vesta.

Rage surges through her as she gets her feet beneath her. Vesta's voice screams, imbued with sudden strength. *Rip him apart! Avenge me!*

The hound doesn't look at Pheir. He and the minotaur stare at Thalea twining flowers into her hair. Sun dapples through her leaves. The minotaur and the hellhound's glances are a puzzling mix of reverence and craving, as if they're scared Thalea will break at the slightest touch — and they're fighting an urge to see it happen.

Pheir recognizes that look. Her chin jerks toward them, angry eyes turning back to Thalea. "What's that about?"

Darker green spreads across Thalea's cheeks. "What do you mean?"

A strange feeling squirms in Pheir's stomach. There's fury, but it's bound with a different sort of confusion. Vesta never looked at Thalea like that. "Your new *Alpha*," Pheir continues. "Don't tell me you're fucking him and his friend."

She sounds like the old Pheir. Good: she needs to hold onto that, to think clearly, to make sense of things.

"Keep your voice down!" Thalea whispers as she collects leftover twine and paper from their meal. "Some of them hear better than we can."

"Are you serious?" Pheir hisses. "Him? Of everyone, you chose the person who killed your mate? The person who —"

"That's *enough*!"

Pheir's mouth clamps in shock. It's the strongest Thalea's sounded, voice resonant and real, as if Pheir's getting a look behind the glaze Thalea was cast in. This is a glimpse at the dryad Thalea grew into, not a whittled version of herself.

"I know it seems simple," Thalea continues, not unkindly. "Like there's a right and a wrong, like everything's black and white, but there are things..." Her eyes dart toward the two Steppes again. "Things you don't understand. Things *I* don't understand. You feel it, too."

Pheir's body freezes like a cornered animal. How can Thalea know that?

Thalea barrels ahead. "When you asked those questions today, I knew it. And when you look at him..." She gestures toward Caius. "Maybe he's not the only one you're thinking about."

There's an urge in Pheir to fight back, to stand staunchly in her belief and refuse anything that contradicts it. She flushes. "I am not —"

"Call it whatever you like." Thalea holds up a gentle hand. For once, Pheir doesn't feel the urge to snap it. "I used to think Vesta and I were like the people in these stories, that she found me by destiny, that love kept me on my toes the same way training did, but it's not..." Thalea thumbs over the arched book spine, shaking her head. "I hope you'll give me the understanding to figure out what life means for me now. What the truth is. Who *I* am. I hope you'll give yourself the same thing."

It's impossible to make sense of that. Pheir stands over Thalea, both of them staring at each other as if they've reached a stalemate. Carefully, Thalea offers Pheir the last of the moonshine.

It's a truce. After a moment, Pheir downs it and shakes the dregs into her mouth.

They gather the rest of the food into the basket. Thalea slips it into Pheir's hands as they approach the truck with Echo and June sitting in the back. The hellhound steps forward, shooting Thalea a coarse look before she nods. Gruffly, he turns back to Pheir.

"Hey. Uh. I wanted to —"

"Asshole," she snaps.

To his credit, he doesn't flinch, nose wrinkling. "Most people use 'Dante'."

Pheir doesn't want to look at him. Instead, she glances beside her to Thalea, who's lifting her brows in a silent plea.

For me?

Pheir doesn't respond — but she doesn't shut Dante down, either. That brings half a smile to Thalea's face. Dante clears his throat and tries again. "I want to clear the air. Not for what happened, but the way it did."

"This is a shitty apology," Pheir notes.

Crossly, Dante grumbles. "Is there an apology you'd accept for me killing someone you cared about?"

Fair. There's no getting past that. As Pheir's mouth twists, she steps toward him. "You know..."

Caius pushes off the truck to intercept her. Dante doesn't move when Pheir stops in front of him, Caius gripping her shoulders to block her body from him. She tilts her eyes up, narrowed and sharp, lifting a dull talon to tap on Dante's sternum.

"I don't want to rip your throat out as much as I expected."

At Pheir's words, Caius breathes a sigh of relief. She turns back to the truck and calls over her shoulder.

"Don't let me catch you alone, though."

Thalea's muffled laughter comes from behind the minotaur. When Pheir slips into the passenger seat, the corner of Dante's lip twitches. "Wouldn't dream of it."

The driver door swings shut as Caius takes his seat. "You're gonna give me a fucking heart attack."

Pheir smirks. "Don't tempt me."

Caius cranks the engine, resting his arm behind Pheir's head. Feathers on her neck stand on end, lips parting as she turns toward him — but he's reversing away from the house. Echo and June make kissing faces through the window.

Pheir tucks her chin to hide her smile. "Why are they riding in the back?"

"Who the hell knows?" When Caius shifts into drive, his arm stays draped behind her shoulders.

The truck turns onto the long path back to the main road. Thalea rises onto her toes to wave, and Pheir watches the rearview until she fades into dusk. Her heart aches to return, to clutch Thalea close and never let go, but when Pheir spots the Timber mountains in the distance, a stronger wanting blooms in her.

She sinks down further in her seat, the back of her head brushing Caius's arm. "Do you think Thalea's ok there with them?"

A laugh barks out of him, as if he knows something Pheir doesn't, *smelled* something she didn't. When his fingers ghost the back of her hair, she forgets her question. He answers it anyway.

"I think your friend's getting along just fine."

FORTY-SIX

Pheir

Without Pheir, the Timber Compound is peaceful. Lev hates it.

Sending Caius to lead reconnaissance was the right choice, but all day, Lev's eyes drift toward the dirt road. What if he runs this time? Worse, what if Pheir turns on him? Things have felt strange since the wedding, like the aftershocks of an earthquake. No matter how Lev tells herself she misread Pheir's feelings, Lev can't forget the way Pheir kissed her. The way she hesitated against Lev's mouth. The way she gasped. The way she tasted —

"Careful." Aren pulls the coffee pot from Lev's hand before she overflows her mug of afternoon caffeine. A smirk plays across his lips. He's been in a chipper mood since his conversation with Caius this morning — if you can call making out like two teenagers "conversation." The thought brings a matching smile to Lev's lips.

Inventory will be a good distraction. Tossing a towel at Aren's head, she makes her way to the root cellar to compare numbers. It takes her mind off things for a few hours, but as she takes her work and her dinner to the library desk, her thoughts drift back to Pheir with the ashes.

It should be an easy image to decipher, one Lev has feared since day one. Of course Pheir stole the vial. Of course she intended to use them; she's told as much to anyone who will listen. But something about that night, that moment, doesn't feel clear at all.

Pheir's expression was off, uncertain what to do with the vial. Caius pinned her, but the look he gave her was betrayal. As if he expected — *hoped* — for something different. Even Aren was confused. And Lev...she can't begin to sort through the emotions bleeding together, impossible to name —

"Bad time?" Caius hovers in the library doorway. Lev's brain doesn't hinder her body as she bounds across the room and flings her arms around his neck.

He's rigid and uncertain, hands hovering off her back. They've never hugged so casually. Maybe she made a mistake in letting intuition tug her closer to him, but it's like her body needed it. Having him under her hands again is more overwhelming than she thought it would be. Her face presses to his chest, squeezing tighter before she prepares to drop her hold — then Caius returns the gesture.

It's tense. It's a little strange, but his body's warm against hers, arms enveloping her completely. She presses her cheek to his shoulder. Both of them exhale a sigh of relief.

"We were only gone for the day." His mouth brushes her ear.

"A day with Pheir has endless possibilities."

Caius's chuckles ghosts Lev's hair. "You're right about that."

It's tempting to stay like that, a moment of closeness that isn't dependent on fighting or fucking. Lev's heart stirs, but she tamps it down, stepping back to look at him. "How was it? Did you find anything of Vesta's?"

"A few things." He steps back out the doorway, hoisting a crate onto a table inside. "Old books. Vesta's real *and* fake journal. It mentions the same shit Rhaiden did, *seeds* and *eggs* and *sleepers*. It's like a code. I didn't get a chance to ask Pheir. She was a little...out of it."

Lev wrings her hands behind her back. "How was it for her, being back there? Did she seem like...?" Lev's not sure what to ask. *Did she mean to take the ashes? Did she seem conflicted? Did she mention the way we kissed?*

Caius's gaze dips guiltily to the ground. "We, uh...talked."

That's not what it smells like — Pheir's scent is light, but it's woven into Caius's fur. More puzzling is that Lev hadn't noticed when he walked in, that she hadn't noticed when she was buried in it herself.

Like Pheir is meant to be there. Like Pheir is one of them.

Caius pulls his shoulders back, prepared to be reprimanded. "Are you upset?"

"No! No." Lev waves her hand. She wants to reach for him, but this is still new. The Caius of days past would shrug out of her touch, so Lev doesn't risk it, leaning into the table beside her. "What did you talk about?"

There go her emotions again, turning into muddy watercolor on murky outlines. Understanding Pheir is hard enough, but Lev can't read herself. Should she feel threatened? Is this another ploy for Pheir to escape? Lev reaches for the feelings that make sense, but she returns with curiosity and timid optimism, a twinge of melancholy for not being there for Caius and Pheir's connection.

Caius's throat bobs with a different tension that has nothing to do with either of them. "History. Where we were before. How we got here. It just sort of came out." Guilt twitches in the corner of his mouth. "I don't know why I told her. I'm sorry —"

"You don't have anything to be sorry for," Lev assures him. Impossible how, a month ago, the four of them were simple. Pheir hated them. They hated her. Marrying Pheir would keep her alive and nothing more. Aren, Lev, and Caius couldn't figure out how to balance each other. Now, Aren and Caius have started to close the space between them. Caius finally recognizes something in Pheir. It's a strange equilibrium, Lev's wife finding her place with the men closest to Lev. Lev has stumbled across a pit of pacing, hungry emotions that are desperate to be fed. Confusing jealousy claws a weakened worry, pride and relief circle with distrust, and a ball of hope curls up in the middle.

Caius shakes his head incredulously, as if he's plucked the words from Lev's thoughts. "It's fucking weird being around her."

An uncertain laugh huffs out of Lev. Caius's mouth pulls back in a smile.

"It *is* fucking weird," Lev agrees. The little ball of hope stretches its paws. "But I think it's good."

"Good that she talked to someone, or good that I did?"

"Both. Is Pheir —" But the question is a betrayal of Pheir's trust, not that there's any to begin with. Lev turns the words over in her mouth before she settles on something safer. "Do you feel like you understand her better?"

Caius considers it for a long time before he answers. "I feel like I understand myself better."

There's an openness to his face that fills Lev, even as sadness settles into her bones. Caius notes the shift in her face. "Are you jealous?"

"No." Lev's mouth twists as soon as she says it. If he's sharing this much with her, the least she can do is put words to whatever it is she's feeling. "Yes...I'm jealous, but not in a way I'm used to."

Caius leans his hip against the table, folding his arms across his chest. There's that possessive flint sparking in his eyes, as if the thought amuses him. "Jealous how?"

Snarling emotions stare up at Lev from the pit. Her voice is quiet and uncertain. "I wish I could do that for you." Her brows knit, trying to decipher the added layers of confusion. "*Both* of you. You and Pheir...I wish I could give you what you give each other. I wish I could give you what you need."

A low chuckle escapes Caius. It surprises Lev, making her blink up at him. He eases a step closer, table creaking as he shifts. "Is that what you think?"

With a swallow, Lev's fur rises on end. Caius stands taller, towering over her until she has to crane her neck back to meet his eyes.

"Before you," he murmurs, "no one protected me. No one looked out for me. Not just my body, but everything else. Things I never considered when all I thought about was surviving." The words seem to come more easily now, as if the last twelve hours of Caius opening up has encouraged him to keep trying. Or maybe it's easier, because they're really talking about *Lev*. "You made the foods I liked. You gave me my own space. Before you, no one cared why I did things. No one cared if I shared with them. Sure as hell no one cared about me finding a home."

She remembers their conversation on his deck days ago, Lev wondering if it would make a difference — but Caius heard all of it.

"I don't think you realize it." He laughs. Affection warms Lev's body. It's the easiest expression of joy he's given, crackling and gruff like dead leaves tossed into the air. "No one else has taken a risk to give me a chance. No one's ever put their body in front of mine. With Singer in the boathouse, you didn't think."

A humble flush heats Lev's neck. "It wasn't a big —"

Caius focuses on her eyes. "You did the same thing when you found me. The same thing when we met Vesta in the orchard. The same thing when you took in Pheir. You didn't listen to the Regents, or the Conclave, or me." His eyes roll with begrudging acceptance. "As much as I *hated* it, I get it. You protected us when no one wanted to."

His hand flexes against the table, stretching toward Lev's. Slowly, her fingers inch forward until they brush the tips of his. There's always been ferality to Caius, lashing out to keep everyone at bay. Now, he restrains himself, giving the barest touch of his fingers. It drives Lev wild, breath short and sharp in her chest.

There's a pulse that begs her to get closer. Her fingers strain toward him, slotting between his before he closes them to keep her locked in place. His voice makes her legs weak, like a sudden roll of thunder.

"You give me exactly what I want. What I *need*."

There's not an inch left between them when he lifts her, sitting her on the table and making space between her legs. A growl vibrates from his chest, snout buried against her throat where her heartbeat jumps under his tongue.

When she reaches for him, he snatches her wrists, pinning them beside her thighs on the table. A whimper claws its way into her throat. Caius licks it from her mouth.

He keeps her pinned. It's like they've switched sides, him holding back as she fights to think past her body chasing temptation. "Please…" Her voice is hoarse. She doesn't know what she wants except to *touch him*.

He lowers himself to her eye-level. "Tell me. You heard what I said. Now I want to hear it from you." It's only fair. The way Caius opened up to her is more than she could ask. He knows it; he's still the same Caius, deliciously cruel grin aimed at her pathetic sounds. "I've got all night, little rabbit. I'm not going anywhere."

A keening sound slips between her lips. The sentiment is more than foreplay. *He isn't leaving. He's staying here.* That promise makes her lose control of the desire she's been too afraid to let herself sink fully into. "You make me…" Her nails dig into the table, breath panting against his mouth. "Lose myself. I get caught up in you, and I forget what I'm supposed to do. Who I'm supposed to be."

When she reaches for him, he lets her, twining her fingers in his fur to pull him closer. Her thighs tighten against his hips until he groans low in his chest.

"You make me feel — like an *animal*," Lev breathes. "Like I want to mark you, and claim you, and make you *mine* —"

The words get away from her, a mindless string too good to stop. It ignites a desire in Lev that she's long tempered, pulsing with *possession* and *hunt* and *take*. The night after the wedding wasn't an accident; it's what Lev wants from all of them. She fights the rock of her hips, but Caius follows them the way he follows her, bared teeth against her mouth. "So make me yours."

When he grinds between her legs, a gasp slips out. No matter how they've fucked before, they've never been this close. Never this intimate, sharing more than their bodies and finally falling into place. His forehead meets hers, eyes slipping shut as if he trusts her to watch over him. Her thumbs trace the scar under his eyes, hands cradling his jaw before she slots their mouths together —

A throat clears by the entry. Lev and Caius pause, but they don't untangle. She drags her gaze over Caius's shoulder, prepared to tell the intruder to *go away* when she recognizes the five Regents in the doorway.

Lev's stomach sinks. Boreas looks triumphant.

"Are we interrupting?"

FORTY-SEVEN

Aren

Aren gave Lev a hard time when Caius and Pheir left for the Eyrie, but at the sight of the truck returned in front of the compound, he takes longer strides. When Caius and Pheir are nowhere to be seen, Aren tries not to let disappointment show on his face.

"Good trip?" he asks, taking a box of dairy from June's arms as he follows her toward the root cellar.

"Very good." Once they're inside, she pulls the cord for the single lightbulb, smirking over her shoulder. "You should ask your *paramours* about it."

Aren fights the twitch of his whiskers, depositing his box on the table behind a row of shelves. "Any idea where they ran off to?"

"Caius went to find Lev." June pries open the top of her box. "Pheir was escorted back to the cottage, last I heard."

Without a thought, Aren moves toward the stairs before he leans back around the shelf to look at June. "I'll be back to help with the supplies."

"If you aren't," June calls over her shoulder as he disappears, "you have to take my dish duty tomorrow!"

He'll let Lev and Caius have their moment. If this morning by the wood pile is any indication, the three of them will have plenty of lost time to make up for tonight. In the meantime, Aren hasn't seen Pheir in days, and a yearning feeling tugs him toward the cottage.

Maybe it's foolish, but the uncertainty of Pheir's reception doesn't bother him. Maybe she'll lash out, like their early days together. Maybe reuniting with her will be as confusing as that night on the island. Or maybe, impossibly, he'll catch a flicker of happiness on her face before she tries to hide it. No matter the case, his chest aches. His footsteps are lighter. He wants to see her.

He's a fool.

His nose barely picks up the unfamiliar scents, too focused on the thought of Pheir. He waves to Echo and Oberon at the firepit as Marius comes barreling out of the main lodge.

"The Regents are here!" they gasp as they trip over their wings.

Behind Mari, the backs of five people stand in the library doors. Aren glances to the moon hanging in the sky and tries to temper his panic. It's barely been a month of Pheir's timeline, but it doesn't matter to them.

"They just showed up." Marius shoves Aren toward the cottage, breathlessly relaying the details. "We tried to make them wait at the entrance, but they waltzed in looking for Lev...and Pheir."

Fuck. Aren steels himself as he picks up the pace. Lev was right about the Regents heading their way. There's two months left before Pheir's time runs out. It can't mean anything good that they're here.

Ice digs into Aren's chest as he runs through his options. He could set Pheir loose to flee, but losing track of her would seal her fate. At least if she's with the Timbers, they can defend her against anything the Regents try.

Aren shoves into the cottage, shouting Pheir's name as he bounds up the stairs. She's crouching under the window of her room, scrambling to toss a blanket over the nest of items stacked around her bed.

"Ever heard of *privacy*?" she blusters.

Aren doesn't have time to question it, tugging her behind him as they make their way back down to the lodge. Pheir nips at his fingers around her arm.

"I expect the roughness from Caius, not you."

"The Regents are here," Aren counters.

Pheir stumbles. Aren keeps her upright as she hisses, "They're here? Why?"

"To check on *you*."

As they approach the main lodge, Pheir keeps pace with Aren. "But there's still —"

"Months left, I know." Aren presses a hand against the small of her back before he catches sight of her wrists. "You're out of cuffs?"

Her cheeks darken, gaze averting at some memory.

"It's fine. It's better," Aren tells himself. "It adds legitimacy." Before they enter the lodge, he turns her to face him, keeping his voice low so no one inside will hear. "You need to play a part, Pheir. Your marriage to Lev has to seem real. It has to look effective. You have to be a part of this pack."

Giving Pheir orders is tempting a slingshot in the opposite direction, but he has to make her understand. A scowl burrows into her face. It's sharp with a need to fight, to be contrary, to shatter something against the ground.

Aren's fingers tighten around her arms. "They will *kill you*, Pheir. That was the agreement. If the Regents don't think you're rehabilitated...if they suspect there's still trouble, they will take the path of least resistance."

In the face of Pheir's detachment, Aren's emotions claw to the surface. She eyes him, giving nothing away in her expression until her body relaxes the slightest bit. Her lips part. His gaze drops to them. They both watch each other until she speaks.

"Why do you care?"

It's curious and uncertain, not the way she would have tormented him before. Standing here now, he could almost believe in the act they've been forced to put on. He could almost believe that Pheir is one of them. That she wants to be here. That she feels the same impossible, puzzling attachment he does.

There's no time. If he truly looks at Pheir, he'll be lost, words building like an avalanche in his throat. He grips a hand behind her neck, pressing his mouth to her forehead before he turns them both to enter the library.

The five Regents turn toward the pair's entrance. Each Regent is a threat in their own right, with physical power and political pull, the Alphas of the largest packs in the Break...and Boreas is at the head. At the center of the room, Lev is flanked by Caius, both their jaws clenched tight.

Unmistakably, they reek of arousal. Aren bites back a weary sigh.

"Impeccable timing" Boreas chortles. When he catches sight of Pheir's bare wrists, he braces with the other Regents. "She's unrestrained?"

Temptation crosses Pheir's face. By some miracle, she refrains from lunging at the Regents. Aren forces his cool disposition back into place. "Pheir is the Alpha's wife." He prays it sounds as certain as he intends. "Of course she's not chained."

"So you *have* performed the vows." Boreas ignores Aren, his griffin eyes cutting back to Lev and Caius. "Then what a compromising position we find you in."

The hackles on Caius's neck are raised. Lev's fingers curl around his wrist. Aren's body wars with his mind as he hovers next to Pheir.

Grab her.

Run.

Stay calm.

He meets Lev's eyes, trying to communicate *something* —

"You started without us." Pheir's voice betrays none of Aren's anxiety when she saunters across the room, passing closer to the Regents than she needs to. They tense uncertainly. Lev's eyes dart toward Pheir, who's well-within reach to gut any of them, but Pheir hoists herself onto the table on Lev's other side. Boredly, she turns back to the Regents.

"Why are you here?" Her tone matches the look on her face, absent of anxiety, not the least bit bothered at the Regent's interruption of their lives.

Boreas regains his footing. "We're here to determine if you've acclimated to the Timbers."

A flicker of the old Pheir rises to the surface. "What happened to the three months you owe me?"

"The Regents received a tip," Boreas sniffs. "From a disgruntled pack member whom Lev dismissed."

Lev's jaw tenses. "Singer?"

"Who reported the concern isn't the issue. After the Broadleaf fiasco, it was necessary to move up the timeline." Boreas turns back to Pheir, a malicious glint in his eyes. "And we've walked in on your *wife* cavorting with one of her combatants."

"You're goading her," Aren growls from across the room. If Pheir lashes out, the Regents will have the excuse they need to be rid of her.

Unbothered, Pheir's legs swing idly beneath her. "Like I said..." She leans toward Lev, who fights not to recoil as Pheir smiles. "You started *without* us."

Realization dawns on all of them. Boreas splutters. Lev swallows her discomfort and leans back next to Pheir, lowering her voice conspiratorially. "You know how Caius is."

His eyes roll as Boreas glances between them in shock. "All three of you are — together?"

"All *four* of us." Pheir's eyes lock on Aren across the room, mischievous and molten. Gods, a look like that... His heart stutters.

Boreas scoffs toward Lev. "Come, now. Your reprobate beta as well? Not even *he* would stoop —"

"What can I say?" Aren crosses to Pheir's other side, avoiding her leg swinging toward his shin when he turns back to the Regents. "We take our jobs very seriously."

The snort that slips out of Pheir is genuine, but her fingers on the back of Aren's neck make his stomach flip. It would be easy access to incapacitate him, but her talons card through his fur instead.

A simper crosses Boreas's face. "You can't expect us to believe a Vestal soldier who would rather *die* than join you has crawled into your bed."

"She's not dead, is she?" Caius folds his arm in effort to keep himself from lunging. "Neither are we. Sounds like the wedding worked."

"Young man, if you think —

Caius interrupts. "You can smell them on me."

Aren's nose twitches. There's no denying it; the scents of Pheir and Lev mingle in Caius's fur, mixed with the smell of Aren from this morning. It's the proof they need. Still, Boreas shakes his head with a sardonic grin. "It's not possible. A month ago, it took multiple creatures to restrain the Vestal when her pack surrendered. She wanted to fight. She wanted *blood*." Boreas's gaze drags over Pheir with disgust. "Even if she's fooled you, you can't truly believe she cares for anyone but Vesta. She doesn't even care about herself."

Pheir stiffens. Lev curls a hand over hers, entwining their fingers to hold both of them back. "We had an agreement," Lev says plainly. "We've held up our end of the bargain. Despite your intrusion, I expect you to do the same."

With a chuckle, Boreas's beak opens. Lev makes him shut it.

"That wasn't a request, Head Regent."

The Regents behind him stand taller, eyes flicking over the Timbers grouped against the table. It wouldn't be a fair fight. Still, Aren and Caius shift onto their feet, watching each other in their periphery. Lev doesn't stand. It'd be too much of an outright threat, but she balances her weight near the edge of the table.

Boreas keeps his gaze on Pheir as he steps forward. "I want to hear it from you."

Aren and Caius angle tighter as Lev's feet meet the floor, all three poised in front of Pheir. An ominous smile creeps up Boreas's face as the other Regents spread out behind him.

"What do you think of what the Timbers have done to you?" Boreas asks. "To Vesta? Do you denounce her?"

His question isn't curiosity; it's an attempt to make Pheir swing. Boreas is close enough that she could reach him, tear at his throat before they could stop her, send their plan catapulting into chaos — but she doesn't move. Not when Boreas tilts his head with a wicked glint, intent to incite Pheir into rage.

She keeps her gaze on him. "No," she finally says. "I don't."

Only the tension keeps Aren's eyes from slipping shut, a sigh threatening to slip between his teeth. Boreas's smile grows as he reaches behind him to gesture the Regents forward —

"But I question her."

The room stills, every eye honed on Pheir. Surely Aren misheard. Surely Pheir isn't walking back her staunchest support. There's a puzzled twist to her mouth that doesn't dissipate as she speaks.

"I question what Vesta told me about the Timbers. About the Conclave. About my old pack. About me." Her brows knit. "I don't know how I feel about her. This is the first time that I've been able to think for myself. To make my own decisions. To see how other people live. Being here is the first time I've questioned what devotion looks like."

"Right: 'brainwashing.'" Boreas's eyes narrow like he still doesn't buy it. "And why do you question it now?"

Pheir chews on her lip. "Because Vesta never would have stood in front of me."

Only now does Aren notice how the three of them circle Pheir, bodies angled outward toward any attack. Their backs align toward her, no thought to the threat she poses, not when the four of them are facing an enemy together.

Boreas notices it, too. After a long moment, he takes a step back, mouth pulls taut. "But you won't indict Vesta. You haven't fully changed."

"Do you really want more mindless loyalty?" Pheir's frustration is real, teeth bared as she flings out her hand. "It's been a fucking month. Do you want someone who obeys by magical force, or would you rather people think for themselves?"

A scowl settles on Boreas's face. Aren holds his breath as Boreas watches Pheir for a long moment before he finally turns back to the Regents. "Fine."

Aren can't stop himself from exhaling relief.

"We'll accept it," Boreas continues, "*for now*. But be warned, we're keeping a close eye on you. *All* of you. Our investigation isn't over." With Boreas's curt nod, the Regents file out the door as he brings up the back.

"While we're issuing warnings..." At Lev's voice, Boreas pauses in the doorway. "The Regents are not welcome on our compound without invitation. Keep that in mind the next time you enter our territory..." Lev's eyes spark like embers. "Or question my wife."

Boreas's mouth twitches before he disappears out the door. Out the window, other Timbers have gathered, prepared to fight. Oberon lifts a hand to Aren, who waves the all-clear. Oberon follows the Regents to ensure they leave the compound.

Only then do the four inside the library let pretense slip, dissolving into laughter as they breathe again.

"Thank the fucking gods." Lev sinks back against the table. "I swore they wouldn't back down."

Caius ruffles a hand through his fur. "At least we made it seem real."

Silence sucks the air from the room. All their bodies prickle with something unfinished.

Pheir doesn't look at them, gathering her thoughts as her legs stop swinging. "Right..." Despite the bravado of her performance, her words hang above her head as if she's not sure she believes them — or didn't realize that she did. "It's artificial. It's manufactured. That's why it felt like..." She sucks in a breath, a bitter smile meeting the shake of her head. "Those wedding bonds are a hell of a drug."

Lev suddenly understands, reaching for Pheir as she pushes off the table. "No, Pheir, they're not —"

Pheir avoids the touch, bursting out the door to the hum of the Timber compound. Then it's gone, just like Pheir's back as the door swings shut.

Of all the fights Pheir has rushed into, this is the first one Aren's seen her run from.

FORTY-EIGHT

Pheir

Pheir runs for the cottage. There's no one gathered around the firepit, save for Darby who jumps to his feet. "Are you escaping?" he shouts, as if she'd answer if she was. He braces to sprint after her.

She slows enough to snap over her shoulder, "*Escort me*, if you're so worried about it!"

Then she's off running again. Darby bounds after her on spindly legs. It takes no time for him to catch her, falling into step as they near the top of the hill. Her jaw is tight. He keeps his distance, watching her warily in his periphery as he lowers his voice like it might prevent the other werecreatures from hearing.

"Did something happen?"

As if they're *friends*. As if she were anyone else in the pack. She can't explain the bubbling feeling inside her. She's weak. Her bonds to Vesta weren't as strong as she thought. The second one of the Timbers touched Pheir like she didn't have to fight for attention, she folded. Worst of all, it's fake. Her feelings are fabricated. So are theirs.

That knowledge doesn't make the hole in Pheir's chest any smaller.

Mercifully, when they reach the cabin, Mari's leaving with a basket of dirty sheets — not the blanket from Pheir's room. She exhales a small relief. As they pass each other, Darby's head swivels to keep his eyes on the bat.

Pheir's hand poises on the cottage door. She wants to be mean, to find her old, familiar cruelty and wear it like a cloak until everything stops hurting. Why is it so hard to find malice when her chest aches like this? She spits the first thing she can think of. "Mari's an asshole."

It's a pathetic attempt at insult, the weakest she's ever managed. Her head swims like the ground beneath her is unsteady. Darby blinks, puzzled but not unkind as if it wasn't an insult at all. "But...*you're* an asshole, too?"

Somehow, it's comforting. At least the wedding bonds haven't altered the way Darby views her. Pheir's head jerks when she realizes she's thinking fondly of him. What the fuck *can't* this magic do? Slamming the front door behind her, she takes the stairs two at a time and shuts herself in her room.

Her face feels pinched. The backs of her eyes burn, stomach contorting inside itself as a chasm opens in her chest. With dull talons, she clutches at her feathers. What the fuck are these *feelings*? They don't make sense. Pheir's never had to contend with this before. There was nothing but rage and vengeance, and now, she's swimming through a sea of conflicting emotion.

Shakily, Pheir crawls onto the mattress on the floor and buries her face against it.

She was using you.

You betrayed me.

You don't have to do this.

They don't love you like I do.

The throbbing in Pheir's head returns, threatening to rip the seams between both sides of her mind, between Vesta's voice and Pheir's. Her mouth stretches into a scream that she muffles against the sheets. Her hands feel for a pillow, pulling it down over the back of her head to stop the throbbing pain.

It's not enough. She reaches for something else, fumbling until her hands land on the edge of a quilt that she jerks around her. Her ears ring. She pulls the blanket tight, covering her body as she inhales for another scream —

It smells like the four of them.

The scream doesn't escape. Feebly, Pheir takes another breath through her nose, letting her eyes slip shut. It's the quilt from the balcony, the four of them intermingling in its threads the same way they did in the library.

She presses the blanket to her nose, resting her cheek against it as she focuses on the scents. Caius is the easiest to pick out, like another version of herself, spicy and commanding. Aren is earthy, a base for the others, so subtle Pheir could miss it. And Lev is dark and sweet and warm. An odd comfort lulls Pheir's heart to slow its pace.

It should have been harder to play her part for the Regents. It should've been impossible, but it was almost easy. Natural. Instinctual.

The Pheir I knew would have ripped Lev's heart out.

Vesta's voice slithers back into Pheir's thoughts. She tightens the blanket around her head. It doesn't stop the truth; Pheir *would* have done that weeks ago. Damn the consequences. Damn death. Damn that fucking rabbit most of all.

Now, Pheir's heart picks up again when she remembers how Aren pressed his mouth to her head. How Caius draped his arm behind her in the truck. How Lev called her her wife.

Which is harder to admit — that her opinions of Aren, Caius and Lev are changing, or that her understanding of Vesta is?

Pheir's skin crawls. She tosses the quilt off, struggling until she's panting under the moonlight. It covers the room from the window beside Pheir. Around her, the floor is chaos, a less-crowded version of her bedroom in the Eyrie. Empty bottles of lemonade line the mattress on the floor, interspersed with blue-checkered wrapping and wilted purple flowers. Beneath her mattress lies a wooden siren figurine next to the woven wedding hoop.

A symbol of the lie they're living. She should destroy it to find some reprieve from the forced emotions that cloud her judgment. Flipping onto her stomach, Pheir feels beneath the mattress, ready to snatch the hoop and snap it like a wishbone...but when her finger close around the wood, it stills her. The hoop is fragile under her hand, a spot already wearing into the arch where Pheir has run her thumb over it again and again. Head resting on the edge of the mattress, she brushes her fingers against the same spot until footsteps approach outside her door.

Her teeth clench. Gods, she can't take more of this. Today has been one whirling blow after another, upheaving everything she thought she knew. She needs to *breathe*. She needs a fucking moment alone to try to find the pieces of her life that have been scattered.

Her heart trips anxiously in her chest. The werecreature outside the door can hear it, whomever they are. Pheir's mouth opens to tell them to *fuck off*, but they don't try to enter. After a moment, the steps fade down the hall until Pheir is left in silence again.

It's a small mercy. She tugs the blanket back around herself. It does nothing to stop her shivering when she remembers three bodies pressed against hers. Heat radiating through their fur, rubbing against her skin and entangling in her feathers. Claws left marks in her body. She wants those marks to scar and stay with her. There is no lullaby of revenge to sing Pheir to sleep this time.

She drifts off to thoughts of Aren, Caius, and Lev hunting her through the forest.

When she wakes, the blanket's kicked off at her feet, her body slick with sweat. Sun beats through the window. That's what overheated her, not the endless visions swirling through her dreams. Not Caius's fur slipping through her fingers. Not Aren's ears twitching at her groans. Not Lev's hair falling over her eyes as she lowered her mouth...

A knock comes at Pheir's door. In her haze, she'd nearly forgotten the nausea roiling in her stomach. It comes rushing back full force along with the events of the previous day. Pheir doesn't bother answering; the door creaks open anyway. Aren stands with two bottles of lemonade between his fingers, surveying the sorry state of her bed.

"Nesting?"

She flushes. That's not what this is. It's *not*. Sniffing, her chin lifts haughtily as she sprawls across the mattress. "Escape requires supplies."

It's a weak excuse. She's losing her touch. Aren doesn't say as much, easing the door shut as the bottles clink gently in his hand. Pheir rolls onto her side so she doesn't have to face him. At her feet, the floor creaks beneath Aren sliding down the wall. "We need to talk about last night."

If Pheir thought being held captive was bad, this is a new form of torture. Her throat dries up. Aren pops the top off one drink with his claw. Bastard: he knows they're her favorite.

"Can you tell me..." His claws *tink* against the glass as if he's afraid his words might frighten her away. "What did you mean about the wedding bonds?"

The feathers on the back of her neck stand on end. She wills her heart to slow its pace. Aren will hear it. It'll tell him something, even if Pheir can't be sure what that is. Her breath comes short and shallow, trying to quell her stomach.

Who is she? Pheir never used to be scared of anything. Now, finding the words to speak is insurmountable. It used to be so fucking easy hating the Timbers, but since she came here...

Aren's silence leaves room for her to speak. She doesn't know how he does that, how he draws her out like he's calling a kitten stuck in a drain.

Her fingers tighten around the blanket. "I don't know. It was just something I said."

She swallows, like it might keep more words from coming. She doesn't want to talk about it. Talking means looking closer; she wants to keep her distance. She wants to fly back to the miserable Eyrie. She wants to burrow under the covers and never come out.

"It's not just something you said," Aren murmurs.

"I have trouble telling what's real anymore." Her mouth betrays her, springing open like a faulty snare. She clenches her eyes shut. "Not just the wedding bullshit." When she blinks, light from the window turns gray against the wall as a cloud drifts over. "I have trouble telling what *was* real, from before. Nothing makes sense."

Rain begins to patter against the window. Liquid sloshes in the lemonade bottle as Aren rests it between his bent knees. "Is there anything you *know* is real?"

What a question. Pheir scoffs as she rifles through her memories and grasps for the firmest pieces. Things that once seemed solid now turn to dust. Vesta hated the Conclave — that seems real, but the 'why' slips through Pheir's fingers. Why did Vesta hate them? She said it was because the Conclave didn't protect any of them. Not Pheir, not Thalea, not Rhaiden. That's why Vesta built their pack — to expose the Conclave. To prove they weren't looking out for anyone but themselves.

Or is there another reason?

Pheir scrubs a hand down her face. It feels like she's been asleep for years, snapping with groggy irritation. "I don't fucking know, ok? I don't know anything."

Spots of light bloom behind her eyelids as she digs her knuckles against them. The ache in her skull begins again, like something scratching to escape. Pheir's talons dig into the back of her head, pressing against the pain —

"Maybe I can help you." When Aren speaks, she clings to his voice like it might drag her out of her murky mind. "I can tell you what I know, and you can see if it makes sense."

A laugh croaks out of her. "What could you possibly know about my life?"

"I don't think Vesta's mission was completely wrong."

FORTY-NINE

Pheir

I don't think Vesta's mission was completely wrong.

Pheir rolls onto her back to get a better look at Aren. He doesn't seem conflicted. He barely responds to the shock on her face as he swirls the open bottle between his fingers.

"In a way, she was right about the Conclave," he admits. "It doesn't live up to its goal. It fails to protect people in the Break time and time again. The Regents are too concerned with reputations or old friendships to address difficult things."

His words are meant to entice Pheir to hear more, to draw her out from the security of her blankets. She knows what he's doing. With a hand, he extends the bottle toward her and waits. Hesitantly, Pheir pushes to sit before she reaches for it. The glass is cool in her hand, condensation slippery as she tips the bottle to her lips. It's as good as last time. She forces herself not to moan as Aren continues.

"The Break used to be full of smaller groups: fledgling packs, unaffiliated townships, larger families. I don't know how much you knew of them. In any case, they're nearly extinct now. The Conclave was more interested in fostering the most powerful packs. Everyone else fell to the wayside."

Pheir presses her teeth to the bottle's rim. It clicks uncomfortably. "Like the Eyrie, before the storm? When it was a village?"

Aren tugs the bottle gently away from her mouth. "There was no one to help them recover. The Conclave invested their supplies and manpower into something else — building a bigger compound for the Head Regent's pack."

So that's why no one returned to the Eyrie. A dark pit forms in Pheir's stomach. It's no excuse for her parents. It makes her hate them more, talons digging into the bottle as Aren's voice softens.

"It wasn't just materials. There were rumors all the time; the smaller the group, the less regulation. If the Conclave never came around, they wouldn't notice bruises or hungry children or signs of trouble." He watches Pheir carefully. She knows what he'll say. It's the same thing Caius said, the same thing Pheir's been struggling with. She braces for his words, but it doesn't make it easier to hear them. "Vesta did notice, though. I think that's how she chose her pack."

Pheir turns her gaze away. Yes, she and Thalea and Rhaiden share similar stories. Things they didn't want to talk about, places they didn't want to go back to, memories that clouded over their faces. Pheir thought Vesta shared that, too, but Vesta never stopped talking about those who'd wronged her. No matter how her story changed. No matter how vague it could be.

Pheir never realized that before.

Her jaw tenses, fist twisting absently around the bottle. "You don't think Vesta was trying to help us. You don't think she chose us to protect us. To teach us to defend ourselves. To stop it from happening again."

It's not a question. Aren answers it honestly, anyway. "I don't think that was the case. I don't think Vesta wanted to fix the

Conclave. She wanted to take its place, and she was willing to sacrifice people to do that."

People like Pheir. Her fingers clamp around the neck of the bottle. Aren lifts it out of her hands, voice slow like he's trying to break it to her gently.

"I think you have trouble determining what's real because Vesta was controlling you for a long time. With her voice, or her presence, or some other magic."

The best magic is a secret.

Blood pulses through Pheir. It's like she can feel her veins forking, feeding separate parts of herself. "No..." She shakes her head. "There's no way."

Aren doesn't say more, like the night after the wedding. Pheir remembers how he looked at her, as if it pained him to tell her the truth. As if he wasn't saying it to be cruel. Pheir wishes he would; it would be easier.

Vesta was controlling you.

It's impossible – but it's also the only thing that makes sense. Pheir pulls her knees up to her chest. Why can't Aren just tell her she was wrong? *You're an evil person,* he could say. *You're as bad as Vesta wanted you to be. You should have died on the battlefield. The Conclave was wrong in sparing you.*

Air is hard to come by, spreading shallowly in Pheir's lungs. She wasn't brainwashed. She wasn't a puppet, because if she was...

"That was ten years of my life." Every confusing emotion Pheir hasn't been able to tame comes flooding back. Her eyes burn. She doesn't know how to cry. "It's not true." She hiccups for breath. "I don't know how to do anything else. I don't know how to *be* anyone else. That's all I have!"

Aren shifts to his knees and kneels in front of her. "That's not all you have."

"Yes, it is!" She crawls back on the mattress, chest heaving. "If that was all fake..."

Everything I think is fake. Everything I feel is fake.

How can she trust any of it? Her hands press to her temples, Vesta's voice screeching in her mind.

"None of it's real," Pheir moans. "It's not real now." That's what she tells herself to soothe Vesta's voice, to slow the frantic tripping of her heart. "It's the wedding bonds. It's more magic."

Pheir wants to claw the voice out of her head. She wants it *out*

—

A hand grips her ankle and yanks her to the edge of the mattress. Aren crushes her against his chest, arms pressing against her back. "Breathe, Pheir."

When she squirms, he holds tighter, head resting on top of hers until she's covered from all sides.

"*Breathe*, Pheir."

The pressure everywhere else eases the pressure in her skull, drowning out Vesta's voice with things Pheir can *feel*: Aren's fur. His whiskers on her face. His chest rising and falling in a gradual rhythm against hers.

It guides her breaths. Slowly, her head drops to Aren's shoulder. Against her back, his claws trace absent patterns with no beginning or end. It reminds her of the tips of Thalea's vines, writing on Pheir's skin after one of them made Vesta angry. *The words are a game*, Thalea insisted as she made Pheir try to guess the words. Pheir knew the real reason they played; touching was comfort, forbidden among Vesta's strongest soldiers. The game was one way to sneak it in.

Carefully, Aren's claws work up to Pheir's scalp, scratching through her hair. No matter how Pheir fights it, her eyes droop as his voice rumbles through his chest. "The wedding was not what you think."

An exhausted laugh squeaks out of Pheir. "You telling me I imagined that whole night, too?"

"No. It happened," Aren admits. "But we didn't complete it. It didn't bind you to the pack, Pheir. It didn't bind you to any of us. There was no magic."

One of Pheir's eyes creaks open. Aren's hands tighten around her, but he doesn't stop the calming motions.

"I know this is a lot to take in," he murmurs. "You can take it one day at a time — one second at a time. But I want you to know there's nothing tying you to us. There's no forced loyalty. You can be angry at us. You can hate us. No magic is stopping you from that."

Blankly, Pheir stares at the wall. There has to be magic. There has to be some supernatural explanation for why she feels this way. Why a swarm of emotions she's never dealt with are suddenly springing to the surface. Why Aren's arms around her comfort the storm of uncertainty inside her. Why her fingers curl into his fur.

Her voice is shaky when it finally comes. "Why would I believe you?"

"You don't have to." It sounds easy when Aren says it, like he doesn't want to push her one way or the other. "You're breaking out of Vesta's hold for the first time. You should take time to see it for yourself. You've been through a lot. You lost an entire pack. You lost someone important to you, whether that was the image of Vesta or Vesta herself."

A lump wells in Pheir's throat, heat pricking behind her eyes. At least this close, Aren can't see it. When she smears her face against his chest, she can pretend there's nothing wet slipping down her cheeks. If she stays close to him, he won't be able to pick up on how off-kilter she is. At least, so she tells herself, an excuse not to pull out of his grip. Exhaustion like Pheir's never felt seeps into her bones. Holding up her body is a struggle, so she leans into him to regain her strength. Just for now. Just for a second.

Uncertainly, her voice slips between them. "Do you hate me?" She doesn't know why she asks. She doesn't know why she wants to know the answer.

A chuckle escapes Aren, blowing strands of her hair. "No, I don't hate you."

Why does that make her throat tight? "Did you ever?"

As he considers it, his fingers move to the nape of her neck. "You frustrated me. There was something about you that wasn't quite *there*. Something I couldn't reach."

With his paws, he smooths down her wings, gently tracing a feather between two fingers until she shudders. "You should be glad *I* couldn't reach you."

His laughter is low from his throat. "I don't suppose I need to ask if you hated me, then."

Pheir pulls back. Tentatively, her knees slot between his, her head turning enough to see his face. This close, she can make out the soft padding of his nose, the white pointed tufts under his chin. "Yeah, I hated you. I hated that you couldn't be provoked. I hated how you watched me. How you always seemed to see more than I was showing you, like I couldn't hide anything."

His eyes stay locked on hers, claws drifting down the backs of her arms. "Do you still hate that?"

Her tongue trails her sticky lips. His eyes follow it when she answers. "I haven't decided yet."

With both hands, he pulls her into his lap, her legs straddled on either side of his as he eases back against the wall. There's no hiding from him now, her body nestled above the long line of his. It leaves her exposed, skin warming as his hands trail up her hips and notch into the dip of her waist.

"I spent a lot of time watching you, Pheir. A lot of time learning you."

He doesn't cover her with his body the way Caius did in the treehouse. Instead, Aren looks up at her and makes her wait as the corner of his mouth ticks up. Impatiently, her fingers curl into his fur. It's thicker now, changing with the season. She doesn't know what she's waiting for, but she wants it *now*. "And what did you see, *beta*?"

The term from her mouth makes his ears flick, grip tightening against her waist. He watches her mouth like he wants to memorize the shape it takes when she calls him that. "Passion.

Loyalty. Anticipation. A girl that wasn't handled with the devotion she gave." He brushes her wrist, dancing against the mark Vesta gave her. He finds Pheir's thundering pulse instead. "More than violence. More than a soldier. Someone about to break free."

She can't stand to hear the words. Or maybe she wants to drink them in, diving against his mouth to see how they taste. They're sweet and tart as lemonade, sharp and lethal as his body when their lips meld like they know each other. Her teeth dig into his lip, chasing the pinprick of blood when he growls deep in his chest. Every hot curl of her tongue is a threat he doesn't shy away from, digging claws into her skin and keeping her close.

She never pulls back for air, dedicated to this feeling until her head starts to swim. He knows her. He's learned all about her, pulling back and tracing the curve of her lips when she gasps for air. When she loses herself, he brings her back, and her mind is finally quiet except for one resounding thought.

This...this could be real.

FIFTY

Aren

Kissing Pheir reminds Aren of kissing Caius. It stirs the same hunger in Aren's chest, awakening parts of himself he hadn't realized were dormant. A passionate, untamed part that forgets everything but what the animal inside him understands.

Want. Need. Mine.

It takes far too long for anything else to register. By the time he hears two Timber guards laughing in the cottage stairwell, Aren has Pheir's leg hitched around his waist as he licks up the pulse in her neck.

Focus, Aren. You have work to do.

She whines when he pulls back, which makes it infinitely harder to will away his desire as the guards' voices fade down the hall.

On the mattress, Pheir stretches like a smug cat. She knows exactly what she does to him. The night of the wedding wasn't a fluke at all. When she sits up, Aren crouches in front of her. "I have some things to check on before the snow blows in. Do you want to help, or are you going to be a distraction?"

Pheir leans closer, innocence dripping from her smile as her tongue presses against her canine. Aren can't fight the amused tilt of his lips when she looks up at him through her lashes. "Why not both?"

Perhaps it's a mistake to bring her along, but it'll give her time to think about everything he's told her. It must be overwhelming. She tortures him slightly as she dresses, bending over to tug up her jeans and arching into her sweater. Aren narrows his eyes before the two of them make their way down the stairs. Aren waves to the guards on rotation before they head down the dirt path to the main compound.

Never did he think Pheir's distractions would take such a turn. The Timbers were well-prepared for her screaming threats, but the curl of her smirk? The stretch of her wings? They draw Aren's attention in brand new ways. They don't feel like diversions. They feel serious. They feel *real.*

Would that be so bad?

It's such an unfamiliar thought, Aren nearly stops in his tracks. The voice is not the calm, assured resonance he's used to. This voice is eager. This voice is hopeful. It's yet another part of Aren that's been awakened since the wedding.

Beside Aren now, Pheir has grown quiet as if she has to stay on guard. Even with Aren at her side, she's not at ease, walking on the outside edge of the path as they approach the center of the compound.

She can sense it, too — the stares they get from the other Timbers. The murmurs as people turn to watch her and Aren walking side by side. It's the first time Pheir's been brought around like this is normal, like she's part of the pack instead of a captive enemy. Aren's shoulders straighten, a pleasant smile across his lips as he nods to the people they pass.

The only way through it is to do it.

Cold fingers brush Aren's back. He turns to see Pheir's hand curled around his tail like a child trying not to lose sight of its mother. It satisfies the little voice in his head. When Pheir realizes what she's done, she jerks away and continues at a quicker pace.

Aren's long strides have no trouble keeping up with her. He leans closer as they walk. "You can hold on, if you want to."

Pheir swats at him as he guides her toward the garage.

It's more of a lean-to than anything, a wooden shelter erected to hold the few vehicles the Timbers have. Out front, the pickup truck sits on safety jack stands. Caius curses from underneath it. Mari and June lean over the open hood, calling down to Caius below, but it's clear they aren't making any progress.

"Need help?" Aren asks as they approach.

Mari steps back with a groan. "*Please*. I don't think he..."

Then they catch sight of Pheir behind Aren. Mari stiffens. June glances between them.

It's the first real trial of Pheir's acceptance into the pack. To her credit, she doesn't hide. She lingers next to Aren's shoulder, mouth clamped as she and Mari stare at each other. Pheir's feathers shiver in the breeze as silence stretches between them. There's a clang of metal beneath the car as Caius rolls out.

"I can't get the fucking oil plug," he grumbles, unaware. His greasy hands smear on a rag as he stalks toward the wooden bench of tools. The others keep staring before Mari speaks shrewdly.

"What did the Regents want last night?"

Caius lifts his head, taking in the sight of Pheir at Aren's side. It won't do any good for them to step in; Caius understands that better than anyone. Pheir could marry the Alpha a thousand times over, but true acceptance is contingent on how *she* interacts. No amount of pushing will bring them together.

June drums her fingers against her lips. Mari's brow lifts sharply, impatient for a response. "Lynx got your tongue?"

"Marius..." Aren scoffs quietly.

"What?" Mari's wings fling up in a shrug. "She's part of the pack now, isn't she? I'd ask any of you the same thing. If she's one of us, then let's act like it." Mari looks scrutinizingly over Pheir. "We know good and well that she can fight her own battles, even against an *asshole*. Isn't that right, Pheir?"

Bewildered, Aren looks toward her. Pheir doesn't seem surprised, cheeks darkening with something like embarrassment as she keeps her gaze locked on Mari.

As much as Aren would like to insulate Pheir, Mari isn't wrong in their assessment of her. Mari doesn't ask Pheir questions out of cruelty. It was Mari who warned Aren of the visitors so he could get to Pheir last night. It was Mari who went to check on the Broadleafs. Under their gruff exterior, Mari cares for the good of the pack. Aren can't begrudge them that.

Pheir's eyes narrow on Marius like she's sizing up a worthy opponent. "They asked me how I feel about Vesta."

There's a hint of pride in Mari's smile. "What did you say?"

Pheir shifts uncomfortably, her chin level. "I don't know how I feel."

Marius's eyes roll. June elbows them and hisses before Pheir's voice snaps out again.

"It's better than when I thought I knew everything, isn't it?"

The bite in Pheir's tone surprises them all. Her hands stuff deeper into her jean pockets as June's eyes widen. Aren tenses for an argument, but when Mari blinks, a satisfied grin tugs at the corner of their lips. "Touché."

Pheir bristles, uncertain if she's risen to the challenge. Mari picks up a crate from next to the truck.

"Come on, June." They jerk their head toward the livestock. "We need to get this feed to the animals before you take off tonight."

June scrambles to hoist another crate against her hip, winking at Aren as they pass. "You know, Mari, we could bring Pheir along. Since you're best friends now."

"Don't get ahead of yourself," Mari gripes.

As the two of them disappear across the field, a smile twitches onto Pheir's lips. It's not camaraderie, but it's something.

Caius whistles through his teeth, twirling the grease rag between his fingers. "That went better than *my* first interaction with Mari."

Tersely, Pheir rolls her neck. "I thought I was gonna have to pay for that 'asshole' comment."

"You made them smile." Aren nudges Pheir. "I'd call that a success."

A different tension permeates the space now that it's the three of them. It's the same uncertainty that filled the gaps last night in the library, like magnets unsure if they should be attracted or repulsed. Caius clears his throat, leaning back against the bench. "I guess you two have talked."

It's not quite a question, but from Caius's wandering eyes, it's clear he wants to know more. After Pheir left the library the night before, Aren stopped the others from following her. It didn't seem like the best time to add more fuel to that fire.

"We did." Aren grabs the socket wrench and lowers himself to the under-car roller. "I told her the truth about the wedding."

Caius blanches. It's the last thing Aren sees before he disappears under the car. From beneath the hood, he can make out Caius and Pheir's feet on opposite sides of him.

"Oh." Caius's voice is audible, but gruff. "Are you...?"

He trails off. There's no sound except Aren's fingers moving against the underside of the truck. By the time he tries the oil plug, Caius hasn't elaborated, weight shifting as if he's struggling for words.

"Don't hurt yourself," Pheir cracks dryly.

The truck stifles Aren's laughter. There's a soft *thwacking* sound before the grease rag falls at Pheir's feet, as if Caius lobbed it at her. There's no disguising the smile in his voice when he grumbles, "Shut the fuck up."

Pheir laughs, a sound so foreign that it gives both men pause. Caius's legs still. Aren's hand curls over the wrench, his head resting back as he listens. Pheir's joy is rusty with disuse, a dirt road that hasn't been traveled in years. It warms a place deep in Aren's chest before he rolls back out from under the truck.

The three of them working together like this is so simple. It's so...*nothing* that Aren sucks in a breath. This is what it could be like: no fighting. No battles. Just idle pack chores and easy conversation, Caius and Pheir settling in to be a part of it. It could be mundane and normal, because they could have it every day — the Alpha, her wife, and their closest confidantes. It could be as natural as the feelings they have for each other. It could be —

"What's the diagnosis?" Caius asks.

Aren tries to remember what he was doing a moment before, holding out a palm toward Caius. "Hand me that pipe."

Caius passes it from the bench. Aren slips the pipe over the wrench handle and wheels back under the car. He focuses on instruction so his voice won't get caught on emotion. "If the plug's too tight, use the pipe for leverage."

When Aren rolls back out, Caius wears half a smile. "Perfect Aren."

Caius extends the drip pan. Aren meets Caius's eyes when he takes it. "You'll get it next time."

Aren hasn't forgotten their conversation from the morning before, when Caius took his frustration out with the axe on the wood. It's not the last time Caius's uncertainties will rear their head, but Aren hopes his presence begins to be a reassurance rather than a threat.

From the softening around Caius's eyes, Aren thinks it is.

Leaning back against the bench, Caius folds his arms as he looks toward Pheir. "To be honest, I'm surprised 'Perfect Aren' got through to you after last night. I wasn't sure how you were gonna feel."

Pheir leans next to him, nudging his hip out of the way. "I'm no moodier than you."

Caius nudges back. "That's not saying much."

Pheir smiles before a thought knits her brow, quizzical eyes turning toward Aren. "Is that why *you* came to my room this morning? You handle the outbursts because you don't react?" Skeptically, her eyes narrow, as if another thought intrigues her. "What's the most upset you've ever been?"

"See?" Caius jerks a thumb toward Pheir. "She noticed it, too." Curiosity gets the better of him, leaning intently on the bench. "What *is* the most pissed you've ever been? And don't say when you met me."

Aren's elbows rest on his knees, staring up at the two of them next to each other. A month ago, Caius and Pheir would never have conceded to the same side. Today, it comes easily. They match each other's' postures, tension ingrained in the same places of their bodies — tight shoulders, tense legs, always aware of what's behind them. They're things Aren will never fully comprehend. These two are reflections of each other. They understand why they move the way they do.

Aren chuckles under his breath. "It was certainly not when I met you."

Caius's weight shifts. "When, then?"

Aren leans back on the roller and slides under the truck. He could lie. He could fabricate some scenario that makes him look better than he was, a situation that doesn't sting with regret. 'Perfect Aren' wasn't always so perfect. He wasn't in control of himself or the world around him.

Maybe it's time they both see that.

Aligning the drip pan underneath the plug, Aren lets out a slow breath. "The most upset I've ever been was after my last pack let me go."

FIFTY-ONE

Aren

Silence looms above the truck. Aren unscrews the bolt, and oil pours out of the car. At least that's a better sound than the quiet. He could stay under here as it drains, avoiding Caius and Pheir's prying eyes and questions. For a moment, he considers it until he rolls back out onto his feet.

Caius and Pheir stare blankly at him. "Your last pack let you go?" Pheir blinks. "Like, kicked you out? Removed you?"

Aren wipes his hands on the rag between them. "Resigned in disgrace' is the term used most often."

Caius's mouth hangs open. "*How*? Why would they do that?"

"Surely you've heard the rumors." Aren leans on Pheir's other side.

They both turn toward him. "*Yeah*," Caius balks, "but I thought they were bullshit. There's no way you'd be forcibly removed. You're..." He gestures at Aren, as if that provides explanation.

Aren shields his eyes against the sun. If he squints, he can see a younger version of himself, directionless and outgrowing his home pack. Back then, there was a lot less gray in his fur and a lot fewer body aches in the winter.

"When I was younger," he sighs, "I was approached by a man. He'd split his pack into pieces to give his grown children their own packs to lead. They didn't vote on Alphas the way the Timbers do; their titles were handed down through descendants."

"So, nepotism," Caius grumbles.

Aren's lip quirks. "The man wanted a beta to temper one of his son's...rambunctiousness." That should have been the first red flag, but Aren accepted the position with the young Alpha, bright-eyed and optimistic. From the second he shook the son's hand, he knew things weren't going to go smoothly. "The son and I couldn't agree on anything — where to invest our time, how to spend resources, who to go to for advice. It didn't take long for the pack to start breaking down."

Who could blame it? The pack members were used to strong leadership, and suddenly, they were being led by two kids with no experience. Breakdown of the pack meant a breakdown of the compound — trash everywhere, living quarters falling into disrepair, chores neglected because people either left or didn't care enough to complete them.

"Outsiders noticed the pack was weakened. They were like vultures circling a dying animal, but my Alpha entertained them like guests." Any occasion for a party was good enough for him. Almost daily, someone new showed up to the compound to feel out the pack's weak points. Aren's Alpha couldn't be bothered to care, giving everyone a front row seat to the unrest.

"So what did you do?" Pheir asks. "You didn't just sit there and take it."

"No," Aren muses, shame creeping up his neck, "but almost. I tried to get help, but every channel was a dead end." His Alpha was too embarrassed to admit they weren't ready to lead. The father refused to speak to Aren directly. Memories of the conversation still make Aren grind his teeth. *Utilize the proper channels. Your Alpha will bring any issues to me.*

"What about the Conclave?" Caius rests his hip against the bench. "They love getting in people's shit."

"They shot me down before I presented my case." Aren huffs a laugh. "Not exactly a shock, since my Alpha's father was the Head Regent."

"*Boreas?*" Caius gawks.

"Boreas's *father*," Aren clarifies. "My Alpha was Boreas's brother. That's how Boreas got his own pack, how he became Head Regent later — family ties."

Caius rolls his eyes. "Fucking asshole."

"Regardless," Aren continues. "I was stuck. Nothing worked. And, if I'm honest...I *did* just take it." His eyes focus on the distance, mouth twisting as he shrugs. "Once I'd tried all the 'sensible' routes, I gave up. I didn't fight. I pulled back and let my Alpha run the pack into the ground."

It was a long time ago, but the memory twinges. That was not the version of Aren he wanted to be. It's not a version he wants to go back to, yet standing next to Caius and Pheir reminds him of what he still lacks. He isn't perfect. Far from it.

In Aren's periphery, Pheir and Caius watch him for a reaction. Aren lets out a slow breath. "Eventually, one of our daily visitors got close with my Alpha. They had more in common — throwing parties, having fun, never telling each other 'no.' They didn't care about rules or responsibilities. It was only a matter of time before the newcomer convinced my Alpha to replace me."

Pheir's nose wrinkles. "Your Alpha took in some random outsider as his beta? Who would do that?"

Caius, however, is quiet. Aren's gaze dips to the ground, foot scuffing the dirt. When Caius speaks, it's lower than Aren expects. "That's what you thought would happen when I came. When I got closer with Lev."

It's hard to look Caius in the face. Harder still for Aren to admit to a fear he's never shared with anyone but Lev. Still, Aren does. "It was something I thought about, yes."

Aren has reminded himself of the truth over the years. *Lev is not the same as your last Alpha. Caius isn't going to replace you.* That didn't keep the thought from recurring in Aren's mind. Maybe it affected the way he treated Caius more than he realized.

Pheir settles back between them. "So that's how you left in disgrace."

Aren braces his hands against the bench. "Not exactly. It was embarrassing to be removed, yes, but hardly anyone outside the pack cared. Not until the fight." His claws dig into the underside of the wood. "I moved off the compound. The pack was in shambles, dwindled to single digits. Only the Alpha and a few others remained. One night, they were drinking. The Alpha and his new beta got into it. No one knows for sure what happened, but the next morning, the Alpha was dead and the beta was gone."

Pheir stares at Aren. "What does that have to do with you? You weren't there."

This time, when Aren smiles, it's not as resentful as it used to be. "Some people just need someone else to take the fall."

Caius leans his weight on one hand. "They *blamed* you? How?"

"It's not hard when your family's full of powerful people. The Head Regent saw to that. It would've been humiliating for them to admit that their son was a shitty judge of character and an even shittier leader. It would've called everyone from that family into question; they'd all been given their titles the same way. It was easier for them to say I hadn't done my part as a beta. I hadn't protected my Alpha. I'd abandoned him. I hadn't sounded the alarm."

"But you did!" Pheir yelps.

Aren gives a noncommittal shrug. "Who would believe me over the Head Regent? Over a family of prominent Alphas? I didn't think it was worth it to fight the accusations."

It's yet another example of the Conclave's failing, just like with Pheir. She chews her lip as she settles back against the bench.

Caius does the same, eyes narrowed contemplatively. "Perfect Aren with a spot on his record."

"*That* was the most upset I've ever been." Aren flexes his fingers. "And I took it. I moved into a house on my own, kept my distance from everyone for years..." He presses a finger into Caius's chest. "From the way you talked at the wedding, it sounds like you wish you were less like yourself — less *of* yourself. Less impulsive, less passionate..." Aren shakes his head. "In my life, I wish I'd been more like you — both of you. I wish I'd trusted my instincts and felt things fully and fought for something."

Comfortable quiet settles around them. The oil finished draining long ago, but none of them move to finish the job. Eventually, Pheir speaks. "After all that, how'd you end up here?"

A smile tugs at Aren's lips. "Lev found me. I tried to warn her about my reputation, but she was stubborn. No amount of rumor mills or common sense could keep her away. It was like she knew something that I didn't."

Fading sunlight reflects off Caius's fangs as he grins. "She has a habit of doing that."

Between them, Pheir folds her arms, mouth twisting as she stares into the trees. Over her head, Aren meets Caius's eyes before both their brows lift. In the past, Aren's questioned Lev about the people she invites in. Standing here now, he's certain the three of them are exactly where they're meant to be. Maybe one day, Pheir will feel that, too.

For now, Aren's content to be here with the two of them.

Caius pushes off the bench. "If you want to be more like *me*..." A cocky grin slips across his face as he turns to Aren. "I can tell you what I would've done with your old Alpha."

"Beat his ass?" Pheir muses.

Caius quirks a brow at Aren. "Have you tried screaming?"

It takes Aren a moment to realize he's serious. A laugh bubbles out of Aren's chest when he turns to glance at Pheir.

Sagely, she nods. "It *does* feel good."

Before Aren can think, Caius grabs him by the backs of his shoulders and moves him closer to the tree line. "You've got to *feel* something, beta." Caius thumps Aren's chest, setting loose a swarm of butterflies. "Get pissed off! Have an emotion! Let that asshole have it!"

As Caius steps back next to Pheir, they wait expectantly. For a moment, Aren's mouth hangs open before he gives a half-hearted bark.

"Come *on*!" Pheir shoves playfully at Aren's chest. "Get fucking *mad*! Let it out! You heard me all those weeks in the cabin!"

Aren tries again. Caius shakes his head, clenching his fists as he howls. Aren screams again. Pheir shuts her eyes and screams louder.

Finally, Aren tips his head back and roars.

Birds scatter from the trees. Caius and Pheir crow happily. They shout toward the treetops until all three of their voices fuse into a round of laughter.

FIFTY-TWO

Lev

Lev should be happy — the Regents have been placated. Pheir grows further from Vesta's influence every day. The Timbers are settling back into a semblance of normality. Yet that same intuitive feeling nags at Lev, a dog nipping at her heels and reminding her something is missing.

She knows what the feeling wants. All these years, she didn't realize that her sudden urges were leading her to the same place. When she felt the motivation to recruit Aren, the impulse that led her into the forest with Caius, the compulsion to draw Pheir away from Vesta. At the time, Lev just thought she was doing the right thing — being an Alpha, providing for her community, giving people a place to call home.

Now, she sees her urges weren't wholly selfless. As Lev helps the youngest Timbers toss feed to the chickens, she realizes where her intuition was guiding her — to a family of her own, gathering the pieces that might one day fit together. Aren, Caius, Pheir, and

Lev started from different points and crossed at different times until they intersected at this moment.

Realizing how the four of them have come together should be more shocking, but to Lev, it's natural. It felt *possible* last night when they were united against the Regents. Lev almost believed the way Pheir leaned against her, their scents twined in Caius's fur as Aren settled on the other side.

Until the Regents left, and the spell broke, and Pheir took off to be alone again.

Who knows if Pheir's ready for the truth of the wedding amidst her withdrawal from Vesta? So Lev doesn't go to her; she's probably the last person Pheir wants to see. If there's one thing Vesta instilled in Pheir, it's a hatred of Lev. Lev's not sure even the siren's tongue will be enough to draw that poison out.

She stood outside Pheir's room last night, despite what Aren said. They needed to give Pheir space, but the thought of her hurting on the other side of the door tugged at Lev's heartstrings. That feeling arose again, reminding Lev what she already knew: *give her some space. Give her some time.* Lev's hand curled into a fist before she lowered it and stepped back.

This morning, Lev left the cottage before first light, avoiding Pheir's bedroom and busying herself with pack business. She tries to sort through the books Caius retrieved from the Eyrie, but she can't focus. She struggles to finish a quilting project, but she keeps jamming her thread. She attempts to help Oberon and Willow with the younglings, but she can't stop glancing up the hill every few minutes.

"Go," Oberon finally urges, two kids hanging from each arm. The children giggle as rain mists around them, but Oberon's knowing smile is for Lev alone. "You're newlyweds. You should be holed up together."

Lev's face heats, but she thanks him and slips up to the cottage.

This time, she goes straight to Pheir's room. It's been almost twenty-four hours. They can talk. Lev can explain the wedding, and Pheir will understand that whatever she feels is not —

But Pheir's room is empty, blankets and objects strewn about under the distinct scent of Aren. Lev's heart sinks as she trudges through the halls and tries to tell herself it's better this way. She can't be what Pheir needs; the hatred is too strong. Aren will explain how the wedding wasn't real, how they didn't force Pheir's bond, how any feelings she has aren't because of the ceremony, but because of...

Lev shakes her head. There's no way Pheir feels anything romantic, least of all for Lev — not after the ashes' incident. But Lev can hardly think of anything else as she sprawls across the main bed.

Once the rain stops, she can't keep still any longer, dismissing the guards from the cottage. They deserve a day off with a jar of moonshine, so Lev hands them out before she grabs one for herself and follows the terrace stairs down to the lake's edge. There's a rocky inlet with a shelf that drops off into deeper water. She wades up to her knees, sinking down to sit and lean back against one side. After the rain, the water should be ice cold, but it bubbles with heat. It's been this way for a long time, a hot spring on the edge of the lake.

Residual magic: impossible to predict.

"Thought I got the first drink from your cup."

The voice makes Lev shiver. When she cracks an eye open, Pheir stands on the ledge across the pool with a blanket wrapped around her sweater and jeans. Lev's heart thumps out of rhythm. She doesn't let it show, tilting her head toward the jar of moonshine. "It's yours, if you want it."

Lev may well be signing her own death warrant. If Pheir shatters the glass and turns it into a weapon...but Pheir doesn't move towards it. Instead, she sinks down to dangle her toes in the water and sets her sights on Lev.

"Aren told me the wedding was fake." Pheir shows no reaction as she speaks. Lev holds her breath, desperate to know what Pheir thinks. Is she angry? Is she glad she hasn't been tied to the Timbers? Does she feel anything else?

Lev settles on a safer question. "Where is Aren?"

Pheir tilts her head back toward the cottage where two figures stand on the deck, watching the two women. Aren and Caius settle their weight against the railing as Pheir leans back on her palms. "I told them I wanted to talk to you myself."

Lev fights to swallow, feet kicking lazily beneath the water. "How do you feel about it? The wedding being fake?"

Pheir's eyes narrow. "I'll ask the questions here."

There's something almost...playful about it. Lev doesn't want to question a good thing. She matches Pheir's expression, fighting the heat spreading up her neck. Pheir's hard enough to read on a good day, but the fading light makes it nearly impossible. There's no way to know what she's really after, so Lev waits silently for Pheir to speak again.

Silence stretches between them until it snaps as Pheir knocks a pebble into the water. "Vesta never explained why she hated you. I mean, I could tell you were fucking annoying, but that wasn't the real reason."

Lev's grin tilts back toward the sky. She can't deny her own curiosity. "What *did* Vesta tell you about me?"

"You were a bitch." The word doesn't feel like an insult from Pheir's mouth. Her toes drag through the water. "You betrayed her before she saved me. You didn't know how to lead. You and I were nothing alike. That was how Vesta knew she could trust me."

Doubt laces Pheir's words. Vesta never trusted, no matter what she said. She bred loyalty the way others might a champion fighter, to ensure she was never betrayed. It would be one thing if Lev learned this in the last few years, gaining insight into Vesta to bring her down, but Lev has known it for a long time. It's ingrained in her bones the same way it's ingrained in Pheir's. Remembering it now brings back the same feelings of fear. Shame. Guilt. Loss. Things Lev never fully contended with. Things she doesn't know if she ever will.

Her shoulders sink down in the water to prevent the chill that has nothing to do with the cool wind. "Vesta came to you — what, ten years ago?"

Pheir nods. Sadness pangs through Lev. Maybe she shouldn't continue. It's not like telling Pheir this story will make a difference. It won't change anything; Vesta still got to Pheir. Vesta still used her as a weapon. Vesta still died. But Pheir deserves a moment of truth in her life, and if Lev can give her nothing else, she can give her that.

"A year before Vesta found you, she came here — to this spot, actually." Bubbles roll under Lev's palms. Maybe it isn't residual Faerie magic that keeps this spring hot; maybe it's something left from Vesta. "My Alpha – the Timber Alpha before me – found Vesta on the shore coughing up water. Vesta said she couldn't remember anything about where she came from, how she got here, what had happened to her. None of the neighboring packs had heard of her. It was like she sprouted fully formed, a lady of the lake."

It's impossible to know where Vesta was before that. Reborn from her ashes on the island in the lake? Flying in from another part of Orena? Sailing into the Break from another continent? Vesta never told the Timbers anything else; it didn't fit her helpless narrative. Back then, Lev thought her Alpha had saved Vesta from death. Looking back, maybe it was all a part of Vesta's plan to lower the Timbers' defenses.

All we can do is rely on the kindness of strangers.

Vesta wove that into her story any chance she got, leaning into the Timber Alpha around the campfire like a damsel rescued from a castle. Lev should have recognized it then, how Vesta feigned helplessness to take advantage of power. But Lev hadn't known any better. How could she?

"We took Vesta in. No one knew much about phoenixes, but she was my age. Teenagers, you know? And Vesta was so...*cool.* Unbothered. Mysterious." Lev's stomach cinches at the memory of firelight flickering across Vesta's iridescent feathers. Across her captivating smile, her clever gaze, her confidence no matter what room she walked into. "I wanted to be her." Lev's eyes go glassy. "Or, I wanted..."

She chews on her lip. It's an admission she hasn't made aloud, not to anyone but Aren and June. *It's nothing to be ashamed of,* they remind her, but how naive could Lev be? How hadn't she realized what would come?

Pheir interrupts Lev's spiral. "You wanted her. However she would let you have her."

Pheir doesn't sneer. Her expression is somber. For once, the two of them understand the same thing, the undeniable gravity of Vesta. Heat pricks behind Lev's eyes, humiliation bound with mourning. It wasn't a simple crush for Lev; it was a desperation to be closer that was dangling out of reach. Vesta teased her with it.

If you really want me, then prove it...

Lev did whatever she asked, but it was never enough. It was never going to *be* enough. When Lev tried to hold Vesta's hand in front of the pack, Vesta busied herself brushing hair from her face, winking at Lev where the others couldn't see.

The best magic is a secret.

"After Vesta noticed me, I felt unstoppable." Lev's arms float in the water, the same weightless feeling Vesta's attention brought. No one could deny Vesta. They gave her extra treats after dinner, let her skip chores and avoid punishments. She batted her lashes. She knew exactly what to say. She won people over. "Vesta always got what she wanted. I should have known I wasn't an exception to that."

On the ledge of the pool, Pheir shifts uncomfortably. That makes something in Lev's chest spike painfully, throat tightening around her voice.

"We talked about running away together and starting our own pack in the wilderness." Vesta's voice rings like a bell in Lev's memory, their fingers intertwined. *Just the two of us. It'll be perfect.* Lev swallows and glances up toward the cottage. "Before that was built, we sat on the edge of that cliff, dreaming up anything you could imagine." Lev remembers it all, but she remembers the warmth most of all — Vesta glowing in the sunlight, wind tossing her hair like sparks as she pressed her hand over Lev's heart.

When the sun starts to dip behind the cottage, Lev can almost see Vesta there again, inclining her head toward Lev. They were saying the same words, but they weren't talking about the same thing. "I was in it for her," Lev murmurs. To do anything with Vesta. To stay with her. To make a life with her. Childish embarrassment heats Lev's face, her gaze dipping to the water. "But Vesta wanted something else. A bigger pack. More people to follow her. More people to love her."

Pheir pulls her legs to her chest, trying to fit the story she knows with the one Lev is telling her. It haunts Lev the same way. If she'd done something differently, would the Vestals still have rebelled? If Lev had given Vesta what she wanted, would the end result have been the same? Would all those people have died? Would Lev have been among them?

"Maybe I did betray Vesta." Lev watches her fingers beneath the water. They seem to change shape beneath the surface as the bubbles rise. "It didn't start as that. It started when our Alpha wanted to train me to lead, to become an Alpha, to take over the pack. It wasn't a sure thing." Lev sounds like she did when she tried to convince Vesta, desperate to appease her. "Our Alpha had taught others before, but that didn't make Vesta feel better. I told her we could do it together, that it would be good for our future pack, but things were different after that."

"Different how?" Pheir asks from her perch.

Vesta's voice hisses through Lev's mind, as fresh as the day she said it. *Do you really think you're cut out for this? The pack will die if we listen to you.* It chilled Lev to her core, spurring questions she'd never had about herself. How could Vesta, as warm as the sun in the sky, be so cold? How could she be wrong when she knew Lev so well? Lev's intuition came in fits and spurts those days, seemingly dormant whenever Vesta was around.

There could only be one answer: Vesta was telling the truth. She was right about Lev. She saw Lev's failings.

"I started second-guessing myself." Lev clears her throat to keep her voice even. "Everything was a competition. Being next to Vesta used to feel like flying, but after that, every compliment was backhanded. I could never do anything right; there was always something she could criticize. She said it was tough love, that she was making me stronger, a better leader —"

"But she was keeping you in your place," Pheir whispers. Her wings curl tighter to her body.

Lev's ears flatten back. "I missed the old days so much it *ached.* I wanted Vesta to trust me again, so I did whatever I could — skipping training, avoiding the Alpha, insisting I didn't want to lead any more. It consumed me, trying to win her back, but it was never enough. The damage was done."

Pheir pulls the blanket tighter around. "That's when Vesta came to me?"

A sad laugh slips from Lev's lips. "No...not quite."

A breeze sneaks through the trees along the shoreline. Steam casts everything in a dim overlay as the sun continues its descent. For a moment, Lev's mind spins back to the moment when she was hopeless and desperate to fix everything.

FIFTY-THREE

Lev

High above the Timber compound, wind rustles through the trees. Leverette braces her feet to keep from sliding. Laughter bubbles out of Vesta until Leverette is giddy too, hoisting herself further along the cliff face.

They could have stopped back where the terrain is flat, but she and Vesta have never let danger stop them. It's a superstition they created a year ago; the higher they go, the less there will be to stop them as they dream up their future.

Maybe it's silly, but it's never led them astray.

As Vesta climbs, her mouth moves, voice lost to the wind.

"What?" Leverette calls after.

Vesta inclines her head back, hair whipping around her face. "I said, it's too loud!"

They both dissolve into giggles as Vesta pulls herself onto the final landing. Leverette grips a sprawling tree root, but Vesta extends her hand and waits for Leverette to take it.

It's been months since they were last here. Months since Vesta has done anything but fight or ice Leverette out with a cold shoulder. When Vesta looks at Leverette now, though, it almost seems like before. Like things could get back to the way they were. Like they could be friends again...

Like they could be more.

Leverette takes her hand. Vesta hoists her up, falling back to the earth from the effort, their limbs entangling blissfully. Leverette tries to unwind their ankles until she looks down at Vesta sprawled against the ground. Her platinum hair shines in the fading sunlight, spread through the grass like rivulets of water, her eyes iridescent around the dark of her pupil. She stares up at Leverette with a fondness that could almost be...

Leverette's heart thumps in her chest. Vesta lifts her hand to it, circling it with a talon as her voice rises above the wind. "You'll stand by me forever, won't you?"

What do teenagers know about forever? All Leverette knows is she can't imagine being without Vesta for one more day. "Always," Leverette breathes. Emotion wells in her throat, scrambling to make itself known before the gap between them spreads again. "I want to stay with you. I don't want to fight any more. We can still make our pack. We can still —"

Vesta places a finger over Leverette's lips to shush her. Leverette's mouth tingles. "We have time, bunny." Vesta's mouth spreads into a smile, fingers brushing fallen hair from Leverette's face. "I just need you to do one thing for me. One thing, and we can forget about everything else. Will you do that for me?"

If one thing will build a bridge across this chasm in their friendship, then Leverette will do it. Anything to repair what was once there. Forget her duty, forget her training; if she can show Vesta an ounce of the feeling she has, maybe the pain of the last few months will disappear.

Leverette nods. Vesta beams, wrapping her arms behind Leverette's neck to pull her closer.

A sticky sweet feeling binds in Leverette's stomach, her eyes dipping to Vesta's mouth. Vesta drifts her lips closer to Leverette's ear.

Leverette's brows knit, but all she caught was the curve of Vesta's smile pressed against her cheek. "Say it again?"

Wind ruffles her fur. It's so hard to hear when Vesta whispers, so Leverette leans closer, shivering at Vesta's warm breath. The feeling alone is so intoxicating, she nearly doesn't hear Vesta when she speaks again:

"Walk off the edge."

Leverette nearly laughs. It pops like a bubble in her mind, weightless and whimsical — but the words tug on her body. Leverette pulls back to look at Vesta's face. She's still smiling, watching Leverette with an eagerness that hasn't been there before. Leverette wants to ask why. Is there something she doesn't understand? Something she can't see?

A strange, reassuring glaze drips over Leverette's mind.

It's fine. You have to prove your trust. She'll swoop down and catch you if you fall.

Leverette rises to her feet.

Glee grows on Vesta's face. Something isn't right. Something is wrong, but when Leverette reaches for it, her hand closes over nothing but air and a voice in the back of her mind.

You'll be fine. Do this once. Do this for her. Do this for *me*. After this, everything can go back to the way it was.

It's Vesta's voice in Leverette's head, but Vesta's mouth doesn't move from its smile. Leverette's feet carry her closer to the ledge. One step. Two. Earth shifts beneath her feet as she draws closer, sending pebbles scattering down the cliff face. Leverette's body screams to stop, holding her in place as she stares at the waves crashing on the rocks below.

Just once. Do this once. Come on, Leverette, do it. Do it. Do it!

"Do it!"

The screech behind Leverette sends her to her knees, clutching for grass to stop herself from slipping. Her body tilts toward the drop off, but she scrambles to keep herself on solid ground. Her heart hammers, chest heaving as she finds Vesta's face.

"What are you doing to me?" Leverette gasps.

In all their time together, she's never seen Vesta like this — vicious and sharp, wild brutality as her eyes glow white-hot.

"One thing!" Vesta hisses. "I ask for one thing, and you won't even do that!" Her claws drag down her jaw, a screech building in her throat. "What kind of power is this?!"

Her scream echoes off the rocks. Leverette can't let go of the grass. Enraged, Vesta stalks closer, lifting her foot to Leverette's shoulder.

"If you really wanted to lead..." Vesta's voice grows until it competes with the wind, wrestling it into submission. "You'd do anything for it. You don't want it like I do." The pressure against Leverette's shoulder builds, her nails scraping the earth as she slides back. "You don't deserve it."

All it would take is one final push. One kick to send Leverette over the edge. A whimper escapes as she claws the ground, eyes widening...

And Vesta hesitates, the taut line of her mouth wavering.

It's the chance Leverette needs to jerk on Vesta's ankle. It knocks her off-balance as Leverette stumbles to her feet and slams her body into Vesta's. They tumble back across the ground, bodies scraped and bruised as they tear at each other. Vesta screams. Leverette digs in her teeth. Fur and feathers fly until Leverette lands on top, panting as she grips her hands around Vesta's throat.

It's a warning. She wants Vesta to stop, but Vesta's snarling mouth keeps snapping. "Do it, then!" Vesta doesn't even look scared, like she's hungry for it. "Prove I was wrong about you. Prove you want it."

She snatches Leverette's wrists, but she doesn't fight her off. She pulls Leverette closer, forcing Leverette's weight against her throat.

Leverette's fingers tighten, blood pulsing through her body as rage spikes inside her. She could do it. She could do it. After all that Vesta's done, all she's put Leverette through, she deserves this…

Vesta stops making sounds, mouth gaping as the corner of her lips curl into a smile. Something wet drops onto her cheek. It leaves a trail down to her mouth, as gentle as a kiss. Leverette's arms tremble until she releases, pulling back to swipe at the tears leaving paths down her face.

Vesta was right about her. She doesn't want it the way Vesta does.

With a gasp, Vesta staggers for breath, pushing Leverette off into the dirt as Leverette tries to stop the world from spinning. Her hands press to her ears, trying to block out the sound of Vesta's voice. Of Vesta's choked breaths. Of Vesta's fading pulse.

"That's your problem, Leverette…" On her hands and knees, Vesta's laugh croaks between her lips. She swipes Leverette's tear off her cheek with disgust, flicking the droplet to the ground. "You don't know how to get your hands dirty."

* * * * *

Only when Lev reaches the end of the memory does she realize she's been speaking without taking a breath. Pheir looks at her with a haunting familiarity reflected in her eyes — the fear of being out of control, careening to the edge to make Vesta happy.

Lev's voice is hoarse when she finds it. "Vesta vanished after that. Ran off to the Eyrie, I guess." All the Timbers felt the loss of losing a pack member. It caused all of them pain. Lev couldn't explain what happened. She couldn't tell them what she'd almost done. It didn't make sense; no matter whose voice seemed to be in

Lev's head, it was Lev who'd walked to the edge. It was Lev who attacked Vesta. How could she explain that?

No matter what Vesta had done to her, Lev still felt the pain of losing her. Lev still wanted her. Lev still missed her the same.

"That's how I knew what she was doing at the battle." Lev stares down into the water clouded with bubbles. "Maybe I was wrong. Maybe she wouldn't have hurt you, but she knew what I would do when I saw her behind you."

You don't know how to get your hands dirty.

"She called you Leverette." Across the spring, Pheir's brows knit, toes dangling in the water. "In the Eyrie, that's what she called you. Never anything else. Just '*Leverette.*'"

Lev's eyes shut. She remembers it like it was yesterday — Vesta leaning close, grin brushing the corner of Lev's mouth...

"That's why I started going by Lev." Her throat aches. "I couldn't take hearing my name anymore."

Replaying the memory always leaves Lev raw, twinging like she's picking at a scab. She braces for it, but recounting the story to Pheir doesn't stir the same emotion. Instead, when Lev inhales, her lungs expand like they can take a full breath for the first time, as if someone's guiding her hand away from an old wound so she can let it heal.

"Vesta chose my name, too." Pheir stares across the lake, a cloud passing over her eyes and making her lips pull taut. "She said 'Pheir' was stronger. Formidable. Intimidating. I wanted to be that for her. I liked hearing her say it."

Pheir's eyes are different than the first time Lev met her. Different than Pheir's first days at the Timbers, when she felt like a hostage. Now, Pheir's eyes are vibrant and clear, fierce and entrancing, a violet rim around her darkened pupil. There's still tension in her shoulders, like she might try to take flight at any moment.

A growing feeling in Lev prays she doesn't. "What do you want us to call you?"

Pheir blinks like she's never considered it. "I don't know." Her mouth twists before another chill snaps through her. "Gods, it's fucking *freezing* out here."

Lev churns the water at her side. "Then get in."

It's the excuse Pheir's been waiting for, slipping out of her blanket and stripping off her clothes. She sinks up to her neck in the hot water, humming as her hair tilts back. It grows a darker shade of mauve, slicked back from her forehead as droplets trail down her neck. Lev's eyes follow them until Pheir speaks.

"You know, I never wanted to like you."

Lev snorts, adrenaline pumping like she's still on the cliff's edge. "No shit."

"Vesta talked about you all the time — sprinkled you in conversation, found any excuse to bring you up." Pheir's arms spread through the water as she drifts closer with a hint of bitterness in her voice. "'*Leverette could never have pulled this off. Leverette never understood me.*'" Behind Pheir, her wings drift out over the water. "Years later, and you were still first in her thoughts. You were always there, hanging above us — the reason Vesta needed revenge, or a pack, or unquestioning loyalty. You were her driving force..." Slowly, Pheir steps closer in the water, her hands rising to the surface. "And she was mine."

It sits leaden in Lev's stomach, throat bobbing when she swallows. "I'm sor-"

"Don't be sorry," Pheir scoffs. "We all made our choices."

"But I don't think you did. I think..." Guilt weighs heavily through Lev's body under the buoyancy of the water. "I think Vesta learned from what happened with me. She learned to plant the seed of control earlier, to spend more time with it. She got better at it."

"Maybe..." Heat from the water wafts across Pheir's cheeks. "For some reason, I'm glad she failed with you." The corners of Pheir's lips twitch before she blanches, coughing as she turns in the water. "It's weird not having the wedding to blame things on."

Slyly, she narrows her eyes over her shoulder. "You're sure it didn't work?"

Lev holds her breath as she looks at Pheir. Pheir's dripping, bare shoulders under droplets clinging to her eyelashes and the corner of her smirk. *Something's* working right now.

"It didn't bind you," Lev confirms, throat raw. "It didn't force any feelings."

Pheir drifts back to the other side of the spring, putting safe distance between them again. "Right. It wasn't real."

"It was *real*," Lev blurts. Gods, she should've kept quiet; things are confusing enough already, but something inside of Lev has been clawing at her mouth to escape. "It was real in that I meant the promises I made. Our marriage is real to me, even if you aren't fully tied to the pack."

Pheir's shoulders drift above the water.

"You're my wife," Lev clarifies. "You have my protection. You have whatever you need." Lev doesn't look away from Pheir. "I don't need magic to fulfill my vows for me."

For once, Pheir is struck silent, eyes wide and unreadable. Beneath the bubbling spring, Lev picks out the quickening pace of Pheir's heart before the harpy shakes her head. "You don't mean that."

"I do."

Pheir's face hardens, a skeptic clinging to safety. "No one offers that without wanting something. We both know that."

The snarky curl of Pheir's tongue makes Lev shudder. Lev's fists clench beneath the water, hot from more than the spring. She's playing with fire, toying with temptation. "Maybe I just want you to tell me what a bitch I am again."

Light flickers in Pheir's eyes, a smile she can't fight back as she leans against the rock wall behind her. She looks down her nose with a wily smirk that makes Lev's knees weak. There's a regality to Pheir, shoulders settling back as she gives Lev a long once-over.

"You know, I thought if I hated you as badly as Vesta did, she and I would be closer than you had been. I played my part: asking her about you, dissecting your strategies, cataloging your weaknesses."

Pheir sets her feet against the bottom of the spring. Lev's toes curl against the sand.

"I couldn't stop watching you, Lev. I couldn't stop thinking about you." Pheir prowls through the water with Lev as her destination. "If I could find *one* way to get under your fur, that would be enough. But you were so sharp. So self-sacrificial. So..." Pheir draws closer, gaze dropping to Lev's mouth. Pheir's words coil like steam between them. "*Visceral.* I couldn't tell Vesta that. I couldn't let myself believe it." Tentatively, Pheir comes to halt in front of Lev. They're inches away now, droplets curving down the line of Pheir's jaw. After a long breath, Pheir pulls her eyes up to Lev's. "I understand why Vesta couldn't shake you."

A coil tightens in Lev's stomach, eyes sparking. "Are you gonna be obsessed with me, too?"

Pheir's hand darts out, clamping around Lev's throat to shove her back against the wall. This could be the end, the death sentence Pheir has always held for her. Lev's heart doesn't thud with fear. Heat pulses under Pheir's palm, her face inching closer until Lev can taste her breath. Until Pheir's mouth is wet against hers, molding over words Lev never thought she'd hear.

"I want you like a grudge I can't let go of. I *am* fucking obsessed with you."

Their push and pull finally collides, bodies slicing through the water, anger and vengeance melted into something else. Lev shifts her weight, pinning Pheir back against the rock with a drag of teeth into her lip. Their breaths meld, wet and hot and traded between their lips.

If this is what Pheir's hate feels like, then Lev wants Pheir to hate her forever.

FIFTY-FOUR

Pheir

Pheir lunges off the rock, sending herself and Lev slicing through the water before she pins Lev on her back in the shallows. This is the moment Pheir has waited years for. It's the scene she's imagined again and again — Lev trapped beneath her, at Pheir's mercy as blood pounds through her ears.

Now the full vision takes shape. Pheir doesn't want to drag her talons across Lev's throat; she wants to bury her mouth against it. Pheir doesn't want to laugh as Lev fights back; she wants Lev's fingers in her feathers, tracing rivulets of water that slip down Pheir's chest. Pheir doesn't want to watch the light drain from Lev's eyes; she wants Lev to look at her like this forever, slow and soft like she would paint Pheir from every angle.

Emotion blossoms in Pheir's chest, too big to be contained. She sits back on her heels as she pants for breath.

"Run."

The word escapes Pheir before she realizes it. Puzzled, Lev pushes up to her elbows as the water laps at her waist.

"Run," Pheir says again, rising to her feet. It's the only thing that makes sense to her carnal mind, past these new emotions she doesn't yet have names for. Her heart flutters as she stares down at Lev with a familiar desire. A coy smile darts across Pheir's lips. "I've been chasing you for long enough. It's about time I catch you."

The animal inside of Pheir rouses, like the night after the wedding when she wanted to give herself to the Timbers completely. The creature inside her is almost giddy, playful, hungry to capture the prey that's always evaded her.

Carefully, Lev pushes to her feet. Damp fur flings to her body, accentuating her curves. "I can run..."

It's useless for Pheir to fight the way her eyes follow the arc of Lev's breasts, the arch of her hips, the muscle of her thighs. Heat pulses through Pheir's stomach when her gaze lands on the devilish curl of Lev's mouth.

"But there's a reason you haven't caught me yet."

Pheir licks her lips. "And what is —"

Before she can finish, Lev bounds toward the trees. Her speed leaves Pheir breathless. Pheir pulls herself out of the spring, but her wings are heavy with water as cold wind raises goosebumps on her skin. "Cheater!"

Lev's laughter echoes off the trees.

Pheir shakes off as much as she can before she sprints after her.

The world feels different. Pheir hurtles through branches and brambles, hissing as they scratch her skin. Her ears perk toward the sound of snapping twigs. In years past, she wouldn't have felt any of it. Her focus would be on taking Lev to the ground. In this moment, Pheir is awash in sensations that make her heart trip as she hunts. Cold earth hardens beneath her feet. Wins bites at her wet skin. Leaves rustle as Lev's white cottontail disappears.

Pheir feels *everything*.

On a rush of adrenaline, she careens through the brush after the pound of Lev's footsteps. As soon as Pheir gets close, the noise disappears, making her grind to a halt in the middle of the forest. Her head twists toward the slightest noises. Is that the sound of fingernails scraping bark, or is it Pheir's imagination?

Her eyes narrow as warm breath puffs from her mouth. She should have known better. Lev is a creature built for stealth; she can move silently through the forest at will. In the fading light, Pheir has no heightened senses to lean on. No smell. No sight. No sound.

She shuts her eyes and tries to listen past the ambient noises of the woods. She shivers, teeth chattering despite the clamp of her jaw. A wolf howls in the distance. An owl takes off from a tree. Pheir's feathers stand on end —

Warm breath teases her ear, making her entire body clench.

Whirling, she springs toward Lev. They crash through the forest, tumbling end over end and holding tight to each other as they slide through a patch of wet earth. Mud splatters across them. Lev's scream turns into a laugh that sparks into Pheir's throat, too.

Straddling Lev's hips, Pheir pins the rabbit's hands by her head. Numbness tingles through Pheir's fingers. From this vantage point, she can survey the damage, flecks of mud clinging to Pheir's feathers and Lev's fur.

With a contented sigh, Lev arches and grinds their hips together. "I gave you that one, birdy."

It's all Pheir can do to keep from seeking friction. Smirking, she leans down to lick a drop of water and a gasp from Lev's lips. "Don't be a sore loser." Cruelty teases into Pheir's voice. Lev squirms hotly as Pheir pouts down at her. "You're gonna make taking my prize so much sweeter."

With one hand, Pheir presses her palm to the mud. Lev realizes her plan, squealing as Pheir leaves a brown handprint over one of Lev's breasts. It looks debaucherous contrasted with the pristine canvas of Lev's fur.

"Mine..." Pheir taunts, struggling to keep Lev in place as she wets her hand again. Mud squishes between her fingers as she grips Lev's hips. "Mine..." When Pheir leans for the ground again, Lev writhes onto her stomach and tries to scramble away. That makes it all the more rewarding when Pheir grabs her ankle and jerks her back. A wet *slap* lands against Lev's ass, muffling her moan as Pheir whistles between her teeth. "*Definitely* mine."

Pheir doesn't need heightened senses to feel the arousal crackling in the air. When Lev glares back at her, Pheir's stomach clenches. She presses her chest along Lev's spine, basking in the warmth radiating from Lev's body. Grabbing the base of Lev's ears, Pheir pulls them back so she can speak against them.

"How does it feel to be captive?" Her breath ruffles Lev's fur. Lev's nails dig into the dirt, hips winding back against Pheir until she gives in and grinds against Lev's ass.

Mud smears between them. Heat blooms through Pheir, making her mind run hungry and wild. With one hand pinning the back of Lev's neck, she forces the Alpha to all fours — face down, ass up, the same way Lev held Pheir the night of the wedding.

"You want to know how bad I hate you?" Pheir asks, sitting back on her heels. It gives her the perfect view of Lev's tail in the air as Pheir spreads the lips of her pussy with both muddy hands.

Of all the ways Pheir's tortured Lev, this is the closest Lev's gotten to delirious. Under Pheir's hands, Lev arches, and Pheir lowers her mouth to Lev's cunt. The air is cold around them, but Pheir runs hot, blowing warm air against Lev's clit. Body bucking, Lev whines and tries to sink back.

Pheir doesn't give her anything. "It's only fair I return your wedding gift, *wifey*." The name snaps from Pheir's mouth, a threat on the tip of her tongue. "You made me fuck my own chains. What should I do to you?"

Lev's tail twitches as Pheir drags her teeth between Lev's thighs, scraping the swell of her ass until Lev groans into the dirt. She could easily turn the tables. Pheir's no match for her Alpha power, but the sounds Lev makes are so submissive. It heats the coil in Pheir's stomach. Aren was right; Lev on her knees sounds *so fucking good.*

Giving Lev her mouth would be too easy, so Pheir flicks her tongue against Lev's clit to see her jump at the sudden stimulation. When Lev eases back for more, Pheir pulls away. Lev's fists clench as she curses in frustration.

"You know what I hate?" Pheir grips both of Lev's hips and pulls her back. "I've never heard you beg — not in a fight. Not on the battlefield. Not when someone's fucking you."

Pheir slots the top of one thigh between Lev's. From this angle, it's barely enough friction, especially when Pheir pulls away as soon as Lev tries to shift back. A whine rips out of Lev's chest, exquisite in its desperation. Pheir has to fight not to rock her hips forward.

"I *hate* that," Pheir breathes. "I hate that I could never catch you. I hate that you always slipped away."

Teeth grit, Pheir edges her thigh against Lev's clit to draw out her moan. Gripping the base of Lev's ears, Pheir holds her in place and sinks lower to the ground. Her hip bone rocks between Lev's legs, rewarded by slick heat that makes Pheir sneer.

"I hate that you're so fucking *hot.*" Her fingers dig into Lev's ass cheeks, talons dragging down the thick meat of Lev's thighs. No wonder Pheir couldn't keep her mind off of Lev. She tormented Pheir from the start, a craving Pheir felt in her bones — and now, Pheir has her. With both hands, Pheir slaps the outside of Lev's thighs. Lev's body jerks forward, rocking back quickly to find the friction of Pheir's body again.

"You gonna beg for me now?" Pheir asks, gripping Lev's hips and grinding her against the juncture of her thigh. It makes Lev shudder, but her mouth stays clamped, dark eyes turned back toward Pheir. There's a neediness in Lev's gaze that hasn't been there before, like the Alpha's losing her grip on control. "No?" Pheir fakes surprise, hands falling away to brace on the ground behind her. Deliberately, she rolls her hip up between Lev's legs. "Guess you're gonna have to fuck yourself on me, then."

It's merciless the way Pheir makes Lev work to get herself off. It's an impossible position with Pheir slotted between her thighs, making Lev lower herself and rock back against the line of Pheir's body.

"I wonder if you did this before." Pheir's head tilts. "In your room all alone, pillow between your legs..." Viciously, Pheir shifts her body out of the way as Lev lowers her hips. With every thrust, Pheir pulls back until Lev squirms in frustration, legs shaking as she lowers herself further. The humiliation makes Pheir's clit ache with need as she teases. "Almost there. You've almost got it..."

Once Pheir can't force Lev to sink any lower, Lev finds a rhythm against her. Lev's hips circle in a delicious pattern, desire smearing against the skin of Pheir's thighs. No one has debased themself before Pheir the way Lev does now. No one has given up their pride to satisfy what Pheir wants.

Lev does it like pleasing Pheir is a reward of its own.

It burrows deep in Pheir's gut, white-hot lust that branches through her like ice cracking on the surface of the lake. The cold around her is long forgotten. All she can remember now is *heat*, rocking her hips forward until Lev groans. Pheir wants that sound again. She chases it like a creature possessed, digging her fingers into Lev's hips and guiding them against her.

"*Gods*, I hate you," Pheir pants, because hate is the only thing this can be. It's the only feeling Pheir knows intimately. It's the only emotion that lingers this long, the only reason Pheir has thought of Lev every day of her life, the only thing that threatens to burn through Pheir until there's nothing left.

If that's not hate, what else could it be?

Pheir tightens her talons into Lev. "I hate that you remind me of the only people I've ever liked." Lev is as kind as Thalea, as clever as Rhaiden, as brilliant as Vesta — but Lev is better. Lev is soft and rough and calm and fierce and every contradiction Pheir never realized a person could hold. Her eyes clench shut as the thought roars through her. "I hate that you look like —"

A goddess. Not one fabricated like Vesta. Spread out on the earth, Lev is a deity of the forest, covered in mud and dirt and leaves. Things that are *real*. Things Pheir can grab between her fingers. Things that ground her and remind her she's the one in control of her body.

And this Pheir doesn't hate anything about Lev. She *craves* her.

Wildly, Pheir shoves Lev onto her back and pries her legs apart. They're a tangle of limbs and cries and dirt as Pheir settles herself over Lev. Their legs intertwined. Both of them gasp when their cunts grind together, clits dragging against each other's' thighs. It's a sloppy mess, desire barreling through Pheir unlike anything she's ever felt. It's obscene the way they move, want building between Pheir's legs when she presses Lev's knee back toward her shoulder.

"I caught you." Pheir closes her fingers around Lev's throat the way she's always longed to. Under Pheir's fingers, Lev's pulse thrums. Pheir doesn't want to let it go. "You're *mine.*"

My wife. My Alpha.

Lev arches into the touch. "I'm yours. I'm yours..." Like it's a promise. Like Lev knows Pheir needs to hear it. Like she knows Pheir's never had anything to call her own. When Lev's head tips back, it's the most breathtaking thing Pheir's ever seen. It's exhilarating, setting loose the desire clawing at her chest. The desire that's begged to be free since Caius kissed her at the top of the trees, since Aren pulled her into his lap, since Pheir caught Lev moments ago.

Under Pheir's hand, Lev's brown eyes find her. Want pours through Pheir, spilling into the depths of Lev's gaze when she parts her lips and begs.

"Please...take it. It's yours. Make me yours."

Electric heat swells and crashes into Pheir as she buries the sounds of her orgasm against Lev's mouth. Lev's nails rake down Pheir's back, hooking on her wings as their whines get lost between each other. Pheir doesn't lose everything, though; she immerses fully in the moment, unfiltered by anyone or anything else.

This belongs to them. There's nothing to dilute it. Pheir holds onto that as fiercely as she holds onto Lev.

Breaths slowing, both their chests press together as their heartbeats stagger. Their ribs dig uncomfortably into each other. Pheir doesn't want to move, eyes shut as her forehead presses to Lev's shoulder. The nails that left marks down Pheir's back now trace shapes between her feathers.

It's a soft touch Pheir doesn't know what to do with. Her body's too exhausted to tense, but Lev recognizes it anyway. She doesn't stop the patterns, tightening an arm around Pheir's waist. "You can tell me more about how you hate me," Lev pants, "if it helps."

A laugh puffs between Pheir's lips, leaving a dazed smile on her face. She digs her teeth into Lev's shoulder enough to make her laugh. It's so comfortable that she doesn't hear the footsteps until they're yards away. When Aren and Caius appear through the trees, Pheir groans and presses her face into Lev's neck.

She can hear the smug smirk in Aren's voice. "Worked some things out, have you?"

FIFTY-FIVE

Aren

Aren always wondered if they'd end up here — Lev on the ground beneath Pheir, breath ragged as they consumed each other. A mutually-assured destruction.

Maybe this was fate after all. Maybe there's an undeniable truth to this that Aren doesn't understand. They were always meant to end up in this clearing, in this position, the two women wrestling for victory. In another world, the ending would be different, but the events would be the same — Pheir's mouth against Lev's pulse, Lev's nails in Pheir's arms, a climax building to a devastating finale.

In this life, though, their chests rise and fall together. Pheir doesn't try to escape the circle of Lev's arms. The smiles on their faces match, lazy and content.

This was meant to be.

Aren crouches down to offer his hand. "Come on. We'll get you warmed up."

"Actually..."

Caius's voice makes Aren's body stiffen when he looks over his shoulder. There's a hot ember in Caius's eye. Never before has Aren understood how his own ever-watchful gaze must feel, a predator lurking in the forest. Instinctually, Aren stands to his full height at the slide of Caius's tongue over his lips. Aren has a good six inches on him, but in this moment, Aren feels like he's on his knees. His stomach twists when Caius cracks his neck and speaks again.

"I want to work some shit out, too."

It's a delicious threat, one that makes Aren's fur rise on end. On the ground behind him, Pheir and Lev hold their breath. There's an entirely new feeling as Caius watches Aren with no one standing between them.

"Caius..." Aren tries to infuse a warning into his tone; it comes out strained and desperate. At the sound of it, Caius's pupils blow wider, like he's on the trail of a weakened animal.

Aren's dick twitches.

"I think it's time you let loose, beta," Caius murmurs.

The honorific shudders through Aren's body. At the edge of the clearing, Caius prowls, broad muscles of his back stretching under his fur. His shoulders shift as he circles the three of them. It makes all of their hearts stutter out of time. In Aren's instinct-driven brain, they're trapped and being hunted...but it's *Aren* that Caius focuses on. It's Aren who Caius pins under his gaze.

"You're tired of living on the sidelines?" Caius rises to his full height, a challenge curling over his lips. "Let's see it, then. Let that animal out."

It's as if Caius recognizes the wild beast that lives in Aren's chest. Despite Aren's attempts to keep it locked away, Caius has discovered it. Caius knows exactly how to entice it. Caius understands the animal. He understands the pieces of Aren he's long kept at bay, the pieces Aren has denied himself.

Caius howls to them to call them out of hiding until they're stampeding into the open.

Caius's weight settles on his feet, poised to attack. Innately, Aren mimics the position, but he's no match for Caius's brute strength. Not when Aren's mind is reeling with desire as Caius's tongue piercings click against his teeth. As if Caius can smell it, he smiles.

"If our Alpha can give control to her worst enemy, surely you can give some to me."

When Caius lunges, Aren almost meets him midair. He almost fights to regain control, but something deep in his stomach stops him. It makes his knees weak. It makes him hesitate. It makes him wonder what it would be like to give himself fully over to something.

Caius collides with him, pinning Aren easily to the ground. Caius tightens his grip to see if Aren will fight back, but the lynx lies still beneath him. It makes Caius growl low in his chest. With one hand, he trails down Aren's jaw and grips his chin. "I want *all* that undivided attention." Then he turns Aren onto his stomach.

Aren tries to push up to his hands and knees, but Caius keeps him trapped in the mud. It coats his limbs and splatters as he struggles. Before Aren, Lev appears, her face reflecting the same dazed desire. If anyone can understand his intrinsic grapple for control, it's her. They've both kept themselves from sliding down the slippery slope of passion. Now, though, she holds Aren's face in her hands with a look far deeper than she's given him before. It's a look of blissful defeat, an acceptance that the two of them can't hold back from Pheir and Caius.

The four of them aren't balanced by staying on opposite sides of the scale; they're balanced by racing to the middle and knowing everything will fall into place around them.

"We don't stand a chance," Lev breathes against Aren's mouth. It startles a laugh out of him, swallowed by the drag of her lips. He reaches for her, but Caius gets a hand around Aren's neck and pins his face to the mud.

"Have you been waiting for this?" Caius's fingers clench on the back of Aren's neck. "For me to give you everything I have? To take you in my hands for once, so you can see if I can handle it?" Caius's voice is patronizing and edgy, warring with arousal like he desperately wants the words to be true. Like he wants Aren to trust him. Leaning forward, Caius breathes against the back of Aren's ears. "You want me to handle you?"

It sparks a new instinct in Aren. He arches into Caius's touch and grinds back. Both men freeze. Aren has always submitted to Lev with ease. With Caius, it's the other way; they fall into pack rankings, Aren in control even when he's on his knees. Giving Caius authority comes so swiftly now that it leaves Aren breathless. Without thinking, he bares his neck to Caius, exposing his stomach as a purr rattles through his throat.

It's not a feeling that can be contained in words; it's a language their bodies speak. Wantonly, Caius's fingers clench. "God*fucking*dammit, Aren." With a circle of Caius's hips, his teeth drag against Aren's ear until Aren has to bite back a moan. There's no fighting the sound that escapes him with Caius in his ear. "I might fucking breed you, too, beta."

Untamed desire in Caius's voice makes Aren whine, and Caius drags his claws down the slope of Aren's back.

"Is that what you want?" Caius pulls back, digging his claws into Aren's hips. "Want me to stuff you full of my cum? Want me to leave you a reminder of whose ass this is?"

Something wet and warm drags over Aren's taint. Before Aren can jerk, Caius's tongue teases against his ass, making his hips rut against nothing but air. Caius's growl vibrates against Aren's sack, the barbels in Caius's tongue toying with him. Aren's claws dig into the earth.

There's no escaping this. There's no denying how badly he wants it. Still, Caius gives him a chance as Caius sits back on his heels and lowers his voice. "It's gonna hurt, Aren. I'm not gonna be gentle."

The words are a jarring reminder, yet Aren's desire-addled mind hadn't considered them. They're in the middle of the forest with no lube, but that animal in Aren's chest is rearing back, enticing his body to rebel. Aren can't remember what he's supposed to do. Pounding desire grows louder with every second.

Take. Mine. Need.

His body arches under Caius's touch, rocking back like an offering, dick leaking pre-cum onto the forest floor. This is the creature Aren has become, as desperate and depraved as Caius believes himself to be. Aren knows he'll take anything as long as Caius gives it to him.

That trust and wanton desire does exactly what Aren wants it to. Ferally, Caius aligns their hips like he might bury himself inside — but he stops.

Aren rocks back, jaw clenched as he buries his face in the ground. "*Caius...*" He whines like a bitch in heat. Fuck the pain. Fuck the ache. Aren *wants* it. He wants Caius buried completely inside and taking everything Aren has. His mind is too far gone to care, but Caius keeps firm hands on the swell of Aren's ass.

"Gotta make sure it's wet," Caius grits before his hands drop. Aren becomes the vicious beast, reaching back and snarling for Caius to finish what he started. On Caius's either side, Lev and Pheir stand, watching how Caius makes Aren kneel for him.

It splatters humiliation in Aren's gut, making his dick grow harder against his stomach. Pheir smirks down at him. Lev is so entranced she doesn't realize that Caius is reaching for her until he pulls her down into his lap. She's light as a feather as he guides her to sit on Aren's upturned ass like it's a chair. Caius keeps her facing him, gripping her hips and moving her with hardly any effort.

"You want to get this cock nice and wet for your beta?" Caius teases. Aren's claws dig into the dirt, shivering every time Caius uses his proper title. He makes Aren lie there, ass presented in the air as Caius spreads Lev's legs on top of him.

When Caius stands, he lines up with Lev. There's no resistance when Caius pushes inside her, swallowing her gasp and forcing Aren to feel every pump of Caius's hips. He uses Aren like a prop, fucking into Lev with Aren beneath her.

It boils Aren's blood. He reaches to get his fist around his dick —

"Don't fucking touch it," Caius snaps. Aren groans. It spurs Caius faster, tugging Lev and Aren toward him with every rhythmic thrust. Aren's dick bobs with the motion until Caius finally pulls out and leaves Lev cursing. Then Caius kneels, followed by the slick sound of his tongue dragging up Lev's cunt. It leaves all of them moaning.

When Caius lets Lev step down, she stumbles. He chuckles and swats her ass before he turns to Pheir. "You gonna get my dick wet, birdy?"

It takes no time for Pheir to take her place behind Aren. This time, she leans down over his back to press her chest against him. Her legs spread, lifting on her toes to set her pussy above Aren's ass. She's doing this to torment him, her voice hot in his ear. "A little payback never hurt anybody."

That makes Aren's hips rock, before Pheir gasps as Caius sinks inside her.

"*Fuck.*" Her teeth dig into Aren's shoulder, not quite hard enough to draw blood. It still makes Aren's head spin when she keens, "He's so fucking *deep*."

Aren bites back his own whine. Her body weight keeps him still. With her hand, she reaches beneath him and brushes his dick with her fingers. He twitches as she fists over him — but only his head. It's torture. Aren can *feel* Caius dragging inside her, his balls slapping Aren's perineum as Caius fucks Pheir.

It shouldn't be this hot. It shouldn't be this fucking filthy, but Aren leaves gouges in the dirt as he and Pheir groan in time.

Then something wet teases Aren's asshole again. It slips between Caius's strokes, making Aren's eyes roll back as he recognizes the wet heat of Lev's mouth. She kneels next to Caius, claws digging into Aren's hips as she trails her tongue against his ass, down to his balls, against the base of his cock and back again. She must be working on Pheir and Caius too, smearing her mouth over the three of them, because Caius curses Lev's name before he shudders and pulls back.

He isn't done, though. He's intent to torment Aren for as long as he can. With one slow thrust, Caius slides into Pheir's lubricated ass.

"It's even wetter than your *cunt*," he groans.

"Your fault," Pheir laughs against Aren's ear before it rolls into a groan as Caius rocks into her. This time, his thrusts are slow and purposeful. Lev's tongue must find Pheir's clit, because there's a sharp sucking sound a second before Pheir writhes and whimpers on Aren's back.

Aren gets no time to bask in it. He can't see anything behind him. He can't be sure what's happening, but then Lev sucks one of his balls into her mouth and makes his body jerk. Pheir nearly topples off of him, but Caius grabs her.

Aren's legs shake. It's not enough. Aren needs *more*. Mercifully, Caius pulls out of Pheir and lands a smack against her ass. "Now, put that smartass mouth to use."

Despite her snarl, her knees hit the ground a second before she swirls her tongue around the rim of Aren's ass. When Lev drags her mouth back to meet Pheir's, it's all Aren can do to keep from shuddering. They take their time, breathy laughter between their lips, slick and wet and *hot*. Aren never knows what's coming next. He never knows what pattern their tongues will take, when they'll pull back to kiss each other and do little more than breathe against Aren. He's trapped in the exquisite turmoil, cursing as they both drip spit down the seam of his ass to coat it thoroughly.

"So fucking ready now, aren't you?" Caius sheaths his claw and circles Aren's ass with one finger. He guides it inside, making Aren moan at the slow stretch, like it's working out a sore muscle. With every pump of Caius's finger, he sinks deeper until he's completely buried inside. Curving his finger, he nudges Aren's prostate, making white-hot stars burst behind Aren's eyes.

"You gonna beg me for it?" Caius works a second finger in, slick with spit and desire from Lev and Pheir. "Gonna thank me for breeding this uptight little hole?"

Aren tries to bite back, but all he can do is meet every thrust of Caius's fingers. Beneath Aren, Lev and Pheir crawl between his legs, whispering so quietly Aren can't understand them. They slip easily through the mud. He peers at them between his thighs before both their mouths are on his dick. He clenches around Caius's fingers, making Caius groan as Lev and Pheir tease Aren's cock. They don't give him the heat of their mouths. There's not enough pressure, not enough covering him, not enough *filling* him. The women whisper and laugh, lips buzzing against his cockhead as Caius pulls his fingers out.

"Beg me, beta," Caius demands.

"*Yes!*" Aren finally shouts. His fist presses into the ground, jaw clamping around words. "Yes, — make it..." Words slip past him, leaving his tongue numb as pleasure pulses in his stomach. Lev and Pheir keep flicking their tongues against his cock.

He can't think. He can't do anything but *feel*, breath ragged and short. His voice disconnects from his head, babbling nonsense.

"Make me your bitch, your anything, *please —*"

That's all it takes for Caius to fuck a groan out of both of them when he buries inside, slick from spit and Lev and Pheir's desire when his hips slam into Aren's. They're both a mess of sounds, Caius holding Aren's tail as he fucks his ass. It sends Aren forward, knees dragging against the ground as his dick slips out of Pheir and Lev's mouths. He stops himself with hands outstretched, back arching as heat radiates off of him.

Aren tries to think, to breathe, when Lev and Pheir crawl out to kneel in front of him. They're both covered in cold mud, Pheir's skin flushed when she holds Aren's chin in her hand.

"Come here, kitty..." She teases when she knows he can't move, trapped by Caius's claws and deep thrusts. Aren is captive to sensation, never given a moment to catch his breath. Caius fills him completely as Lev kneels behind Pheir, hands tracing down the feathers of Pheir's body and outlining the curves of her breasts.

When Lev twists Pheir's nipples, it draws out a hiss, but Pheir's head lolls back against Lev's shoulder. Pheir's letting herself be used. It's a sight Aren never thought he'd see, Pheir giving herself over for the Timbers to enjoy. It burns through him so quickly that he doesn't realize he's trying to crawl toward them.

"You always took your job so seriously," Lev murmurs to Aren as she continues playing with her wife. The curve of Pheir's waist earns a scratch of Lev's nails, Pheir's hair pulled taut in Lev's hand, Pheir's hips winding in search of Lev's fingers. Aren can't tear his eyes away. Caius grinds into him, making Aren gasp at the stretch. Lev clicks her tongue. "The perfect beta. You let everyone have a turn with you, don't you? That's what you're here for — to take care of the Alpha and the pack."

It sends Aren's eyes shut, overwhelmed with sensation rocketing through his stomach. It *is* what he's meant to do, but it's debaucherous in Lev's mouth, making Aren fuck back over Caius without warning. Cursing, Caius grips Aren's hips before Caius picks up the pace and drags deep inside.

"We've shared everything, Aren," Lev breathes. "They say nothing is closer to an Alpha than her beta, but I think we can get closer than that." A lascivious look passes over Lev's face as she edges Pheir closer, moving Pheir's knees with her own. "You want to share this, too? You want to share my wife? My combatant?"

At the sight of Pheir kneeling before him, Aren leans forward, desperate to drag his tongue over her bare pussy — but Caius and Lev work together, holding Aren and Pheir back until they both groan. Lev uses one finger to tease Pheir's clit, circling for a second before she pulls away. Pheir's body bucks against Lev's restraint. Aren's helpless to reach her.

"If you want it to be yours…" Lev drags her tongue up Pheir's neck, following the thrum of her pulse. Aren can feel it in his body, his ears, the sounds of all their heartbeats building to a fever pitch. Pheir arches in Lev's grip, her eyes on Aren as Lev drags her teeth against Pheir's shoulder. "Show me, beta." Lev's lips brush Pheir's skin. "*Take it.*"

Restraints break through Aren's body, his nerves pulled tight before they snap. He can't find his thoughts. There's primal heat when he snatches Pheir's leg, dragging her to the ground beneath him. She screams as blood blooms on his tongue.

Wet. Hot. Mine. Ours. Ours. Ours.

He doesn't realize what he's done until Lev gasps. Caius stills behind him. Aren's mind tries to understand. Pheir's neck is in his mouth, flooding his senses with *her*. Her body's trapped beneath him, her fingers in his fur.

Panic darts through him. Has he hurt her? Has he *killed* her? No, that isn't what his primal mind wants. He's tasting her. He's marking her. He's making her his. It's what his body yearned for the night of the wedding, but there are now vows to stop him now. Now, he can sate his carnal desire and give it what it craves.

Pheir clutches Aren tighter, a groan slipping past her lips as her arousal floods over Aren's tongue. He laves at her blood and the marks he's left in her skin. Finally, the beast in him can do what it's been begging for.

Making her his. Making *all* of them his. Leaving an impression they can't get out.

It rushes through all four of them like the night of the ceremony, desire combusting and leaving nothing but carnal beings in its wake. Caius snarls, bearing down harder to fuck Aren like the monsters they are. Pheir scratches, knees locking around

Aren's hips to pull him toward her. She arches her throat deeper into his mouth.

Aren digs in his teeth until Pheir screams. Her orgasm tears through her without a touch, neck arching into Aren's mouth like she has no fear, like she trusts her life in the jaws of a beast. The sight and smell of it sends Caius over the edge. There's no warning when he snaps his hips, burying into Aren and filling him. Cum leaks out around Caius's cock, but he holds Aren in place. With every thrust, Caius works deeper, fucking in cum like he never wants Aren to get the scent out.

Blood trails from Pheir's throat to the ground, but Pheir is still flush with life. She reaches above her for Lev. Aren doesn't think, grabbing his Alpha and pulling her down, too. He and Pheir bury their mouths on either side of Lev's neck, turning her gasp into a groan as they break through her fur.

Blood pricks into Aren's mouth, making him salivate as he leaves his mark in Lev. She clutches both of them as Pheir smears her lips with blood and tongues at the mark she left.

Only then does Caius pull out, diving down amongst them to lick Lev's blood from Pheir's mouth, to taste Pheir on Aren's tongue before his teeth find Aren. There's no telling where their mouths go, dragging against each other through blood and mud and cum until everyone wears three sets of teeth prints.

Desire heightens the possession. Once they've left their marks, they grab for each other's bodies, not caring where their mouths land. Tongues drag between legs, hard dicks rutting against each other, slipping between hands and mouths and cunts, covering each other in every way they can. They're a mess of bodies and limbs, claws and talons and fangs digging into each other and never letting go.

In another lifetime, a different kind of blood would be spilled. This time, though, blood mingles on their tongues, lost in the scent of arousal and assurance and devotion. Beneath them, the ground hums a symphony. A chain of teeth marks link around Pheir's neck, a perfect vision of what the animal in Aren craves. His nose fills with the smell of it as he buries his face between the others.

There are not four scents any longer. There's only one — the scent of *them*. The scent of home.

FIFTY-SIX

Caius

The forest is still. In the distance, frogs croak at the edge of the lake, trees rustling in the breeze overhead. There's a chill in the air, but it's nothing the weres' fur can't handle. Nothing Pheir can't handle when they're all stretched out on the ground, bodies pressed together.

With a smug smile, she closes her eyes, tipping her head back onto Caius's stomach. It's the first time they've all been this close without her head on a swivel, Caius stretched perpendicular as the other three lay against his body.

It means something that Caius is the one wrapped around the others. That Aren hasn't taken his place. That Caius is the one trusted to be on guard, watching their backs as well as the sated exhaustion in their bodies.

Caius has never felt this sore. No day of labor compares to the contented ache in his bones, the gratified twinge when Aren stretches against his thighs.

"I didn't think you could get any quieter," Caius teases as he tugs the fur of Aren's head. Caius's hips rock at the memory of Aren finally giving himself to them. It felt natural, as simple as bracing their backs together in battle.

When Caius's fingers tighten in Aren's fur, Aren whines. Pheir tilts her smirk toward him. "Oh, he's *definitely* saying something..."

Aren digs his claws into her hip until she laughs and rolls over to face Lev on her other side. Their Alpha is seconds from sleep, eyelids heavy, cheek pressed to Caius's chest where he stretches out above them. Between his fingers, he strokes Lev's ear. "I've never seen her this relaxed." With his other hand, he tugs down Pheir's chin to get a look at her tongue. "You must have magic in that mouth of yours."

"I don't need magic," Pheir murmurs, like she's heard it before. Her gaze stays on Lev like the cat that finally caught the mouse and wants to keep it. With her teeth, Pheir digs into Caius's thumb. He doesn't flinch. She drags her tongue over the wound and holds his gaze. "Maybe you'll find out what else my mouth can do."

Comfortably, Caius rolls onto his back. Touching other people this softly has never been simple, but it's easier when Caius focuses on the moment. On the pressure Pheir applies with her teeth, enough to turn his snarl to a smile. On Pheir's fingers dancing over the mark she left in Lev. On Aren draping his arm around Pheir's waist as he tongues the teeth-prints in her skin.

There's intimacy in being physically close, Caius knows, but he understands now that it's nothing next to the intimacy of being known. They can drag their bodies together, but it'll never be half as close as the feeling that surges between them. This is solid. This is chosen. This is magic of its own, whether they need it or not.

In the silence, their breathing settles into a rhythm. Aren's paw brushes a path down Pheir's side, drifting through the smattering of feathers on her hips and thighs. Despite the gentle touch, her body stiffens, as if the calm unsettles her. Caius understands that. Quiet forests have always meant someone's waiting to strike.

She turns her head to look at Aren, her voice little more than a whisper. "Is this real?"

The question strikes Caius as strange, but Aren curls his hand around her and pulls her back against his chest. "It's real," his voice rumbles. "Give it time." It's almost like Aren could be speaking to Caius, too. This comfort, this closeness, this whole *world* is steeped in history that will take more than a few weeks to unravel.

If Caius thinks about it too intently, the worry seeps in, spreading its jaws until it could swallow him whole. *You think you deserve this? You think this can last? Let your guard down, and you'll see what people do to fools that trust them.* But Caius doesn't want to listen to his father's voice any longer. Instead, he lifts his nose toward the air and sniffs. "Smells like snow."

Stars prick through the trees. Pheir shivers as cold finally sets in. Wearily, Aren pries himself to his feet and extends his hand. "We should get you warmed up. Clean ourselves up. Find some food."

Pheir grumbles but allows Aren to hoist her to her feet. Caius rouses Lev with a grin as he murmurs against her ear. "I think we've all had *plenty* to eat."

Groggily, Lev swats him as he lifts her over his shoulder. They make their way back to the shoreline and slip into the large beach shower stall at the bottom of the stairs. As Aren takes Lev off Caius's shoulder, Caius cranks the hand-pump to draw hot water in.

It's almost unbelievable that they're together, the people who spent years trying to kill each other now caring for each other. When Pheir watches them, it's not with the vicious plans of before. It's not intentional, her eyes soft and distracted as Aren begins to wash Lev's fur. Caius settles behind Pheir and drags a soapy hand down her stomach.

She shoots him a poor excuse for a glare. "I don't need help."

His cold nose brushes behind her ear until she shivers. "You sure about that?" When his arms loosen, she grabs them both and tucks them tighter around her. His hands trail down to her thighs, lathering before he walks them both under one of the sprays. Pheir turns in his arms, tilting her head back as water rushes over her body.

Never has he appreciated *skin* like this, fingers tracing the places where her feathers fade. Her body tastes different than fur, too, dynamic on the end of his tongue. He lowers his mouth to her shoulder, licking droplets roughly until her fingers curl into his fur.

Her teeth chatter, but it's not from cold. Gruffly, she pulls him closer, lifting on her toes to seek his mouth. "Don't fucking smile," she mutters against his teeth.

"Or what?" Caius challenges, biting into the laughter she tries to disguise.

Bathing takes longer than usual. They all find excuses to linger under the spray of the water. When Caius shakes dry, he splatters the rest of them wet again. Aren "accidentally" drizzles Caius with soap so he has to rinse for a second time, with Aren's mouth against his neck. Lev drapes her arms over Pheir's shoulders from behind as they ask the men for help cleaning their backs. The devilish look in their eyes comes to fruition, and by the time they've cleaned up, they're all dirty again.

Eventually, they make it back up the stairs to the cabin and set off on the cliffside path toward the main lodge. The night is cloudy. In the distance, the firepit is lively with voices and song.

"We still *reek* of sex," Caius notes, but he's far from complaining. He's never been in such a giddy mood, sticking out his leg to trip Aren so their bodies collide as dust kicks up around them.

"We just showered!" Lev laughs. A white dot drifts through the air, winking in the dark before it lands on the path. Another speck falls in Lev's fur, blending into the light patches before another catches on the end of Aren's nose.

Lev sticks out her tongue, and the white flake melts as soon as it lands. "First snow." She stares up toward the haze of sky before she remembers. "It's Pheir's first snow ever! You know, they say —
"

When Lev turns, there's no one behind them, nothing but snow swirling through the air where Pheir should be.

Caius's eyes dart toward the forest lining the path, ears pricking to hear past the trees scraping together. His heart thuds as his nose twitches for a scent. There's nothing but snow and smoke and the fresh smell of soap...until the camouflage fades. Until Caius makes out the shadows back by the cottage door, and the scent of a fox overtakes everything else.

Two forms take shape as Caius's eyes adjust — Pheir standing in front, chin forced into the air by the claws pressed to her throat. Another hand cages her heart, digging into her skin beneath a flash of white fur. Behind Pheir, two eyes reflect the moonlight, illuminating the wicked flash of Singer's teeth as they press to the back of Pheir's neck.

"You're one tough bitch to kill, birdy."

FIFTY-SEVEN

Pheir

Pheir has lost blood a thousand times. It's clogged her nose, scent overpowering as it suffocated her. She's swallowed it down. She's spit it between her teeth. She's gagged on it, choked on it —

But it's never turned her stomach like it does now.

Blood rises under the pinpricks of Singer's claws, tiny droplets Pheir can barely feel. It's nothing like the blood she spilled an hour ago under Aren and Lev and Caius's teeth. Those were a connection forged together, binding Pheir to the people she chose. These new marks are a reminder of how easily they can be torn apart.

Snow spins lazily around them, blurring the space between her and the others. A flake lands on her eyelashes. She blinks, and the flake dissolves into nothing.

She is not invincible. She is not the untouchable assailant Vesta taught her she was — and still, Pheir fights back.

"I'll kick your fucking ass!" She jerks against Singer's restraint. The claws over her heart sink deeper, strangling her scream under the pain thudding through her.

Lev steps closer, the same way she did across the battlefield. That makes Singer clutch Pheir tighter, hoisting her back against his chest.

Pheir's breath puffs into the air as she tries to catch Singer in the corner of her eye. What can she do? The one way she knows how to fight is impossible now. She's the last line of defense, meant to throw herself at danger for someone else. If she can't...

Who will?

Yards away, Lev approaches, flanked on either side by Aren and Caius. As they draw closer, the space between the Timbers grows as snow flurries around them. Lev creeps toward Singer head-on, trying to keep his attention. On her left side, Caius takes a long path that stretches out before it bends back toward Singer. Aren does the same on the other side.

Singer doesn't miss it. His claws tighten against Pheir's neck so sharply that she chokes, his shout ringing in her ear. "Stop fucking moving!"

The Timbers grind to a halt. Their eyes cling to the blood blooming from Pheir's throat

Lev keeps her gaze level. "Let's talk, Singer. You don't need to do this."

On his back, his wings beat, smile curling against Pheir's cheek. "I'm gonna have to disagree."

An angry snort comes from Caius, hackles raised as he surges forward.

"Call off your fucking wolverine!" Singer shouts to Lev, dragging Pheir's body toward him like a shield.

Lev doesn't have to speak. Caius stops in his tracks, grinding the balls of his feet into the dirt as he snarls. "It's three against one! We can kill you in a second!"

Singer's claw taps against Pheir's jugular. "Not before I kill her."

"What do you want?" Aren grits. He's no longer the tranquil man Pheir is used to. His lips pull back over his teeth, claws flicking out from his hands. "We'll give you whatever it is: food, supplies, transportation. Take it. Start your life over somewhere else."

It doesn't matter if the offer is true. Singer doesn't care. His claws twist into Pheir's chest, ripping a groan past the clench of her teeth.

Caius nearly lunges again. Lev shouts his name. He keeps distance between them, prowling back and forth through the dusting of snow.

Singer's smile spreads against the back of Pheir's head at the control he wields. "Anything I want?" Lev gives a sharp jerk of her chin. Singer laughs and shrugs his shoulders. "I want Vesta back."

Pain makes Pheir's head spin. The whistle of wind takes Singer's words and distorts them. Pheir can't be thinking straight, but the others wear matching confused expressions. Pheir sucks in a breath through her teeth, trying to piece together the words. "What are you talking about?"

Mockingly, Singer's face tilts in her periphery, his breath hot against her face. "*So important*, Pheir. That's what Vesta always said about you. But without me, you'd be nothing, wouldn't you? A shell with no purpose."

His claws dig into Pheir's chest. She screams, struggling in his arms. Lev edges closer, fur rising in frustration as she shouts above the snow. "You hated Vesta! You said everyone who fell for her were weak —"

Singer smirks. "I've been practicing for a while."

Ice spreads through Pheir's veins, colder than the snow. It doesn't make sense. Feathers bristle on her back. "What does that *mean*?" she yells. "Stop playing games! What the fuck do you *want*?"

When she struggles, Singer tightens his arms around her and rips off one of his boxing wraps. Those ugly fucking wraps, always around his wrists...but buried in his white fur is a discolored patch of hair in the shape of a "V."

Breath stills in Pheir's lungs. Singer's teeth scrape her ear, his voice raking down her spine. "You're not the only one Vesta trusted."

Nothing makes sense. Pheir's mind whirls to understand. Singer was a stranger to her. She never heard his name, never knew he existed...

Because Vesta *hadn't* trusted her with everything.

Nausea roils in Pheir's stomach. All those days Vesta left the rest of them at the Eyrie, she was going somewhere else. Pheir believed her excuses. Pheir made excuses *for* her, nodding along with everything Vesta said.

I'm making investments for the future. People who will sing my praises for years to come.

Pheir fights the urge to vomit. It's so fucking obvious, like Vesta was playing with them, dropping hints all along.

Realization dawns in Caius's eyes as he looks at Singer. "You're the sleeper. From Vesta's journal. You were part of her plan —"

"Killing Pheir won't bring Vesta back!" Aren voice cuts in above the howling wind, body battered by snow. Pheir can hardly make him out through the dark storm. "It won't bring your pack back. It won't change anything."

Singer's laugh sets Pheir's teeth on edge as his claws line up over her heart. "We all have our purpose. Since the Regents aren't going to do this for me..."

"Wait!"

It's the desperation that stops him, straining through her voice like she's already dying — but it isn't Pheir who spoke. Her heart pounds under Singer's hand, finding Lev's face in the moonlight.

She's the one that shouted, eyes wet as fear reflects through the tears gathering there.

"Please..." Lev's lip trembles. Snow swirls erratically around them. This storm can't be controlled any more than Singer can, but Lev tries. Pheir hears her beg. Lev's voice cracks when she swallows. "She's *ours*."

When Pheir looks at Lev, she recognizes something bigger than herself. The same look crosses Aren and Caius, too. This look is more than the vengeance Singer is after, more than the revenge Pheir cared about for so long. *You're nothing like them*, Vesta always told her, but Pheir is reflected in the Timbers now. She understands that desperation, the willingness to sacrifice anything to protect someone else.

A feeling comes to life in Pheir, deeper than Singer's claws and stronger than his hate. It's the feeling she always wanted from Vesta that she could never get.

Love.

Singer's claws drive completely into Pheir's chest. She screams, body finally tearing in two the way it's been begging to. Blood rushes through her ears above the roaring pain, wind howling as Singer's voice rises. "She's Vesta's. And she always will be."

Then Singer tears out Pheir's heart.

Something explodes from her chest. It sends Pheir flying, eyes clamping shut against the heat before her body thuds along the dirt. Her head pounds. Her eyelashes cling together, caked with soot as she squints against the light. Heat presses in from all sides. Fire swirls around her and roars through her ears. She tries to get her legs under her, but they give out, collapsing as she searches through the wall of flames for the others.

Past the line of fire, three figures struggle toward each other. At the edge of the cliff, Caius's claws dig into the earth, slipping every time he tries to pull himself back onto solid earth. Aren bleeds from a deep cut above his eye, grabbing for Caius's forearm as Lev scrambles to help.

Pheir reaches for them — but they're too far, lost behind the flames. Her head tilts as she looks down at the damage to her chest. Blood trickles from her body, heart thudding haphazardly in her chest. It's still there. *It's still there.* With one hand, she presses against her wound to staunch the flow of blood before she realizes that rainbow flames are pouring through her fingers.

Maybe she hit her head harder than she realized. Flames continue swirling from her chest, spreading rapidly around her. Her eyes follow the trail to a body a few yards behind her, white fur matted with blood and ash. Flames eat away at Singer's open eyes. He doesn't move. He doesn't scream.

He's dead.

"He never could keep up."

It's the voice from Pheir's head, the one that kept its talons in her. She tries to will it away. Pain screams through her body, threatening to split her in half. Through the raging fire, a figure appears, glowing and iridescent. Vesta extends her hand, tracing the curve of Pheir's cheek.

She jerks — but the touch doesn't burn her. It licks softly over her skin like a brush of eyelashes. Out of every other overwhelming feeling, this feels so real. So delicate. A comfort in the chaos.

Pheir's eyes slip shut in disbelief. The touch is still there, gentle and warm.

"Not like you." Vesta's voice echoes. "My best and most loyal soldier."

It clenches in Pheir's stomach. They're words she's longed to hear, words she spent her life striving for. Now, Vesta drapes them over Pheir like a cloak after a never-ending war. Vesta trails her fingers down to the wound in Pheir's chest that's still spilling flames.

"I knew you'd keep me safe."

Pheir clenches her hand against her chest. "You were — here?" Her skin smolders. Her stomach turns, but Vesta lifts Pheir's chin on a finger to draw her eyes away from the injury.

"Of course. I never left you." Wind sweeps the flames in a circle around them, blowing back Pheir's feathers on a warm breeze. "I always have a backup plan."

Vesta's soft smile twists in Pheir's gut. It's like Vesta never left, regaling Pheir with her stories and waiting for her captive audience to be struck with awe. Pheir heaves for breath, sinking back on her heels as Vesta's voice vibrates through her skull.

"You don't get to be the most infamous immortal creature with only one way to return. It took a few lives to perfect. Patience. Trial and error..." Subtly, her eyes cut toward Lev who's still struggling to drag Caius back onto solid ground. "There were a few failed attempts, but every life, I grew stronger...until you." With a talon, Vesta draws a flaming X over Pheir's heart. "My perfect soldier. My perfect shell."

Over the roar of the flames, someone shouts from a distance. Pheir's eyes flit toward the voice. Vesta jerks Pheir's chin back, brows knit with rage before she smooths them out into a grateful smile.

"Thank you, Pheir, for everything you've done." Vesta brushes a hand through Pheir's hair, fingers weaving through the strands. Pheir's eyes slip shut. Vesta's never touched her like this, with such open adoration. Pride radiates from every syllable of Vesta's words. "Every scar. Every obedience. Every sacrifice. There's only one more thing that I require from you."

Dried blood matts feathers to Pheir's chest. Breathlessly, she tries to lift onto her knees, but they wobble. "What do you mean?"

Vesta tucks a lock of hair behind Pheir's ear, a sad smile tilting onto her mouth. "You're dying, Pheir." She says it as simply as she would note the weather. "We can't both survive this. Only one can remain intact: the shell or the phoenix. Now you can do what you've always wanted. You can save me. You can bring me back.

You can give everything to me." Holding Pheir's face in both hands, Vesta leans closer until her smile warms Pheir's face.

Grass singes beneath Pheir's knees. Smoke billows toward the night sky and blacks out the clouds. Vesta never looks away from Pheir. There's a cold calculation in Vesta's gaze, so absent of the concern Pheir expected – the concern Pheir *wanted*. Vesta's smile is still in place as she looks over Pheir's dying body.

Is this what it would have been like? If Pheir had thrown herself in front of Vesta on the battlefield, is this the last thing she would have seen? The image of Vesta's wild eyes and depraved grin with a hint of impatience that Pheir doesn't have the decency to die quickly.

The realization snaps into place like a bone breaking.

"This was your plan." Pheir's throat dries, recognition seeping in. Sweat drips down the back of her neck. "This was always your plan, wasn't it? From the moment we met. That's why you stayed with me. That's why you saved me."

FIFTY-EIGHT

Pheir

Every memory swarming through Pheir's head grows rows of sharpened teeth.

You're the most important person in my world.

You'd never leave me, would you?

It's always going to be you and me.

Every time Vesta pressed a hand over Pheir's heart, and Pheir clung to the memory for days, basking in the warmth of that single touch. It was only to protect whatever Vesta had implanted in her.

"You never cared," Pheir realizes dimly.

Vesta coos like a wounded bird, but Pheir's not sure it's a denial. "There was no one more willing to protect me, Pheir. To carry my flame until the time was right. It was always meant to be you." Vesta says it like Pheir should be proud. Like she should be *grateful.*

Pheir can't breathe. Smoke clogs her lungs, her fingers digging into the earth as her chest tightens with pain. The truth hurts as much as the wound, her head shaking as she tilts in place.

"Why didn't you tell me?" Pheir gasps. "I would have done anything for you. I would have *killed* myself if you asked me to."

With a pout, Vesta clucks her tongue. "That's not how the magic works, kid. Believe me, I tried." Kneeling, she cups Pheir's face in her hands. "*The best magic is a secret.* That's the phoenix way. If I told you what needed to be done, the seed wouldn't have taken. It's not about a willing sacrifice; it's about loyalty when you don't know the price — and you were always willing to pay it."

Nausea roils in Pheir's stomach. She pulls her face from Vesta's grasp, gulping air to soothe her. Soot spreads into her throat and chokes her until she coughs. "That's — why you found Singer? You trained him to kill me. My whole life, you knew what he would do to me."

Vesta's eyes narrow. "Consider it a failsafe." She returns to her full height. Despite the flames, a chill shudders through Pheir as Vesta looks down her nose. "People think a sacrifice should be given, but it's much more effective when it's taken."

Past the wall of fire, Lev calls Pheir's name, pulling herself onto a pile of fallen rocks to get a better vantage. Beside Lev, Aren searches for a way through the flames. Caius jerks his hand back when fire catches on his fur.

"You know, *Pheir*..." Vesta's snap takes on a bitter edge. She blocks Pheir's view of the Timbers with her body. "You're going to die. It's inevitable. But I can make it quick and painless." Vesta's features soften again, ethereal and kind. She extends a hand to Pheir's broken body. "I'll take care of you when you go. Just give me what's left of you."

"Pheir!"

Aren's voice rises above the chaos, but Pheir can't make out any more of his words. Caius screams beside him as dread fills Lev's eyes, the same way she must have felt the last time she was on this cliff's edge with Vesta.

Suddenly, the flames spin wider, scattering the Timbers as fire scorches the earth. Pheir can't hear their screams, but the wall of flames bears down under the direction of Vesta's wings.

Pheir scrambles to grab ahold of Vesta's leg. "Stop!"

It does little more than throw Vesta off-balance. "If you aren't going to give yourself willingly…" Through the fire, Vesta finds Lev and sharpens her flames to a point. "Then maybe you need a little convincing. It's about time I give that bunny bitch what's coming to her, wouldn't you say?"

Fire blocks Aren and Caius on one side. On the other, Lev scrambles away from the flames, slipping on the cliff's edge as she grapples for something to hold onto.

"*Stop!*" Pheir screams, using every bit of strength she has to dig her talons into Vesta's leg.

Delighted, Vesta's wild eyes glow as wickedness courses through her smile. "You want to do it yourself? You want to get your hands dirty?"

Vesta's hair billows around her like a gnarled crown. This is the Vesta Pheir remembers, barbaric in the heat of battle, as fierce and rampant as a wildfire. She turns to Pheir, the broken soldier with no strength to fight back. Yet when Vesta speaks, it ricochets through Pheir's body.

"Stand up."

Uncontrollably, Pheir's feet find the ground, pushing her up despite the scream that breaks through her teeth. Pain throbs through every part of her, but she stands straight and tall, following Vesta's orders as if Pheir's body is not her own.

Gleefully, Vesta clears a path through the flames. It leads straight to Aren and Caius, who sprint toward Pheir. She can't move. Can't open her mouth to stop them. Can't take in a breath to scream before Vesta flicks a careless hand in their direction.

"Kill them."

Everything in Pheir wails for her to stop, but her body springs and collides with Aren in midair. They tumble to the ground, Aren's head smacking the earth as Pheir pins him on his back.

Her talons find his chest, digging in as deeply as she can. No hesitation. No mercy. With a groan, Aren grabs her wrists and tries to keep from hurting her. Pheir doesn't have that worry. Her hands dig into Aren until she draws blood. The Pheir inside her head screams to stop, but her body doesn't listen, clenching until Aren gasps.

"It's not you," he groans, hands locked around her wrists. They both shake with the effort, a stalemate she can't push past. Desperately, he searches her eyes. "She's doing this to you. You can fight her!"

Pheir wants to sob. Her body keeps pressing down into Aren. Hopelessly, pain radiates through her limbs. She's not strong enough to stand, yet Vesta forces her body past its limits. It's disconnected from the pain, driving Pheir to bear it alone as her body becomes the soldier it was always meant to be.

Pheir can't fight Vesta's control. It's been years in the making, buried inside Pheir before she had a chance. Tears stream down her cheeks as she bears her weight down on both hands.

She has *always* been Vesta's. Now, she always will be.

A weight collides with Pheir's back, knocking her to the dirt as she scrabbles beneath it. Claws and talons fight for control, scraping each other like the first day in the orchard. Caius's fingers clamp around her wrists, pinning them beside her head no matter how she bucks and fights against him.

"It's not you, Pheir!"

Her body screams along with her mind, two factions warring with each other. No matter how she struggles, he doesn't let her go, gritting his teeth against the scrape of her talons. He leans closer. She tries to ram her head into his, but he presses his forehead down to hers, keeping her trapped beneath him.

"You don't need magic!" he shouts. "You know that! You're not hers — you're ours! You're *yours*!"

A flame blasts him across the grass. Vesta's laughter shrieks as she floats closer to Pheir. "Don't tell me you believe that," Vesta chides, staring down at Pheir with a shake of her head. "They don't know you. *No one* knows you like I do."

From Vesta's mouth, another flame barrels toward Caius. It knocks him back and forces a scream between his teeth. Fire eats through his fur as he tries to put out the flames. Lev rushes through the fire to help Aren struggle to his feet.

Vesta steps toward them. Pheir crawls on the ground before her, the last thing between Vesta and the Timbers. Beaten and bloody, Aren, Caius, and Lev stand side by side. Vesta smiles cruelly at them, but their eyes are on Pheir, a solemn comfort in their final moments. They hold each other upright, Lev limping to the front to use her body as the last buffer.

Hot tears streak down Pheir's face and hiss on the burning ground. Her body quivers, still captive to Vesta's control. It's useless. It's hopeless. Pheir can't fight Vesta; she never could.

No matter how many times you get knocked down, you always get back up for more.

It's the memory that reminds Pheir. It takes all of her strength to find her feet, weighed down by pain and Vesta's control screaming through her. Pheir's legs wobble, but she stands, staggering sideways as Vesta swirls in a storm of fire.

Fury lashes across Vesta's face. "Come on. You *really* think they care about you? You think anybody in this world cares about you the way I do?" With both wings, she pours flames toward the Timbers. Screams of pain spread like smoke into the air. Vesta's voice rises above them. "Who was there when you had no one? Who made you what you are? Your parents didn't want you. *I* did. *I'm* the one who made you special."

The words threaten to drag Pheir back to the ground, but she refuses to give in. There's one thing her body knows how to do, one instinct that overrides every thought, one thing she spent her whole life preparing for.

She puts her body in front of Vesta.

Vesta's flames ricochet off of Pheir's chest, blocking the Timbers from the heat, her wings flapping to spin the fire back toward Vesta. Stunned rage rises in Vesta's eyes. She doesn't withdraw her power, jaw setting in a grim line as fire blasts against Pheir's front. "If you don't give in, I will make this hurt, Pheir."

At Vesta's words, pain slices through Pheir, flames licking over her with renewed force. As if the fire was always burning her, but Vesta hadn't let her feel it. As if Vesta blocked Pheir's mind from the truth so Pheir would give her what she wanted. Pheir grits her teeth, fists clenching at her sides. Her voice is thick with smoke, but it's *hers*. "I'll kill you before I let you hurt them."

Deliriously, Vesta tips her head back and cackles. Flames whirl around them like the eye of a tornado. Pheir can't see past the wall of fire. When Vesta steps toward her, the force of the flames grows, shooting from her wings directly at their target. Directly at Pheir. "You have no purpose without me," Vesta snarls. With every word, the fire beats down harder. "You were trapped in a *crawl space* before I found you. You'll die as nothing. You *are* nothing."

Agony rattles through Pheir's bones. It threatens to sweep her legs out from beneath her — but she stands. Feathers float to ash as she pushes forward, squinting against Vesta's brilliant light. Pheir is as close to Vesta as she's ever been, both their teeth grit as they bear down toward each other. Finally, Pheir sees the truth of Vesta — there's no warmth, only blazing heat. Only searing destruction.

"And without me," Pheir gasps, "what are you?"

Vesta screams like Pheir has never heard before Vesta's hands clamp over Pheir's heart. It combusts, spraying fire as Pheir is blasted down the path. Her body skips against the ground, no sound but ringing in her ears. Her entire world is on fire. The smell of burning skin hits her nostrils, chest heaving as her breath comes ragged and wounded.

The rhythm of her heart slows.

Her vision blooms black. Every nerve inside her screams, desperate to be free of pain. Shouts come from a distance. They're muffled by the dark spreading to her ears. It envelopes her like furs pressed against her body, every ache soothed into the memory of teeth leaving imprints in her skin.

Inside her, Vesta's light flickers out.

FIFTY-NINE

Lev

The worst moments of Lev's life happen on this cliff.

Her body aches. She can't see through the smoke, feeling along the ground to find the others. Everything is hot and stifling. A scream swells to her right, followed by another blast that sends heat cascading over her.

Lev's heart trips. Where is Pheir? Where are Aren and Caius? They stood beside each other, prepared for Vesta to finish what she started — but Pheir got in the way. Pheir pulled all her strength together and stood on her feet. Pheir took the brunt of Vesta's blast and stared her down as flames scorched her body.

Past the pounding in Lev's head, fire crackles and splits through wood. In the distance, the cottage burns, the rest of the forest saved by the stone surrounding the foundation. Rainbow flames eat down the stairway toward the spring where she and Pheir sat hours before.

Lev tries to stand, hissing as she puts out a patch of flaming fur on her hip. Someone gets their arms under hers.

"I've got you." Caius's throat is clogged with soot, but he lifts her to her feet. "I've got you, come on..."

Lev tries to make sense of what remains in the chaos. There's no sign of Singer. Nothing left of Vesta but ashes drifting through the wind and mixing with the snow. None of the trees have caught fire, but the flames billowing through the cottage are as bright as the sun.

Where is Pheir?

Further down the trail, Aren kneels, his hands ghosting over something but never quite touching it.

Lev's heart drops into her stomach. Pheir doesn't stay down. In battle, she refused to stop, rage fueling her as she took hit after hit. Right now, Pheir lies limp and motionless with smoke curling off her charred body.

Staggering over, Lev and Caius drop to their knees. Even in the dark, Pheir's skin is an angry red, wings nothing but a few rows of scorched feathers. The worst is on her chest, blisters and shorn skin surrounding her heart where Singer dug in his claws. At least the flames have cauterized it and stopped the bleeding.

A ringing starts in Lev's ears. It must be from the blast, but the sound rises up from the earth. It vibrates beneath her feet. Her eyes blur, her world spinning off its axis. It's not real; the earth is not moving. But Pheir's body trembles where she lays on the ground, pebbles jittering as Lev leans closer.

"Don't die for Vesta," Lev hisses. Her ribs ache. She finds a patch of Pheir's skin that isn't mangled and clenches her fingers around Pheir's wrist. Despite everywhere else the fire touched Pheir, the V scar is still raised against her skin. There's a tiny flutter under Lev's fingers. She can't tell if it's Pheir's pulse or an echo of her own when her voice cracks. "Do not *fucking* die for her."

Footsteps thunder up the trail toward them, mingled with a chorus of shouts. Lev tries to get her thoughts straight. She's the Alpha. She needs to lead her pack, but the panic in her chest at seeing Pheir like this is worse than the pain.

Darby's the first to approach with a horrified expression as Lev grabs his arm. "Get the others to help us carry her. Tell Oberon to prep everything in the medical supply — everything we have, everything we've been saving." When Marius skids to a halt behind Darby, Lev's eyes lock frantically on them. "Send for Thalea and Rhaiden. Tell them Pheir's been burned by Vesta. *Hurry!*"

Mari takes flight as Darby sprints back toward the lodge, shouting directions as he goes. It's an effort to carry Pheir even with other Timbers lifting her, but they burst through the door to the main lodge and spread her on a cot in the cramped medical space. Lev's throat tightens. Under the lights from the generator, Pheir looks frailer. Oberon lumbers in with a bag as Echo rushes to assemble its contents on the table at the foot of the bed

"I need to clean her wounds." Oberon is gentle but somber. Lev, Aren, and Caius nod, crowding the space next to Pheir. It's then that Lev realizes what Oberon means, her frantic eyes finding his.

"We can't leave, we —"

Gingerly, he maneuvers them away from the bed, careful not to touch their injuries. "I need you to step outside. There's not enough space."

His tone brooks no arguments. Lev rises on her toes, trying to see past him as Echo begins to clean Pheir's wounds. Pheir still hasn't moved. A crack forms in Lev's voice. "Is she...?"

Lev can't say it. She can't ask the question she's not sure she wants the answer to. Oberon understands. "We have some potions for burns." The uncertain slant of his face sends Lev's heart plummeting no matter how softly he tries to say it. "I need you to step outside. Let me do what I can."

The last look Lev gets is Oberon murmuring hurriedly to Echo before the door swings shut. Lev strains to make out any sounds from Pheir through the wood, but among the bustle of bandages and glass vials, there's nothing.

Lev steps back. Aren and Caius stand on either side, watching the door as if it will give them an answer. It doesn't move. Pain begins to sink in, coursing through Lev's body like she's still on fire. Aren guides her onto the bench outside the medical door.

"Vesta really got you, huh?" he whispers. Despite his injuries, he checks over Lev's body with the same care he'd taken after they returned from battle a month ago. Lev's throat burns, head tilting back to rest against the wall. Her body's exhausted. She wants to sleep. She wants to stay awake for any news of Pheir. She never wants to think about Vesta again.

"She always does," Lev croaks.

Caius sinks to the ground beside her, burying his head in his hands.

Who knows how long the three of them take turns pacing before Echo steps out of the medical room.

"What's happening?" Caius asks, pushing brusquely to his feet. "How is she?"

Lev and Aren flood Echo with a barrage of questions before she lifts the bandages in her hands. "Oberon's still working on her. I don't have any news. I need to get the three of you patched up."

They allow Echo to work, hissing when the salves burn, legs bouncing anxiously as they watch the medical door. After some time, June appears from the corridor, cursing Lev in every way she can think as she flings her arms around her. June drags across Lev's injuries, but Lev winces and bears it. Once June is satisfied that Lev will make it, she plies the three of them with water, returning from the kitchen with her arms filled with bottles.

"This is why I don't take a night off," June grumbles, brushing Lev's ears back from her face. "Of all the girls in the Break, you marry the one harboring your dead ex inside her."

It hurts to laugh. The sound breaks through Lev's chapped lips, but it disappears quickly when she remembers Pheir on the other side of the door. June sees the worry on Lev's face and moves on to mothering Caius.

When he tries to drink the water himself, June swats his hand away, nervously tipping the jug to his mouth. "Let me do it," she hisses. It's an excuse to have something to do with her hands as she worries. When Oberon emerges from the medical room, Caius coughs and pries himself out of June's grip.

Oberon cleans his hand on a wet rag. Lev and the others struggle to their feet.

"Pheir is unconscious but stable — for now. I can't really explain why." Oberon shakes his head, gaze distant. "Her injuries should be worse, but there's no sign of infection yet. Hopefully Thalea and Rhaiden have a better knowledge of these types of burns. It'll be a long road to recovery, if Pheir makes it."

It's not promising. Lev swallows her disappointment, trying to *believe* through the fear. She clings to the shred of emotion that she's not sure is intuition or false hope. *Pheir is alive. She's still here. She can make it.* "Thank you, Oberon."

He steps aside, gesturing toward the open door with a tired smile. "Do you want to see her?"

The three of them file in and crowd around Pheir's bed. She lays on her back, seemingly sleeping as bandages crisscross her body. Now that she's cleaned, she looks worse than before. The patches of skin that they can see are bright and angry, but Pheir's chest rises and falls beneath the most concentrated swell of gauze.

She's still alive. She's still here.

Lev exhales a breath of relief, sinking into the windowsill as Caius and Aren slide down the wall beside her. They're too tired to do anything but watch Pheir's ragged breathing. Every time her chest falls, Lev holds her breath, counting the seconds and wondering if it's Pheir's last — but Pheir's chest always rises again.

The window is cool against Lev's back, snow pattering gently against it. Past the sound of flakes falling and Pheir's shallow breathing, the ringing in Lev's ears starts again. It reminds her of the day she arrived at the Broadleaf camp, quiet and ashen as something churned beneath the ground. It reminds her of the patch of wildflowers sprouting green and fresh through the charred earth. It sounds like life. It sounds like growth.

It sounds like magic.

"Do you hear that?" Caius's ears flick. The sound buzzes deep in the earth, a frequency that's almost impossible to make out.

Aren lets his head fall back against the wall. "We should get some rest. That blast probably damaged our hearing."

"You first." Caius rests his cheek against Aren's shoulder where Lev's calf drapes over it. She tries to shift out of the way, but Caius holds her in place until the three of them settle into silence once more. After a long moment, Aren tilts his head to rest against the top of Caius's. Caius's breathing doesn't change. He doesn't flinch. Aren shoots Lev a raised brow before he tentatively drags his tongue over the top of Caius's head, cleaning away remnants of soot.

Caius stiffens before he turns to catch Aren's eye. "Are you *grooming* me?"

Aren licks at the lightest of Caius's wounds until Caius finally huffs a laugh. His body gives up the urge to fight, settling into exhaustion as he rests against the two of them. It's quiet for a long moment before Caius speaks, his voice so low Lev almost can't hear it.

"No one's done that for me in a long time."

He tries to hide the way he leans against Aren's mouth, Caius's eyes slipping shut under the rough swipe of Aren's tongue. Aren doesn't change his rhythm as Lev reaches down, brushing her nails gently through the tangles in Caius's fur.

"When was the last time?" she asks. It's a question she wouldn't have braved before, certainly not in front of Aren. The Caius of days past would have tensed. That Caius would never have offered a glimpse of his past at all.

But it's a past he never has to return to, a history that can't touch the home he has. The three of them sit in silence for long minutes, Aren licking Caius clean as Lev unwinds the brambles from his fur. They don't press Caius for more. They don't do anything but linger beside each other, touching in the soft ways that they can.

Caius watches Pheir on the bed beside them. No matter how still she is, she's fighting a battle with her wounds. Always the warrior, refusing to give into anything that tries to drag her under. She's braver than the things that try to destroy her — and so is Caius.

Finally, he begins to tell his story.

SIXTY

Pheir

Turns out being "nothing" feels pretty good, aside from the searing pain.

Everything is dark. Soot lingers in Pheir's nostrils until her mind flows away on a lazy river. It's hard to keep her head above water, but sinking under the surface is less like drowning and more like sleep. Somewhere deep below her, the earth hums an ancient song that stirs waves against her body. It cools her as she drifts, wet plants clinging to her skin as she bobs through reeds and shallows

"So this is what Vesta does to her favorite soldier."

Rhaiden's voice vibrates through the water, buzzing against Pheir's skin. She can't see Rhaiden. She can't see anything. She must have drifted back to the Eyrie, to the time when they lived there together. If Pheir pretends, she can picture the treetops branching out above her as she floats in the sea and waits for Rhaiden to swim up from the depths to dunk her under.

Plants coat her body. Pheir sighs in relief. The seaweed is like fingers covering her wounds in salves like Thalea used to. Pheir can hear Thalea's voice now, almost like she's floating in the water beside her.

"Vesta had one favorite. It wasn't any of us."

If Pheir kicks her feet, maybe she can splash Rhaiden. Maybe she can make Thalea laugh. Pheir's right here. She can hear them, but she can't move, so she's content to drift next to them like she used to.

Being here with them is nice, but Pheir yearns for something else. Sunlight beats down on her face, warming the sea until it's like bathwater that stings with salt. She misses gray clouds threatening rain. She wants the icy chill of a lake. She craves the scent of pine and lemonade and candles burning in the forest.

Words ripple through her mind, different than the voice of Vesta that Pheir grew used to.

"It's been two days."

"Thalea said recovery would take time, if ever."

"Don't say that: 'if ever.' Believe in something."

Pheir knows those voices. They pull her through the water like a fish on a line until the ocean is long behind her. The cool Timber lake rocks her gently, pressing in on all sides like three sets of fur.

For once, Pheir doesn't think about what used to be. She imagines things that haven't happened, a future she never entertained before. There are no visions of Vesta's grandiose power or Pheir at her side. These new vignettes are simple, small enough for Pheir to hold in her mind's eye. She sits on Caius's shoulders as they knock Aren and Lev into the lake. She dries her feathers on the bank as she falls asleep pressed to the rumble of Aren's chest. She chases Lev up to the cliff's edge where they sit pressed against each other and look out as far as the eye can see.

It feels better than the thoughts of Vesta ever did.

It isn't always calm in Pheir's mind, though. Sometimes, the lake turns to fire, eating away at her skin as Vesta holds Lev off the edge of the cliff. Other times, Aren and Caius reach for Pheir before they crumble to ash and drift away to the sound of Vesta's laughter.

Pheir's not sure how long it takes for the nightmares to stop. Eventually, she drifts to shore, and one of her crusted eyelids cracks open. This isn't one of her visions. This is the real world, bright and blurry as her eyes sting from disuse. It takes a minute to adjust before she can make out the shapes in the room.

It's somewhere she hasn't been before, wooden floors and walls like the Timber lodge. Overhead, footsteps scamper across the second floor as children laugh. One side of Pheir's small room is lined with glass-front cabinets full of vials and bottles. On the table by her cot, tucked among ointments and bandages and a water glass, is a vase of purple wildflowers.

There's a hum of voices outside the door, but there's no sound from Caius slumped in the chair next to her bed. His arm's in a sling, fur regrowing from scorched patches scattered across his body.

Pheir's throat is too parched to make a sound. She tries to speak, but all that comes out is a crackle. It's enough to make Caius stir. Blearily, he shifts in his seat, blinking before he realizes Pheir's awake. His mouth falls open.

She gets the first croaked word as her eyes tilt toward the flowers. "Sappy."

"Shut up." He blinks in shock before he calls toward the door. "She's awake!"

The voices in the corridor stop, followed by a scramble to the door. Aren and Lev appear with their fur blackened in parts, but their eyes are bright as the they crowd the bed.

"You made it," Lev breathes as if she can hardly believe it, fingers drifting over Pheir's hand. Lev doesn't touch down, as if she's scared she might hurt Pheir...or that this might not be real.

Aren checks Pheir's bandages. "How are you feeling?"

She's delirious with pain, sleep, and impossible happiness. "Shitty."

Their laughter sounds more like a sigh of relief. Pheir's smile fades, head pounding as memories claw to the surface of her mind. The last thing that happened was snow, and flames, and betrayal. "Did Vesta...?" Pheir's teeth scrape her lip before she winces at how chapped they are. She doesn't know what to ask. Blame it on her dry mouth and how brittle the air in her windpipe is.

Aren sinks onto the end of the bed with the same care with which he watches Pheir. Carefully, he touches the tips of his fingers to hers. "We think she's gone for good."

The feeling crushes Pheir's chest. She doesn't know how to explain it. She doesn't know why her eyes prick with pain, why the thought of Vesta vanishing makes her want to fall back asleep. Vesta is the reason she's lying here. Vesta is the reason the others are beaten and broken. Still, Pheir stares at the ceiling and tries to work out if the ache in her throat is from the fire or something else.

"We're not sure what reuniting the vials of ashes could do," Aren admits, "but she vanished after you denied her. No one's seen any sign of her since."

Sorrow claws at Pheir's chest, but there are other feelings, too, relief and rage and hurt. Bliss at seeing Lev, and Aren, and Caius. Guilt that there's not more grief for losing Vesta. Emotions overrun each other until Pheir loses track of them. It's dizzying, feeling more than one thing.

"Wh-" Her voice cracks. Aren guides the water from her nightstand to her lips, holding it as she drinks. She pulls back and licks her lips to speak. "Could you hear...what Vesta said?"

Aren and Caius look toward Lev, who sinks down on the arm of Caius's chair. The heavy look she gives Pheir tells her all she needs to know. "Some of it," Lev answers finally.

"And Singer is...dead?" Pheir croaks.

Lev nods.

"Fucking *dick*." Caius shifts lower in his chair.

It would be easy to agree. A spike of anger rises into Pheir at the memory of his claws in her chest. At the same time, she can't deny their similarities, trapped under Vesta's power for years. Assigned a purpose and never told what the end result would be. Dedicated to Vesta until it would have killed them.

Still, it's hard to feel bad for him when the hole in Pheir's chest aches. One thought pulses in her head. "Vesta was...going to kill me. She was always...going to kill me."

The others are quiet. When Pheir blinks, her vision grows wet and blurry. If she struggled to place her emotions before, she's completely lost now, spinning back through the decade she spent with Vesta. Did Vesta plant the seed the day they met? Did Pheir ever have a chance to escape?

Her fingers clench in the sheets, skin stretching over bone, like a different pain might give her something else to focus on.

"It was strange..." Lev's voice pulls Pheir from the whirl of her thoughts. "Until you and Vesta blew apart at the end, it looked like the flames were washing over you. Even when they burned us, they rolled right off of you."

Pheir tries and fails to clear her throat. "That wasn't...her full power. It's not like she was...fully *real*. She was...more like a mirage than a person. A fraction of herself."

There's a hopeful feeling in Pheir's chest that needs to be deflated, a temptation to cling to old lies. *Vesta kept the flames from hurting you because she cared. She cauterized your wound when she could have killed you.* Nervously, Pheir's eyes flick to Aren. She needs something to ground her, to bring her back to earth, to keep her from falling into comfort that only hurts her in the end.

As if he understands, Aren offers her another drink. She takes it greedily, gulping water until he lowers the cup back to the nightstand. "I do think Vesta was holding back." At his words, Pheir's heart spasms, but he keeps a steadying hand on her. "Not for sentimentality. Because she thought, in the end, you would still submit."

It leaves a sour taste in Pheir's mouth, but she's grateful for it. The bitter truth is better than the sweet lies she's used to. With a nod, she digs past the things she was told for the things she *knows*. Vesta was looking out for herself. That's why she didn't incinerate Pheir from the beginning. Vesta was protecting her vessel as she had been since the moment they met.

It's painful, but it's real. That's all Pheir can ask for.

Lev's mouth twists in understanding. Her burns are harsher than everyone but Pheir's, as if Vesta still hadn't let go of that age-old grudge. At least someone else understands the confusing mess of emotions Pheir struggles with. It brings a small smile to her face. Lev leans forward, brushing away a strand of hair that sticks to Pheir's bandages.

This warm feeling is real, too, and it's not painful at all.

"Truthfully, Pheir…" Aren rests his paw on Pheir's leg, enough pressure to show he's there. "I'm not sure how you survived. Even if everything else is true, most of your burns were first degree. The worst of the ones on your chest were second. Compared to what we got on the sidelines, you should have been much worse."

Pheir swears the earth hums again. Lev tucks a knee up to her chest like she's beginning to understand something. "Residual magic has a way of showing up when you least expect it."

When Lev gives Pheir a secretive smile, Pheir can't fight a grin of her own. She wants to stay like this, looking over the three of them like it's the first time. Like she's seeing them as they are, without pretense, without any emotions but her own.

This is hers. *They're* hers.

It's strange how something she would have sworn she hated has become the thing she wants…and something she nearly lost without realizing it. A lump wells in Pheir's throat. This time, her hoarseness isn't solely from the burns. "I'm sorry…for what happened."

Caius shakes his head. "You couldn't have known —"

"Before that." Pheir fights back wetness pooling in her eyes. "I'm sorry for everything...that she did. Everything *I* did...to you. To other people."

The scar on Caius's face won't vanish with time. Neither will the years of torment and Pheir's attempts to bring Vesta back. In the end, Pheir did what she set out to do, just not in the way she expected.

Lev reaches for Pheir's hand, careful to touch only the bandaged parts. Aren squeezes Pheir's knee. Caius rolls his eyes, but he leans back, propping one foot on the bed to knock gently against Pheir's. They're all strange reflections of each other, lives aligning to send them on a collision course. They're different in ways they never expected, similar in places they thought impossible, tipping the scales into perfect balance.

"Vesta caused a lot of damage." Lev lifts her fingers to the curve of Pheir's cheek. "We'll take it one day at a time. Of all the things she got wrong, I hope we can fix at least one of them."

When Lev brushes Pheir's face, it doesn't feel like a touch from Vesta. Lev doesn't stare through Pheir. Lev doesn't look for what Pheir can do for her. Lev's palm rests against the healthy skin of Pheir's cheek. "You were never nothing. You are...everything." Lev traces the hollow under Pheir's eye. "I hope you'll let us show you that."

A furtive tear streaks down Pheir's cheek. A knock comes on the door as June leans into the doorway. "Thalea wants to see her and change her bandages."

Pheir swipes at her eye with one hand. Aren squeezes her ankle as he rises with Lev close behind, pausing in the doorway. "We'll be back. Spend some time with your friend."

As they exit, June steps further into the room, tilting her head toward the vase. Her hands tuck behind her back. "*So*...do you like your flowers?"

"She said they were sappy," Caius grumbles. Pheir tries to flip him off but struggles with the bandages.

There's amusement in the narrow of June's eyes, on the precipice of a truce. "There's no impressing you, is there? Just like an in-law." With that, she turns on her heel with a cheeky grin and slips out the door.

Only Caius remains, lingering near the bed like looking away from Pheir might change her outcome. She does her best to sneer toward his injured arm. "You think you'll make it?"

He adjusts his sling. "I'll be back to kicking your ass in no time."

Pheir scoffs, throat scratchy. "You must still be asleep, 'cause you're dreaming."

When Caius nudges her thigh, she hisses in pain. An apology darts across his face before she smirks.

"Sappy. I told you."

Growling, he leans down to press their foreheads together, two unstoppable forces that move for each other. He pulls away and disappears out the door. Pheir's body radiates warmth. She's not sure if it's from the burns or the people, but when Thalea appears in the doorway, Pheir knows the answer.

Thalea's face is pinched under tracks of dried tears, a smile stretching across her lips. Pheir rolls her eyes, fighting the emotion bubbling in her chest. "Don't start, Thalea."

"I'm *not*," Thalea sniffles, dabbing at her face with a flower as she stands next to Pheir's bed. Thalea worries the petals in her hand like a handkerchief. "I'm really glad you're ok."

"Thanks to you."

Thalea lifts vials from the end table, pouring them into a mortar to mix. "Who knew studying Vesta's burns in training would save your life?" There's a hitch when Thalea says the name, a sob that she bites down on.

Pheir averts her gaze. "I'm really sorry...about what happened."

Thalea unwinds a strip of bandages, hands trembling as she moves. She tries to keep her voice cheery, but sadness dips into it. "What for?"

Words spring onto Pheir's tongue. *I killed your mate. She chose me to bring her back instead of you.* None of the answers feel sufficient. None of the reasoning makes sense. Pheir shrugs, flinching at the scrape of skin against the sheets, guilt and sadness returning. "I don't know. All of it. After everything, it still feels...wrong to do that to her. To betray her like that. To deny her."

Pestle in hand, Thalea pauses, staring at the poultice forming at the bottom of the bowl. "You didn't choose what happened, Pheir. Even if you had..." She doesn't finish the thought, shaking her head as she undresses Pheir's wounds. "*I'm* sorry."

"For what?"

"Vesta is a hard person to get over." Thalea's eyes are focused on her work, but her gaze is distant, mouth twisting in thought. "I don't know if we'll ever really be free of her. In the end, she got what she always wanted. She left her mark. I don't think we owe her more than that. I don't know if we owe her anything."

Quietly, Thalea cleans Pheir's wounds before she applies new treatment. It reminds Pheir of their days in the Eyrie, when Thalea tended to her after Rhaiden got the best of her.

Pheir huffs a laugh at the memory. "Guess Rhaiden will be disappointed I made it."

She tries to make it sound like a joke, but Thalea's head shakes soberly. "She was here, actually."

Pain zings through Pheir as she jolts upright. "She was?"

"*Easy*, please..." Thalea eases Pheir back into a better position before she continues. "She got here before me. Brought some of the materials I needed." With her fingers, Thalea instructs Pheir to readjust so she can wind the bandage around Pheir's chest. "She and Caius had a few words, but by the end, they were both sleeping in here."

The surprise distracts Pheir from discomfort. Once Thalea tucks the last bandage into place, she steps back to take in Pheir in her entirety — charred wings, sunken cheeks, shallow breathing. Pheir's a shadow of who she was, but Thalea tips her head thoughtfully.

"You look different, Pheir. I mean…" Her flowers blush bright pink. "Obviously you look — I mean, you're injured, of course, but you *seem* different. Like there's more of you. Not *physically*, but…" Her hands move through the air, outlining Pheir's shape before Thalea sighs and lets her hands drop. "I don't know what I'm trying to say, but it's good."

Somehow, Pheir understands. There's more of herself now, emotions and thoughts and desires she never fully grasped before. It's staggering to think about what she might discover as time goes on, so overwhelming Pheir almost wishes for the days when she felt one thing — but not quite.

We'll take it one day at a time.

"Thanks." Pheir settles back against the pillows. "I think there's more of you, too."

Thalea smiles. It wavers as she shifts on her feet, like there's someone else watching them in the room. Remnants of smoke linger in Pheir's nose, an echo of Vesta hanging over them. Even in death, she finds a way to stick around.

I don't know if we'll ever really be free of her.

Thalea clears her throat, gaze dipping to the floor. "I'll let you get some rest."

"Will you stay?"

Thalea stops in her path toward the door. She turns back toward Pheir, as if she's not sure how to move. The old Pheir never would have asked for this. It's strange to connect when there's no Vesta uniting them. They have no task to carry out. No mission to execute. No battle plans to discuss. It's just the two of them fumbling through what Vesta has left them with.

Maybe that's good enough to start.

Pheir pats the bed beside her. The smoke in her nose clears enough to breathe through. "We can talk, and, I don't know..." Pheir shrugs her shoulders, cringing at unfamiliar words. "'Hang out'? Is that what people do?"

With a laugh, Thalea crawls onto the bed beside her, and they sit in silence. A long minute passes before Pheir blurts: "So, what's *really* going on between you, Dante, and the minotaur?"

As the hours stretch on, they find their way to topics that don't involve Vesta or strategy or vengeance. It's awkward. It's strange. It's nice. It's a brand-new world neither of them has experienced.

Pheir thinks she might like it here.

SIXTY-ONE

Aren

3 weeks after Vesta's (second) death

"I can't take all of them."

"Of course you can!" June adds another bunch of wildflowers to the wooden crate on the table. It hardly makes a dent in the ten other vases adorning Pheir's temporary bedroom.

Pheir glowers. Aren nudges her, and she tries to hide her smile. "How big do you think my new room is, June?"

At least the crate will be filled with *something*. Aside from the flowers June keeps well-stocked, Pheir has few sentimental items to speak of. The ones she did have were lost in the cottage fire. She hasn't mentioned them, but Aren remembers the nest that was forming around her bed, mementos and keepsakes that can't be easily replicated.

They'll have to make new memories with her.

A knock comes as Oberon eases open the door. "Last checkup?"

Pheir pushes up from the bed, wincing as she unzips her jacket. It's clear she's not completely comfortable among the Timbers yet, keeping wary eyes on Oberon as he checks over her. She glances at Aren, who gives a reassuring nod that eases her shoulders the slightest bit. For someone who would have gladly slaughtered the Timbers two months ago, she's making progress.

So is the pack. It's not a seamless transition, but the more Pheir unlearns about Vesta, the more the Timbers learn about Pheir. Not everyone in the Break is willing to believe in Pheir's rehabilitation, but Aren's familiar with that. It helps that the Timbers witnessed it firsthand. She's a different person than the one that arrived here in shackles, even if she isn't sure who that person is yet.

Oberon examines her fading wounds as June bustles around the room. The black bear gives a pleased nod. "Happy to say I think you'll make a full recovery."

Pheir zips her jacket. Her eyes slip to Aren for support before she turns to Oberon. "Thank you. I know I wasn't..."

In the weeks since Vesta's death, Pheir's memories have become a minefield. Things that once brought her undisputed joy now fill her with confusion and regret. They take it one day at a time, sorting through the rubble of her life as delicately as they can. Fortunately, there's always one of them to sit beside her — Lev to round out the picture of Vesta, Caius to commiserate, Aren to ask her guiding questions.

Sometimes it's easier to focus on the present, for Pheir to try and make amends. She's still learning. The words don't always come out right, but Aren encourages her. Over Oberon's shoulder, he nods again, and Pheir wets her lips to finish. "I haven't always appreciated your help. But thank you."

Oberon lifts a brow towards Aren before he gives Pheir a squeeze of her arm, which is more than a week ago. It's a start. As Oberon leaves, June follows him out the door, setting the overflowing crate of flowers on the bed. "Carry those for your girl, will you?"

Before Aren can move toward them, Pheir shifts the box to her hip. "I've got it."

There's that same proud lift of her chin that never fails to make Aren smile. He sidles up next to her, dusting his fingers across hers as he lowers his mouth to her ear. "What if you let me?"

The Pheir of days past would have refused out of spite. Now, she keeps the same defiant posture, but her grip loosens on the box. A hint of her desire tangs the air. Aren smirks and lifts the box from her arms.

"You're welcome," she sniffs.

His whiskers brush her neck, making her feathers ruffle. He's missed being this close while she's healed. "Let me properly express my gratitude," he purrs, tracing his wet nose against her earlobe. She laughs and shoves him toward the staircase.

They make their way through the main lodge, dodging the chaos in the living area as they step out onto the field. Lev and Caius wait among the cabins, watching the two of them approach. "Wow," Lev admires, "she let you carry the box."

"Barely." Aren lifts it out of Pheir's reach, narrowly avoiding her growing talons.

She bares her teeth at him before she turns back to Lev. "Aren't you supposed to be with the Conclave? If one of the Regents is being replaced..."

Pheir trails off as she notices the A-frame cabin before her. Both sides are made of multiple transparent panes that hinge outward over the small deck. Stunned, Pheir steps onto the platform and stares up through the panes. The view to the sky is perfect.

It's a small space, but the hinged sides allow easy outdoor access. A large bed takes up the single room of the cabin, draped with a blanket the four of them have shared. One of Thalea's harvested vines grows from the dirt outside, twining around the structure like two arms squeezing tight. From the bed, the lake and the mountains are clear in the distance.

Lev steps up shyly next to Pheir. "Caius said you might like something more open. It's yours, if you want it."

Pheir toes the threshold. "All of it?"

"Every Timber gets their own space."

Every Timber. Aren shivers to remember that Pheir is one of them — or, she can be, one day. Impossibly, it settles into his bones like a piece that was missing.

Pheir's fingers clench as if she feels it too, teeth scraping her lip. "What if I don't want to be by myself?"

Aren can't help the twitch of his smile. Despite Pheir's recovery process, the four of them have found ways to squeeze into the same bed. They've been careful of her wounds, but Oberon had to run them out of the medical room more than once.

"Your new bed should fit a few people," Lev assures her, tilting her head toward Aren's and Caius's cabins a few yards away. "And your *neighbors* will annoy the shit out of you, don't worry about that." Lev's voice softens as she lets her hand hang between them, brushing Pheir's fingers with her own. "My cabin is always yours, but I want you to have a place that you can go. A place you can make your own. Somewhere you can get away from everything else, if you want to."

Pheir's eyes follow their hands, pressing their fingertips together. Soft touches are still new, but the brightness that flits across her face is worth it. She looks back over her cabin. "It's so...pristine."

Lev's ears twitch uncertainly. "Is that bad?"

A wicked smile curls Pheir's lips, reminiscent of the girl they knew. "We should break it in."

"You're still healing," Aren admonishes.

Caius flops onto the bed and props his hands behind his head. "And you can barely smell us, anyway."

Despite her injuries, Pheir pins him as her wings spread behind her, feathers growing back into place. She leans close to taunt him, flicking his snout. "Trust me, you smell strong enough for even *my* nose."

Caius rolls Pheir carefully beneath him. Aren doesn't chide him, setting down the crate and climbing onto the bed on Pheir's other side. From behind Pheir, Caius wraps his arms around her, smirking at Aren over her shoulder. "Now everyone has a bird's-eye view to Pheir getting her ass handed to her in bed. Thank you, *Alpha.*"

"There are curtains." Lev's eyes roll, but a smile settles onto her face as the three of them curl around each other. It's too cold to leave the sides of the cabin open, so Lev closes them and climbs into the space between Aren and Pheir.

No matter how tenuous everything else is, this physical closeness grows easier by the day. As the sun sinks, crickets chirp outside, and the four of them settle in together. Caius drapes his arm over Pheir's waist. Aren runs his claws against her knee, and Lev brushes the hair out of her face.

"What about the cottage?" Pheir finally whispers.

There's nothing left on the cliffside besides charred marks and rubble. It pangs in Aren's chest, knowing Lev built it to replace the memories of Vesta, but Vesta destroyed it all the same. He wraps his arm around her waist.

Her smile is tight, but it's real. "We'll build something new." She traces a quilted shape on the blanket. "I think we'll call it the Nest."

Pheir's cheeks heat a darker shade. Her fingers follow the same path on the quilt, outlining the same abstract shape before she speaks. "My wedding hoop was in there, before it burned down."

It's impossible to tell what Pheir's expression means, as if she's not quite sure herself, working through her puzzling emotions. Aren hadn't realized she'd kept the wedding hoop.

Apparently, neither did Lev, settling her hand next to Pheir's. "Oh, Pheir...I'm sorry." Their fingers spread to make space for each other, never quite touching, but close enough for comfort.

Pheir's heartbeat picks up. The weres hear it, sharing glances over her shoulder. She keeps her eyes trained on the quilt. When Aren looks closely, he realizes the shape she's tracing is an infinite figure-eight curving back and forth over itself.

"What if we made another?" Pheir murmurs.

It takes a moment for the words to register. Lev's brows knit. "What do you mean?"

Caius props himself on one arm to get a better look at Pheir's face. Aren's hand settles on her leg. All of them watch as she follows the infinite pattern with her finger. "As twisted as it is, the first time I had a choice for myself was here — in chains." She huffs a laugh, but she doesn't lift her eyes, heart tripping nervously. "I didn't know what to do with that. I didn't know how to think for myself, to *want* things for myself. I missed dedicating everything to one person, but now I feel like..." Words get caught in her throat before she clears it. "You all make me feel like it's something I could want. You make me want to question things. You make me feel like I'm more than what I can do for someone else."

"You are." Lev squeezes Pheir's hand. "You don't have to do that again. You can be a Timber for as long as you want to be."

"What if I want it forever?"

"It's yours," Aren assures Pheir.

Earnestly, she lifts her gaze and locks eyes with Lev. "And if I want *you* forever? All of you?"

It stuns them into silence. Anxiously, Pheir rushes to fill it.

"You don't have to say yes. There's a lot of my life I don't understand, but I want to. I want the truth. I want you with me while I figure it out. You make me feel like..." Her eyes slip shut, heartbeat slowing as she breathes through her nose. She exhales, sorting through her emotions the way Aren taught her. "I've always felt strongly about the three of you — but it's different now." Her eyes slip open, certain and sure. It sends a thrill down Aren's spine. "It's different, not weaker."

The same feeling burgeons in Aren's chest, swelling until it threatens to burst. It's passion that can't be contained when it's all of them together. All his time spent rationing his emotions didn't prepare him for their four lives converging. No amount of reasoning explains how they fit together. They're carved from different trees, discolored wood with knots and grains that don't align, pieces broken and mismatched, yet the sanding and shaping of their lives has worn down the grooves until they join perfectly. Like the four of them were in the world's plan all along. Like this moment between them was created by something bigger, long before they knew each other.

Maybe it *is* magic.

Lev extends her hand, tracing gently over the burn that peeks beneath Pheir's collar. It matches the scar that Lev has on her shoulder. "Of course we'll be here, Pheir. But you deserve a time in your life when you're not beholden to anyone." With a finger, Lev presses against Pheir's sternum. "Time to figure out who *you* are when you're not tied to anyone. If we're going to do this, I think..." Lev sucks in a breath, like the words pain her even as she knows they're the right ones. "We need to start from the beginning. You need to get to know the pack and make sure it's the right fit. The four of us need to slow down — stop sharing the same bed every night. Stop having sex."

Caius and Pheir groan, heads flopping back in sync. Aren can't help but laugh despite the twinge in his stomach. Taking a step back from this will be hard, but he can't disagree that it's the right choice. What could be worse than freeing Pheir from Vesta's hold to see her dive into someone else again?

"We don't *have* to," Lev acknowledges, tracing the line of Pheir's jaw. "But I think it could help you figure things out without getting caught up in something else. I want you to have breathing room, time and space to choose us of your own volition, if you choose us at all."

Pheir tightens her fingers around Lev's. "I *will* choose you."

With a wet laugh, Lev fights the ache in her voice. "But you don't *have* to. That's the most important thing. It's your choice."

Contemplatively, Pheir runs her fingers through Lev's fur. Never before has Aren seen Pheir give anything careful consideration, even if it is short-lived. "*Fine*," she begrudgingly agrees. "It sounds like something Rhaiden would do, so it must be smart."

"Don't side with them!" Caius moans. "Don't start using your head."

Pheir rolls onto her side, draping a teasing leg over his hip. "The only heads I'm gonna use are yours and Aren's…" Her hand slips lower, talons scraping his chest.

Aren exhales slowly. "Not to be a killjoy —"

Caius drags a hand down his face. "Don't say it."

"I think the rest of us should do the same so Pheir's on equal footing."

"You mean celibacy?" Caius blanches at Aren. "For *all* of us?"

Aren winces as he tries to soften the blow. "There might be slip-ups, but…consider it courting."

"Courting," Caius repeats flatly, as if he's never heard a more offensive term.

"It won't be easy," Aren acknowledges. "None of this has been, but I think it's worth it if it gives us a chance to make sure this is what we really want. *All* of us."

Pheir rolls onto her back to match Lev and Aren. The weight of their decision settles in, the four of them staring up through the windows as the moon shines through the roof.

"I've never done that before." Pheir's mouth curls over the foreign word. "*Courting*."

The whispered word makes heat spread in Aren's stomach. What will courting them be like? Presenting Pheir with trinkets to tuck into her new nest. Sharing his thermos with Lev and watching her mouth press to the place his has been. Lingering goodnights with Caius in front of his cabin when neither of them wants to part.

Arousal taints the air, a smothering scent from all of them.

"Gods, this is gonna be torture." Caius rolls onto his stomach so he can hide his hardening desire.

Pheir turns toward Caius again. "I'll do it." She wrinkles her nose in challenge. "It's one more thing I can beat you at."

Aren's mouth opens. "I don't think that's —"

Caius pushes up to his knees, lifting a cackling Pheir and tossing her onto the others. He flops on top of them with an exaggerated sigh, draping over their bodies as they laugh. "Fine," Caius grumbles. "I'm in."

They settle into quiet again as night spreads across the sky. Caius stretches out to cover them all like a blanket. With one finger, Lev twirls Pheir's hair.

"You didn't really get to enjoy your first snow," Lev murmurs.

Pheir buries her smile against Aren's purring chest, curled between them like it's where she belongs. Where she's always belonged. "Guess I'll have to stick around for next year's."

EPILOGUE

Caius

2 months after Vesta's (second) death

Turns out staying away from each other is as harder when they aren't trying to kill each other.

Caius understands the reasoning. Clearly, he's been spending too much time with Aren if he gets *why* Pheir needs time to herself. She has to "reconcile her past before she creates her future." She "needs space to choose for herself." She "deserves a chance at a real home" — or whatever else Aren says.

If Caius didn't know any better, he'd think Aren was talking about what Caius needs, too.

None of that stops the possessive animal from prowling in Caius's chest, snarling for the three people who belong to him. After the chaos of the last two years — last *lifetime*, for some of them — the physical distance between them is an opportunity. "Put yourself first," Aren reminds them with a pointed look toward Caius. The thing Caius wants to put first is Aren's ass in front of him while Lev and Pheir mark up his neck, but Aren would say that's a "method of distraction" or a "coping mechanism."

Caius doesn't care what it is, because it fills his thoughts every moment they aren't together. They have their own cabins and chores and duties, but the absence doesn't make him want them any less. Gods, no. It drives him to distraction in the middle of the night, picturing the four of them as fear creeps into the back of his thoughts.

Without sex, how will he tell them how he feels? Without a physical reminder, how will he know if they stop wanting him — *when* they stop wanting him?

The thought sucks him down like a black hole. He stares up at the ceiling, breath tight until the door to his cabin eases open. Caius shoots up in bed, claws bared and teeth on edge until he recognizes Aren's scent.

The lynx's fur is ruffled with sleep, eyelids heavy as he shuts the door behind him. When Aren approaches the bed, Caius yearns for contact. Without thought, he slips to the floor on his knees and reaches for Aren's hips. He'll show Aren what he's missing. He'll prove why Aren shouldn't forget about him —

But Aren guides Caius's hands away. "Get back in bed, Caius." Aren's voice is thick with sleep, doing nothing to dampen the heat in Caius's stomach. Puzzled, he shifts back to sit on the mattress as Aren climbs into bed behind him.

When Aren wraps his arms around Caius's waist, embarrassed heat creeps up Caius's throat. His body shifts uncomfortably. If there's no sex as a distraction for his racing thoughts, what's he supposed to do? Just lay here? Aren seems unbothered by the prospect, nuzzling against Caius and sighing.

"Bit late for a stroll," Caius grunts in the dark.

"Your cabin reeks of worry," Aren murmurs into the back of Caius's neck. "It's hard enough smelling you when you're horny."

The thought makes Caius shiver. Gruffly, he turns in Aren's arms, doing his best to maintain a surly expression. It's difficult to look Aren in the face when Caius's hackles are up, but this is a "time to get to know himself." A time to *try* to use his words. They fizzle on his tongue until he finally speaks. "You should've been asleep hours ago."

Tentatively, Aren's claw traces Caius's ears. They flick under his touch, so responsive that Aren's pupils dilate. "Believe it or not, Caius, I'm always looking out for you."

Emotions wells in Caius's chest. What the fuck's he supposed to do with that if not kiss Aren? So, Caius tries, but Aren redirects him with fingers on his lips.

"Mm, no — let's talk."

It's tempting for Caius to withdraw, to roll onto his side or take off on a bullshit excuse. Instead, he snorts through his nose, warring with tension in his body. Aren smooths down the fur on the back of Caius's neck. Finally, Caius's voice escapes, raw and quiet.

"Do you think Pheir will choose us at the end of this?"

It's a worry he hasn't expressed, one that plagues him like the others. Now that Pheir moves freely about the camp, there are no chains to keep her here. When she takes practice flights on her regrowing wings, Caius almost forgets he's holding his breath and wrestling with the thought that she might leave and never return.

Funny how he's ended up on the receiving end of that.

Aren cards his hand through Caius's fur. "I don't know," Aren admits, a solemn knit in his brow. "I hope she does. I wonder about that, too."

Somehow, hearing Aren's doubts makes Caius more secure. A smile flickers on his face. Aren trusts him with this. Aren does feel something after all.

Aren drags his claws through the fur on Caius's neck the way he likes. "I hope you choose us, too."

It's laughable that Aren could think anything else could come of this. Despite himself, Caius's smile deepens, brushing Aren's snout with his own. "Are *you* gonna choose us, old man?"

Aren tightens his arms and pulls Caius as close as they can get, dragging his tongue over the cowlick on Caius's head. "You say that like I could do anything else."

It's the first time the two of them have been this close without fucking, and the first time Caius forgets all his worries.

Pheir

3 months after Vesta's (second) death

Thank the gods for Pheir's cabin. She needs an escape.

No matter how ferocious she was before, life with the Timbers is terrifying. It's like being immersed in a new language you never knew existed. The Timbers laugh. They joke. They aren't constantly at each other's throats. When they do argue, nobody ends up with a black eye.

It's madness.

Pheir would take a bloody nose over the way her throat locks up when any of them ask her a simple question. Caius understands, but he's fallen in with them faster than Pheir has. Turns out when he isn't baring his teeth at everyone, people are actually nice to him.

"It still took me years, Pheir." He knocks her knee as they sit on the dock, trying and failing to fish. "We didn't start on equal footing. It'll happen; I promise."

At least the chores are similar enough to Vestal life that Pheir can handle them. It gives her plenty of time to think. After a decade of using a miniscule amount of her brain, it's probably good to give it some exercise. Slowly, Lev, Aren, and Caius reintroduce Pheir to things that she'd once thought she understood. It's painful how much of it can be found in Vesta's journal. Siren's tongue. Her true goal. Rhaiden's subversion. Things Pheir had access to all that time, but her loyalty prevented her from seeing it.

One day, Pheir wants to go to the Broadleaf territory. She trusts the stories Lev tells her, but Pheir needs to see it for herself. To make amends. To help the earth continue to regrow. To put names and histories to the people Pheir never realized they were hurting. It's a small step, but a necessary one. In all of this, Pheir has not forgotten her duty. That's one part of herself she still recognizes, even if the focus has changed.

Eventually, thinking through her chores isn't enough to occupy her mind. Through the windows of her cabin, she sees a small group gathered around the campfire as dusk begins to fall. Uncertainty clenches in her chest. It's the most unsettling of her unearthed emotions. Everything with Vesta was unquestionable and easy. Pheir was always confident. She misses that simplicity — but that brings back the fire of familiar anger. Fuck Vesta. *Fuck Vesta* for the years Pheir wasted. Fuck Vesta for leaving Pheir floundering so hopelessly.

Resolutely, Pheir pulls on a fleece jacket from Lev and stalks over to the gathering.

As she draws closer, the wind slips out of her sails. Her footsteps drag through the dirt as her mouth twists. She should go back. Today's not a good day. Maybe tomorrow —

"Pheir!"

The voice makes her body tight with fear and light with hopefulness. Willow waves as Oberon smiles. Mari scowls.

Two out of three ain't bad.

Cautiously, Pheir trudges to the campfire. Willow's brows lift, like she knows what Pheir's avoiding. Willow gestures to the seat across from her and Oberon. "Sit with us."

Pheir swallows and eyes the wooden chair. How the fuck do people talk to each other when they're not bickering? No matter how Lev and Aren have tried to help her, Pheir's been avoiding the actual practice of it. Lev and Aren can't do this for her. Sucking in cold air through her nose, her eyes dart to the window of the library

In the fading light, two rabbit ears appear haloed by the lanterns hanging from the walls. Lev wanders the floor, paging through books and taking a bite from a stick of celery. There's a gap between Lev's front teeth. It's one of many things Vesta never mentioned that Pheir's become preoccupied with, like the tensing muscles in Lev's thighs when she lifts boxes, the cinch in her brow when she discusses plans, the snuffle of her nose when she laughs.

Once, Pheir's hate for Lev would have been enough to forget everything else. Now, a different feeling pulls Pheir's attention, glowing like embers in her stomach. Lev's gaze lifts to the window as if she knows someone's watching. A smile tugs on her lips when she realizes it's Pheir — then Lev takes in the others around her. Cheerfully, Lev gestures with her celery and mouths the words.

You can do it!

Pheir bites back a laugh. Gods, what was she scared of? In this moment, it's hard to remember any feeling but the ardor she has for Lev. Emotions that were once as overwhelming as a raging fire are now as freeing as a summer breeze. Pheir doesn't have to burn her way out of a corner; she's no longer trapped in one.

Scuffing her foot, Pheir turns back to the group. They watch her warily.

"Do you *want* to join us?" Oberon asks.

Pheir tucks her hands into her pockets and rocks on her toes. "Last time I joined a cult, it turned out pretty poorly."

It's an attempt at levity, one Pheir isn't sure will land; she still hasn't gotten the hang of what constitutes a joke. The others blink for a long moment before Mari ducks their head and chuckles into their shoulder. Willow's giggle comes after, followed by Oberon's roaring laugh as he slaps his knee. A smile cracks across Pheir's face like a chick breaking through an egg.

"Sit down," Mari instructs, shaking their head as they hold out a half-drunk bottle of moonshine. Pheir climbs into the offered seat, tucking her feet beneath her. In the window, Lev lifts her celery in a proud toast. Pheir does the same with the bottle before she tips it back, and warmth spread through her entire body.

Aren

5 months after Vesta's (second) death

The teasing starts the second Aren enters the kitchen.

It's not like he can blame the rest of the pack. He isn't subtle; none of the four of them are, hanging back after every meal to get a moment alone. Once Lev, Aren, Caius, and Pheir got through a few months of giving each other space, courting was a natural progression. They're still celibate, but they move with intention — gifts left on doorsteps. Strolls around the lake together. Lingering kisses that leave their knees weak.

When the campfire dies down for the night, they're always the last to leave, huddled under blankets and watching each other for a sign. Air crackles with untapped energy as they wander to their cabins, making excuses to stay out longer. Their goodnights take no less than an hour, the four of them dawdling on their separate decks to flirt with each other long after the rest of the compound turns in for the night.

Tonight will be no different. It's still not quite time for them to be together. They're starting to get to know each other again, watching Caius and Pheir slot into place among the pack. As the rest of the Timbers file out of the kitchen, Mari makes kissing noises as June coos and wiggles her fingers. Caius elbows the door shut as Mari calls back to Pheir, "Don't be up all night! We have scouting tomorrow." Then their laughter disappears across the field.

The four of them stand among the remnants of dinner. The food has long gone cold. There's nothing but scraps left, but Aren can't bring himself to care when he's finally alone with the people he craves most.

Lev pulls open cabinets to search for something that can serve as a meal. "Hungry?"

Pheir's eyes follow Lev's ass as she lifts on her toes. "Not for *food.*"

A sensual warmth slips into the space between them. It's a common occurrence now. Aren hasn't gone a day since this started without a desperate need to get himself off. The vow of celibacy is tougher than he thought, especially when the four of them live in such close quarters. Every night, one of their arousals saturates the space between their cabins, and the others are helpless to do anything but take care of themselves alongside each other.

It's impressive they've lasted this long. Not that there haven't been lapses in judgment...

Heat flares in Aren's stomach. He finds a piece of jerky on a cutting board, tearing off a bite with his teeth. "Speaking of: Pheir and I have something to confess."

Lev and Caius's ears perk as Pheir groans. "Do you have to tell them? It's humiliating."

Caius nudges her aside, leaning into the island as he rips a piece from Aren's jerky. "I want to fucking hear it."

Aren clears his throat. "When we checked the outer territory borders today, we got back in the truck and started talking." He can't remember what they spoke about. Conversation between them comes so effortlessly now, slipping easily into a different type of communication — Pheir's hand on his thigh, her eyelashes brushing her cheek as she looked up at him with that wicked grin...

It's no wonder they ended up with his hand in her hair and his dick in her mouth.

The kitchen is silent as he retells it. Lev and Caius stare, pupils so wide their eyes are nearly black. Thank the gods the other Timbers have left, because the scent of arousal is stifling as Caius adjusts himself beneath the counter.

When Lev looks at Pheir, the Alpha's voice is tight, subtly shifting her thighs. "How is that humiliating for you?"

"Because I stopped it!" Pheir digs a handful of leftover carrots from a bowl. "I was the responsible one. I'm turning into Aren."

A laugh rumbles out of him. "Tell them *how* you stopped it."

With a shrug, Pheir drags the carrot innocently against her lips. "I asked Aren what my wife and confidante would think if they knew I was sucking off their beta."

Lev and Caius groan, heads lowering to the counter as they try to stifle their desire. Smugly, Pheir pops the carrot into her mouth and bites down with a crunch.

"While we're confessing…" Caius lifts his head, "Lev and I slipped earlier, too."

"It wasn't…" Lev scratches the back of her head and averts her gaze. "I don't know how it happened."

Aren can guess how it happened. Between the spring muscle Lev's put on in her thighs and the comfortable bulk Caius has settled into, Aren hasn't been able to look at them without wanting them. Neither has Pheir, licking peanut butter from a knife as the blade drags against her tongue.

"It was after we met in the library this morning." Caius gestures across the island to Lev and Aren. "Aren left, and I remembered the day the Regents came for Pheir all those months ago, when we were pretending this was real…" There's a dreamy glaze in his eyes before he shakes it away, falling back into surliness to hide his infatuation. "I mean, what the fuck am I supposed to do? Now that you two include me in the pack planning, and ask me what I think, and set the schedule around me, how am I *not* supposed to get turned on?"

An unmistakable twinge lingers in the air. Lev's teeth drag into her lip. Pheir's eyes are dark. Caius's fingers curl around the edge of the counter. It's almost enough for Aren to forget the rules, to close the space and give them all what they're yearning for. It's a fight to keep his feet planted on the ground as he straightens his spine.

"If we all go back to one cabin…" Contemplatively, his claws click on the counter. Lev, Caius, and Pheir watch his fingers. "We could take care of ourselves at the same time. In the same room."

It's a ruthless, torturous plan. The idea alone surges through Aren's veins. Call it a loophole. Call it whatever you want, but it's been five months of being unable to touch any of them. Five months dreaming of the moment they'll smell like each other again. Five months of fucking into his fist every time one of them so much as smiles at him.

Pheir's eyes are bright and wild. "Extreme edging."

Lev's gaze dips to Aren's mouth. "Feeling spontaneous, huh?"

He laughs low in his chest. It's strange being the one to give into temptation, but Pheir's right. It's become a give and take. As Pheir and Caius learn restraint, Lev and Aren have begun to enjoy impulsiveness.

Caius's fur stands on end, weight pressed on his toes like he's ready to pounce. "You think we're gonna get ourselves off together and manage *not* to fuck each other?"

"Surely you can resist." A smirk slips across Aren's lips. Caius bares his teeth like he wants to fuck it off. Aimlessly, Aren takes a few steps toward the screen door, hands clasped behind his back. "If you need anything, I'll be in my bed. Alone. Waiting."

He barely makes it outside before the others sprint after him toward his cabin.

Lev

8 months after Vesta's (second) death

"I've had some time to think," Pheir announces.

At the cliff's edge, she steps onto the foundation of the new cottage. Beneath her, the scorched grass has regrown lush and tall, covered in a picnic blanket big enough for the four of them. Sunlight filters through the trees, washing Pheir in a golden glow that highlights her regrown feathers.

It could easily remind Lev of Vesta, but lately, Lev has better things to think of — Aren's chest against her back, Caius's body draped over her legs, Pheir's coy smile behind the rim of her lemonade bottle.

Lev wants to make her smile like that a thousand more times. Lev's head tilts fondly. "What have you been thinking?"

Pheir's back straightens. "As a former hostage, I think I'm entitled to compensation." There's a teasing lilt to her voice, one that's become more prominent in the months since the fire. Hard to believe the girl that screamed for attention now stands before them, trusting that she can ask for exactly what she wants.

Aren's smile spreads against the back of Lev's neck. "What are your demands?"

Theatrically, Pheir paces until Caius snatches for her ankle. She avoids him and lifts her chin. "I want to be brought fully into the Timber pack."

Lev's heart skips a beat. Caius sits upright as Aren's fingers clench around Lev's arms. Is it happening? Is this the moment they've waited for?

"You're sure?" Lev breathes. Butterflies swarm her stomach like they might lift her straight off the ground.

With a smirk, Pheir lifts a finger. "I'm not finished. This is a negotiation, *Alpha*."

The spark in her eye heats Lev's entire body. With Aren's arms around her waist, Lev's nails dig into his him.

Pheir continues nonchalantly, as if she isn't changing their world for the better. "I want all of you in my bed, every night. I'll make concessions for pack business, but that's as far as I'll extend that compromise."

Lev grins until her cheeks hurt. Pheir matches it as she looks down on the three of them. Nothing controls her any longer. Nothing forces her desires. She makes choices for herself, and she chooses the three of them freely, without expectation. As much as Caius needed Lev and Aren to want him to stay, Pheir needed freedom, and now, she has it.

"There's one more piece I'm not willing to bend on." Pheir steps off the platform toward the blanket. When she reaches it, she sinks to her knees and traces her talon in a circle around Lev's heart. It's a touch they've reclaimed from Vesta, one so natural that Lev hardly believes it belonged to anyone else. "There's a way to bind me to the pack," Pheir whispers. "A way that would bring all four of us together. I want that. I want to wear your marks. I want to go back to the island and make it real."

It's exactly like a younger Lev dreamed it would be. When she fantasized about her marriage, this is what it felt like — incandescent happiness. Immeasurable comfort. Solace that swarms her from all sides.

"Do you agree to my terms?" Pheir asks cheekily.

"*Yes!*" Lev gasps as Aren and Caius tug Pheir into the pile atop them. It's a knot of limbs and mouths and laughter. They've earned it. This is a promise of what they deserve, and Lev trusts the humming ground beneath them will see it through.

Caius tugs Pheir back against his chest and nips at her ear. "Never thought *Pheir* would be the one proposing."

Tranquilly, her eyes slip shut, her smile brighter than the

setting sun. "Call me Pheira."

* * * * *

THANK YOU for reading *Vicious Devotion*!

Want more Caius, Lev, Aren, & Pheir as well as Thalea and Rhaiden's stories? Sign up for my NEWSLETTER to get an exclusive bonus epilogue, and join my PATREON for extra scenes!

AVEDAVICE.COM/NEWSLETTER
PATREON.COM/AVEDAVICE
FACEBOOK.COM/GROUPS/AVEDAVICE

Want Flint and his partners' happily ever after? Begin their story with *Skin*!

This monster is the only one who can touch her...

The last time Harbinger felt someone's touch was years ago. Cursed with the ability to soak up information through her skin, she focuses on loaning out her services and keeping the world at arm's length. Easier said than done when she's partnered with the gargoyle Jasper Flint.

But when a routine mission turns into an ambush, Flint shields her from a spray of bullets...and brushes against her in the process. Now, she can feel everything he does — including his growing attraction to her. Flint tries to keep things professional, but Harbin doesn't want to miss the chance to finally feel someone against her skin.

And if Flint's the only one who can put his hands on her...he's going to make it worth her while.

Read Skin now!

About the Author

Aveda Vice is the author of sinful stories and infernal paranormal romances. In her books, you'll find a weakness for monsters and polyamorous pairings. She researches true crime, decorates every day like it's Halloween, and is going to hell.

AVEDAVICE.COM

Sign up for Aveda Vice's NEWSLETTER and PATREON to stay up-to-date on new releases, special offers, and bonus content.

Follow @AVEDAVICE on TWITTER and INSTAGRAM for sneak peaks and promotions.

Join the FANGS WITH BENEFITS FACEBOOK READER GROUP for community chats and posts.

Leave a review for this book on AMAZON and GOODREADS.

Acknowledgements

After I finished writing *Inextricably Tied*, I said, "I don't want to write anything that long again." Then, *Vicious Devotion* became almost double that length. Well, guess what: I'M STILL SAYING IT! I don't want to write anything this long again, but for this story, it was necessary. Adding all those extra words transformed this into a book I'm proud of. Exploring and balancing four people in a relationship is hard, but it was worth it to tell these characters' story.

This book may not follow the typical beats of romance, but it explores a journey to a happy ending. These characters learn about themselves, grow into the people they want to be, and work to heal from their trauma. They find acceptance within themselves and each other. They make a home for themselves. They find happiness and contentment. Their love grows so much stronger than their hate. This may not be the romance people expect, but it is the romance these characters need; I can't think of anything more beautiful than that.

Thank you to my beta readers, who read this book when it was half the story it is today. For *Bound:* Michael, Gab, Whitney, Cam, Heather, Jacque. For *Vicious Devotion:* Whitney (once again), Ames, Freydís. My lovely Steph, who always makes me believe that I can keep doing this. And special thanks to Amanda, who understood what I was trying to do with this book in its very early stages. You saw beautiful things in these characters even when my words were clumsy, and that gave me the faith to keep writing, even when it was hard. Even when it took so much more work than I expected. For that, I thank you immensely.

Rabbit, it's your (and Lev's) year. I hope it's the best one yet.